Potter's Field is the middle [...] paranoiac undertow of con[...] *Cathedral* – and the final v[...] is concerned with guilt, resp[...] and tragedy.

In this disturbing and black-humoured novel the families of Theódóra, Vilhelmína and Dagný are variously linked by blood, guilt and greed in a world divided between wealth and poverty, and between political power and political impotence. In contrast, the Roman Catholic priest, Father Bernhardur, though doubting his vocation and his faith, is a humane and dedicated man. Through the three wives and their children, including a Serbian child in Theódóra's foster care, he becomes intricately involved in the problems and conflicts within their families. Linda, Theódóra's religious and visionary stepdaughter, alone embodies Gudmundsson's belief in the possibility of redemption and transcendence in tragedy.

The book is written with the author's customary precision both in the complexities of characterization and in the expression of inner truth through extreme and violent action. It is the combination of family trauma and seemingly random external events that produces paranoia and despair – and tentative hope.

In this fascinating novel, which I found impossible to put down, Ólafur Gunnarsson tackles many of the classical themes of great literature in an idiosyncratic way. *Potter's Field* takes some of the Icelandic political intrigues from earlier this century and brilliantly reworks them in a contemporary international context. The action and rich characterization would ring true anywhere in the world. The novel has a wonderful feel for the absurd and grotesque that lie at the heart of human endeavour and aspiration.

Vigdís Finnbogadóttir
President of Iceland, 1980–96

For details of Mare's Nest books, please see pages 483–9.

POTTER'S FIELD

Published in 1999
by Mare's Nest Publishing
41 Addison Gardens London W11 0DP

Potter's Field
Ólafur Gunnarsson

Cover photography and design Squid Inc.
Author photograph Valdimar Sverrisson
Typeset by Agnesi Text Hadleigh Suffolk
Printed and bound by Antony Rowe Ltd Chippenham Wiltshire

ISBN 1 899197 55 9

Blódakur was originally published by Forlagid, Reykjavík, 1996.
This translation is published by agreement with Forlagid,
to whom the publishers are grateful.

This book is published with the financial assistance
of the Arts Council of England.

Potter's Field has been translated with the financial support
of the European Commission under the Ariane programme for 1998.

Potter's Field

Ólafur Gunnarsson

TRANSLATED FROM THE ICELANDIC
BY ÓLAFUR GUNNARSSON AND JILL BURROWS

MARE'S NEST

REYKJAVÍK

Town Centre and Eastern Suburbs

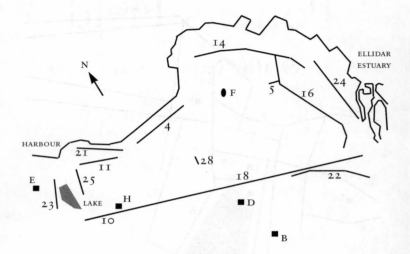

REYKJAVÍK

Town Centre

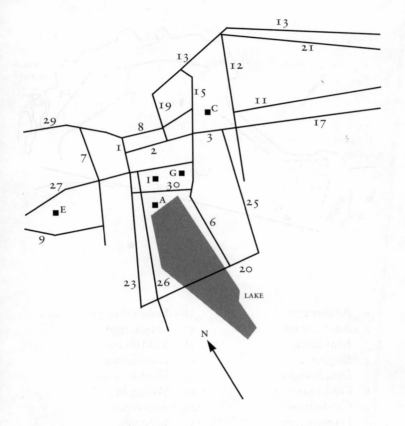

A City Hall
B City Hospital
C Government House
D Kringla Shopping Centre
E Landakot Church
F Laugardalur Stadium
G Lutheran Cathedral
H National Hospital
I Parliament Building

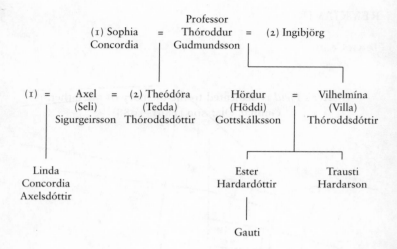

```
                              Professor
              (1) Sophia   =   Thóroddur   =   (2) Ingibjörg
              Concordia       Gudmundsson

(1) =    Axel    =   (2) Theódóra      Hördur      =   Vilhelmína
         (Seli)         (Tedda)        (Höddi)          (Villa)
      Sigurgeirsson  Thóroddsdóttir  Gottskálksson   Thóroddsdóttir

      Linda                          Ester          Trausti
      Concordia                    Hardardóttir    Hardarson
      Axelsdóttir

                                      Gauti
```

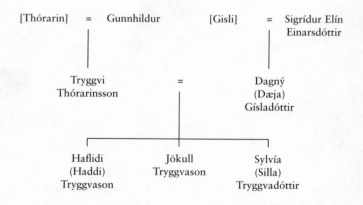

```
[Thórarin]   =   Gunnhildur      [Gisli]   =   Sigrídur Elín
                                                Einarsdóttir

        Tryggvi              =              Dagný
      Thórarinsson                          (Dæja)
                                          Gísladóttir

      Haflidi            Jökull            Sylvía
      (Haddi)          Tryggvason          (Silla)
      Tryggvason                        Tryggvadóttir
```

Potter's Field is dedicated to the memory of my father,
Gunnar Olafsson (1891–1988)

And then Judas, which had betrayed him, when he saw that he was condemned, repented himself, and brought again the thirty pieces of silver to the chief priests and elders.

Saying, I have sinned in that I have betrayed the innocent blood. And they said, What is that to us? see thou to that.

And he cast down the pieces of silver in the temple, and departed, and went and hanged himself.

And the chief priests took the silver pieces, and said, It is not lawful for to put them into the treasury, because it is the price of blood.

And they took counsel, and bought with them the potter's field, to bury strangers in.

Wherefore that field was called, The field of blood, unto this day.

Then was fulfilled that which was spoken by Jeremy the prophet, saying, And they took the thirty pieces of silver, the price of him that was valued, whom they of the children of Israel did value;

And gave them for the potter's field, as the Lord appointed me.

Matthew 27:3–10

INTRODUCTION

I used to edit *Weekend*, and then I got fired. Everyone remembers the old scandal sheet. We all claimed to be above such things but we read it just the same. In my time as editor, I used to survey the current scene and pick out things I considered worth covering. So, as I see it, I'm ideally placed to give a full account of what happened in Reykjavík the December before last. At the time some people were even considering calling on the NATO Defence Force for assistance but, thank God, it didn't quite come to that. For a few days back then I could be found dashing from place to place, picking up what scraps of information I could – even though I didn't have a magazine to edit any more. So, I've decided to write up what really happened in book form. My name is not important. (But then, of course, actually everybody does know my name.) If this tale were to be read a thousand years from now, just like any other Icelandic Saga, then it would fall into the same distinguished tradition of anonymous authorship. In that selfsame spirit, I shall try to keep myself well out of the spotlight.

Probably the best place to start is with a few words about Thóroddur Gudmundsson. I shall save myself a lot of bother if I simply give a brief outline of the salient points and don't try to write the man's biography as such. In any case, the contents of *that* particular book are only too familiar, as the moment it arrived in the bookshops the brown stuff well and truly hit the fan. When Professor Thóroddur's daughters, Theódóra and Vilhelmína, hired a writer to tell his story, the doctor had already been dead for some years. Now, it just so happens that I know the writer involved personally. He's written a number of books along the same lines and they've all been bestsellers. The daughters planned to 'bathe their father's memory in a golden glow' as someone once said, but the writer demanded complete freedom of expression. He was sick and tired of churning out saccharine hagiographies for the upper classes.

3

For some extraordinary reason the sisters agreed to his terms. They allowed him access to documents, personal letters and photographs, and they gave him introductions to lots of people to assist him in his researches into their father's life. He let them have sight of carefully chosen passages before publication, but he held back the juicier bits in case they insisted on cuts. When the book came out, they both went mad. I read it myself and couldn't see what all the fuss was about. It emerged that the doctor had used heroin for a while after he returned to Iceland having completed his education overseas. So what? Every other young person you come across these days is into drugs. The book claimed he brought his mistress into the household and his wife hadn't had the guts to leave him. This would have been in 1950 or thereabouts. It's my contention that the way we view these things has changed a lot over the years. The doctor found himself a younger woman – a trophy wife, if you like. No one would think twice about it today. The sisters did all they could to stop publication and in the resulting kerfuffle the writer took to his bed. (All this silliness meant that *A Doctor's Life* got far more publicity than it otherwise would have done.) The book was a bestseller. And there I was, in a perfect position to watch events unfold. *Weekend* devoted many column inches to the affair, both in its supplement and on the front page.

According to the book, Professor Thóroddur was clearly not a bundle of laughs. The doctor was known to hurl instruments at the wall during surgery if he was handed the wrong item. Reading between the lines, it was obvious that the second wife had his measure rather better than the first had done. Her late husband had been a car importer. She brought a considerable fortune to that marriage, and then watched her investment grow while she kept a firm eye on the management of her late husband's company well into her considerable old age.

I read somewhere that in choosing a spouse a woman is subconsciously seeking her father and a man is subconsciously seeking his mother. I'm not sure how much truth there is in this: the sisters could hardly have found two more contrasting husbands. I incline rather to the opinion that in choosing a man, a woman is subconsciously seeking her *mother*. Theódóra married Axel Sigurgeirsson, who, for all I know, may have been kind-hearted and easy-going,

4

even though he was a director of the family firm. The younger sister chose the iron-willed Hördur Gottskálksson, who, I have to concede, was indeed a surgeon, just as her father had been, so perhaps my theory doesn't hold water . . . As Hamlet put it, 'There are more things in heaven and earth, Horatio, than are dreamt of in our philosophy.'

I was acquainted with both Axel and Hördur as we were all members of the same luncheon club. We would meet at the round table at Hotel Borg: Axel, Hördur, a few lawyers, members of parliament and various other society figures. Even the Prime Minister occasionally graced us with his presence. I was the youngest by a long chalk and felt a bit of an outsider, but so long as I was the editor of *Weekend* no one wanted to risk getting on the wrong side of me.

The spring day my story begins Hördur Gottskálksson was expected back from overseas. I had fixed an interview with him, and lined up a photographer, as soon as he was back in town. He had done a stint with *Médecins sans frontières* and was returning from some trip to foreign parts. Hördur had suggested the interview himself – this way of doing things is much more common than people generally think. That very morning the entire editorial board got the sack. Out of the blue I lost my job. In all the consequent hoohah I clean forgot I was meant to be meeting the doctor and I found out later in the day that he had been asking for me. As it happened, Hördur's return flight to Iceland was to produce plenty of material for *Weekend*'s front page. Indeed, a train of events was set in motion that would occupy the front page weeks after a new editorial board had been appointed.

You may well wonder how I come to have such detailed information about something that happened on board a plane heading towards Keflavík Airport. In the old days I would have come over all mysterious and said, 'Ah-ha! Nothing escapes a good nose for news.' But nowadays I no longer feel like playing that sort of game. It just so happened that I was engaged for a while to a stewardess who saw everything that occurred on that flight. However, the really newsworthy event – something that later was to put a metaphorical bomb under the city of Reyjavík – went completely unnoticed by her.

5

PART I

The plane had just begun its descent east of Iceland when a
stewardess, walking down the aisle checking that all seatbelts were
fastened, noticed that one of the passengers, a fat young man with
a deathly pale face and bushy red eyebrows, was staring straight
ahead with his mouth open in abject terror. She looked at him for
a moment. He put her in mind of a fish. She asked him to fasten his
seatbelt, but he did not seem to hear her. She touched his shoulder
and repeated her request. The man opened and closed his mouth as
if about to say something, but no words came and his eyes rolled
in his head. She eased herself between the seats, lifted his seatbelt,
fastened its across his paunch and gently patted the back of his
hand. 'There's nothing to be afraid of,' she said. 'We're in good
hands.'

The plane was approaching the Westmann Islands, swiftly and
steadily losing height. The stewardess returned to the back of the
plane, bracing herself to counteract the angle. In the aisle seat in
the back row there was a very handsome middle-aged man fast
asleep. She thought she recognized his face. She whispered, 'Please
fasten your seatbelt. We'll soon be landing.'

The man opened his eyes and it seemed to take him a moment
to remember where he was. Suddenly she could put a name to the
face: Hördur Gottskálksson, the surgeon who'd made such a public
fuss when he'd been dismissed by the National Hospital. The
stewardess moved towards the front of the plane, passing the small
number of passengers, most of them foreigners, dotted about the
cabin.

The angle of the wing flaps changed, exposing the mechanism
inside. At the wing tip a stony shoreline was visible. A little way
out a fishing boat was going about its business, its net like an
inflated balloon in the green sea.

The stewardess steadied herself by holding on to the back of a seat and asked a drunk who was demanding more whisky to hand her his plastic glass. 'I'm sorry, it's not possible. We're about to land.'

In the seats beyond the drunk, there were two young men, lovers by the look of them. She had seen them with their fingers entwined. They were the only two passengers who had watched the film. She took a step back and they handed her the earphones. One of them was affected by the changing pressure in the cabin, reached a hand to his ear, rubbed it vigorously and yawned.

The second time she passed the fat man by the emergency exit, his body seemed to jerk. He was white as a sheet, his skin was glistening with sweat and his breathing was rapid. 'God,' she thought, 'why does this always have to happen on my flights?' She prodded his shoulder. 'Is anything the matter?'

He opened his eyes and she had seldom seen greater terror.

'Can you hear me?'

The man nodded. He could be scarcely more than thirty, so it was unlikely that he was having a heart attack.

'Are you ill?'

He half closed his eyes but said nothing.

'Do you have a history of heart disease? Are you diabetic?'

Still he said nothing and she looked out of the window. The crevices and clefts of the flat-topped cliffs of the Reykjanes were now clearly in view. There was still snow in the meadows and in the gulleys, even though May was drawing to a close.

Then the man said something. 'I believe I'm dying.'

She looked at him and didn't know what to think. From the way he looked, it could be true. 'What's the matter with you?'

'I feel so ill.'

She spoke more loudly. 'What do you think is wrong with you?'

'I think I've got ebola.'

'What?'

'Ebola fever.'

She had read in the papers about the terrifying epidemic sweeping across Africa. The virus consumed the body from within, and its victims bled to death through every orifice. Medicine was powerless to defeat the virus. 'No, it can't be that bad.' She tried to smile.

'No,' he whispered. 'I was trying to bring up a bit of dried cod.'

Another, older stewardess had come to her assistance. 'What's up?'

'He thinks he's got ebola fever.' The younger woman rolled her eyes and sighed. 'What can we do? Is he drunk?'

'I didn't bring him any spirits. Did you?'

The other stewardess shook her head.

There was a noise like thunder, metal grinding against metal, as the plane lowered its undercarriage and the floor juddered. The younger stewardess turned to the sick passenger, sitting there with his mouth open in terror. She said, 'We'll be landing shortly. I'm sure there's nothing wrong with you.'

His lips moved as he tried to speak.

She asked him to repeat it.

'Don't go,' the man mumbled and his shoulders stirred as if he was trying to lift up an arm but did not have the strength to do so. He raised his head for a moment and then let it fall back on the head rest. 'Don't go.'

She put a comforting hand on his shoulder. 'No. I'm not going anywhere. She glanced towards the back of the plane and saw the top of the doctor's head. 'We're in luck. We have a doctor on board,' she said loudly. 'Shall I go and get him? I'm sure you don't have ebola fever.'

'Don't touch me, or you'll die too,' sighed the young man. His head jerked and then fell back against his shoulder. His eyes were rolling. She withdrew her hand.

She struggled down the sloping floor, holding on to the backs of seats, keeping her eye on the doctor. 'Excuse me, but aren't you Hördur Gottskálksson, the doctor?'

Hördur nodded and looked at her suspiciously.

'The thing is there's a young man at the front of the plane who says he's quite poorly. Would you be kind enough to have a word with him once we've landed?'

'What's the matter with him?'

'I'm afraid I really don't know.' She was finding the doctor rather standoffish. 'He thinks he's got ebola fever.'

'Ebola fever,' repeated Hördur and a faint smile played on his lips. 'I'll be damned. Where's he come from?'

'I don't know.'

'OK, I'll see him when we've landed.'

The stewardess walked back to her colleague and waited for the plane to land. She braced herself against the metal cabinet where the passengers' meals were stored. It was her least favourite place in the plane. Standing there always brought back the same memory: fourteen years earlier she had been on a chartered flight carrying pilgrims when the Icelandair plane had crashed in Sri Lanka. The roof was torn away at the front and some of the passengers hadn't been quick enough to duck. She could never get what she had seen out of her mind: decapitated heads bouncing across the hunched backs of the other passengers. The plane landed with a judder and the brakes screamed. The stewardess started making her way forward as soon as the wheels touched the runway. It was light outside, an Icelandic light, grey and naked – light like nowhere else in the world, she thought. The older stewardess emerged from the cockpit and they met by the sick man's seat. 'I've informed the captain, Stella. They'll have to call a doctor out to the plane.'

'There's a doctor on board. I've just had a word with him. Tell them up front so they won't need to call out a doctor from Keflavík.'

The plane had landed on the runway furthest from the terminal. It taxied quite a long way, its wings bouncing gently, the lights at the tips flickering. There were two Hercules transport planes from the US base parked closely together, fat and solemn, on another runway. One of them was being unloaded, with its vast rear doors standing open. As the plane approached the Leif Erickson Building a small buggy appeared pulling an empty trailer behind it. Another, loaded up with passengers' luggage, was driving in the opposite direction. The older stewardess's voice came over the PA system: 'Welcome home to Iceland. We have now landed at Keflavík. The weather is fair, cloudy, with a slight breeze. It's a bit cold: the temperature is . . .' The precise details of the temperature were drowned by crackling. She gave the same information in English. The younger stewardess looked at the sick man. He was breathing through his open mouth but his earlier panic had gone. 'Are you feeling any better?'

The man opened his eyes immediately but did not say anything.

The captain was speaking: 'Passengers are requested to stay in their seats until the illuminated signs have been extinguished. Thank you.'

Hördur Gottskálksson stood up. He was tall. His face was sharp-featured and his skin was leathery, like a golfer's who's spent long hours in the open air. His hair was beginning to turn grey, but it was still thick, blond and shoulder-length. His eyes were blue. He was wearing a white suit. He walked towards the front of the plane and looked down at his patient. In his long professional career he had seen a very great deal. His first instinct was to approach a patient with profound suspicion. He jabbed a finger at the man who seemed to be asleep and asked in quite a rough tone of voice, 'And what's the matter with you?'

Startled, the man opened his eyes and looked at Hördur.

'He's a doctor,' said the young stewardess. She was aware of people in the plane craning their necks to see what was happening.

The young man burst into tears but immediately, in Hördur's presence, became quite talkative. His name was Haraldur Sumarlidason. He was returning from Zaire. As everyone knew, it was a while since the Africans had bought any dried fish. Then this horrible illness had broken out. Hadn't the doctor heard about it? Hördur nodded.

'Four hundred dead.' Haraldur Sumarlidason wiped his face with the 'Wash 'n' Wipe' tissue the stewardess handed him.

'Do you have a fever?'

'Last night I had a fever and was talking rubbish.'

'Yes, but you do not have ebola fever, old chap,' the doctor laughed. 'There's no possibility of that. Were you staying in the area where there was the first outbreak of the plague?'

'No. The army surrounded the city and no one was allowed to leave.'

'Well, there you are.' The doctor looked round, pleased with himself.

Haraldur burst out, 'But people were running away. I could have caught it from them.'

Hördur shook his head. The plane eased itself towards the terminal doors and the engines shut down. People were standing up, a few getting down their hand luggage. The captain came out of the cockpit into the cabin. He was middle-aged. He was wearing a white shirt and blue trousers. He looked rather sour. Hördur went to meet him. 'What's wrong?'

'He's got it into his head he's got a dangerous infection, ebola fever,' said Hördur with a faint smile.

'What makes him think that?' The captain scanned the plane suspiciously.

'He's on his way back from Zaire.'

'Did he come into contact with anyone infected?'

'It seems unlikely, in my opinion.'

'But can you be sure?' The captain was in a bad mood. 'We have to observe the very strict rules laid down by the health authorities in cases like this.'

'This man doesn't need to be examined. It's all rubbish.'

'Are you a specialist in viral infections?'

'No, I'm a heart surgeon.'

'Then your special field of expertise is hardly appropriate here,' said the captain with considerable authority. 'Anna,' he said to the older stewardess, 'run to the cockpit and ask Sigthor to tell the passengers to stay in their seats.'

'What are you going to do?'

'Get another doctor, of course! It's the only thing I can do. Get in a specialist. I have to take responsibility.'

A little later a friendly voice came over the PA: 'Passengers are requested to remain in their seats for the time being. Due to factors beyond our control there will be a short delay before disembarkation.' The engines roared and the plane reversed a distance of about thirty yards. The passengers sat down again and a few who had taken their hand luggage out of the overhead lockers put their bags back. The captain returned to the cockpit.

Hördur kept an eye on the patient. The likeliest explanation was that he had caught a cold in London after the hot African climate. He had quickly arrived at a diagnosis for himself. Flu, that was all it was. Flu. Shivering. His temperature would be about 38.5. 'He's simply hysterical,' he thought, 'and as for all this "specialist" rubbish!' He asked, 'Was anyone else at the hotel sick?'

'Yes. The Swedes.'

'What was the matter with them?'

14

'Some of them had flu,' said Haraldur Sumarlidason. He was about to burst into tears again.

Hördur grinned, pleased with himself.

'Talk to me.' Haraldur lifted his hand and beckoned the doctor to bend closer. 'You've got to give someone a message for me.'

'What message? Who for?' Hördur did not sound at all friendly.

'Gudjón Sigtryggsson.'

'And who might Gudjón Sigtryggsson be?'

'He's a company director. The address is 16 Silkibakki. Just go and ring the bell.'

'And say what?'

'Tell him there are certain people . . . bend down so I can whisper in your ear . . . Tell him there are certain people – he knows who they are – who want to sell their United shares for next to nothing . . . peanuts . . . just to get out . . . They won't be bossed about any more . . . He can pick up a controlling interest in a company worth 2 billion for chickenfeed. Greet him from Halli Sumarlida . . . with gratitude for . . .' The expression on Haraldur Sumarlidason's face indicated the imminent approach of death. 'He knows what for.'

'United what?'

'United Fisheries.' The invalid seemed surprised by the question.

'Of course I'll be your messenger boy,' mocked Hördur. 'Don't you worry. It won't be long before a *proper* doctor'll come and see you.'

The doctor walked to the back of the plane and sat down. He did not realize the implications of what he had just been told. He was not really taking it seriously. If he had, he might well have told me, if we had done the interview later in the day as arranged. I would immediately have realized what was going on and that this was explosive front-page stuff. How I found out about it is my little secret. I don't name my sources – any more than I did when I still worked on the magazine.

'What's the problem?' asked a man on the other side of the aisle.

'Nothing much. The usual Icelandic rubbish.'

'It's what you get the moment you set foot on *terra firma*,' said the man morosely. 'There's never a moment's relief from stupidity in this country. And Icelandic stupidity's the worst in the world!

When it comes down to it, it's probably the only thing we're really good at.'

'You're absolutely right, my friend,' said the doctor, in complete agreement.

'Well, you're little rays of sunshine, I must say,' said a jolly voice from a couple of seats in front of them.

'No, we're just being realistic. Take me, for instance. I make furniture. I'd be the first to say I'm dimmer than the average Icelander.' The carpenter grabbed the back of a seat in his earnestness and stuck his head out into the aisle to see whom he was addressing. 'I ordered some veneers from overseas and started making rococo furniture with just one aim: to bring hard currency into the country and to keep myself in work. But guess what?' he exclaimed. 'People turned their noses up at it because it wasn't imported – even though it was much better quality than the stuff that gets brought into the country. No, Icelandic stupidity and narrow-mindedness take some beating.' The carpenter sat back in his seat and looked at Hördur. 'There are people in Iceland who could do unbelievable things in their chosen professions, unbelievable things. But they're just not allowed to.'

The surgeon nodded.

'It seems to me that the only firms showing any common sense these days are the ones with women at the helm. Women are setting up their own small businesses all over the place. Women are much more reliable in business than men.'

'And now they're taking over politics as well,' said a voice from the front.

The carpenter pulled himself up again, had a look and raised his voice. 'That's what I'm saying! Did you see the Independent Party is putting up a woman in the election? An experienced business-woman. Theódóra of Heidnaberg. Now she's personally worth more than 2 billion. Everyone's convinced it'll be a good year for the party. In my opinion she should be given an important government job straightaway if they get in. In my opinion, that is.'

'I don't see it myself,' said Hördur, frowning. 'Theódóra! She's a hard-nosed cow. She can't see anybody's point of view except her own. I just hope, for the sake of the country as a whole, that she doesn't get elected.'

'Come off it, don't be like that,' said the man at the front. 'You've got to let the women have a go these days, in just about everything.'

'Listen to the man,' the carpenter said to Hördur. 'There's a died-in-the-wool Independent Party member for you! Theódóra'll soon have the economy sorted out. The present lot are spending money right, left and centre, like it's going out of fashion.' The carpenter looked at Hördur and a malevolent gleam could be detected in his eye. 'You can bet on it. Thousands'll vote for the party tomorrow for that one reason, and not only the women. I bet they'll get that eleventh seat. I'd stake my factory on it.'

'You do that, my friend, gamble it away,' muttered Hördur. He had lost all respect for his fellow passenger. He fumbled in the seat pocket in front of him for the 'Wash 'n' Wipe' tissue he had saved from the lunch tray. He ripped open the sachet, spread out the tissue and put it up to his face. The dampness gave a momentary relief. 'Two billion,' he thought, suddenly feeling very weary. An amount like that could make quite a difference. With that sort of money, a man like me, in my sixties, well, I could give up the night locum work and stop having to write out prescriptions for junkies. He lifted the 'Wash 'n' Wipe' from his face. Some of the signs were flashing. The stewardesses were scurrying to and fro. Many of the passengers had become impatient. Most felt uncomfortably hot and the delay was irritating them. 'Do you think they'll hold the Reykjavík bus for us?' a woman asked.

The drunk with the plastic glass was demanding more whisky. The older stewardess was getting cross.

The door next to the cockpit opened letting fresh air into the cabin. The carpenter loosened his tie. Hördur walked to the front of the plane and glanced at the invalid out of the corner of his eye. He looked much the same. The man was half asleep and his breath was coming in shallow gasps. Steps were pushed up towards the door. The ice-cold wind blew sleet across the asphalt. A young man bounded up the steps. He waited at the top as they were pushed into place and then he strode aboard. An older man was immediately behind him, with a nurse on his heels. The captain and the co-pilot came out of the cockpit.

'Hördur Gottskalksson, a professional colleague of yours.' The surgeon held out his hand.

'How do you do?' The young doctor had an unusually long face and wore his hair in a crew cut. 'Finnbogi Sigurdsson. Strange meeting you like this!'

'Yes. I've just got back from London.' Hördur could not recall having met the man before but assumed the chap knew all about him from the dispute at the National Hospital. He had become famous among doctors. He remembered a headline from *Today*: 'Dismissed from Cardiac Surgery. "I'll see you in court," says heart doctor.' 'Are viral infections your speciality?' he asked, drily.

'I wouldn't go as far as to say that. How's the patient?' the young doctor asked quietly.

'He reckons he's got ebola fever.'

'He's imagining things.' The young doctor spoke slowly and raised his eyebrows. He glanced at Haraldur Sumarlidason. 'Where's he come from?'

'Zaire, he says.'

'From the infected areas?'

'I don't think so. Some damn Swede at the same hotel had flu.'

The stewardess was attending to the invalid. She dabbed at his face with a 'Wash 'n' Wipe'. His eyes were wide open.

'Are you feeling very poorly?' asked the doctor.

'A while back I thought I was dying,' said Haraldur. He was clearly a lot more relaxed. He looked at the faces of the people gazing down at him.

'I'd better check you over.' The doctor put his bag on to the seat and took out a small torch and a spatula. 'Let me look at your tongue.'

The patient stuck out his tongue. It was large and furred, a witness to his not having been sparing with alcohol on his travels. The doctor placed his spatula on it.

'Now let me see your eyes.'

Haraldur leaned his head back on the headrest and opened his eyes as wide as he could.

'I think', said the doctor as he pulled down the patient's lower lid and shone light into the iris, 'that if there was something seriously wrong the symptoms would be quite different and much more devastating. An illness like that is usually accompanied by a high temperature, vomiting, diarrhoea and loss of balance. He put the little torch away in his bag and laid a hand on the invalid's forehead. 'I think you are running a bit of a temperature, though.'

'He thinks I've got the flu, that's what he thinks.' The invalid pointed at Hördur.

'He's been around a long time and he ought to know.'

'You're perfectly OK, just like I said,' said the younger stewardess, relieved. The captain sighed heavily and returned to the cockpit.

'Shouldn't we take him with us back to Keflavík and give him a thorough examination?' asked the nurse and the orderly nodded.

'I don't think that'll be necessary.' The patient sat up. 'I started thinking about the plague as we were approaching Iceland. One thing led to another and in the end I convinced myself I was going to die. I've never heard of a more horrendous illness.' He took a copy of *Time* out of the seat pocket and showed them the photograph of a sick man on the cover. He looked at them all rather sheepishly. Some colour had returned to his large, pale cheeks. 'I think I'm almost all right now,' he said.

Hördur walked off the plane and into the Duty Free shop. He bought some sweets for his daughter's son, cosmetics for Vilhelmína and a bottle of whisky for himself. The ebola patient was piling his basket high with sweets and alcohol. His face looked completely normal but as he was wearing a heavy black overcoat and a snow-white shirt, he still gave the impression of being rather pale. His fiery-red eyebrows exaggerated this effect. He was a tall man, enormously fat, and he took small mincing steps. He stayed close to Hördur. When the doctor met his eye, Haraldur seized the opportunity and spoke to him. 'Please don't tell a soul what I said about the United Fisheries shares. If it got out I'd be strung up.'

'I wouldn't want anything bad to happen to you,' mocked the doctor.

Haraldur Sumarlidason carried on putting things into his basket.

Hördur was about to reach for a bottle of White Horse on a shelf at eye level. Then he noticed that it bore the label of the Icelandic importer: Heidnaberg. 'Damn me if I'll line Seli's and

Theódóra's pockets any more,' he thought and he took down a bottle of twelve-year Chivas Regal instead.

Hördur had expected his son Trausti or his daughter Ester to meet him, but when he emerged from the terminal building with his bags, the white Chrysler was nowhere to be seen.

There was no one waiting for him when he got off the airport bus and walked into the foyer at the Icelandair Hotel. He glanced at the clock on the wall. It was well after three o'clock and he reset his watch to Icelandic time. He picked up his bag and and left the hotel. A taxi-driver put his bag into the boot and Hördur sat in the back seat holding the plastic Duty Free bag. He lived only a little way from the hotel and it annoyed him to have to take a taxi. He leaned forward as the house came into view.

The house where Hördur lived was divided into three flats. It dated from around 1960, was built in stone and painted white. The green roof with its tilted gable end looked slightly Chinese. A large veranda gave on to the street. The reception rooms were large and light and the rooms at the back were small and neat. The door frames were of an expensive inlaid hardwood. He was profoundly proud of his flat. It had once been the property of a wealthy restaurateur who had spent a lot of money on it. Nevertheless Vilhelmína had been pestering him for years to buy a house. Her older sister, Theódóra, owned one of the most beautiful buildings in Reykjavík, the house that had once belonged to their parents.

Hördur looked up at the veranda. No one was standing at the window. His car was not in its usual place. He swore to himself. There were buds on many of the trees in the garden, despite the cold.

Hördur walked up the steps and pressed the entryphone. No one answered. He put his bag down and fumbled in his pockets. He didn't have his keys with him. He walked round to the garden. His daughter Ester had a room in the basement flat with her three-year-old son. Four months ago she had walked out of her secretarial job with the family firm. She claimed she had been sexually harassed by Vilhjálmur, the managing director. The wretched man, who had worked his way up from being an errand boy, swore his innocence. Her father suspected she was simply too lazy to hold down a job.

The doctor tapped on the window. There was no one in. It must have been Ester who had taken the car. He'd have to ask the neighbours to let him in. He walked down the steps to the basement and found the door was unlocked. He walked through the dimly lit basement and up into the main house. He opened the front door and picked up his bag. Up on the third floor landing a flower pot stood on the windowsill and he kept a key to the flat hidden under it. He lifted the flower pot with both hands. The key was there. He opened the door and, although he knew there was no one home, he called out, 'Hello, everyone', and walked through to the kitchen. There were newspapers on the table and a plate of dried-up corn-flakes. He picked up one of the newspapers, glanced at the back page and read, 'Next Saturday, 28 May 1994, Iceland holds its parliamentary election.' He threw the paper down and looked out of the kitchen window. The man next door caught his eye. His neighbour was tidying up the garden. Hördur liked watching the man. He had been watching him for years, although they did not know each other. His neighbour had three daughters and it would seem that they all bullied him mercilessly. Hördur felt a strong sympathetic bond with this man and often cited him in the middle of family arguments. 'Yes,' he'd say on these occasions. 'I know you want to treat me just like those girls over the way treat their poor father. They say his heart's giving up with the strain. I was standing in the queue at the shop behind him the other day. He was buying a single cigar, whispering to the girl behind the counter and his eyes were just like a beaten dog's. He stood all hunched up in the rain behind the shop to smoke it.'

The doctor went into the sitting room and put the Duty Free bag down on the table. He unpacked the treats. He hung up his over-coat and sat by the phone table in the corridor. He wanted to phone to find out about his car but he didn't know who to ring. The phone rang. A man was asking anxiously about Ester.

'She's not at home,' her father said, ' but I'm thinking of hiring a secretary to deal with you lot. If you do see her, you might ask her to bring my car back.'

He had hardly put the phone down before it rang again. The Reykjavík night locum service needed a doctor for the evening shift. The chap who was meant to be doing it was suddenly unavailable and the secretary was doing all she could to find a replacement. Hördur explained he had only just walked through the door after a trip overseas. 'I was working in darkest Africa. Ring me back if you can't find anyone else. I'll see if I can do it then.'

At that moment he heard a key turn in the lock. It was Vilhelmína. He could tell at once that she'd been drinking.

'I'll be . . . home already!' Vilhelmína stared at him.

'Yes, Villa, and I can't say the welcome's up to much.'

'But . . . I thought you were due back yesterday.' She walked into the corridor, thin and upright, casually fingering her shoulder-length red hair and arching her neck – all to make it seem as if she wasn't drunk. He would have preferred it if she had just let herself go. 'I rang the airline. There were no planes from Copenhagen today.' She came close to him and put her hand on his shoulder. 'I needed to talk to you, Höddi. It's Mother, she's passed away. She died last night.'

'I got a connecting flight in London,' he said. He did not stand up nor did he show any sign of having taken in her news. 'Would you like a drink, Villa? And, please, for God's sake, don't call me "Höddi". I wouldn't give a dog a name like that.'

'Why should I want a drink? Why now?' She took two steps backwards and looked at him in amazement. 'Didn't you hear what I just said? My mother's dead.'

'Don't get upset. I can see you're drunk.' He said nothing about her news but he flushed as red as a beetroot and there was a twinkle in his eye.

'That's rubbish. A few of us girls met for lunch and we had a glass or two of red wine. That's all. I can't understand them, they're going to vote for the Women's Party.'

'And who are you going to vote for?'

'The correct way, of course. I shall vote for the Independent Party and for my sister Tedda. I'm surprised you need to ask. Not everybody has a sister who stands head and shoulders above everyone else and gets herself elected to Parliament. It's almost certain she'll be part of the next government. What do you say to that?' Vilhelmína glared triumphantly at her husband, her watery blue eyes shining.

22

'"Head and shoulders above everyone else",' said the doctor, scornfully. 'They've got money, that's all.'

'They've worked hard and deserve everything they've got,' said Vilhelmína haughtily.

'"Worked hard"!' Hördur snorted. 'And aren't you pleased your mother's dead? You should be happy the poor woman'll have some peace at last. And what's all this "worked hard" rubbish?' He sounded almost friendly. 'Axel and Theódóra took over the company when your mother was too old and sick to run it. They've kept the whole thing to themselves, all the time I was studying and we were overseas. They've never let you see so much as a farthing of your parents' money. Tedda's only Ingibjörg's stepdaughter, in any case. Isn't the house on Dyngjuvegur half yours by rights? Why do you stand up for them? Isn't Heidnaberg, one of the biggest companies in Iceland, half yours? If you had a fraction of the money that's owed to you, we could get that dream house of yours and stop living from hand to mouth like this.' He stood up.

'That's rubbish!' She tore off her coat and threw it on the sofa. 'Tedda gave me money towards the deposit on this flat.'

He shook his head with well-intentioned kindness. 'No. The time's come to get things straight. These are substantial assets and they're your assets, our assets, Vilhelmína! And the children's, of course. You'll get your house; Trausti and Ester will be able to buy their own flats. Our home life will be a lot happier. I can move my surgery from the old town centre out to the new suburbs and all our problems will be at an end. Your share should be something like a hundred million kroner, maybe more, who knows?'

'I've no idea.' She looked uncomfortable. 'I really don't want to discuss it so soon after my mother's death. It just doesn't seem right somehow.'

'You let me sort out Theódóra. Where's the car?'

'I don't know. I think Ester's got it. Did you offer me a drink?'

He went into the sitting room and took a crystal glass from the cabinet. He took a bottle of whisky from the Duty Free bag and poured her a drink. 'Be my guest. I regret now not getting the bottle with "Heidnaberg" on the label.' He grinned. 'How was I to know I'd be paying myself?'

'What are you on about?' She took the glass, sipped the whisky and tossed her head. She was more drunk than he had realized.

'You've really been pouring it down your throats, you girls, haven't you!' He was getting angry now. 'You're really out of it, aren't you? If I have a cognac with my coffee, it's a binge; when you get plastered, it's women's rights.'

'What? What are you on about? I'm not drunk! A woman shouldn't be spoken to in that tone of voice.' Vilhelmína went into the kitchen with her head held high. 'Never, ever, did I see my father treat my mother like that!'

'Well, no, you wouldn't. All he did was keep his mistress in the same house for years and years while he was still married to your mother.'

'I'm not listening to this, Hördur,' she said. 'The fact of the matter is that my father was a much better, more distinguished and altogether more remarkable doctor than you'll ever be!'

He followed her into the kitchen. She raised her glass but it never reached her lips. He took two strides towards her and knocked it out of her hand. He aimed to send the glass and its contents into the sink. That's where the glass ended up but most of the liquid soaked the right sleeve of his jacket. 'You bloody idiot!' he shouted. 'Can't you even stay sober when I'm expected back from overseas?'

'Well, that'd mean being teetotal, you're away so much,' she said, smoothing her dress to wipe away liquid that wasn't there; she'd escaped the shower of whisky. 'You know I can't bear it when you threaten me like that.'

He laughed. 'I've never hit you, not once, even though there have been times when you deserved it.'

'Does a women ever deserve to be treated with violence? Do I deserve it, the day after my mother's died?'

'The way you talk, anyone'd think I'd been beating you year in and year out. Both of us know I've never laid a finger on you. The day that happens, neither of us is going to forget it. And if you keep going on about your father like that, it'll happen, you mark my words.'

She leaned against the kitchen table and looked at him scornfully. 'The only reason you blow your top like that is not because you're a better or a worse doctor than my father. It's simply that you can't bear being reminded that the money for this flat' – she waved her hand – 'and the money for us to live overseas, that it all came from my family.'

'I'm not listening to this rubbish.'

'And where's your surgery, Hördur? Eh? It's in my parents' old house on Skólabrú. A prime town-centre site. What have you got to complain about?'

'If you want me to pack my things and clear out of there, I can be gone tonight.'

Her voice changed. 'No, don't go getting upset, darling. You'll have to change your clothes, Hördur. You stink of alcohol.'

'I'll be damned if I'll let you organize my wardrobe for me!' he snapped and went in to the guest bathroom off the corridor. He dampened a towel and rubbed at his sleeve to get rid of the whisky. It had soaked through to his skin. He squeezed the towel, dampened it again and rubbed harder at his sleeve, sniffing it. The jacket stank of whisky. The phone rang. He glanced at his watch. It was ten past five. He could hear Vilhelmína using her 'serious' voice: 'Yes, just a moment. The doctor is in. I'll go and get him.'

'I'm just coming. Ask her to wait a moment,' called Hördur.

She had put down the receiver when he came out into the corridor. 'She asked me to tell you the doctor's car's on its way. There are eight calls already. How come you agreed to do a shift now? You've only just got back. Aren't you worn out?'

'There wasn't anybody else,' he mumbled. 'They've got problems.' He put his jacket back on, picked up his overcoat from the back of the chair, fetched his doctor's bag from his study and shut the front door behind him without saying goodbye and ran swiftly down the stairs.

2

Axel Sigurgeirsson, Chairman of Heidnaberg, felt his heart give an extra beat. All it took was the steps from the garden path to the pavement. He stopped still, took a deep breath, looked at his car, unable to make up his mind, and took his own pulse with one eye on his watch. Seventy-nine.

Tumi, the family doctor, had instructed him to walk to work. 'That way your posture will improve and you'll get rid of that paunch. The ladies will fancy you again, Seli, old chap.' 'Tumi hit the nail on the head,' Axel thought, solemnly. He gently pressed his thumbs and index fingers together in the way he'd seen walkers do, and marched smartly off down Dyngjuvegur.

At the corner of Langholtsvegur Axel met a girl and started thinking about women in general. He was as excited as a child that his wife had got on the list of candidates for the Independent Party. Her position had been described as 'iconic', particularly as she was standing for the seat that would decide the election. She stood no chance of getting in and she had already decided to turn her back on politics anyway. 'It wouldn't come as much of a surprise to me if Tedda were to be elected president one day,' Axel thought. He fantasized about the groaning board at Bessastadir, the roast game, the bowls of fruit, the distinguished foreign guests. He swallowed and shook his head fondly as he thought about Tumi the doctor, who kept himself slim and dyed his hair and was always eyeing up the girls. Tumi had even gone so far as to read a book on body language so he could work out whether a girl fancied him or not. If their hips sway slightly when you're talking to them, then they like the look of you. And if they blush! Well, your luck's in and they want to jump into bed with you! 'You're too old for all this, Tumi, old chap,' Axel had said. They were sitting one on each side of the desk in the doctor's surgery. Tumi was taking his friend's blood pressure. It was high, far too high.

Axel was aware of his heartbeat as he walked. It was even and natural. Perhaps a little too quick. He hadn't been able to resist a slice of cake and a glass of ice-cold milk before he left home. He was pleased to think the Heidnaberg complex would soon appear ahead of him on the other side of the bay. There was a lot of construction work at the northern end. The company had grown so quickly there were times when he found himself wishing it was still on the old town-centre site. 'In Iceland it's much more fun when a company's just starting up than when everyone's pretending they're on Wall Street and trying to get inside knowledge about share values,' he thought. 'And I'm so ham-fisted with computers. I touch a key and everything disappears from the screen or it freezes or it asks you a stupid question. In the old days you could simply walk over to the filing cabinet and find out anything you wanted to know. But these days a hundred million kroner could be wiped off the value of the company and I wouldn't be any the wiser,' Axel thought, irritated. 'And courtesy's a thing of the past, in society and in business. My colleagues in the Chamber of Commerce are like birds of prey sharpening their talons on each other. If they got wind of my heart condition, they'd be firing off letters to Toyota and Saltykov before you could say knife. It's lucky Tedda can help a bit with the running of Heidnaberg. It's getting too much for me.' He stood still a moment and listened to the beating of his heart.

Four months earlier he had hired a secretary to take some of the pressure off him and since then had been more or less free of this tedious symptom of the extra heartbeat. He was pleased to be shot of Ester, who was not very efficient. He had trusted his intuition when making the appointment and he had been lucky. Dagný was on top of the job in no time at all.

Axel felt his pulse. He had developed the habit of feeling his pulse when he was thinking. It got on the nerves of his nearest and dearest, so he tried to avoid doing it much at home. At work no one noticed him do it. Recently Theódóra had taken to looking irritated whenever he mentioned Dagný. Surely she didn't think he fancied the girl. Tedda couldn't be that stupid.

Even so he decided to observe his assistant's body language when he arrived at the office. It couldn't do any harm. You might as well know where you stood.

He took a shortcut through the Súdarvogur industrial estate. The grassy bank stretched along by the sea as far as the old bridge over the river Ellidaár. It was a good place for a stroll. There was the smell of seaweed from the shore. Spring was here and the grass was shooting up. The grass and the dandelions and buttercups trembled in the gentle breeze. He slowed down and bent awkwardly to pick a buttercup and smell it. He took large strides down the steep bank. He felt the strain on the muscles of his thighs and his heart speeding up. He stopped on the bridge, panting proudly, and checked his physical condition. No extra heartbeats! He looked contentedly around. A duck was flying in from the shore. As it flew under the bridge its wings seemed to whisper. Axel turned to watch the bird follow the course of the river and disappear in the distance. Cars zipped all around him. It made good sense not to stuff oneself with sausages, potatoes and white sauce. Much better to eat one's greens and get rid of the paunch. But devil take it if I'm going to start chasing after young girls. Tumi is talking rubbish. Axel looked at the company buildings, with the Toyota flag flapping in the breeze. The windows were full of blue banners bearing the letters XD in white. On the right was his wife's face, on the left an identical study of the Prime Minister. Axel took a moment to enjoy surveying his kingdom. Whatever anyone said, the business world was a game for gentlemen.

When Axel entered the showroom, Vilhjálmur was nowhere to be seen. There were used cars everywhere, in the showroom itself and out on the forecourt. They'd do better to shift all this junk at a car auction. He bounded up the stairs and through the offices, nodding happily to the staff, and headed for his office – the office Theódóra commandeered when she came and worked at Heidnaberg, sorting everything and everybody out. Outside the door to his office Dagný sat at her computer. 'How are we today, Dagný?' asked Axel as he walked into his office. 'Any messages?'

'Your wife rang. She's just left the house.'

Axel hung up his overcoat by the door. 'Do you know what about?'

'Something to do with the election.'

'Any sales so far today?'

'Yes. Just the one car.'

On his desk there were some papers awaiting his signature. His heart gave an extra beat. Surprised, Axel rubbed his chest. What was making him feel anxious? He was considering taking over another company. But why the tension? He was used to handling things like this, or so he thought. Was it the imminent meeting with his daughter that was bothering him? Or was it the portraits on the ground floor of the two people most dear to him in all the world that was causing it? Probably.

He sat down, put a finger to his wrist and counted the beats with his eye on the clock that had been presented to him by one of the Toyota directors. It showed nearly midday. The clock's mechanism was visible under a glass dome. Axel had sent the Toyota director a barrel of herring by way of a return gift. Everyone knew how crazy the Japanese were about fish. They wanted it raw. He could imagine the Toyota chairman swallowing a herring whole straight off the fishing boats, head, tail, guts and all. He grimaced at the thought.

Dagný brought the post in for him.

'Have you got a minute, Dagný?' Axel stood up straight, took a deep breath, gripped the sleeves of his jacket, puffed out his chest and waited for some physical response from the woman. She did not budge an inch. He gave it up as a bad job and walked over to the drinks shelf and took down a bottle of brandy. He studied it closely while his secretary watched him and then he replaced it on the shelf. 'Have you ever had this brandy?' Axel inclined his head towards the shelf, folded his arms across his chest and stood with his feet a little apart. He waited anxiously. Would the woman sway her hips sensually? Blush, even? He looked at her, pleased with what he saw. She had quite large breasts, but a very slender waist. He had not believed that such women existed outside the pages of the kind of magazines he did not have the courage to buy but occasionally tried to flick through surreptitiously in newsagents. What a bird! No, nobody called attractive women 'birds' any more. He leaned towards the shelf and looked at her, almost imploringly.

Dagný walked over to him, read the label on the bottle, and then stood up straight without paying the slightest attention to the body language of the company chairman. 'This brandy? No. Why?'

Axel ran his fingers through his hair, hoping desperately that she would follow suit. She ignored it. She didn't move her feet slightly apart, blush, or run her fingers through her hair.

'I don't do anything for her,' he thought and felt hurt. 'Still, what's it matter, I wasn't going to do anything about it anyway.' 'The distillery was wanting us to handle it for them.' Axel reached for the bottle and gave it to her, 'Do take it home and let me know what you think. Would you ask callers to ring back after lunch, please. I've an important decision to make on that bloody pots and pans outfit.'

He sat down and pushed his post to one side. She left the room and closed the door behind her, having thanked him for his gift.

In the middle of May he had been approached with a view to a friendly takeover of IceTeflo, a small factory in Ólafsfjördur with cash-flow difficulties. He had said he would make a decision as soon as the elections were over. He flicked through the papers. IceTeflo manufactured kitchenware and had a substantial overseas market share. Sales were good and future prospects looked even more promising, he was convinced of it. The company's losses could be set against Heidnaberg profits. But he still found it difficult to come to a decision. What did he know about pots and pans? It would be best to let Tedda take a look at it. He pushed the papers away and yawned.

Half the office wall was glass and he could see into the outer office. The venetian blind was up. He glanced across at Dagný's profile. She was staring blankly at her desk.

He meant to press the intercom and ask her to get hold of Tumi, the doctor, but she moved her head suddenly as if she was listening to someone beside her. Curious, Axel moved to one side. There was a man in a blue anorak standing at the corner of Dagný's desk. He was waving his arms about and seemed very agitated. He was fair-haired, rather good-looking, with a cleft in his chin. Dagný did not seem to be paying him much attention. She was typing at her computer keyboard. 'Best not to disturb her. The customer comes first,' thought Axel sleepily. 'The customer always comes first.' He leaned back in his chair and felt even more sleepy. It was too bright in his office. The sun was shining in the window. He couldn't be bothered to go and draw the blind.

Suddenly her distorted voice came over the intercom. 'Vilhjálmur's on the phone.'

'Villi's always got some problem or other,' muttered Axel, irritated. Vilhjálmur was no exception to the rule that employees were given freedom to work in their own way, but recently he had taken to demanding confidential meetings with Axel. Usually to discuss matters of the utmost banality. The young man was obsessed with the company, desperate to become chairman and there were times when Axel considered calling it a day and handing over the reins to him. He was tired of running the company and longed for a quieter life. 'Yes, what is it?'

'I have to talk to you. It's urgent.'

'Oh well, pop into the office.'

Axel swung his chair round and stood up. He looked into the outer office. The fair-haired man was still standing by Dagný's desk, staring at her. Axel opened the window, sat down and turned on his computer. This time he was going to show it who's boss! He prodded a few keys and was amazed and delighted to find himself at the system interface. He beamed with satisfaction as various icons appeared on the screen. Eventually the computer asked if there were any other applications running apart from Windows.

With no hesitation, Axel pressed the 'N' key. Now he was inside Heidnaberg's brain. He decided to go no further before Vilhjálmur arrived. He suspected Dagný of being a bit sweet on Vilhjálmur. It was only natural, he was an extremely handsome man. It was strange, this antipathy Ester had developed towards Vilhjálmur. But then Dagný . . . Come to think of it, he could distinctly remember her swaying her hips when Vilhjálmur talked to her. She might even have blushed. There had been sixteen applicants for the job. He had interviewed five, of which the front-runner was an A-grade student from the Commercial College. He always favoured students from his old school, but there was something in Dagný's face that appealed to him the moment he saw her. She seemed so independent and smart. She was the oldest applicant, a graduate of the theatre school with considerable experience of office work. He asked her about her last position. He knew the company. 'And why did you leave?'

'I got involved with a man and had my children.'

'And who is your husband?'

'We're divorced,' she said quickly. 'He lives overseas.'

'Why aren't you acting at the National Theatre or the City Playhouse instead of applying for a job like this?'

'I never get the parts,' she said, embarrassed. 'The competition's very tough.'

'Would it be all right if I phone you tomorrow or the day after? I've got a lot of people to see. It's going to be a difficult decision. The city's full of girls applying for this job.'

'Yes, and the ones without children are always at the top of the list,' she said with some bitterness.

Whenever Axel of Heidnaberg made up his mind about something he did it quickly and was guided more by intuition than reason. Dagný started work the next day and was quickly on top of the job. He did not have to worry about her at all. It was as if whatever task he gave her seemed to be accomplished without him noticing. 'A good work force, it's a gift from God,' he said to Theódóra one evening. 'I never have to tell that girl anything more than once. It almost makes me believe that saying you have, about God taking a hand in the affairs of us mere mortals, no matter how small they may be. My heart condition's certainly on the mend.'

Theódóra had been embarrassed by this.

He drummed his fingers on the desk a few times, fidgeted in his chair and looked out of the window. The man in the outer office stood stock still and stared at the woman. It was as if they were in different rooms, although there was no wall between them. Axel stood up and went to the door. Dagný usually looked up as he opened the door to his office, but not this time. There was something strange going on. Axel looked the man up and down. 'Good morning. Can I help you at all?'

The man looked at him, surprised. And without so much as a shake of the head to indicate he had heard the question, he turned on his heel and walked out. Axel watched him go. There were very few people at work in the office. 'Who's he when he's at home?'

'My ex-husband.'

'I thought he was overseas.'

'He's come back.'

'And does he have a name?'

'Tryggvi.'

Axel looked at Dagný's profile. She did not look too happy about the reunion. He had thought an actress would be better able to hide her feelings. Axel walked across to the window. He had half expected Tryggvi to be standing on the pavement staring up at the window, but there was no one there.

Vilhjálmur arrived a little later and apologized for the delay. A customer had just turned up unexpectedly. The car sales were improving now that spring had arrived. Vilhjálmur sat down.

'What do you want this time? I'm terribly busy, Villi.'

'I just got a whiff of a potential killing.'

'And what killing's this, old chap?' Axel was suspicious and looked closely at Villi.

Vilhjálmur looked round, got up and closed the door, sat down again and said, *sotto voce*, 'I've just heard from a reliable source that some United Fisheries shares, a controlling interest, may be coming on the market. And it's nothing to do with Hannes's people.' Vilhjálmur leaned back in his chair and looked at his chairman to see how he was taking the news.

'Where did you get this from?' said Axel, blinking nervously.

'Whoever gets their hands on those shares will hold the balance of power, they could line up with either faction on the board and control the company,' said Vilhjálmur excitedly.

Axel didn't say anything.

'Shall we go for it?'

Axel of Heidnaberg looked in amazement at his employee. 'You can't be serious. Do you expect me to commit professional suicide? I wouldn't touch anything like that with a barge pole. Everyone involved is a personal friend of mine. Hannes is a key shareholder. Do you imagine our Prime Minister would take kindly to being undermined like that? Do you think that's the way to treat power-ful people? It's insane.' Axel smiled. 'Don't even think about it, Villi. Are you really serious about this? Are you out of your mind? I'd rather give Heidnaberg to charity. The world of business is a gentleman's world.'

'Well, I'm a salesman through and through and it's difficult to let a deal this sweet slip through your fingers.' Vilhjálmur rubbed his hands.

'We're not touching it,' said Axel, now anxious. 'People mean more to me than profit. We're doing just fine as it is.'

'"We"!' Vilhjálmur laughed. 'I'm only on a monthly salary, like everybody else. If I was sitting on a few million I'd go for it.'

'It's asking for trouble,' Axel insisted. 'Just forget all about it and don't say anything to anybody. What do you think the people in the Independent Party would say if they heard about it?'

'They'll ditch Theódóra, I'm sure of it,' said Vilhjálmur, sulkily.

'Ditch her?'

Vilhjálmur looked at Axel kindly. 'Don't you read the papers? They say they'll ditch her when they form a government. That's if the Independent Party gets to form the government, and that's a foregone conclusion.'

'That's rubbish! They won't get enough candidates elected in Reykjavík. It's not going to happen.' Axel slammed his hand down on the keyboard and a dinosaur trotted across the screen. 'They were simply paying her an enormous compliment when they invited her to stand in that seat. No one expects her to actually win that far down the list. She plans to get out of politics after this. Look!' He pointed at the dinosaur. 'There's that blasted animal again.'

Vilhjálmur slowly shook his head, with great patience. 'Seli,' he said, 'if only you got up a bit earlier you'd know what was happening around town. She stands every chance of getting in. The last Gallup poll showed the party in a surprisingly good position. Much better than anyone expected: between 46 and 48 per cent. People are talking about a landslide tomorrow. More than 50 per cent! And we've got her to thank for it. People can see she's taking a risk and it's going down enormously well with women. They've been fed up with the Women's Party for a long time now. And that's leaving aside how highly regarded she is by the women in the Independent Party and people all over the country. They see her risking everything and they admire her for it. If the Gallup poll's anything to go by, she could well be offered a ministry. They wouldn't have any choice! There's a tide in the affairs of men, Seli,' he said with excitement. 'Just take my word for it. Winds of change and all that!'

Axel's heart gave an extra beat. Tedda in the government! 'For the love of God, don't say this to anyone. There's no way they can get eleven candidates elected. And don't say anything to Tedda about these shares. Please, Villi, for my sake. Look,' he said, pointing to the screen, 'it's stuck.'

Vilhjálmur went over to the desk. His fingers moved quickly over the keyboard and the computer responded at once. The sales department was paging him: 'Message for Vilhjálmur Kalmannson; please go to sales immediately.' He hurried out of the office, leaving the door open behind him.

When Axel looked into the outer office, the fair-haired man was back again, staring at Dagný. Axel stood up and went to the door. 'Can I help you?'

Tryggvi looked at him and their eyes met. This time Tryggvi did not turn on his heel, but stared at him without saying anything.

'I'm sorry, my friend, but you'll have to leave. If you don't go, I shall have to call the police.'

Tryggvi looked to the heavens, as if this was some kind of joke. He looked at his wife to see if she too was finding it funny that this strange man should be meddling in their affairs. Dagný stopped work, rested her elbows on the desk and put her face in her hands.

'Dagný, please be good enough to tell this man he can't hang about here. This is a place of work.'

'I'm thinking about getting a new car,' said Tryggvi forcefully. 'I was under the impression you sold cars here.'

'You can get all the information you need down in the sales department,' said Dagný wearily.

'I'd rather get it here,' said Tryggvi, menacingly.

'Right,' Axel said. 'We can't have this. I'm going to phone the police.' He walked quickly into his office and pulled open the top drawer of his desk. To his surprise the phone book wasn't there. Dagný dealt with all his calls. He felt murderous. There was a fire extinguisher in the corner by a filing cabinet and he grabbed it, intending to hit the man with it, but when he went back into the outer office Tryggvi had gone. The clock showed five to twelve. Everyone had gone for lunch and there was no one to see what was happening. 'When Theódóra's here,' he thought, 'everyone stops at twelve o'clock and is then back at their desk on the dot of one.' 'What kind of bastard is this?' he said. He was panting and did not want the girl to see how short of breath he was. She was white as a sheet. He went to the rest room and brought her some cold water. Just as she was drinking it the sun broke through the clouds. In the sudden brightness his eye was caught by a crucifix hanging from a chain around her neck. Dagný had freckles on her neck and across her throat.

'I don't know what to do.' She lowered the glass. There was a tiny drop of water in the corner of her mouth. 'I don't get a moment's peace. I'm terrified he'll harm our little daughter.' The colour was returning to Dagný's face.

'Can you go to the police?'

'Go to the police?' She laughed. 'Don't be ridiculous!'

Axel felt hurt. She had never spoken to him like that before.

'I've been to people all over the city. I've seen the Chief Physician, the Chief of Police, the Ombudsman, Social Services, but everywhere I turn it's just hopeless. No one will help me.'

Axel went back into his office without saying anything and sat down. He looked at the screen and was puzzled to find the dinosaur wandering gracefully to and fro. 'I've got enough to deal with without this,' he thought. 'I can't cope with this. I wish Tedda were here.' He always turned to his wife in times of trouble and she sometimes looked to the New Testament for guidance. 'What would Christ do in my position?' wondered Axel. The man always seemed to know what to do, how to handle things, and he was never at a loss for the right word. But nothing occurred to Axel. After a while it came to him: Christ would have driven the evil spirit out of the man. 'That would have been worth seeing,' thought Axel of Heidnaberg and suddenly felt very hungry.

The majority of Heidnaberg's work force went home for lunch or made do with a yoghurt in the rest room. Axel despised such food. He was given to calling it 'Viking curd thinned with whey'. He had an agreement with Mulacafé to provide food at lunchtime. He owned part of the Mulacafé site and the food was in lieu of rent. A pink plastic tray was sent over in a taxi – good, wholesome, home-cooked, Icelandic food. It was a cause of daily pleasure to him to lift the lid of the container and see what was inside. 'Gusti at Mulacafé always provides generous helpings,' he thought happily.

Dagný never commented on his diet or tried to force health food on him and he respected her for it. He had not been nosey enough to enquire what she had for lunch, but his opinion of her was so high that he naturally assumed she would be eating good Icelandic food and not some high-fibre snack.

At ten past twelve the driver arrived with the food tray. Dagný was concentrating on her work. It was plain she wasn't going out for lunch. Axel lifted the lid with high expectations and found large portions of sausage and white sauce. 'Perhaps I can offer you a bite or two, Dagný,' he called. 'It's sausage today.'

She swung her chair round, looked at him, amazed, and asked him to repeat what he had just said. He renewed his offer. 'Sausage, oh, God, no,' she said and put a hand over her mouth. 'That traditional Icelandic food is so bad for you. I usually have a yoghurt at lunchtime.' Axel frowned. He could smell sweat. It was his own. He was surprised to discover what a sheltered life he must be leading if the man's visit had upset him so much.

'Yoghurt,' he muttered, irritated, and looked at his sausage. The white sauce was getting cold. 'I only hope I'll be left in peace to eat this,' he thought. 'I only hope there are no more visitors.' And he bent over his food.

3

A little before five, after he had failed to raise Tumi, Axel decided to phone his brother-in-law, Hördur Gottskálksson. Hördur didn't answer at the surgery, so he rang the Vatnsholt number. Ester answered and told him her father was doing a night locum shift, but she would ring the agency and tell him to go to the Heidnaberg complex. 'I'll be here until six o'clock,' Axel said. 'If he's any later, tell him to go to Dyngjuvegur.' He glanced at the outer office. Dagný was still at her desk, although everyone else had gone home.

The door opened a crack a few minutes later. Axel looked up and saw Hördur's profile. Hördur Gottskálksson was resting his hand on the door knob and smiling at Dagný. 'First, Seli floods the market with White Horse whisky and Viceroy cigarettes. The next thing you know he's flogging the hospital equipment to cope with the outbreak of cirrhosis of the liver and lung cancer.'

Hördur looked at the medical equipment displayed by the window as he walked into Axel's office. 'I saw the Red Cross presenting one of the those to the City Hospital the other day. The doctors were posing one on each side of it. First I thought they were running a hotdog stand and were showing off some new cooking utensil.'

'Hello, Hördur,' said Axel, amiably. 'Did you mention cirrhosis of the liver? You do realize you have to drink an awful lot to get that? It didn't take you long to get here.'

'I received an order from a higher authority to bring my stethoscope. We were near by, us night locums, out and about saving people's lives, so the driver ran me over here in next to no time.' Hördur was looking at the papers on Axel's desk. 'Still forcing everyone else into bankruptcy, are you?'

'It's good to see you,' said Axel.

The doctor put his bag on the desk, opened it and took out his sphygmomanometer. He held Axel's arm and barked at him, 'Undo your shirt, man, are you asleep?' Axel undid the button and Hördur rolled up his shirt sleeve, revealing a pale-skinned, fleshy forearm. Then Hördur placed the cuff around his arm and pumped it tight. The mercury column rose. Hördur Gottskálksson glowered at the measure in mock seriousness. He released the pressure. Axel followed the process with mounting distress.

'It's bad, isn't it?'

'As far as I can tell, "The cold grave gapes open at your feet,"' quoted Hördur.

'Don't joke about it,' said Axel, hurt.

'Your blood pressure is through the roof. It's two hundred over a hundred. Has something upset you? An outstanding invoice, perhaps? An investment not showing an acceptable profit margin?' Hördur grinned. 'Being bossed about by the wife?' He bent down towards Axel and whispered in his ear, with one eye on the door, 'An uncontrollable mistress?'

'"An uncontrollable mistress"!' snorted Axel. 'If only that was it. What do you think Tedda would say if I got tangled up with some woman? No, there was a man here earlier. He caused a scene and, like a fool, I got myself worked up about it. It's no good, getting worked up like that,' he said, sunk in thought. 'And certainly not when it's a complete stranger. It's a bad business.'

Hördur removed the cuff from Axel's arm, took his stethoscope out of the bag and listened to the swiftly beating heart. 'Take a deep breath, Seli. I must congratulate you on being the talk of the town. You need a broad back to be married to the next minister of finance. They'll soon be calling you the minister's wife. Perhaps Tedda'll be prime minister next, who knows?'

'What's all this rubbish? Who's spreading stories about Theódóra wanting to be a minister? It's just not going to happen.'

'Why not?' This time Hördur genuinely had no idea what Axel

meant and did not have to pretend. 'No false modesty, now. It's all over town.'

'Tedda told me she's getting out,' he said. 'She's been a member of parliament for long enough.'

Hördur Gottskálksson squinted at him, keeping the stethoscope in position. 'Getting out, my foot! Goodness me, she's modesty incarnate these days. This is news to me, I must say. They say she'll be the star of the election. Don't be such a fool, Seli,' Hördur said to him firmly. 'She'll get the Ministry of Education at the very least.'

The heart lurched painfully. 'Did you hear that?' Axel asked but the doctor didn't say anything and kept on listening.

'They haven't counted the votes yet,' said Axel. 'I think people are getting a bit ahead of themselves.' He obeyed Hördur's instruction to bend forward and pull up his shirt at the back. Hördur listened again, moving the stethoscope across Axel's back and then folding it up. Axel tucked in his shirt. 'Perhaps I'd better go and get myself checked out at the City Hospital?' The truth was that he had already been there, but he did not dare confess this to Hördur.

'You don't want to bother with that,' the doctor said, rather aggressively, and put his stethoscope back into the bag. 'The idiots over there can't do anything I can't do in my surgery. You just take things easy and try not to get agitated about the bloody company. If you don't trim your sails a bit, you'll drop down dead. Piss in a bottle, I'll take some blood and we'll do some tests.'

'But how can I take it easy, Hördur, old chap?' Axel pointed to an easy chair under the drinks shelf. 'One day a man comes running in here, throws his bag under the chair and says there are some documents in it relating to the bankruptcy of Hafskip Shipping and will I hold on to them for him. The Fraud Squad's after him. Then he dashes off again. Five minutes later an old pal of mine who often drops in for a gossip comes by, sits down in that very chair and do you know the first thing he says? "The Hafskip bankruptcy's reaching into some very dark corners."'

Hördur cleared his throat. 'Mother-in-law's popped her clogs, then.'

'Yes,' said Axel solemnly, and tilted his head to one side as if meditating. Then he looked at Hördur as if he wanted to be let off

39

the hook; he had a hunch Hördur wanted to discuss the division of the estate. He said, 'Why do you feel so strongly about the National Hospital? There are some good people working there.'

'I got thrown out,' said Hördur, frowning.

'Your pal Tumi Sæmundar wants me to have a check up at the Cardiac Clinic.'

Hördur's reply was instant. 'Tumi's an idiot.'

'Don't say things like that, Hördur.'

'It's true. I know him. We were students together.'

Looking worried, Axel went to a chest of drawers and took out a bottle of medicine. He handed it to Hördur.

Hördur read the label with a solemn expression on his face. Then he walked over to the small washbasin in the corner of the office, unscrewed the cap and poured the contents of the bottle away. 'What kind of poison's this? Is the fool trying to kill you? I'll give you a prescription for something that'll sort you out.'

He sat down and wrote the prescription. 'I've never understood why you have Tumi as your family doctor when you've got someone much more highly qualified in the family,' he said, as he filled out the form.

'He's been our doctor a long time,' said Axel nervously. 'Since the time you and Villa were overseas. I can't just drop him. Surely you understand that, Hördur? And it's not just my decision.'

'I don't give a damn what quack you go to,' the doctor said. He was in an evil mood.

As Axel took the prescription he wondered whether Hördur had prescribed exactly the same medicine he had just poured down the sink.

'You can do me a favour,' Hördur said, deep in thought.

'What?'

Hördur looked at him, mocking. 'That chap whose photo you've got in all the windows downstairs. The Prime Minister. He's a friend of yours, isn't he?'

'He most certainly is.' And Axel smiled broadly.

'There might be something I could do with his help over.'

'What's that?'

'If they're going to try to bury me alive in this city, then I have to fight for my rights. That Head of Nursing at the National

Hospital, I've got to pay her back for what she did to me.'

'Why are you always fighting with women?' asked Axel, bemused. 'We should love and honour our womenfolk.'

'Let's not get into that today. Could you talk to the Prime Minister and set up a meeting?'

'I should think so. What do you want him to do?'

'He's the Prime Minister, isn't he?'

'Yes.'

'Well, he can pull some strings for me. That's what he's there for.'

'I'm not sure it'll be an easy matter to get Hannes to do your bidding,' Axel said carefully. And he changed the subject. 'You're going to have some company downtown soon.'

'Company?'

'Linda's going to move into the top flat at my old office on Skólabrú. She rang me yesterday to tell me.'

'When is she coming?'

'After the weekend. Theódóra's popping over to England to bring her home.'

'Whatever for? Can't she fly on her own?'

'You know how close she was to her grandmother. It seemed a bit rough to Tedda not to go and give her some support now the old lady's died. It's not easy to grieve on your own. She'd have gone today, but of course she's tied up with the election. And then there's the charity thing she's involved with. She's got a boy coming over as an exchange student, I think.' Axel looked round anxiously as if he was worried someone might overhear. He pointed his index finger to his temple and said quietly, 'Tedda's going because she thinks Linda's gone mad. The girl thinks God is talking to her.' He looked straight at Hördur, to see how he would react, but when no reaction came, he continued, 'So you can expect her around the house. Do me a favour and keep an eye on her, would you? I'm so cack-handed with women. But is it so strange for God to speak to someone once in a while?' Axel looked to his brother-in-law for confirmation. 'He used to in olden times.'

'I have no patience at all with religious fanatics,' said Hördur sharply. 'But I'm sure the apple of your eye and yours truly will get along together just fine,' he added, with the suggestion of a smile. When he saw this did not go down well with Axel he indicated the outer office with his head and said, 'You're not without help, then?'

'Dagný? That girl's taken so much pressure off me. I don't know how I'd manage without her. My heart's been perfectly OK since she's been here.'

Hördur smiled a thin smile.

As they walked through the door Axel said, 'Dagný hasn't been feeling too well lately.'

'No, no, it's not worth mentioning,' the woman said.

'What's the problem?'

She looked at the doctor. 'Nothing much. I've had a headache and I've been feeling a bit run down. I'll be fine. My daughter's the one who's poorly. She complains about a pain in her ears.'

'Dagný is an actress,' said Axel proudly.

'Come to my surgery at one o'clock sharp tomorrow,' said Hördur, cutting across him.

'But it's Saturday.'

'I never take a day off,' said the doctor solemnly.

Axel nodded. 'Hördur is one of the world's great doctors,' he boasted. 'He was a member of the team that did the first heart transplant in the States.'

'Then perhaps you could have a look at my mother. My ex-husband came here earlier. My mother still lives in the same house as he does. I've just not been able to find a flat big enough for her to come and live with me. She has trouble with her heart and she's in a bad way – and at least that's what Tryggvi says. If he's telling the truth, of course,' she added.

'Dagný's moved out,' said Axel. 'Her husband came here making trouble.'

'I'm on the city locum list,' said Hördur. 'Just ring and ask for a visit and we'll look in on you. But, as Seli's been talking about me in such glowing terms, did you know he once gave 200 million kroner to the nation for a new prison?'

'That's double the actual figure,' said Axel, looking rather proud of himself. 'And most of what we gave was in kind, in building materials.'

'I know that, Axel, I'm only teasing you.' Hördur walked off, through the rows of office desks. When he reached the middle of the large room, he turned and shouted, 'Come to the surgery next week and I'll take some samples of your waste products.'

'I'll come and see you, Hördur, old pal,' said Axel and then thought to himself, rather anxiously, 'What do I say to Tumi? He is my doctor, after all. I can't avoid hurting his feelings.' Axel looked at Dagný. 'Well, I must be off. The nightwatchmen will be here soon.'

'Is it that late, already?' Dagný looked at her watch in surprise.

'Perhaps you're not feeling up to going home?' he asked carefully.

'Of course I am. I've made an appointment with a solicitor for after the weekend. I'm going to take out an injunction against Tryggvi. I'm not letting him get away with this.'

'I'll just make sure you get into your car all right. Then I'll know everything's OK.'

He waited at the window. The official locum doctor's car was still waiting while Dagný had a brief conversation with Hördur. She looked up at Axel, winked and got into the little white Toyota. Axel nodded and waved back. The locum car reversed away from the building. Axel opened the window and let in the fresh air. The window was fixed at the middle and swung open vertically. As he turned round again his eye was caught by the fire extinguisher. He put it back in its proper place. 'I could probably have smashed his skull with it,' he thought and felt quite excited. He was shocked to realize he had half hoped the intruder would attack him. He sat down at the desk. When he looked up he found Tryggvi standing in the doorway looking at him. He had changed into smart clothes.

'She's gone.' Axel looked at the clock on the wall. It was five to six.

Uninvited, Tryggvi walked into the office and stared sullenly at the desk. His nose was so big it made his eyes look closer together. Axel took a deep breath. Suddenly he was seriously afraid of having a heart attack. 'Listen, old chap, whatever your name is, whatever's been going on between the pair of you . . .'

'My name is Tryggvi.'

'Why do you treat her like this, Tryggvi?' said Axel, in a soothing voice. He was hoping he could keep the man calm.

'"Treat her like this",' parroted the man, speaking slowly and angrily. 'She's my wife and she doesn't want anything to do with you.'

'What?'

'She doesn't want anything to do with you.'

Axel was so taken aback, he couldn't bring himself to speak. Eventually he managed to stammer, 'I beg your pardon. I'm a married man.' This was all that came into his head. He was finding it difficult to breathe and he clutched at his throat.

'I want to give Dagný some money. There's a lot I want to do for that girl.' Tryggvi looked at the wall, excited. There was a photograph of a red jeep; year of manufacture: 1995. It was not yet on the market. 'I know a bit about cars,' Tryggvi said, looking at the photograph. 'I work at GM Service over the other side of the bay.'

'Ah, you work at Einar's. We're good friends, Einar and me. But, my dear fellow, she doesn't want to have anything to do with you, now does she?'

'It's down to you, mate.' Tryggvi nodded to the outer office. 'You! You, with all your dough. You're famous, you are,' he said bitterly. 'Don't you think I know who you are?' he said, eagerly. 'I've read all about you in *Weekend*.'

'Some idiot kid got it all wrong,' said Axel. (He was, in fact, referring to me, the narrator of this saga. He blamed me – although actually I had no part in it – for a series of articles blowing the lid off corruption in the large Icelandic conglomerates. I swear on my honour as an editor and a journalist that the one about Heidnaberg simply slipped by me.)

'It's the money Dagný's after,' Tryggvi said. 'She's hoping your wife'll snuff it so she can marry you.' His eyes were wide. 'I can see you don't believe me, but it's the God's honest truth.' He rubbed his fingers and thumb together. 'Money, money, money, that's what she's after. I don't bring in enough to satisfy her. She says you've got good taste in clothes.' Tryggvi stared at Axel's shirt. 'I don't see anything special. Dagný's meant to have really good taste, but I'm rubbish, of course.' His face was contorted with anger. 'She calls herself liberated. All the women in Iceland, they're oh-so-liberated now. None of them bothers with cooking and they're never satisfied. Look.' He opened his black coat to reveal a dark suit beneath. 'Italian. The best. The most expensive. None of your charity-shop rubbish. I look good, don't I? I just bought it.'

Axel nodded. The suit fitted Tryggvi very well.

'And the shoes. Hugo Boss.' He took a step to the side of the desk so Axel could see them properly. He looked at Axel and an unpleasant smile spread across his face. 'I can give Dagný one or two things you can't. Dagný's sorted, I tell you,' he said triumphantly.

'What the devil do you mean by that?'

Tryggvi grinned.

'Do you mean you've got your own business?' Axel asked stupidly and tried to seem interested, although he knew perfectly well what the man meant. He could feel a burning sensation in the heel of his hand and a dull pain in his chest, as if a paving stone were lying on it. He rubbed his chest.

Tryggvi rubbed his chest as well. Axel was surprised by the physical echo. 'My own business?' Tryggvi imitated him, stressing the word 'business' over and over again. 'A business? No, I don't have my own business. But I've never gone short.'

'She applied for the job here,' said Axel firmly. 'And she was the best candidate.'

Tryggvi smiled mockingly and said slowly, 'But of course she was the best candidate. I wasn't the only one after her in the old days. I know what's going on in that brain of yours, but there ain't no one going to take my wife off me. I love that girl.' He looked straight into Axel's eyes, giving weight to his words.

Axel knew that the worst thing to do would be to let Tryggvi know how scared he was. He banged on the table and said angrily, 'What the hell are you on about? Isn't it enough to wreck your own home? Do you have to come and wreck things here as well? I hired the girl to do a job, that's all. And that's all I care about.'

At this the intruder gave a hollow laugh. 'It doesn't wash with me, mate. I knew straightaway there was something going on between the pair of you. I could smell it.' And with this, he left the office.

When Tryggvi had gone, Axel picked up the phone in order to sack Dagný. 'How dare she have a madman like that following her about and then get herself taken on here?' he thought. He was furious. He didn't even try to count his heartbeats. His heart was racing. He rubbed his chest hard and his anger turned on his own body. Suddenly it seemed cowardly to fire her. He decided to think about it over the weekend and he thought, 'If only Tedda wasn't

45

tied up with the election and could sort this out for me.' Then, the thought formed: ' Is there something going on between me and my secretary that I haven't noticed but that her husband has?'

4

I expect my readers are wondering what on earth the wretched chap is thinking about, maundering on for a whole chapter about Hördur Gottskálksson's locum night shift when he promised quite unequivocally to recount straightforwardly and without unnecessary deviation what we all want to know: what really happened in Reykjavík around Christmas the year before last and is still a matter for some conjecture. Why doesn't the bloke get to the point? Why's he wasting our time? Does he have no regard for the splendid alternatives to which we could put our leisure time?

I should assure you that any apparent deviation is indeed necessary and that I shall get to the point and reveal the nub of the matter at the right point in the narrative at the right time. Don't worry about it. As editor of *Weekend* I was often sued by angry, outraged financiers and members of the upper classes, but never because I didn't get to the point and was unclear in any way when it came to blowing the lid off their shady dealings.

As Hördur walked down the steps he looked up at the façade of the Heidnaberg complex. As a student he had supported himself by occasionally working as a debt collector for a number of wholesalers and as a consequence whenever he entered an office building he still found himself feeling anxious, try to master it as he might. He saw Gunnar Bragason, his driver, was dozing with his head resting against the windscreen. As Hördur passed him he tapped on the window with the knuckle of his index finger. Gunnar Bragason woke with a start. He was the laziest of all the drivers.

Gunnar saw Hördur walk round the front of the car grinning at him. He was fed up to the back teeth with this doctor. He hardly knew him, even though they had done night shifts together for several years now. When Hördur had returned from America he wanted to sit in the back seat. No one else had ever wanted to do that. Generally doctors were well disposed towards the common herd.

Ten more house calls had come in while Hördur had been at Heidnaberg. There was flu going the rounds, particularly among children. They threw up, ran a bit of a temperature and their ears hurt.

'I don't know what things are coming to, flu at this time of the year,' the doctor muttered. Once he was settled the car reversed.

Hördur grumbled to himself as he read the list of house calls. 'They're all up on Golan Heights,' he said. It was the nickname for Reykjavík's Breidholt district. 'Step on it. Let's get this wreck on the road.'

'I plan a more dignified end for myself than coming to grief in this load of old junk,' said Gunnar laconically. It was at this moment that Dagný came down the steps and Hörder wound down the window. As she was turning the key in the lock of her car, Hördur said, 'Listen, where did you say you lived? I'll pop in now.'

'Twenty-eight, Thingholtstræti. My mother's name's Sigrídur Einarsdóttir.'

'We'll be there this evening.'

'Oh, thank you so much. But I won't be there myself. My husband and I have divorced recently and I very rarely go to the house.'

Gunnar Bragason drove at snail's pace towards Reykjavík's Golan Heights. He'd been driving doctors around for so long he knew all there was to know about illness. He could speak with authority about myocardial infarction, appendicitis, meningitis, diabetes and salpingitis. From his years experiencing the state of health of the city's inhabitants he had derived a standard biography for the average Reykjavík citizen. The first time the average citizen made use of the locum service, he was recently married and had just become a father. He was living in a cellar, over the moon about his new wife and new child, but the standard of the accommodation was not good and the child would have a cold. Grandmother and Grandfather would have come for dinner and Grandmother would have made an almighty fuss and insisted on calling out the night doctor. Next time the typical family would have moved into

47

a block of flats. The whole place would be in uproar and fights would have broken out on the stairways. The wife would be lying on the kitchen floor having some sort of fit. The doctor would give her an injection to calm her down. Finally they would have moved from the flat into a terraced house. The man would now be in his thirties or forties and believed he was having a heart attack. Debt and overwork would have brought on an attack of 'flu'. The service would be summoned in the night to a newly built villa rising like a cliff from out of the sea. A massive boulder would stand in the middle of the lawn. The master of the house would be showing the first symptoms of clogged arteries. At dawn the locum car would arrive at the final house. The boulder on the lawn would now be weathered by wind and rain and would give no sign after years decorating the front lawn that it had until recently lain beneath the soil since the beginning of time. The man of the house would be dead.

The doctor's car stopped at a red light and the driver glanced at Hördur out of the corner of his eye. He was chain-smoking and seemed agitated. Probably he'd had a fight with his old lady. It was the driver's opinion that that particular marriage left a lot to be desired. Gunnar thought he could smell alcohol. He bent over the glove compartment, pretending to be looking for something, but concentrating on the smell. Definitely alcohol! No doubt about it. The doctor was drunk. In other circumstances he would have driven the doctor home and sorted out another duty doctor for himself, but he did not dare suggest it with this man. At last the traffic started moving again. Gunnar drove to the house in the Seljahverfi district and the doctor disappeared into a basement. The driver leant his head against the windscreen and dozed off again.

There were a lot of stories about Hördur Gottskálksson going the rounds of the night service. They said he was always reminding the doctors he had worked with at the City Hospital how much better educated he was than they were. Even Gunnar knew the doctor had worked on the first heart transplant in the States in 1968. His arrogance made for a lot of bad feeling. How could doctors with an ordinary education and a second-class degree from some Swedish hospital be expected to put up with this sort of thing? All the same Hördur was not entirely unpopular. Outside the door of the Director of Surgery at the National Hospital, one on each side, stood two vending machines, full of sandwiches. The Director of Surgery was generally held to be a pompous prig. One day as silence had fallen in the hospital dining room, Hördur had asked, his voice cold with irony, 'Tell me, Director, is it true you stay up all night making sandwiches for the machines?'

While Hördur was inside the basement, four more house calls came in. Gunnar Bragason lowered the window and waited. He turned on the radio and listened to the weather forecast. The weather was going to be good for the election. The damp air smelled fresh. There was an air of expectancy about the city. Hördur came up the basement steps, sat in the car and said, through clenched teeth, 'Bloody grandmothers. They're always having hysterics. There's nothing the matter with those brats. Just a bit of a cold and a runny nose.'

Gunnar Bragason nodded. 'And it costs the city millions to deal with this nonsense.'

A gang of kids surrounded the car. One knocked on the window and said, 'Go on, man, turn on the syringe!'

'It's called a siren,' said Hördur. 'Can't you see this car doesn't have a siren. It's only got lights.'

'Oh, really?' said the child and looked at the roof, disappointed.

The voice of the girl operating the radio came through, sounding agitated. 'Gunnar, are you there? I've got a house call in the old town.'

'What are the details?'

'It's a woman with an acute infarct. Sigrídur Einarsdóttir, aged seventy-eight. Severe chest pain and pain down the arm. She's complaining of nausea.'

'Where exactly in the old town?'

'Twenty-eight, Thingholtstræti. The woman who made the call said she'd spoken to you earlier. Shall I send the crash team?'

Gunnar looked at Hördur Gottskálksson. He knew the doctor hated having to send patients to hospital since he had been dismissed from the National Hospital. Hördur grabbed the microphone, pressed the button with his thumb and said, 'I've got the details, I'll take the call. Old Gunni and I are in the vicinity. I spoke to the woman a little earlier. I'll send the patient to hospital if it's necessary. Anything else?'

'Yes, there's a house call on Sogavegur.'

'Let me write it down.' Hördur released the button and turned to the driver. 'Get this heap of junk on the road, Gunnar.'

Gunnar Bragason put the car in gear and drove as fast as he possibly could. Meanwhile Hörder scribbed down the details of the housecall on Sogavegur. The driver listened in. A man in his sixties. Bad stomach pains. Diarrhoea. They were worried in case a stomach ulcer was haemorrhaging.

Hördur put the microphone back. 'Drop me off on Sogavegur first. The call on Thingholtstræti is just a domestic. There's no rush. The woman's turned her back on it all and has left her old mother in the care of her husband. No doubt the place'll be full of crying brats. That's why the grandmother's having difficulty breathing. I tell you, I'm getting pretty used to that sort of riffraff.'

The doctor was at the house on Sogavegur for a long time. The request for a visit to the house on Thingholtstræti was repeated. Just at that moment Hördur emerged. 'Me and the doc, we're just round the corner,' said Gunnar Bragason.

Hördur got into the car and fumed. 'A haemorrhaging stomach ulcer indeed! The damn fool had been eating rhubarb pudding.'

There was a traffic jam on Miklubraut and Gunnar switched on the red light. The flashing only made matters worse as the cars tried and failed to get out of the way of the emergency vehicle. Gunnar and the doctor were held up by traffic around Mikletún. A little girl looked out of the back window of the car in front of them, pointing to the flashing light. Her father looked over his shoulder and tried desperately to get out of the way.

'What were those children saying? "Why don't you have a syringe?"' asked Hördur.

Gunnar Bragason had no answer to this. In the old days the doctor's car did have a siren, just like any other official car that needed to get to its destination quickly, but the night locum service had lost this privilege. As it happened, Gunnar used to turn on the siren whenever he was heading back to the City Hospital for his supper. It didn't go unnoticed and one day the police were waiting for him.

'Where are you off to in such a hurry?' the cops asked.

'For my supper,' said Gunnar Bragason. He wasn't given to lying.

'And has the hospital canteen laid on something particularly tasty this evening?'

'It's sheep's head,' answered the doctor's driver. 'I'm partial to sheep's head.' It was this reply that had cost the night locum service its sirens.

They crawled along Miklubraut in the dense traffic with the light flashing and could not escape until Gunnar could turn off towards Laufásvegur. The driver was later to make a statement to the effect that the woman had already been dead a long time and it had taken them thirty-five minutes to get to the address from the Golan Heights.

The door at 28 Thingholtstræti was standing wide open when they drove up to the house, with the light still flashing. Dagný's car was parked outside the house, half on the pavement. A well-built, fair-haired man was standing on the steps, indicating to the doctor to get a move on. Hördur took his bag from the back of the car and went inside. The house was old. It was built of wood, with corrugated-iron cladding. There were two floors and a loft room. The doctor commented to Tryggvi on the unusually good quality of the renovation. The stairs led straight up from the hallway. Two solemn-looking boys of perhaps fourteen and sixteen stood looking down at them. Suddenly a little girl appeared at the top of the stairs and burst into tears.

'Tryggvi, will you please go and see to Sylvía,' hissed Dagný. She then addressed the doctor: 'My mother is in here.'

Dagný took the doctor into the boys' room, where the patient was lying on a settee below a large picture of the group Metallica. There was a vacuum cleaner on the floor. On the walls there were pictures of basketball players glistening with sweat. The varnished redwood floor shone. Hördur put his bag on a chest of drawers and looked at the old lady for a moment. Her skin was suffused with a deathly blush and her features were pinched. 'There's nothing I can do,' he said.

Dagný looked at him in disbelief. 'But it was only a moment or so ago she lost consciousness.'

'My speciality is heart disease. I'm a surgeon. It's too late to do anything.'

'But it's over an hour since Tryggvi phoned them the second time and told them it was urgent. Aren't you even going to try to do anything for her?'

'She's not the only patient in the city.' Hördur picked up his bag from the chest of drawers and went into the parlour. He sat down at the table, took out a pad of invoice forms and filled one out. 'It'll be fifteen hundred kroner.'

Dagný stood in the doorway, looking at her mother in bewilderment. 'Aren't you going to try and bring her round?'

Hördur shook his head. 'The patient is dead. I'm so sorry.' He looked at Dagný more closely. She wasn't just attractive; she was a real beauty. Her cheekbones were high and her blond hair was long. Her strength of character was apparent. 'Obviously a fighter for the rights of women,' he thought. 'A feminist.' He looked in his wallet for a fifty-kroner coin to give to her.

'It's OK,' said Tryggvi, sounding embarrassed.

Hördur found a hundred-kroner coin. He put it on the table, saying, 'No, I insist.'

When he came out, Gunnar asked, 'Did you phone for the crash team?'

The doctor shook his head.

'Oh, she was dead, was she?'

'Just about.'

'Didn't you try to resuscitate her?' asked Gunnar, surprised.

'No,' the doctor said. 'I didn't resuscitate her. It would only' – and he used the English phrase – 'prolong her suffering.'

They dealt with two calls on the west side of town. While Hördur was visiting one patient, yet another was added to the list. Gunnar was worried about missing his supper. The City Hospital canteen, where the night locum service personnel were allowed to eat, would close at eight o'clock. And some of the doctors were too greedy to allow the night locums and the ancillary staff time to eat. To Gunnar's joy, when Hördur returned to the car he said, 'Come on, Gunnsi, let's go and find that sheep's head. There's no point taking calls on an empty stomach. Just don't go putting the "syringe" on.'

It was a strange coincidence that on the menu that night there was indeed sheep's head. This was a rare occurrence. Gunnar

52

Bragason sat down to his half a sheep's head and kept his eye on the nurses at the next table. Over the years he had seen them treat the food appallingly. Sometimes they would just eat the tongue and leave the rest. Hördur, however, enjoyed the whole dish. He eased the eye out of its socket and ate it with relish. When he had finished, he lit a cigarette and sat there, hunched up and silent for a long time.

They were having a coffee and discussing the election when a young doctor came over to the table and whispered something that Gunnar Bragason did not quite catch, even though he tried as best he could. The expression on the young man's face showed he hoped he could get away with saying what he had to say without Hördur making a scene.

'The woman was dead,' said Hördur, as if he was spelling something out to a child. 'There was nothing to be done. It was an instantaneous infarct. You can put that on the death certificate.'

When they set off again the traffic was much lighter. The doctor came away from the next patient furious that 'a crazy old woman' had said he stank of booze. 'Can you smell alcohol?' The driver decided the wisest course was to shake his head. But anyway Hördur insisted in being driven to his surgery, where he changed into a fresh suit. The shift was over at midnight. Gunnar Bragason drove the doctor to Skólabrú and was relieved to be shot of him.

Hördur decided to sleep at the surgery. He sometimes did this after a night shift to get some peace and quiet. He used to share this house with his mother-in-law. They had got on well, as they had shared a violent temper and a healthy mutual respect. When the doctor arrived at the empty house he had still not recovered from the woman screaming at him that he was drunk. 'I am a doctor!' he said out loud, still furious. 'How dare she!' He rinsed his face in cold water. He was too agitated to sleep immediately. He decided to go to a bar and have a couple of stiff drinks. He'd sleep better then.

There were surprisingly few people in the bar. He asked for a double whisky, downed it in one gulp and asked for the same again.

A group of people came in, talking loudly among themselves

about the election. Hördur drained his glass, left the bar and walked down Hafnarstræti. It was deserted. He paused by the antiquarian bookshop and looked at the trusty old tomes. Neatly typed notes on white paper protruded from the volumes, giving odd scraps of information. The rare-book dealer composed them for his own pleasure and the pleasure of others. Hördur sometimes stopped to read the notes. He was aware of a teenager taking up a position beside him and looking in the window. Another, shorter boy stood on the other side of him. There was a book open in the window at a picture of Joseph Stalin. In the photograph Stalin assumed an air of respectable authority and his moustache was large and bushy. The note beside the book read: 'Delightful speeches from a much-loved and caring politician. An extremely rare item.' The doctor grinned. At this moment the shorter of the two boys kicked his thigh without any warning and called out in a high-pitched voice, 'He's laughing at me!'

Hördur fell to the ground and the other boy immediately kicked him in exactly the same place. The pain was excruciating and sent cramp-like spasms through his body. He was seized by a paralysing fear. He thought, 'I should not be treated like this.'

There was a single stone slab in the doorway of the antiquarian bookshop. He eased himself over to this step and heaved himself halfway upright. The fear turned into uncontrollable anger. The teenagers looked at the doctor. The larger one had fair hair and a long, pimply face. The shorter one was fat and there was an ugly, evil expression on his face. They were both drunk. Hatred for these repulsive creatures flared up inside him. He pulled himself up to his full height, and said in a voice, that to his great distress sounded both unsteady and whining, 'You're ugly and stupid, the pair of you!'

'Look at him! He's crying,' said the younger boy. 'Knock the old geezer out.'

When Hördur had been a student in the States he had done a bit of boxing. He had a swift and powerful punch. He had had very few fights because he was so afraid of losing, but now the experience stood him in good stead. He stumbled back out on to the pavement despite the pain in his thigh and put his fists up like a professional boxer. The smaller one closed in with his right hand held up ready to punch. There was a knuckleduster on his fist. As the teenager came within his reach, Hördur leapt forward and knocked him out. The fair-haired boy looked down at his mate in surprise.

'Come on, you rotten little punk,' Hördur hissed and stumbled towards him. He stared at the pimply face. The mouth was like a red slash and the fair hair was oily.

The boy turned on his heel and ran away.

Hördur stumbled back to the boy lying on the ground. He wasn't much older than his son Trausti. His face was strangely white and he was unconscious. He was wearing a leather jacket, jeans and a black T-shirt. He had a black tie with yellow spots knotted around his neck. Presumably he had stolen it from his father and now wore it to make fun of good, honest citizens. Hördur kicked the boy's leg. Twice. He was seized with an urge to strangle the boy with the tie. He grabbed it and twisted it until the boy started to make choking noises. The boy was beginning to turn blue when he released his grip and dragged him to the corner of the house, still holding on to the tie. A few steps led down into the square. He dragged the boy down the steps. A man heading towards Vesturgata crossed Ingólfstorg. The man stopped and looked at him. Hördur let the boy go and kicked him hard in the shoulder. Then he stumbled across Austurstræti. In Ingólfstorg there was gateway into Austurvöllur, another square.

The doctor looked back over his shoulder from Austurvöllur. No one was following him. He unlocked the door at Skólabrú. He took a sedative from the old white cabinet that had once belonged to his father-in-law and gave himself an injection in the thigh. He suspected a damaged nerve. He was not used to fighting, but he was surprisingly calm, even light-hearted. He hoped he had broken the boy's cheekbone. He yanked the telephone line from the socket, lay down on the couch in the surgery, pulled a blanket around him and fell asleep.

Hördur slept fitfully. Dream after dream chased across his mind's eye. Sometimes he would be half awake, tossing and turning, then he would fall asleep and dream again. Somewhere around dawn he woke with a start, remembered the fight and sat up. He immediately felt a sharp pain in his thigh and hobbled about the room testing whether his leg would take his weight. He lay down on the couch again and dozed for another half-hour. He was awoken by a stream of cars sounding their horns in unison. He hopped over to the desk and plugged the phone back in. It rang just once. He was not sure whether to answer it or not.

'God, I'm glad you answered,' said Vilhelmína. 'Where have you been?'

'I had a night shift. I thought you knew.'

'Why didn't you sleep at home?'

'I often kip here after a night shift. You know that.'

'Shall I ask Ester to come and get you?'

'No. Ask her to bring the car over and leave the keys in the glove compartment.'

'She'll come straight over.'

Hördur washed his face in the washbasin. He found a comb and dragged it through his hair. He was white as a sheet and his eyes were bloodshot. He poked out his tongue. It was furred. His foot was throbbing. He remembered the boy he had left unconscious in the street and devoutly hoped he had caught his death of cold. He unzipped his trousers and lowered them to see the livid bruise on his thigh. The muscle was swollen. It would undoubtedly get worse. The boys had known what they were doing. Hördur kept a black suit at the surgery. It was in a chest of drawers in his mother-in-law's old flat. He hobbled upstairs and changed. Then he selected a light-coloured coat from the coatstand in the waiting room.

The waiting room was dingy. The lower half of the walls, up to shoulder height, was clad in plywood, with thin strips of wood covering the joins. The doctor himself had varnished the wood, and the rest of the room was painted green. The ceiling, once white, had yellowed. There was a row of stainless-steel chairs with worn leather seats and backs along one wall. A round wooden table stood under the window by the radiator. There were a lot of magazines on the shelf under the table. The door to the hall was open.

The Bank of Iceland building overshadowed the house and even though it was a bright day, the hall was gloomy. The surgery windows looked out over the garden but the reception area was on the Skólabrú side of the building. The ground floor was divided in two. Before Heidnaberg moved out from Hverfisgata, Axel had had his office there, with a view facing the Cathedral and Kirkjustræti. Although Axel had not worked there for years, he still had not had time to clear the room out. The door was standing ajar and an ancient advertising poster with a picture of beautiful young people sitting by a roaring fire drinking Scotch was lying on the floor. Hördur walked across the room and peeped through the Venetian blinds but could not see his car anywhere in Kirkjustræti.

Ester would be there any moment. He picked up his medicine bag, opened the front door and stepped out on to the steps. At the last moment he whipped his hand away from the doorknob to avoid the two fish that were hanging there. He nearly ran backwards down the steps. There was a pool of fish slime on the top step. One fish was heavier than the other and had pulled the lighter one right up to the doorknob. The doctor stared at the fish.

For several weeks the doctors had almost been waging a war. They stood accused of raking in money from all sides, that they received an exorbitant salary, that they were cheating the state and the people. A system of referrals was about to be introduced. Hördur was against it. He did not have any paid work in the hospitals or apart from running his own surgery and the occasional night locum shift. Until now he had considered his income rather modest. However, it was now obvious that person or persons unknown did not share that view. He took a deep breath and looked down at the steps. Moisture was still dripping off the fishtails. Whoever the perpetrator was he or she could not be far away. The doctor turned round quickly, glanced up and down the street, but he could not see the culprit. He noticed a man standing in the sunshine on the lawn in front of Reykjavík High School. It seemed to him that the man was looking in his direction. Hördur stood stock still and stared at him. The shadow of the school building stretched far across the sloping lawn and the man was standing at the very corner of the shadow. He was too far away for the doctor to be sure whether the man was studying him or not. He looked back at the door. The cold fish slime stank. He was of a mind to call the police and make a real fuss. The man on the school lawn was now looking in the opposite direction. He put his hands in his pockets and sauntered off. Suddenly Hördur realized that the ridiculousness of the incident rendered his anger risible. This made him all the more angry. 'So the bastards are not even going to allow me a subsistence wage now,' he thought. Then he said out loud, 'I can't leave the door like this. I'll just have to deal with it later in the day.' He lifted the fish from the doorknob with his index finger. The string tying them together felt wet. He marched quickly round the side of the house. On Kirkjustræti he met a woman pushing a pram. She seemed to notice nothing unusual in his behaviour. Hördur walked round to the back of the house, lifted the dustbin lid and dropped the fish on top of some cotton and rags and other rubbish from the surgery. Now he needed to wash his hands. One of his eyes hurt. There was a steady, hard throbbing behind the eyeball from all the tension. In an inside pocket he found a key to the back door and opened it.

He walked slowly into the waiting room and peeped through the net curtains across to the house opposite. It was a specialist fish restaurant and did not open until the evening. There was no sign of activity. He looked at the Hotel Borg to see if anyone was watching him from a window but it was impossible to be sure. From Axel's room he could see no one acting suspiciously on Austurvöllur. He went into the surgery, closed the door behind him and washed his hands thoroughly, snatching up a nailbrush and scrubbing his fingers. He took a glass from the shelf above the washbasin, filled it with water and took two Valium. He sat down at his desk and massaged his temples. Opposite the desk was the old ottoman on which he had spent the night. The head of the couch was raised, the leather fixed in place with gilt studs. Looking at the yellow studs did not make him feel any better and he tried to master his anger.

There was an eerie silence in the surgery, as if he was sitting inside an enclosed, sheltered world. Reykjavík felt a long way away, even though the window was open and the sound of the traffic could be heard clearly in the silent house. When he had recovered sufficiently he picked up his medicine bag and walked through to the front of the building. His eyes widened in surprise. Dagný was sitting in the waiting room with her daughter Sylvía. They looked as if they had been waiting for some time.

'What! You!' exclaimed the doctor. He had not heard them come in.

'You said to come at one o'clock,' she said, sounding equally surprised. 'Had you forgotten?'

'Yes,' he said guardedly, under his breath, remembering the visit to 28 Thingholtstræti in every detail.

'I'm sorry if I'm making a nuisance of myself,' she said shyly.

'It doesn't matter.' Hördur invited her into the surgery and closed the door behind mother and daughter. 'I'll do whatever I can for my brother-in-law,' he mumbled and sat down. 'Seli and I have always got on well. So this is the patient?' He did not wait for an answer but leaned forward in his chair and looked at Sylvía. The girl had a long face and almond-shaped eyes.

'Yes.'

'And how old is she?'

'Sylvía, tell the doctor how old you are.'

'I'm eleven.'

'A bit short for your age. Now, what's the matter?' He opened his big hands.

'She complains of headaches and she's got a nasty cough.'

'Let's have a look at you, my dear.' Hördur took the child's hands into his own for a moment, tilted her cheekbones slightly with his long thin fingers and asked her to open her mouth. 'Open wide, my dear. Her throat's a bit red but it doesn't look as if it's anything serious. Nothing to spoil this nice bright day.' He went over to a drawer and took out his stethoscope. 'Is it OK with you, Sylvía, if I use my stethoscope?'

Dagný removed her daughter's sweater and pulled up her vest. All this while Sylvía was looking at the doctor's face with curiosity. She jumped when the cold metal touched her chest.

'Now would she like to turn round?'

Sylvía crossed her arms and held her vest up. 'You don't have to

59

hold it, Mother.' Her thick brown hair fell over her shoulders. She lowered her head.

'You get bad headaches, do you, poppet?' the doctor said in his strong deep voice.

'Yes,' the girl's thin voice replied.

Hördur placed the middle finger of his left hand on her back, over her left lung, and tapped his knuckle with the middle finger of his right hand. Then he moved across to the right lung and did the same. He warmed the stethoscope in his hand before putting it on her back. He looked kindly at the mother and removed the stethoscope from his ears. 'I can't hear anything the matter with her lungs. Does she get enough sleep?'

'Yes.' Dagný seemed to hesitate. 'Yes, I would think so.'

'And you take your cod-liver oil every day?' Again he took Sylvía's hands in his.

'There's no way I can get her to take it,' said Dagný.

'Do as your mother tells you. Take your cod-liver oil and go to bed at a decent time,' he said, letting go of the girl's hands. 'Then your head will feel better.' He looked at Dagný. 'I'll give you a prescription for some cough medicine, just to be on the safe side. Give her half a painkiller before she goes to bed for a few nights. She's fine. Come and see me again after the holiday if the headaches don't get any better.'

Sylvía put her sweater back on and went into the waiting room. She sat down beside the magazine rack. She left the door open.

'I expect the reason she gets these headaches is because we never get a moment's peace. We're harassed from morning to night. Did Axel tell you?'

'Harassed? Who by?'

'My ex-husband.' Dagný crossed her legs and started gabbling. 'I can hardly get in and out of my own flat. He follows me all round town. He sits on the stairs and waits for me. He stuffs bits of matchstick into the keyhole so I can't open the door. And now I've got this job he hangs around at Heidnaberg like a madman or comes into the office and makes a nuisance of himself. He works at the GM garage on Sudarvogur. He's trying to get me fired. That's what he wants.'

Hördur leaned back in his chair and folded his hands across his stomach. 'No, Seli didn't say a word to me about all this.'

'I thought there was probably nothing wrong with the child, but I just wanted to make sure.'

The doctor waited, smiling a thin smile.

Suddenly she spoke again, words pouring out of her in an uncontrollable torrent. 'It's awful. Do you know what happened last night? I just felt I couldn't go on any more. I decided to kill the child and then kill myself. I thought if I got the sack and had to go hunting all over town for another job, with Tryggvi following me everywhere, I'd rather be dead. So I took Sylvía in my arms and went out on to the balcony. We live in a top-floor flat on Skúlagata. I opened the door on to the balcony above the back yard. I decided I'd throw the child over and then cut my wrists in the bath. The summer night was so bright, but you could see the moon. Suddenly it seemed as if a voice was ordering me to throw her over. I was just going to do it when I thought better of it. The thing was I was feeling so agitated because my mother had died that evening.' Dagný looked over her shoulder and to her irritation saw Sylvía standing in the doorway looking into the surgery. She indicated firmly to her daughter to close the door. 'Couldn't you use your stethoscope on me? I can feel a kind of surging sensation in my chest.'

'Yes, of course. If you like to undress. I'll just write out a prescription for the girl while I remember.' He took a fountain pen from the chest of drawers, delved into his bag and tossed a prescription pad on to the desk. When he had finished writing he looked in amazement at Dagný. 'I only meant for you to unbutton your blouse.'

She was stark naked, with her long legs and her magnificent body and her hair falling round her shoulders. She was just about to step out of her knickers. She laughed. 'I don't know what's the matter with me today.'

'Well, life's like that.' He sounded friendly. 'And if you've all these domestic worries, it's no wonder you feel under the weather. Mind you, I've got a good few worries of my own.' He frowned. 'Really, the way some men get away with treating their women,' he muttered darkly, deep in thought. 'Can't someone have a word with him?'

She shook her head, unable to speak.

'Where do you live?'

'Fifty-eight, Skúlagata.'

'And where's your daughter when you're at work?' He scribbled the address down on a scrap of paper.

'At the moment the woman in the flat opposite looks after her sometimes. There's a chance I may be able to get her a place in a day-care centre for after school in the new year.'

He tore off the prescription, folded it and put it on the corner of his desk. She fastened her clothing. He stood up and placed the stethoscope in various places on her back. The flesh was firm and there was a pleasant scent on her skin. The pale blond hair glistened on her scalp. 'Would you be so kind, my dear, as to turn round?' He put the stethoscope on her breast. 'Well, so far as I can tell, you're perfectly fine. Your lungs as well as your heart.' He folded the stethoscope.

'What do I owe you?'

'Nothing. It'll go on Seli's account.' He looked at her face. Her lips were strange, almost as if they had been carved out of marble.

'You're so kind.' Dagný put her blouse back on and lifted her hair, letting it fall over her shoulders.

He folded his hands together and stood facing her, slightly hunched. 'I was sorry about your mother. I did what I thought was right.' He shook his head sadly, as if it were he who had lost the close relative. 'It would have been cruel to, as they say in the profession, "prolong her suffering".'

He walked through the waiting room into Axel's room. He could see his car parked in Kirkjustræti.

Dagný took her jacket from the back of the chair and put it on.

Sylvía was thumbing through a magazine and swinging her feet. She looked towards the surgery. 'You're weird, Dagný.'

'Put your coat on,' said her mother.

Mother and daughter put on their coats and went out into the corridor. Hördur was there before them. He said goodbye abstractedly. There was a patch of fish scales on the door. It had begun to dry and looked like flaking skin. He heard the telephone ring in the surgery and quickly went to answer it. It was Vilhelmína.

'I forgot to say. You must call in on Tedda.'

'Must I?' Hördur retorted. 'What does she want?'

'I haven't the faintest idea, Hördur. It must be something to do with Mummy. It has to be.'

'What can we say about one dead human being?'

'I don't know. Won't there have to be an autopsy? Perhaps we all need to know the results.'

'Every damn fool in Iceland has an autopsy,' said the doctor, irritated. 'You're talking rubbish. Did she say anything about the will?'

'No. But then again perhaps Tedda's blood pressure's up. The election's today. I haven't got the faintest idea what she wants with you. Don't take it out on me.'

The keys were in the glove compartment. On Skúlagata Hördur looked out across the bay. The sea shone like a polished mirror. A little way out from the shore an enormous Russian tourist ship lay at anchor. The long wide arc of a motorboat curved up to the side of the white ship where people were waiting on a platform at sea level. The name of the ship could be easily read from the shore: FYODOR DOSTOEVSKY. Hördur knew this was the name of a Russian writer. He had once read part of one of his books, but he found the characters so extreme, and the tumultuous events so numerous, that the story became in consequence unbelievable. Suddenly the clouds moved away from the sun. The surface of the sea was a brilliant green and the *Fyodor Dostoevsky* gleamed from stem to stern. The brightness hurt the doctor's eyes and he turned his gaze from the ship. There was a sharp pain in his thigh. He stretched out his leg in the footwell and gently massaged the bruised area. 'Damn it, it's really painful. I hope to God I killed the bastard that kicked me.'

He parked in front of 4 Dyngjuvegur.

He reached home in Vatnsholt after the meeting with Theódóra about an hour later. He caught sight of himself in the hall mirror and was surprised to see his forehead beaded with sweat. The meeting with that woman had disturbed him deeply. 'Treating me like that!' He walked into the parlour, cursing to himself, and took a cigarette from a pack on the living-room table. There was a bottle of wine without its cork standing on a shelf. Vilhelmína was sleeping. As he smoked and calmed down, he gazed at the big black-

and-white photograph of his father-in-law in the frame above the sideboard.

It had been taken when the professor had been in his prime. Hördur had seen many similar photos of Thóroddur. In each one the professor held his head high and squinted slightly. Got off heroin all by himself! 'You need a will of iron for that,' said his autobiography. 'He's certainly keeping an eye on his daughter's bottle,' the doctor thought and he grinned.

Neither of the sisters could accept that he was a better doctor than their father, more highly qualified and with a sounder grounding. That he was vastly more skilled as a surgeon. They needed only to look at the examinations he had passed. His diploma from the hospital at Stanford recording that he, among others, had assisted Norman Shumway at the first heart transplant in the United States of America in 1968. And his name in the English-language encyclopaedia, 'assistant surgeon in the pioneering US heart transplant team'. But neither Theódóra nor Vilhelmína paid the least attention to it. None of it meant anything to either of them. According to them, the highlight of their family history was when their father took part in a conference in 1936 with the German physician Dr Sauerbruch. (At the beginning of the century he had pioneered the surgical technique that allowed surgeons to work successfully inside the ribcage. This is all covered in *A Doctor's Life*.) They still looked on their father as the greatest doctor Iceland had ever produced. 'All Vilhelmína has to do', thought Hördur Gottskálksson, 'is to admit that I'm a better doctor than her father was. If she could only do that it would make no end of a difference to our marriage.' But to elevate him in that way was the last thing the woman could do.

He idly remembered the time when as a young man he had visited 4 Dyngjuvegur for the first time. It would have been some time in 1964. He was a second-year medical student. He was invited into the parlour, nervous at the prospect of meeting his idol, the famous doctor. Professor Thóroddur lowered his newspaper into his lap so that his fine aristocratic features and handlebar moustache came into view. His glasses rested on the very tip of his nose. He resembled, surprisingly, a horse. 'Father, this is Hördur Gottskálksson,' said Vilhelmína quietly and shyly. Her father the doctor rose and greeted Hördur with an outstretched hand and said in a loud voice that rang round the room, 'So this is the young man you were telling me about, my dear. And he intends to become a surgeon.' Thóroddur grasped the hand of his future son-in-law. 'And he can't wait to start operating himself and kick us old men out of the way. That's what I like to see!' Hördur could not remember what he mumbled by way of reply. There was a gap in his memory. In all probability he would have been offered coffee. All he could remember was his own awkwardness, him a country lad, being invited to meet this famous man in his magnificent house. Suddenly he smelled a familiar smell he had certainly not expected. Horse manure? In desperation, he thought, 'Is it me?' He sniffed as cautiously as he could. 'Can you smell the horses?' asked the doctor, getting to his feet. 'I keep horses in the basement.'

They went down to the basement together and there were two of them in the stall, a coal-black stallion called Dark and the other one, much paler in colour, not quite so big, called Light. Light nuzzled the doctor's pocket. Thóroddur stroked his chin with his long fingers. There were black hairs on the back of his hand. The horses were the cause of endless disputes with the neighbours because the sewers in the Laugarás district were forever being blocked with horse manure. They were also up in arms about the nature of the household. For a long time the first wife had simply refused to move out and had lived in a single room in the basement next to the horses. As time went by she became a maidservant to her former husband and his new wife. This was something Theódóra could not forgive her father. 'But was it poor Professor Thóroddur's fault if the Danish bint wouldn't move out?' Hördur thought. 'So what if the poor old sod kept two women and injected heroin once in a while to clear a hangover? They're all dead and gone now and anyway who's business was it but theirs? Would the old goat have crept down to the basement even though he had a new model upstairs?' Hördur looked intently at the photograph. 'Of course he would!'

Vilhelmína came into the sitting room looking very sleepy.

'He was a fine fellow, your father!' said Hördur loudly. 'One hell of a good chap!'

'What did Tedda want to talk about? Did she mention the will?'

'No, she didn't mention the will,' he said, imitating her. 'It was something quite different. She wanted to talk about Axel's illness.'

'Yes, it's meant to be really serious. Does she want you to do the operation?'

'No. As a matter of fact she doesn't. I don't think it even enters her head that I might be capable of such a procedure. But she thought it appropriate to have me drive over there so I could suggest a suitable surgeon.' Hördur shook his head. There was something dangerous about him. 'You just don't treat people like that. That's how you treat a dog. Your sister doesn't have an ounce of common decent humanity. All you've got to do is look at Axel. His heart's swollen up and it's putting pressure on his lungs. There's fluid in his lungs and his arteries are clogged up. He's in a bad way. Why the hell didn't your sister talk to her family doctor? Why summon me? Anyway they went to the Cardiac Clinic without consulting me. It was obvious that's where they'd been.'

'Poor Seli.' The woman looked rather arch. 'I'm not sure his condition is entirely Tedda's fault. Do you know what *Weekend* did to him while you were abroad?'

Vilhelmína opened a drawer, took out a magazine and put it on the edge of the table. Hördur stubbed out his cigarette and picked up the magazine. His brother-in-law was on the front page. He had been snapped coming out of the house on Dyngjuvegur glaring evilly with narrowed eyes at the photographer. His hair was grey, thinning and all over the place. His face looked puffy and pale. Underneath the picture the caption read, 'How does this man make ends meet?' Featured in a box at the bottom of the front page were photos of four square office buildings Hördur had no idea Theódóra and Axel owned. *Weekend* claimed that Axel of Heidnaberg paid no more income tax than a humble cleaner. Heidnaberg was described as 'one of the fangs in the mouth of the Icelandic financial monster'.

Hördur whistled to himself. 'Well, the poor old chap is certainly having a torrid time of it.'

'He certainly is. Of course it's just a way of getting at Tedda because of the election.'

'She'll be passed over after the election. That's what everyone's saying. But then Seli told me she was thinking of getting out anyway.'

'Getting out? She hasn't said anything of the kind to me. I know the women will vote for her in droves. She wanted to take her chance. She's got fighting spirit. You are going to vote for her, aren't you, Hördur?'

Hördur began to tremble all over. He tried to stop but it was impossible. His face turned red and before he knew what was happening he had burst out laughing. The woman looked at him in amazement. He had to lean forward in his chair and cover his face with his hands. Tears ran down between his fingers. His body was shaking violently.

'What's the matter with you?'

'Oh!' he said but it was impossible to speak for laughing. When he had laughed himself to a standstill, he said, 'I've just realized the fish tied to my door at Skólabrú that made me so mad and had me tiptoeing round to the dustbin, they weren't meant for me. They were meant for Tedda and poor old Seli. I was covered in fish scales and had to wash my hands twice.' He pointed to the front page, full of joy. 'You see, here, they talk about how little income tax a cleaner pays. You remember the old custom of giving servants a free fish for the pot?' He wiped his tears and opened the magazine.

The article was spread across the centre pages. A photograph of the villa was placed prominently at the foot of the page, taken from the garden. The photographer must have sneaked in there and lain down on the grass. The angle made 4 Dyngjuvegur look as high as a mansion. The balcony supports looked like pillars and the reflection of the sun in the windows made it seem as if the whole façade was made of glass. The steep blue roof did not appear in the photo and neither did the high chimney faced with the shiny black lava known as 'raven stone'. The house was valued at 42 million kroner and Heidnaberg at 2.5 billion. 'There should be something in this for us all,' said the doctor, flicking a fish scale from his index finger with his thumb.

'Why didn't you say anything to her?'

'I didn't think it was appropriate, with your mother not yet cold in her grave. I have some sense of decorum even if your sister doesn't.'

The telephone rang.

'Oh yes, there's some woman keeps ringing and asking for you,' said Vilhelmína.

He strode quickly into the corridor and picked up the receiver. An ice-cold voice asked, 'Are you God?'

'Wrong number.'

There was a short pause and then the caller continued, in a sing-song voice, 'I'm not so sure that this is a wrong number. I smelled alcohol on you last night. Had you been drinking?'

The doctor deliberately sounded angry. 'Who is this? Who do you want? My name is Hörður Gottskálksson.'

'You thought there was no point looking at my mother.' The voice turned sad. 'I thought I was dreaming. I thought I must have gone mad. But you admitted it just now.'

'That's incorrect,' said the doctor, getting agitated. 'Your mother was dead when I got there. Just be careful what you say, woman.'

'You're lying,' screamed Dagný. 'She had a heart attack. It's happened lots of times before. But you didn't think it was worth trying to save her. I'm going to phone the police.'

The doctor rubbed his face. They were both silent.

'I want to know what I owe you so I can settle up for the visit to your surgery,' she yelled.

'Eleven hundred kroner.'

'You still haven't answered my question.'

'What question was that, my good woman?'

'Tell me, are you God?' There was strange mingling in her voice of mockery and sensuality.

'There's no point in our continuing this ridiculous conversation. I'm going to hang up.'

'And I'm going to press charges against you, you bloody murderer,' the woman screamed, out of control now.

He put the receiver down on the sound of her screaming.

6

On election night there were stranger things going on than the results of the ballot. Anyone who says I don't know what I'm talking about can look up the relevant issues of *Weekend* and read it there in black and white. The article was in the first issue produced under the new editorial board: BURGLARY AT LANDAKOT CHURCH.

That year there were quite a number of burglaries in churches. I can remember a church at Selfoss being robbed, although possibly not by the same people. Items taken from the church were found a few days later out in the middle of nowhere by one of the pillars of the Ölfursár bridge.

The Friday before the burglary, the day Hördur returned from abroad, I was walking up to Landakot, the Catholic parish, early in the morning. I wanted to tie up a few loose ends on quite a different matter, something that had also featured in the pages of *Weekend*. The Catholic Church had found itself in court because the will of a man who had left the Church a house was being contested. The verdict had gone in favour of the Church. I wanted a comment from Bishop Lambert. When I phoned he was too busy to give me an interview, but said, 'But I'm sending someone over to have a look at the house. Father Bernhardur.'

I decided to go myself. It's a good idea to get out of the office occasionally and take time to think. I saw Father Bernhardur in the distance. He was walking down Túngata and I waited for him on the corner. He pretended not to recognize me and walked across the car park in order to avoid me. 'Father Bernhardur, wait a moment,' I called.

He looked at me, quite sullenly, and did not answer. I had on one occasion discussed religion with him and given him my opinion of the behaviour of the Catholic Church through the ages. The argument became so heated that he ended up spluttering incoherently.

'Are you going to have a look at the house on Sudurgata?'

He answered in the affirmative and strode off round the corner. I trotted after him. As this priest will have a large part to play in our story, I shall take the liberty of giving a brief description of him at this point. He was a tall man of some thirty-five summers. He had black tousled hair and a full beard. His nose was massive. He often seemed a little absent-minded and when he was preoccupied with something he had the habit of tugging at the beard with his right hand. For that reason the beard growing on his right cheek was somewhat bedraggled.

'Congratulations on winning the case. At *Weekend* we were

keeping a close eye on proceedings, as you may remember, Father Bernhardur. We were right behind you!' I grinned at him.

He said nothing.

I was not about to let him get the better of me, of course. Suddenly he whirled round and stared at me really fiercely. I can still remember him clear as day, his mouth like a thin line, the wind in his hair, his eyes hard. He asked, 'What make of car do you drive?'

'Car!' I repeated. 'I don't have a car. Why? Why ask me that? Do you want a lift somewhere?'

'No. But I've been given permission to buy a new one and I don't know whether to get a Toyota or a Volvo.'

'Go for a Toyota.'

'Why?'

'More fun and they're easy to handle. They're better in the snow and the price is more reasonable.'

'Father Otto wants me to get a Subaru. But the Volvo's a four-wheel drive too.' He tugged at his beard, deep in thought.

It was at that very moment that Axel of Heidnaberg came into my mind. 'Listen,' I said. 'I know Axel Sigurgeirsson. We used to take coffee together for years at Hotel Borg.'

'Who's this Axel?'

'Seli. Seli of Heidnaberg?' I was amazed he did not know the name. 'You've never heard of him? One of the richest men in the country! He imports Toyotas. He's a personal friend of mine. Let me have a word with Seli for you.'

Father Bernhardur took quite long strides. I had to skip every third step or so to keep up.

'I think I'm perfectly capable of managing my own affairs.'

'Of course you are, but if you mention my name, he might well knock something off the price.'

'We'll see.'

The spring sun was high in the sky, like a shield of light.

Father Bernhardur stopped and put his hand on the gatepost of 14 Sudurgata. It was a big wooden house painted yellow, and stood out from Reykjavík houses of a similar style, even though it had corrugated-iron cladding like all the others. The imposing house stood within its own grounds at the top of a steep slope. There was carved wood on the shutters and in the left-hand corner an Italian-style arched window. By this window there was a door with another small window, built in the same arched style above it. The porch had railings round it. The priest walked up into the garden and felt in his pocket for the keys. I followed him.

I was about to ask, 'Do you intend holding on to the house?' when my mobile phone rang and I was informed that my employment at the paper was terminated forthwith. After this bitter blow I stood there on the garden path in shock. I immediately knew why this had happened. I had lost credibility with the proprietor and I had never quite regained my position after asking for paternity leave three years earlier. I had to get going at once and protect my rights. I have already told the story of my parting company with the paper and as I would not want the reader to think I am in any way obsessed with it, I shall return to the matter of the purchase of Father Bernhardur's car as it is essential to my tale.

After I had made my hurried departure, Father Bernhardur looked at 14 Sudurgata and thought long and hard. The greater part of the front of the house was in the shade of an ancient tree in full bloom. It was hot; there was a wonderful fragrance from the trees and the terns were crying across the lake. Should he recommend the sale of the house? Was it right for the Church to keep it? Could it be used as somewhere for young people? It was so easy these days for young people to get mixed up in all sorts of unsavoury things. He bounded up the path with the scent of fresh grass and moist bark in his nostrils. He felt his cassock swing round his knees as he jumped up the wooden steps and found himself at the door, with his long pale face and the beard as sharp as a spear. He peeped through one of the tiny panes of the stained-glass window and saw a room that had once been used as a sun lounge. He put a key in the lock but it was not the right key. He looked round the garden and felt quite at home. On the other side of the road he could see the tower of the old Reykjavík fire station. In a gap between the houses he could see part of the old villa on the corner of Fríkirkjuvegur and Skothúsvegur on the far side of the lake.

Father Bernhardur ran down the steps and walked round the north corner of the building. There was another pair of doors. The key fitted the lock. He opened the door and closed it behind him.

71

A door in the corridor stood open to the sun lounge and the morning sun had warmed the floor. He listened intently for a moment. He liked the atmosphere of the place immediately. On the floor there were all sorts of bits of paper, a complete mess, price lists, pages of accounts, letters. It looked as if the police had made a thorough search. A wholesale business had been run from the house. The wholesaler had been an elderly man and had surprised everyone by bequeathing the house to the Catholic Church when to the best knowledge of everyone concerned he had never so much as entered the church porch and had certainly not been baptized a Catholic. All the same, Father Bernhardur thought he could remember once seeing the man sitting all alone in a pew deep in thought. The priest thought he recognized him from the photograph in *Weekend* when it ran an article about the bequest and all the fuss when the relatives had contested the will.

Father Bernhardur walked from one reception room to another. There was rubbish all over the place. On the lower ground floor there was a kitchen that had been used for a long time as a coffee room. Upstairs there was a large living room, a number of smaller rooms and an airing cupboard. You had to lift a hatch to get into it. It was bright and spacious upstairs. He went to a window and looked out over the garden. He could see the Thingholt district. He decided to recommend that 14 Sudurgata should not be sold but used as a young people's home in accordance with the Bishop's suggestion. Father Bernhardur went downstairs, walked out of the house and closed the door behind him.

He strode up Túngata trying to decide whether to buy a Toyota or a Volvo. He entered the Church of Christ and crossed himself before the altar, sat down in the front pew and prayed. As he said a Hail Mary he realized that if he recommended keeping the house, the correct course of action would be to buy the cheaper car, the Toyota, and to use the money that would be thereby saved to subsidize the conversion of the young people's home. Father Bernhardur smiled and gave thanks to God for guiding him to his decision. Father Otto would be overjoyed.

The Skoda was parked on the Hávallagata side of the church. The engine coughed when he tried to start it. A few boys playing basketball by the presbytery stopped and looked in his direction.

The engine spluttered again and Father Bernhardur tried it for the third time. The Skoda sparked into life, the boys shouted with delight and Father Bernhardur waved at them. One of them scored a perfect goal.

He had imagined the Heidnaberg complex as a skyscraper, but it was long rather than tall, only two storeys high, the lower almost completely glass with a vast number of cars on display both inside and outside the building. The name was prominently announced on the roof: HEIDNABERG. Father Bernhardur stroked his beard thoughtfully and went in through the main doors.

He saw his reflection in the glass door and smiled his thin smile. He always aroused curiosity walking about Reykjavík in his cassock.

He went into the showroom, which seemed even bigger than it had done from the street. There was no one else buying a car. A salesman approached him and wished him good day.

'I want to buy a car.'

'New or secondhand?'

'New.'

'Then we have a variety of makes and models to choose from.'

'The smallest you have. A Toyota. The most economical on petrol. The one that's best in snow. The cheapest.'

The salesman smiled. 'That's it!' he exclaimed. 'I have the very thing. You describe it so well. I couldn't have put it better myself.' He led the priest between scores of old cars and new cars and then opened the door of a small white vehicle with plastic-covered seats. The little car seemed quite attractive. Father Bernhardur sat in the driving seat.

'This is the cheapest model. You could pay a little more for extras such as automatic transmission . . .'

'This is fine just as it is.' The priest stroked the seat and put both hands on the wheel. 'I'll take it.'

'Bingo! Just like that!' The salesman held on to the top of the open door and rested his chin on his hands.

'That's right. Instant decision!'

'You don't hang about, do you?'

Father Bernhardur looked around. 'Can I take it straight home?'

'I don't see why not,' said the salesman with a smile. 'If you will just be good enough to come with me.' He walked over to a desk. The priest followed. 'Now how do you want to pay?' He sat down at a computer terminal.

'By cheque.' Father Bernhardur had his chequebook in his breast pocket.

The salesman tapped away at the keyboard and the computer produced an invoice. 'What shall I put? "The Catholic Church, one Toyota, paid in full"?' He smiled.

Then Father Bernhardur told the salesman he thought he should be eligible for a cash discount. The salesman sighed and it was apparent from his expression that he had feared something like this might happen, that the priest had come to such a quick decision, there would be bound to be something go wrong. 'This is the standard price,' he said, looking solemn and withdrawing his hands from the keyboard as if the deal were off. 'It's not negotiable. If you pay in instalments, then it'll cost you more.'

Father Bernhardur was not to be deflected. He even implied that if he did not get his discount he might take his business elsewhere. The salesman pushed his intercom button and asked for Gudmundur. Gudmundur was not in his office.

'Who is there, then?'

'What's it about?'

'There's a chap wanting to buy a car and he wants a discount for cash.'

'I'll check it out, Vilhjálmur. Just a moment.'

While they were waiting, Vilhjálmur asked about the Church. He seemed to have got the idea that the Catholic Church was a sect, a branch of the Jehovah's Witnesses with a few lunatic members. Father Bernhardur said his parish was not very large, only about two thousand people. He was about to mention that the worldwide community of the Catholic Church numbered some 2 billion, when the voice on the intercom said, 'Theódóra's in.'

'Oh, right,' said Vilhjálmur and it seemed to the priest that he was a little taken aback.

'She wants to talk to your customer. Please send him up.'

'The managing director will have a word with you,' whispered Vilhjálmur. He pointed. 'Just go up those stairs over there.'

Upstairs there was a large open-plan office with lots of cubicles.

People were working at computers and above one of the desks was a sign reading, INFORMATION. He asked where he should go and the door was pointed out to him. He walked over to it. Dagný was sitting at her desk. Before he could open his mouth she asked, 'Are you the gentleman enquiring about a discount?'

'Yes.' He felt like a criminal.

Dagný pushed a button. 'Theódóra, the gentleman is here.' She indicated for him to go through, pointing with her thumb over her shoulder.

He knocked on the door and opened it. There was a woman sitting at a desk in a large office. She looked up when he came in and smiled. She would be about fifty. Her long auburn hair contrasted with her face, which was beginning to show signs of ageing. She was wearing a grey jacket and the cuffs of her white blouse peeped out at her wrists. There was a gold watch with a fine strap on her left wrist.

'But you're a priest!' she said in surprise, getting to her feet. She was tall and slender. She held out her small hand. 'A Catholic priest!' She sounded even more surprised, taking in his cassock. 'Well, I couldn't be more surprised to be reading my own obituary! Do you always go around dressed like that?'

'No,' he said. 'I was a bit distracted and forgot to get changed. I was thinking about buying a car.'

'And you'd like a discount? Are you sure God would want you to spend so much time thinking about money, Father . . .?'

'Bernhardur.'

She waved the priest to a chair.

'Yes. What's so strange about that?' And Father Bernhardur smiled in return.

'I thought you holy men never thought about money.' The woman leaned back in her chair and waited.

Father Bernhardur was quite used to dealing with people. He looked directly into the woman's eyes and, although her expression was serious, she seemed amused as well.

'Such an extraordinarily handsome man too. Forgive me bringing it up, but why ever did you choose celibacy? I am right in thinking you Catholic priests aren't allowed to get married?'

'That's right. And by accepting that the priest makes a

75

considerable personal sacrifice, if I might say so.'

Her eyebrows arched in surprise.

'The sacrifice of denying oneself a family, I mean. If I had married, had a wife and children . . . Well . . . I don't know . . .' He couldn't find the right words. 'I would have loved them so much!'

Theódóra turned her head, smiling a tight smile and looking out of the window. She picked up a pen and twice tapped the point of her chin thoughtfully. He found her expression difficult to read and when she turned back to him, she said, 'It seems to me that you priests get off lightly. It's the rest of us who have to cope with all the problems. That's how I see it, when it comes to families, my own included.'

'Do I know you? Have we met somewhere before? Have you come to the church?'

She shook her head. 'No.'

'May I ask your name?'

'Theódóra Thóroddsdóttir.'

He thought a moment. 'Yes. I'm sure I've heard that name somewhere before.'

'Who knows?' She smiled her sweet smile. 'And how do you intend using the discount?'

He explained it all to her quickly. She nodded. She knew the house in question. She had read about the court case. 'The ruling was in your favour, wasn't it?'

'Yes, and we planned to sell. But then the Bishop was considering opening a young people's home. There are thousands of young people in the town centre at weekends, getting up to all sorts, as the saying goes, getting drunk, getting into fights, and worse. The Catholic Church wants very much to reach out to people, to serve them better. The house has obvious advantages. Fourteen Sudurgata is only a short walk from the presbytery and the town centre. But we always have money worries . . .'

'Didn't you get 500 million kroner from the sale of Landakot Hospital?'

'That money's long been spent. I wanted to be able to put whatever discount I might get here into the coffers.'

She leaned back in her chair. 'It's a worthy impulse. Tell me, Father Bernhardur, what's so special about the Catholic Church?

What makes it so much better than our good old Lutheran Church?'

'Do you like fine wine?'

'I like some wines very much. I sell quite a range of them.' She pointed to the display shelf where there were dozens of bottles.

'Which is your favourite?'

She considered the array on the shelf. 'A red wine.' She smiled. 'A Mouton Rothschild '86. It's a great wine and I intend to see in the Millennium with it.'

'Let's say for a moment that you came to a great feast, in a palace say, or perhaps at a table in the open air, in a bright clearing in a forest. Jesus is sitting there and invites you to eat with him and has his best wine brought for you. You are allowed to choose between one glass, half full in the way people of taste and discretion like it, and the other with only a little in the bottom of the glass. Which do you choose?'

'It's the same wine in both glasses?'

'Yes.'

'Then I would choose the one that's half full,' the woman said. 'Really, what a thing to ask!'

'Of course you would. And so would I. So would anyone unless they wanted to appear ridiculously humble.'

'And what do the two glasses of wine symbolize?'

'The glasses are the Lutheran Church and the Catholic Church. The Catholic Church is the church Christ established on earth.' Father Bernhardur took a small Bible from his pocket, flicked through it and then started reading: '"Jesus asked his disciples, saying, Whom do men say that I the Son of man am? And they said, Some say that thou art John the Baptist: some, Elias; and others, Jeremias, or one of the prophets. He saith unto them, But whom say ye that I am? And Simon Peter answered and said, Thou art the Christ, the Son of the living God. And Jesus answered and said unto him, Blessed art thou, Simon Barjona: for flesh and blood hath not revealed it unto thee, but my Father which is in heaven. And I say also unto thee, That thou art Peter, and upon this rock I will build my church; and the gates of hell shall not prevail against it. And I will give unto thee the keys of the kingdom of heaven: and whatsoever thou shalt bind on earth shall be bound in heaven: and whatsoever thou shalt loose on earth shall be loosed in heaven. Then charged he his disciples that they should tell no man that he was Jesus the Christ."' Father Bernardur threw wide his arms. 'When Luther changed the way people understand the Eucharist and said that although Christ's true presence is in the Sacrament, there is no Transsubstantiation, he took away the mystery of the Mass. Jesus said, "He that eateth my flesh, and drinketh my blood, dwelleth in me, and I in him."'

The priest looked at the woman and put the Bible back in his pocket. His cheeks were flushed. 'Jesus intended that literally. The living body of Christ is the glass with more wine in it. Jesus is within the man who asks him to dwell within him and since that is what Christ said, the thing to do is to take him at his word – that is the essence of faith!'

'Now, now, calm down, Father Bernhardur. You scare me half to death getting all excited like that,' said the woman. She did not know what to think. 'I don't understand what you're saying but I'm going to give you your discount anyway. Would 10 per cent be acceptable?'

He nodded.

She pressed the button on the intercom. 'Vilhjálmur, what is the book price on that car?' When she had got the information she required she pressed a few keys on her calculator. 'Ninety-seven thousand, six hundred and twenty-one.' She looked at him questioningly.

'That's very good!'

'Let's say a round hundred thousand kroner.' She pressed a button on the intercom. 'Vilhjálmur, would you kindly arrange a hundred thousand kroner discount for the priest when he comes downstairs?'

'Yes,' the intercom replied.

'Who knows? Perhaps one day I'll look in on you at the church,' she said, stood up and held out her hand. 'If I were a Catholic and hadn't been to Mass for a long time, I'm sure you'd be the one to bring me back into the fold,' she said pleasantly. 'Are you pleased with your discount?'

He nodded and smiled and shook her hand warmly. 'Very pleased and deeply grateful. It would be good to see you. You don't have to be Catholic to look in on us at Landakot and attend Mass.'

'I'll think about it,' the woman said, but there was a hint of impatience in her voice and the priest felt it was time for him to go. They said goodbye and he hurried downstairs to see the little white car he was already rather fond of.

Straight after supper Father Otto and Father Bernhardur went to fetch the Skoda that Father Bernhardur had left at Heidnaberg when he drove away in the Toyota. Father Otto was in his eighties. He was German, small, quite dashing, and he had served the Church all over the world. He was cross that the younger priest had not followed his advice.

'I got a good discount.'

'And who you it give?' asked Father Otto, whose command of the language left much to be desired. For some reason he had seemed quite reluctant to come with Father Bernhardur.

'The managing director.'

'Naturally the managing director it would be.'

'A woman.'

'Naturally a woman she would be,' said Father Otto, without the least expression in his voice.

'Don't you think that's unusual?'

'No,' said Father Otto without further explanation. Father Bernhardur waited. He knew an explanation would in fact be forthcoming. They drove on in silence until Father Otto suddenly burst out, 'The reason be that women be free and that woman be so free because, if I not mistake, soon she the Prime Minister as well as a managing director be. You read a newspaper never, my boy? You watch the television never?'

It was then that Father Bernhardur placed Theódóra Thóroddsdóttir. He laughed. 'Yes, I've seen her on television and in the papers. I am a fool. That's why I recognized the name!'

'This a very intelligent conversation not be,' said Father Otto, frowning. He was a bit moody and had an unpredictable temper. Father Bernhardur could not guess the cause of his grumpiness. It could scarcely be the purchase of the car. When they arrived at Heidnaberg Vilhjálmur was taking down the pictures of Theódóra with the Prime Minister from the windows. 'You too inside

79

yourself be. It dangerous for a priest be,' said Father Otto sharply. 'Did you not the pictures of the woman in the windows see?'

Father Otto refused to drive the Skoda back to the west side of town. Father Bernhardur followed the Toyota back to Landakot, fretting all the way about Father Otto's erratic driving.

When Father Bernhardur had parked he could not resist walking round the new Toyota patting it here and there. Then he checked that the car was properly locked and went into the presbytery. Father Otto was watching football on the television. The old man was very fond of his football and woe betide any soul who came between him and a game. He had missed more than half the match, which explained his foul mood. Father Bernhardur went up to his room, lay on his bed and picked up the Bible from his bedside table. He read a passage every evening before settling down to sleep. For some time he had neglected the Book of Revelation, the terrible vision God had afforded to St John. There had been innumerable theories proposed about the Book, but no one could fully interpret the vision with any certainty. Over the centuries it had caused many a man to lose his mind. Sects had persuaded themselves of the literal truth of the prophecies coming true around them. A quotation from the Bible floated into Father Bernhardur's mind: 'Take heed that ye be not deceived: for many shall come in my name, saying, I am *Christ*; and the time draweth near: go ye not therefore after them.'

He followed the words but his mind was not on the text. Suddenly he remembered where he had seen Theódóra's name. It wasn't on television, nor in the newspapers. A few days previously he had been checking the parish register against the electoral roll to check whether anyone had recently become a Catholic. Such conversions sometimes went unnoticed and it was a matter of some importance for the Church that the relevant state subsidy was claimed. He seemed to remember coming across the name 'Theódóra Thóroddsdóttir'. Has the woman recently converted to Catholicism? Could it be possible? He had to know for sure. He went downstairs to the office and looked up the list. 'Theódóra Thóroddsdóttir, 4 Dyngjuvegur, Reykjavík. Born 17 May 1940. Baptized into the Catholic faith 23 May.' His eyes were wide. 'This is just what I suspected,' he muttered. 'The woman is a baptized Catholic and she gives no sign of it when she has a Catholic priest standing there in front of her on her own carpet. Doesn't she realize what Church she belongs to? I'm not the only one to let things slip my mind.' Father Bernardur decided he would get to the bottom of it as soon as the election was over.

7

When Father Bernhardur approached the altar early on Sunday morning to prepare for Mass, he felt a gust of wind travel the length of the church. He looked back to the door and saw it was open. He looked round. There was no one sitting in the pews. 'Hello? Is there anyone there?' he called loudly, but there was no answer. Over the previous few weeks, gentlemen of the road had been seeking shelter in the church at Landakot. Sometimes they were drunk and the Bishop himself had been obliged to have a sharp word with them. When that had no effect, it had been decided to keep the church locked overnight. Father Bernhardur was anxious in case he came across some poor drunk sleeping it off. He checked the rows of pews from the altar to the west door and to his relief found there was nobody there. He closed the door.

Only a few people had turned up when he, attended by an altar-boy, began the service. Probably everyone had been up late with the election. When he came to that point in the Mass when the officiant turns to the Tabernacle, the golden casket containing the body of Christ, he found it was not in its rightful place. The Tabernacle was gone and the two plaster angels guarding it had been moved. One of them lay smashed on the floor. Father Bernhardur thought it was almost incredible that he had not noticed this before now. He hurried into the vestry where the Eucharist was kept in a metal box when it was not in the church itself. The Chalice was not there. The congregation was expecting the body of Christ; they were kneeling at the altar rail, but Father Bernhardur's hands were empty. The priest left the altar and walked through the church whispering to them what had happened. He moved through the congregation: 'I'm sorry. I'm unable to give you the Eucharist today.' The people stood up in the pews and exchanged a few subdued words with each other about it.

He removed his vestments and hurried into the presbytery to find out if Bishop Lambert or one of the other priests knew how this might have happened. Then he suddenly remembered that it was he who had said Mass the previous evening and it would have been his responsibility to see that the church was locked. He'd forgotten all about it. He walked round the outside of the church. The green at Landakot had not been cut and the tall grass had been trampled where someone had walked through it. Father Bernhardur followed the trail and came upon the round copper box lying there in the early-morning sunshine. The Eucharist was scattered all around. The thieves had forced the catch on the Tabernacle with a screwdriver or a knife and tiny copper flakes glinted in the moss. The Chalice was nowhere to be seen. With great care the priest collected the damp pieces of bread. He spent a long time searching before he was sure he had found them all. He took the body of Christ into the church but asked the altarboy to guard the Tabernacle itself.

When Father Bernhardur told Father Lambert the news the Bishop phoned the police. Then he went back with Father Bernhardur to examine the scene of the crime. The police came quickly. They took photographs of the Tabernacle and questioned the priest. A policeman accompanied the Bishop to the altar and was shown where the Tabernacle should have been. One of them looked around and said, 'This is nothing like a Lutheran Church. It's much more fancy.'

His colleague looked round.

Father Bernhardur had put the angel back in its place. A wing tip had been broken off and there was plaster dust in the red carpet. They asked him to put the angel back on the floor, exactly how he had found it, and then they took photographs. They promised to be in touch as soon as there was any news. Father Bernhardur followed them out to the car. The altarboy was still waiting patiently on the lawn in his full vestments. Father Bernhardur carried the Tabernacle into the church. Coming into the dark interior from the bright sunlight outside, he could hardly see where he was going.

He felt guilty about not having locked up. He shared his misery with his Bishop. Lambert could sometimes make a real fuss about minor things but when it was something serious it was quite a different matter. He comforted the priest. Even as a child Father Bernhardur had had a lot of respect for the Bishop. I remember hearing a story about him. Father Bernhardur was a small boy. He was travelling home by bus when out of the blue Lambert got on the bus. There were just the two of them on the bus with the driver. Even so, the boy offered the Bishop his seat.

Father Bernhardur half expected to hear from the police straightaway and when two hours had passed without the telephone ringing he decided to go and visit Theódóra Thóroddsdóttir. He was going to remind her which denomination of the Church she belonged to and ask whether she might consider coming to Mass. He had watched television the previous night and felt a certain pride when he saw her on the screen at the election-night party at Hotel Saga. The Independent Party was winning by a landslide and most of the credit was being given to Theódóra. There was a great shout from the gathering when it became clear that the eleventh candidate on the list (Theódóra) had polled enough votes. She parried the inquisition of an aggressive journalist adeptly. Did she expect to be in the cabinet? 'I will just quote Hallgerdur Long-Trousers from the Sagas: "I'm not a lady to sit in the chimney corner."' A few women behind her applauded.

It did not occur to Father Bernhardur that the woman might have any other demands on her time that morning.

He parked the Toyota on Dyngjuvegur and looked down the street towards the house. There was a stained-glass window above the front entrance beneath the gable end and a big brass knocker on the door. He knocked abstractedly and was startled when a woman opened the door almost immediately. Theódóra frowned at him. She seemed irritated, as if she had been expecting someone else. 'Perhaps she thinks I'm going to ask her for money or try and convert her to Catholicism,' he thought and smiled broadly. 'Hello! I hope I'm not disturbing you.' He glanced at the pair of glasses she was holding in one hand.

'I thought you were my husband, Axel. I'm expecting him to bring some people.'

'Congratulations on your success in the election.'

'Thank you. But that won't be your reason for being here.'

'No. That's right. I'm here to inform you that you are a Catholic.'

'Me? A Catholic!' She looked taken aback. 'What in God's name do you mean?'

'Did you not know?' He smiled at her.

She shook her head.

'Iceland is a wonderful country,' he said, and laughed. 'In no other country in the world could people be Catholic and not know about it.'

'How do you know?'

'From the parish register.' He shifted his weight from one foot to the other. Wasn't she going to ask him in?

'Yes, my God, now I remember.' She put two fingers to her forehead. 'It's not that much of a mystery. I must have been baptized at Landakot.' She drummed her fingers on her temple. 'It's ridiculous. My mother was Catholic. Well, at least she was baptized a Catholic. She was Danish. They met when my father was overseas studying.' She looked at him solemnly and shook her head. 'I didn't want to remember all that. Still, I always go to church at Christmas and Easter.'

He looked down at his shoes. She did not invite him in. The shoes had large toecaps with a pattern in the leather. He looked at her.

'Won't you come in?'

'Yes, thank you.'

She stepped back from the doorway and let him into the hall. He ducked as he entered the hall although there was little chance of him knocking his head on the ceiling. He could see into the large living room. The spring sun was shining on the gleaming parquet floor. The light in the hallway was bluish. 'Tell me,' said Theódóra suddenly as she reached the foot of the stairs. 'The stained-glass window: do you know what it is?'

Father Bernhardur studied the window. 'It's Salome being presented with the head of John the Baptist on a salver. It's very unusual.'

'Yes. God, I don't know what on earth my father was thinking of. I used to be scared of it when I was a child. But my daughter Linda thinks it's absolutely wonderful.' She sighed. 'Come into the living room. How lovely the sun is when it starts shining on us again!'

She drew the full-length white velour curtains in the living room. They hung on wooden rings from a rail. She opened the doors on to the veranda and cool air swept into the room. She waved him to a comfortable leather chair by the window. 'Tea? Coffee?'

'Tea, if it's not too much trouble.'

She looked at him. 'This the first time I've ever had a priest as a guest.' She stopped talking and folded her hands together. 'Is the new car all right?'

'It's fantastic. I couldn't have got anything better.' He tugged abstractedly at his beard and did not say anything. She went through to the kitchen and from his chair he could see her midriff between a cabinet and the table below. She was wearing a thin black leather belt with a gilt buckle. The curtains did not quite meet and a strip of sunlight bisected the parquet floor. He could feel the draught from the veranda on his back and ankles. He pulled up his socks gingerly. He remembered his negligence in not having locked the church. There was a strange perturbation in his soul. He closed his eyes and rubbed his face.

Father Bernhardur had heard of priests who were in such close communion with the divine that it was said they had been touched by God. He had never felt such a presence and was not even sure that it was something to be desired. In his opinion a priest should rely only on his common sense, his faith and the Word of God as it is revealed in Holy Scripture. He should serve to the best of his ability. That was vocation enough. Suddenly he felt very alone in that living room.

'How sad you look, Father Bernhardur.' Theódóra was standing in front of him holding a tray.

He looked up. 'And you in politics! What a victory in the election! I should have realized when I saw you in your office on Friday. But perhaps I don't pay enough attention to worldly matters. Was it a surprise?' he asked, genuinely interested.

'Yes, I suppose it was.' She put the tray down and said with some pride, 'I was given a seat that was thought to be quite hopeless, but the Icelandic women rallied round me.' He thought she was looking rather anxious.

'What happens now?'

'The next thing is to form a government.' She lowered her eyes and looked serious, stroking the coffee table anxiously.

'I don't know much about politics. But you must be in a key position. So perhaps you'll be a cabinet minister?' He looked at her with admiration.

'I don't know about that,' she said, drily.

'I was just thinking about getting this young people's home at Sudurgata up and running,' he said eagerly. 'I'd like to think we could look to you for support if you were in a position of power.'

She did not reply but remained silent for a moment. Then she looked up sharply and said, with half a smile, 'What do you think Jesus would say if he could see me living like this?'

The interior of the house was not extravagantly furnished but it was tasteful and attractive. There was a chair of some reddish wood in the living room and a set of chairs with yellow seats. There were paintings by Icelandic masters on the walls. The priest examined one of them: a horse on a mountain road, the red road leading across the white moorland wilderness and the sun sinking into the white expanse. Another smaller reception room led off the one they were in. He could see a green sofa and chairs with unusually high seats. The living room did not strike him as so grand or forbidding you would be too nervous to sit down. It was obviously somewhere people lived. But who were they? He said, 'I'm sure that if Jesus came and visited you he would look around in surprise and say, "How well you live! Theódóra, your home is a palace!"'

She smiled and sat down.

'But didn't Christ say we should give everything we own to the needy?' She poured him a cup of tea.

'We all have to do our best in the service of God,' he said quietly.

'But who can say what our limitations are?'

'No one. We have to find that out for ourselves.'

Theódóra stirred her cup meditatively. 'Perhaps I should give away my business. There are people here in Iceland not knowing where their next meal's coming from.' She lifted her cup to her lips and took a sip. She said sadly, 'God knows it would be a burden off our shoulders.'

'Then do it,' he said, teasing her.

'Then what would become of all the people we employ?' She looked at him sternly.

All he could do was smile from ear to ear. The smile was so warm and good-natured that she did not get angry. He said, 'The chances are, Theódóra, that it's God's will for you to keep on giving these people employment. If you become a cabinet minister, think of all the good you can achieve.'

The woman clasped her knees. 'Tell me what you would have done if you'd been with Christ at that last Passover? All the fools and idiots who write religious columns in the papers saying St Peter was a coward irritate me so much. Or the priests puffing themselves up in their pulpits and accusing him of being weak!' She looked at him beadily. 'Would you have denied him, like Peter did, before the cock crowed twice? Or are you so brave you'd've said, "Yes, I'm one of his disciples." And then, probably, they'd've crucified you.'

'Absolutely! Absolutely! It's outrageous to blame Peter.' He grew thoughtful and she smiled at his large features. 'Would I have denied Christ or not? How can I know the answer to that?'

She smiled as if she had led him into a trap. 'I think your pride is getting the better of you.'

'I would have been no less proud if I'd given you a different answer. As soon as anyone says, "I'm so humble", he's the proudest of the proud.' He tugged gently at his beard. 'And they did crucify Peter.'

'Did they?' she said, surprised.

'Yes. It was when Peter was quite old and he knew what was coming with the Roman persecution of the Christians. He was fleeing from Rome when Jesus appeared to him and said, "Do I have to be crucified a second time?" Then Peter understood what Jesus had meant when after he had risen from the dead he had asked him three times, "Do you love me?" He was indicating by what manner of death Peter should glorify God. Peter returned to the city and asked to be crucified upside-down so that he would not be likened to his master.'

The phone rang. She let it ring a couple of times without seeming to hear it, as if she were expecting a secretary to answer. 'Have a look at the photographs,' she said and left him.

There were two albums one on top of the other on the coffee table. Father Bernhardur took the bottom one, the older album, laid it on his lap and opened it. The pages were thick and there was not room for many photographs. It was the family ancestors. There was a stiff-backed farmer in a dark suit, looking astonishingly like the actor Sean Connery. Beside him in a chair was a woman, looking much older in the face. She was wearing Icelandic national dress with the tassled bonnet. The priest turned the pages. Old photos taken overseas. A young man in a white robe standing on a gravel path – Professor Thóroddur. Large tree trunks in a garden with the fort-like hospital in the background. He lifted the album up to his face to read the name of a liner on a postcard: ICELAND. Another photograph took up the whole page: a fair-haired young woman in the full bloom of youth. Was this the Danish lady? On the opposite page there was the doctor, looking older now and with a long straggly beard like a billy goat. He wore riding boots and looked at the camera haughtily. Father Bernhardur flicked through the newer of the two albums. A small girl holding her father's hand on National Day, waving a flag. On the photo someone had written in white ink, 'Tedda and Dada, 17 June 1948'. He turned a few more pages. A lot of black-and-white photographs of a house at Hverfisgata, Heidnaberg's former offices. A young woman standing by a car looking shy. The sun must have been in her eyes.

'Yes, thank you very much. I'm sure we'll know what's happening in a few days,' he heard Theódóra saying. 'Yes. Goodbye.'

She came back into the room and looked at the photograph. 'That's me. I always worked at the office in the summer.' She took the album on to her own lap. 'This must have been taken in 1962. Judging by the car. Look at this! My father with my mother and my stepmother. My mother's the blonde.'

The doctor, his hair now thinning, lay on a grassy slope. There were two women beside him. The new one was quite serious-looking. Her nose was extremely thin and her hair was swept up and pinned in a bun on the back of her head. The Danish woman was ruffling his hair and laughing.

The telephone rang. 'Goodness, there's never a moment's peace in this house.' She put the album away and ran to grab the phone. Now there was tension in her voice. 'Yes, how are you? But, good God, you've known all this for years. Listen, there's someone here. I can't talk at the moment. Yes, by all means do that, darling, as soon as you know anything. Yes. OK. Goodbye. What? No, I really don't know what can be done about that. Well, what do you expect? What? No, there's nothing definite at all yet. They should be here any minute. I must go. I'll ring later. Goodbye.'

She came back into the living room and stood close to the priest without sitting down.

'That was my sister. She rings me at least ten times a day. Quite simply, her husband is killing her. He's a doctor, Hördur Gottskálksson. Perhaps you know him?'

Father Bernhardur shook his head.

Theódóra pointed to a photograph. 'Look! This is my step-daughter, Linda. She's about three in this photograph, sitting in her mother's lap. She used to live in the Western Fjörds . . .'

There was the sound of a key in the lock and they both turned to face the hallway as the front door opened. Somehow the priest had expected an ugly and violent-looking man to enter. But the first man to set foot on the parquet floor was a man of average height, kindly looking with a double chin and a paunch. 'This is my husband, Axel Sigurgeirsson,' said Theódóra. Father Bernhardur stood up to shake his hand.

There were three men and a woman with Axel of Heidnaberg. The priest recognized the most handsome of the men immediately. It was the Prime Minister himself, Hannes Pálmason.

The priest quickly said his goodbyes and she saw him to the door.

'It was great fun getting to know you,' Theódóra said.

He felt their short acquaintanceship was now at an end. He made one last effort to bring her in to the Church. He said, 'You know where to find me if you ever need me.'

She brightened. 'I may need you now. My brother-in-law, Hördur, has got himself into a spot of bother, with my own hus-band's excellent assistance. A girl who works for us is threatening to sue him for negligence. It makes no difference to me if he's struck off, but it would make my sister's life hell. It's for her sake that I'd like you to go and visit this woman if you've got a moment and see if you can talk her into dropping the charge. Reasoning with her seems to have no effect. I rang her yesterday and had a chat. Quite frankly, for two pins I'd sack her. Her name's Dagný Gisladóttir and she lives at 28 Thingholtsstræti. She's left her husband, but I think she's spending a lot of time at Thingholtsstræti because of the recent death of her mother. She'll tell you all about it if you go and see her. If she wants to know who sent you, it's all right to mention my name.'

He promised to do everything he could and walked down the steps to the pavement. Heavy clouds were billowing around the sun, trying to blot out the pale yellow disk. The edges were livid with red-gold fire.

Father Bernhardur looked in on Thingholtsstræti but no one was at home, so he drove west back to Landakot. There was no more news about the burglary. He drank his tea and listened to the news on the local radio station. It was speculating about the make up of the new government. The Prime Minister was quoted as saying it would reflect well on Iceland if a woman were to be given the Foreign Office.

8

The priest thought he would go for a walk and see if Dagný was at home. The sun was shining on the wet streets. He had not taken much notice of the house on his first visit but now he could see that it had been beautifully renovated. There was a name plate beside the door. On the ground floor lived Tryggvi, Dagný, Jökull, Haflidi and Sylvía. Upstairs there was just the one female name: Sigrídur. He rang the doorbell, heard footsteps inside the house and then the door was opened. An attractive young woman looked suspiciously at Father Bernhardur and waited for him to say something. During his visit to Heidnaberg he had been preoccupied with the discount and had not noticed her.

'Dagný?' he said, unconsciously putting his hand to his beard.

'Yes. What do you want?' she snapped. 'I don't like the god squad on my doorstep.'

'Actually I'm from the Catholic Church,' said Father Bernhardur. 'I'm not here to preach at you. Theódóra Thóroddsdóttir, the managing director and member of parliament, asked me to come and see you. She said you would know what it's about. She wanted me to see whether there was some amicable way of solving this difficulty, as so much is at stake.'

'"Know what it's about"?' the woman snapped. 'Is this a joke? "Some amicable solution"?' Dagný folded her arms across her midriff. '"So much at stake"? Who for? These people are monsters, they think they can get away with anything just because they pay your wages. You don't ask much, do you? Do you realize what you're expecting me to do?'

The priest hesitated a moment, uncertain what to say.

'I'm not dropping the case. I'll tell you that straightaway. That bloody doctor, he's a madman. He killed my mother.'

Father Bernhardur looked at her in amazement. 'He killed your mother?'

'I'm beginning to think you haven't got any idea what you've got yourself into. Is this your way of paying for the discount?' she mocked him.

He let the comment go. 'It's true. I don't know what happened. Won't you tell me?'

'I'm not sure I want to talk about it any more just now. I've just phoned the Medical Council. And I've spoken to the Medical Practitioners' Union. And I've talked to a solicitor, and the Director of the Reykjavík Medical Service. And *Weekend*. So the old girl's trying to buy me off, is she? If she thinks she can do that, she's got another think coming.'

'Would you consider dropping the case out of Christian charity?'

'Listen, you, what is it with you?' Dagný was gasping for breath. 'Didn't you hear what I said? He killed my mother!' She looked at him searchingly, trying to work out whether he was serious, and when she saw that he was confused, she said, 'He couldn't be bothered to try and save my mother and then the next day I went along to his surgery like some dumb sheep because I didn't want to believe what had happened. I took all my clothes off in front of him. Have you ever heard anything like it?'

'Would you let me come in and then I can get the full story?'

The woman seemed not to hear him.

'The doctor's wife is some kind of invalid. It'll be very hard on her.'

'Yes, I gather he treats her like some sort of slave.' Dagný began to soften a little. 'How can she live with such a bastard?'

'It's all very difficult. That's why her sister is so concerned to get something sorted out.'

'Sorry,' said Dagný, 'it's just that I don't make deals when my mother's been murdered.'

'What is it you want?' asked the priest. He was hoping that bit by bit everything would become clear.

'Justice! I want justice! I can't let this man carry on deciding who's going to live and who's going to die. I want to see him in court! I've gone to the newspapers, you know.'

'Can't you let me come in and tell me all about it?' Father Bernhardur stood on the front step, immovable.

'You won't let it go, will you?'

He expected Dagný to slam the door in his face but instead she stepped back into the hallway and opened the living-room door. Two long-haired boys were sitting at the table looking at a magazine. The priest thought he caught sight of pictures of cars and stereo systems.

He sat down. The table was varnished red with not a scratch to be seen. The floor was highly polished, red and yellow. The walls were painted white and the lintels were a dark red. There was a doorway dividing the room and the door frame was also dark red. The frames of the many small windows had been freshly lacquered white. The skirting board was blue. 'Well,' said Father Bernhardur when the lady of the house had gone into the kitchen to make coffee, 'and how are you two boys today?' It sounded awkward and beneath the boys' dignity. The older boy grinned, but the younger one tried to smile at him. They continued flicking through their magazines. Dagný came back with the coffee. Father Bernhardur was about to lift the cup to his lips when the door into the hall opened and a girl came in. She had a strangely adult face. She was pale, with large eyes, emphasized by the dark circles beneath them. Her hair was plaited in a style that might have been current at the turn of the century. She looked at the priest. 'Who are you?'

'I am a Catholic priest.'

'Why are you here?'

'I invited him in, Sylvía,' said her mother. 'Just be polite.'

'And what's your name?' asked the priest.

'My name is Sylvía Tryggvadóttir.' The girl held her hand out. 'How are you?' She turned to her mother. 'Is he here because of Granny?'

'How come an Icelander gets to be a Catholic priest?' asked the younger boy, Jökull, puzzled.

'Because of the overwhelming injustice in the world,' said Father Bernhardur.

'Huh!' said the girl dismissively. 'You ought to think about the injustice of a doctor, a complete stranger, coming here and letting my grandmother die.'

'He just burst in the door,' said the older boy, Haflidi, looking shocked. 'He scarcely even glanced at my grandmother lying there.' The boy pointed to a closed door. 'Then he just wanders out again without trying to do anything, sits where you're sitting and writes out a bill. Dad paid up and didn't say a word. I'd've told him what was what. I'd've given him a punch in the mouth.'

'He didn't even try to bring her round,' said Jökull.

'Mother's going to make his life a misery,' said Sylvía solemnly, slowly shaking her head. 'This doctor isn't going to know what hit him.'

'Was that really how it was?' the priest asked their mother.

Dagný nodded impatiently. 'Let's change the subject, children.'

'Don't you think that constitutes an injustice?' said the girl, sounding very grown up.

'Oh, Sylvía, stop being such a drama queen,' said Haflidi.

'Are you going to be an actress when you grow up?' asked Father Bernhardur, sounding interested.

'No, not me, it's Mother who's the actress.'

Father Bernhardur noticed this information seemed to make the woman uncomfortable, so he looked around him and said, 'This is a beautiful place to live.'

'Yes, we live in a beautiful place,' said Dagný with a graceful sweep of her arm. 'Or should I say "lived"? We don't own a single plank of this building. My ex-husband took out a large loan for the renovations. If there isn't some sort of miracle he'll lose this place. My mother lived upstairs. We bought it jointly with her.'

'Can't you get an acting job?' nagged the daughter meanly.

'Oh, do stop going on.' Dagný looked at the priest. 'There's no work in the theatre. There's twenty actors after every role.'

'Last job she had was as a crocodile,' said Haflidi, grinning.

'Stop it,' said Dagný. 'Last autumn I was in *Medea* and well you know it.'

'I shall pray for you to get a job of some sort,' said Father Bernhardur.

Dagný screwed up her eyes but decided not to say anything when she saw that the priest really meant it.

'There's always some scandal round you Catholic priests,' said Sylvía with contempt.

'What do you mean?'

'Overseas, anyway. You read about it in the papers. Terrible things to do with children. Aren't all Catholic priests gay?'

They all looked at Father Bernhardur and waited for his answer.

'Well, I'm not gay,' said the priest and smiled. 'And if I was I wouldn't be ashamed of it. You can't control how you feel.'

'I never go to church,' said Haflidi. He had long fair hair hanging down his back. He was thin and his features were quite delicate. 'I can't bear the hypocrisy.'

'The Church can always handle one more hypocrite,' said the priest. 'Be my guest.'

The boy pulled a face and the mother, brother and sister laughed. Father Bernhardur turned to Sylvía. 'God's Church on earth may be run by men, but nevertheless it is still God's Church. It can never be better than the men who run it. If it was perfect, then we wouldn't need it, because we'd be perfect. Remember that, Sylvía.'

'This is all too heavy for me,' said the girl. 'Tell me, who should be master in the home, the man or the woman?'

'A woman should obey her husband. It say so in the Bible.'

'Watch it,' said Haflidi. 'Mother's a feminist.'

Dagný was looking at the priest. 'Where does it say that?'

'God created man,' said Father Bernhardur, and smiled. 'Then he created woman from one of his ribs.'

'You won't find anyone in the twentieth century believing that.' Dagný's eyes were large with pity. 'It's high time people had a new conception of the Almighty. God's a woman just as much as a man.'

'Mother one, priest nil.' said Haflidi, laughing. 'One day God's going to wake up to his worst nightmare. He'll be sitting on his throne mulling things over and then jump when someone nudges his leg and says, "Sorry, but if it's all right with you, could you move along. That's my seat." And when he looks round, he'll see Mother tugging at his robe.'

'Stop that,' said his mother firmly. 'Doesn't it say somewhere, "Thou shalt not take the name of the Lord thy God in vain"?'

'Yes, but to take his name in vain, you've got to believe in him first.' said Haflidi.

As Dagný followed the priest to the door, she said, 'Tell Theódóra I don't want to say anything else about my mother's death until we get to court. It'll all be in *Weekend* on Wednesday. You'll find out all about it then.'

When Father Bernhardur took Mass that morning, there was still no news about the stolen artefacts. The Bishop had found a new Chalice for the Sacrament. At the end of the Mass, he lifted his hands, blessed the congregation and asked everyone to go in peace.

He looked down into the well of the church and a warm feeling took hold of him. Theódóra was standing in the furthest pew, looking towards him. The west door was open behind her and the sun was shining out in the street. Whenever he managed to persuade someone to come to the church it made him intensely happy.

He walked quickly to her and took her hand. She looked round. 'It does look very familiar,' she said, 'but I haven't been here since I was a baby.'

'You're a little late. Mass is at eight o'clock sharp.'

'I didn't come for Mass. I wanted to talk to you.'

'Then let's go into the presbytery,' said Father Bernhardur. She followed him through the vestry and out of the church. He opened a door for her and they went into a small room with an old table in the middle with six chairs round it. There was a picture of Pope John Paul II on the wall and a bookcase along one wall. She glanced at the titles and was surprised to find that the greater part of them concerned the writings of Martin Luther. Above the bookcase was a photograph of the old wooden church, its flag stiff in the wind, a metal cockerel as a weather vane on the roof. A sad old horse was waiting, hunched over, by a potato field bordered by a rough stone wall. People were coming out of church. Theódóra turned away from the photograph quickly and said, quite firmly, 'What should one do when one's prayers are not answered?'

'Remember the word of the angel, after the Resurrection: "Tell Peter and the disciples that he is risen from the dead; and, behold, he goeth before you into Galilee; there you shall see him."' He made a special point of mentioning Peter.

'Not everyone is capable of that.'

'One has to do one's best.'

'Did you go and see the family in Thingholtstræti as I asked you?'

'Yes.'

She waited.

'Dagný doesn't want to make peace. She's too angry.'

'Then that's that,' said Theódóra and she became subdued. 'If she doesn't want to make peace then it'll have to run its course. There's nothing more I can do for Villa in the circumstances. What a mess,' she said, irritated. 'I don't see how we can continue having this woman working for us.'

'Does this dispute have to affect her employment?'

'I could say no. But then . . .' Theódóra shook her head. 'I don't see how we can make it work.'

'How can I help?' He moved a chair for her to sit on and waited, wondering what she would say.

'The thing is, I've received some information that means I have the opportunity to make a very large profit for very little outlay. Next to nothing, in fact.'

'And?'

'I don't know whether I should take it up.'

'What kind of thing is involved?'

'It would mean buying some shares.'

'They're for sale?'

'Yes.'

'What's the difficulty if these shares are for sale? What would be wrong about buying them?'

'If I take up these shares, it will give me a lot of power. Other people might feel that their holding is worthless.'

'And they would lose what power they had?'

'Yes.'

'Then all that matters is whether you intend to use that power for good or ill.'

'Father Bernhardur, I'm not planning to exercise that power to an evil end,' Theódóra said, with a hint of irritation.

'That's not what I meant. Bear with me. I don't know very much about business. Would you be ruining someone?'

'No.'

'You have enough money already, don't you?'

'Yes, as things stand. But many Icelandic companies are a bit rocky at the moment, as you may have heard. One tries to consolidate one's position. That is what security is all about. Business is business.'

Father Bernhardur thought about it and tried to find a suitable biblical quotation. Suddenly his features broke into a smile. 'Christ would have said, "Render unto Caesar the things that are Caesar's."'

She looked down and smiled. He did not know what to make of this smile, so he smiled again himself.

'Have I understood you aright?'

'I trust so.'

'If this venture is profitable,' she said, 'then I shall remember the Church.'

'I wasn't touting for custom.' He laughed.

'Don't be like that, Father Bernhardur. I've been in business long enough to be a pretty good judge of character. And your business sense is perfectly sound. Just like the rest of us.'

'Well,' he said, 'so be it. I would like you to remember me. Would you like to make a confession?'

'Not at the moment, I think,' she said, awkwardly. 'I might later.'

'Why the delay? Christ doesn't want anyone "lukewarm, neither hot nor cold". Make your confession and then attend Mass regularly.'

She looked straight into his eyes. 'Now I know who it is you remind me of, though you're as different as chalk and cheese!'

'Who?'

'Linda, my stepdaughter.'

'Who?' Then the priest remembered a photograph in the album. 'She's a beautiful girl. I'm afraid I'm thought to be terribly ugly.'

'I didn't mean how you looked. The way you are.'

'And what way is that?'

Theódóra laughed. 'Perhaps you will meet each other. Then you'll see. I'm flying to London tomorrow to collect her.'

'What's she doing over there?'

'Trying to "find herself", as they say. One day she wants to become a pianist, the next a painter. Now she wants to make films.'

'Are you going to be a minister?'

She looked out of the window, apparently as if it was far from her thoughts. 'It's not quite settled yet.'

9

A man sitting a few rows in front of her on the plane stared at her as he put his coat in the overhead locker. A couple of hours later, as he passed her seat on his way to the back of the plane, he leant towards her for a moment and whispered, 'Didn't you have the bottle to go through with it? I thought it was disgusting.'

Theódóra had said nothing.

The whole nation now knew she had been passed over when the government had been formed. Everyone knew it would have been only right, that she'd played a key role, that it would have been only fair in the light of the election result. That was why the women of Iceland had voted for her! Everybody knew she had been passed over. She had risked her parliamentary seat and this was the way they repaid her.

They had sorted it all out really quickly when it came to it, the

Prime Minister and his cronies, when they had come to the house. 'Theódóra,' the Prime Minister had said in his firm manly voice with his usual show of courtesy, 'we've got to build a coalition with the Left. Would you settle for chairing the Parliamentary Foreign Affairs Committee?' A tense silence fell around the table and Gudrún Samúelsdóttir gave her an encouraging look as if to say, 'You deserve more than this. You've got to say no. Say no, for God's sake, woman.' Axel looked imploringly at his wife.

'No, I won't accept that,' said Theódóra, with great dignity.

There was an uneasy silence. Axel looked anxious. Gudrún looked at her, flushed with pride. 'Theódóra, could we just have a word?' said Axel and stood up.

They went out into the hall and his eyes pleaded with her. His face was tinged blue from the stained-glass window. He whispered, 'I've been thinking this over these last few days. None of us really expected those results. It would be an enormous strain for you as a woman to take on a ministry. You know how my health is. I just don't think I'd be up to all the aggro you'd have to cope with. Of course, Hannes has no option but to remain as prime minister. But think what it would mean if you became minister of health with all the budget cuts that are in the pipeline. You'd be in the middle of such a political storm it would be hell here. And then we've got to consider the business. I'll have to have this heart operation before the autumn.' Unconsciously his hand moved over his heart. 'I'm not sure my health's up to it. I think it could kill me. Just think the effect all that filth in *Weekend* had on me. Anyway, I thought you were going to get out of politics.'

'I didn't think this was going to happen, Axel.' She was silent for a moment, deep in thought. 'Chairing the Parliamentary Foreign Affairs Committee, yes, it sounds OK,' she heard herself saying, listlessly, although she could scarcely believe it. She returned to the room, sat down and accepted the Prime Minister's invitation. Gudrún gasped in shock.

'Why did I let them do this to me?' she thought, with a feeling of real hatred, and then she remembered what the stranger had said, 'I thought it was disgusting.' 'Why did I? Of course, they'd planned it all.' When she thought about it she could see Axel had all but learned his lines by heart.

Theódóra looked out of the window. Far below them, above the clouds, another jet was crossing their path. It looked like a toy. Theódóra felt relieved to be getting out of the country. 'Axel, asking me to give up political office!' she thought.

The previous evening she had nearly asked Vilhjálmur to buy the shares in United Fisheries. She knew the Prime Minister was involved with the company. If she bought the shares it would have a major impact on him. Why should she always be taking other people into consideration when they never thought twice about her? Those men never gave her a second thought. They'd hardly waited for her to give her assent before she was out of the negotiations altogether and there they were discussing this option and that option, at her table, in her home, and with her husband, the much respected company chairman, tiptoeing around with coffee and nibbles, his cheeks pink with the pleasure of having delivered exactly what the power-brokers wanted. 'Yes, Hannes; no, Hannes; three bags full, Hannes.' The Prime Minister had never entered 4 Dyngjuvegur before seeking a favour and that Sunday it had taken him no time at all to get his own way. They'd be in for a surprise if it ever came out about who it was who actually ran Heidnaberg. Who it was who had worked so hard to build it up from that little wooden hut on Hverfisgata into the great concern it now was. For two decades Axel had done little but sip coffee in Hotel Borg! When Theódóra thought about the company, she remembered the man who had lain in wait for her outside Heidnaberg. She had just been about to get into her car when he had come over to her, in what was intended to seem a respectful manner. He was a fair-haired man with a large nose and his eyebrows met in the middle. He introduced himself as Dagný's husband. 'My name is Tryggvi.' And he leered at her. 'I just wanted to say, ma'am, that you and me, we've got to look out for our common interests.' 'Common interests?' she'd asked, surprised. He raised his eyes to heaven. 'Can't you see what's going on, woman? It's all around us.' Just for a moment Theódóra wondered if he was an Independent Party activist trying to warn her about something, but then he said, 'There's something going on between my Dagný and your husband.' Theódóra got into her car quickly and refused to enter into a discussion with Tryggvi. He stood and watched as she backed out of her parking space. It was as if he had only just realized that she was a woman.

Theódóra had planned to sleep during the flight to London, but every time she was about to drop off she was suddenly wide awake again. In the terminal building a man had come straight up to her with a questionnaire. How much money did she expect to spend in England? 'As much as I possibly can,' she said with a thin smile.

She put her suitcase down on the pavement. It was a five-storey Victorian terraced house. There was a row of ants marching across the step, disappearing into a crack in the marble. There must have been hundreds of them. There were very few people about. There was the sound of hammering in the distance. She went up the steps, taking care not to tread on the ants. She rang the doorbell and heard light easy steps as if someone was running upstairs. 'Is the girl living in the basement?' she thought.

Linda was tall and blond and got excited very easily. Then her eyes would fill with tears and her sharp little nose go red at the tip. She did not immediately fling her arms around Theódóra but instead stood there in the porch, drumming her feet on the ground, laughing, clenching her fists and then gnawing at her palm. Theódóra took her by the shoulders and kissed her. 'It's good to see you, darling.'

'Yes,' said Linda and her eyes filled with tears. 'Me too! No, I mean, it's good to see you.' She laughed. 'How did Granny die?'

'She just slipped away in her sleep, thank God.'

'Was anyone with her?'

'No.'

'Oh, I wish I'd been there.' Linda sighed. 'People shouldn't have to die on their own.'

'Then you'd've had to have sat with her for the last three years. She's not really been with us, has she?' Theódóra was going to fetch her suitcase to cover her irritation, but Linda ran down the steps and brought it inside.

The hall was large and high-ceilinged. It was painted pink. A window looked out on a big tree in the back garden. There was a wooden shed that had seen better days, beginning to rot and with patches of moss on it. A cat was basking lazily on the roof. The door to the living room was open. There was a piano against the wall. Theódóra noticed another, closed door, but assumed that neither of these rooms were her stepdaughter's and made as if to go upstairs.

'I'm in the basement flat, Mother.'

'The basement! But, Linda, you know I can't stand basements.'

'Well, that's where I live,' said her daughter, sounding irritated and pursing her lips.

There was a narrow spiral staircase winding its way down to the basement. It had been painted white and the paint was flaking off. Linda carried the suitcase and they found themselves in a dark corridor. 'The house needs a lot doing to it, but it's a nice place to live,' said the girl as she felt for the doorknob in the dark. 'It's only twenty minutes from the centre of town by tube.' She showed Theódóra into her room, which extended across nearly the whole basement area. The windows were larger than they had seemed to Theódóra. Spring flowers were blooming against the windows. She nearly said, 'This is a lot better than I thought', but she bit it back and said instead, 'This must be the brightest and most comfortable basement flat I've ever seen.' She looked up. 'The ceilings are high in here too. If you could find a glass, we could have some port. She took the port from the Duty Free bag, tore off the plastic seal and eased out the cork.

'How's Dad? When he rang to tell me I could go and get the ticket for the plane he said his heart wasn't so good.'

Theódóra could not stop herself smiling coldly. 'Well, there's no way he's going to change his diet. Eating horse-meat sausages before he goes to bed! If he's running the risk of having a heart attack, don't you think it's a bit strange for him to ignore the doctor's advice? Your father will carry on eating until his eyes pop out of his head.' She shook her head.

'Mother,' said the girl reproachfully, 'sometimes I think you don't love him at all.'

Theódóra was taken aback. 'Linda! I adore your father. It's just that I don't think this is the way to carry on.'

'Well, he can be pig-headed, but perhaps that's why he is who he is.'

'What do you mean?'

'Well, look at the way he's built up the business.'

'She can't be serious?' thought Theódóra and shrugged it off. 'It's lovely you're coming home in time for his sixtieth birthday. Your father and I . . . well, we've a bit of a surprise for you. You're not to know yet,' she added when she saw how excited the girl was getting. 'I was so exhausted after the election, you wouldn't believe it.'

'Weren't you going to become a minister?' Linda asked innocently.

'Whatever gave you that idea?' Theódóra stirred her cup.

'I rather gathered that from Father when he rang.'

'Was he boasting about it? Well, that's news to me. I thought he was lining up with the people who wanted me to quietly disappear.'

'What's this?'

'Nothing. The old bastards will inherit the earth,' Theódóra said crossly. 'It's lovely to see you,' she said, sounding affectionate and resting her hand over her daughter's.

'What brings you to London, Mama?'

'Just to see you, my pet. And have a break from politics. I had to meet Steven at Saltykov. We're expecting to have a boy from India come and stay with us in Iceland for a few months. The "Lions" arranged it. I wondered if you'd like to help me look after him for the first few days. You know, until he can find his way round Reykjavík on his own.'

'Of course, I'd love to. Do you want to see your room? The landlady's lent it to us. Let's go upstairs.'

Upstairs the window looked out over the top of the tree. 'I want us to have dinner together tonight. And not some awful heavy Icelandic-type meal! But now you must have a nap.' Linda turned back the bed to make it looked welcoming for her mother.

Theódóra lay awake a long time without falling asleep. The wallpaper looked old. It was obvious the room hadn't been decorated for many years. 'Probably nothing's been touched for decades,' she thought and turned her mind to the Greek islands. Whenever she had trouble getting to sleep she thought of the Greek islands. It was there she and Axel had gone on their honeymoon. He was ten years older then her and had had raven black hair. She had been a fool and smiled at Greeks who then thought she was looking for company. She was getting drowsy. She remembered a man with a terrific body who had come and sat at their table. Now she could see the islands, the sea lapping at the cliffs that were so white in the sun it hurt to look at them. She dozed, full of sadness and anxiety, and angry with her own body for beginning to show signs of ageing. She had always felt there was something missing because she couldn't have a child of her own. Sometimes Axel and Linda seemed so close she felt she wasn't wanted.

She heard light steps going up the stairs. Someone was moving about the house. It seemed much larger and more complicated than the spiral staircase and the five storeys had led her to believe. There were doors everywhere. How many people actually lived here? Axel had put on a lot of weight since they had first met. Now he had taken to cooking really unhealthy things for himself at home, fat salted meat in white sauce. 'He really loves being left in peace to eat alone,' she thought, irritated. She rolled on to her side and curled up. She lay like that a long time, dozing. She felt her life had gone too quickly and been wasted. Then she thought about her stepdaughter and it seemed as if she had already moved into the basement room at Dyngjuvegur where her own mother had lived like some kind of housemaid. She could see all her mother's furniture out on the lawn. 'Linda will never make me clear out Mother's room. It'll never happen,' thought Theódóra, clenched her fists and fell asleep.

It seemed as if she was at home in Iceland taking a walk in the old part of town. A man was walking on her left. She could not see who it was, but felt it might be the Catholic priest. He had come to ask her a favour. She did not know what the favour was and did not need to ask. She could not see his face. They walked together to 14 Sudurgata and looked at the house. The sun shone on the yellow corrugated iron and was reflected in a small window under the eaves. Suddenly the window exploded and flames burst out of it. The house on Sudurgata was on fire. There was something strange. Although the fire was burning fiercely, the house was not consumed by the flames. Then she noticed something even more strange. The house surrounded by fire was not 14 Sudurgata; it was her own house.

She sat up straight with a foul taste in her mouth. She was

wrung out with exhaustion. She had no appetite at all and could not face the thought of eating out.

Linda was sitting at her desk reading when Theódóra came down into the basement. There was a small lamp on. The girl's long hair fell on to the pages of the open book. 'You're awake?' Linda slammed the book shut. 'Good. I was just coming upstairs to wake you.'

'I'd rather stay in tonight. I much more tired than I thought.'

'You'll feel better in a bit. We've got so much to talk about, Mother. I know a super Vietnamese place. Something light'll do you good.'

Linda waved to a taxi. It was quite hot outside. A heatwave was about to descend on London. They drove along a long straight street in heavy traffic. Suddenly the houses on the right stopped and a large park came into view: Hyde Park. At the Oxford Street corner there was a large crowd gathered beneath the trees. Here and there people were standing on boxes above the crowd. 'It's Whitsun,' said Linda. 'I'd completely forgotten. We must go to Speakers' Corner.' She sounded excited. 'Usually there's nothing going on there, but on Sundays anyone can say anything they like.' Linda tapped on the glass behind the driver's head. He drove round a corner and let them out of the taxi.

10

There was light-coloured gravel scattered on the ground. A warm breeze wafted across the grass and moved gently through the crowd. The tall trees moved slightly, as if their branches were fans cooling the people below. The speakers were set a fair distance apart and the crowd comprised many different nationalities. Two policemen patrolled discreetly with radios tucked into their belts. Another two police officers sat on horses, unmoving among the crowd. On the grass a group of Muslims was facing Mecca and praying. A pale man with a long face was walking around carrying a placard: THE BLOOD OF CHRIST.

'Is everyone here a religious maniac?' asked Theódóra.

'Pretty much.'

A small black woman stood on a box behind a pulpit so high she had to stretch to reach it. She had small features and her face was set into a grimace. She was wearing a blue dress and a blue hat. She waved the Bible in the air and pounded it over and over again with her clenched fist. 'This is the Word . . . the Word of the Lord. Whosoever believeth not, he has already tasted death!'

A young black man could not resist this. He freed himself from the crowd and, outraged, hopped up and down in front of her, shouting out in his falsetto voice, 'Death!' He wagged his finger at her. 'How can you say that, sister? I want to show you something. I've got here written down some quotations from the Christian Book.' He pulled out a piece of paper covered in writing and tried to put it on the pulpit. The people crowded round. He tried to push the piece of paper towards the woman but she was having none it. She treated it as if were written by the devil himself, and screamed, 'Answer me! Do you believe Jesus was who he said he was?'

The young man pulled a face and did not answer. He tried to get her to take the piece of paper but she was resolute and demanded an answer: 'Was he who he said he was?'

'Can a man be God?' He was so outraged he could scarcely speak. 'Can some man be God? God was spirit!'

The little woman pounded the Bible with her fist and yelled, 'You read this book. Read, read, read this book!'

'It's a slaves' book. It's a book they've used to keep us enslaved for centuries.'

'You will go to hell and you are already dead, dead, dead!'

'How can you say such a thing, sister?' The man sounded shocked and amazed. 'Nobody can say he is God.' He was shouting now. 'They've been lying to us. Didn't Alexander the Great say, "I'm God"? Then Christ came. And God is meant to have turned into a man. No!' he shouted wildly. 'No! According to the laws of the time, the Jews were right to kill Jesus.'

'You'll burn in hell!' shouted the woman.

Now a fat black woman had had enough. She ran in front of the pulpit and shook her fist in the atheist's face, wailing, 'But Jesus is God. He is God. Jesus is God!'

Linda tugged her mother's arm. Behind them a young Muslim wearing a black robe and with a white scarf round his neck was standing on a box. He wanted to show the crowd a innocuous-looking Englishman who had embraced his religion. A tall young man, most likely a Christian, positioned himself immediately in front of the speaker and threw a fit whenever the Arab tried to speak. He waved his arms around like propellers and shouted, 'Oi! Just ask him what they do to people who nick something, no matter how little it's worth. They cut their hands off!'

The Arab jumped down from the box. He struggled with his English. 'You let me speak,' he stammered. 'Be gentleman. Show you are Christian! Be a gentlemen, good sir,' he begged, patting the Christian on the chest with the palm of his hand.

It did not have the slightest effect on the other man. The Arab talked quietly to his companions and wanted the police called over. A group of black Muslims stared threateningly at the white boy.

Another speaker was extolling the virtues of family life. He was elderly and kindly and wanted an international police force set up to bring about peace anywhere in the world at short notice.

'Excuse me, are you an arms dealer?' someone called out and people laughed.

On the next box there was an American in a ten-gallon hat telling people how he had been saved. It had happened on the evening of 23 March 1969, at exactly five past six.

'Why did you bring me here?' Theódóra asked Linda.

'To demonstrate to you that I'm not mad. Let's go now.'

The trees swayed gently above the crowd as if they would like to throw away their fans and pat the people's heads.

They were sitting in the Vietnamese restaurant. Linda ordered fish and rice for herself and oysters for her mother.

'Oysters! Let me choose for myself. I've never had oysters.'

'Then it's about time you did.'

Theódóra asked for water but her daughter wanted lager.

'Is Father killing himself working too hard?'

'He took on a secretary the other day, but she's no good and I think I'll have to let her go,' Theódóra said wearily. 'I'm going to sort out somebody better when I get back. It's so difficult to find the right people even with unemployment so high.'

'You're just jealous,' laughed Linda. 'Is the girl you want to fire pretty?'

'Yes.'

'The old bugger!'

'It's not like that, Linda. Don't say things like that. Your father isn't much of a one for the ladies.'

'No, of course not.' Her daughter sipped her lager and looked at her. 'But I'll just say this. I'll bet she's go fair hair and a great figure. You know Father's always had a weakness for blondes with great figures. Look at your own hair.'

'But I'm flat as a pancake.' Theódóra looked at the mirror behind her daughter and saw that her hair was more silvery now, even though there were still auburn lights in it. She must have been looking sad because Linda said gently, 'Don't worry. I was only teasing.'

The food was served. Theódóra put an oyster in her mouth and waited in anticipation. As she eased the flesh apart with her tongue and teeth, she was struck with such a strong taste of the sea she had a mental image of an old wooden pier covered in fish slime. 'Good God! I can't eat that!' She swallowed and grimaced.

Linda picked up some fish and rice with her chopsticks and said, 'I'd like you to let me live at Skólabrú.'

Theódóra looked at her in surprise and took a deep breath. 'You know it's just not possible. That's where Hördur has his office. I've got your old room back just how it was.'

'I meant the top floor. Grandmother's dead.'

'Nothing's been decided about the house.'

'Then I'll just have to rent somewhere in town.' Linda frowned. '"Put my old room back how it was"! I can't live there with you like that any more. I'm an adult now.'

'I don't think your father will be very happy if you move out as soon as you get back home.'

'He knows I want to move out and he's got nothing to say about it. He just hasn't dared mention it to you. Isn't it about time you did something with that basement flat? It's got it's own front door anyway. Can't I live there?'

'I can't bear to think about it. I can't.'

'It's over twenty years since Sophia Concordia died.'

'If I cleared out that furniture it would feel as if I was betraying my mother. I just can't do it.'

'It sounds insane to me,' said the daughter calmly. 'You're like Miss Havisham in Dickens's *Great Expectations*. Like the old lady sitting in the great hall with her wedding cake all those years.'

'So?'

'But there's nowhere for me to go.'

'Your father and I have put your old room to rights. I don't want to talk about it any more.' Theódóra was getting angry.

There was high colour in Linda's cheeks but she calmed enough to say, 'Well, someone'll get Skólabrú.'

'Yes. Isn't it only right for Hördur and Villa to have it?'

Linda put her elbows on the table, interlaced her fingers and raised an eyebrow at her mother. 'Do you really think they'll settle for that?'

'What do you mean?'

'How long have you been in politics?' Linda asked satirically.

'I don't know what you mean.'

'Obviously they'll insist on Heidnaberg being sold. Or at least divided up between the heirs. Or to have a bigger say.'

'Why should they want that?' asked Theódóra grandly. 'It's my company. I built it up.'

Linda stopped pretending her father had anything to do with it. 'My God, Mother, you're such an innocent! Vilhelmína will inherit, jointly with you. After all Ingibjörg was her mother.'

'It was Ingibjörg's wish that Villa and Hördur shouldn't get their hands on Heidnaberg. It was all agreed five years ago. She was convinced they'd want to sell up.'

'So were they cut out of the will?'

'Not exactly. They'll get some shares. This is confidential,' she whispered. 'Nobody but you and I knows anything about this.'

'So who gets the money? Who gets Heidnaberg?'

'I do.'

'But you and Grandmother weren't really getting on.'

'No, but she knew I was the only one who could keep the company from falling apart.'

Linda grinned. 'That's something to look forward to: the look on Vilhelmína Thóroddsdóttir's and Hördur Gottskálksson's faces when they hear that. But I can tell you one thing. They're not going to be happy with just one solitary old house.'

'Everyone is trying to drag me under. My colleagues in the party. The Prime Minister. My husband . . .' Theódóra looked at the girl fiercely. 'And now you. I can see I'm going to have to defend myself.'

Linda sat up in her chair. 'How come you let them trample all over you when they were forming the government?'

'Linda, I've come to London to get some rest.'

'You've never been able to forgive Father for having had me and you not being able to have any children. The truth is that as a child I was always left on my own, ignored, abandoned.' said Linda coldly.

Theódóra did not answer but looked down at the table to hide how she felt.

Linda saw this and was sorry for what she'd said, but could not bring herself to apologize. She ordered a bottle of white wine and Theódóra had a glass. They finished their meal and gradually the tension between them slipped away.

The daughter drank most of the bottle as she talked about the Italian painter Caravaggio. She had just seen a film in which the director had tried to unify film and painting. And it had come off! 'You ought to see it, Mother,' she said enthusiastically. 'It's fantastic when the actors move and what you thought was a painting comes to life.'

'Is this one of those films where nothing happens? I always fall asleep in that sort of film. I thought you were keen on music?'

'I haven't made up my mind yet.'

'So, what have you been doing with yourself?'

'Oh, this and that. Mostly just trying to find out about myself. Let's go to a pub. There's one round here.'

It was getting dark but cooler. It was very crowded in the pub and there was lots of noise. They found a space by a small high round table.

'What are these revelations you told your father about on the phone?' asked Theódóra as she sipped her brandy. 'Is God speaking to you?' She looked at her stepdaughter with a serious expression.

'Well, somebody is.'

'Is this in your dreams?'

'No, not always. I sometimes see visions. God has saved me, Mother. I feel his spirit enter me and my surroundings fall away and for a few seconds it's as if I'm transported somewhere. I can't describe it any other way. It's much more like reality than a dream. Last time it happened it was as if I was standing in the middle of a lavafield back home in Iceland and I saw a demon so large it blotted out the sun. I knew it was the beast from the Book of Revelation that has the voice of a dragon and the horns of a ram. There was a multitude surrounding the beast. I knew that it was the nations of the world bowing down and worshipping the beast and the beast set his seal on the foreheads and hands of all those who belonged to him. And I heard a voice like thunder saying, "Linda Concordia Axelsdóttir, you must fight this beast." And suddenly the lavafield pulled us together and I was standing in front of the beast and I saw it stretching out its hand towards me. It wanted to touch my head or my hand and I could not escape it. A dark, evil group of people stood behind me, pushing me closer to it. We were surrounded by the darkness, a living, breathing darkness. Then, instead of the beast, there was a man in a leather garment with a hood standing in front of me. His face was bony and covered in sweat. His eyes were as cold as the eyes of a fish. He stretched out his hand and touched me. I felt a sharp pain on my forehead and came back to consciousness.'

The girl rubbed her forehead.

'This is all nonsense!' said Theódóra, full of anxiety. 'Are you insane? What has God got to do with this? You've seen some horror film in the cinema or on TV and it's affected you, that's all.'

The girl sipped her Campari through a straw and seemed hurt.

There were lots of people in the pub talking at the tops of their voices. Theódóra was silent for a moment, watching them. Finally she said, 'I'm not even sure that God exists. How can you be so sure of it?'

'He has revealed himself to me.' Linda looked at her mother solemnly. 'I have read the whole Bible while I've been so lonely here and there it says that whomsoever he chooses, he shall draw unto himself.'

Theódóra went off to buy some peanuts. When she returned Linda was deep in conversation with a tall young black man wearing sunglasses. The man was very calm. His shirt was opened at the neck and the hairs on his chest were even blacker than his skin.

'Is this a friend of yours?' asked Theódóra when there was a gap in the conversation.

'No. We've only just met.'

'Linda, I want to go home.'

'Can't we stay a bit longer?'

'I'll get myself a taxi then.'

'I'll come with you.'

But the girl's conversation with the man continued until Theódóra was tired of waiting and left in a temper. At the next corner she found a taxi rank in the gathering dusk. She had to ring the door-bell and explain her presence to the landlady.

When she was in her room and had pulled the blanket over her, she thought, 'If she can take care of herself for months and years on end, she scarcely needs me to wait up for her.' She dozed and woke when the front door slammed. Not long after someone left the house but she could not see through the trees whether or not it was the black man. 'Well, she's not getting that basement flat at the house,' thought Theódóra angrily. 'God saved her! Who from? Filled her with his spirit. It's all rubbish. Doesn't it say somewhere, '"Thou shalt not commit adultery"?'

She remembered the man who had spoken to her on the plane and punched the pillow angrily. She meant to let her mind wander off to the Greek Islands, but found herself thinking of her mother. They had stopped over in Copenhagen before flying on to Athens. She remembered the bright red trams crisscrossing the town in their efficient way like so many toys. It was in the Year of Our Lord Nineteen Hundred and Seventy-Six. The beautifully cut stone slabs in the streets were polished by the passing traffic of human feet and horses' hoofs. They took a train to Roskilde. She wanted to see Sophia Concordia in Sankt Hans Hospital. It was a lunatic asylum. She sat with her face up against the window watching the redbrick houses with their neat little gardens and brown roofs hurtling by. They drank coffee in a restaurant on the main street. There were a few round tables inside, the stained-glass windows were arch-shaped. She looked at the parrots in a shop window. One of them was old and angry and had dirt on its breast feathers. The bird kept jerkily lifting its knotted talons up to its beak. It twisted its neck and said its name over and over again: 'Jesper! Jesper!' Why did one remember such insignificant details with such clarity, as if this was some momentous event?

What would Sophia Concordia look like? She was considered dangerous. Theódóra dreaded seeing the staring eyes and open mouth. She did not want to have to face it alone. 'Will she know me?' she thought and felt like a condemned criminal. She walked towards Roskilde Cathedral with its twin towers and its walls covered in foliage. She walked down a wooded slope. On a wall there was a stone satyr's head spewing water into a stone trough. A fat dog came and drank and wagged its stubby tail. She walked on down the path. There was a lot of greenery and the trees were tall and strong. Birds were singing everywhere. She did not know their names. There was the sound of running water. The heat was stifling and insects hovered in the air. She sat down on a bench and looked at the hard dry ground and the green grass. She was sitting under a tall tree. There was cool and eerie silence in its shade. A black bird with a white breast flew into the tree and perched there as if he'd done it a hundred times before. He rocked on the branch, looking around him, ignoring her completely. She walked on and came to some solidly built houses, painted white, with small windows. There was a high stone wall around them. Theódóra walked to and fro outside the gates for some time. Finally she walked back up into the wood and sat beneath the same tree. The bird had gone. She waited there for an hour and then walked back into town. Axel was sitting outside a pavement café, fortifying himself with a cognac until her return. His cheeks were flushed and he looked happy. He stood up as she joined him. 'Did you see your mother?' 'Yes.' 'How was she, Tedda?' he asked kindly. 'Oh,' she said. 'Don't ask. I'll tell you later. I will say one thing, though. It was quite a shock.' She looked at him, surprised he did not realize she was lying. He seemed relieved not to have to talk about Sophia Concordia and never asked about her again. She could remember the evening train to Copenhagen. The green of the train grew darker in the twilight.

Theódóra did not get to sleep until there was a grey light in the window. She seemed to have dozed a little, then she woke and hunted for her wristwatch. It was seven. She had slept for about two hours. She fell asleep again and awoke with a start at half past nine. She had a meeting with one of the directors of Saltykov at eleven.

The Saltykov offices were in a new hexagonal dark grey building. Theódóra was met by Steven Williams. He was an ebullient young man with a ginger moustache. He had visited Iceland and was a friend of Axel's. He showed her some photographs, pictures of the Indian children. One of the presidents of an American corporation prominent in the 'Lions' had asked the European distributors to work together with him on this humanitarian project. 'What those children have suffered is appalling! All their fathers were ill-treated while they were in custody. I can't say more than that at present. Terrible things were done. I'll post the information on to you. Would you like to choose a child?' He seemed slightly embarrassed, as if the question were inappropriate somehow.

She counted the photographs. There were fourteen. Boys and girls. Her eye was caught by a dark-skinned boy of about ten. The child looked like some adult whose steadfastness and loyalty God had hazarded in some unspeakable bet with Satan. 'I'll take little Job,' she said and pointed to the child.

'Good!' Steven took the photograph out of the album and looked at the name on the back. 'So in the autumn he'll come to you in Iceland for a year?'

She nodded. 'It's a pleasure to be able to help.'

'And he'll be staying with you?'

'Either with us or I'll find him a good home.'

They had a light lunch in a restaurant. Theódóra was meeting her daughter on the steps of the National Gallery at two o'clock sharp.

She looked round as she arrived but Linda was nowhere to be seen. First she takes a man home with her and now she makes her mother wait. Did the girl have no respect? She felt an ice-cold anger. It was nearly three by the time Linda deigned to put in an appearance.

Theódóra did not try to hide her irritation and greeted her coldly. Linda acted as if nothing had happened the night before. The highly polished floor and the slight echo in the gallery put Theódóra in mind of a gym. Linda walked straight towards the painting. 'This is Christ at Emmaeus by Caravaggio. The greatest of all painters. It was done in 1604. This is the painter I mentioned to you yesterday.' The girl explained the painting. 'It's called *The Road to Emmaeus*. After the Resurrection, Christ met the apostles on the road but they did not recognize him until they sat down to eat. The painting shows that moment, Mother. Look, Jesus has an almost female beauty. He stretches out his hands to bless the bread, the meat and the fruit. He disappeared the moment they realized who he was.'

On the table there was a flask of wine catching a square of bright crystalline light. Behind Jesus was a disciple gazing intently at the lower half of the Saviour's face. Two were sitting with Christ, one of them a young man, astonished and about to leap out of his chair, the older sitting in stunned amazement on the other side of the table.

'I like to think the one on the right's Peter. Look how startled he is.'

The Apostle Peter had grey hair and a full beard.

'Look at him, Mother. Look at him stretching out his hands. Caravaggio is telling us that Peter will be crucified.'

'There's a man I'm going to introduce you to when we get back.'

'Who's that?'

'His name is Father Bernhardur. He's a Catholic priest.'

'Jesus! I've no desire to meet any Catholic priest.'

'Could you find a phone for me?' said Theódóra as if her mind was on something else. 'I ought to ring and speak to Vilhjálmur.'

'Something important?'

'Yes it is. It's very important.'

I spent most of Tuesday trying to get in touch with Axel. I was trying to set up a new magazine in competition with *Weekend*. As often happens after an election the town seemed a bit drowsy, but most of us, with the exception of Seli, were at Hotel Borg for lunch. I was greeted with an icy silence at the round table. A stranger had been invited to take my chair and I could see that news had got round that I was no longer editor. I managed to raise Seli by phone just before three o'clock. I was lucky to catch him as he was rarely in the office after three and went to the cinema at five nearly every day. I asked him if he wanted to invest in my new venture. I can't understand how I could have been so stupid. All my connections were severed. I was experiencing the truth of the old saying that a person might laugh at your jokes but that doesn't make him your friend. He asked me coldly if I really thought he would consider investing in a magazine that would libel him.

I looked everywhere for investment but doors kept being slammed in my face. No one wanted to put up money for a new magazine. They all thought the market was saturated. Late that evening I was so desperate that I went to Dyngjuvegur to try and talk sense into Seli. There was no one there as, believe or not, he'd gone to the cinema for the seven o'clock screening.

Axel arrived at the cinema just before seven. People were standing in line waiting to buy tickets. He did not feel like joining the queue so drove down to the ice-cream parlour at Hagamelur and bought an ice-cream with hot chocolate sauce and ate it in the car. When he came back the cinema was full. He went to Hotel Holt, ordered a salad, drank water from a wine glass and thought how proud Theódóra would be of him.

When he got back to the car he found he was dreading returning to the empty house on Dyngjuvegur. Instead of taking the coast road he turned off into Skúlagata and glanced at Dagný's windows. Was she home? She had rung in and said she would not be able to come to work for a few days after her mother had died. Her sons would need her, at least during the day when their father was at work. 'Poor woman,' thought Axel and decided to call and offer his condolences.

On her doorstep he hesitated and was about to change his mind about visiting her. The entryphone wasn't working and the door was ajar. When he got to the third floor his heart was beating rapidly, but he didn't know whether it was stress or excitement. He paused on the half-landing and took a few deep breaths. He left it a moment before knocking. He did not want Dagný to see him huffing and puffing. He looked at the keyhole and imagined it blocked up with bits of broken matches. He looked down at the stairs and imagined Tryggvi sitting on the step looking up at him. He shuddered when he thought of the expression in his eyes. He thought that it was a great blessing not to be born a woman and then he knocked on the door. There was a peephole.

He could hear rustling on the other side of the door. Someone screamed. There was such terror in the scream that it seemed to rob the person of all human dignity. Axel stood there a moment paralysed. Then he hammered desperately on the door. He tried to shout, 'Dagný!' The sound of her name was drowned out by the noise now coming from inside the flat. He heard someone shout for help and knew that the woman was shouting out of the window into the street below. He carried on hammering on the door, although he knew it was pointless. He heard the door on the landing opposite open and a fair-haired elderly woman with a puffy face, sagging cheeks and a lizard's protruding eyes stood there staring at him accusingly. 'Are you all crazy?' she asked. 'What's going on?'

Axel ran down the stairs to the window on the half-landing and pressed his face to the glass. He could see Dagný leaning out above him with the sash window resting across her shoulders. The catch swung to and fro as she waved and shouted. A stranger paused by a shop front on the other side of the street and looked up at her. Axel hit the glass several times with the palm of his hand and shouted, 'Dagný!'

'Bastard!' hissed the woman on the landing.

Shouting had no effect on her at all. For a moment he glanced across the street below and out to sea. At that very moment the evening sun caught the surface of the sea, setting it on fire as if it was dried tinder.

Axel ran upstairs heavily and rang the klaxon-like doorbell. He could hear a child crying. 'Damn it all!' he shouted. He was both angry and afraid. 'Everyone'll get to hear about it. I'm not used to this sort of thing!'

The woman in the doorway was still looking at him, shocked. 'Have you no shame?' she said.

Axel hammered on the door and rang the bell. No one opened the door. He ran downstairs. A thin, dark-haired man was standing on the second-floor landing. The door to his flat was open and he looked at Axel with contempt. Axel thought he was drunk. 'When are you going to stop making trouble here?' said the man. 'You don't give us a moment's peace.'

He hardly knew why he was going downstairs but it now struck him it would be a good idea to get to his mobile phone, get Dagný's number from directory enquiries and ring her. Anyway get into his car and put some distance between him and the flat. For the life of him he couldn't remember Dagný's family name. He pushed open the door to the street and walked out for all the world as if everything was perfectly all right. But at that moment the police drove up in their white Volvo. He remembered the police approaching Toyota for a deal. The policeman in the passenger seat looked at him pityingly. The driver leaned forward in order to see better. Axel thought himself a free man and began to cross the street but both policemen got out and the driver barred his way.

The dark-haired man from the house had come out on to the steps with another man, who now declared, 'He was beating up his wife. We can't get any peace in this house for the pair of them.' Axel looked up at the window. It was not secured and the catch was hanging down against the glass. Axel turned to the policemen and smiled at them. He was wanting to show how ridiculous the whole thing was. The policemen did not seem to be on his side but stared at him blankly. Neither had yet spoken. Axel introduced himself. 'My name is Axel Sigurgeirsson and I own Heidnaberg. I'm the Toyota importer. At one time the police were considering buying Toyotas. I can't now remember the name of the chap I was dealing with.' Axel looked into the face of one of the policemen. He shrugged his shoulders and hitched up his trousers. He stood on his toes for an instant and laughed, but the laughter did not reach his eyes. 'This is my car.' He pointed to it. 'The new Toyota Land Cruiser 1995 over there. It's a show-room model. It's not on the market yet.' Axel felt he was being tested on his catechism. 'My wife's name is Theódóra Thóroddsdóttir.' He scratched his head. 'She won a tremendous victory in the elections and the Prime Minister is a good friend of mine.' When nothing seemed to be having any effect he added, 'He's been a great friend for years! He's a good chap, Hannes Pálmason.'

'He's been here every day acting like a maniac,' said the dark-haired man, losing his balance.

Suddenly Dagný appeared. She ran straight over to the police-man and tugged his sleeve. 'He doesn't even look like Tryggvi!' she shouted. The policemen looked at each other and then one of them cleared his throat. 'This is the man that's disturbing you then?'

'God, no. I'm so sorry. My ex has been making my life a misery,' she said quickly. 'I've phoned the police over and over again and you never come. My ex has a coat like this. That's why I was so scared. But this man is my employer.'

The police returned to their Volvo and the crowd of curious onlookers drove off or melted away one by one into their own flats. Dagný stood on the pavement looking pale and anguished. There was grid of small windows in the front door and her daughter Sylvía was looking through one of them. Axel opened his mouth but before he could say anything Dagný interrupted. 'How was I to know it was you?' she asked pitifully.

The little girl was trying to open the door and eventually did so.

'Mother, come indoors,' she pleaded.

'Let me invite you in,' pleaded Dagný.

'I wasn't here for any particular reason. I was just out for a drive. I was going to the cinema but it was full and I found myself wondering how you were. Tedda's overseas and I was feeling a bit lonely,' he stammered.

He followed her upstairs with his hat in his hand. Sylvía ran ahead of them.

The woman on the fifth floor opened the door and peeped out into the corridor as soon as she heard the sound of footsteps. 'It's OK, Halldóra,' said Dagný.

'I just wanted to have a private chat,' puffed Axel. He rummaged in his pockets for some change to give the girl for sweets but couldn't find any. He was keen to be alone with the woman. 'Something struck me the day before yesterday after you had gone home.' He surprised himself by getting to the point so quickly.

She invited him into the kitchen. It was a long time since he had been in a room like that. It was little more than a galley. It looked comfy, with a small table with a striped plastic tablecloth and tall cupboards painted white with brass handles. She opened a cupboard and took out a bowl of sugar. He could see the shelves were covered in vinyl with the edges secured with drawing pins. 'Tea or coffee?' she asked. She was out of breath. There was a transfer of a pear decorating the bottom of the cupboard door. She bent down to get out two cups and he stared at her arse. 'No, thank you.'

'There must be something I can get you?'

'I want to talk to you.'

Sylvía was looking at him accusingly and silently. It was clear to Axel it would be very difficult for him to discuss the matter in these circumstances. The mother turned to her daughter. 'Go and play, Sylvía.' She turned back to Axel. 'Shall we go through into the sitting room?'

The sitting room was chilly, like a summer home that was heated only once in a while. There was an old green sofa and two chairs, the arms painted with black lacquer, set against the wall. She sat on the sofa and he sat down beside her. 'What would she look like topless?' he wondered. And the answer came at once. She'd be like a page torn from *Playboy* or *Hustler* or *Knave*. He wanted to put his arm round her. Her scent was driving him mad.

Sylvía found something to play with out in the hall. He could sense she had her ears on stalks.

'What did you want to say to me? I can't wait.' The kettle wailed in the kitchen.

'It struck me I could help you with your current difficulties,' he said, blushing and sweating. 'I've been mulling it all over ever since your husband came to Heidnaberg. It so happens' – he had forgotten for the moment about his daughter Linda – 'that the second-floor flat on Skólabrú will soon be available. To be quite frank it's better than this by a long chalk.' He looked round him. 'I think you would be perfectly safe there. Hördur would be downstairs nearly all the time and he'd take care of you if Tryggvi came calling. And, I assure you, Hörder Gottskálksson is no pushover.' He paused a moment. 'The police station in the customs house is close by if Tryggvi bothered you in the evening. I think you'd be very well set up on Skólabrú.' Axel looked happy. 'It's only a step to the National Theatre and the Idno Theatre and you are an actress, aren't you?' He could feel his heart cantering, but it was a pleasant canter. 'Well, what do you say, Dagný?'

Sylvía leaned against the door jamb and stared at her mother and her mother's guest.

While Axel had been talking Dagný had been nodding thoughtfully, looking a little disturbed, but now she burst out, with her face flushed, 'The bloody man. The bloody bastard! I could kill him! At first I used to pity Tryggvi but I don't any more. If there's any justice in this world, he'll pay for it! I'm completely defenceless. Does someone have to die before the authorities take anything seriously? And what about the girl?' She flung out an arm in Sylvía's direction. 'I know you mean well. But there's no way I could live so close to that doctor. Haven't you heard? I'm having him charged with manslaughter. Honestly, I thought it was him at the door. That's why I screamed. I was terrified. You wear the same clothes. Why's that?'

'It's what the sisters gave us last Christmas. I don't know why Tedda and Villa chose things so similar. Probably as a joke.' He stroked the black coat thoughtfully as if he was admiring the quality of the wool. Then he suddenly seemed to realize what she'd said. 'You're going to have Hördur charged?' He was flabbergasted. 'What do you mean? I hadn't heard. Manslaughter! Nobody tells me anything. But that shouldn't make any difference to you having a look at the flat. The estate will be shared out and Hördur and Vilhelmína will be considerably better off. Hördur won't want to have his surgery in the old town. He'll be gone before the summer, you'll see.'

'I can't bear the thought of living there. The man disgusts me. I'm terrified of him.'

Axel had thought everything out very carefully but now his plans had come to nought. Sylvía looked at him scornfully, with a cold smile. As she looked at him Axel said quickly, 'Actually, I have another flat.'

'It's very kind of you, I must say. I can't stay here much longer. The flat belongs to a friend and she's due back at the end of next week.' Dagný waited to hear what Axel had got to say.

'There's a very good basement flat at Dyngjuvegur. It's empty at the moment. Two rooms and a kitchen, with its own access.'

'How does that sound to you?' Dagný asked her daughter. 'Would you like living on that side of town?'

The girl shrugged.

'Let's go and have a look at it,' said Axel.

Sylvía objected, but Dagný was worried in case Tryggvi came and she asked the woman in the next flat to look after her daughter. The lizard eyes inspected Axel in minute detail. It felt like a dream, walking downstairs with Dagný. By the time he opened the car door for her, Theódóra had ceased to exist. He felt terrific walking beside her up to the door at Dyngjuvegur. He opened the door, invited her into the hall and indicated for her to go in front of him down into the basement. He pushed open the door of his mother-in-law's flat. He was beside himself with excitement. They went into the living room.

'What wonderful furniture!' She clapped her hands together.

'This old junk?' he said, surprised.

She stroked the mirrored cupboard and caressed a jug and the washbasin. 'Junk?' she said, admiringly. 'These are wonderful old things.'

'To be honest, I think this is the most appalling old rubbish.' He walked over to the window and drew back the curtain with a sharp tug. The curtains smelt musty.

'Not in my opinion,' she said decisively and wandered round the room touching objects as if she was examining the contents of a treasure chest. She walked across to the mirror and looked at herself, stroking her hair as it fell down by her cheek. He walked up behind her and looked over her shoulder. She looked different in the mirror. The face was reversed and the look in the eyes was different. He was almost tempted to put his arms round her but he controlled himself.

'You look so strange in the mirror,' she said, blushing.

'I've never been what you'd call good-looking.'

'You're a handsome man,' said Dagný.

'Let's have a look at the kitchen,' said Axel, happy.

'Is it a long time since the old lady died?'

'An eternity. But Theódóra couldn't bear any suggestion of touching anything in here. Until now, that is,' he lied. He went into the kitchen and opened a cupboard. There was a terracotta milk jug and an odd assortment of cups. There was a foul smell coming from the sink. He turned the tap and rusty green water spurted out. He let it run.

'You could have a fridge over there. There's a point for it in the corner. I don't know what happened to the old one. The whole place needs airing.' He tried to open a window in the kitchen and had to hit the catch hard to release it. 'Well, what you think?'

'I think it's marvellous.'

'Let me show you the bedroom.'

They walked through the living room and he opened a door. The old bed was still made up. Without thinking he opened a wardrobe. As he looked towards the bed, he suddenly saw in his mind's eye Dagný pulling up the quilt to cover a breast, revealing a naked leg. He shut his eyes tight. That's what you get for seeing too many films. Suddenly he had a thought. 'Was old Professor Thóroddur carrying on with the both of them?' he asked, his voice shaking slightly. 'The bathroom is at the end of the hall.'

She turned round a full 360 degrees before they walked through to the bathroom. Under the window there was a Westinghouse washing machine and spin drier. Axel looked at Dagný.

'Could I use this?' she asked eagerly.

'I don't see why not.'

'It would be wonderful. I was intending to buy these things for myself.'

'Don't go spending your money like that.' He patted the washing machine. 'There's plenty of life left in this. These machines were built to last. A machine like this would make light work of anything you and your daughter could throw at it.'

'What are you going to do with all those things in the flat?'

'Put them into storage or give them away.' It occurred to him that she might like to have some of the things herself. Even so, he did not think it right to offer her anything until he had had a chance to talk it over with his wife. He mentally formed a sentence: 'Tedda, would it matter to you if Dagný had some of mother-in-law's old junk?'

He tried to imagine his wife's reply but found it impossible. Suddenly he realized Dagný was looking at him tenderly.

'It's no good,' she said. 'We both know I could never move in here. Perhaps we were both a little insane.' She laughed and her eyes misted over. 'But thank you for being so kind. You're so sweet.' She gave him a quick kiss on the cheek. 'Now drive me home.'

12

They got a taxi home from Keflavík Airport and when it drew up at the house Linda saw Vilhjálmur standing on the steps ready to welcome them. Axel had come outside smoking a cigar, looking excited and rather foolish. Linda ran into her father's arms. 'Don't you want to see what I've got you, Father?' she said, the moment they embraced. She was laughing with happiness. 'Villi, please put my bags in the living room. What am I doing! Ordering you about like Mother. I'm perfectly capable of carrying my own bags.' She picked up both her suitcases and hurried inside with them. She threw one of them on to the sofa under the living-room window and opened it. As she straightened up she could see Laugardals stadium through the window. It was like an old friend. 'Don't you think you'll look good in this, Father?'

'What are you doing buying me shirts?' Axel was astonished by the gift.

'Careful, you'll burn a hole in it,' said his daughter and snatched the cigar out of his mouth.

'Linda,' said Axel, sounding worried, 'what was it you were saying to me the other day on the phone about God talking to you?'

'That's right, Daddy.' She continued taking things out of the case. 'Just like he does to everyone else.'

Axel stood in the middle of the living room, looking happily at his shirt. Then Linda tossed five pairs of underpants at him, each with its own little blue hanger. Then he found himself holding a pair of light-brown trousers. And then some socks. 'I don't think I'll be able to get into these,' he said, examining the trousers. 'I've got so bloody fat.'

'Go and try them on. I spent all day yesterday in Oxford Street.'

He looked around in surprise. 'What happened to your mother and Villi?'

'I expect they're having some secret meeting about the stock market as usual. Stop worrying about it. All they think about is money. Think about me instead, Daddy.' She sat down on the sofa and rummaged around in the suitcase. When she looked up her father was standing in the middle of the room like a stork, trying to get one leg into his new trousers. 'God, just look at you! Oughtn't you to do that in private? Do you always take off your clothes when there are ladies present?' Linda stood up, folded her arms across her chest and put her head on one side. 'You really do look good.'

With considerable difficulty, Axel managed to pull up the trouser leg. He leant on the living-room table for a moment before making an assault on the other leg. He reached out for his cigar and had a puff. Then he carried on from where he had left off, trying to get the trousers on. 'Do you think they suit me?' He was trying to fasten them over his stomach.

'Yes. Those are for summer. You look fine. Mother didn't want to get them, but for once I put my foot down. I want you to look good, Daddy.' She kept taking things out of the case in great excitement.

Theódóra bustled in. 'Your father's far too old for clothes like that!'

'Oh Mother, you always give people things you really want yourself,' said Linda impatiently. 'I chose this for Daddy.'

'Now, girls, be nice to each other. I think I'll try on the shirt too.' Axel picked up the brown and blue striped casual shirt. 'This'll go well with the trousers. Perfect for the summer home.'

'That's why I got them!' Linda threw a Tyrolean hat with a small pale-green feather in the band at him.

'And a hat! How do you like that!' He started to unbutton his shirt but suddenly felt awkward exposing his bare chest to the women and left the room, carrying his shirt in one hand and wearing his hat on his head. When he had left the room, his daughter's manner changed and became serious. She asked, 'That's your last word, is it, Mother? I'm not to have the top flat at Skólabrú?'

'You know I can't make a decision now, Linda. Can we just put it on hold for a while?' Theódóra rubbed her temples. 'I'm getting a headache.'

'Why not? I don't understand.'

'I don't think you're old enough yet. The town centre is full of drunks at the weekend. Your grandmother's only just died. And I haven't had a chance to speak to Vilhelmína about what's going to happen to the house.'

At that moment Axel returned. He had tucked the shirt firmly into his trousers. He was wearing the hat.

'And here are your slippers.' said Linda crossly and threw them on the floor.

'I reckon I could pass for a film star. Doesn't Daddy look good?' He looked at mother and daughter and eased his feet into the slippers. 'Aren't you going to make films?'

'Yes,' said Linda sullenly.

'What about?'

'I'm going to make a documentary about women in Iceland. About the position of women today.'

'Well it's a good position, isn't it? Icelanders have always loved and respected their womenfolk!'

Linda shuddered and her father had no idea why.

She lifted her head, letting her hair fall down her back, and looked at him seriously. 'What you think, Daddy? Can't I go and live in town like we agreed?'

Axel swallowed. 'But that's my office. I just don't see how I can do without it.'

'You haven't set foot in that office for a million years. Anyway I don't want to live in your office. I just think the best plan is to clear the top flat. Are her things to be left to sit there like in some ghastly museum? Just like the basement downstairs. I'm not allowed to move in there either. What do you reckon?'

'I don't know what to say.'

'So you're against it then?' Linda was looking at him, hurt and betrayed.

'That's not what I'm saying.' Axel glanced at Theódóra.

'Then what are you saying?'

'It's just that you're so young.' He hesitated. 'I don't feel it's right for you to move out so soon. You're only just twenty.'

'So you're against it?'

'I think I'm going to have to say no. I agree with your mother.' Axel sounded embarrassed. 'And there's something else,' he added, suddenly brightening. 'These days young people want to live at home until they're getting on for thirty.'

Theódóra found it hard to suppress a smile.

His daughter stood up. Her face was stormy. 'You're bastards, the pair of you,' she hissed and stomped out of the room.

'I was planning on giving you a new Toyota,' Axel called after her.

'Yes. That's the surprise I mentioned,' called Theódóra.

'You can take your Toyota and shove it up your arse,' came the yell from down the hall.

'Listen, young lady.' Theódóra's voice was heavy with anger. 'Come back here this instant!'

The daughter slammed her bedroom door.

Axel started to go to her.

'No, Axel, leave her be,' said Theódóra firmly, sat down and sighed. 'All this is killing me. Perhaps we should let her have the top flat at Skólabrú?'

'It's up to you and your sister.'

Theódóra stood up and went down to the basement.

She opened a drawer in her mother's flat where she kept photographs, letters and odd bits and pieces. She had managed to retrieve the medical notes from the Sankt Hans Hospital with a great deal of difficulty. She flicked through the pages and came to '21 March 1967'. 'On arrival the patient was drunk. A journalist by profession. Had worked at the Royal Porcelain Factory in her youth. Communist. Loose morals. Predisposed towards promiscuous sexual behaviour. Blames everything and everyone.'

'January 1969. Rude. Uncontrollable. Amenable between attacks. Sent to the punishment cell. Good at sewing and cleaning when she sets her mind to it. Teaches the others. Had to be confined to the punishment cell at Christmas for attacking a nursing assistant.'

'21 August 1970. Sophia Concordia unsettled. Shouts out of the window at passers by. Insists on her Communist convictions. Sharp tongue. Able to curb her language if threatened with a cold shower. Was allowed to go into town yesterday where she drank coffee with a man and has since been very grateful.'

'18 July 1971. She has begun to work in the laundry and joined the choir, but then takes the opportunity to shout and scream. Behaves as if she knows everything. Politics. Religion. Patronizes the other patients.'

'31 March 1972. Preoccupied with thoughts of violence and seems unable to control herself. High opinion of herself. Says: "Trust little Sophia." Claims to have the strength of three when it comes to work.'

Theódóra turned the pages. In 1975 there was just one single word: 'Insane.'

'1976. Confined. More or less OK after a month. Able to work.'

Then came the final entry, which Theódóra knew by heart: '8 December 1977. At about two o'clock in the afternoon, Sophia Concordia entered the kitchen on Ward K and asked for a glass of water. Everything appeared normal. She had only just drunk the water when blood suddenly spurted out of her mouth and she dropped down dead.'

Theódóra looked round. Perhaps it was time to pack up her mother's things. Then she noticed that the bowl on the table had been moved. She checked the rest of the flat and peeped into the kitchen. Nothing else seemed to have been touched. She put the bowl back in its place. She walked into the corridor and could almost sense the big warm horses there in the darkness. One Christmas her father had been called out to castrate a mental defective who had raped his own mother. The operation had been performed in the cellar of the police station in Pósthússstræti. In her mind's eye she could see the snow-covered streets and the Christmas tree on Austurvollur in all its glory. The image of the mental defective flashed into her mind. She had followed her father down into the cells. It couldn't have been the day of the operation. The cell door was open. The mental defective's trousers were caked with blood at he crotch and he was staring ahead of him as if he did not understand what was happening. She saw her father hunched over his medicine bag, rummaging in it. 'Go upstairs immediately, child!' he said when he realized she was there. A policeman came and stood in the doorway.

'Axel, did you go into the basement while I was away?' Theódóra asked when she came back upstairs.

He flushed and stuttered. 'What happened, Tedda, was that I went for a drive.' He took a deep breath. 'I was going to go to the cinema but it was full so I bought some ice-cream at the Mela shop and who do you think I met on the way home?'

'I've no idea.'

'Dagný, you know, who works in the office. She was out in the rain with her little daughter. The poor woman looked so miserable . . .' He glanced at Theódóra. 'I gave her a lift. The poor thing needs somewhere to live. Her husband is destroying her. I suggested Skólabrú first of all but she's so scared of Hördur that's not an option so I drove her here and showed her where mother-in-law used to live.' Axel smiled wryly. 'Isn't it about time we sorted out all her things and brought some fresh life into this house. Is there any reason to put it off?' He looked at his wife, hoping for mercy.

'Get rid of my mother's things?' She said, repeating the words slowly and staring at him. 'Are you insane?'

'Yes. That's what Dagný said. She said it would never work.'

Theódóra stood for a moment, rooted to the spot. 'Well, she's got common sense, I'll give her that,' she said at last. 'I just can't believe what you're saying. You do realize this woman is taking my sister and her husband to court? You do realize I'm a member of parliament? Why didn't you just screw her outside the walls of Parliament and have done with it? Dragging that tart into my mother's room! So much for your heart condition.'

'I didn't drag her anywhere. She was simply unhappy, Tedda, and I wanted to be kind to her. Don't you understand?' Axel looked balefully at Theódóra with his large trusting eyes and then caught sight of Linda standing, shocked, in the doorway. She walked slowly into the room, her mouth hanging open. She drew close to her father without taking her eyes off him for a second. 'Were you inviting some woman, some stranger, to come and live downstairs, in Granny's flat? Don't you understand what Granny had to put up with? Are you picking up where Grandfather left off? Why not get some horses and put them in the basement? It's OK for strangers to live there but not your own flesh and blood.' She looked from one parent to the other.

Axel did not know what to say. 'So what do you reckon, Linda?' He said at last and scratched his stomach. 'Is Daddy going mad?'

'I don't know about that,' said his daughter. 'But I do know you've hurt Mother and me very deeply.'

13

The office of the Prime Minister was acquiring a new Buick and GM Service at Súdarvogur had been subcontracted to check the vehicle over before it was delivered.

Tryggvi Thórarinsson opened the driver's door and quickly slipped into the plastic-wrapped seat behind the wheel. He backed the car out with great style and then slammed on the brakes just for the fun of it, letting the engine pull against the brake. When Einar came out to pull the garage door down again he released the brake and the Buick jumped across the garage forecourt with a yowl. In the rearview mirror he could see the foreman glance up at the car and shake his head. The car was to be delivered to the Acquisitions Agency before midday. Tryggvi saw the clock said ten to twelve. He drummed his fingers on the wheel, put his foot flat on the floor and hurtled along Kleppsvegur. Dagný had called on him after midnight the previous night bringing a friend for protection and had thrown one of her tantrums. She was losing her job.

The boys didn't dare come downstairs. Tryggvi frowned. Why was she making such a fuss? And Dagný was hinting at stuff. As he saw it, he was being held personally responsible for his mother-in-law's death. Actually he and the old lady had always got on well together and that was what Dagný found so hard to stomach. Now her friend Jóna was back in town and needed her flat back. Tryggvi smiled. His girl was coming home. Dagný, the queen of his bed, threatening him with divorce! She couldn't live without him. It was all talk. Where could she go anyway? She'd got no qualifications.

Tryggvi really enjoyed sitting behind the wheel of expensive cars. He turned on the radio and switched on the windscreen wipers. They moved gracefully to and fro like the wings of a swan. He put his foot down a fraction and the Buick accelerated. It was so responsive! All this snobbery about Japanese and European cars didn't wash with Tryggvi Thórarinsson. You couldn't beat an American car. He glanced at his watch and decided, just for the hell of it, to head down town and drive up Lækjargata like a boy racer, putting his foot down as he passed Government House. The ministers, in the middle of handing out the usual old baloney to the television reporters on the balcony, would stand there like stunned mullets with their mouths open. He stepped on the gas a little more and the power was almost too much for the car. There were three men standing on the steps of Government House. He hoped they would look at him but a bus was in the way. Damn it! When he reached the Bank of Iceland he turned the power steering with one finger and executed a U-turn with a great screaming of tyres. He looked in the mirror. It was a bloody shame the tyres weren't smoking. It would be fun to pop home to Thingholtstræti and take the boys, Jökull and Haflidi, out for a ride. Or, better still, pick up a girl on the Lækjargata. Honk your horn at her shivering arse, just like in the old days, let the car crawl along the edge of the pavement, bring the electric window down slowly. 'Got any plans for the weekend, darling?'

The lights at Bankastræti changed to amber and he shot across the street and past Government House. Fuck! There was no one there. Kalkofnsvegur was closed at Arnarholl. He had no option but to drive down Hverfisgata. He came to a grinding halt at the Reykjavík Shopping Mall. Hverfisgata was solid with traffic as far as the eye could see. Tryggvi looked at the old stone building while he waited. It looked so sad and dilapidated. Nobody shopped in the old town centre any more, let alone here. An iron ball swung slowly like a pendulum above the crumbling shopping centre. Tryggvi could not resist gunning the engine a little to show off the

Buick's horsepower. Beside him there was a white Lancia, a smart-looking car even if it was Italian, with a redhead behind the wheel with her nose in the air. Tryggvi was watching her surreptitiously, glancing in the mirror and now and then scratching the cleft in his chin and sometimes turning his head so a lock of blond hair fell across his forehead. The Lancia slowly edged forward. Tryggvi gave the bird a chance to give him the once over but she declined, damn the bitch. Fuck it. At long last and not before time the grid-lock of cars started moving. At that moment the iron ball landed on the shopping centre and a fine cement dust rose into the air. He was lucky to get away before the dust settled on the fancy government car. Tryggvi reached the shelter of the Bjarnarborg estate and looked round for the bird. One Saturday Dagný had taken the kids and her mother to a circus. He had seized the opportunity to laze around watching videos. Had a really nice time on his own in the house watching porn, fairly hard core, as he was a free man for a few hours. The bird in the Lancia reminded him of the leading actress in the film who'd thought nothing of taking on two studs at the same time. The column of cars suddenly ground to a halt. It was so slow. He drummed on the wheel. The Acquisitions Agency closed at twelve sharp so they could go and stuff themselves with salt cod and porridge in the canteen. He indicated left. And who should let him in but the redhead? She smiled at him. She smiled! Of course she did. Of course she smiled, buddy boy! Tryggvi grinned back at her. She couldn't be much more than twenty. The bitches always liked to looked flash but deep down they all want-ed the same thing. However Tryggvi Thórarinsson was not about to go chasing after a bit of skirt. He looked serious. He was a one-woman man. He wasn't about to screw some kid like an idiot. Many a bloke had had to pay through the nose for a mistake like that. What a woman Dagný was. She wasn't even aware of it. She thought she was too fat. Too tall. Too this, too that. Her breasts were too big. Women had no idea how gorgeous they were, what power it gave them simply being what they were. Women! What was the phrase when you had a weak spot about something? Tryggvi had to stop at the red light on Snorrabraut and looked round. He was thrilled to find the man beside him looking envi-ously at the Buick. Tryggvi really stepped on it when the lights changed and zoomed past the police station. At last he had managed to get the tyres smoking. Achilles heel! The phrase popped into his head. Women had the Achilles heel of simply not realizing how sexy they were. They wanted to be skinny and look like those bags of bones on the catwalk. 'Twiggy' or whatever they called themselves. But it wasn't true. Not as far as men were concerned. No. Birgitta Nielsen, that was more like it. Stallone a was prize idiot for not holding on to her. Tryggvi looked towards Mount Skardsheidi. It lay on the horizon, black with rain, like some black bint on a beach – that perpetual Icelandic male fantasy. Oh, to drive out of the town into the wilderness. Reach the north in a flash. Pick up some bird in the Shalli and making a sex-sodden night of it in the Hotel Kea. Why not grab freedom by the balls? That old road out of Reykjavík had a tremendous pull. Why be afraid of the good things in life? But he was flat broke. Suddenly Tryggvi remembered he owed 17 million kroner on the Thingholtstræti house. He instantly broke out in a cold sweat. What was going on? How had this happened to him? And now Dagný threatening to divorce him. 'Tryg*veee*! You killed my mother,' she'd screamed. 'You took her last kroner!' 'Stole from your mother, me? I didn't take anything off her. Did somebody twist her arm? She came in with us of her own free will and now she's gone most of it's yours!' 'Most of what?' she'd screamed. 'We don't own a plank of this rotten house!' Rotten house? Now he was really hurt. One of the most impressive buildings in the country! Constructed from driftwood from the *Jamestown* of Boston. Why couldn't she pronounce his name right when she was angry? Tryggvi grimaced and muttered, 'Trygg*veee*.'

He looked in the rearview mirror. The Lancia was nowhere to be seen. 'I'm not going to hold it against Dagný, her moving out, but if anyone should carry the can for my mother-in-law's death, she's the most likely candidate, leaving her husband and children like that, rather than that poor sod of a doctor,' thought Tryggvi and indicated he was turning right into the Acquisitions Agency. At that point a rusty white Lada scooted past almost scraping the left-hand side of the Buick. To Tryggvi this was sacrilege. Were there any witnesses? Overtaking a government car like that! Was the man insane? Have people no respect? Don't the idiots know how to drive any more? Was the man a raving lunatic? He was just about to drive after him, catch up with him at a red light and knock him senseless. Just imagine, a 5-million kroner car being smashed up by a 5000-kroner old banger. It was unbelievable how disrespectful people could be. Tryggvi looked in the mirror and slowly guided the car into the car park.

It was ten past twelve and the bloke was out of his pram. 'What the hell are you doing here? The car should have been delivered to the Prime Minister's home.'

'Nobody told me,' said Tryggvi, snorting with anger.

'Well, get it there. It's nothing to do with me.' The man refused to take the keys.

'I'm not taking orders from you, mate. Or from the Prime Minister for that matter. You've neither of you got any right to boss me about,' said Tryggvi, feeling chuffed with himself. He opened the car door, put the key in the ignition and walked away. He had half a mind to ask the man to drive him to Súdarvogur but there was obviously no point. Well, sod it, it would do him good to walk. He wondered about sauntering up to Skúlagata to see if Dagný's Toyota was parked outside the house, but it would only look as if he wanted to make up. Better play your cards a bit closer to your chest. Dagný would have to come crawling back home to Thingholtstræti when her friend Jóna threw her out.

As Tryggvi turned into Borgartún he could feel the mild sea breeze. 'I've a sailor's soul,' he thought and zipped up his blue anorak, put his hands in his pockets and walked briskly along the grass strip in the middle of the road parallel with the sea. He hunched his shoulders and shivered in the drizzle. Sometimes he broke into a trot. A taxi drove by slowly on the look out for passengers. Actually Tryggvi could have taken a taxi and charged it to the Acquisitions Agency or to the Prime Minister's office, but then a stroll does you good, gives you a bit of chance to think things through. Twenty-eight Thingholtstræti was soaking up a fortune; it was like throwing money on a bonfire. He couldn't stop thinking about it. Tryggvi whistled to himself as he thought about the way life did the dirty on you. What chance did anyone have? What was happening to this country anyway? He was like a cabin boy on a ship trying to avoid talking to the captain. You can walk to and fro on the deck but sooner or later you're going to have to go up on the bridge, because the ship's in the middle of the bloody ocean.

Dagný had an appointment with a lawyer at two o'clock. She was going to press charges against Hördur Gottskálksson, take him to court, ruin him, make sure he was struck off. She had dark circles under her eyes and was edgy from lack of sleep. When she had turned up for work, that feeble yes-man Vilhjálmur met her and said she needn't come back the following day. 'Don't I get three months' notice like everybody else?' 'No, you were still in your probationary period.' 'Is Axel in?' 'No, he's ill.' 'Theódóra?' 'No.'

Dagný decided to walk out there and then. She went back down-stairs and heard the automatic doors shut behind her. She stood outside Heidnaberg for a moment feeling dazed. There was a note waiting for her on the kitchen table at Skúlagata: 'Went outside to play. Back soon. Sylvía.' Dagny phoned Thingholtstræti. Haflidi was at home and told her Tryggvi had gone off to work early. 'Then it should be OK for me to call in,' she thought. 'My final salary payment, a hundred thousand kroner, goes into the bank today.' She wrote a message on the back of Sylvía's note: 'Gone home. Mummy.'

No one was in at Thingholtstræti. She needed a good hot shower. She stood in the shower for a long time, letting the water run over her skin. Her body was firm. She knew she was a magnificent woman. She had become aware of it as a teenager when she noticed the way men were with her, how they looked at her with a kind of aggressive, hostile hunger. She soon learned how to get them to do what she wanted. She soaped her body, her long muscular legs, her firm stomach and her breasts. She poured shampoo into her palm and rubbed it into her scalp with the tips of her fingers. In spite of the shower she still did not feel good. She was still cold, despite the warmth of the water. She rinsed the shampoo out of her hair and washed her face twice. She let the water rinse away all the soap, turned the water off and stepped out of the shower. Still she felt cold. She listened. The three floors of the house were silent. A few drops of water fell from the shower head and made a strangely intense ringing sound as they landed in the base of the shower. Dagný opened a window and the spring air rushed in.

She wiped the condensation from the long mirror and looked at herself. Her wet hair spread over her shoulders like unravelled rope. The evening before she had half watched a film about expensive call girls in Los Angeles. The clients were young men, tall and handsome, with long hair tied in a pony tail at the back of their heads. Their backs were muscular and sunburned. Dagný looked down her body. Even when she pressed her thighs together, there was still a triangular sail-shaped gap between them. 'The place that was made for only me,' Tryggvi used to say. 'Don't be so sure,' thought the woman. 'I should have married Halldór Ragnarsson the lawyer.'

She picked up a towel from the shelf, dried herself, put on a bathrobe and walked barefooted into the kitchen. As she entered the living room she rubbed her hair vigorously. The bedroom was large and airy with an old varnished wardrobe that just about reached the ceiling. She sorted through some clothes. She wanted to look smart for the appointment with the lawyer. Perhaps I should have taken his advice before talking to the newspaper? She chose a white blouse and then saw there was a tear in the armhole. She had never really mastered the sewing machine and, without thinking, was about to go upstairs to ask her mother to mend it. She looked out of the window and remembered there was no one upstairs. The garden was lawn down as far as Miðstræti. The grass was long and trembled in the gentle breeze. Further down, beyond the lawn, there was a gravel parking space where a piece of blue glass glittered in the sun. At that moment she realized her mother was dead.

She walked over to the window and saw the pile of bits of wood against the wall of the house. It was rubbish that Tryggvi had thrown out when he was working on the loft conversion. All around it was some horrible-looking grey fibre, stuff that had disintegrated with the weather and coloured the earth. 'Why is this man always restoring things?' she thought. Old cars, old houses. Suddenly she wanted the house dead. She would have enjoyed seeing flames burst out of the windows and snatch at the black roof beams.

It was nearly twelve. The boys were out. What blessed peace. She opened the wardrobe doors and looked at her clothes. There was nothing she wanted to wear. She put on her jeans and a light-weight white sweater. She found the hair-drier and used it. She wanted to get herself something pretty. Spend a bit of time on herself. 'I've nothing to wear,' she muttered. She took the car keys from the crystal bowl on the mantelpiece. It was nearly twelve. Would she manage to get away before the boys came back? She was panicking. She looked around for her bag with her purse and credit cards but then the doorbell rang. 'Oh my God, I knew it,' she muttered and went towards the door. But suddenly she was overcome with anxiety. It had to be either Tryggvi or Hördur out to hurt her. The bastard doctor would get quite a shock when he saw *Weekend* later that day. Sylvía was standing outside. 'Where were you?'

'Nowhere,' mumbled the girl sulkily. 'Out playing. Why did you come home without me?'

'I didn't have time to hang about waiting for you.' Her daughter's sour tone had irritated her.

'Where are you going?'

'There's somewhere I have to be.'

'Can I come too?'

'No. For God's sake, I need to be on my own. Anyway someone has to stay here to let your brothers in. They never take a key with them, no matter how much I nag them.'

'Jökull always has his key.'

'I want to be alone. There's a packet of cornflakes on the kitchen table and milk in the fridge.'

'I'm not hungry,' said her daughter, sulkily. She sat down at the living-room table and reached for the paper.

'I'm certainly not paying the next instalment on the car,' Dagný muttered to herself as she sat behind the wheel. She cursed Axel of Heidnaberg. 'What a bastard! How feeble can you get? What would the old girl have said if I'd moved into her basement? And he never did any work. The old girl did it all.' Dagný drove fast down the road. She thought she could see the boys making their way up Bokhlödustigurinn so she decided not to go that way and drove off out of their sight.

She took Bankastræti into town and Miklabraut out of it. She drove round the Kringla multistorey for quite a while looking for somewhere to park. It was quite chilly on the second floor of that grey vault out of the sun. Crowds of people were milling round the shopping mall. She wandered from shop to shop but didn't find anything she fancied. She stepped on to the escalator. There was an old man sitting by the fountain with a stream of snuff running down his face. He looked like something out of the nineteenth century. Dagny saw herself reflected faintly in a shop window. She turned round. A middle-aged man, shabbily dressed, was looking at her with that hungry look. She smiled tightly to herself and took the next escalator up. She found a murderously expensive shop. Dresses hung from rails. She had a sudden urge to buy something way out. She tried on four dresses and chose a full-length yellow dress with a white collar. She bought a white hat to go with the dress. And a black umbrella. Was it some queen who stared back at her from the mirror, with hair cascading down to her nipples and red cheeks? She blew some hair away from her face. 'I'll wear this to mother's funeral,' she thought and said to the shop assistant who was looking at her in the mirror, 'I'll take this one.'

'And the umbrella and hat?'

'Yes.'

'They don't quite go together somehow.'

'So what?' said Dagny tetchily.

'Nothing,' said the girl quickly.

Dagný went into the changing room. The girl waited outside and took the dress from her. When Dagný emerged she was folding it into a white box. 'Is it all right if I put the hat on top?' There was a snooty tone in her voice, as if she was being obliged to deal with someone entirely devoid of taste.

Dagný got out her credit card and the girl swiped it through the machine. There were two women waiting at the counter with small purchases. The girl looked straight through them all. The machine made a noise and disgorged a slip of paper. She tore it off. 'I'm afraid this transaction has been refused,' she said frostily.

'What?'

'This transaction has been refused. Insufficient funds.' She put the slip on the counter for Dagný to see.

'But that can't be right,' said Dagný, bewildered. 'Isn't it the second of June today? My salary should have been paid in.'

'I'll try one more time,' said the girl without expression. 'Please may I have your credit card?'

Dagný fumbled for it. But the same thing happened. 'Could you put these things by for me? I'll have to go to the bank and sort it out.'

The shop assistant put the box on the floor without comment and turned to the other women. Dagný walked out. How could her salary not have been paid into her account? Was the witch keeping it back to set against the payments on her car? *Weekend* must be on the streets by now. Was the article about the doctor in it? The editor had been delighted to hear from her when she rang. He came and saw her himself to interview her for the article. He was a sharp-eyed young man with shiny black hair combed straight back from his forehead, chuffed to bits to be allowed to take it on, to lance the boil, new to the job, the callow bloody idiot. (It's not always easy for me to remain entirely objective as a narrator.) Dagný went into a bookshop. Newspapers were stuffed into a rack. She took a copy of *Weekend*. There was a photograph of the house at Skólabrú with a caption saying that Hördur Gottskálksson's surgery was on the first floor. Beside the picture of the house there was a picture of a man. It was Hördur and she could remember the arrogance in his voice: 'She isn't the only patient in Reykjavík.' On an inside page there was a photograph of a wrecked car and the caption: 'The doctor smashed up his girlfriend's car.'

And I stripped naked in front of this man. I must be mad. She scanned the article, learning many new things about the doctor's difficulties in his relationships with his fellow doctors at the hospital. *Weekend* also pointed out that Hördur's sister-in-law was Theódóra Thóroddsdóttir, whose political ambitions the women of Iceland had recently supported so whole-heartedly in the hope that she would become a government minister. Dagný smiled with satisfaction. It was good she hadn't managed to get into the cabinet, damn her. On another inside page there was a photograph of the selfsame member of parliament accompanied by a column headed 'On the downward slope: Tedda of Heidnaberg. Prime Minister to give her the push.'

As soon as Dagný folded the paper her pleasure in Theódóra's lack of success evaporated. She felt exhausted and confused by the

crowds of people and the noise and the bright lights. She thought
about buying a copy of the magazine but it felt as if she would soil
the car if she brought a photograph of Hördur Gottskálksson into
it, so she squeezed the copy back into the rack.

She drove towards Heidnaberg to demand her salary, but when
she saw the building in the distance her courage failed her. 'I ought
to pop in and see Tryggvi,' she thought. Maybe we could transfer
some money from his account into mine. I'll be all right as long as
Einar is there. No, Tryggvi never has any money and if I go and see
him he'll stick to me like glue.'

A sudden shower, warm spring rain, fell on the car. The windscreen wipers eased the wetness away. All the same she headed for the
garage. Water dripped from the corners of the sign: GM SERVICE.
A steady stream of water fell from a hole in the rusted gutter and
glistened in the sunshine.

She opened the door. Einar was rolling a tyre towards a high-
bonneted army-surplus truck. He bent down on one knee and
looked over his shoulder. 'Hi.'

'Hi. Where's Tryggvi?'

Einar did not answer her but prepared the tyre, squatting down
on his haunches and lifting it up in one smooth movement. He had
to lean across the tyre as he eased it on to the wheel and his cheeks
puffed out. He stood up. He was small and stocky and, surprisingly,
not out of breath. He said in a sarcastic tone, 'Tryggvi has gone
into town and been temporarily held up by the flash new car the
Prime Minister's getting to put under his bum. As far as I'm concerned they could come and get it themselves but, no, they're far
too grand for that. Then two gentlemen of a rather different background came asking for him. In my opinion those two were not in
the best of moods.'

'Isn't this too much for you to do on your own?' she asked,
looking at the wheel.

He walked across to her. 'I expect one day I'll just drop down
dead in all the oil and dirt and it'll be a fitting end.' He wiped his
hands on a rag. 'I was sorry to hear about your mother.'

She looked over to the corner. Yet another of Tryggvi's junk heaps
was up on the ramp under the dirty windows. She looked ven-
omously at the car. The clock in the coffee room said ten to two.

'Oh my God, I'm meeting someone at two.'

'Trading in for a new model?'

'No, it's a bit more urgent than that.'

She had chosen the lawyer almost at random. It was the only name she recognized as she scanned the list in the phone book. She parked her Toyota quickly. The building rose like a stone finger out of the new town centre. From the lift she walked straight into the offices of Ólafur Sigthórsson, licensed to practise in the High Court.

'He's waiting for you in there,' said the receptionist.

The door to the lawyer's office was standing open. The office faced Kópavogur and the winding seashore could be seen through the window. The sea shimmered in the sunlight. The man had made himself comfortable in his chair. She had seen him several times on television. He looked much younger in the flesh. He had hung his jacket on the back of the chair he invited her to sit in. They introduced themselves. 'Yes, it's a bad business.' He sat down again.

She looked at his desk. *Weekend* was nowhere to be seen.

'Cases like this are notoriously tricky,' he said as he flicked some invisible dust from the surface of his desk. Although he was frowning, his attitude was authoritative and friendly. 'The burden of proof would be on us if we were to sue. What evidence do we have of culpable negligence? There are also implications arising from professional codes of practice and individual human rights.'

'What about my mother's rights? The man didn't even examine her.'

'This is no great surprise to me,' said Ólafur. 'I'm already rather familiar with this particular character.'

She looked at his face, feeling suddenly optimistic. Did he know something that would substantiate the claim for negligence? 'Oh?' she said, carefully.

'Oh, it's nothing. But in this kind of case there are many elements to consider.' Ólafur looked as if the case were already lost. 'Why wasn't the emergency ambulance called out?'

Dagný shifted in her chair nervously. 'I don't know. It didn't occur to us.'

'I can imagine the other party saying it should have been contemplated as the delay was considerable, far beyond any reasonable period of time.'

'It was up to me to think of that?' she asked in disbelief.

'I'm not saying that,' said the lawyer firmly, spreading his strong arms out across the desk and revealing his massive and manly chest. 'I'm just trying to imagine what the opposition will come up with. Cases like this are notoriously difficult. No one takes the city or the state to court without a very sound reason.'

'Why does it have to be the city or the state? Why can't it be him personally?'

'Just between the two of us, so I know what I'm dealing with, what are you looking to get out of this? You want to get the better of him?'

She did not answer directly and said quickly, 'It's not the money. It's justice! I simply can't let him get away with it. He can't just walk into my flat, look at my mother as if he has the power of life and death over her and then walk out with a paltry fifteen hundred kroner in hard cash and treat us like dirt.'

He thought about this for a moment and then said, 'I'm not sure that there would be any compensation worth mentioning. I can't think of a single precedent.'

'Should we give up then?'

'No, I think we should at least try. Were you dependent on your mother?'

'Dependent?'

'If we can show you suffering financial loss as a result of this, our position would be that much stronger.'

'No,' she said. 'My loss is entirely different and much worse.' Dagný cleared her throat, crossed her legs and clasped her knees.

Ólafur reached under his desk for his copy of *Weekend* and said, accusingly, 'Why is this already in the papers?'

'I rang them and told them about it.'

'Wasn't that a bit over hasty?' said the lawyer, looking at Dagný as if she had committed some terrible crime. 'The media will make hay with this in the next few weeks. You and I have hardly even started to discuss it. If we lose the case we're in trouble. You need proof before you make serious allegations like this. The man is innocent until proved guilty. There is something called "the right to privacy". This way *he* could end up taking *you* to court.'

For a second she was afraid. Nothing of this had occurred to her. 'It might have been stupid of me to go rushing off to *Weekend*, but I haven't been myself since my mother died,' she said anxiously. She thought of asking him whether it was legal to fire her on the spot, or whether she should have been given notice like everyone else. Ought she to tell him she'd stripped naked in front of the doctor and gone to see that poky basement flat in the chairman's house, when she was out of her mind. Some inner voice warned her it was best not to mention it.

'I'm not sure of the best way to tackle this,' said the lawyer, mulling it over. 'I think perhaps taking Reykjavík Medical Service to court. They have to take some responsibility for the people they employ. I think that would be the first step. If nothing comes of that, we can consider future alternatives, but I should warn you, things like this take time and it is as likely as not that nothing will come of it. Doctors' errors are far more common than people think. And there's another thing.' He looked out of the window, his chin set. He relished addressing the room as if he were winning a case in court. 'You could lose. It could be that it might become obvious to us, a year or two down the road, that it was not worth continuing with the case and by that time you might well owe me a considerable sum. I don't come cheap.' He looked at her.

'I do realize that,' said Dagný, who even so had not considered the possibility of losing or that she would have legal expenses to meet. 'A year or two? Could it really go on for that long?'

'Perhaps longer.'

'Could we see if he wanted to settle out of court?'

The solicitor smiled.

She understood the smile immediately and realized the truth of the matter herself. It was not justice she was after but money. She needed the compensation in order to get free of Tryggvi and pay off her debts. She had to get out of the flat on Thingholtstræti to get her life back, to get her spirit back.

Ólafur did not rub her nose in the fact that she had not after all come in to his office with nothing but her own high-mindedness. He said, 'We won't get a kroner out of this chap.'

'Why not?'

'I know the type.'

'Do you know him personally?'

'He was at the same school, a couple of years ahead of me. I vaguely remember him.' He leaned back in his chair, his paunch threatening to burst his shirt buttons. 'He played a trick on a friend of mine, one of his colleagues, once. They were hardly more than kids. They were medical students, a long time ago now. This would probably be the summer of 1966.' Ólafur cleared his throat. 'This friend of mine, my old schoolfriend, he was into the fashions of the day and had let his hair grow long.' The solicitor put one hand up to his shoulder to indicate the length of his friend's hair. 'For all I know he might even have played the drums a little. Well, this good doctor that we're up against, he stole some stationery from the hospital and sent his colleague a formal letter, forging the signature of the head of the department, to the effect that the student should make sure his hair was of an acceptable length when he next entered the hospital or else he would be dismissed.'

'And the student was taken in?'

'He got a crewcut that very day.' The solicitor was not smiling. However, there was a slight twinkle in his eye.

'My God,' said Dagný and smiled in spite of herself. 'That's appalling!'

'That's how it was in those days.'

'It's dreadful. What a shit! Well, it's no surprise to me.'

'All right, my dear. I'll see what I can do. It's best to take this a step at a time. I'll make a start by writing to the Reykjavík Medical Service and have a letter couriered to them today. I'll contact you as soon as I have their response.'

Dagný stood up. Outside the door there was a big-built man. He seemed nervous. His bulging eyes glanced to and fro. Dagný could recognize the expression on his face. This was a man heavily in debt.

At reception she phoned Vilhjálmur at Heidnaberg. Talking to the solicitor had given her courage. Vilhjálmur came to the phone. 'Hi. This is the woman you sacked this morning.'

'Oh, hi!' He tried to sound as if they were friends.

'Why hasn't my salary been paid into my account?'

'Hasn't it been?'

'No. That's why I'm ringing.'

'I'll sort it out straightaway.'

'Thank you. Straightaway, please.' She replaced the receiver, not giving him the opportunity to say anything else or be the first to say goodbye. 'And the creep was coming on to me,' she thought in the lift on the way down again. Then she drove over to the Háaleitis-braut branch of the Bank of Iceland. Nothing had gone into her account. There was a telephone for customers' use in one corner. She picked up the receiver and dialled Tryggvi. He had to have some cash on him. As she listened to it ringing she realized she had forgotten to mention her divorce to the lawyer. 'There must be something wrong with me,' she thought. Einar picked up the phone. Tryggvi had come back but he had gone out again. 'Where to?'

'To buy spare parts at Bilanaust.'

'Could you ask him to transfer thirty thousand kroner into my account as soon as he comes back? It's money he owes me.'

'Yes,' he said, sounding irritated. 'But he hasn't got a kroner to his name.'

'Why are you being so mean?'

'Can't the pair of you sort out your divorce outside working hours? I need to get some work out of the man.'

'Oh, excuse me!' She slammed down the receiver. She asked the cashier to check the account again. Still no payment.

And two years to wait for compensation, even if she got anything, and maybe more than two years. And no acting jobs. Even actresses famous throughout the country didn't get enough work. If you wanted work you had to be better than Helga Bachmann and that was impossible. She hated working as a secretary. Acting was all she really knew. What the hell could she do? She couldn't go on being married to that idiot. But then who would look after the boys? How could she support two growing lads? I married beneath me, that's what Mother always said anyway. And it was horrible having her in the house, keeping her beady eye on everything. And Tryggvi lying awake at night thinking about her shares in Eimskip. She remembered the lawyer who had proposed to her. She could remember his voice on the phone. She thought him short and ugly. At the time Tryggvi had seemed irresistible.

The shares in the Eimskip Steamship Company. Whenever they were mentioned the boys faces glowed like Easter lilies with sheer wonder. The Eimskip shares! One day Haflidi – this was before he had long hair and taken to staying out all night – had asked her, 'Mother, don't you think we could buy the Empire State Building in New York with the Eimskip shares?'

Dagný stood in the middle of the floor as if rooted to the spot. People milled around her. Her face was flushed, there was a humming in her ears and she felt dizzy. Her face felt puffy, she could not control the thoughts whirling round her head and as she looked around her she was overcome by a longing to do something outrageous, to scream and wail, to pull faces at the dopey sheep queuing up to pay their bills.

The Eimskip shares would be her passport out of the hell of her marriage. Perhaps it was not quite the done thing to cash them in only a few days after her mother had died but that was what she was going to do. Her need outweighed social niceties. She strode out of the bank.

14

Suddenly Tryggvi stopped dead in his tracks and in the middle of the road. A wave of joy surged through him and he spread his arms out to embrace the city. The Eimskip shares! The old lady had some shares. Blessings on her memory. The shares had been bought when the Eimskip Steamship Company, the child the nation held in its heart of hearts, was founded. Tryggvi slapped his forehead with the palm of his hand. How could he have forgotten? His mother-in-law, a woman of great foresight, what a useful woman to have about the place. Tryggvi tapped his brow. Now where were those shares? It ought to be possible to stave off the most unrelenting of moneylenders until the national lottery coughed up the big one.

Yes. Now where *were* those shares? Just think, mate, think. Tryggvi racked his memory like a man possessed. Then a house buried in a dark corner of his mind appeared to him, a newly built house in traditional Icelandic farmhouse style. That's where the shares were, in the safe at the Moneystock Market Company on Lækjargata. The old duck had waddled off and handed them over

146

for safe keeping. She had a head on her shoulders. How could I have forgotten! He remembered some yuppy calculating the present-day value of the shares: a couple of years ago it had been 2 million kroner. Just pop over there and pick up the dough, nothing to it. There'd be time out in this endless battle with the debt collectors. Dagný wouldn't know. She'd got her mind on other things. That old fart of a doctor had it coming, barging in and turning his back on people who needed him. Dead right of Dagný to sort him out. The bloody bastards thought they were a cut above ordinary decent folk and they could always rely on each other to cover up their murders, but this time the devil had met his match.

Their education's paid for by ordinary people's taxes. They laughed when devaluation all but wiped out their student debt repayments. And who kept them going? Seamen like us. Tryggvi looked out to sea. A shiny white liner lay at anchor out in the bay. Much better to be at sea. Away from the endless arguments. Laze about on deck with a drink in one hand and a dusky maiden in the other. Suddenly he remembered the deck of the *Thorkell Máni* with the sea rising up above it and crashing over the stern. They had been fishing off Newfoundland. He was a lad of sixteen at sea for the very first time, with the trawler *June* fishing the same grounds. His old dad looking after the *June*'s engine. His father had wanted them to sail together so he could keep an eye on him but Tryggvi's mother had begged them not to go together. 'If something happens, I don't want to lose you both.' It was back in 1959 and his parents had just built themselves a house on Kópavogur. They got caught in the famous storm off Newfoundland. A whole book could be written about it. Both ships were full to the gunnels with fish. The sky turned leaden and black, the barometer was plunging and there was a heavy swell. Then there was an explosion. You had to have been there; you couldn't imagine it. He'd often tried to describe it to people, the blinding flash in the sky and the waves leaping up as high as ten-storey houses. They thought he was exaggerating. The only person who hadn't was a meteorologist he had met by sheer chance once in a bar. He'd bought the man a drink, he was so grateful. All the water landing on the deck began to freeze immediately. Turned into thick dough. A disgusting gluey slime covering everything. The metal hawsers were half a yard thick with ice and the ship was getting heavier every second. Five days of madness, hacking at the ice with anything you could lay hands on. He wept with fear. Then Bragi the mechanic talked some courage into him. He could bend a wrench with his bare hands just for the hell of it. What guys they were! Heroes of the sea. And then, with the ship in dock, they turned into bums on the streets. Drunks people crossed the road to avoid. But they were Iceland's heroes, although no one realized it except for Tryggvi Thórarinsson the car mechanic who had himself lived that life. They worked like slaves for days on end trying to keep the ship afloat. The second day someone worked out how to use the welding gear to free the boathooks. Twelve hours on deck. The winch looking like some iceberg. The snow so thick you couldn't see the rail. When the boathooks fell overboard the ship righted itself. What a ship! The *Bismarck* of the Icelandic fleet! 'Don't you worry about your old man, Tryggvi lad,' someone said. Tryggvi made it up on to the bridge to ask, 'Is there any news of the *June*?' Captain Marteinn, a hero himself, had frowned and said, 'We're getting no signal over the radio.' It's strange how everything stands still around you when you hear news like that. Tryggvi stood there in the street, biting his lip, feeling full of emotion, shaking his head and clenching his fists. The *June* went down like a stone when the wave hit it. Thirty hands lost, damn it, some of them boys.

When they sailed into Reykjavík harbour, the deck of the *Máni* looked as if a war had been fought on it. Half the town was standing on the dockside to welcome them home. Tryggvi had his hands in his pockets, fingering a penknife his father had given him. He treated that knife like a religious relic.

And here I am in Skúlagata, flat broke. I've wasted my life with filth and rubbish and what have I got to show for it? Nothing. A wife who despises me and who's taken off with my only daughter, the apple of my eye. She's always rubbing salt in the wound, saying she ought to have married some lawyer who wanted to marry her before she took up with me and then she screeches like some prima donna, 'I must have been craz*eee* not to marry him.' 'Yeah, well, why didn't you marry the bugger?' 'I was a fool to marry you, Tryggvi. I married beneath me.' Tryggvi had said, as quick as a flash, 'Dagný, there isn't a woman in Iceland didn't marry beneath her.'

He looked across the street and waited for a gap in the traffic. What's Dagný ever done but fart about at her acting and make a prat of herself, because she's no more an actress than a hen's arse in a storm. Then she swans about in my Ford taking coffee here and going to sales there with her bloody mates while I drive myself into the ground working all hours and then restoring one of the most extraordinary houses in Iceland to its original glory. Pine throughout. No, I've earned the right to borrow those shares.

He ran across Skúlagata with his hands in his pockets. The spring weather was bloody cold. This country is tundra on the edge of the habitable world. He jogged past the National Bank. Don't worry about it, mate. Dagný hasn't divorced me yet even though she's threatening to. She's just trying to put the wind up me and take away all my pleasure in life.

He glanced at his watch and crossed Hverfisgata by the National Library. The endless stream of cars driving out of town. The poor shop-keepers on Austurstræti. Everybody shopped at Kringla these days. A 1972 Mercedes drove slowly past. Probably the only job that was secure was fixing up those bloody heaps of junk. You weren't about to join the ranks of the unemployed if you were in Tryggvi's trade.

In Hafnarstræti he bought some red roses. The right thing to do would be to drop in on her this evening and say, 'I just wanted to give you these flowers, Dagný darling, with my condolences on the death of your mother.' A box of chocolates too? No, that would be over the top. He would have played all his aces then, she would see straight through that. It's not good to show weakness when you're dealing with a woman. Then they get the upper hand. It's better to be firm and unbending. Oh, to hell with it, he bought the choco-lates anyway. He was feeble in matters of the heart. And some port from the state-run off-licence on Austurstræti.

He walked south down Lækjargata. The financial whizkids would already have earned their smart suits over lunch in Hotel Holt. If he won't hand over the shares or tell me how to cash them, I'll hit him. Tryggvi blew on his fingers, even though it wasn't cold, pushed open the glass door in its brass frame and walked into the marble foyer. There was a board listing the impressive company names. The Moneystock Market Company was on the third floor. He ran up the steps to the entrance.

There was a dark-haired bird at reception. She smiled at him. In this sort of place it was difficult to know what a smile like that meant, probably nothing, but you never knew. 'I have to see an agent. I met him the spring before last. He's holding some bonds for me in the Steamship Company.' Tryggvi jigged from one foot to the other, put his things on the counter and scratched his head. 'I can't remember the chap's name.'

'Who is the registered share-owner?'

'The owner? My mother-in-law. She's just passed away. I have to check this out on behalf of her heirs.'

'And what was her name?'

'What was Sirry's name?' Tryggvi lifted himself up on to his toes and looked around as if the question was ridiculous. 'Well, I am in a position to tell you that her name was Sigrídur Einarsdóttir,' he said, sounding very confident and behaving as if he was doing the girl a great favour by revealing this mystery.

'Identity number?'

'170518–2365.'

The girl keyed something into her computer, squinted at the screen and said, 'It's all here.' She pushed a button. Her nails were sharp and red. 'Kristján, there's a gentleman here to see you.' She turned to Tryggvi and pointed. 'Turn left. It's the door at the end of the corridor.'

When Tryggvi picked up the roses, the box of chocolates and the bottle of port, she said seductively, 'Oh, are you taking those with you? How boring. I thought they were for me.'

He gave her the sweetest of looks. He knew he had the face of an angel and that the lock of hair falling over his forehead pointed straight down to the cleft in his chin. He said in his deep husky voice, 'If only, love, if only.'

As he walked down the corridor it became obvious to him that he meant it. He was dog tired of the nagging and the arguments. Perhaps it would be better if Dagný didn't come home? He tapped on the door. In the room there was a boy sitting at a computer. It wasn't the same lad he'd given the shares to for safe keeping. Tryggvi wondered why he hadn't put his foot down in the first place years ago and simply insisted that mother and daughter put those shares into the general – and eternally failing – family exchequer. Everyone else at 28 Thingholtstræti hung on to their own money and he was under the cosh. He put his things down and sat opposite the boy. A bag of acid drops was lying on the desk.

'OK if I have one?'

'Go ahead.' The boy looked up from his papers. 'And what can I do for you?'

'I've come to have a word about the Eimskip shares my mother-in-law deposited with you.'

'And what do you want to know?'

'What they're worth.'

'Have you got written authorization?'

'Authorization?'

'Yes, clearly you have to have authorization. We can't have just anybody walking in off the street and asking to see anything he's a mind to.' The young man looked at him with his steady business eyes and smiled with what seemed like pity. 'We would not be looking after our clients' business very well if we did that, now would we?'

Tryggvi was becoming confused. People in banks and offices had a way of getting you all mixed up in no time. They started by giving themselves airs, calling themselves things like 'authorized agents' and then they yabbered on about shares to the value of a ratio of one in ten and it being their intention to bring taxes into line with the private sector as it should be borne in mind that . . . They depended on ordinary people not understanding a word of it. You had to be as canny as a snake to deal with buggers like that and not be ground down. 'I'm not just anybody,' said Tryggvi, firm as a rock. 'This woman lived in my home for years. It was her registered domicile!' He narrowed his eyes. 'It's my mother-in-law we're talking about.' Tryggvi sat up straight in his chair.

And, what do you know, the creepy little yuppy turned back to his computer. 'And what's her name?'

'Sigrídur Elín Einarsdóttir was her full name. As I said a moment ago, she's recently passed away.'

The computer didn't need long to produce the name. 'Yes. Those shares are held here. Their nominal value is three hundred thousand kroner.'

'And what', said Tryggvi, crossing his legs and letting his foot swing, rubbing thumb and forefinger together, 'is that in real money?'

The yuppy tapped away on his computer. 'Two million, seven hundred and seventy thousand kroner.'

Tryggvi stared at him. 'Can I withdraw it?'

'No, I'm afraid it's not as simple as that.' The bastard yuppy smiled as if he was handling a lunatic. 'I can't just hand it over without the proper documents.'

'What documents?' Tryggvi was feeling less sure of himself.

'Probate documents,' said the yuppy politely. 'Once probate is granted I could hand the shares straight over to you or sell them on your behalf.'

'I haven't got those papers. But I'll get them.' He leaned forward in his chair, smiling broadly and whispered, 'Can I interest you in a little killing?'

'What kind of a "killing"?' The boy looked suspicious.

Tryggvi whispered, 'Cash those shares now. I'll sign a document on behalf of my wife as lawful heir and then I'll give you something for your trouble.' He glanced round to make sure no one was listening. 'Your boss needn't know anything about it. Let's say forty thousand kroner. That's not to be sneezed at.'

The young man laughed an ugly laugh. 'Are you quite mad? That would be breaking the law. And anyway there's no way that such a thing could be done. I'd lose my job on the spot. There are people in this town who'd give their right arm for this job.'

'Straight from the shoulder?' Tryggvi snorted angrily.

'What?' The yuppy looked nonplussed.

Trygvi could see he was getting nowhere with the young man and stood up. The boy did not shake hands.

He walked briskly down the corridor with the flowers, the confectionery and the bottle. Sometimes life ran like clockwork and sometimes it didn't. He was a gambler. Tryggvi Thórarinson the gambler, the best poker-player in the old gang. Probably he had misconstrued what the girl on reception meant. She didn't even bother to look at him as he strode past her.

And what about this ridiculous business with the flowers? To beg Dagný's forgiveness? What for? He was shocked by his own behaviour. He looked at his watch. All he could do now was to take a taxi to Súdarvogur. It was nearly two o'clock. Einar would be furious. The best thing would be to give him the flowers. Tryggvi asked the taxi-driver to stop at a kiosk and he bought Einar a cigar.

Tryggvi arrived at the garage as large as life and chucked some money at the driver. Einar was standing on the fender of the Dodge truck. It was a six-wheel vehicle dating from the American 'occupation'. The bonnet was up. He looked over his shoulder. 'Where were you then?'

'They weren't going to give me a lift at the Acquisitions Agency and in the end I had to get a taxi. Tryggvi looked admiringly at the Dodge. 'Those trucks are indestructible, even after half a century. The Yanks knew a thing or two about making cars.'

'They knew more than a thing or two about making babies with the local girls,' said Einar, grinning.

'That was before my time,' said Tryggvi and gazed lovingly at the Dodge.

Einar was welding a hole in the cooling system. 'Get back to work then!'

'All right, all right! I just wanted to give you a cigar.' Tryggvi put the flowers down. 'Don't be such an old miseryguts, Haven't you got over the election yet? You lefties, you're sore as hell, going around frowning at everybody.' He pushed the little paper bag with the cigars towards Einar, who stepped off the fender and lit up.

'I've never been able to work it out,' said Einar, puffing away at the cigar, 'an intelligent man like you, Tryggvi, voting for the Independent Party, it just doesn't make sense.'

'I've been a member of the Independent Party since I was in nappies.' Tryggvi smoked his own cigar and spat proudly on the floor. 'I drank in the Independent spirit with my mother's milk, mate.' He grew serious, as if he was trying to persuade Einar of something important. 'You can see the Prime Minister is doing great things. He's steering this rackety old trawler of a nation into calmer waters.'

'OK, back to work. There's hardly anything left of the day. Oh, there was something.' Einar scratched his head. 'Two men came asking for you. They wanted to have a word. They weren't exactly choirboys. And not in a very good temper. A bit after that Dagný was looking for you. Half Reykjavík's after you.'

'What? Dagný? What did the men want? What did they look like?'

'Bit musclebound if I can put it like that. In a filthy temper. They all use steroids, don't they?'

'What did they want?' Tryggvi, like an idiot, wanted to be told, even though he knew perfectly well what they wanted.

'Don't ask me. They were waiting out there in their car for getting on for an hour.'

Heavies. Damn it! You couldn't trust anyone. They'd given him three days to pay up.

15

She'd just take her clothes, that's all. The boys were grown up now. They'd have to fend for themselves. She couldn't sacrifice her life for them. In ten years' time she'd be fifty. It was high time to make a move. Suddenly she felt her entire life had been wasted and soon it would be all over.

She found a kiosk and bought *Weekend* and *Today*. There was no shortage of accommodation in the small ads section in *Today*, but you had to put in an offer in a sealed envelope at the newspaper's reception desk marked something like 'Sobriety 1994' or something equally idiotic. At the bottom of the page there was an advert for a letting agency.

She went back into the bank to make a phone call.

A man with a deep voice answered and was keen to help. She needed a flat? No problem. But it wasn't going to be cheap. 'What kind of flat are you looking for?'

'Well, two or three rooms.'

'And whereabouts?'

'Not in the old town centre.'

'Hang on a moment, I'll see what we've got on the computer.' He came back a minute later. 'There's a two-room flat on the eighth floor on Asparfell. I looked it over the day before yesterday. Great views. It's a two-year lease, preferably paying four to six months in advance.'

'What's the monthly rent?'

'Not that much. Thirty-five thousand.'

'As much as that?'

'It's very reasonable.'

'What else have you got?'

'A two-room flat on Laufásvegur.'

'No, that's no good.'

'Two on Kópavogur, one on Grafarvogur and there's a three-room flat in Árbær.'

'When could I view the one on Asparfell?'

'The office closes at four. We could meet at a quarter past.'

She looked at the clock in the bank. It was half past three. 'Let's meet there then,' she said. 'What number?'

'Eighteen.'

She replaced the receiver and checked again with the cashier whether Vilhjálmur had transferred the money into her account. Not a single kroner! She tried ringing Heidnaberg but it was constantly engaged. She drove up the hill to Asparfell. The house had a penthouse flat. It was grey and not very well maintained. Just looking at it made her feel depressed. She went up to the front door but it was locked. She looked through the window but there was nothing to see except a yellow carpet and a row of mailboxes on a wall. Junk mail was sticking out of some of them. She was about to lose heart. Wasn't it madness to swap the gleaming floors of Thingholtstræti for this dump? But I can't bear Tryggvi!

She had quite a long time to kill. She looking down across the town. The wind was warm. The sun was shining but on the slopes of Mount Esja there was a single square area of shadow, almost like a cemetery. She gazed at the dark square and found herself almost wishing she could be laid to rest there. A white-sailed yacht was sailing near Videy island. It must be strange not to be short of money. Some people had money coming out of their ears and never had to think for a moment about spending it. Watching the yacht calmed her. Everything would be all right once she got a divorce! She could meet a man who owned a boat like that and he'd ask her to go round the world with him. They'd make love on deck beneath the flapping mainsail with the sea spray on their skin and it would be as if they'd invented sex. She could not stop her imagination and before she knew it she had a steady relationship with this imaginary yacht owner. She was pregnant and weighed down with a multitude of problems, grizzling children in every room, up to her neck in debt.

'No,' she thought, 'I'm going to make it. I'm going to get out of this marriage even if I have to kill Sylvía and the boys.'

A classic American car pulled up at the house. A tall, ginger-haired man got out and looked at her shyly. They shook hands and got into the lift. He showed her round the flat. Two reception rooms, a small bedroom. The view was fantastic. 'Yes,' she said. 'I'll take it.'

'You sure you don't want longer to think about it?'

'No. I'm getting divorced and I need somewhere to live.'

'Can you pop into the office tomorrow and we'll deal with the paperwork?'

'Yes, fine.'

He took out his pocket calculator. 'It'll be two hundred and twenty-three thousand kroner on signature of the contract.'

'No problem,' said Dagny. Somehow her words did not carry conviction.

He looked at her solemnly. He had a long neck and a gold filling in a front tooth. 'We've got to be sure about this. There's always someone with ready cash. It creates problem if I've already made a verbal agreement on the flat.'

'It's definite,' she said. 'I've already spoken to the bank. It'll be OK if I pay a hundred thousand kroner tomorrow and the rest after the weekend, won't it?'

'That should be all right.'

She opened the door to the bathroom. There was no window.

'Have you got any family?' asked the man brightly.

'No. Just a daughter. She's eleven. I told you I was getting divorced.'

'Well,' he said, glancing towards the door, 'I'm afraid I'm in a bit of a hurry.'

'What's the time?'

'Twenty to five.'

She drove to the old town centre and parked in front of the Bank of Iceland. She was planning to go to the Moneystock Market Company and find out how long it would take to cash the shares. She would have to manage on her salary until then. She got a statement. The money had gone in: 98,677 kroner. It was seven minutes to five. She pushed the door at the Moneystock Market Company. As luck would have it it was still open. She ran up the stairs.

Tryggvi kept one eye on the doors until he and Einar left around six o'clock. He expected the heavies to burst in any minute. As it got nearer to going-home time he wondered whether to stay on and work on the Chevy he was restoring but he didn't fancy being in the garage all on his own, defenceless. And he didn't dare go home. It felt like sitting on a bomb. He looked out of the window and his mood lightened. His Ford, sprayed a deep scarlet with the spare tyre in a silver drum on the back was waiting out in the car park. He would rather die than lose that car. He left with the bunch of roses, the chocolates and the port, put them on the back seat and sat at the wheel without starting the car. The district was quiet. A few raindrops were falling on the windscreen. Where should he go? What should he do? It was good news that the doctor who had killed his mother-in-law was connected to one of the richest families in the country. They should be able to milk the toffs.

He drove into town. The white liner was still far out in the bay. He turned into Tryggvagata and drove east down Hafnarstræti. Drop in on the Harbour Bar? He looked round. Nowhere to park. He couldn't find anywhere to park until he was in Gardarstræti. Would the car be safe? Everywhere you went there were vandals scratching cars. He took the flowers and the chocolates and the bottle and walked into town. It wasn't advisable to leave anything in a locked car. The vermin would break in. The streets were bathed in the spring sun and there was a strong smell from the sea. That sort of thing touched the old sailor in him. He opened the door of the Harbour Bar. It was bloody winos' place. He wanted somewhere light and warm with leather chairs and a bit of human company. How did the poet Dagur put it? 'Why leave all the

flowers to be plucked by fools?' He walked into a bar on Tryggvagata carrying the bag with the bottle and the bouquet close to his
chest. Here everyone would be in a party mood. But not a bit of it.
There was nobody there. He sat on a stool and asked the barman
to look after his things. His sons, Haddi and Jökull, would have to
fix themselves something to eat. Think what it would be like if you
had lots of bread like that old fart at Heidnaberg. He was shitting
himself when I was telling him to lay off Dagný. Suddenly Tryggvi
got an idea. Get her to make the old man guarantee a bank loan.
It was sweet.

He looked at himself in the mirror. He was still quite tasty. He
could still cut it with the birds. A tall, fair-haired girl was standing
at the bar not far from him. Drop-dead gorgeous. About twenty.
Where had she come from? He hadn't noticed her coming in. 'Well,
hello, you gorgeous blonde,' he thought. God, what a weakness he
had for blondes. Tryggvi asked for a double gin and cola. Girls like
that were meant to go for older men. No boys wet behind the ears
for them. They got fed up with the groping and nervous, sweaty
fumbling. Suddenly a tall man with his ginger hair tied in a pony
tail sat between them. He looked at Tryggvi. 'Can I get you a
drink?'

'Yes, thanks, mate.'

'What's your poison?'

'Gin and cola.'

'Where're you from?' The barman looked curiously at Tryggvi.

Tryggvi stared at the man. 'Right here. Reykjavík. Why do you
ask?'

'No one's asked for gin in years. Are you one of those hippy
types from the sixties?'

'No, mate, I was born long before the war.' The barman took
the joke as the gospel truth and Tryggvi was hurt. He looked at the
girl. Her expression hadn't changed, so he looked over his shoulder, out into the street, so she couldn't flatter herself thinking he
was looking at her. The ginger guy asked for a Campari. Tryggvi
could tell from his voice that he'd already put a few away. Tryggvi
watched him out of the corner of his eye. He had strong cheekbones and the roots of his beard were deep red. He was a bit taller
than Tryggvi and more thickset. Their eyes met. Why did they look

into each other's eyes for so long? For all he knew the other guy's pupils were enlarging. A pony tail, eh? A bit of a poofter. Was he coming on to me when he offered me a drink?

Tryggvi stroked his cheek and turned his head this way and that in the mirror. The hair was trimmed a bit too close at the side of his head. He sipped his gin. A drink you could trust.

There were tables and chairs in a corner by the bar. Everything seemed to be yellow. The yellow of rotten teeth. He looked up at the ceiling. In some places the yellow had come off, revealing a different, older yellow beneath. Where the original yellow showed through it was beginning to turn bronze. In the corner there was a billiard table beneath a single lightbulb, a 'Russian chandelier' as they say. There was a sun-yellow corona around the bulb. Suddenly the green of the baize seemed ugly and unpleasant. Tryggvi rubbed his cheeks with his palms. The colour oppressed him. He was finding it difficult to concentrate. Perhaps it was the heat. Or the heavies waiting for him in town. Yes! And at home for that matter! That bloody stockbroker and his refusal to cash the shares. The poofter turned to him. 'What do you do for a living?'

'Who? Me?'

'Well, there's only the two of us drinking.'

'No, there's the blonde as well.' Tryggvi laughed. He didn't expect the poofter to take much notice of her. He saw the girl in the mirror sitting over her glass twiddling the cocktail stick. Her fair hair brushed the counter. She did not seem to have heard.

'Don't you want to tell me what line you're in?'

'I'm a mechanic.'

'And where do you work?'

'GM Service.'

'GM?'

'We service General Motors cars for the importer. Chevrolet, Buick, Oldsmobile. General repairs on other models.' Tryggvi was quoting word for word from the card Einar sometimes gave to customers.

The poofter twisted the glass of Campari between his fingers. 'Shall we sit down? Have a chat?'

This came as no surprise. Tryggvi shuddered. The man was making a pass at him. It was disgusting. 'Shouldn't we ask the little lady to join us?' He looked at the girl.

The poofter looked at the blonde. 'No, thanks. I've had it with women.'

'What's the matter with you? Have you got something against women? Are you the other way?'

The poofter looked at him a moment but it seemed as if he didn't dare mix it with him. 'I've just got divorced. The woman I love chucked me out.'

'What bitches they can be.' Tryggvi looked sympathetic. 'Perhaps I've misjudged him,' he thought. 'But he does look like a poofter.'

The poofter suddenly frowned, realizing the slight. 'Gay? Are you accusing me of being gay? I talk to you, man to man, offer you a drink and you insult me.'

'Sorry, mate.' They were both silent and Tryggvi saw out of the corner of his eye that the man was looking at him with little drunk piggy eyes. 'Why did I even think of offering that yuppy money so I could get my hands on those shares?' thought Tryggvi. The gin made him see things clearly and now it seemed utter madness. Suddenly the poofter hit him in the head. Tryggvi fell off his stool and almost lost consciousness. The poofter kicked him in the shoulder. What an outrage, kicking a man when he's down! Tryggvi marvelled at this despite the pain and being laid out on the floor. He fought to stop himself losing consciousness.

'Now then, lads, I'll call the police if you don't pack it in!' shouted the barman.

When Tryggvi tried to stand he got kicked in the thigh. Around them was a deep silence tinged with hatred and fear. Tryggvi scrambled to his knees and held out his hand. He did not want to fight. The poofter hit his hand. 'I do weight training,' said the poofter.

'You don't say,' puffed Tryggvi and hit the man hard in the face. The poofter stumbled backwards against the bar looking surprised. Tryggvi's thighs and the side of his head hurt. He punched the poofter in the chest. The poofter looked at him with complete loathing and punched him in the face sending him staggering backwards. It was a heavy punch but nothing like as bad as the first one. The girl sat on her stool, sipping her drink through a straw, strangely unmoved by what was happening around her. Tryggvi landed a single punch on the poofter's stomach and pinioned him in a half-nelson. He wanted to strangle him. But the other man twisted free of the hold so Tryggvi could not maintain his grip. He was punched in the abdomen and then, heavily, over the heart. To his horror he realized the strength was draining from him. He stumbled backwards through the door and fell on his back on the pavement. The poofter staggered after him and tried to kick him but missed. A few passers-by stopped to watch.

Tryggvi pulled himself up by holding on to a railing and threw a punch in the air. The poofter clasped him round the waist and they fell down with Tryggvi on his stomach. The poofter was clutching him from behind like some Graeco-Roman wrestler and Tryggvi couldn't move an inch. The poofter was panting and holding on tighter and tighter, his breath rasping. Tryggvi realized the man was trying to kill him. He clapped him twice on the shoulder to show he was submitting. This made no difference to the poofter. 'Why isn't anyone helping me?' Tryggvi thought mournfully and his mind wandered to tender thoughts of his family. Especially of Haflidi. A firm inner voice said, 'I don't think Haddi would be very pleased to see his father being treated like this.' He could hear himself choking. At that moment he managed to get hold of his precious knife, open the blade and shove it into the man's side. His clothes gave him no protection. The knife went in. The man screamed and loosened his hold. A second stab forced him to let go completely. The third caught him in the upper arm. The poofter stumbled to his feet clutching himself. Tryggvi swung his arm intending to plunge the knife into the man's neck but missed. Before he got another chance to try two men grabbed him under the arms and yanked him to his feet. One of them took the knife off him. Tryggvi staggered away from them, walked drunkenly over to the poofter, grabbed hold of his shirt at the neck, flung him on the ground on his back, sat on top of him and let the blood from his nose drip on to the man's face. 'That's how we did it in the old days, us seamen of Iceland.' He was panting hard. 'We didn't beat people up just for the sake of it.'

'Let the man go,' someone said.

Tryggvi stumbled to his feet. 'My knife. Give me my knife.'

Somebody handed him the folded knife and another brushed down his clothes. He took the flowers, the chocolates and the port in his arms. He could barely keep hold of them. 'Let me be!' he said in a gruff, breathless voice and staggered past the door of the bar where the girl was standing looking at him with cold eyes. 'Let me be!'

'Did you stab him?' asked an old man, trying to hold on to Tryggvi. 'Did you stab him? Are you out of your mind?'

Tryggvi shook the old man off and walked unsteadily along Tryggvagata. He did not feel up to making it to his car. He walked, exhausted, into Lækjartorg. It was strangely tempting to lie on the lawn in front of Government House. He sat down on a bench. The evening sun was shining on the square. Suddenly he could see clearly how ridiculous it was to ask Dagný to get Axel of Heidnaberg to guarantee a bank loan. He found himself wishing intently that the heavies would show up and kill him.

He conceived the wonderful plan of going home to his mother in Kópavogur and asking if he could stay the night. He would be safe there. He would ask Dagný for the shares tomorrow, make it plain she had no choice in the matter. Perhaps everything would be all right? He remembered the stone house at Kópavogur. It was a two-storey house and his mother owned the lower half. He had inherited the top floor from his father and sold it long since. Dagný and he had started their married life there. Dagný and his mother had fought like cat and dog. Tryggvi had often hinted that he wanted to use the lower floor as collateral but his mother would hear none of it. The idea of suicide crossed his mind.

He took a taxi to Kópavogur. His face was covered in blood. The driver didn't say anything about his appearance. The silence became too much for Tryggvi and he told him all about the fight. He walked straight through to his mother's kitchen. There was nobody there. He called up the corridor, 'Mama!'

'Yes. Is that you, Tryggvi?' His mother leaned over the banister and looked down the stairs. She had a large face. Her dark hair was cut in a fringe and her eyes were black. 'I'm having coffee and doughnuts up here with Ágústa. I'll be down in a minute. Make yourself comfortable in the kitchen.' Then he heard her on the stairs. 'Whatever happened? You look terrible. Is something wrong? God, you look so miserable.'

'Yes. I'm not going to argue with that. It was only today that it hit me that my mother-in-law's dead. There was a fellow not show-ing proper respect to her memory and I wasn't going to let him get away with it. That's why I look like this.' He listened to himself and was shocked by the sentimental rubbish.

'There, there, my dear,' she said, stroking his cheek. 'It'll get better in time.'

It comforted him to have his mother's hand stroking him and suddenly there were tears falling down his cheeks.

'What's the matter, son? Is Dagný trying to kill you? Has she left you again?'

'No, no.'

'You can't fool me, Tryggvi.'

'Everything's fine between me and Dagný, Mother.'

'Of course it's not fine. She's slowly killing you. Let me get a damp flannel.' She returned with a flannel wet with cold water and dabbed at his face.

'Mother, I've been meaning to say for ages that you should come and live with us. You wanted to when I bought the house on Thórs-gata, but there wasn't enough room. Well, now you can, because the upstairs flat's empty, as you know. Do you want to think about it?' He looked up, full of hope. 'You could do worse than live in the old town centre and didn't you tell me the other day you wanted to move? I know the kids would love to have you there and so would I.' He decided not to mention that his mother would need to sell her flat in the Kópavogur house and continued, 'I wouldn't want much in the way of rent. I bought these for you, to make you happy.' He took the flowers and the chocolates and the port from the kitchen table and laid them tenderly in her arms.

He was too on edge to stay overnight with his mother. Later in the evening he decided to go home, whatever happened, even though the heavies would probably cripple him.

163

16

As Tryggvi opened the door to the living room, Dagný picked up the crystal bowl from the table and flung it at him without a second's hesitation. She aimed for his head and her aim was true. The bowl caught his cheekbone, drawing blood, broke against the door frame and shattered against the wall under the stairs in the hall. Jökull and Haflidi leapt up from the table and stared at the spectacle, rooted to the spot. Blood was pouring down Tryggvi's cheek. He was swaying slightly but still kept on heading for his chair at the top of the table, pulled it out, sat down and said, panting, 'Dagný, I want us to move out to the country. There's a garage in Seydisfjörd I know I can get cheap.'

'Shut your mouth or so help me I'll kill you, you rotten drunk,' screeched the woman. 'Were you trying to get your filthy paws on Mother's shares?'

He gulped in air through his open mouth, looking ridiculous. She pitied him when she saw what a state he was in. She rested her fists on the other end of the table, looked at him and said, her voice now completely different, 'Just look at you.'

He felt the cheekbone under the half-closed eye that looked like a prune in the socket. 'It's nothing.' He tipped his head back so his family could see his face properly and tried to grin. 'Two debt collectors gave me going over,' he lied. 'It's no big deal. I've seen worse.' Tryggvi focused on his wife with his right eye. 'I have to get a hundred thousand kroner. Otherwise it's good-night Vienna.' He felt his chest. 'I think they might have broken a rib.'

Haflidi went to the head of the table and made a professional assessment of his father's condition. 'How'd it happen? How could they knock out my old man?'

'I had one of them down on the street and then the other bugger kicked my head in.'

'Where were you fighting?'

'Just outside. On the corner. Didn't you hear anything? I tried to call out for you, Haddi.'

'You look awful. Your nose could be broken or your cheekbone.' Haflidi looked at his mother. 'Don't you think we should phone the night doctor?'

'Didn't we have enough of that last time?' Tryggvi sighed sadly. 'Your grandmother's dead and gone. But don't you worry. I'll defend the family honour. I had one of the bastards on the ground. These were eighteen-, nineteen-stone guys. But they forgot they were dealing with an old sea dog. A good Icelandic upper cut can do more damage than karate, you just remember that.' Tryggvi put up his fists and shadow boxed but he had scarcely any strength left. He let his arms fall. 'Those guys'll come back. I've got to get some money from somewhere, Dagný,' he said, agitated.

'What debts are these? Don't you lie to me, you toad.'

'I bought the Chevy I'm doing up on a bill of exchange and they must have picked it up.'

'Are you a complete fool? You spend a hundred thousand kroner on a pile of junk when we haven't got food to put on the table?'

Tryggvi rested his elbows on the table and put his face gingerly into his hands. The black eye peeped out between his index and middle fingers. He let his forehead rest on one hand and felt his lip.

'Shouldn't we call the police?' Jökull frowned at his father. 'Isn't your nose broken? They can't get away with something like that.'

'You're all making such a fuss.' Tryggvi looked at Haflidi and caught him smiling. Probably he had already spotted that the story did not quite hang together.

The front door opened.

'Careful, Sylvía!' called Haflidi. 'There's broken glass all over the hall.' Sylvía stared at the floor and tiptoed through the doorway.

Jökull sat down. It hurt him to see his father like that and he was irritated to see his brother shadow boxing around the room like some idiot. Sylvía went over to Tryggvi and tenderly stroked his cheek. 'I love you, Father,' she said.

Dagný put a folded flannel to her husband's face, then stood back with her hands on her hips and looked at him. She seemed more friendly. Haflidi aimed two karate chops in quick succession at his brother's face.

'Arsehole!' screamed Jökull. 'I'm sick of all this macho stuff.'

Tryggvi held the flannel to his face and told them about the fight. Haflidi rained questions down on his father's head, trying to dignify the story. 'How did you knock him down? Do you think you broke his jaw? I wish I'd been there. I'd've killed the other bloke. It's not just about strength. It's speed and aggression that's more important.'

'Haflidi, leave your father alone. Can't you see he's in pain?'

'It's OK, Dagný,' said the man of the house, sounding a little frail. 'Dæja darling, this flannel's not cold any more.'

'Do you want some ice-cubes?'

'Yes, please, would you?'

Dagný got some ice-cubes from the ice-box. She wrapped them in the flannel and held it to her husband's eye. She held his head against her stomach and he rested there peacefully. He lifted a hand and squeezed hers. She did not pull it away.

Haflidi was still shadow boxing. 'We're tough guys, aren't we, Dad! We've both got bashed-in faces. That was some fight I had the day before yesterday. I'm always hoping someone'll cut my cheek with a knife. I could really do with a good scar.'

'Honestly, this family!' sighed Sylvía, affecting boredom.

Jökull fetched a broom from the bathroom and swept up the broken glass into a dustpan. The solid base of the bowl had flown between the banisters and was standing on a stair. Jökull shook out the doormat in the garden.

'Close the door so your father isn't in a draught and then get the vacuum cleaner.'

Jökull closed his eyes and clenched his teeth when he heard the concern in his mother's voice. He shut the door to the living room. He went upstairs carefully and then brushed each step twice on the way down to make sure he'd caught all the glass splinters. He put the base in the dustpan, put on some shoes and went out to the dustbin. As he let the glass slide out of the dustpan he looked back at the house. He imagined 28 Thingholtstræti metamorphosing into a large clipper. The timber in the house had come from a famous shipwreck. He imagined three tall masts rising out of the roof in the Year of Our Lord eighteen hundred and seventy-seven. He could see the sailors climbing the topmast, edging their way out sideways along the spar, releasing the sails one by one. One sailor continued climbing to the very top of the mast to stand guard. The

Jamestown out of Boston, one of the largest clippers in the world, heads slowly out to sea from harbour in Mexico with its holds full of redwood and silver-ore ballast. The boy walks to the stern and looks out across the sea.

As he came through to the hall he could hear happy laughter. He wasn't sure he'd got every splinter of glass but he couldn't bear to go back in to fetch the vacuum cleaner. He left the dustpan and broom in the hall where his mother would be sure to see them and went up to his grandmother's flat.

When his father had started restoring the Thingholtstræti house he had torn down an old wall of rotten timber in the cellar and the digits '1882' had been revealed carved in the stonework. He summoned his family and they had all marvelled at it as if it were some freshly discovered altarpiece. 'I didn't expect the house to be that old,' said Tryggvi, his eyes shining as if some great good fortune had befallen him. He began to research the history of the house and discovered that a farmer's son from the Sudurnes had built it out of driftwood. When he'd torn up the linoleum and underfelt he set to work with the wood-polisher and the old redwood floor shone once more.

Twenty-eight Thingholtstræti was the third house Tryggvi had restored from the foundations upwards. He drove out to the south coast with Jökull to find out about the shipwreck. Perhaps he'd come across some old shed people were planning to pull down constructed out of the same driftwood and he could cannibalize it. It was best to use original wood for restoration.

The ship had foundered in Hafnar district. They were pointed in the direction of a man who knew all about local history and he invited them into his parlour and told them all about the wreck. The *Jamestown* was known as 'The Timber Ship'. A lot of houses along the south coast and in Reykjavík had been built from its wood. The man showed them a stone church and told them the wreck was associated with the church. There was a story about it. He'd written a book about Hafnar district and they could read it there.

'While the stone church was being built, the farmer pondered the construction of the pulpit. He had read in a foreign newspaper that the great cathedrals of Europe all used pine for their pulpits. There was nowhere on the south coast one could lay hands on such a wood. He made inquiries in Reykjavík. Not even a splinter. The plan was to consecrate the church that summer on the Feast of Saint Thorlákur. On the Whitsun Eve 1881 he knelt in prayer in the church: "O God, I have built you a new house. The old one was nothing but a leaking shed. Until now I have not sought your help with so much as a nail. Please now provide me with some redwood by any means at your disposal so that this building may be to your glory." He listened with his eyes closed. He experienced the silence of God.

'When he had been studying his catechism with the priest before his confirmation he had read in the Psalms of David that God heard all the thoughts of mankind, so there was no point in dissembling. "Perhaps I have built this church for my glory and not yours?" he suggested to God. "Now are you going to give me the wood?" The farmer still did not sense the presence of his creator, despite his honesty.

'"O God," he prayed, "we both know it. I have committed the sin of pride here in Hafnar district, but it is still true that it will be not me but your son whom people will praise in this house for centuries to come. I'm holding you responsible for providing me with the redwood."

'When he had finished praying he felt he had cleansed his soul before the Lord and he went into his farmhouse and fell asleep. On Whitsun morning 1881 there was a commotion outside his house: "Shipwreck! Shipwreck!" Everyone ran to the window. A great black ship was rolling in the waves just offshore. The *Jamestown* had been lost at sea three years earlier. In its hold were a hundred thousand planks of redwood.

'In the autumn the ship broke in two where it lay and the timber was scattered along the shore. The farmer's son got some of the hull as his share. He tore it apart, plank by plank, and sailed the ship's timber, along with a lot of the redwood for good measure round the coast to Reykjavík, where he built a house on Thingholtstræti. He had enough timber left over to pay for labour, braces, bricks for the chimney and glass for the windows.'

The boy lay down on his grandmother's sofa. The clipper *Jamestown* had been a hundred and thirty-six yards from stem to stern and thirty yards in the beam. He could imagine the mainmast rising from the rooftop, a hundred and twenty feet high. The house frame was constructed of timber from the masts. Two men stretching round the mast could not touch fingers. When the iron rings were hammered away, the mast split into many separate beams, all free of knot holes and smeared with oil. He closes his eyes and he sees the *Jamestown* keel over in a fierce gale. The terrorstricken crew tries to cut down the aft mast. The sails are dipping into the sea and they cannot hack through the mast. He can see the crew scurrying for the lifeboats. The aft mast breaks with a sound like thunder, the ship rights itself, picks up speed and heads out to sea without its crew. Jökull laid his hand against the wall. It was strange to think of the things that wood had witnessed a hundred years before he was born. Perhaps the full force of the gale had struck this particular plank. He sat up and touched the redwood of the floor with his toes. History said, 'What great good fortune when the Good Lord sent such a large load of timber to the south coast, the greatest cargo in the history of the country.' He looked at the clock and thought he could see it sliding along the chest of drawers. The *Jamestown* was keeling over into the sea. He stood up and the great ship righted itself again and the two masts lifted out of the sea.

He heard the ceiling above him creaking. There was no one living up there. No one wanted to sleep in the loft room. Forty years ago a man had hanged himself in that room. It was said that his ghost attacked people. Lots of people had tried to rent the room but they had all been driven away. Haflidi had let himself be talked into sleeping there one night. He saw nothing and his dead grandmother had said it was because he had no soul.

When Jökull was sure everyone was in bed he crept downstairs and went to his bed. Haflidi was asleep and had turned his face to the wall. Usually Sylvía slept in her mother's room but now she was sleeping on the sofa in the living room. No sooner had Jökull got into bed than he heard creaking coming from his parents' bedroom. He recognized the sound. Once he had accidentally opened the door to their room and found his father glaring at him, shocked and angry. He shouted, 'Shut the door, boy!' Jökull squeezed his eyes tight shut and tried to imagine the regular sound was the creaking of the spar. But the image in his mind of his parents would not go away. 'Shut the door, boy!' He crept back up to the second floor and settled on the sofa in the living room. As he went upstairs a sliver of glass cut his foot.

And still he thinks of the *Jamestown* . . . The wooden ship drifts slowly with wind and weather towards the coast of Iceland, nearer and nearer to the Reykjanes. For him it is a secret hiding place. But tonight it does not bend to his will. The ship keels to one side, alone on the ocean, its sails torn and tattered and the rats scurrying and squealing in the dining room. He sees the *Jamestown* lit up from stem to stern like a jack-o'-lantern in a choppy sea. He sees it beneath a frozen moon, in unimaginable chill, white with snow, with not a soul aboard in the mid-Atlantic with its decks covered in a thin film of ice. And with that vision in his mind he slept.

17

Recently too many people had taken to doing their weekly shop in Hagkaup on a Thursday so Hördur and Vilhelmína had switched to a Friday. When they had finished shopping Vilhelmína pushed the trolley to the checkout and Hördur went to look at the magazines. As he scanned the rack he found his own face on the front page of *Weekend*. He wasn't surprised. He glared at himself coldly. He looked around slowly and then took the magazine in its Cellophane wrapper and went to the checkouts, found Vilhelmína and tossed it, face down, into her trolley. Just by the checkout there was a rack for newspapers and magazines, positioned to encourage customers to pick one up on the way out. His face was there too. He looked at his wife. She hadn't seen his familiar features. He did not need to read it to know what it was about. That bloody tart from 28 Thingholtstræti was out to get him. Now his colleagues would have a field day. This was what they'd all been waiting for. Vilhelmína picked up a pair of socks from the trolley for her daughter's son and put them on the conveyor belt. He watched the socks glide by towards the cashier. There was a lot of noise and bustle, people getting their shopping out of their trolleys and glancing at each others' goods. Fridays were just as bad as Thursdays, the doctor decided and got out his Visa card. He suddenly wanted to get out of the place and read the magazine.

'Just a moment,' said Vilhelmína and grabbed the socks the girl had just scanned. The girl looked at her. 'Weren't those socks on offer?'

'I don't know.'

'I thought they were reduced. I got them from a table. It said ninety kroner a pair.'

Hördur Gottskálksson looked at the till above the conveyor belt. It said a hundred and seventeen kroner. He looked at Vilhelmína and could have killed her. 'It's only twenty kroner, woman, let it go.' His voice sounded harsh with suppressed tension.

'No,' said Vilhelmína, 'it's only right.'

'We can't keep all these people waiting,' said the doctor. He tried to look natural, turning round and smiling at the considerable queue that had formed behind him. Some people looked away, embarrassed.

'It's OK, I'll go and check it out,' said the cashier.

'That really isn't necessary,' said Hördur firmly.

A few people behind them in the queue had taken their trolleys to other checkouts.

'Of course it's necessary,' insisted Vilhelmína. 'I wouldn't have bought those socks at full price.'

Suddenly it seemed to Hördur that fate was conspiring against him. His medical triumphs overseas were ignored by his colleagues; his face was plastered over the front page of grubby newspapers; at home he had a daughter who thought it her divine feminist duty to contradict him on everything; he had a son who wanted to be a film director just like everyone else, and to cap it all he was married to a woman who habitually acted the fool in public. And it had to happen now, just when he needed to slip away to a quiet corner and read the damned magazine. He picked up *Weekend* from the trolley and chucked it to the front of the pile of shopping on the belt. He was careful, however, to ensure his picture was still face down so Vilhelmína couldn't draw everyone's attention to it, as she was bound to do. He cast his mind back to those areas of his life that did give him some satisfaction. Well, they had managed to get Trausti to take a job.

The girl returned. Yes, the socks were on offer and she corrected the error. Ninety-seven kroner. 'I do apologize.'

Once *Weekend* had gone through the scanner, Hördur picked it up and left the supermarket. He sat in the car and tore off the wrapper. The whole business was set out in some detail. On an inside page there was even a photograph of the driver, Gunnar Bragason, standing by the doctor's car. From the traitor's expression it was clear he hadn't taken much persuading to pose for the camera. In a small box was the lie that Hördur Gottskálksson had been fired from the National Hospital. There was a sentimental paragraph, perhaps designed to soften *Weekend*'s attack, recounting that he had been born a farmer's son in the Landbrot, brought up in poverty, which might account for his abrasive attitude. They had even got their hands on a photograph of the old farmhouse, a shack with corrugated-iron cladding. On another page there was a photograph of his surgery on Skólabrú. The caption read: '*Weekend* has ears everywhere and we hear it can damage your health to set foot beyond the doors of this house.' In a thick black frame readers were reminded of an old story by a photograph of a wrecked car. Hördur used to tell anyone who would listen exactly what had happened. 'I gave my car to that bitch. A brand-new Chrysler Imperial, a wonderful car that cost 4 million kroner near enough and did she thank me?' Ten years earlier he had moved in with his receptionist for ten days. It wasn't a great success as the doctor had old-fashioned attitudes and expected her to cook and clean and do his laundry. When the girl threw him out she refused to return the car, even though Theódóra, at Vilhelmína's request, looked into the matter. She told the simple unvarnished truth: 'Hördur gave it to me. I'm not giving it back.'

The car was parked in a rundown district of Reykjavík, outside a garage where it was due for a service. In the dead of night the doctor had taken a sledgehammer to it. *Today* printed a photograph of the car. So did we at *Weekend*. I went to the scene myself. I was just an ordinary office boy in those days. Hördur had made a thorough job of it. It must have taken at least half an hour. The Chrysler was sold for scrap.

'Now I will go and see the Prime Minister,' muttered the doctor, overwhelmed by an urge to commit murder. 'It's all I've got left. If he can't do anything for me, I'll have to take matters into my own hands. And it'll add up to something a bit more serious than smashing up a car. Hördur folded up the magazine and put it in the glove compartment. His mind was all over the place and he couldn't face his wife reading the article on the way home.

'As the scalpel enters the flesh one perceives the body as a machine,' Hördur Gottskálksson had started one of the few articles he had ever written for a newspaper. The rest of the piece was in the same vein, dry, distant, cold. There is no need for me to quote from it at length, although I have a photocopy beside me as I write.

Hördur did not exactly shine at school. It was not that he was any worse than the other pupils. It was that the only thing that interested him was the human body, its illnesses and the inexorable decay that plagued this machine.

When the other first-year medical students were out partying, enjoying being young, Hördur would be sitting in his digs studying and studying. 'I'm going to be a doctor!' he would mutter to himself.

By the time the bright kids from school were finding it all too tough and dropping out of university, Hördur was getting top grades in his first-year exams.

He was brought up in the countryside and had to support himself through his training. Whatever the truth of it, he never tired of telling his family the hardships he had suffered.

Trausti, his son, however, was of the opinion that there was not much point in going to university. His father could not for the life of him understand such a lackadaisical attitude. Trausti had done his best to keep his nose in his books while at school. He struggled from term to term, finding it difficult because he felt so tired all the time. The names of dead kings and queens, the finer points of mathematics, accurate spelling, everything was a trial to him and he found it difficult to see the relevance of any of it to human existence. When he looked at the world around him it seemed fairly obvious that all that mattered was having money. Lots of it. And on that score his uncle Axel had done much better than his father.

Trausti knew his father wanted him to become a doctor. When Trausti was a child Hördur had sometimes taken him with him to the hospital but the place made Trausti feel depressed. Once he had happened to flick through one of his father's old medical books. It was a pathology instruction manual and even now the thought of it revolted him. Another was on forensics and that had not been much better.

Getting your hands on a lot of money was what gave life meaning. But how to set about it? It was easy enough for people who made money to persuade other people and themselves that what they had to sell was the best of its kind, whether it was shares, planes or wine. But Trausti thought he wasn't interested in commerce. He didn't want to work. He saw no point in working with little or nothing to show for it while other people raked in the millions and sat on their backsides smoking cigars. 'Uncle Seli hasn't done an honest day's work in his life,' he thought. Trausti tried to explain this when his parents were fixing him up with that job at the Heidnaberg construction site. Hördur had said he wouldn't put up with any nonsense. Vilhelmína advised him not to be too familiar in the office during working hours. 'It'll get on Aunt Tedda's nerves to have you hanging about there. Have your coffee in the shed with the other men.' 'Don't we have shares in this company?' Trausti had asked. 'I thought we were just as good as them. Do I have to take this job?' 'You've got no ambition, my lad,' said Hördur. 'And remember, money has got nothing to do with how good a person you are.'

Was his father the remarkable person he claimed to be? Were there actually any witnesses to the world-famous heart transplant he was supposed to have taken part in in 1968? Hadn't he provided *Who's Who* with that information himself? Why was Hördur never in photographs with wealthy benefactors and the equipment they were donating? Why did they still live in such an ordinary flat? He stood in the pouring rain yanking nails out of recycled timber thinking about life in general while the Ellidar river, heavy with spring silt, swirled murkily around Geirsnef island and out into the estuary. 'I shall kill myself,' thought the boy. 'I can't live like this.'

The funeral of his grandmother Ingibjörg was a heavenly oasis in the midst of the disgusting building work. He sat in the front pew with Linda, who was looking pale and sad. Her nose peeped out of her blond hair, slightly redder at the tip than usual. He listened to the priest casually recounting the main points of Ingibjörg's life. Naturally the story lacked the main decisive event of her life when she had moved into the Skólabrú house while Theódóra's mother was still living there. Trausti didn't care tuppence about all that. He dozed as the familiar hymns were sung and did not come to himself until Linda dug him in the ribs and it was time to carry the shiny white coffin containing the old lady festooned with flowers out of the church. He was one of the pallbearers. On television that evening he saw himself sliding the old lady into the undertaker's hearse. It was considered newsworthy when the majority shareholder in Heidnaberg went to her grave.

The next day he walked away from the pile of timber never to return. Someone called after him, 'Where are you off to, my lad?' He neither looked over his shoulder nor made any reply. It was lucky there was no one home at Vatnsholt. He lay in the bath for a long time. He planned to be out of the house at four o'clock when his father was expected home from the surgery. He stood up and wrapped a towel round his waist. He was short and stocky, his hair as yellow as the sun and his eyes as blue as water, his cheeks firm. He put on a Nirvana CD and smoked some blow out on the balcony where no one would smell it.

His father had watched a film on the video the night before and the cassette was still in the machine. He drew the curtains, curled up in an easy chair in the middle of the floor. *Happy Days in the Wild Wild West*. He thought the film unutterably funny. Many happy thoughts floated in and out of his mind unbidden thanks to the dope. He thought about 'The Tale of the Jeep', a story he had been told since early childhood. His father's brother bought a jeep but old Grandad made him take it back because 'out in the Landbrot, we use either our legs or our four-legged servant, which was his way of referring to the horse'. 'And my brother got rid of the jeep,' Hördur Gottskálksson used to say, his voice quivering. Trausti imitated his father: 'He did not have the strength of character to stand up to our father. But I wasn't going to be treated like some farmyard animal, so I went off to Reykjavík and I had to

175

make ends meet by collecting debts for a wholesaler while I got myself an education.' 'Make ends meet!' laughed Trausti. 'Now I always wanted to be a doctor,' he said in his father's voice, 'but your ambition, Trausti, is to do nothing!'

He fell silent and started getting involved in the film. A shrink was trying to talk some madwoman out of throwing herself off a skyscraper. She was wearing cowboy boots and a ten-gallon hat. Apparently her fiancé, a Country-and-Western singer, had fallen in love with someone else. The skyscraper was higher than the cliff face on Lomagnupur mountain. Trausti found himself hoping the woman would jump. He heard someone in the hall. His mother must be home. His mind wandered to the Landbrot, which he had visited several times. Last time had been to pick up a home-killed steer. The meat was for his parents. His uncle had thrown the heart down for the dog and Trausti remembered the dog's big tongue pushing at the heart, playing with it. The dog's tongue explored the nooks and crannies of the heart. Then the dog settled down and ate it. Trausti reached for the bottle of Pepsi and took a gulp. Suddenly he remembered a dream he had a few weeks back. He was looking at himself in a long mirror. He was wearing a dress and had long blond hair cascading over his shoulders. The dress was red silk. He smiled at himself. This body fitted him like a glove, he had known it in the dream. 'Wow!' said the boy as his stoned mind considered the dream. Then he realized he was a woman trapped in a man's body.

The phone rang. He was going to struggle to his feet and answer but he was surprised to hear somebody speaking. It was Ester. She'd come home! 'Father, for you!' she called. 'It's the Director of the Medical Service.'

Trausti froze with terror. They'd all come home, the whole lot of them. And here he was, out of his skull.

Hördur put his bags on the floor and picked up the phone.

'Hello, Bárdur, old friend.' He waited while the other man cleared his throat. 'What's new?'

'We've received a complaint. That's what's new.'

'A complaint!' Hördur sounded as if he hadn't a clue what the man meant.

'Someone rang and accused you of making no attempt to save

her mother from imminent death. And I've just received a letter by courier from Ólafur Sigthórsson the lawyer.'

'"Making no attempt to save her mother from imminent death",' parroted Hördur.

'Yes. Those are her exact words.'

'I'm in some difficulty as to the point of all this.'

'The point is, old friend, that you made a call to 28 Thingholt-stræti at about half past five on Thursday. You were driven by Gunnar Bragason . . .'

'Oh, that! I know all about that,' interrupted Hördur. 'The patient was dead as far as I was concerned. I considered it unlikely that any attempt to resuscitate her would have any effect. My assessment was that although it might have been possible to get the heart beating again it would only have "prolonged her suffering".'

'"Prolonged her suffering",' said Bárdur in his bass voice, deep in thought. 'That's it exactly. Those are the precise words quoted in the letter.'

'The guy on duty at A. & E. told me the old woman had been brought in to the hospital many times,' said Hördur. 'The last time only a fortnight before she died.'

They talked about it for a while. To Hördur's surprise Bárdur seemed to be siding with the opposition. Finally the Director said in a neutral voice, 'I have the phone number. Perhaps you might calm these good people down?'

Hördur bumbled around the telephone table but could not find a scrap of paper on which to write down the number. He got the receipt book from his medicine bag, wedged the phone against his shoulder and wrote down the number. 'What was the lawyer after?'

'He's planning to take us to the cleaner's.'

'What can we do?'

'I'll think about it over the weekend. I'll write to him early next week. I can't see that this is any business of the Reykjavík Medical Service.'

They said their goodbyes and Hördur rang the number. A boy answered. 'Is this 28 Thingholtstræti?' The boy conceded that it was. 'Could you fetch your mother to the phone?'

'Yes. Just a sec.'

Hördur looked at his watch. Quarter past six.

'Hello. Dagný speaking.'

'It's the night locum service doctor here. First of all I want to thank you for that phone call the other day.'

'There's nothing to thank me for,' said the woman, sounding rather sheepish.

'I would have thought that would have been the end of the matter.'

'Well, we're just not happy about it,' she said quickly and nervously.

'Not happy about what?'

'The way you dealt with things.'

'Do you have medical training?'

'No. Why?'

'In my opinion I am well qualified to know how to "deal with things", as you put it.'

'Why was no attempt made to save my mother?'

'How old was she?'

'Seventy-eight.'

'She was skin and bone and looked in a bad way. She had suffered heart failure and had probably sustained some brain damage. I saw no reason to prolong her suffering. She had had a heart attack only a fortnight before.'

'How do you know that?'

'I was told by the A. and E. Department at the City Hospital.'

'But you couldn't have taken that into account when you assessed her.'

'I could see at once what her condition was.'

'How long do they reckon it takes before there's brain damage?'

'Three or four minutes.'

'It can't have been more than a couple of minutes between her losing consciousness and you getting here.'

Hördur had some difficulty framing his next sentence. 'I judged the situation, that it would be wrong to resuscitate this lady. For her own sake. And yours.'

'I've already made a formal complaint.'

'Oh, have you?' said Hördur. 'You're determined to squeeze some money out of this, aren't you? Well, that pleasure will be denied you. And you went running to the papers.' His voice sounded almost gentle. 'Now what was all that in aid of? Just you listen to me. You've got yourself into more trouble than you realize. You won't even be able to withdraw the complaint now.'

'Are you threatening me?'

'Maybe I am.'

Trausti had sensed the comings and goings in the flat with mounting paranoia. He could no longer make head nor tail of the film. A horse was being killed and blood was spurting everywhere. The slaughter caused Trausti great distress. At one moment it seemed as if the living room had turned into the farm at Landbrot and that the dog was in the middle of the floor ripping the heart apart. He had no convenient excuse to explain his presence at home. He had driven his mother and sister out of the living room with his temper while Hördur was still on the phone but now the door opened and his father was standing there in the doorway. His greying hair seemed almost transparent and dangled lifelessly around his ears. 'What! You here!' roared Hördur, his voice making the flat vibrate.

The lump of meat in Trausti's mouth, his tongue, made an affirming sound.

'Why aren't you at work?' His father walked into the living room, turned on the light and pulled back the curtain. Trausti got out of the easy chair and turned off the television. It took an effort of concentration. He hadn't realized just how stoned he was. 'We ran out of cement.'

'You ran out of cement.'

'Yes.'

'Nonsense.' Hördur sat on the sofa, the leather creaking beneath him.

'Why's it nonsense?' Trausti risked asking. He said it to try and make things normal but it was difficult getting the words out. He could scarcely get his breath in his father's presence.

'Isn't the foreman's job to make sure the men have got everything they need to keep on working?' asked his father as if he was one of the Heidnaberg directors. Out! I've got to get out of here! Trausti could hardly stand. The phone rang.

'You get it.' said his father.

The floor beneath the boy's feet was like the waves of the sea.

'Yes. This is the police,' said the voice on the telephone.

Trausti clutched the receiver, dumb with terror. In the marijuana haze anything was possible. How had they found out about his little bit of blow?

'Hello? Is anybody there?' asked the police constable.

'Do you want to talk to me?' the bewildered Trausti finally managed to say it seemed like ten thousand years later.

'If your name is Hördur Gottskálksson, yes.'

'No. This is his son.'

'Then put me on to your father, would you, lad?'

'Dad, the cops want to talk to you,' said the boy, almost singing with delight at being let off the hook.

'Tell them to go boil their heads,' said his father angrily.

'I can't,' said the boy, looking at the receiver in alarm. 'I can't . . . do . . . that . . . Dad.'

'Then hang up. I'm not speaking to them and if they ring again, don't answer.'

'I've got to go out for a bit, Father,' Trausti said with considerable effort. The phone rang again almost as soon as he had hung up. He heard Vilhelmína answer and call to Hördur.

He went to the bog for a piss. It went on for ever. He was afraid he'd piss away all his innards and end up like a burst balloon on the bathroom floor. The shapes in the hall were all out of proportion and he went downstairs leaning against the wall for support.

When Hördur had agreed to go and make a statement at the police station, he pulled the phone out of its socket and went into his study.

'Father, I need to use the phone,' called Ester.

'It'll have to wait.'

He reconnected the phone and rang Dyngjuvegur. Axel answered. He was eating as usual.

'What are you eating, Seli?'

'Dried fish.'

'Well, we're blood brothers now all right.'

'Hördur, we've been that for a long time.'

'Have you seen that filth in *Weekend*?'

'No.'

'I'm on the cover.'

'What's all this about?' As far as Hördur could tell Axel was finding this highly amusing.

'I want you to speak to the Prime Minister for me,' said the doctor firmly. 'Arrange a meeting for me with Hannes Pálmason, so I can fill him in.'

'What dirty tricks are they up to?'

'It's all lies. They got me "excommunicated" at the hospital. Now they're trying to get me struck off. Your secretary's made a complaint against me.'

'Dagný?' Axel sounded stunned. 'Is this true? I haven't seen *Weekend*, but shouldn't you get legal advice before you go rushing off to see the Prime Minister?'

'Don't you have the guts to speak to him?'

'Of course I do. But why don't you approach him yourself?'

'Because you're involved with him in the Independent Party already and I'm not. He'll be all the more helpful if he knows I'm related to you. Isn't that the way the world works? They're trying to deprive me of the one source of income I have left, Seli. That's what it amounts to.'

'I'll try and reach him, Hördur, either this evening or tomorrow and then I'll get back to you,' said Axel, feeling that the conversation was getting uncomfortably near the matter of his mother-in-law's estate.

Hördur left the copy of *Weekend* on the desk where he was sure they would soon find it. He had got a migraine headache and went out into the garden and walked round the lawn hoping the pain would recede. One eye felt warm in its socket and his vision was obscured by a multicoloured tapestry.

Downstairs at Vatnsholt lived a couple with two sons. The younger was nineteen. The boy suffered from depression. He was good-looking, but his face was puffy and there were dark rings under his eyes. As the doctor went upstairs the boy was standing in the gloaming in the hall with the door to his parents' flat ajar. He was beaming from ear to ear. 'And you're always fixing up people!' Before Hördur could say anything he burst out laughing.

The doctor walked upstairs without saying a word. Vilhelmína had found the magazine and read the article. 'Whatever shall we do?' she asked forlornly.

'Do?'

'You'll lose your practice!'

'Not necessarily.' He tried to seem strong and in control even though his head was destroying him.

'I rang *Weekend*.'

'Whatever for?' He stared at her with his mouth open like some idiot.

'To get the address of the woman who made the complaint against you.' She was almost shouting. 'Why else would I do that? I phoned that woman at Thingholtstræti.'

He screwed up his eyes. 'You spoke to that woman? Are you mad?' He couldn't control his anger any more. 'Have you gone stark staring mad? And what did the journalist get out of you?'

'Why shouldn't I ring her?' screeched Vilhelmína. 'Perhaps she'll drop the complaint and get you out of this mess you've got yourself into and at least then we can put food on the table.' Her voice was getting louder and louder. 'Have I got to get a job on the checkout at Hagkaup? Is that what you want? Or do we have to sell up and move somewhere cheaper? And I didn't let the journalist get anything out of me.'

Hördur hit the living-room table where *Weekend* was lying open. 'Insist that Theódóra gives us our cut right now! What did the woman say to you?' He began to sound calmer. 'You women always gang up these days.'

'She said she was very sorry but things had gone so far now there was nothing she could do to stop it. It's with the Medical Service.' Looking tired and serious, Vilhelmína said, 'Why do you always rub people up the wrong way? Father would never have got himself into a mess like this.'

Suddenly Hördur raised his fist and took a step towards her.

His daughter intervened. 'Father, you're not to treat Mother like this,' she hissed. 'Didn't you see what it said in *Weekend*? Smashing up his girlfriend's car!'

The doctor slumped on to a kitchen chair and put one hand over his eye where the colours were shimmering like oil on the surface of water. 'Working on the checkout at Hagkaup?' he said out loud. 'Would you really do that, my dear?'

'Yes, or I would,' said Ester.

'I don't think that'll be necessary, Ester,' said Hördur slowly.

'Why? Why not?' She faced him, hands on hips. She had Vilhelmína's red hair. She was quite plump. Her face was freckled and her nose turned up a little at the tip. Her hair was a mass of tight curls.

He said, 'I think I'll get taken on there myself.'

18

'Hannes, someone on the phone for you.'

'Who?'

'Axel Sigurgeirsson.'

'Could you ask him to ring back in about half an hour?'

I shall take just a minute to provide a brief description of the Prime Minister. Hannes Pálmason was one of the tallest men in Parliament. Although he was only in his mid-sixties, his hair was completely white. He reminded one of a bust of Roman emperor. He was a died-in-the-wool Independent. 'I am so Independent, I'm probably a Social Democrat at heart,' he once told me when we were having a drink in Naust restaurant after an interview.

Sometimes as he sat all alone in his office at Government House he would look up at the paintings of his predecessors and think it quite extraordinary that he was now numbered among them. He spread his hands out on his desk and found it strange that they were indeed his hands. The day his own portrait was hung there it would be evident to all the world that he was the most handsome of the lot of them. He was stronger looking than Hannes Hafstein and more aristocratic that his hero, Ólafur Thors. Yet he did not feel that within himself he held the seeds of greatness. Perhaps this insecurity was his strength? Perhaps having one's feet on the ground is a leader's crowning glory? But although Hannes was accounted handsome, many found something to dread in his face. His wife sometimes teased him that when he was deep in thought he had the fiercest of expressions. He had to guard against that expression if a journalist or television interviewer asked some outrageous question. He did not know himself where this look came from.

Hannes Pálmason knew how to comport himself in the company of the great and good. Not seeming too enthusiastic, not bowing too deeply, not trying to curry favour with the powerful. The thing to do is to let the French President bend a little. Iceland's international role needed to become more important. A Prime Minister should not behave like a peasant or a factotum. He often thought back to the time when Leonid Brezhnev announced he would touch down in Iceland and the whole government went scuttling off to Keflavík Airport while the Secretary of the Communist Party flew straight over the island. Hannes wouldn't have been seen dead doing something like that. He would have waited for Brezhnev at the Government House.

The Prime Minister sat in his office. It was Friday, 8 June 1994. A man was striding across Lækjartorg. He disappeared around the corner of Austurstræti. The Prime Minister gazed at the portrait of Ólafur Thors looking down on him from the opposite wall. Ólafur Thors had been his role model when he was a young man and now here he was sitting in his chair. Ólafur had built himself a house on Gardarstræti. When the house had come on the market, Hannes was all set to buy it. His wife liked it and he wanted to live there himself but the more he thought about it the clearer it became that if he went ahead with the purchase he would only open himself to mockery and derision. 'I can't go into politics on Ólafur Thors's coat tails,' he said to himself. 'It must be by my own good offices. We can get something in the same district later.' And when a house had come on the market on Hólavallagata three years later he snapped it up immediately. It was on two floors, a black box in the 1940s 'Fúnkís' style, and more or less in its original condition. As he walked to work in the mornings, whether to the Parliament building, to Government House or to the offices at Arnarhváll, he tried to resist the temptation to see himself in some way as the all-wise father of the nation. 'If I think of myself as some kind of patriarch, the vanity of it will show in my face,' he thought. 'If, however, I consider myself unworthy of the honour bestowed upon me, then my face will glow with humility.'

The Prime Minister received visits from the general public

between the hours of nine and ten on a Friday morning. The intercom said, 'Hannes?'

'Yes.'

'Are you ready to meet the people?'

'Are there many of them?'

'There's one man waiting. A priest.'

'A priest! What's he want?'

'I'm afraid I didn't ask.'

This answer irritated Hannes Pálmason but there was no point in complaining. You weren't allowed to say anything that might offend women these days. He controlled himself.

'Your wife's on the phone.'

'I haven't time to speak to her. Is Haraldur Sumarlidason in the building?'

'I don't know. Do you want me to find out?'

'Yes, please,' said Hannes rather grumpily. 'Could you send him in as soon as you locate him?'

'Is the priest to come in now?'

'Just a minute.'

'Women,' he muttered to himself. Was it the habit of office girls in the days of Ólafur Thors to neglect to ascertain a visitor's business? Would Ólafur's wife be ringing Government House at all hours? No, she would be preparing salt cod for lunch in case Ólafur took it into his head to bring guests home. The Prime Minister swung his chair round to face Ólafur and rubbed his face with both hands. These last two days he'd been on edge and absent-minded. Talks with the Left about forming a coalition had been arduous and he'd received a blow from the quarter he'd least expected: his own party. Those women! He was not easily unsettled. Unfair accusations in Parliament, that was OK. Dirty tricks on the path to power, that was only to be expected. For years he had trained himself to look on disaster with equanimity, in preparation for the day of his own downfall. A old saying floated into his mind: the boxer never sees the blow that knocks him out. Because if he saw it, he'd avoid being knocked out, he'd outsmart his opponent, wouldn't he?

But the women in the party. They were livid because they weren't allowed more of a say. They were forever on at him over every little thing. It hurt. The animosity because Theódóra Thóroddsdóttir hadn't been given a ministry was incredible. 'Why didn't I make the bloody woman Minister of the Environment?' he thought and the answer came immediately. 'Because I couldn't bear the thought of it.' You can't criticize a woman nowadays without being accused of prejudice and sexism. They're all singing from the same hymn sheet and we're all over the shop. What is it the French say? *Cherchez la femme*? If men were fighting among themselves, the French had just about got it right. *Cherchez la femme*, indeed.

He found himself thinking about Haraldur Sumarlidason, that fox. He knew Haraldur was wily and treated everyone equally badly, but that was exactly why he needed him. Haraldur had an excellent memory and reported all the useful party gossip to the Prime Minister. Sometimes people rose through the ranks at great speed and Hannes had played his part in the rise of Haraldur Sumarlidason. He had even taken to sending him overseas to do little jobs for him. The Prime Minister kept thinking about Theódóra. Everyone knew it was Theódóra who ran Heidnaberg and that when it came down to it Axel was nothing but a good-natured buffoon. But he was as faithful as a sheep. Sometimes his devotion got on Hannes's nerves when he saw the adoration in Axel's eyes. Theódóra on the other hand was made of sterner stuff. Sharp as a needle, always able to come up with the unforeseen solution, a legal education behind her, she was a dangerous woman. Still, it was even worse to have her in the government than out of it, thought the Prime Minister. Everyone had been taken by surprise by her personal following. It almost looked as if she would have a government post by right. Hannes hadn't wanted to pursue this thought to its logical conclusion because then he would have had to work alongside her for four long years, with her opposing him at every turn with her own ideas. He had been her lawyer in the past and could envisage the endless arguments. He had offered her the eleventh seat when he heard she was thinking of getting out of politics anyway, so he could make sure of seeing the back of her. He was convinced she wouldn't be able to stand the excitement. She had said yes straightaway. It had been Haraldur Sumarlidason's bright idea. This was almost the first time Hannes had felt himself not entirely in control of his own life, just at the moment when the results were clear and he should have been celebrating. Who could have foreseen such a personal following?

He had decided not to hold the meeting with her in Government House, nor in the ski lodge at Hveradalir, nor in the Independent Party office at the Parliament building. He went and saw Seli and Theódóra at their home on Dyngjuvegur. He had not been feeling very steady that day. He had gone there with his colleague who was newly returned from overseas. Haraldur had been oddly tetchy and nervous, a bit shame-faced, as if he had committed some reprehensible act. He kept glancing at Hannes as if he wanted to seek his forgiveness for some offence. Hannes had tried to get to the bottom of it. Was the man sympathetic to the women's caucus in the Party? Was there some conspiracy brewing? Or was Haraldur simply anxious about some orgy on foreign soil he didn't want made public knowledge in Iceland? To the amazement of them both, Theódóra had agreed almost unconditionally to step down after discussing the matter with Seli. Hannes had been so relieved that he'd taken his eye off the ball and blundered. He gave her the chairmanship of the Foreign Affairs Committee out of sheer gratitude. He had expected her to insist of being Minister for Foreign Affairs. Poor old Seli of Heidnaberg, the poor bastard, he'd crept about petrified his wife wouldn't do the decent thing, terrified of not being able to deliver what his friend wanted. 'Perhaps the opposition had struck home without me realizing it?' wondered Hannes Pálmason. 'But how? And what's up with Haraldur? Was it a serious error of judgement to sideline the woman?'

'Hannes,' said the intercom. 'There someone on the phone for you.'

'Who is it?'

'Axel Sigurgeirsson.'

'Put him through.'

'The priest's waiting.'

The door opened and the Prime Minister caught a glimpse of a man in a long black robe. He raised his hand and called, 'Just a minute.'

The Prime Minister picked up the receiver. 'Yes, how are you, Axel? What can I do for you? Let me give you my condolences again on the death of your mother-in-law. She was a fine woman, and a member of the Independent Party through and through, just like you and me.'

'My brother-in-law's driving me round the bend,' said Axel and filled Hannes in on the whole story. 'It would be dreadful if he was struck off. Would you have a word with him?'

'He ought to speak to the Minister of Health rather than to me.'

'It's you he wants to see,' begged Axel.

'Tell him to pop in and see me on the eighteenth after National Day. I'm up to my eyes otherwise. Yes, thank you, Axel, that's fine. On the eighteenth, that's definite. Then we can go on together to the Hotel Saga party. You're the only person I know with the same birthday as Jón Sigurdsson, the President. Yes, Axel, you see, I know all about it. Do give your wife my warmest regards.'

He looked up from his desk and called, 'Come!'

The door opened and a tall man with a prominent nose and mass of tangled black curly hair came in. The Prime Minister stood up to shake his hand. The man introduced himself, 'Bernhardur Tómasson.'

'Haven't we met before?' asked the Prime Minister without sitting down. 'I never forget a face. You're a priest?'

Father Bernhardur nodded.

'At the Cathedral?' But the Prime Minister knew that was not where he had met the priest. He had seen him a day or so earlier, during the election campaign, but then he had shaken thousands of hands and met so many people he couldn't place the priest.

'It was at Theódóra Thóroddsdóttir's and Axel Sigurgeirsson's house.'

'I was having a word with Seli on the phone just now.' The Prime Minister offered his guest a seat, sat down himself, cleared his throat and crossed his ankles. 'How do you come to know Seli?'

'I hardly know them at all.'

'Good old Seli,' said the Prime Minister in his deep, manly voice. 'He's done all right for himself.'

'Yes, God has seen fit to bless his endeavours.'

The Prime Minister looked quizzically at the priest, perhaps a little frostily. 'And how may I help you?'

Father Bernhardur gave as brief an account as possible of the matter in hand. He had decided from the off to go straight to the top. He was planning to open a young people's home in town. A youth centre. Somewhere for young people to live. God knew there was a need for it. Thousands of teenagers hanging about the town centre at weekends. The unpleasantness and fighting were awful. Some of them, scarcely more than kids, wandering about the streets drunk. The Prime Minister nodded his head enthusiastically. 'They need some structure in their lives,' said the priest. 'And some of them need somewhere permanent to live. Would the government support such a scheme?'

'It's certainly worth consideration,' said the Prime Minister. 'Perhaps you should speak to the Domestic Affairs Minister or the Mayor of Reykjavík. Have you sought business sponsorship at all?'

'I took it to Heidnaberg. Theódóra's offered some support. I thought the woman would be keen on the idea.'

Hannes was feeling irritated. 'Perhaps young people wouldn't be like this if their mothers didn't go out to work. If they were in a position to stay at home, that is. Those kids are running wild. No one looks after them; no one disciplines them. That's the source of all this anarchy, right there. It's all very well for women to insist on equal rights, but it's the human being who needs equal rights. Men are suffering, just like the womenfolk, all over the continent, here in Iceland, throughout Europe, and further afield as well. Women are always going on about the past, the nineteenth century when their sisters were meant to have had such a bad time of it. But who was out there catching the fish, eh? You tell me that,' roared the Prime Minister. 'Icelandic men drowned in their hundreds. And somehow I don't think it was such a cosy life in the fishermen's turf huts in a hard frost.' He looked at Father Bernhardur as if he expected him to disagree. 'Women,' he muttered as the priest remained silent. 'Some men are so under the thumb they daren't even taste their own cooking.' The Prime Minister was getting angry.

Father Bernhardur laughed. 'I think there's a little more to it than that. If I preached like that from the pulpit I'd have no women in my congregation, except perhaps for a few nuns. If a politician in Iceland today started expressing those views in public, his female supporters could be counted on the fingers of one hand.'

'I'll see what I can do,' said the Prime Minister, more gently. 'But the problem is there's no money available. Are you thinking of somewhere the kids can enjoy themselves? The City of Reykjavík runs something like that in Ólafur Thors's childhood home at 11 Fríkirkjuvegur. It's an amazing place. That would be more a matter for the City or the Domestic Affairs Ministry.'

'What I was thinking, or rather what the Bishop was thinking, was that the Church should show the way and perhaps set up a home for a few young people, not many, say five or six. It's only a drop in the ocean, but it's better than nothing. If it went well, we could expand.'

'The Church's not strapped for cash, is it? As I recall, we bought Landakot Hospital off you for 500 million kroner.'

'That money's nearly all spent.'

'And how are you going to select the children?'

'I think I need to talk to the Domestic Affairs office and take on the worst cases. But probably Divine Providence will guide us to the children.'

'How much did you have in mind?'

'One or 2 million kroner.'

'And where is this town-centre site?'

'Fourteen Sudurgata.'

The Prime Minister looked at the priest but nothing could be discerned from the politician's expression. There were enough problems in the town centre at weekends and no call to fill a house near his own home full of trouble-makers. But that was no way to think with the thing all but a *fait accompli*. If some filthy rag got hold of what he was thinking, the editor would think all his Christmases had come at once. 'You can't do much with a million.'

'The house is in good condition. All we plan to do is give it a lick of paint, buy some furniture and a music centre and a few bits and pieces just to make it seem like home. The outside's been painted fairly recently.'

'I know the house. It's the yellow one, isn't it?

The intercom spoke: 'I've got Haraldur Sumarlidason with me.'

'Yes. Send him in in a minute.'

Father Bernhardur got to his feet.

'Well, I'll look into it and see what I can do. And if the City can't do anything I'll have a chat with some of my colleagues and see if they can't chip in since my old friend Seli's already agreed to help.'

Hannes looked up. The meeting was at an end. 'You'll be hearing from me in a week or so.'

'Thank you so much.' Father Bernhardur shook the out-stretched hand and inclined his head.

The priest met Haraldur Sumarlidason in the doorway. Haraldur was looked ashen and agitated. 'I wouldn't want to be a politician,' thought Father Bernhardur. 'They always look so worried.'

'Look at yourself, Haraldur,' Hannes said loudly once the priest had closed the door. 'You're always so down in the mouth these days. Anyone would think you're about to join the Progressive Party. I've forgiven you for that brilliant piece of advice the other day. Has the Progressive Party made you a better offer or something? Is this how you pay me back for all the kindness I've shown you?' The Prime Minister smiled.

'Your wife just rang,' said Haraldur and sat down without the remotest of smiles touching his lips. He unbuttoned his jacket to reveal his paunch, loosened his tie and sighed deeply.

'Surely a conversation with my wife can't have had such a devastating effect on you?'

'Yes. She told me something rather distressing.' Hannes face twitched with tension.

Hannes looked at his assistant. He prepared himself for the worst. The worst was something having happened to his son.

'News from the stock market,' muttered Haraldur, pulling a face and glancing at first one corner of the ceiling and then at another. His eyes flicked only occasionally towards the Prime Minister.

'Spit it out, man,' said the Prime Minister fiercely. 'I can take it.'

'A 7 million kroner holding in United Fisheries has changed hands.'

'So what?'

'"So what?"' gulped Haraldur, '"So what?"'

'Answer me, man.'

'Whoever's picked up those shares will acquire a majority hold-ing and can control the company.'

Hannes looked blankly at his assistant. There was a pause. 'Who's buying?'

'I don't know.'

'Did Gerdur know who it was?'

'No.'

'Have you rung Moneystock?'

'Yes, but they wouldn't tell me anything. They wouldn't tell Gerdur anything either.'

'We'll see about that. I'm not letting them manage 300 million kroner of mine, raking in commission, and then have them not play ball.' He put his hand on the telephone and then withdrew it. It wasn't advisable for the Prime Minister himself to ring from Government House and ask questions about the stock market. He looked at Haraldur. 'How come? How can this have happened?'

The corners of Haraldur's mouth twisted. 'There're so many leaks, Hannes, it's unbelievable. Everyone knows everything about everyone else. Those shares came up with no warning.'

'What's it going to mean for you and me? I've got family money tied up in the company.'

'I'm afraid things aren't looking too good from a financial point of view. At present, anyway.'

'What do you mean?'

Haraldur Sumarlidason fidgeted in his chair. 'Well, the share value depends on the demand . . .'

'So it's all so much worthless paper.'

Haraldur nodded. 'Except that the new majority shareholder will be working alongside you. Anyone buying in is your ally.'

Silence fell. Hannes Pálmason said, 'Let's hope they're well disposed towards us.'

The only sound was the throbbing of an engine as a bus left the square. Haraldur noticed a yellow roof disappearing out of his field of vision. 'Was it wise to tie up all that cash in the one concern?' asked Haraldur.

'I can't answer that. Losing money isn't the worst thing that can happen as far as I'm concerned. The worst thing that can happen to me is for people to prove themselves unworthy of the confidence I place in them. I'm now going to ask you to earn my trust by finding out who's bought these shares. But tread gently. It's always as well to know who you're dealing with. It may not be a knock-out punch.' He thought a moment and then said, 'But if this is political, there'll be a full fifteen rounds to go.'

'It's not certain the money's lost.'

'It's lost.'

The Prime Minister spoke with dreadful calm. Haraldur knew that tone. It was how Hannes Pálmason protected himself when under attack in Parliament. But in that situation he generally knew where the danger lay.

When Haraldur had gone the Prime Minister paced about the room. At length he stopped by the window overlooking the square. He stood there deep in thought for a long time with his hands clasped behind his back. Three hundred million kroner scattered to the four winds!

His father-in-law had owned a cardboard-box factory that had dominated the Icelandic market. When the old man died, the company passed to his daughter and Hannes became a member of parliament. They sold the company for a tidy sum. He put that money into shares. Shares did not shout from the rooftops. Shares worked quietly, in secret. Compared with all the big noises in the Icelandic business world, he could be said to keep a low profile.

The Prime Minister turned and gazed at the portrait of Ólafur Thors. Had Ólafur ever been lonely, disappointed, tired? Probably, but still he fought his corner and kept them all on their toes with his brilliance.

'Hannes,' said the intercom, 'Channel 2 wants to do an interview with you on the front steps.'

On television that evening it would not be apparent from the Prime Minister's expression that the dogged news reporter had caught him off-balance.

19

As the priest left Government House and walked down the steps he was suddenly seized with a feeling of intense isolation and anguish. He whispered, 'O God, help me.'

Father Bernhardur had a secret. Like a number of his parishioners, he sometimes doubted the existence of God. He often asked God to come near to him, even if it meant trial by fire.

He stood still a moment and tried to control his anguish. He looked down at his black robe, at the wide-toed shoes, and he felt ridiculous, as if his becoming a priest had been a hasty and impetuous decision. He asked himself, 'However did I become a priest? And here am I on the steps of Government House! Who do I think I am to go barging in there, talking to people on equal terms?' He trotted down the steps and walked home along the harbour road. That way there was less chance of meeting anyone.

On the way home to Landakot he prayed intensely, trying to shift his melancholy. For a long time he had felt as if something ominous was about to happen. Some conspiracy or occurrence was about to appear out of the blue and take away his ability to serve God. It seemed to him as if someone might catch him off guard and he would deny his Saviour. Hadn't the woman tried to tempt him in that way? It struck him that the burglary of the church was another link in this invisible chain. But what was the trap? Wasn't it just all in his mind? 'This is all rubbish,' he thought desperately. 'Just stop it!'

'Copy of *Weekend*, mister?'

'Mister.' He hadn't been addressed like that for years. Father Bernhardur immediately felt better. A girl of about ten was standing on the pavement looking up at him solemnly. 'No, thanks.' He was about to walk on when the girl said, 'There's lots of really juicy scandals in it.'

'Good. And one day you will doubtless become a busy entrepreneur, but I've got no money.'

'Oh.' She lost interest and went on her way with the yellow bag full of magazines hanging from her shoulder, shouting, '*Weekend*! Jóhannes Sigurdsson the lawyer steals hundred of millions of kroner from his clients! The Public Prosecutor calls for a custodial sentence!'

'I didn't see the child!' the priest muttered, shocked. 'I'm so tied up in myself I didn't see the child, let alone notice where I am!' He looked towards the north. A grey finger-shaped cloud hovered above Mount Esja and pointed at him. The sea hadn't noticed it was spring and the waves stirred in their usual autumnal fashion. A sudden flash of sunlight broke through the cavernous dome of the sky. For a second a cloud seemed to catch and hold it before it spilled over the edge and turned a small area of sea's surface a brilliant green. 'Now I can choose whether or not God is speaking to me,' thought Father Bernhardur. 'If he is, then he is telling me what Jesus told people long ago, that the Kingdom of God is within you but you cannot see it!'

The roof of the sky closed and the sea returned to its autumnal mood. But within Father Bernhardur it did not grow dark again. He thought that the Prime Minister himself had as good as promised him support. He decided to gather a few people together to paint 14 Sudurgata.

At Landakot he was told that a boy had come to see him. The boy had not given his name but had decided to take a walk and come back a bit later. Perhaps it was one of the boys who had broken into the church? Perhaps he had come to a realization of his sin and was now repentant? When the doorbell rang Father Bernhardur jumped up and hurried to open the front door. He immediately recognized his guest. It was the younger boy from 28 Thingholtstræti.

'Well! And how are you? You're . . .?' He held out his hand. 'Just for the moment I can't remember your name.' He smiled apologetically.

'Jökull,' said the boy quietly. His hand was slender and soft and cold.

'And what can I do for you?'

'I want to talk to you.' Jökull had stepped into the hall.

'Feel free. The pleasure is all mine! We can talk about anything you like, in heaven or on earth.' Father Bernhardur opened the door to the room where he had talked with Theódóra.

He offered Jökull a chair. 'You wouldn't be thinking about converting to Catholicism?' he asked brightly.

'No.' Jökull was slow in answering. 'I wanted to talk to you about what's going on at home.'

'Is it bad?'

'You know Grandmother died?'

'Yes. And it's quite natural that you should all feel sad.'

'I don't think the feeling sad has got much to do with Grandmother. They don't think about anybody but themselves. They've got into a mess because of the house. They can't talk about anything but debts. And to make things worse, Grandmother had shares in the Steamship Company. And now everything's gone crazy because of it.'

'Why's that?'

'Father needed the shares to save the house. And he also needed Mother's final salary of a hundred thousand kroner to pay off some blokes that were out to get him. And now the idea is for my other grandmother from Kópavogur to come and live with us and that's pushed Mother over the edge. She can't bear the idea of living in the same house as her. Grandmother's sold her flat in Kópavogur. She was lucky, it went just like that. And now that money's meant to make everything right.'

'Won't time sort all this out?' asked Father Bernhardur, sounding concerned.

'I don't know. Grandmother from Kópavogur says she would never have agreed to it if Tryggvi hadn't told her Mother had left the house for good. Mother says she'd never have let Tryggvi get his hands on the shares if she suspected that Grandmother was moving in. They were fighting. He beat her up.'

'That's bad,' said the priest, frowning.

'Yes.'

'Does that happen a lot?'

'Only when he loses it.'

'Where's your brother at the moment?'

'Haddi? I've no idea. He doesn't care. None of it affects him at all. It's only Silla and me that get upset.'

'What do you want me to do?'

'I want you to come back with me and get them to make it up.'

'I'm not sure that's the right way to go about it. I'm a Catholic priest. You aren't Catholics. Where were you confirmed?'

'Hallgrímur Church.'

'Then that's where you should go for help.' The priest put his large hands on the table and interlaced the fingers.

'I don't know about that. I thought you seemed to be a good influence on Mother. I'm sure you could help us.'

'I don't know what your parents would say if I started interfering in your family life,' said Father Bernhardur. He didn't know what to do.

'Why did you come and see us then?'

'I was asked to,' said the priest, a bit shamefaced.

'Well, now I'm asking you to.' Jökull was flushed and sweating.

'Oh, well,' sighed Father Bernhardur. 'If it's so important to you, I'll come. But I still think it would be better if you turned to your own parish priest.'

'But I don't know him. You're the only priest I know. And if I went to the police when they were fighting I don't think my father would ever forgive me. My brother once rang the police when they were having a fight and Father's never forgiven him for it. Come this evening, please,' pleaded Jökull. 'Please. Perhaps some day I'll be able to return the favour.'

The wind was snatching at the trees on the lawn at Landakot. Father Bernhardur looked out of the window and thought it over. 'There's a chance you could give me a hand later on. Do you like decorating?'

'Not particularly, but I can give it a go.'

'Good, I need some young people to help me. If you and your brother showed up after the weekend in overalls, then I might be able to help you.'

'OK. I'll have a word with Haddi. But I can't promise he'll come. He's awfully lazy. When will you come?'

'When do you want me to come?'

'This evening they'll both be there.'

'OK, I'll come this evening then.'

When Jökull had gone, Father Bernhardur sat down at the table in the living room. He regretted letting Theódóra send him over to the house. I didn't argue, just trotted over there like some poodle, but now some teenager comes and asks me, I try and wriggle out of it. Did I let her send me all over town just because I could hear her money talking? Because she's a big wheel in fashionable society? And then I storm in to see the Prime Minister as if I'm a person of real consequence. Only because I'd been kind of introduced to the man in passing. What an idiot I am! He scarcely remembered me.

There was a bowl of shiny red apples on the snow-white table-cloth. Some things he heard in confession you might think people made up. He remembered a man in the congregation coming to him the week before and telling him he had been having a love affair with another man for years. The man came to confession regularly but had always left that particular sin out, even though it was a serious matter not making a full confession. Lying to God! 'How many Sundays have I given this man Holy Communion?' thought the priest. And his wife doesn't suspect a thing. The next time the couple came to Mass Father Bernhardur thought there was something different about the man. And this was in spite of the duty on the priest never to let the sins of his parishioners affect his attitude to them. They were all equal in the eyes of God and he was the humble servant of God who had been given the task of looking after them. He had reprimanded the man severely before he had given him absolution.

Father Bernhardur came back to himself and focused on the bowl of apples. One of the apples was going rotten. He carefully lifted it up and saw it was leaking a sickly sweet liquid, smearing the other apples in the bowl. 'I am not humble enough to be a priest,' thought Father Bernhardur. 'I'm not patient enough.' I'm too much like everybody else. There are times when I ache for the pretty girls in the parish. I dream of them naked. My God, how did I ever come to be doing this job? My intention was to serve others, but I have difficulty in serving others because my faith is not strong enough.' Suddenly he registered an anger against Jesus Christ and even against God. 'Couldn't God just do the one small thing of strengthening my faith when, in spite of all the difficulties, I've decided to dedicate my life to him?' he thought angrily. 'Since I am doing this of my own free will, can't he give me more love for my fellow man?' Father Bernhardur felt so consumed with anger that had he not been able to control himself a curse would have passed his lips. He fell to his knees in prayer and whispered, 'O God, help me! Holy Mary look mercifully upon me. If this continues, I am lost. Give me faith at least, please, O God. Even if it brings me suffering.'

He closed his eyes and gazed into the darkness. That afternoon he was due to celebrate Mass and he did not feel right about handling the Holy Sacrament without making his confession, since he had thought bitter thoughts towards God.

Bishop Lambert was his Father Confessor. The Bishop's study

was in the south wing of the presbytery. Lambert was a short, stocky man. He had a handsome face and wore a small goatee. He had a fondness for playing practical jokes on his congregation. He had lived in Iceland for forty years and spoke the language perfectly. When Father Bernhardur entered his study the Bishop immediately leapt into a boxing pose and swung a fist up under his chin. 'Uppercut! Caught you off guard!'

'The whole world catches me off guard.'

'Let me guess,' said Lambert and raised a finger. 'You went trout fishing over the weekend. You caught three and now you are worried sick about the trouts' orphaned children and you want absolution now this instant!' The Bishop looked solemnly at Father Bernhardur.

Father Bernhardur was too preoccupied with his own troubles to smile. 'It's worse than that.'

'What's this? Tell me all. I can't wait.' Lambert closed the door, walked round behind his desk and sat down.

'I want to sleep with some of the women in the congregation.'

'Are you still having difficulty with that temptation?' There was warmth and patience in Lambert's eyes.

'Yes.'

'We cannot control our thoughts and feelings. We are human beings. Temptations do not damage us unless we consciously invite them into our souls. And you have not done any such thing. Without will there can be no sin.' Lambert looked solemnly at the priest. 'You're struggling against this?'

Father Bernhardur stared down at the floor with his arms resting on his knees and his hands folded. 'There is something worse.'

'What is that, my son?'

'I have felt anger towards the Lord.'

'And that kind of feeling causes you pain, doesn't it?'

'Yes.'

'Jesus is tempering you like steel. He is refining you in the fire of the Holy Spirit so that in due course he can call you closer to him.'

'You think so?'

'Yes. You cannot forge metal without first putting it into the fire. Ask the Lord your God to spare you this bitterness if it becomes unbearable. Otherwise try to be thankful for the pain it causes you, because there can be no God without suffering.'

'But these thoughts take away all my calmness of soul.' He looked up in distress. 'Sometimes I lose my faith.'

'Fear of God is good. It is essential. But it has to be moderated by stability and joy in the soul. The knowledge that you are loved by God. If the fear is too great it is generated by evil. Fear of God brings peace. Be confident that God loves you as he loves your fellow man. If you feel that you are losing your faith, then you can be sure that God is pushing you away from him for a moment, only to draw you closer to him later. He is testing you because he loves you. Take it as a sign. He chastises those he loves. Those who in later life became holy men and women he put through terrible suffering. Nobody profits from a life without discipline. He is a good parent.'

'And there is another sin.'

'What is that?'

Father Bernhardur was embarrassed. 'There are times when I would rather turn to you than turn to Jesus.'

'Would you do everything that Christ asked of you?'

'Yes.'

'Would you obey him absolutely?'

'Yes.'

'I am considering asking you to do me a favour later today.'

'What is it?'

Lambert pointed towards the town centre. 'To walk to Government House, knock on the door and demand to see the Prime Minister of this country. Then sock him one on the jaw.' The Bishop raised a clenched fist.

Father Bernhardur looked at him anxiously. 'But I couldn't do it.'

'Why not?'

'Because that would not be acceptable to God. I would not be behaving in a Christian way.'

'And do you imagine Jesus would send you on such a task?'

'No. Never.'

'See! But I could. You will never be able to turn to me more than you turn to him. Now kneel and I shall grant you absolution.'

When he had said Mass Father Bernhardur walked over to Thingholtstræti. It had been raining earlier but now the air was still

200

and the evening sun was drying the streets. The house looked rather desolate and there was no sign of life in the windows. He looked at the façade and it struck him it would be good to involve the head of the family in the renovations at Sudurgata. 'I just hope he won't get violent,' thought the priest with trepidation as he rang the doorbell. He had expected Dagný to come to the door, black and blue and with one eye puffy and closed, but it wasn't the woman who opened the door. Tryggvi looked surprised to see the priest.

'Is Dagný in?'

'No.'

'How about Jökull? Is he your son? Tryggvi, isn't it?'

'The boys went off somewhere with their mother. Yes, I'm Tryggvi.' Father Bernhardur studied the man. He had imagined him differently. This man was nervy, mild, subdued. His face was covered in scratches and he had a black eye that was beginning to heal. 'Can I take a message?'

'The thing is I was here a few days ago. Perhaps you heard?' He looked at Tryggvi and Tryggvi slowly shook his head.

'It was because of the passing of your mother-in-law. I am a priest. And today your son Jökull came to see me.'

'What's the matter with him?'

'He was upset about the situation at home. He said you and your wife had had a fight.'

'So, my younger boy calls a priest and my older boy calls the police.' Tryggvi smiled thinly. 'Won't you come in?'

'Yes, thank you.' The priest stepped into the hall. 'It's getting a bit chilly,' he said, rubbing his hands together.

'I'm afraid it'll be just as cold in here,' said Tryggvi, a bit put out. 'They came and cut off the electricity today, even though they'd promised to hold off for a bit, because I have been settling all my bills these last few days.'

Father Bernhardur followed the man into the sitting room. He carried on rubbing his hands together, but more from embarrassment than from the cold.

'Sit down.'

'Thank you.' The priest sat where he had sat on his first visit.

'I lost control. Perhaps the boy told you?'

'Yes.'

'Dagný's threatening to divorce me.' Tryggvi sat opposite him at the head of the table. 'I don't know when to believe her any more. She's always making threats like that. And we're always arguing over money. I'm never allowed to mention our debts. She wants to go off with her credit card zooming around the sales. If I ever suggest I can't earn enough to cover it all she loses her rag. And now she's lost the job that was meant to make things easier for us. Of course that's down to me as well. All the bills are my responsibility but I don't have any say in anything else. There's something wrong here, isn't there?' He leaned across the table and stared into the priest's face.

'Of course a family must stick together in difficult times. How did she come to lose her job?'

'The old girl gave her the push. Theódóra. That's what they're like. It doesn't matter what they say come the elections. There's just no way to keep a family together on less than three hundred and fifty thousand kroner a month. I just don't earn that kind of money.'

'Three hundred and fifty thousand?' Father Bernhardur whispered the amount. 'Is that really what it takes?' He whistled in surprise.

'Where have you been? You're meant to serve the people and you haven't the foggiest what an ordinary family needs to live on.'

'It's true. I'm beginning to feel my life's a bit too sheltered.'

This answer surprised Tryggvi and took the wind out of his sails. 'Of course I can squander money too.' He looked up at the ceiling and waved his arms around. 'I've been doing up this house. And that doesn't come cheap. I have a weakness for classic cars and I've been rebuilding some as a hobby when I get the time. But that's mostly in my spare time and it doesn't cost all that much.' He scratched his chin. 'Dagný brought her mother into the house like it was the most natural thing in the world but now I want my mother to move into the same flat she goes beserk. What's going on? Last winter she took this course called "Women, Be Your Own Boss" or something just as ridiculous. "Women, Be Your Own Boss"!' sneered Tryggvi and looked in bewilderment at the priest. 'She's always been her own boss and she's been my boss into the bargain! She's always told me what to do. I don't think the Pope would get very far with her.' Tryggvi looked at the priest. 'Why should a woman exist on a higher level than a man? Why is a woman a better human being? Tell me that!'

'But is that the case?'

'It's what they say,' said Tryggvi, getting animated and looking excitedly at the priest. 'Don't tell me you haven't heard. There was even a kid on the television the other night, saying it in as many words. I heard it myself. The guy whose show it was just laughed. "Women are better than men"!' Tryggvi stared at Father Bernhardur. 'Don't you think it must make for an easy life being born in the right? To be the perfect sex and to be incapable of ever doing or saying anything wrong? It must be wonderful to be like that. I wish I could be like that. But it's different for us blokes, isn't it?'

'Do you feel that badly about it?'

'Where have you been? I feel how I'm meant to feel. A second-class human being! What's the Bible got to say about this then?'

'It says men and women should respect each other.'

'Does the Bible say women are better than men?'

The priest shook his head.

'I knew it!' Tryggvi clenched his large fist in triumph. 'And neither do the Sagas. In the Sagas the old hags are just as vile as you and me.'

'But there is never any justification for physical violence,' pleaded the priest. 'That was what brought your son to me. That's why he asked me to come and see you. He felt bad about it.'

Suddenly the air in the living room was electric. Father Bernhardur expected the man to jump to his feet but nothing happened. What did happen was that Tryggvi's face turned beetroot. 'It was only that I lost control when she threatened to take Silla away again, when they'd only just come back home. You can't treat a child like that. That's all! I didn't know what I was doing until it was all over.' Tryggvi waved his hand across the living-room table. 'Dagný can do whatever she wants. It's the God's honest truth that she's got everything here just how she wants it. When I make a mistake like this it's a living hell. It'll take months for us to get back to how we were just because I raised my hand to her. It was hardly anything.' He looked at Father Bernhardur. 'The timid mouse isn't always as perfect as she looks, as they say. I envy Einar. The chap I work with. He's not married. The father's always the dustbin of the family.'

'Is Jökull a handful then?'

'No, the other boy is though.'

'Haflidi?'

'He's a hard nut,' said his father proudly. 'Do you know the only thing the man of the house is fit for these days?'

'No,' said the priest nervously.

Tryggvi rubbed his thumb and index finger together. 'This!' he said. 'Bringing in the dough. That's the only thing we're fit for and it's impossible to do because there's no money in this world of ours. It's all been stolen.' He leaned back in his chair, as if he had said his piece. 'I'm sorry about this business with Dagný, but if I'm being really honest, hand on heart, I reckon she was asking for a bit of a slap.'

'Nobody asks to be beaten up,' said Father Bernhardur firmly. His eyes met Tryggvi's. The man looked hot and excited. 'The Lord God remembers every blow.'

'Well he must have some memory to remember every blow anyone's ever given anyone else since this country of ours was first settled, because I tell you there's a good few jaws been broken over the years.' Suddenly a smile started to spread across Tryggvi's face, then just as quickly it was gone. The priest had often seen this happen. Someone had been about to use God's name in vain but then had thought better of it. The solemn look bore witness to the person's religious faith. Even when he did not quite realize it himself.

'What can I do?'

'Ask her forgiveness.'

Tryggvi shook his head and smiled bitterly.

'Why don't you all come to Mass?'

'Mass? Where?'

'Up at Landakot.'

'Why there?'

'Because I'm inviting you.'

'But we aren't Catholic.'

'Come anyway.'

After a while Tryggvi said, 'Perhaps it would be a good idea.'

'I'll need your advice about something at the same time.'

'It's not your car? I get enough of that in the week without sorting out some junk heap at the weekend.'

'No. I'd like to ask you to take a look at a house we own. It's a timber building on Sudurgata. I'm not asking you to start working on the house, just to tell me what needs doing to it. I've never renovated a house and you know what you're doing.' He looked round the living room. 'And I can see you've made quite a success of this place.'

'Yes, sure, I can do that for you. That's fine. But I'm not sure I can come to Mass though. Perhaps later. Somehow I don't feel I need it. I get close to my God in my own way without anyone else getting in the way. But there is something you could do for me.'

'What's that?'

'Talk to Dagný and get her to drop this stuff about leaving again. I'd even be prepared to tell my mother there's no way she can move in upstairs. I love Dagný. I love the woman!' Tryggvi laughed with embarrassment but then looked at the priest, deadly serious, and said, 'If she leaves me, I'll . . . well, I don't know what I'll do, but . . .' He stared at Father Bernhardur, who was startled by the look in his eyes, and then he said, 'I'll do something. Haven't you read about those guys overseas who just get up one day and start shooting at everyone?'

20

It was 17 June 1994. Axel of Heidnaberg's sixtieth birthday. He was as excited as a child. When he was a boy it had always seemed that the coincidence spoiled the day, stopping him from claiming it as his own, but now that the Republic was fifty years old, it seemed rather satisfying that he should share his birthday with the late Jón Sigurdsson, the first President of Iceland.

He woke, sat up and watched the wind stirring the topmost branches of the two aspens. The leaves fluttered in the wind, twisting this way and that with a soft susurrus. It filled him with joy and tenderness. He wanted to ring up all his friends and tell them how much he loved them.

'The seventeenth of June. Sixty today. Today's my birthday!' Axel pushed back the duvet, slipped his feet into his slippers, picked up the red bathrobe from the back of the chair, put it on and walked downstairs to the living room. There was nobody about. Great! The television was already broadcasting the ceremony at Thingvellir live. He thought about how his birthday would be. Theódóra and Linda had gone to Thingvellir with Vilhjálmur, who was test-driving a new jeep. They'd be back about three. The plan was that the family would visit between three and five. All other things being equal he would have thrown an enormous party for lots of people but that wasn't possible on this occasion. The party at Hotel Saga would have to do. Something was very odd, thought Axel. They hadn't received an invitation. Perhaps it had seemed ridiculous to send a formal invitation to such obvious guests as themselves.

The road out to Thingvellir was one continuous stream of cars. The camera panned to the main area for the festivities. There were lots of people. The television coverage cut to a glass booth on the edge of the Almannagjár ravine for an interview with the Minister of Foreign Affairs and his wife. Axel had met the man a few times. On those occasions he had always been impressed by Hannes, because he had never seen the Minister of Foreign Affairs get the better of Hannes in an argument. Axel was thinking about Hannes Pálmason when the phone rang. He was almost sure it would be the Prime Minister of Iceland phoning to wish him happy birthday. It was Hördur Gottskálksson. He only ever rang when he wanted something and that was the case this time. It was the 'mercy killing' and Weekend again.

'Don't you ever read the papers, Hördur? Haven't you noticed it's the seventeenth of June? A lot of international bigwigs are here celebrating with us. The Prime Minister's got better things on his mind than dealing with you and me. Haven't I already told you he's going to see you once he's got the seventeenth out of the way?' Hördur grumbled on and Axel waited for his brother-in-law to remember the true significance of the day, but they said their good-byes without Axel's birthday being mentioned. The doorbell rang. Perhaps it would be the invitation?

It was a basket of flowers. A small white van was waiting for the driver with its engine running. The basket was so big Axel had to ask the lad to carry it into the living room. There was a bottle of cognac and two bottles of champagne nestling in among the blooms. It was accompanied by a card from the Heidnaberg work force: 'On 17 June, a few years apart, Iceland acquired two wonderful sons. You, dear Axel Sigurgeirsson, are the other one! From your employees.'

He sat down in front of the television. The flags under Lögberg cliffs were whipping in the wind. There were fathers carrying children on their shoulders, members of parliament, the Bishop, the President of Iceland, a number of foreign guests. Axel read the card twice and his eyes misted over. There was a shot of Hannes on the screen chatting with the Queen of Denmark.

Axel brewed some coffee and buttered a slice of bread and put cheese on it. The doorbell rang again. There were lots of telegrams! The morning paper was lying on the hall floor. It had come at last. He sat down and hunted through the paper. He found the photograph of himself: 'Axel Sigurgeirsson, company chairman, sixty today.' He thought guiltily of Dagný. What an appalling coward I was, staying home the day my secretary got fired. I only hope her husband won't come and shout at me. He looked at the paper. Three of his closest friends had written appreciations, one of them the Prime Minister. Axel's heart raced with sheer joy. Now he was convinced it was a mistake that they hadn't received an invitation. The Prime Minister's piece was short, to the point, and Axel thought it flowed elegantly. Hannes mentioned that, as a young lawyer, he had held in trust some of Axel's finances, that they were political allies, firm friends since time immemorial. That many a time he had been privileged to be a guest at the magnificent Dyngjuvegur home of Axel and his wife. The Hotel Borg lacked that certain something on days when Seli was absent, and that was the general consensus among the habitués of the goodly round table in that particular establishment. 'He's a fine chap, Hannes,' said Axel out loud and read the article again. 'I must remind Tedda to cut this out of the paper,' he thought.

The doorbell again! 'It would have been useful to have a woman here this morning,' he said chirpily on his way to the hall. The same lad was standing on the doorstep. 'More flowers?' he said, amazed. 'Are you quite mad?' This time he carried the basket in himself and sat down in front of the television. The queue of cars hadn't budged. He'd been right about how bad the traffic would be. A young man jumped out of his car and shook his fist at a policeman. The camera panned slowly along the line of cars. Out of force of habit Axel counted the Toyotas and before the camera looked elsewhere was overjoyed to see that he'd been responsible for importing six of the gridlocked cars. There was an aerial view over Grimsness crater. It was too far away to make out the models of the cars, except for the jeeps. He leaned forward and tried to spot Heidnaberg's new model but there were so many jeeps it was hopeless. Axel beamed broadly as the presenter recommended people to approach the area via Mosfells valley, as the traffic was lighter there. 'What a horrible person I am,' he thought, gratified that his wife and daughter were suffering the consequences of ignoring his advice. Next was a shot of the Prime Minister and Axel gazed at him adoringly. He smiled when he remembered the page 3 girl in *Weekend* putting Hannes at the top of her list of men she'd most like to go to bed with. He'd pushed a famous pop star into second place. 'There's not a human being on the face of the planet that Hannes can't win over with his charm when he puts his mind to it,' thought Axel, looking at his friend's imperial visage. The camera panned across the stands full of foreign leaders and their representatives: the Queen of Denmark, the Vice President of the United States, the French Minister of Culture. All the top brass from the Independent Party. Axel frowned when he saw a fair number that he considered of lower status than Theódóra. The screen reverted to the glass booth and the face of the Prime Minister. The Prime Minister was saying how all these distinguished visitors would be attending the evening festivities and Axel of Heidnaberg's head nodded with anticipation and he half rose from his chair. Wasn't the chap going to mention that today was also the birthday of a good friend of his and that this friend would also be an honoured guest at Hotel Saga? 'It must be a mistake, not sending me an invitation,' he thought morosely. 'No, my presence is such a foregone conclusion, Hannes would think it a waste to send me an invitation,' he muttered to himself and relaxed again. The transmission changed back to the view of Lögberg cliffs.

The phone rang, 'Probably it'll be the Prime Minister's office reminding me about the party,' thought Axel.

'You bastard. You've ruined me.'

'Hello, who is this? This is Axel Sigurgeirsson at 4 Dyngjuvegur, Reykjavík.'

'Yes. I know who you are and I know where you live, you bastard. You've destroyed me and now I'm going to kill you.'

'Hello? Who is this?'

'Don't play the innocent with me.'

'What?'

'Is your family never satisfied?'

The speaker slammed down the phone and Axel listened, shocked, to the dialling tone. 'I haven't ruined anyone,' he said to himself. He put his hand to his chest and took a deep breath. 'This isn't the kind of birthday present I wanted.' He was hurt. 'I've always been above board in all my business dealings. The man must have got the wrong number.' Nevertheless he couldn't think of a single Axel apart from himself who was prominent in Icelandic commerce.

There was a chocolate cake on a plate in one of the kitchen cupboards. Axel ate two large slices before falling asleep in his chair.

Axel woke with a start and looked at the television. There was a clock showing the time as a quarter past four. He had an acid stomach from eating too much cake and he didn't find the traffic jam so amusing this time. He said out loud, 'No one's coming to my birthday.' Then he heard a car engine being turned off outside. He went through to the hall and peeped through the curtains. Had the chap on the phone come to kill him? He was very surprised to see the Catholic priest from Landakot. He opened the front door and waited for Father Bernhardur.

'She's not in,' he said as the priest walked up to the front door.

'It wasn't her I came to see.'

'Then who, my good man?'

The priest smiled. 'I've been invited to your birthday. Theódóra wanted me to meet your daughter.'

Another car drove up as the priest stepped into the hall. Hördur,

Villa, Ester, Trausti. Hördur was the first to arrive at the door. 'And who's His Eminence?'

'A friend of Tedda's. A priest.'

'I didn't know Theódóra was much of a one for religion,' said a surprised Vilhelmína.

Hördur Gottskálksson studied Father Bernhardur's robes. 'You're not Lutheran?'

'Catholicism's very trendy just now,' said Ester scornfully.

'Isn't church attendance throughout the country steadily rising?' asked Vilhelmína politely. 'God only knows, there are times when I could do with having a priest to talk to.'

Hördur looked at his wife and said drily, 'I don't think Icelanders find much call for Catholicism.' He looked at Father Bernhardur, expecting him to come to the defence of his Church. The priest remained silent.

'What a fine young man you're turning into, Trausti,' said Axel as they shook hands. 'That's because of all your hard work at the construction site, I expect,' he said approvingly.

'I quit a fortnight ago,' said the boy and glanced at his parents.

'And where's little Gauti?' asked Axel.

'A friend of mine's looking after him at her place,' said Ester.

Vilhelmína turned a full circle in the middle of the living room. 'It always seems so odd to come and visit the house I grew up in.' She looked at the baskets of flowers, blazing in the sunlight. 'Oh, what lovely gifts people have sent! Trausti, run out to the car and fetch our present.'

'I didn't invite anybody,' said Axel, glowing with happiness, 'because of the do at Hotel Saga. Even so, presents have been turning up for days on end. Theódóra's tucked them away in the little room off the sitting room. You can tell Trausti to leave it there.'

'So you'll be going to Hotel Saga?'

'We're to be there at seven sharp,' said Axel proudly.

At about this point there was a flurry of activity in the hall. Axel was relieved to find it was Vilhjálmur, Linda and Theódóra returning. 'God, I wished I'd stayed at home,' said Theódóra. 'I thought we'd never get back. We've been stuck there for seven hours.' She looked sharply at her husband. 'Axel, are you still in your bathrobe? Will you please be so good as to nip upstairs and get dressed.

This is my stepdaughter, the girl I told you about,' said Theódóra to the priest as soon as she walked in and stretched her hand out towards Linda.

'God speaks to man via dreams and visions. That's true, isn't it?' Linda asked excitedly, standing in front of the priest.

'Yes, that has been known to happen,' said Father Bernhardur, carefully. 'But the Holy Church warns us against paying too much attention to dreams. It can be dangerous.'

'The Catholics think the devil's behind it,' mocked Hördur.

Father Bernhardur nodded. 'That's it exactly. The Church is also very careful when it comes to visions. You can never be sure what's caused them.'

Trausti had taken on himself to pour the white wine and was out in the kitchen pouring it down his own throat. Theódóra and Vilhelmína were soon a little tipsy. Vilhelmína was anxious that there should be no row over the estate and her older sister was simply exhausted after her outing to Thingvellir. Trausti passed Linda a long-stemmed glass and sat down beside her, whispering, 'The old girls get plastered on half a glass. Look at Villi,' he said admiringly. 'He's so handsome. He's got such big hands and he bites his nails to the quick. I think that's a sign of a real man. Just imagine being a woman and having hands like that wandering over your naked body.'

Suddenly the dream came into Trausti's mind and he knew the answer to all his problems. 'I'm gay,' he thought. 'Gay!' He closed his eyes and conjured up the dream again, the vision he had half stifled but now allowed to burst into his consciousness and wash around him like pleasantly warm water: he was wearing a full-length red dress and his long hair cascaded about his shoulders. He was afraid he would be rent asunder; somewhere deep in his consciousness and will a scream was forming, ready to force itself to the surface and he had to use all his inner strength to strangle it. He heard a noise in the room, a noise like a kind of sob. Vilhelmína, drunk and stupid, wearing far too much make-up, looked at him.

'What's the matter, Trausti?' she asked, concerned.

'Nothing, Mother,' he said, suddenly suffused with joy.

Vilhjálmur was standing in the middle of the room. He picked up a cube of cheese on a stick and then said, 'I took a party of Japanese up into the interior. They see limitless opportunities for trade between Iceland and Japan.'

'What did you give them to eat?' asked Axel.

'Fish, of course! Like you told me.' Axel ate his cube of cheese.

'And didn't the Japs enjoy their fish?' asked Axel keenly.

'They were in seventh heaven. We agreed to get a new marketing initiative off the ground.' Vilhjálmur spread out his hands. 'I want us to take on the environment. We show an Icelandic waterfall in all its glory and then a plastic bottle or some bit of garbage on the seashore and the voiceover says, "Let's look after Nature."' Vilhjálmur waved his hand. His eyes were on Ester. 'Then you get the name across the whole screen – Heidnaberg – with perhaps Drangey island in the background in bright sunshine. Then, and only then, a 1995 Land Cruiser drives into shot and obscures the island.' Vilhjálmur looked round at the assembled family. 'It's a play on the meaning of "Heidnaberg". Heidnaberg: "Heathen Cliff". The real Heidnaberg's on Drangey. The place Bishop Gudmundur the Good didn't bless because a great hand came out of the cliff and a strange, hoarse voice threatened to cut his rope and the holy Bishop would have fallen and been killed on the rocks below. Well, what do you think?'

Ester rolled her eyes.

'Eh?' asked the man whose birthday it was. 'Didn't he want to bless Heidnaberg?'

Trausti sniggered.

'No,' said Vilhjálmur and turned pink. 'The monster in the cliff said there had to be somewhere for evil to live. Haven't you ever heard the Heidnaberg story, Seli?' Vilhjálmur looked in surprise at Axel. 'Do you know this story?' he asked Father Bernhardur.

Father Bernhardur smiled and nodded. He sipped his Coke.

'I am a woman trapped in the body of a man,' thought Trausti and laughed quietly to himself. 'At long, long last I understand the truth about myself. This dream has revealed the truth to me.' Trausti looked at his father and realized that Hördur had been watching him. 'I'm meeting a few mates in town,' he said. 'Linda, could you ring for a taxi?'

'Seli, remember me when you meet the Prime Minister this evening, won't you?' roared Hördur.

'All those lovely things he said about you in the paper,' said Vilhelmína.

'What's this about Axel talking to the Prime Minister?' asked Theódóra crisply. She looked at her husband. 'I thought you'd run enough errands for the man.'

'It's not important, just something I need to have a word with Hannes about,' said Axel carefully and glanced across at his brother-in-law.

'Somehow I've got to stop retreating and go on the attack with that crazy woman Seli made me go and see,' roared Hördur. 'She's stitched me up in *Weekend* and now she's trying to take me to court. I've got to defend myself. Vilhelmína and I have to eat! I'm always profoundly beholden to you two, it's true,' he added.

'And what business is it of the Prime Minister if you make mistakes?' asked Theódóra loudly.

'I didn't come here to argue with you, Theódóra. I came to celebrate with Seli because it's his sixtieth birthday. As for your precious Prime Minister, I think he can look after himself, don't you?' He grinned and picked up a packet of cigarettes.

'It never ceases to amaze me how a grown man, and a doctor at that, can smoke,' said Theódóra, feigning astonishment.

'I was not first in line when they were handing out willpower,' said Hördur, grinning maliciously.

If she recognized the quotation from *A Doctor's Life*, the biography of her father, she did not show it.

'Doesn't smoking damage the heart? Aren't you supposed to be a cardiologist?'

'My heart's as tough as tensile steel,' he said. 'It has little or no effect on me. At least I know how to make the best of the good things in this world and nicotine is one of them. Would you believe it! I've just had a sudden revelation,' he said, lighting his cigarette. 'That Dagný. She's the dead spit of your mother, Tedda. Two peas in a pod!' He flexed his fingers like a magician about to pull off a spectacular trick. 'Go and get the family album. They could have been sisters.'

'What rubbish!' snapped Tedda.

'It's true, Tedda,' said Axel, taking the cigar from his mouth. 'They do look alike.'

'Perhaps that's why you took her on,' spat Theódóra. 'Just to upset me.'

'Oh Mother, do stop it,' said Linda.

'There isn't a single person in the whole wide world, not a soul, who ever thinks for a second about Sauerbruch and the low-pressure cabinet – except, of course, for you and Vilhelmína,' mocked the doctor. 'I am one of the most skilled heart surgeons you'll find anywhere and none of you is in the least interested.'

'Gosh, how super to be told after all this time what a great man we have in our family!' laughed Tedda.

'Father Bernhardur, please do something,' pleaded the anguished Vilhelmína. 'It's Axel's birthday.'

'Linda, how are you fixed for charlie? You couldn't let me have a line?' whispered Trausti, as he sat next to his cousin. 'All this is driving me insane.'

'No. I had it up to here with that filth when I was in London. Do you want a lift into town?'

When they had gone into the hall, Hördur whispered to his daughter, Ester, 'What's up with Trausti? Why's he keep staring at Vilhjálmur like that?'

'He's gay, isn't he?' said Ester loudly. 'It's nothing to whisper about. Don't tell me you hadn't realized?'

'Oh, really?' said Hördur, frostily. And then, more slowly, 'Well, I suppose it's a good thing that someone in the family is taking an interest in Vilhjálmur.'

Vilhjálmur had been listening to this and now turned bright beetroot.

'What are you talking about?' asked Vilhelmína, looking round her family as if it was the first time she clapped eyes on them.

'I was just telling Father that Trausti's gay. I've known for ages.'

'Oh, Lord in Heaven help me!' said Vilhelmína. She was completely at a loss. 'I can't cope any longer.' She appealed to Father Bernhardur. 'Do something!'

'There's absolutely nothing for you to "cope" with, Mother,' said Ester, thoroughly annoyed now.

Hördur smashed his fist down on the table. 'We have a claim on the largest fortune in this country, Vilhelmína and I, but we can hardly make ends meet. I insist on Heidnaberg being divided between us!'

214

'Our parents wanted to keep the business together,' said Theódóra.

'Your father hadn't got the first idea about business,' roared Hördur.

'Do you think Mother wanted to see me disinherited?' shouted Vilhelmína.

'No. But she didn't want to see the business she'd spent her life building up go down the plughole either. Heidnaberg will never be broken up for the simple reason that Ingibjörg did not consider you fit people to run it!'

'"Fit people"!' Hördur took the cigarette from his lips and stared at her with his mouth open. 'What do you mean?'

'You'd better ask your old secretary that, Father,' said Ester. 'The one who pinched your car. Your bloody bit on the side!'

Hördur shook his fist at his daughter, then remembered where he was. He spread his arms wide and said, 'This house we're in. Why did it come to you? It's all part of Villa's inheritance.'

'Please, children, behave yourselves,' said Axel, sounding anxious. 'It's my birthday. There really is plenty for all of us.'

'I thought my mother had suffered enough insults in this house,' said Theódóra, catching her breath and grimacing with fury.

'What insults?' asked Ester, laughing.

'Having to wait on your grandmother Ingibjörg hand and foot like some servant. Are you trying to make out you don't know?'

'What's all this rubbish?' shouted Ester. 'I can't stand the hypocrisy. Grandfather lived with them both, long before the hippies and free love. They all got on like a house on fire! They shared him, I'm sure of it. From what I hear both the old dears were over the moon with the arrangement. Our family tragedy is that there is no family tragedy. I'm sure that if anyone suffered as a result of their set-up it was poor old Grandad. I gather from people who should know that they were both unfaithful to him.' Ester caught Axel's eye and saw he was smiling.

'I think Father only went downstairs to see to the horses,' said Vilhelmína pathetically. 'I'll never forget Light. He was so beautiful. He always lowered his head into my arms.'

'"To see to the horses"!' Ester laughed coldly. 'Mother, don't be ridiculous.'

'Ester, I don't need this!' shouted Theódóra. 'Do you think my mother would have agreed to put up with such humiliation and shame? She worked as a servant in his household and lost her mind because of it! And you don't have to sit there, grinning away like some evil genius, Hördur. Our father was a much greater man than you'll ever be.'

'Darling Tedda, it's all in your mind, your mother suffering in this house.' Ester allowed Axel to pour some more white wine into her glass. 'I'm not surprised you get screwed over in politics when your private life's such a mess. She worked in the Danish porcelain factories when she was a girl and got lead poisoning. That's why she went mad. Grandfather told me all about it. He must have said something to you! He knew what he was talking about. He was a doctor, after all.'

'I was just remembering the day Father got his teeth stuck in the caramel cake,' said Vilhelmína out loud, but it was said almost tragically to herself.

Father Bernhardur stood in the centre of the room like some elf in the company of humans, studying the family around him. From time to time he opened his mouth as if to say something and then closed it again.

'Oh, yes, poor chap. He spent ages trying to work it loose before he ended up taking his dentures out with the cake still stuck to them,' laughed Hördur. 'He was a great man, a decent man was Professor Thóróddur,' he said solemnly. 'A great and decent man! And it wouldn't surprise me at all if those old bats had bumped him off between them!'

'Sometimes I find myself wishing that we were married to each other.' Theódóra looked at him with contempt.

'Married! You and me? Whatever for?' He looked at her in amazement.

'Because then I could grind you into the dust.'

'Oh, there's no knowing which way that would go, who'd be doing the grinding,' said the doctor grimly. 'I can't make Axel out. Here he is, a handsome man like that, and he still hasn't got himself a mistress and told you to take a running jump,' he said. 'You're stark, staring mad.' Hördur pointed at Axel and raised his voice. 'Just look at Seli! See what you've reduced him to! He's on his last legs. Turn your back a moment, and he'll drop down dead.'

'My dear Hördur, I'm perfectly all right,' said Axel.

'Father, you disgust me,' shouted Ester.

Theódóra glared at the doctor and said nothing.

'Shall I take your blood pressure, Tedda?' teased Hördur. He felt much better seeing how agitated she was.

'No need. Just treat my sister properly and it'll go down of its own accord.'

'Oh, how I wish I was a child again! Father Bernhardur, won't you please say something?' Vilhelmína turned to the priest in her anguish.

'In the year 1672, Christ appeared to Saint Margaret Mary Alacoque,' said Father Bernhardur hastily. 'He showed her his sacred heart crowned with thorns with the cross above it.' Without realizing it, the priest opened his jacket. '"My heart", said Jesus, "so burns with the love of man that the flames may scarcely be contained. It must manifest itself to mankind so that man may profit from the wealth within it. I have chosen you to undertake this task. From this moment on, you will be called the Blessed Apostle of my Sacred Heart." And one of his promises was that he would grant unto all sinners his boundless mercy.'

Once the priest had spoken there was a pause while they all looked at him in amazement. Linda had been standing listening in the doorway and now went to Trausti out in the hall. Vilhelmína unsteadily followed Theódóra into the kitchen. Vilhjálmur sat in a chair and tried to stifle a yawn. It was Hördur who broke the silence. 'In our different ways the priest and I both minister to the heart of man. I read recently in a scientific journal that evolution seems to have progressed haphazardly, making wild guesses in every direction. I've not thought much about it, but if God has anything to do with it, then it's quite obvious he's not got the first idea of what he's doing. I'm not saying God and his son don't exist. On the contrary, I think it's quite likely, it's just that I've not come to a conclusion on the matter as yet, well no more than any Icelander has. But if I were God, I'd destroy the whole world as if it were some failed experiment. There's a basic flaw in the design. The human body, its decay and its illnesses, make my point for me.' The doctor laughed dismissively. 'Three hundred millions years wasted on the dinosaur!'

'And yet here we are,' said the priest with a smile.

Hördur smiled back. 'But don't you think the results are a bit iffy, Father Bernhardur? You look to me like someone struggling with himself. You need a break from that holy life of yours.' When he saw that the priest was indeed troubled, he continued, 'In the old days, as you probably know, there was a custom throughout Europe of electing a Lord of Misrule just before Christmas. Even the priests were allowed to commit sacrilege in the church. When they'd all let themselves go for a day or two, they could be good men once again for the rest of the year.'

'Tell me, Hördur, why is it that everyone always seems obsessed by dinosaurs?' asked Axel.

'Trausti, are you sure you've got enough money for the taxi?' asked Linda out in the hall. She held his face in her hands and kissed his lips. She was so like a mother, so warm, that he felt he loved her and had always loved her, ever since they were both children and had snogged in secret when no one was looking. He put his hand in his breast pocket. There were some notes there.

'Are you sure I can't drive you? It seems silly to let you go off in a taxi.'

'No,' he said sadly. 'I'd rather be on my own. I don't belong in this family.'

'Of course you do, Trausti. You and me, we've always been such good friends.'

'Yes,' he said, trying to find the right word, 'we're . . .'

He was going to finish the sentence, but she did it for him. 'Soulmates,' she said.

The taxi beeped its horn.

21

Suddenly they all jumped. Someone was throwing stones at the window. The father of Ester's child had shown up. For a while she had been very much in love with him but then she ditched him. The poor guy was wandering drunkenly to and fro across the lawn, furiously shouting over and over again, as if there was some doubt about it, 'I'm a man too! I'm a man too!' Vilhjálmur went out on to the balcony to try and calm him down, but to no avail. The child's father threw handfuls of earth up at the balcony. Luckily there were very few stones lying around. Little Gauti was the dead spit of this chap. Ester appeared on the balcony and looked at her ex with hatred.

I can still remember the look in her eyes, even though I was completely pissed.

Vilhjálmur went indoors to phone the police. They came soon after and picked me up off the lawn. You'll remember I promised to take a back seat in this story, but there are limits. Ester had used the article about Heidnaberg in *Weekend* as a final excuse to cut all contact with me.

'Whatever have you got against the poor chap?' laughed Hördur once the police had taken me away. 'Haven't you forgiven him for the fish on the Skólabrú door?'

'Fish? What's all this about fish?' asked Theódóra, all fired up. 'And, Ester, how on earth can you be safe from that kind of thing in the middle of town?'

Then Ester and Linda rowed about the Skólabrú house. Ester had been angling for the flat and Linda hadn't been told about it. Father Bernhardur tried unsuccessfully to restore peace. Ester talked her parents into going out to the car. Vilhelmína was pale and shivering. 'I never imagined you could be so selfish, Linda,' said Ester, sarcastically, 'trying to get your hands on Granny's flat.'

'Fuck off!' screamed Linda.

Axel trailed after Theódóra round the living room trying every conceivable argument to persuade her to go with him to the party at Hotel Saga but she was adamant. She had gone white as a sheet and her mouth was a fine horizontal line. 'You fool! Don't you think they'd've sent us an invitation if they expected us there! I wasn't invited to Thingvellir! And you offered that girl – Dagný – the flat in town without discussing it with me first! Your heart was OK then! What do you think people would have said if she'd moved in? I'm sure it's all over town as it is. And then you brought her here! I simply can't look people in the face.' She looked at Axel, furious with him. 'Perhaps you did it because she reminded you of my mother.'

'Please, darling, don't be like this. We both know there's nothing to it. Please, Tedda.'

She went up to her room and locked the door.

Axel took a taxi all by himself to Hotel Saga at around ten. He'd put on his tuxedo. He was upset about missing the celebratory dinner. The woman was being ridiculous, he thought. Of course they'd been invited! In the taxi he chatted about the traffic jam. Everyone was talking about it. 'I heard the royals were brought back to Reykjavík by helicopter,' said the driver. 'There'd have been no party otherwise.'

There were a few guests standing outside Hotel Saga, getting some fresh air, as Axel arrived. I hadn't quite sobered up and wanted to gatecrash the party and march straight through the foyer but I was stopped and asked for my journalist's accreditation. I still had my pass, but one of the security guys knew I'd lost my job because the scumbag put his great fat paw on my chest to stop me getting in. Then I saw Axel of Heidnaberg struggling out of the taxi. He wasn't too pleased to see me. I ran across to him, planning to slip in to the party in his wake. 'Let me tell you,' he said, poking me in the chest, 'everything's all to pot at home because of you. Hördur, my brother-in-law, he saw that article you wrote. There was some property mentioned there that he didn't even know existed. The sisters, Tedda and Villa, are at each other's throats. I've got you to thank for the wonderful birthday I'm having. You always have to go over the top, don't you?' He poked me again. 'You and Ester, you sort this custody business out somewhere other than in the Dyngjuvegur garden, OK?'

It made no difference explaining to him that it wasn't me who wrote the article. He wouldn't listen.

'So, you're driving me out,' I said.

He smiled at my misfortune. It was the one and only time I saw that happen. 'You're not going to get your hands on the Heidnaberg money, if that's what you're after,' he said, belligerently. 'You're not going to get a bean!'

'Next time we meet, I'm not even going to say hello,' I said.

'And what a relief that'll be!'

Axel walked through the foyer and up to the first floor with no problem at all, even though he didn't have an invitation. He saw the Prime Minister and went to greet him. The Prime Minister's dark tuxedo made his hair seem almost phosporous white.

'How are you, Hannes?' said Axel and held out his hand.

Hannes continued talking to his companion, turning side on to Axel and behaving as if he hadn't seen him.

'Thank you for that birthday greeting in *Morgunbladid*. It was a kind thought.'

'I couldn't get to them in time to stop them running it,' said the Prime Minister icily.

'What?' Axel stared at him. 'What . . . what do you mean?'

'I don't talk to thieves,' said Hannes.

Hannes's companion was embarrassment personified. Axel looked round and slowly let his hand drop. He heard the words but could not work out why they were being addressed to him. There was chatter all around him but he felt as if he and the Prime Minister were standing alone in an empty, silent circle. There were party lights above the bar and they were disturbing him. 'What?' asked Axel. 'What did you say?' He was clinging to the hope that Hannes had been addressing the other man.

'You heard.'

'Me? A thief? I don't understand.' Axel's ears were buzzing and the room beyond the circle containing him became dark and distant. The Prime Minister walked away into this darkness. Axel was finding it difficult to keep upright. 'I had a little too much champagne earlier,' he said, trying to excuse himself to the man who had been talking to the Prime Minister, someone he didn't recognize. 'What was Hannes talking about?'

The other man mumbled something in his embarrassment and disappeared. Another man came and stood directly in front of Axel and stared at him grimly. 'Is this some kind of joke?' thought Axel of Heidnaberg and laughed. He was under such stress that he couldn't remember the name of the man in front of him. He knew he'd seen him on a number of occasions. He was tall and fat. His skin was so fair that his eyebrows gave him a demonic look. Then he got a grip on himself. It was Haraldur Sumarlidason.

'Hannes was only telling you the truth.'

'What truth?'

'Who told you?' asked Haraldur aggressively.

'Told me what?'

'That the shares were coming up. There were only two or three people who knew about it.'

'I've no idea what you're talking about.'

'It's down to the old girl, is it?'

'What old girl?'

'Theódóra.'

Axel was too taken aback to spring to his wife's defence.

'She's grabbed the majority holding in United Fisheries,' said Haraldur fiercely. He almost pitied the poor bastard standing in front of him, white as a sheet and gulping like a fish. 'You bought in to United Fisheries. At a rock-bottom price! That arsehole Vilhjálmur fixed it while the old girl was overseas. You must have known about it.'

Axel stared at the man. He felt his heart lurch.

'You should have thought again.' Haraldur's face was contorted with bitterness. 'Heidnaberg is hardly a charity case. I don't see you in the queue for the soup kitchen. You might be a bit vulnerable on the fish-farming side of the business, even if you think nothing can touch you. How did you hear you could pick up United Fisheries for next to nothing?' he asked again, roughly.

'This is the first I've heard of it,' said Axel quietly.

'Do you mean to tell me you've no idea when your company's involved in a takeover deal?'

Axel shook his head. 'Perhaps there's some misunderstanding? I'd vetoed the purchase of those shares.'

'So, at least you'd discussed it then! You do know about it!' Haraldur Sumarlidason smiled evilly and raised his glass. He gripped the glass, almost as if it was a tonne weight. There was a napkin round the glass so that Haraldur's hand would not feel the cold. The corners of his mouth tensed as he swallowed and his look took in the whole room as if Axel of Heidnaberg had betrayed everyone there. 'No, there's no mistake,' he said. 'You've stolen everything people have worked for all their lives, all their savings. Why do you think Hannes was so angry?'

'I told Vilhjálmur not to get involved,' said Axel, with childlike insistence.

'If that's true, I shall have to ask you to make sure that your wife

222

sells her shares to the people whose entire livelihood is tied up with the company. About 800 million kroner has been knocked off the market value.'

Axel looked round for a chair. He had to sit down. Otherwise he thought he might collapse. There was a row of chairs by the main table. Most of them were occupied but he could see an empty chair and headed for it.

His feet felt like plasticine but he made it and sat down. He looked about him. To his left there was a distinguished-looking gentleman with an enormous nose and raven-black hair. On the man's left was a very attractive blonde. She looked at Axel as if he was some gatecrasher. The man seemed friendly enough. He lifted an eyebrow and asked in English, 'And who might you be?'

Then Axel recognized him. He was sitting beside the Vice President of the United States. Axel introduced himself. He remembered reading that the Vice President took a great interest in the environment and he began to tell him about Vilhjálmur's idea for a television commercial. Talking came remarkably easily to Axel in spite of all the stress. The Vice President paid close attention to Vilhjálmur's ideas and nodded enthusiastically. But he seemed to lose interest the moment Axel paused for breath and he turned back to his companion. Axel was gradually running out of steam. He tried to summon up the energy to tell the Vice President that at one time Heidnaberg had been the Icelandic agent for General Motors, but the words did not quite make it to his lips. All he was aware of was this: that Hannes Pálmason had cut him dead and called him a thief. 'I've got to get out of here,' he thought. 'I've got to find a bit of peace and quiet and collect my thoughts.' He sat quite still on the chair for some considerable time. He noticed a man in a black tuxedo, perhaps a caterer, eyeing him closely.

There was a terrible babble of voices from the guests at the dinner and it seemed to be getting louder and louder as he sat there. He was suddenly stricken with terror that he might have to be carried from the room. He managed to stand up, swayed a little as he took the first step and, without thinking, grabbed the back of the Vice President's chair. The Vice President glanced sharply over his shoulder and said, 'Careful!'

Axel stopped, swaying to and fro as he stood there. He wanted

223

to say something in return but the sentence would not come out. He tried to smile, set off towards the staircase and was relieved to find himself feeling stronger with every step. He was confident of making it downstairs without anyone having to help him. He gulped down two large whiskies at Mimi's Bar. There was a nasty pain in his heart, but the alcohol dulled it a little. He needed the toilet. And from there he left the hotel. He walked along Sudurgata into the town centre with his shirt sticking out of his trousers. Occasionally he stumbled a little. He walked like men do when they are dead drunk, and he hung his head.

There were lots of people milling around the town centre as the fine weather had lasted into the evening. He was hungry and wanted a hotdog. He found one of the temporary kiosks scattered about town for National Day. He walked north towards Lækjargata eating his hotdog. A gang of youths surrounded him. One of them seemed out of it, his eyes flicking backwards and forwards in their sockets. The others were laughing. Axel kept calm and serious. He looked from one to another, from face to face. 'I'm sure you don't see yourselves as successful businessmen,' he said. 'You're idiots,' he spat out. 'You know nothing!'

He was hoping that the gang would turn on him and kill him. A little way away two policemen were standing watching. The youngsters melted away like the good children they were. Axel of Heidnaberg ate what was left of his hotdog and looked around for a taxi.

The policemen had something else to think about. They were amazed to see a large van being driven right into the town centre. By this time I had reached the town centre as well. I was standing on the corner of Pósthússstræti at the very moment the van was parked there. I didn't fade away into the background when the whole town went wild. I just danced along with the kids. When that unauthorized truck swept into the centre, neither I nor anyone else could guess what was coming.

The drummer was waiting in the dark. He listened out for the other members of the band and heard them giggle with the tension. The drummer and lead singer of the Assassins was impatient to get going. The driver pulled open the side doors as agreed and there it all was, a free concert for everyone in honour of National Day, 17 June. Kids gathered, curious, and the drummer battered the skins. They started with a Metallica song, 'Enter Sandman'. The song crackled overhead like a whip and the crowd started to dance in front of the truck. The drummer felt he could control the whole of the town centre with his drumming. A drumroll spun into a cymbal crash. The people in the streets jumped up and down along with the beat. Heads rolled like the waves of the sea in a gale. The lead guitarist leapt about at the front following the drumbeat. All the members of the Assassins obeyed the beat; the city obeyed the beat; the sky obeyed the beat. With his drumsticks he could command the sea out in the bay to rise. He could make Mount Esja crumble; he could roll back the summer night sky; he could banish the white night sun and summon the moon . . .There was no end to what he could achieve as he felt his hair swing round his head and the sweat spray from his temples in a glittering arc, exactly like in the colour photograph of him that appeared later in *Icelandic Review* under the headline: 'Viking Orgy on National Day'. Another photograph, in black and white, showed him in the custody of the police being pushed into their car, the white helmets of the police bobbing in time to his beat.

Axel took a taxi to Heidnaberg and sent the nightwatchman home. It was good to be alone in the vast empty building. He opened a window and sat at his desk. Gulls were circling the bay on the summer night. This was the place, in spite of everything, where he felt most at home. He took a bottle of port from the display shelf and drank straight from the bottle. Suddenly the fax machine sprang to life and brought forth a sheet of paper. He stared drunkenly for a moment at this demonstration of life without doing anything. Then he tore off the message and read it. The fax was from Shadrak Inc. in the United States. The company was planning to acquire Bloodaxe Vodka of Finland. Negotiations were going to be held in Iceland. Heidnaberg was requested to arrange a pleasant private venue and a seafood meal at 16.30 hours on 6 September 1994.

On the dot of half past four that morning, Axel gazed across his office and said out loud, 'So, they want to eat on the dot of half-past four. They can bloody well starve!' He crumpled up the fax and threw it in the bin.

22

When Axel woke the veins at the back of his skull were throbbing and the memory of the evening at Hotel Saga came hurtling back. He decided to punish Theódóra for letting him down like that. 'I shan't talk to Tedda for a week,' he thought angrily, but he soon realized he was not the kind of man who could stick to something like that. Sometimes Theódóra could drive him mad by not speaking for days on end. He was always the first to crack.

For some years now they had slept in separate rooms. This was because of Axel's snoring. He was naturally an early riser but now he made a vow not to call her down to breakfast as he usually did. He rearranged the little pillow beneath his head to ease the pain but it made little difference. The phone beside his bed rang. It was a very polite journalist from *Weekend* requesting an interview.

'An interview about what, eh? *Weekend* treated me so abominably badly last time I gave you an interview.'

'Oh, last time. That was under a different editor. This is a whole new ball game. We're giving you a chance to set the record straight.'

'Well, OK then, but no photographer if you don't mind.'

Wincing and groaning, Axel managed to sit up. He rang Heidnaberg and asked for Vilhjálmur.

'I only did what I was told. I'm not in charge here, you know that,' said Vilhjálmur.

'But didn't you know Hannes held shares in the company? We'd talked it over, you and me. Hannes and I are friends. I just can't understand you doing something like that!'

'You'd better speak to your wife.' Vilhjálmur had transferred the call before Axel could say no. Was it as late as that? Was Theódóra at Heidnaberg already? Axel listened to her extension ring twice before he lost his nerve and put the receiver down. He just caught his wife's voice saying, 'Hello?'

He got out of bed. He mustn't let the doorbell wake Linda. He opened the door out on to the shady garden path so he would hear footsteps outside. The sun was shining further down the street. He took some orange juice out of the fridge and drank two full glasses. Then he heard footsteps. The journalist had not respected his wish not to have a photographer there. Axel was rather cross but showed them into the living room, pointed to some chairs and sat down where he could keep an eye on the camera.

Facing him sat a handsome young man, rather short, with a small chin, a high, poetic forehead and shiny black hair gelled solid into a baroque quiff. The journalist tossed his head as he spoke and showed his subject very little in the way of common courtesy.

Linda was woken by the sound of the visitors. She had been dreaming of being back at school. She was studying Icelandic. The classroom was nearly full and there was no space for her. She was sitting an examination and knew nothing about the subject. Suddenly there seemed to be piles of dead bodies in the classroom. Blood seeped from the beneath the bodies.

She woke. What a revolting, trivial dream! She was exhausted, in spite of having slept for ten hours. They had all been arguing the night before. This confused dream was the result. She left her room and looked into the living room. Her father was sitting there with some men. Who were they? Journalists? What were they getting out of him? What had they already got out of him? She had to put a stop to this nonsense immediately. She called out, lightly, 'Father, can I have a word?'

'Later, Linda. I've got people here.'

'I can see that.'

'Yes, it's all right, darling. Pardon?' she heard her father say. 'Do we export pullovers?'

'Yes, to Russia. To St Petersburg! Don't you know about it?'

The journalist's eyes were very deep set and his face was like a death mask. He looked at Axel steadily, 'You do know you have major fish-farming interests?'

'Yes, of course, I know that,' said Axel, offended. 'We are one of the few companies still running a profitable fish-farming operation. Tedda wanted us to diversify into fish-farming because we have such good relations with the Japs through Toyota.'

'Father! I really must speak with you!'

'Yes, in a moment, sweetheart.' Axel looked round for a cigar. 'We used to use the Flying Tigers to deliver the fish, but the Icelandair monopoly put paid to that. There's nothing to say about it really.

Business is business.' He wondered what he should say next, and decided to pay the Prime Minister a compliment. 'Hannes was once my lawyer, you know.' Axel's face assumed an expression of glowing affection. He stretched across for a cigar from one of the nest of inlaid tables, bit off the end and spat it out into an ashtray. 'The legal problem he couldn't disentangle didn't exist. Would you like a cigar?' They declined. 'The best way to describe Hannes . . .' He hunted for the right phrase and silently found it: 'a wily old fox'. Instead, out loud, he said, 'He's sharp. Of course, that isn't something you can say in an interview, is it?' He grimaced and then stretched out his hand and looked at his fingers as if he wanted to correct his own quotation. 'Find the right words for me, would you? Are you new to *Weekend*? Has it been taken over or something? I don't remember having met you before. The last editor was the most terrible shit. I'm personally acquainted with him, you see.' (Here he was maligning the present writer.) 'It still rankles, how you turned me over a few weeks back. You made me sound like some mean, swindling old man,' he said, solemnly. 'How could you think that?' He turned to the photographer. 'And as for you. Don't take any photographs. I don't like being photographed. I had quite enough of that last time. I looked like an exhumed corpse. You really shouldn't do it.' He looked at them, bewildered. 'People ought to be nice to each other.'

'Like I said, it's all different now,' said the journalist coldly. 'We had nothing to do with all that. A few years back you gave a charity donation to help with prison construction?' he asked out of the blue.

Axel of Heidnaberg stood, with difficulty. His expression was more kindly, but standing up set off his headache again. 'That's absolutely correct!' He walked over to a cupboard and took out a little flagpole on a golden stand. His name was engraved on the base. He looked fondly at the object, stroking it. 'When the new prison at Höfdabakki was opened, they gave me this. Here, take a look, they had my name engraved on it.' The journalist and the photographer took the little flagpole and passed it between them. There was a solid trim round the base and the whole thing stood on four golden balls. At this moment, Linda called again, 'Father, could you just come into the kitchen for a minute? Now, please!'

'This gift is exactly the kind of thing I want to discuss,' said the journalist. 'Quite frankly, the reason I'm here is to ask about this donation . . .'

'Really?' said Axel, surprised. 'I thought we were here to talk about that article in *Weekend* a few weeks back, but you just fire away, my friend.'

'Is it true that the donation made Heidnaberg eligible for major tax breaks?'

'Possibly, possibly, I don't really know about that side of things. I'm a bit of an idiot when it comes to doing my tax return.'

'And isn't it correct to say that the donation took the form of building supplies, which the company at that time was itself importing?'

'Yes, Tedda and I owned Timber Trading at that period. But it ran at a loss. Buying and selling sticks of wood bores me.'

'And isn't it true to say that the declared figures, the apparent purchase price of the supplies, had been subject to a considerable mark up?'

'I wouldn't know anything about that.'

'And the commission payment was squirrelled away into some bank account?'

'Can't help you there either.'

The journalist's manner had acquired a dangerous edge to it. 'No, but the fact remains that when you take various factors into account: the tax allowance set against company profits; the mark up on the declared value of the supplies; the commission payment; your insistence on subcontracting your own workers to build the prison and the considerable cost to the state of continuing interest payments, then when it comes to calculating the real value of the donation' – the journalist leaned forward in his chair with a finger in the air and stared steadily at Axel – 'it doesn't seem to be quite so altruistic. Perhaps it's not as magnificent as it appears at first glance. It's hardly worth anything in fact. Then there were the delays in the construction work, because the subcontractors did not meet the deadlines as they were busy laying the foundations for Heidnaberg's complex at Ellidavogur. I got an accountant to take a look at the figures.' The journalist delved into his case. 'His assessment is really rather interesting. It demonstrates that when all is said and done the cost to the taxpayer of your donation runs to tens of millions. I would like to hear your reaction to this.' He smiled a thin smile. 'What do you say now about this donation? After all, you played a part in all this, didn't you?'

'What do you mean?'

'Were you aware that this donation involved a net cost to the state rather than a clear benefit?'

'No, that can't be right, old chap,' said Axel, suddenly frightened. 'The whole country's known for ten or fifteen years that I donated getting on for a hundred million kroner. Do you think they'd've given me that flag if I was making a profit on the deal myself?' Axel felt hurt. 'This is all rubbish, really it is.'

'The precise figure is 73 million kroner.'

Axel's eyes widened. 'That's my profit on this?'

'No, that's the cost to the state.'

'What?' Axel couldn't believe it.

'This report shows that the only person to have benefited from this donation was you. Do you want to read it?' He handed Axel the bound report.

Axel of Heidnaberg took the report. It was labelled 'Audited at the office of Haraldur Haraldsson, 186 Hverfisgata'. The figures stretched across some forty pages and there was index as well. He glanced at an odd page here and there but could not make head or tail of it and threw it down on the inlaid table. 'Is this accountant sick in the head or something? Is it OK if I hang on to this? I need to ask Villi or Tedda to take a look at it.'

'I'm sorry, that's the only copy, but I'll get one sent over to you after lunch.'

'Father, will you please come and talk to me!'

'Yes, I'm coming.' Axel looked at the journalist. 'You got it all down verbatim, did you? Facts are sacred, remember.'

'Yes, it's all there.' The journalist smiled tightly.

He stood up to see them out. As he was going, the journalist pointed to the photograph of Professor Thóroddur which dominated the living room. 'Who's that then?'

'That's Professor Thóroddur, my late father-in-law. A marvellous old boy, with a will like iron. It's almost beyond belief, how strong willed he could be. Didn't you see his biography when it came out last year?'

Linda was standing in the kitchen doorway in her white night-shirt, showing her muscular calves and her large feet. Her cheeks were flushed and she was pushing her hair back from her face.

'Some reporters here for a chat, Linda my dear,' said her father. Then he added, proudly, 'This is my daughter. Linda Concordia Axelsdóttir. 'Concordia' for her grandmother. She was Danish. But you don't use the name now, or do you, Linda?'

'No, I never use it, Father.'

'Now what was it your grandfather got away with? Hashish, was it?'

'No, it wasn't such a big deal in the West in those days, Father,' said the girl, and shivered slightly.

'I'm so stupid about things like that.'

The journalist shook Linda's hand and bowed his head with a little shake.

'Hey,' said Axel, giggling, 'you're just like a poet I was at college with. He used to shake his head just like you when he shook hands. Oh, what was his name? He's often on television.' Axel thought a moment and his guests waited in anticipation. As Linda slipped away into the kitchen, he said, 'Linda, do you know who I mean?'

'I haven't the foggiest, Father,' she called, irritated.

'And did you pass?'

'Did I pass?' asked Axel.

'Yes.'

'Did I pass what?'

'The college exams.' Both visitors were grinning.

'Of course I passed. The year of '54. But the poet got better grades than I did.'

'Then it's thank you and goodbye from us.'

'How can you let fools like that insult you, Father?' Linda stood there with her fists clenched as the door slammed to behind them. 'What did they trick you into saying?'

'What do you mean, "insult me", "trick me"? Linda, darling, what are you talking about? They were very decent chaps. We were just having a bit of a chat.'

'A chat about what?'

'I don't want to talk about it. Well, you heard some of it.'

'No, I mean before that.'

'Oh, nothing.'

'Does Mother know about them coming?'

'No, she doesn't know anything about it. I am capable of doing things on my own, you know.'

'That man was making out you were so stupid you couldn't pass your college exams.'

'You and your mother, you always think the worst of people,' said Axel, hurt. 'I didn't hear them say that.'

The girl shuddered. 'Father, please go upstairs and leave me in peace.'

'Linda,' said Axel hesitantly, 'your mother told me you had hurt her quite badly when you were in London.'

'Hurt her? How?'

'You took a man home with you. I don't understand. Haven't we always been good to you?'

'Yes, of course you have.' Linda stood up straight and looked him in the eye. 'What if I did take a man home? That's my affair. As it happened I didn't. He was just a boy making a film and he was fun to talk to. Father, please don't take it out on me because Mother bought those shares.'

'Linda, I can't be doing with all this. I don't want to be spoken to like that. You all went crazy last night.'

'Of course we went crazy. You're going to hang on to that money. Do you think Hördur and Villa will put up with it? Father, sometimes I think you're living on another planet.'

'What do you mean?'

'What do I mean? Well, for one thing, you have no idea what's happening in your own company. Those journalists know more about it than you do.'

'Oh, really! And I only built it up from nothing!'

'You've never done a stroke of work there and well you know it.' She stamped her foot on the kitchen floor. 'Will you go back to your room before I scream?'

Axel went upstairs and left the door to his bedroom ajar so he could hear the doorbell. He was expecting a messenger from *Weekend* with a copy of the auditor's report.

Linda pulled out the phone and went back to sleep. She woke at about three, took a quick shower and got dressed, firm in her resolve to get out of the house before her mother came home and everything went mad. What would Theódóra say when she heard reporters had been there pumping her father? For the second time in almost as many weeks!

In the shower she thought about the little journalist. She had taken an immediate fancy to him. She thought he was sweet. 'I wouldn't mind shagging him,' she thought as she dried her hair, 'if we'd met under different circumstances.'

She drove into town and parked in the car park on Hverfisgata and went window shopping. She couldn't see her face reflected in the windows. The wind was tossing her hair all around her head like eruptions on the surface of the sun.

A man came out of a shop. He was wearing a dark blue sweater and had pushed the sleeves up. His forearms were sinewy and covered in dark hair growing in little circle patterns. He was handsome, with thin lips and a high forehead. She opened her purse and looked for her credit card. 'I shan't go home until gone midnight,' she thought. 'I'm in no hurry to go home. The next ten hours are all mine. And in the autumn I'll go back to England.' She had decided what she wanted to do with her life. She would leave filmmaking to Trausti. Her thing was going to be the piano. She'd work hard, religiously practising ten hours every day . . . God only knew how far she'd get!

The sun warmed the pavement and bounced off the cars driving along Laugavegur. She couldn't stop thinking about that little journalist. Would he be at Solon? Perhaps she'd get a chance to speak to him and get him to tone down some of the garbage she'd heard him drag out of her father. Linda Concordia Axelsdóttir. Perhaps the time had come to acknowledge her middle name. The name of a Catholic who turned feminist and communist. She hadn't dared use it at school, afraid of being teased. At Solon Islandus nearly every table was occupied. She went up to the bar, wondering whether or not to have a cake. No. She asked for a milky coffee and picked up *Weekend* to see if she could work out what kind of article they would write about her father. She didn't need to guess because Axel Sigurgeirsson was plastered all over the front page. They must have been holding the press while the little bastard was fitting him up.

The photograph of her father seemed strangely frightening. He looked grey. He was outside the house, holding up a hand to fend off the photographer. He hadn't gone outside this morning, so this must have been taken on an earlier occasion. 'He used dirty tricks to get UF shares, but denies it all. Axel of Heidnaberg answers our questions.' She read the interview quickly. The Prime Minister wasn't mentioned, nor was the donation towards the building of the prison. On the other hand, Theódóra was mentioned. Axel spelt it out: 'Tedda and Villi are responsible for the whole damn thing.' The magazine ended by summarizing its previous examination of Heidnaberg's affairs.

'So this is what he was telling them before I got up. I need to get away from all the madness at 4 Dyngjuvegur tonight,' thought Linda. She glanced round the café, but did not recognize anyone, no journalists nor anyone else. She finished her coffee, feeling upset, and looked round for a phone so she could tell the little black-haired weasel what she thought of him, but then thought better of it. Her father would have to deal with his own mess. 'Why isn't anyone left alone if they own property in Iceland?' she thought. 'Why are people so horrible, why are people always so snide and envious?'

She walked out into the sunshine. Axel had offered to buy her a small flat but she wouldn't hear of it. The way she was feeling she might as well go back to England straightaway. She suddenly remembered the way her classmates at school used to make fun of the little white sign propped against the window on Skólabrú. It was always dark and empty but her father was allowed to play at being a businessman so the Heidnaberg staff would be left in peace to get on with their work. ICELAND TRADING: IMPORT–EXPORT, it said. Poor father, how ashamed and embarrassed she'd been. And he'd always been so kind to her, so good. She remembered a trunk with some of her father's samples, a few sad packets of soup, in the bottom. 'We should support Icelandic business, Linda, my dear.' He always bought things for himself at the most expensive places so that his fellow merchants would get the benefit and yet he thought himself no end of a sharp operator when it came to business affairs.

She waited at a red light at Lækjargata, crossed at the corner of Austurstræti in a crowd of people, and ran into an old schoolfriend. They were enormously excited to see each other and their lack of control began to get embarrassing. In actual fact they had detested the sight of each other at school, but even so they stood there like idiots exchanging all the gossip. 'I need somewhere to get away from it all,' said Linda, finding it hard to meet the other girl's eye. 'I need a chance to be on my own, a bit of peace and quiet to think things over.' She pretended to ignore the way the other girl was smiling. 'That's why I went overseas. But I've not been doing anything special. I haven't a clue what I want to do.' The other girl was smiling dangerously, as if she knew everything. As they said goodbye, Linda realized she hadn't thought to ask the other girl how she was and what she was up to. She was surprised to find she couldn't remember the girl's name.

London suddenly seemed very boring. Playing the piano didn't mean anything. She racked her memory desperately trying to conjure up other cities she'd visited: Paris, Rome, Athens, New York, Tokyo. She didn't want to spend time in any of them. What did interest her? She didn't know. Was this why people killed themselves? They killed themselves out of boredom! She thought she'd have a look at the Skólabrú flat. Perhaps Hördur would be in his surgery. He'd let her look around upstairs. She'd make sure she'd be allowed to move in!

There was a van parked outside the house. She crossed the street, looked into the van and recognized her grandmother's furniture. The door was standing open. Hördur was nowhere to be seen but the door to the waiting room was ajar. Ester appeared on the stairs. 'Oh, hi. I wasn't expecting you.'

'Obviously not,' said Linda, feeling aggrieved. 'What's going on?'

'Your mother rang this morning and said it was perfectly OK if I wanted the flat.'

'Oh, did she?'

'Didn't you know?'

'No, I never thought she'd just go ahead and do it like that.'

'I can't see anything wrong with me moving in.'

'Ester, please stop messing about. You knew I wanted to live here.'

'You! I really do feel Mother and Father are entitled to their share. Honestly I do.'

Linda ran out of the house. She glanced over her shoulder when she reached the other side of the street. The faithful old sign, ICELAND TRADING, was still in its rightful place. She went into Hotel Borg, upset and angry, and asked for a large Campari. She had a boundless capacity for alcohol. At college she was nick-named 'Bottomless Pit' by the boys. She had rather enjoyed that. The most hardened drinkers in the college had tried to drink her under the table, but they never got very far. By the time they were seeing 'The Pit' in triplicate, she'd be lighting a cigarillo as calmly as you please with a near-empty bottle of vodka in front of her.

And it came to pass that her mind's eye beheld the beast stalking the horizon. It was so mighty that the ram's horns upon its head obscured the sun itself. She heard herself summoned to fight with the beast, to conquer or lose her mind in the attempt. Or had the summons come too late? Was the battle already lost? What sin had she committed too terrible for forgiveness? What have I done? She could not fathom the transgression and neither could she drive the night-world from the recesses of her mind. She rubbed her forehead hard where she was marked with the mark of the beast. She could almost feel anew the searing pain that had come upon her when he had triumphed over her and branded her flesh. Was there a hell? The Bible said that there was. And why should the Bible not speak true on this matter when on all others it spoke true? Was there a place where men and women floated helplessly trapped by fire and agony, a place from which there was no escape? The enemies of God! Who among us truly knew God? Jesus himself had warned against offending the Father. 'Fear him, which after he hath killed hath power to cast into hell.' Was it possible to transgress so pro-foundly to become an abomination in the eyes of God? She closed her eyes and saw the man in the robe from her vision saying that she now belonged to him. When he had touched her it was as if he had struck a nail into her forehead right into the bone.

She was seized with an intense fear and prayed for a vision, for the spirit of God to carry her away and show her that she was saved. She waited for a while with her eyes closed but no vision came. Was God demanding complete and boundless trust of her? Suddenly the thought came to her: perhaps it was not God who had spoken to her. Perhaps it was some evil being trying to rob her of her sanity.

The dark and threatening world suddenly receded. She finished her drink and ordered another. The liquor comforted her. She stared into the glass, swirling the drink round, the ice cubes chiming against the side of the glass, floating in the red liquid. She soon ordered a third. The waiter gave a look from the bar when he went to fetch it.

'Excuse me. Is it OK if I sit here?' She looked up. A rather good-looking man was standing by her table staring at her. She shook her head crossly.

'Why not?'

'Because I say so. Do you want me to call the waiter?'

The man left.

She could feel warm clay around her feet and remembered as a small child paddling by the shore at Lake Thingvellir. Perhaps she should drive out to the summer home and stay the night there? She could easily break in if she couldn't lay hands on the keys. Surely she was allowed to sleep one night there?

She looked at her watch. It was nearly seven. Time went fast when you were sitting over a drink, you didn't always realize. She stood up. She was too drunk to drive. She settled the bill and left. The sun was more gentle, a warm breeze was blowing in from the harbour, there were fewer people about. She licked the traces of Campari from her lips. She almost wanted to walk to the corner and throw stones at the Skólabrú windows, make an awful scene. Now her parents had seen to it that she'd never have any of Granny Ingibjörg's furniture. Once the Vatnsholt lot got their hands on something, you never saw it again.

There was a Russian clipper in the harbour with masts soaring up into the sky and a sturdy bowsprit. The public were being shown over the ship and she went on board. The sailors were selling red babushka dolls and various souvenirs. She saw one of her old teachers there. He was sitting in a chair with his head up, as if the deck was his classroom. The gentle breeze stirred his hair. He had taught them history one winter. The class had taken against him and driven him away. He had been destroyed by drink and hadn't a tooth in his head. He nodded when, rather awkwardly, she introduced herself but it was obvious he didn't recognize her.

She hurried off the ship and went into the Café Paris, staying there an hour sitting over a coffee and a cognac. Then she went on to a bar and sat there for most of the evening enjoying the feeling of having alcohol in her system.

Suddenly everything seemed brighter. All her crazy thoughts now seemed funny. 'How could I let some ridiculous fantasy like that knock me for six?' she thought. She fell in with a crowd who were going to the National Theatre Cellar. It was full to bursting.

She got herself a drink and stood watching the band and the people on the dance floor. A young man came up to her and said, 'Hello, darling, you're looking really sexy. Fancy a shag?'

'Drop dead!' she said in English.

She was standing at the bar with one foot on the footrail sipping a large Campari through a straw when she saw the man in the mirror behind the bar. He was very masculine, grey-haired, and decades older than her. She just about managed to hear him say he was a pilot above the noise of the band. 'He's probably married,' she thought. 'But then, so what?'

He was frightfully charming. She took him home with her to Dyngjuvegur a bit before four. Young people were thronging the streets. The sky was more overcast now. It was strangely dark for a June night. At the front door she put her finger to her lips. He had to be at least fifty! 'I must be going mad,' she thought. The night lights in the floor were on in the hall. She took his hand and led him into her bedroom. She started to undress him almost immediately. Then he put his hand on hers and said, 'I'm sorry, I can't do it just like that. I don't like the woman taking the lead. Leave it to me, do you understand?' The brown forehead was lined below the harsh grey crewcut.

'No, I don't understand,' she whispered.

He opened the door to the hall.

'No, don't go, my friend,' she said tenderly and locked the door. 'Try and relax.'

Much later there was a hand on the doorknob. 'Linda, dear, are you in?' asked a voice in the corridor. 'I need to talk to you for a moment.' Her guest was getting dressed. She peeped round the door. Axel was standing there in his pants, the night lights illuminating his stork-like legs.

'Good evening.' The man – she hadn't even thought to ask his name – walked past her father.

'Yes. Good evening.'

Axel stumbled off and stared at the departing visitor. Linda locked her door and slipped on a nightgown. She heard the front door slam shut. She felt she should go out to her father. Axel was standing in the living room looking out over the city. 'Linda, I'm not happy about you bringing a stranger home without telling me. And he was so old!' He thought a moment, trying to find the right words. 'Never in all my life have I seen such a repulsive old man!'

'No, you're wrong. He was very good-looking.'

'This is meant to hurt me, is it? Well, I can tell you, it doesn't.'

'Oh Father, this is ridiculous,' said the girl wearily. She went back into her room and crept under the duvet.

23

'This is worse than a doctor's waiting room,' said the man.

'Don't mention those bastards to me,' said Hördur. 'I had to go and see a surgeon the other day. I was very busy and the man kept me hanging about for nearly an hour. They seem to think it's perfectly all right,' he said, frowning, 'but if you keep them waiting five minutes they hit the roof.'

'Are you going to have an operation?'

'There's something wrong with my colon,' lied Hördur, 'but they haven't found out what it is yet.'

'Huh!' said the man contemptuously. 'They don't know anything.'

'You're right there, my friend.'

'I once had an operation on my back and it only made things worse.' The man had sharp features and sunken cheeks. His greying hair was cut short at the temples. He was waiting for Hördur's question, so the doctor politely obliged: 'And what was the problem?'

'My back's permanently damaged. I was in the swimming pool

239

when an old girl weighing twenty-odd stone jumped off the top diving board straight on to my back.' He was talking quite loudly, ignoring the girl on reception who glanced in their direction. 'Several of the vertebrae simply snapped.' He didn't get any further because the girl said, 'Gudmundur, the Prime Minister will see you now.'

Gudmundur got up from his chair and walked stiffly towards the Prime Minister's office. Hördur would have to wait a while longer. He kept an eye on the door. Gudmundur was inside for a long time. The doctor felt for a cigarette.

'I'm sorry, you aren't allowed to smoke in here,' said the girl before he managed to extract a cigarette from the packet. Hördur went outside.

Out on Lækjartorg there were groups of workmen dismantling the bandstand and clearing up after the celebrations. He had half smoked the cigarette when the man with the bad back came out. 'Best of luck for your operation,' said Gudmundur.

'I doubt very much I'll let the murdering swine anywhere near me,' said Hördur and tossed the half-smoked cigarette out on to the lawn.

'The Prime Minister is waiting for you,' said the girl.

Hördur walked into the office. The Prime Minister rose to greet him. They both sat down. The room had a high ceiling and a pine floor. The walls were painted white. There were two leather armchairs by the window. The chair in front of the desk was on a level with the Prime Minister's chair. Hannes did not need the psychological advantage of looking down on people. The Prime Minister looked enquiringly at Hördur.

'Axel Sigurgeirsson of Heidnaberg sent me over. We're related by marriage. He wants to make peace with you if that's at all possible.'

'Yes, I thought I recognized your face,' said the Prime Minister, 'but I couldn't quite place you.' He put both hands on the table and then brought them together. He radiated calm. '"Make peace"?'

'Yes. Clearly we both know what this is all about. He's been on the phone to me morning, noon and night. The poor chap's simply devastated.'

The Prime Minister looked hard at Hördur as if assessing him. 'How come I don't remember you from all those years when I was their lawyer?'

Hördur met his eyes and decided to play it as if they'd never met. The truth was the Prime Minister was perfectly well aware of who he was. Of course he was! Some time before Hannes had reached the exalted heights of his present office, he had been stopped by the police, suspected of drink-driving. Axel of Heidna-berg had had a quiet word with his brother-in-law. Hördur had gone to the City Hospital and substituted another blood sample. 'My wife and I lived overseas for quite some time,' said Hördur Gottskálksson. 'I was studying. Besides, it's chiefly on my own account I'm here.' He found himself relaxing into the conversation. He told the Prime Minister all his troubles with the National Hospital and his current woes with Dagný's frontal assault. Hadn't the Prime Minister seen the business referred to in the papers? Hannes Pálmason sighed and recalled having read the article in *Weekend*. At the same time he vaguely remembered something else about Hördur: wasn't this the lunatic who'd smashed up his car with a sledgehammer?

'I think there's no doubt,' said the doctor, 'that the woman is only after my money. But she's doomed to disappointment. To be perfectly frank, Theódóra has taken all her sister's money. My wife came off badly before, the poor dear,' he muttered, 'and I can't see that she's going to do much better this time round. Her mother died in the spring, so there's a considerable estate to be settled. But, as I said, Seli wants to make peace.'

'So, there we are,' said the Prime Minister and he became more friendly. 'And how much does he want for the shares?'

'I'm not sure they're for sale. As far as I know, he hasn't dis-cussed the matter with Theódóra yet. He just wants you to know that he had nothing whatsoever to do with it.'

The Prime Minister leaned back in his chair. It was hard to read his expression; it could go either way. He brought the tips of his fingers together. From outside the sound of an air-compressor could be heard. Work on the foundations of the new Courts of Justice had begun. 'She's quite something is Theódóra,' said Hannes slowly, having thought it over thoroughly. It was possible to discern a degree of warmth in his voice. 'You've got to admire the woman.'

'And what about the matter I raised?'

'Which is?'

'The potential injustice.'

'Isn't that more a matter for the Chief Physician or the Minister of Health rather than me?'

'The Chief Physician!' Hördur frowned and made a dismissive noise. 'I don't trust him. A few years ago he invoiced the Health Service for giving himself an rectal examination,' he said, grinning. 'No, I want to go straight to the top on this.'

'How far has the case got?' Hannes folded his fingers behind his head and looked at Hördur.

'They'll take witness statements in the autumn.'

'There's no way that a process like that can be interferred with. It must take its course.' Hannes suddenly leant forward in his chair, rested his elbows on the edge of the table and tapped the tips of his fingers together over and over again. 'But don't worry. You've nothing to fear. You can have complete faith in the Icelandic legal system.'

Hördur said nothing.

'You doctors, it's quite a Mafia you've got going between you!' said the Prime Minister with a grin. 'If anything, you're even worse than us politicians.'

Hördur looked at him sharply. There was an edge to his voice. 'You bet there is. I came back from overseas with the best qualifications from the best hospitals and I'm given next to nothing to do, I'm driven out of the National Hospital where I'm working, and the place is left to charlatans, taking perfectly healthy organs out of perfectly healthy patients.'

'Well,' said the Prime Minister, as if he had suddenly remembered he had a lot of work to be getting on with, 'we'll see what happens.'

As he reached the door, Hördur turned round and said, 'What shall I say to Axel?'

The Prime Minister looked up from his vast desk. 'Just while I think of it, where do you stand politically, Hördur? Do you take an active part in politics?'

'Not until now.'

'Tell Seli the party looks after its own.'

The Prime Minister busied himself with his papers and the doctor closed the door silently. He met a man mincing his way down the corridor. Haraldur Sumarlidason looked at the doctor. He was appalled at the prospect of this reunion. 'What, you here!'

'Yes. How are you, old chap? How are you feeling?' Hördur tried to look serious.

'I've been more or less OK.' Haraldur shrugged as they shook hands and looked sharply at Hördur. 'What business have you got here?' His nerves were on edge and he didn't take his eyes from the doctor.

'I've been treated most unfairly! Perhaps you've seen the papers? Some bitch is trying to ruin my reputation.' They had still not let go of each other's hands. Haraldur tried to read the doctor's eyes. It was obvious to Hördur what was concerning him. 'No, my friend, I haven't broken your confidence,' he whispered. He was unable to suppress the twinkle in his eye.

'Good. That's good,' said Haraldur. 'Do let me know if there's anything I can do for you.'

'There is something! I was looking for justice from the Prime Minister. He seemed quite sympathetic. I'd really appreciate it if you would have a word about it with him and back my case.'

'I'll ask round and see what I can do.' Haraldur gave a little goodbye wave on parting and walked to Hannes's door. Before going in he glared with evil intent at the departing doctor's back.

Hördur Gottskálksson did not drive directly back to his surgery. He turned up Veghúsastígur and into Thingholtstræti, letting the car coast past number 28. He didn't quite know what he was doing there, but he found it strangely exciting and enjoyable to be so close to his adversary.

24

About halfway through the holiday season someone lent me a cottage and I camped out there for a few weeks. As the summer had gone on it became more and more obvious to me that it would take quite a while to raise the capital to get a new magazine up and running. Nevertheless I began to make notes which were to come in handy later when I sat down to write up this narrative. By the beginning of the autumn I was quite serious about it. Then something happened that is still a matter of conjecture. I'm not sure that we'll ever get to the bottom of it, although naturally I do have my own ideas. Of course Axel did lay on a spread for that foreign company even though he had screwed up the fax and thrown it in the bin. I have had some difficulty ascertaining exactly what followed from that but I think I have got the whole story and can give an accurate picture of what happened.

On the way to Thingvellir, Axel asked the pilot to fly over the Laugarnes valley as he wanted to show the foreign guests his home in Reykjavík. The helicopter slid over the stadium, its shadow rippling across the seating, jumping the fences and travelling across the grass along Laugarasvegur. He pointed and shouted above the roar of the rotor-blades, 'That's where I live, over there!'

The three foreign visitors looked out but there was no way for them to work out which house he meant. They were thin, expressionless men with raven-black hair. They had landed at Reykjavík Airport in a nifty-looking private white jet, which was waiting for them there now, glistening in the sun, with the red lettering on its side: SHADRAK. Their spokesman was wearing a white silk suit. Another was wearing sunglasses. He was the friendliest of the three and had let his foot tap non-stop on the metal floor of the helicopter. He nodded and shouted in English, 'You have a very nice home!'

'Shall I go round again?' called the pilot.

'No,' shouted Axel.

He took another quick look at the house before it disappeared. The black, raven stone on the chimney was glittering in the sun. It was strange to think how long he had lived there. 'You used your heart condition as an excuse to betray me,' Theódóra had said. 'And then, to cap it all, you went to the press.'

Now he could see the shadow of the helicopter on the flat green surface of Kollafjördur. The helicopter described a wide arc as it turned towards the Mosfells valley.

'Shark?' asked the man in the silk suit.

Axel asked him to repeat the question.

This irritated the foreign guest. Axel felt he had seen the man before. Had seen them all before. Had met them somewhere. But it was impossible to remember where.

'No. There's no danger of sharks so close to the shore,' he shouted. 'The water's too warm. They're further out.' He hunted for the correct word in English for this particular species of shark but couldn't remember it. Bone shark? Was that it? He wanted to tell them about Icelanders hunting sharks and gutting them and hanging them in wooden sheds. How meat cured this way was considered a great delicacy. 'Traditional food,' he said loudly, but they didn't realize he had said anything and he decided against trying to scream this information at them.

Where had he seen the man before? Where? He looked at them closely. The foreign guests nodded at him.

The helicopter flew over Mosfells heath, hurtling over a chasm, sliding over flat grasslands. There was a single raven flying by. It was autumn now and the heather and grass were turning pale. Then the shadow of the helicopter was pitch black on the silver surface of Thingvellir lake. To Axel's relief he could see that there were two cars parked in the space under the trees. Vilhjálmur had met up with the Finns and the caterers. 'It's that building over there,' shouted Axel.

'Where's a good place to land?' called the pilot.

'On the west side, on the grass,' Axel called back.

The helicopter made a wide circle to the east. There was no wind to disturb the surface of the lake. Water birds were swimming, their wakes growing ever wider behind them. The helicopter reduced its height, buffeting the tops of the trees, and landed on the grass surrounded by birch trees with their bronze and golden leaves.

Vilhjálmur was standing by the cars watching the helicopter

land. When the rotor-blades had stopped turning, he welcomed the guests one by one as they got out. He was quick and energetic. Axel felt as if a heavy weight had been taken off his shoulders. 'This'll be rather a long wait for you, I'm afraid,' he said as he struggled awkwardly out of the helicopter.

'Oh well, I'm getting paid for it,' said the pilot happily enough. 'Who are they?'

'They're worth 17 billion dollars, so they can afford to keep you waiting.'

'How much is that in real money? You can never grasp figures like that.'

'Just multiply by sixty-five and that'll give you the value in kroner.'

'Seli? Are you coming?' called Vilhjálmur from the veranda.

Axel's eye was caught by the white plastic family boat on the shore. He thought how nice it would be to be out here by himself and take a quick trip out on the lake. The thought took him aback. 'But I've never taken a boat out all on my own.' The water suddenly stirred in the sun, as if a shoal of herring had risen from the depths.

He went in through the kitchen entrance where two chefs from Hotel Saga were setting up. Two girls in waitress uniform were leaning across the table under the cupboards. He was able to inspect the menu: shark, clams, redfish, ray, small halibut, sea urchin. Suddenly he felt it had not been a good idea to make his own summer home available for this meeting. It was a thoughtless and stupidly grandiloquent gesture. He tried to multiply 17 billion by sixty-five in his head and failed. He went into the sitting room to say hello to the Finns. They were sitting in armchairs and had already started negotiating with the Americans. When Axel had welcomed them, he and Vilhjálmur stepped back and stood awkwardly in the background shifting their weight from one foot to the other.

'We're not needed here,' said Vilhjálmur. They went out on the veranda. 'What's up with Theódóra? Why didn't she want to come?'

'I don't know,' said Axel. He put both hands on the wooden railing and looked out over the large shield-shaped lake.

'You should make it up, husband and wife.'

'She's still cross with me. She thinks I'm a terrible coward because I didn't just button my lip. But I didn't buy those shares. You did.'

'She's just as cross with the party leadership,' said Vilhjálmur guardedly. 'I don't think stuff in the press bothers her too much.'

Axel gazed sadly over the lake. A powerful yellow speedboat was out near the island. It was turning in narrow circles, almost spinning on its own axis. The sun was lower in the sky. The shadows on the island were growing longer.

'Oh, there are lots of things that trouble me, Villi. Hannes was my friend. You should have stopped Tedda going ahead with it and told me what was going on. You treat me like some snotty kid.' He cleared his throat and looked hurt. 'The success of the company is nearly all down to her. We both know that. But even so . . . And what about my daughter? What do you think of her?' He looked from the lake now afire with golden light to Vilhjálmur.

'What about Linda?'

'I'm worried for her. Her mother was an alcoholic and committed suicide.'

'It doesn't mean anything. There are alcoholics in all families.'

'And you're not making any progress with Ester?' He tried to look jolly and bring a twinkle to his eye.

'No. She seems very cold towards me,' said Vilhjálmur and sighed.

One of the Finns, red-faced, came lumbering out on to the veranda looking very happy. 'Well, that's sorted,' he said. 'We've shaken on it.'

'You seem very pleased,' said Axel in English.

'I am indeed,' said the Finn emphatically. 'I most certainly am.'

The Finns were all very cheerful but the Americans were more low key, sitting on the sofa quietly discussing something among themselves. Smiling, Axel did his Brando impression: 'We'll make them an offer they can't refuse.'

The girls brought in cocktails and Axel looked at his watch. It was ten past four.

The chef appeared in the kitchen doorway wanting a word with him. 'We're a little behind with the food. It'll be ready at about five.'

'I'd better tell them.' He said apologetically to the Americans, 'The meal will be a little late. We'll be eating at about five.'

The man in the silk suit looked at him blankly as if he did not understand what he was saying.

Axel repeated himself.

The American looked at him very calmly. 'No,' he said coldly. 'I think you have made a mistake. The meal will be served at sixteen thirty.'

Vilhjálmur watched this exchange uncomfortably. He flushed beetroot and stepped out on to the veranda hoping the breeze would cool the redness from his face. Axel wanted to tell this sun-tanned, shade-wearing son of a bitch to go to the devil. He wanted to pick up the dish of fish delicacies and throw it over his fine silk suit. The Finns were aware of the awkwardness and waited in silence. There was considerable tension in the room. Too much money was at stake, far too much money. Axel turned and walked quickly into the kitchen. 'Robbi, they're insisting on eating at half past four. If they can't have it at half past four you can chuck the whole lot out on to the lavafield.' In the kitchen the caterers went berserk.

The guests had come out on to the veranda, where there was peace and quiet. 'I was telling them you were involved in politics,' said one of the Finns.

'That's not quite right,' said Axel grumpily.

'I told them your wife was a government minister.'

'No, there was some talk of it but it all came to nothing,' muttered Axel. 'She's a congressman.'

'A congressman, well I'll be damned!' said one of the Americans. '"My wife's a congressman,"' he told his colleagues. 'How do you like that?'

At half past four the dishes of seafood were laid out on the table and Vilhjálmur asked the guests to help themselves. The waitresses stood stiffly at each end of the table but now it turned out the Americans weren't interested in eating at all. The food stayed untouched until seven minutes to five when Axel could contain himself no longer and served himself. He was careful not to put too much on his plate. One of the girls was helping an American to choose some food. The sunglasses were on the tip of his nose and his jet-black hair was brushed back from his forehead.

248

When they had finished the meal the man in the silk suit asked Axel to take a photograph of them all on the veranda. He studied them one by one as he was focusing the lens. He could not help smiling inanely. He had realized where he had seen them all before. It was in the movies! Not these actual people, but the same types. They had been strangely amused when he had quoted from *The Godfather*.

As he got the focus right and the camera shutter clicked, it struck him: 'I'm dining with the Mafia!'

25

As the helicopter lifted the corporate vice-presidents of Shadrak Inc. up into the air, Axel saw Linda appearing out of the whirlwind produced by the rotor-blades. She ran up to the veranda and into the summer home with a magazine folded under her arm. The headline on the front page read: 'Höfdabakki Prison Donation. Axel of Heidnaberg's vast profit on 100m kroner "gift"'. The photograph showed him holding the ornamental flagpole. There was a cigar in his mouth. It was taken from below, making his stomach seem huge. He read the article. The 'gift' made a decade ago had cost the country an incredible amount of money, said *Weekend*. The word 'donation' itself insulted ordinary taxpayers.

He had been hoping that this interview was dead and buried. That it would not see the light of day. Suddenly he realized who was behind its publication. The man he had at one time most revered in all the world. He rubbed his temples. 'Why did you bring me this, Linda?'

'I thought you'd want to see it as soon as possible.' She look worried. 'Did I get it wrong?'

'Just leave me alone,' he snapped at her. 'Can't you go for a walk or something?'

'Why don't you come out for a walk instead and do some fishing?' she said sullenly. 'It'll cheer you up.'

They walked through the undergrowth together. An icy wind

was blowing from the east and the lake had turned grey. Axel said nothing and gripped the rod awkwardly. There was a place he knew, a lava ridge, where you could walk a long way out into the lake. He took slow measured strides along it, still carrying his rod. 'Careful you don't fall in, Father,' she called, sounding anxious.

'No risk of that,' he whispered, raising a finger to his lips. 'I know every pebble along here. Shush! Don't talk so loudly. It scares off the fish.'

The water was waist deep. Linda sat on a slab of lava and watched her father as he turned sharply to the east. He rose up as if he was walking on invisible underwater steps. He paused and waved at her. Linda was hunched up, with her hands in her armpits and her feet braced against the ridged slab of lava sloping down into the water.

She looked back at the house built on a slope. Behind it tall pine trees rose up out of the birches. The house was a little too close to the edge of the water. Hadn't it been built with children in mind? All this water so close to the house. 'We were never allowed to play here,' she thought bitterly. Her father cast his line. He looked rather quaint with the Tyrolean hat she'd given him on his head, standing there in the water. There were ripples everywhere, scurrying to and fro across the bay, lapping around his feet and running up the shore. She remembered that he used to be rather afraid of water. 'He used to stand on the shore when I was a girl with a cigar in his mouth and his stomach sticking out, telling people to be careful if they dared to go more than a foot or two from the shore.'

The line went taut and he reeled it in furiously, hunched awkwardly over the rod. It was a big trout and he smashed its head on the ridge. Recently he had seemed so distant, as if nothing mattered, as if he didn't care about her any more. At any rate he seemed not to have mentioned the night visitor to her mother.

She heard footsteps behind her and glanced over her shoulder. Oh God, it was Gudni from the next summer home. She stood up. Gudni had appointed himself leader of the little community and had become indispensable to Axel and Theódóra. He was a large man in his sixties, overweight and red-faced. Linda had the feeling he had come along to express his understanding and sympathy and he gave it away immediately by his awkward, embarrassed manner, which he tried to hide by turning his face into the strong wind. He was nervous and secretly pleased both at the same time and shuffled his weight from one foot to the other.

'Has he caught anything?'

'Yes, a trout,' she said, irritated.

'It's too windy.'

'And far too cold.' She turned away from him and looked out over the lake, shivering with cold. The clouds slowly parted and for a moment they were standing in a column of fire, with the autumn sky ablaze, the surface flashing with light and her father walking on the water. He neared the shore, sank up to his waist, carving his way through the lake, holding his rod high in his right hand and showing off the trout in his left. 'This is a fair old size,' he said as he came up the bank.

'It certainly is.' Gudni laughed.

'He was waiting for me,' bragged Axel. 'He just didn't want to take the bait.'

'Didn't you have a fly?'

'Oh, I caught him with a fly,' boasted Axel.

'This is a four-pound fish!'

The mossy ground came alive in the sunshine. 'What did I say to you, Linda? We'll have trout for supper tonight, my girl. There was no need to shop.' Linda found something artificial in all the jollity. She was ready to protect her father, to make sure Gudni didn't get a chance to bring up the scandal.

'I bought potatoes and butter,' she said sulkily. She had also bought something else, something special to make him happy, his favourite cheese.

'Of course you have to have Icelandic butter with fresh trout,' said Gudni, trying to keep things light, keeping his eyes constantly on Axel and scarcely able to contain himself.

The men set off in the direction of the houses. Her father was talking too much; he was talking too loudly. Gudni was nodding and not getting the opportunity to get a word in edgeways. It looked to Linda from the expression on his face that he was trying to stifle an evil grin. The path through the lava narrowed and the men were walking shoulder to shoulder. Suddenly her father turned round and handed the trout to her without comment. She inserted a finger into the gills. The sun dipped behind a cloud, but it was only for a moment. Then it was shining on the east end of the lake, then, just as suddenly, on the west end of the island, setting the black sand ablaze. She listened to the conversation and could hear her father on the defensive. Yet Gudni hadn't said anything. His manner was provocation enough. Axel was talking about some annoying hold-up with the import-tax officials, and no it didn't apply only to him. 'No, it's not just me, Gudni,' he said, seeming to excuse himself. 'There's a lot of other people caught up in this.' The other man was laughing continuously, as if he could not suppress his merriment, and was clumsily honing the anecdote for his wife on his return home: 'He's a wreck, the poor sod. And as for the daughter, she just clings to him all the time, just like the old girl.' Linda took in Gudni's appearance, the green anorak, the trainers. It was obvious he'd got dressed in a hurry because he'd neglected to tuck one trouser leg into the woollen sock. They had arrived at the gate. Her father rested a hand on it. He had always been easily hurt and the expression in his eyes showed how vulnerable he was. Linda felt he was about to unburden himself of all these confidential matters, lay it all on his neighbour, look to Gudni for comfort. She couldn't bear to watch. She went up to the gate and opened it. 'Well, here we are,' she said brightly. 'Father, I'm so hungry, I'm absolutely starving. Nice seeing you again, Gudni. Say hello to your wife for us.'

It was good to be in the safety of one's own garden in the shade of the trees. The fir trees swayed in the wind, just like animated trees in a cartoon. It would come as no surprise if they were to tear themselves up by the roots, gather round the roof and strike up a conversation. Linda went up to the veranda. There were two ravens cawing above the house. They hovered above the waves and there was a brilliant sheen on their plumage. Linda opened the front door. The oven was alight. The smell that was the soul of the summer home came wafting towards her. She put the trout on the kitchen table. It was almost dusk and the thick electric element in the oven glowed bright in the gloaming. She looked out into the garden and saw the old red-painted swing frame and her father's face. It was as if all he could do was defend himself. The trees around him swayed to and fro. His mouth was moving all the time.

'He's talking all sense out of himself,' she thought. 'I'll have to call him.'

She went out on to the veranda. 'Father!' she shouted but he did not hear her. She cupped her hands round her mouth and yelled, 'Father!'

He turned round. She did not feel she could shout again and beckoned him indoors. He behaved as if he hadn't noticed, turned back to Gudni and carried on talking, talking, talking. Anger boiled up within her. 'Yackety, yackety, yack.' She grimaced, cupped her hands round her mouth again and screamed, 'Father!'

The wind carried the cry to him and at long last he started to close the gate, not looking towards the house, still saying a few more words to his neighbour. Almost apologetically he pulled the gate to and inclined his head towards his neighbour. She ran into the house and watched him come up the path. Suddenly she realized that her coming would have brought him additional stress.

She heard him walking on to the veranda. He opened the door and said, sounding worried and annoyed, 'What's all the fuss, Linda? Why are you shouting at me like this, girl?'

'Girl' was the word he used when he was telling her off, to show her that although she might be his only daughter, even the only woman in his life, there were some things she couldn't get away with. 'I could see the old fool was wearing you out.'

'That's ridiculous. Gudni's a good sort. What's all this about? What time is it?'

'Getting on for eight.'

'Your mother should have been here by now,' he said, sounding anxious.

The cold wind blew through the house. 'Father, you must close the door. We'll lose all the warmth.'

He closed it from the outside and walked past the windows. She knew he was looking at the parking space, listening for the sounds of traffic on the gravel road. He reappeared in the next window, sat down on a garden chair on the veranda and struggled to pull his boots off. He propped his fishing rod up in a corner. The lake behind him was grey. The wind was whipping up the surface of the water and clouds were scurrying around the mountain peaks.

He had managed to lighten his mood and was relaxed and

talkative. 'Well, Linda, wasn't it a good idea to come out to the summer home and meet your old dad?'

'Yes. Shall we eat? I'm famished.'

'I think we ought to wait for your mother.' He glanced at his watch.

'Yes, but at least I could put the potatoes on to boil,' she said stubbornly, teasing him. 'I want to eat right away!'

He gave in. 'OK, you do what you like, my dear. But I've had quite enough fish for one day myself.'

She turned on the gas and put a pink saucepan on the hob. She put potatoes into the saucepan. They floated in the water, looking rather lonely. Her father cut the head off the trout, slit it open, gutted it, rubbed along the spine with his thumb and then neatly cut it into pieces. Night was falling swiftly and the autumn darkness covered the wood on the far side of the lake, painting the island black. The wind lashed the trees. Outside the window there was a small yellow square of light from Gudni's house. Axel opened the fridge and was pleased to find a bottle of white wine. 'I'd intended your mother to be sharing this with us.'

'Father,' she said, 'I've brought some cheese for you and me. Camembert, your favourite! It's nice and runny. Let's have a glass of wine and eat together. I think, father and daughter, we've earned the right to have a nice time together.'

Grudgingly he looked round for a corkscrew. While he was doing so he talked about the wine. He told her where in France it was produced. 'I passed through there a few years ago. It's an excellent wine. Good people to do business with. They told me a strange story from the Second World War. A French division and a German division met in the valley. And what do you think? Instead of driving through the vineyards, the tanks made a detour round them and fought to one side. Yes, human beings can be weird, Linda.' For some reason the story seemed to make him sad.

He found two long-stemmed glasses, ran them under the tap and shook the water off them. He sat beside her at the table. The candlelight drew deep lines on his face. She noticed a small black scab on his scalp just on the hairline. He poured the wine into the glasses, swung it round and sipped it like an experienced wine-taster. He was looking tired and a little puffy in the face. It was darker now and the wind had grown even stronger. Linda sipped the wine. It had a good, clean taste. There were no bitter overtones. The aftertaste was fruity. She found traces of apples and pears. Her father disagreed. 'No, this is pure grape,' he said. 'Quite outstanding! But I still haven't managed to get it taken up by the state monopoly.' He pointed to the bottle. 'This is a sample.'

'Well,' she said, 'I'll be off abroad any day now to pursue my education.'

'It's going to be lonely at Dyngjuvegur without you.'

'Don't forget I'll be back. I've made my decision. It's going to be the piano.'

'Ah, so that's it, you're going to study the piano.' He was taking no interest whatsoever.

'What's the matter, Father? Is it the stuff in the papers?'

He shook his head and topped up the glasses. 'No, my skin's thicker than that.'

'What is it then?'

'I think it's just that I'm getting old, Linda. I don't get any pleasure from the business any more.'

She looked pensively into her glass. 'Is it Mother?'

'Among other things,' he admitted finally and made a face. 'It's always been like a shadow between us that she couldn't have a child and that I already had you. But you must be aware of that?'

She nodded, looking solemn. She was glad that he seemed more relaxed and that they were talking about something other than the shares. 'Yes, I think I've always known it.'

'She thinks I've betrayed her by being honest about it,' he said, suddenly animated again. 'But what could I do? They didn't discuss it with me before they went ahead and bought them.'

'Bought them! Bought them! Bought them!' thought Linda. Bought the shares. It was always the same thing. Now it was pitch black outside. The clouds had cleared. A yellow beam of light stretched from the moon straight across the lake and over the island. It was so dark that was all that could be seen of the lake.

'Mother is so ambitious. She hasn't achieved what she wanted as a politician. What is this shame you're meant to have brought on her? She seems to forget how highly the Prime Minister thought of you. She just wanted to take her revenge. She was ignored. What woman can put up with that?'

Without saying anything he poured some more wine into her glass and the rest into his own. Then he said, 'The truth is Hannes was afraid of Theódóra. He must have thought she'd use that business years ago when I got Hördur to substitute the blood sample at the City Hospital when he was accused of drink-driving. But I never told Tedda about it. It never occurred to me to do so. The thing is your mother had decided to get out of politics and then she changed her mind.'

'Oh God!' She leapt up and ran into the kitchen. 'The potatoes must be boiled dry.' She turned on the light above the hob and lifted the saucepan lid. The skins had burst and started peeling away from the flesh. She picked up a dishcloth and moved the saucepan across to another ring. She filled another pan with water. All the time the gas was hissing viciously. She picked up the breadboard with the trout on it and let the fish slide into the water. She grabbed the salt cellar and shook salt over it. Her father stood up, surprisingly drunk. 'I think I'm just going to pop over to Gudni's, Linda, my dear, and give him back a bottle of wine I borrowed last spring.'

'The trout'll be ready in no time,' she pleaded.

'I won't be a moment.'

He slipped his feet into some shoes and put on an overcoat. He took the torch from the shelf by the window and took a bottle out of the coolbox. He opened the door and the icy gale ripped through the house. 'It'll be on the table in fifteen minutes,' she shouted.

In the darkness she watched the beam of light dancing down the garden path, disappearing when it was masked by the undergrowth and she could make out neither man nor trees. Then the light appeared again by the gate, darted about the mossy ground and set off for Gudni's summer home. Then she could see her father again by the light of the moon. The water was coming to the boil and she reduced the heat under the trout. She felt physically light and easy, pleasantly aware of her own body. The wine had done her good. She looked in the fridge. There was another bottle. He wouldn't mind if she opened it. She found the corkscrew, cut away the plastic seal, pushed the metal spike down into the cork and then pulled as hard as she could. At first the cork would not give and then at last it began to slide out with a quiet sucking sound. She sat down and poured herself half a glass. Theódóra would not be coming. It was inevitable that her father would have got himself involved in some endless conversation with Gudni. Her pride stopped her from going and fetching him back. She wouldn't be able to avoid being asked in by Gudni and the old lady and the trout would end up as fish broth. Linda took the saucepan off the heat and set it down on the breadboard. She lifted the lid and the smell filled the living room. The butter was burning and had begun to turn black. She quickly lifted the pan with the white handle, turned off the hob and walked across to the window. The lights were burning bright in the neighbouring house. God only knew when her father would come back. Probably he was trying to shed new light on the matter, laying all his cards on the table, trying to get those people to understand that he was OK really. 'I hate the lot of them,' she said under her breath.

She drained the fish and the potatoes. It'll serve him right if it's cold. Not her fault. She sat down and poured some wine into her glass and then tipped the glass down her throat. He had hardly touched the cheese. She drank another glass, brooding the while. It was nearly ten o'clock when she came back to herself. She was drunk. She was irritated to find she'd lost her appetite. She picked at the fish, letting it stand on the table. He'd see the plate when he came back, he'd see that even this, the one solitary meal they'd share before she left the country, had come to nought. The gas heater was humming in the dark. She blew out the candle. Outside the lake was boiling like a storm-tossed sea. The moon was tinged with pink and touched the waves with a cold, yellow light. She enjoyed moving about the house in the dark. She opened her bedroom door and felt for her bed. She found it, found the sleeping bag and the duvet, the blanket. It was all cold to the touch and the blanket was coarse and furry. A draught of cold air shot into the living room. The branch of a tree was beating on the roof and she found the sound comforting. She unfastened her shoes and put them on the floor. It was a tiled floor. The action was familiar to her. She snuggled down into the sleeping bag, covering herself with the duvet and the blanket, zipped the sleeping bag up to her shoulder. She was shivering with cold. She crossed her arms over her breast and crossed her legs. She tried to summon up some erotic fantasy but was too tired. Her mind was whirling round, full of some nonsense or other, until she could hardly tell the difference between dream and reality. 'A mistress!' she heard her mother scream, her voice like a raging tempest. It was all the same to her if she could be heard out in the street. The girl was afraid of the memory. 'What do you think people will think when they see you bringing a young woman into the house!' Linda was nearly asleep and murmuring something to herself. She had heard rumours about the Prime Minister since she was little girl. How can Father let this get to him? Hannes Pálmason had often come to the parties at Dyngjuvegur. His hands were big and warm, unlike many of the other guests, whose hands were always cold. He has a habit of holding his glass in his left hand with a napkin round it. 'So this is Linda! This is our little Linda! I've heard so much about her. And now she's nineteen!' And he takes the time to talk to her. Nods dismissively at some lesser mortal, irritated at being interrupted. The air between them is electric. Linda keeps one eye on her mother, moving gracefully from room to room.

Did she hear tyres on gravel and an engine turned off or was it a dream? Was she awake or was she sleeping while quiet voices talked in the living room? Did she hear the bed creak in the room next door as her parents settled down, or was it only her father lying down on his own? Perhaps no one came into the house? Did her mother sit up waiting through the long reaches of the night? Did she see her in a dream, sitting at the table, looking grey, haggard, sad? The woman who did not become a government minister. The woman who was insulted in public. I must comfort my mother. She reaches down for her shoes and her hands are met by the cold tiles. It is pitch black in the house. The air is dense, tastes sour. She is lying on the floor. She has crawled out of the sleeping bag and is coughing. Her face is near the tiles, gulping for air. There is sharp bitter smoke in her eyes. She wants to stand up but she can't. Where's the door? Where's the window? I've got to get out! I don't want to die here! Her hand searches wildly and finds the radiator. She must be under the window; she knows where to aim for. She crawls on her stomach over to the door but the door is shut. A lizard flies across the floor, right by her face, she can feel its tail hit her cheek. She does not remember shutting the door when she crawled into bed but the door is definitely locked. She gets to her knees, grabs the doorknob, manages to open the door and suddenly she knows the house is on fire. The living room is black, full of dense, sour smoke, deadly and terrifying. There is no time, no chance of saving anybody. I've got to get out, oh God, oh God, oh God, I don't want to die. Jesus Christ, Jesus Christ, I don't want to die. She crawls across the floor, making hissing, sucking sounds and reaches the living-room table. There is something warm and heavy there. Her lungs are full of smoke, an agonizing smoke, it is like a knife being driven into her lungs, like barbed wire deep in her lungs with someone trying to drag it out through her back or out through her throat, but it's stuck and won't budge. She rolls on to the veranda, coughing and groaning. It is bright dawn. She crawls a little way and collapses on the grass, nearly blinded and coughing, coughing. Black smoke pours out of the door. She must get back inside, save her father, save her father! She tries to stand up but everything is happening so quickly. As the smoke is pouring out of the house, oxygen is being sucked back in. There is an explosion. The house is a crystal of pure fire as dawn is breaking. At the living-room table she can see a human being burning brightly. It is the woman who was unable to have a child. The intense heat pinions her upright. It seems to Linda as if the short hair in the nape of Theódóra's neck suddenly flares. Fire is leaping out of the windows. The house crackles with the heat. She backs away down the slope. There is almost no space left for her on solid ground because of the heat. She backs away down to the edge of the lake. All this water so close to the fire! She leans against the old swing frame and coughs up her liver and her lungs. She feels the cold wind off the lake at her back.

And she is standing there when Gudni comes running up to her, fussing away. He looks funny hopping about in the grass in his nightshirt with shoes and no socks. Some of the trees have caught alight. The living-room table is burning intensely although no one can be seen sitting there.

'Did you escape unscathed?' asks Gudni. 'Is everybody safe? I can't find my lizard.' He looks at her, strangely offhand. 'Your father's been so happy since you wore that engagement ring at the National Theatre Cellar in the spring.'

Linda does not answer. She does not understand what he means. She looks at the water. It looks different. It is azure blue. The beach is white. An old man in a long robe is standing there. Linda snatches up some of the white sand in her hands and kneads it into a lump of clay that takes on a life of its own, separate from her fingers and her palms. The clay has become a bird that shakes itself alive and flies out of her hands. And the old man who has been watching from afar says, 'Jesus Christ does not come for the clay. He moulds it.'

At these words the girl woke up in the dark and unzipped her sleeping bag. She was shaken and sweating. She went through to the living room where the gas heater with its yellow and blue flame was humming. Her father wasn't in the living room. She opened the door on to the veranda. The trees were tossing wildly in the darkness. She picked up her watch from the living-room table. It was midnight. She peeped into Axel's bedroom. There was no one there. She got dressed quickly, grabbed an overcoat off a peg, walked through the undergrowth across to Gudni's summer home. It was all in darkness. She hesitated to disturb them. Where the hell could her father be? Was the man fishing in the dark? She walked along the lake, the wind tearing at her hair. The wind had turned southerly and the moon was bright. She reached the bay and saw their boat had drifted ashore. Its stern was stuck on the bank of lava and the water was lashing it furiously. The lake was like the open sea with breakers catching the light of the moon in the darkness. She cupped her hands to her mouth and called twice, 'Father!' She could scarcely hear her own voice above the storm.

The girl stands there for some time, looking at the boat which should not be here, abandoned and battered against the shore, when it should be safely beached by the house. Then she prepares herself to address the whole business of growing up and the promises the dream made her by dragging the boat up the shore to safety.

PART II

26

When I think back to the autumn of 1994 and the events that, in my opinion, led to the death of Axel Sigurgeirsson, I maintain that I knew all along who was responsible for the attacks on him. Having once been an editor, I was not entirely innocent of such extreme measures myself. Rumour soon spread the name in question all over town, even though there was no likelihood of conclusive proof.

The editor of *Weekend* at the time was obliged to resign. It went even further than that. He was advised to leave the country. Several of Axel's friends simply threatened to kill him at the Lief Ericksson Terminal should he dare to return in the foreseeable future. The question of whether Seli had had a heart attack or died by his own hand was never satisfactorily resolved. I rather incline to the view that it was an accident. The lake was certainly rough that night.

Axel's funeral was held with great pomp and ceremony at Hallgrímskirkja. He was laid to rest at Gufunes. A long cortege headed by the undertaker's hearse drove slowly up Ártúnbrekka. When they drew level with the Heidnaberg complex, the cars slowed to a halt and paused while the flag was first raised and allowed to fall to half-mast.

Morgunbladid printed a double-page spread of obituaries. All sorts of people appeared there saying good things about Axel. He had solved so many people's problems. He had even been kindly disposed towards begging letters. Telegrams arrived from overseas. Toyota sent a representative. Hallgrímskirkja was packed and a host of people followed on to the graveside – including me. Theódóra had no idea that Axel had been so popular. There was talk of raising a monument to him, but, in view of Heidnaberg's extraordinary wealth, setting up a memorial appeal fund did not seem appropriate. At the time of writing, there has been no further progress on the matter of a public monument.

Theódóra invited the mourners for coffee at the Pearl restaurant. People had to wait to be seated. As she gazed across the room she realized Axel Sigurgeirsson had been in the wrong line of business. He should have gone into politics. The thought made her sad. There was never an adequate explanation of why five hundred attended the burial service but seven hundred took coffee at Pearl, although I'm sure this would have delighted Seli, with his fondness for food. It was a warm autumn day and the sea round the Álftanes shimmered in the sunshine.

A week later Hördur Gottskálksson appeared in the Reykjavík Magistrate's Court. The case had attracted a lot of public attention. Channel 2 filmed the doctor arriving. Vilhelmína caught the item on that evening's news bulletin and, contrary to her natural inclinations, felt a degree of pride. Hördur entered the building with his head slightly bowed, running his fingers through his long hair. He had exactly the same posture as when he was pretending to be completely innocent in the course of some marital dispute. 'He knows he's in the wrong,' she thought. A court usher glanced down the corridor and looked into the camera lens before closing the door of Court 301.

The defendant, Hördur Gottskálksson, was represented by the Defence Counsel, Ásgeir Bjarnson. The Prosecuting Counsel faced the Defence and the senior judge and his accompanying magistrates sat at one end of the courtroom wearing long black silk robes. Rows of chairs were tightly wedged from the entrance to the window corner. Dagný sat by the window and Hördur sat beside his counsel. The first witness to be called was Gunnar Bragason, the doctor's driver. All Hördur needed to do was take one look at him to know his evidence would not be helpful. The previous evening he had rung Gunnar to suggest he did not mention the visit to the house on Sogavegur. There was, in any case, no record of the fact that they had made the Sogavegur call a priority.

Gunnar Bragason fidgeted throughout his time in the witness box. He announced that Hördur had insisted on them going to Sogavegur before they went to Thingholtstræti, even though he had kept on telling the doctor they should answer the call to the possible heart attack immediately.

The Prosecuting Counsel stabbed at his papers with his pen impatiently. 'And what was the doctor on call's response?'

'He used the word "hysteria".'

'Hysteria?'

'Yes.'

'How long did the doctor on call spend with the patient at Sogavegur?'

'Ten or fifteen minutes. We thought it might be a bleeding stomach ulcer but the patient had eaten too much rhubarb pudding.' Gunnar glanced at Hördur. He was hoping the rhubarb pudding would help the doctor's case. However, judging from the Prosecuting Counsel's expression, it didn't seem to be having the desired effect.

'Did the doctor on call smell of alcohol?'

Gunnar nodded.

'Will the witness please answer the question?'

'Yes.'

'I would like the witness's response to that question to be noted,' said the Prosecuting Counsel, looking stern.

Gunnar Bragason left the court without having the courage to look in Hördur's direction. Hördur had stared at Gunnar through-out his evidence. Witnesses were called one by one. First Dagný, then Tryggvi. She recounted in great detail everything that had already been said about Hördur's visit to 28 Thingholtstræti. Tryggvi fidgeted nervously in his seat and backed up her evidence. A clerk recorded the information on a computer. When Hördur himself went into the witness box, he tried to justify his actions with his now familiar reasoning. Out of the corner of his eye he could see Dagný looking at him with a triumphant grin.

'How could it even occur to someone to assess a heart patient over the radio?' asked the Prosecution aggressively. He stared at Hördur Gottskálksson unblinkingly. 'The defendant ought to be ashamed of himself.'

Hördur looked at the magistrates, amazed that neither his counsel nor the senior judge should intervene and put a stop to statements such as this. The verdict was announced around the middle of October and the doctor decided immediately to lodge an appeal to the High Court. His sentence was two years' imprisonment, suspended for two years. He was found guilty of manslaughter by reason of recklessness and his licence to practise was withdrawn. However, he could continue to practise pending the outcome of the appeal. Damages were not considered at this time in order to reach a swift verdict. Dagný decided to go for a private prosecution.

Hördur could not believe it. Was there no justice in Iceland? He felt the prosecution was aimed not solely at him, but at the medical profession as a whole, that the general downturn in economic conditions meant that the public was being encouraged to scrutinize the actions of the profession unjustifiably. He was confident the Medical Union would make public declarations in the media in support of his case. The day after the verdict his photograph was taken as he got out of his car on Kirkjustræti. He turned to face the photographer, who promptly took another picture. He did not have to ask what publication it was for. 'You killed Seli,' he thought coldly. 'But you won't kill me.' Hördur smiled. He surprised himself. People thought he would crack under the pressure. He had even half expected it himself. But the stronger the opposition, the better he felt. If he lost the appeal in the High Court he would have to sell his flat. Then Vilhelmína would really have to fight her corner with regard to her stepmother's estate. These last few weeks Theódóra had used Axel's death as an excuse to avoid dealing with it.

On the front steps at Skólabrú stood a little girl waiting for him. She was armed with a toy rifle. 'I've come for my mother's prescription. Her name's Ásta. She rang you yesterday.'

Hördur went into the waiting room, sat down, calmly took off his shoes and stretched out for his sandals. The child followed him indoors and said, 'Bang!' He looked up. The girl was standing in the doorway holding the rifle and looking at him solemnly. She had greasy fair hair hanging down to her shoulders and chubby cheeks. She pointed the rifle at him. 'Bang!' The doctor fell back in his chair, limp. His legs stretched and twitched. Then his head slumped forward on to his chest.

The girl dropped her rifle. 'There was a woman here but I told her you hadn't come yet. She said she'd come back later.'

The doctor didn't answer.

The girl repeated what she'd said and came up to him. She poked him with the rifle. 'Say something.'

He opened one of his eyes, grinned and said, pleased with himself, 'I can't. I'm dead.'

'But you're talking.'

'That's only because I'm a ghost.' As quick as lightning, he grabbed the rifle, pointed it at the little girl and blasted away at her furiously. 'Bang! Bang! Bang! Now you're dead! I shot you with my last breath!'

'No,' she said. 'I'm still standing.'

'I see. When you shoot me I'm supposed to drop down dead. But when I shoot you the rules have changed,' he said, in a filthy temper. 'God, you're all the same!'

'It's my game. I make up the rules.'

'Oh, get out!' he said, bored with the whole thing. 'Tell your mother I don't write prescriptions for junkies.' The girl made for the door. He changed his mind. 'No, on second thoughts, come here, you poor little thing. Victims like us ought to stick together.'

The phone rang a bit later and he let it ring a long time. He was sure it was Vilhelmína asking about the verdict. But when the phone went on and on ringing he picked up the receiver. It was a female journalist from *Weekend*. She wanted to know how Hördur felt. Although he felt inclined to threaten to break every bone in her body, he knew it was vitally important to keep calm. If he slammed down the phone it would be easy for the magazine to turn it into a triumph. He told her he would be appealing.

'And what if you lose the case in the High Court?'

'Perhaps we should wait and see what happens.'

'Do you think the Medical Union will support you? The Chief Physician perhaps?' Behind her voice he could hear the noise and bustle of the press room.

'I would certainly expect so.'

'I think perhaps you ought to check that out. I was just talking to them and it's not a foregone conclusion by any means. The Chief Physician said that although there isn't a precedent for withdrawing a doctor's licence to practise in cases such as this, it's quite common overseas. And it seemed to me that the Medical Union wasn't at all interested.'

'As I say,' said Hördur, tried to control the hostility in his voice, 'let's wait and see what the High Court has to say. It's still the country's supreme court. I did only what doctors throughout the world do as a matter of course. Thank you, but I don't intend prolonging this conversation.' He put down the receiver.

He looked outside. It was beginning to get dark even though it wasn't yet three o'clock. As dusk fell it began to rain and the temperature dropped. A cold wintery sleet began to freeze on the window. The door to the waiting room was open. He heard a noise and went to the door. There was an old woman who had kept faith with him for a long time sitting in the waiting room. 'And how are you, my dear Gudrún?' asked the doctor. 'What's the matter?'

She began to rock backwards and forwards in her chair as soon as he spoke to her. 'I hurt all over, my dear Hördur.'

'I think that's how we all feel,' he said and smiled. 'Would you like to come in?' She walked into the surgery and sat facing him at his desk. He listened with half an ear to the catalogue of symptoms that hadn't changed at all over the years. A burst blood vessel. A headache. 'Do you want the ones with stripes or the ones with spots?'

'Give me what you gave me last time.'

He got out his pad and quickly wrote her a prescription.

'People treat you so badly,' she said.

'So, you read the papers, do you, Gudrún?'

'Yes. And I can tell you, Hördur,' the old woman said, 'that it doesn't matter to me what they say. You'd always be welcome to cut me open. Even if you were dead drunk.' She looked at him solemnly. 'You are my doctor and I shall always put my faith in you. I put my life in your hands.'

'It's good to know that I've got the support of decent people,' he said, and smiled. 'Now, if you'll just sign your name here and then I can take the chitty over to the Reykjavík Health Service and get some butter to put on my bread.'

The old woman scribbled her name and he showed her out. The weather had settled again and the streets were shimmering with frost. It was nearly five. He sat at his desk and lit a cigarette. Suddenly it struck him that the journalist had been right. It was unlikely anyone would speak up for him, not the Medical Union nor the Chief Physician. They'd been waiting for years for the chance to ditch him. 'They're fools,' he thought and remembered the one and only time he'd gone to the annual Doctors' Ball and conjured up the faces of his colleagues, laughing, clutching their glasses, leaning on the bar, talking nonsense. Arseholes educated in Sweden. 'I lost so much when I lost Axel,' he thought. 'Is it possible the Prime Minister was behind the attacks on Seli? Surely it can't be. Wasn't it Theódóra's doing? Everyone says he took his own life. The man holding the country's highest office just doesn't take risks like that. Seli was a damn fool anyway, a fine fellow but a damn fool. Now it's time for me to put a little pressure on that prat Haraldur Sumarlidason.' He derived considerable pleasure from remembering Haraldur half dead with fright in the plane. 'That shower don't seem to have managed to do too much for me as yet. Perhaps it's understandable. The Prime Minister doesn't seem to be having too good a time of it at the moment.'

There seemed to be a serious rift in the government coalition. The Radical Left was insisting on investment interest being taxed. It was also asking for paper profits on shares to be taxed. The Independent Party was flatly refusing to consider this. The trade unions were agitating as well and it looked as if strikes were looming. Hördur had seen Hannes in the street. He looked pale and tired. 'Poor Prime Minister,' thought Hördur. 'It's not only me that's got troubles.'

Suddenly he came back to himself. The cigarette had burned down to his fingers. He looked at it. The long grey column of ash balanced precariously. On the news the previous evening there had been an item about a boy going beserk in a small town in France. He had murdered his brother, his mother and his stepfather with a hammer and then he'd gone out with a rifle and killed nine people on the street before shooting himself in the head. It was fascinating to wonder what was behind it. Hördur sat at the table for a long time. He found the silence in the house comforting. 'Would I be capable of something like that?' he thought and imagined Gunnar Bragason's head exploding with the blast from a shotgun. The Judge and the Prosecuting Counsel went the same way. Bam! Bam! Straight in the chest as they opened their front doors. Why not do something spectacular like that? Shuffle the world like you'd shuffle a pack of cards?

He could hear someone. It was Ester coming home. A lot later he heard banging on the front door. He listened. It didn't seem as if Ester was going to come downstairs and open the door. She often couldn't be bothered, the lazy girl. There was another bang. He stood up stiffly and went and opened the door.

He stared, dumbstruck, at the Prime Minister himself.

27

The Prime Minister wasn't wearing anything on his head. He smiled broadly, revealing a small gap between his front teeth. His cheeks were red with the cold and he was carrying a briefcase. 'Hello there!' he roared.

Hördur didn't budge from the doorway.

'I clean forgot to ask you the other day whether you'd mind just giving me a quick once over if you'd got a moment. There's something odd going on with my heart.' The Prime Minister shuffled to and fro on the step. 'It's so convenient to be able to drop in on you like this. You're only a stone's throw from the parliament building.' He raised his voice. 'Let me in, man! I'm freezing out here.'

Hördur moved back from the door. 'Be my guest.' As he turned he saw Ester standing halfway up the stairs.

'Who is it, Father?'

'It's OK,' said Hördur. 'It's for me.' He'd scarcely been able to grasp what was going on.

The Prime Minister had walked into the hall. He nodded at Ester who came downstairs to shake his hand. She ran back upstairs.

'Seli was always telling me there was no one in the country better qualified than you.' The Prime Minister was looking over the waiting room like a carpenter who can't help appraising the woodwork whenever he visits his friends.

Hördur nodded. The friendly down-to-earth manner of the most important man in the country was making a good impression on him.

'Qualifications from the best teaching hospitals! Hands-on

270

experience in the best hospitals! That's the way to do it.' The Prime Minister put his briefcase on a chair.

'I took part in the first heart transplant done in the United States.'

'So Seli told me.' The Prime Minister smiled. 'You realize we haven't shaken hands yet!'

They shook hands. The Prime Minister's hand was large and hot and rough. Hördur's hand was cold, something that always annoyed him. He had had poor circulation all his life. All the stresses and strains of his life went straight to his hands. If the Prime Minister noticed anything he didn't show it. 'We Icelanders don't make the best use of our own people,' he said, and turned taking off his overcoat into a great performance. 'It's a national trait. It's a curse. Every time someone shows a bit of natural ability, we try and cut him down to size. All independent endeavour in Iceland is smashed by simple envy. It's how it's always been and I dare say how it always will be. The national character is nothing to write home about, but don't tell anyone I said so.' He hung up his overcoat and looked at Hördur.

'What the hell does the man want?' thought the doctor and tried to steady his nerves. The unexpected visit had disturbed him. 'After all that's gone on you've got to give him credit for his guts. Doesn't he realize I'm Theódóra's brother-in-law and could pass on everything he says to her? Doesn't it worry him that more than half the country thinks he had a hand in Seli's death? Does he know my sister-in-law and I don't exactly get on? Has he heard the outcome of the court case already? Perhaps he thinks I'm nearly done for and this is a good chance to exploit me in some way. I've heard that's how he goes about things.' He decided to tread very carefully and to go on the offensive. 'Everyone seems to have got it in for me these days,' he said, with a edgy smile.

He thought the Prime Minister would either ignore this completely or contradict it vehemently, but his reply took him by surprise. 'Yes. I thought it might be appropriate to see what I could do on your behalf, offer a bit of first aid as it were. That's more or less why I've come. There's a rumour that the fair sex is thinking of setting up a new political grouping on the far right.' Hannes was waiting politely outside the surgery door. Hördur went ahead of him and pointed to a chair.

'I really don't know why I haven't been to see you before now,' the Prime Minister said as he sat down. He looked almost boyish. 'You're only a stone's throw away! I love the old town centre. I live in Hólavallagata. I don't see any reason to dash off to the new town just for a check-up. I was only saying to my wife at lunch, we should take our ailments to Dr Hördur Gottskálksson. People are trying to destroy his reputation at the moment so he's bound to understand if I tell him these rumours doing the rounds about Axel are nothing to do with me.' The Prime Minister looked up. 'Now how may I help you? You came to see me the other day.'

'What!' Hördur was taken completely by surprise.

'You came and saw me in the spring and told me something of your problems. I suggested you contact the Minister of Health and I regret to say that was not sound advice. I'm not entirely without influence myself, you know.' Hannes poked his tongue into his cheek and looked meaningfully at the doctor. Then he shook his head sadly. 'But just between you and me, the Minister of Health's a bastard.'

Hördur pretended to recall all his troubles as if they weren't already in the forefront of his mind. 'Everybody's out to get me these days,' he said. 'I lost a court case today.' And to his surprise he found himself opening his heart to this complete stranger. He felt as if he had known him for a long time, so familiar did the Prime Minister's face seem from the television. He talked about his background and his education while the Prime Minister rolled up his sleeve to have his blood pressure taken. It had been so hard for him, a country lad from the Landbrot, coming to Reykjavík and supporting himself with casual jobs here and there while he got himself an education. 'I used to be a debt collector. My guts still knot up every single time I go into an office building. That's because of how we used to be received then. I can imagine what people then would have to say about young people nowadays wanting to live with their parents well into their forties.' He told Hannes all the difficulties he had had to overcome to get an education, how he'd made all the spoiled brats of daddy's boys look like prats when he got top marks in the examinations. 'And then when I came back to Iceland,' said the doctor and he frowned and paused. 'I had planned to put my education to good use. But shall we say I got a rather hot reception. It was as if I'd been excommunicated!'

Hördur squeezed the rubber ball. The needle rose and fell on the sphygmomanometer. The lower measurement was a little on the high side. He squeezed again. 'I don't much like the look of this,' he said, looking worried. 'Your blood pressure's up. The lower reading is far too high.'

'Well, that's only to be expected, I suppose.'

'She's giving you a hard time, is she, my sister-in-law?' said Hördur, moving to and fro and looking at him out of the corner of his eye. 'That's how it is, isn't it?'

'Tedda?' The Prime Minister looked at him and seemed to be genuinely surprised. He took his white vest off over his head in one swift movement and sat facing the doctor who had not asked him to get undressed. He was a big-built man and his skin was very white. His chest was unusually flat. 'Theódóra's no more bother than anyone else,' he said. 'The women in this country have gone bonkers. She's no worse than the rest of them. At least you know where you are with her. But you know her a far sight better than I do.' The Minister glanced sideways at Hördur. 'I've heard she's planning to split the party. To stage a walk-out with the other ladies and set up a party of her own. That's what tends to happen when people don't get their own way.'

'You've only got to look at all the schisms and factions in the Church, spreading like salmonella,' said Hördur, feeling philosophical. 'In the end the faithful say, "There's nowhere in the Church good enough for true believers like us. We'll establish our own!"'

'Exactly,' said the Prime Minister. 'I haven't heard it put better.'

Hördur placed his stethoscope over the heart. He always found this deeply affecting. It didn't matter how often he listened to the beating of different hearts, of the young or of the old, of criminals or of the great and the good, he was always moved to hear this thundering powerhouse of life. The heart was almost like an autonomous living creature within the body. If the heart was strong, then the patient was strong. The heart reflected any sickness, whether of the body or of the soul. And now The Prime Minister's heart skipped a beat. The Prime Minister looked up, like a child, and said, 'You see!'

Hördur took away the stethoscope and folded it up. 'If you were my patient, I would certainly recommend you to take a bit of time away from work.' He looked down at the Prime Minister's body. A single grey hair grew from one nipple. 'And get rid of the spare tyre.' He grinned and looked at Hannes. Usually a remark like that irritated his patients. But nothing seem to affect this man, even though his blood pressure told a different story.

'Yes, my dear wife's always on at me to eat her health food and go jogging, but I've no intention of having the Workers' Union or the Opposition see me in a tracksuit,' roared the Prime Minister. 'And all this muesli stuff, grit and powder in skimmed milk, no that's not me at all. I like brown sugar on it. But I can lose the weight.' The Prime Minister picked up his vest and dived into it head first. 'No sweat. There's only one answer to being fat.' He looked at Hördur who had now sat down. 'Eat less!' The doctor nodded his agreement. Hannes buttoned up his shirt. 'I'm not impressed by lack of willpower. I'm not going to spend billions of kroner to stop people drinking. There's only one solution for drunkenness: stop pouring whisky down your throat. And if you advise me to lose some weight, you just see, I'll be like a stick insect in no time. And I don't need some publicly funded programme to do it either. No jogging, no acupuncture, no drinking some slimy horrible mushroom concoction.'

'My God, you've taken the words right out of my mouth,' said the delighted doctor. 'I can't imagine more disgusting operations than stapling up stomachs or sucking out the fat from overweight women. Just imagine, asking a man of the highest education to do that! And what's the point of stapling the stomach? To be able to eat more. So everything goes through the body faster.' The doctor looked out of the window. 'When you look at it like that, I ought to be glad they elbowed me out of the hospitals. And then my wife's got this thing about reincarnation. I think she reckons she was the mistress of Genghis Khan in a previous existence. Mind you, that would explain the way she carries on!' He grinned. 'I have to say that, as far as I'm concerned, if I have to listen to any more of this feminist rubbish then I hope there *is* something to this reincarnation business and I can come back completely ignorant of the world as it is, because I really can't bear listening to the ladies any longer.

I've heard more than enough of that garbage to last me a lifetime.'

'You should have brought your problems to me sooner,' said Hannes Pálmason and brought his tightly clenched fist down on the desk. 'Sometimes it's possible to clip someone's wings, even when it's the Head of Surgery in a hospital. A Head of Surgery isn't Almighty God,' he roared angrily. Then he suddenly turned jovial. 'I must be going mad. That bloody rag *Weekend*.' The Prime Minister raised his index finger and pretended he was having trouble remembering the details of the article. 'Weren't you having a spot of bother with . . . er . . .' He clicked his fingers.

'With a madwoman.' Hördur finished the sentence for him. 'I decided not to resuscitate her mother when she was on the point of death. I was exercising my professional judgement. She had heart disease. She had been unconscious for a long time. She had a chronic condition. Braincells cannot last long without oxygen. The family were going to be lumbered with a vegetable. But what's behind it all is an attempt to extort money from me. Those people think I'm connected to Heidnaberg and I've got money coming out of my ears.' Hördur Gottskálksson looked solemnly at the Prime Minister. 'But that's not true.'

'Shouldn't you have taken a blood sample from me?'

'Whatever for?'

'Cholesterol level?'

'I really don't think that's necessary,' said the doctor. 'It's simply stress. The political life.'

'That's what I think. Might I use your phone?'

'Please do.'

The Prime Minister phoned home. 'Hello, darling. I popped in to see Dr Hördur Gottskálksson. No, everything's fine. Just need to take things a bit easy, the doctor says. The extra heartbeats are nothing to worry about.' The Prime Minister fell silent as his wife did all the talking. 'Well, what did he want?' Hannes scratched his chin as his wife carried on talking. The doctor wondered whether he should let the Prime Minister pay for the visit or not. It hardly seemed right to charge him if he was going to need his help himself over the next few days. Still it smacked of flattery and patronage to let him walk away without paying. 'And, God knows, I could do with the money,' he thought.

'What's for dinner?' The Prime Minister frowned. 'You said we were going to have lamb curry. Are you going to aerobics?' He looked at his watch. 'It's nearly six. No, don't worry, I'll get something myself.' He put down the receiver. 'No proper meal tonight,' he thundered. 'Oh well, I suppose I can start my diet. And it's high time I cut down on the stress.' He looked Hördur Gottskálksson up and down. 'You don't look like a man who'd say no to alcohol. Would you like a drink?'

'Why not?' Hördur abandoned all hope of being paid.

They went outside. There was a sharp frost. They walked past the parliament building. 'He's going to invite me to Naust restaurant,' thought Hördur.

But as they past the corner of Adalstræti without the Prime Minister turning down it, Hördur thought, 'Can he really be inviting me to his own home?' In spite of himself he felt proud to be out walking with the great man. They met an elderly couple and Hördur saw out of the corner of his eye that they were looking at them with some curiosity. He tried hard not to look in their direction just as if it was the most natural thing in the world to be out walking with the Prime Minister of Iceland talking about this and that and the good of the country. 'Where are we going?' asked Hördur as they passed the crossroads of Gardarstræti and Túngata.

'We're going to my home of course,' said Hannes as if it were perfectly natural.

Hannes's house was strong square stone box with windows at each corner. There was a faint light from the sitting room and a light shining in an upstairs room. The Prime Minister walked up the flight of wide steps at the front of the house and opened the door into the warmth. Hördur looked back over his shoulder from the top of the steps. The clouds had parted over the city. There was a pale moon. The stars were shining. They went in. In spite of himself, Hördur was full of admiration. There were lots of framed photographs on the staircase wall but he could not make out the faces in the dim light. 'No, don't bother taking off your shoes,' said the Prime Minister. Hördur was angry with himself for his exaggerated respect, but he could still not prevent himself from feeling a sense of humility as the Prime Minister pointed the way through the dining room to some leather chairs. The sitting room doubled as a library.

'There is one thing to be said for the women going off jogging and doing aerobics. A man can have his whisky in peace.' He went to the drinks cabinet. He reached in his jacket for his wallet. 'I clean forgot to pay you earlier.' He put a 5000-kroner note on the table by the sofa.

Hördur Gottskálksson picked up the note. 'Now, listen. This is far too much.'

The Prime Minister looked surprised.

'This. The charge is 600 kroner and about the same again on your health insurance.'

'Health insurance is against my principles.' Hannes poured generous slugs of whisky into both glasses. The front of the cabinet opened outwards to become a little table hanging from golden chains. 'People should pay their way at the doctor's.'

'Even without the health insurance this is still far too much.'

'It's not a single kroner too much,' said the Prime Minister and sipped from the cut-crystal tumbler. 'Aren't you one of the best heart specialists in the country, perhaps *the* best?'

'Well, it's not for me . . .'

'Icelandic doctors have a good reputation the world over.' The Prime Minister put down his glass in front of him on a small round glass table and sat in a creaking leather chair. 'That's what I've gathered when I've been travelling overseas. We Icelanders have doctors who are considered among the best in the world.'

Hördur knew the man was flattering him. There had to be some hidden agenda, but try as he might the doctor could not work out what it was.

He drank about half his glass and the cares of the day slipped surprisingly quickly from his limbs. He was irritated to find his slight intoxication immediately evident in the slurring of his speech. 'Is he trying to get some kind of hold over me?' he thought, beginning to get angry. 'Does he take me for a fool? Does he know I told Theódóra about the shares? Does he know I met his assistant on the plane?' The memory brought a smile to his face.

'How are things?' asked the Prime Minister suddenly, sitting forward in his chair and grimacing as he swallowed his whisky. 'Won't the question of the inheritance be enormously complicated now that Seli's no longer with us?'

'The old girl keeps it all for herself and she's somehow so . . .' Hördur sipped his whisky. 'My wife's got no backbone. She won't confront her sister.'

'But what about the Southshore Fish Farm?'

'Well, that's part of the estate. There's a lot of property all over town.'

'There are enormous debts. Quite incredible sums.'

'Really?' asked Hördur, surprised. 'Is the fish farm in trouble?'

'If all the debts were called in immediately, even Heidnaberg itself would be in danger of going to the wall. I've had many a scrap with Theódóra and she's no mean opponent.' Hannes glanced quickly at his guest. 'Have you heard her say she's going to split the party in half like Albert did before her all those years ago? That's what people are saying. There's rumours of a new Citizen's Party.'

'I've heard nothing about it.' Hördur shook his head and sipped his drink. The banknote lay on the table untouched. The Prime Minister noticed it when he got up to get them more whisky and encouraged the doctor to take the money. In the end Hördur relented, folded the note and put it in his breast pocket.

'I wouldn't speak ill of a woman closely related to you and an old political ally of mine.' The Prime Minister voice was sonorous. He added a splash of soda from a syphon to both glasses. 'I'm just having a drink and talking man to man.' The Prime Minister pushed the glass towards Hördur. The bottom was wet and a note rang out as the tumbler slid across the glass tabletop.

Hördur felt a pleasant fluttering in his eyelids. He gazed at Hannes's face. It was incredible that he should be sitting here having a friendly drink with this man. He sipped his whisky. It was strong and good and wrapped itself around his tongue. 'You can be quite frank with me about how you feel about her,' said the doctor.

'She might have bitten off more than she can chew if she's intending a full-frontal attack on the party itself. It would be as well if Theódóra were to realize that,' said the Prime Minister, pondering deeply. 'That might be what she's planning. Has she offered you any support in your little legal difficulty?'

Hördur allowed the hand holding the tumbler to move slowly down between his legs and rest on the seat of the chair. He gazed around the sitting room in surprise. 'Help me? Theódóra? I'd never turn to her for help. It just wouldn't occur to me.'

The Prime Minister suddenly lunged towards the doctor's chair and brought a hand down on to the doctor's knee to affirm their comradeship. 'I might be able to come up with something. I promise you I won't make Theódóra's sister suffer for it, even if Tedda does behave abominably towards me.' And the Prime Minister stood up to recharge their glasses for the third time.

'The verdict of the District Magistrate was a bad day for justice in this country,' said Hördur as soon as he had his glass in his hand again and felt he could take the Prime Minister into his confidence.

Hannes sat down. 'I believe you know Haraldur Sumarlidason?' he asked suddenly.

'No,' said Hördur immediately and behaved as if he had no idea who the Prime Minister meant. 'Who might that be?'

'I know you've met,' said the Prime Minister and looked at him gently. 'I know what happened in the plane. I know Halli let it slip about the shares coming on the market unexpectedly. I know it was you who told Theódóra.'

Hördur put down his glass. He was feeling a bit dizzy. 'Yes, that's right. Oh, him! Is he one of your chaps then?'

'Haraldur? Of course he is!' The Prime Minister looked at him in surprise. 'Haraldur can be a hard man sometimes but I need him.'

Hördur Gottskálksson was suddenly very angry. He was on the point of jumping to his feet. 'I say whatever I want to anybody!' he said, furious, but then slumped down again in his chair.

'And that's how it ought to be,' said the Prime Minister and did not press the point. Neither was he at all taken aback. 'Take your glass off the table. I just wanted to know what kind of a man you are before I ask you formally to become the family doctor. If you'd told me immediately everything you'd heard on the plane, it would have shown you weren't to be trusted.' The Prime Minister laughed. 'But you decided to keep quiet about it and I like that.' The Prime Minister raised his voice. 'I am now going to ask you to take on the responsibility for the health of this family until such time as I am laid to rest in Gufunes Cemetery.' He waved his hand.

'Tell me, my friend, did Halli really believe he'd caught some virus? Did he really believe he was dying of ebola fever?' The Prime Minister waited for an answer with his mouth hanging open.

Hördur nodded. 'He was close to giving up the ghost out of pure terror.'

The Prime Minister laughed soundlessly but his shoulders were shaking and there were tears in his eyes. 'Oh, Halli,' he said. 'How dull life would be without him.'

Suddenly they heard the front door opening. 'Oops, the wife's back.' Hannes wiped his eyes with the palm of his hand. 'Now I'll get told off for not using the coasters.'

Hannes's wife came into the hall and standing there in the light she seemed to the doctor like a woman in a dream, with her thick red hair and pink cheeks, glowing with exercise and full of youth and well-being. She came into the sitting room and put her sports bag on the table. 'I have a guest,' said the Prime Minister.

'And who's this?'

'It's Hördur Gottskálksson, the heart surgeon.'

'Yes, how do you do?' She held out a delicate hand. Hördur did not have the nous to stand up but simply sat there smiling like a beached whale. He was more drunk than he realized.

'We've just been having a drink, my love,' said the Prime Minister. 'And we've been discussing some very important matters. Like brothers. Like two good Icelanders together. Like two members of the Independent Party.'

'I think it's probably time I got going,' said Hördur after Hannes's wife had gone.

'Now, you wait there, my friend,' said Hannes Pálmason. 'I'm sure my wife won't consider it beneath her dignity to butter a slice of bread for us. Isn't there some smoked salmon in the fridge?' he shouted loudly.

When the taxi sounded its horn, the Prime Minister accompanied his guest out on to the steps and patted his shoulder in farewell. Hördur was now so drunk he lost his footing halfway down the steps. He managed to grab on to the railing. As he fell he glanced back at the door. The Prime Minister was looking down at him with an evil grin.

'You lucky sod!'

'I know the safe places to walk,' said the doctor and laughed, although he thought his reply sounded stupid.

'We'll hold each other up in the storm to come,' said the Prime Minister. 'Good sense comes with the passing of the years.'

The taxi driver lent forward to catch a glimpse of the house as he drove off but said nothing.

Vilhelmína was watching television when the doctor got home. There was a pot of tea standing on the living-room table. 'Who's been?'

'Father Bernhardur.'

Hördur looked extremely surprised. 'What did he want with us?'

'He wanted to talk to me.'

'What about?'

'I asked him to come. I'm thinking about becoming a Catholic, like Theódóra.'

'Don't go letting any of those witchdoctors get their claws into you, Vilhelmína,' said Hördur and the alcohol could be heard in his voice. He was in too good a mood to start an argument about religion with his wife.

'I've been thinking about it for a long time,' she said.

Hördur sat down and watched the news. The Workers' Union spokesman said they were determined to tear up all existing wage agreements. In response to this, the Prime Minister gave an interview. He had positioned himself in front of the portrait of Ólafur Thors. 'I simply cannot believe that they all want to see an end to the steady increase in the standard of living that we've managed to achieve,' said the Prime Minister and looked furiously at the female interviewer as if the whole crisis was her fault.

'Where were you?' asked Vilhelmína. 'I caught a glimpse of you on Channel 2. It was a very harsh verdict. How can people be so unfair? What will happen to us?'

'Everything'll be OK, don't worry.'

'Have you had anything to eat?'

Hördur couldn't take his eyes off the Prime Minister who was not about to let the female interviewer trip him up.

'I just said, Hördur, have you eaten? There's fish and potatoes in the kitchen.'

'I'm not hungry,' said the doctor and pointed to the television. 'I had something to eat with him a while back.'

It didn't even occur to Vilhelmína that he could be serious and she didn't say anything more to her husband. When the doctor realized, he decided not to humiliate himself further by telling her about the visit.

28

Nobody but Haflidi had dared to sleep in the loft room at 28 Thingholtstræti but now Sylvía had moved up there. She was completely unaware of the ghost. When he thought about it, Haflidi reckoned he had seen it: a small, evil, mean-looking old man with dried chickenshit on his rubber boots who had tried to attack him on the stairs claiming to be the master of the house.

Sylvía risked moving in there now because her grandmother, Gunnhildur, was living on the floor below with all her furniture and things. She'd come running up immediately if the old chickenshit man appeared. Half the house was now in her grandmother's name. Dagný's uncle from the Eastern Fjörds had come over when they cleared the flat and to Sylvía's amazement her mother had insisted on him taking everything except for one painting. 'I want to be shot of the lot of it,' said Dagný. 'Then Tryggvi can't get his hands on it and sell it to a junk shop for next to nothing.'

'It's taking that boy quite a while to grow up,' said the uncle and drove off with a truckload of stuff.

Sylvía heard voices in the hall and sat upright listening. Were Dagný and Tryggvi having a fight? Hardly. Tryggvi would have left for work hours ago. Sylvía tiptoed out on to the landing to listen, but it was too late, the front door was shut. She walked back to her bed and noticed that the first snow of winter was falling over Reykjavík. She leaned on the windowsill and looked across the town. The snow was fluttering down over the roofs, falling steadily on to the Thingholt district and turning the streets and gardens sparkling white. The lake in the centre of town was disappearing behind a veil of snow, the houses to the west had disappeared and Midstræti was completely white.

She lay down. The two brothers and their sister had started at a new school, the old Midbæjarskóli, which had been taken over by a group of teachers who were running it as a private school. 'How are you going to pay the fees?' Tyggvi had asked. 'I shall find a way,' Dagný had said. 'It'll sort itself out. The children shouldn't have to suffer because of all this.' '"Sort itself out"?' said Tryggvi. 'Everything's always supposed to "sort itself out"!' 'Haflidi's already had to repeat a term,' said Dagný firmly. 'Yes, but that's not for lack of money. That's because he's lazy, and thick with it,' said Tryggvi, and then they had a fight.

Sylvía caressed an old familiar knothole in the wall. The wood was reddish in colour. Suppose the story Jökull was obsessed with were true. No wonder the kids at school called him a nerd. One day he'd taken his sister down to the basement, cut a sliver of wood from a beam and showed her the red colour of the wood. 'Just think of it, Silla!'

She looked at the alarm clock. It was nearly ten. She got dressed and went downstairs, carefully tiptoeing past the closed door of her grandmother's flat so she wouldn't be called on to run an errand.

Dagný was sitting at the table reading *Morgunbladid*. 'Up already?' The girl looked at her mother. Dagný yawned.

'Why so happy?'

'I spoke to the lawyer this morning and when I pushed him he seemed fairly confident we'd win the private prosecution.'

'Won't the doctor appeal to the High Court?'

'He can do that as often as he likes, the poor sap,' said Dagný brightly. 'I know I'll win there too.' There was the sound of footsteps on the floor above, the boards creaking. Dagný listened. The footsteps moved out on to the landing and then on to the stairs . . .

'Here, take the old lady her paper.' Dagny pushed it across the table. 'I can't bear her coming in here asking me for it.'

Sylvía ran halfway up the stairs and gave the newspaper to her grandmother. The old woman reached for it with a low moan. Sylvía ran downstairs again, sat down and fiddled with the tablecloth pensively. Dagný looked at her daughter. 'You don't believe me? It won't do the doctor any good appealing. It's as good as over. He's lost.'

Her daughter didn't answer, but simply frowned.

'What's on your mind? Spit it out.'

Sylvía sighed. 'I'm thinking about that saying, "Don't count your chickens until they're hatched."'

'That's not how it is.' Dagný sighed. 'There's something you ought to know. I'm thinking of divorcing your father.' She looked at her daughter meaningfully, as if it was a secret.

Her daughter rolled her eyes. 'Not again!' Then, in English, 'My God!' She continued, 'I mean it! Have you started all this up again? Why did we move back home? How many times is it now?'

'I'm serious this time. You'll have to choose. Me or your father. I'm going to let the boys make their choice as soon as they get home.'

'I want to live with you. You know that.' The girl thought for a moment. 'But I don't think we'll be going anywhere,' she said to wind her mother up.

'I want you to change your name.'

'What?'

'I want you to take your family name from me.'

'Take my name from you? What do you mean?'

'I want you to be known as Sylvía Dagnýardóttir.'

Her daughter laughed out loud. 'You are joking?'

Her mother ignored the laughter. 'You see this painting?' She pointed to the wall.

'The old painting from Granny's. Yes.'

'It's the only thing of hers I've kept and there's a very important reason for it. When your grandmother was a girl she worked at Framtidin, the woollen mill. The boss used to give his employees a painting as a wedding present. For some reason he only gave my mother a bowl. I suppose he thought their house would be too small to go hanging paintings on the walls. Now when my parents bought the flat on Fjólugata he came to the flat-warming. There were high ceilings there.' Dagný stretched her arms up. 'Higher than here. Father and Mother had no money, they'd only just set up together and the walls were screaming out for a painting. The boss looked round but he didn't say anything. A few days later he called Mother into his office. He asked her to look after a painting for him. He'd ask for it back when he wanted it. She looked after it for forty years. The week before she died, she said to me, "If the heirs ask you about the painting, you must give it to them without any argument." I promised I would. It's the only thing my mother entrusted me with because we can't make any claim on the painting. It's not ours. Everything she owned I wanted out of here.'

'But how can you imagine the heirs will want the painting back now?'

'Sylvía, that's exactly what I asked Mother. And this is what she said: "People remember where they left their money."' Dagný looked at her daughter and nodded her head self-importantly. 'They could come any day.' She glanced across to the window and the door. 'Any moment now.'

'That's hardly likely!' Sylvía looked at the painting on the wall.

The painting was of the island of Videy, with Mount Esja and the reef, before the lake was filled in. A small fishing boat was heading straight for the reef.

'There's something wrong with this,' said Sylvía. 'That boat's far too close to the shore.'

'When Haflidi was young he threw a knife at it during one of his mad turns. The year before Father died. Father took it back to the artist and the poor guy fixed it for free. He was talking so much when he was working on it, he painted the boat the wrong way round. It should be sailing out to sea.'

'Is the stupid thing worth anything?'

'No, it's not worth much. You might get fifteen thousand kroner for it if you were lucky.'

'Then why take all this trouble?'

'I know the painting's not worth much and it's not even very good, but that isn't what matters,' said Dagný calmly. 'I promised Mother I'd look after it and that's what I'm going to do.'

After a silence the girl said, 'I'd rather keep my old name. I like it. It's got sentimental value.' She got up from the table.

'Have you done your homework?'

'There wasn't any.'

'Why not?'

'It's a teachers' study day.'

'Don't you want any breakfast?'

'No thanks, I'm not hungry. I'm going to go and see a friend.'

'Well, wrap up warm and don't be long.'

As she set off she started chanting, 'My name's Sylvía Dagnýjardóttir not Sylvía Tryggvadóttir.'

She caught a bus in the square in the town centre to go and see her father to find out what he thought about what was going on. The bus stopped not far from the garage. The snow was deep enough to cover her shoes. The red Ford was in the car park. Tryggvi had spent four years fixing up that car. When he first met Dagný he had just done up a 1921 Model Ford. Oh, they were the sweetest couple in town, driving round the centre in the cool of the evening, drop-dead gorgeous in their sweet old Ford. There was a photograph of them in the Ford hanging in their bedroom. Under it was written, 'The sweetest couple in town, 1968.'

Tryggvi was sitting in the staff room at the garage drinking coffee. 'Hello you! Something up?'

'I'm thinking about changing my name.'

'Changing your name? What are you on about? Have you taken a fancy to one of the old snobbish names like Thoroddsen or Nordal or Rist or something like that?'

'No, I'm going to name myself for my mother. That's what people are doing these days. I'm going to be known as Sylvía Dagnýjardóttir. I just thought you ought to know, Father.' The girl looked at her father's face, his fair hair and the deep cleft in his chin.

'What garbage is this?' Tryggvi started flicking quickly through a newspaper, agitatedly fidgeting in his seat.

'It's such garbage,' said Einar cheerfully, 'that they're all doing it. Just look at the paper! Will you kindly take a seat, Sylvía *Dagnýjardóttir*?'

She sat down. The icy winter wind blew through the garage where two cars were up on the ramps. Her father leaped to his feet. 'Take away my name! No, never! She's done quite enough to be going on with. Take my name away from me! My name is my name. Isn't that worth something?'

'Please don't be like that, Father. You're frightening me.'

Tryggvi looked tenderly at his daughter. 'You mustn't get upset when your mother and I fight.'

'Aren't you getting a divorce, yet again?'

286

'No, no. We're just arguing over money. Your mother's got it into her head she's going to win that compensation case against the doctor but she doesn't want to use any of the money to help with our financial problems. I just ask her straight, "Do you want us out on the streets?"' Tryggvi sat down and looked at his daughter with his eyes wide. 'A bird in the hand, Silla. We can't count on your mother winning.'

Tears began to trickle down Sylvía's cheeks.

Einar got up and wandered out into the garage. Tryggvi moved closer to Sylvía and stroked her cheek with a large finger. 'Were your brothers OK? Had Haddi woken up?'

'Yes, he's gone out.'

'Well, there's a surprise. He just floats through life, that boy.' Tryggvi scratched his chin. He moved his chair without standing up and reached for a box of biscuits. 'I should offer you some refreshment. It's not every day that such a fine young lady visits our humble garage. Fancy a biscuit?'

'No,' said Sylvía so quietly she was scarcely audible. She sniffed and let her legs dangle. 'Dad,' she said, looking at her father. 'I don't want to change my name. Not really. Mother wanted me to.'

'So, there we are, Sylvía my pet,' said Tryggvi. 'Of course. I never thought for a moment you wanted to betray me.' He poured some coffee into a mug and ate a biscuit. The girl watched the strong line of his jaw as he munched the cracker. Tryggvi's eyelids were twitching nervously. 'Well, Dagný can look to the future with a smile on her face,' he said and drummed his fingers on the table. 'She'll win the private prosecution and the doctor'll have to pay her. Then our lives'll change for the better. Just smile for me, that's right. Well, what are you up to today?'

'I've got the day off. Are you going to get that computer for Jökull for Christmas? The boys do nothing but talk about it.'

'Who knows? I might. We'll have to see how he does in his exams.'

The phone rang and Tryggvi dashed off to answer it. Einar hit a rusted bolt on a brake drum. Sylvía came to the doorway. On the other ramp there was a Subaru with its bonnet up. A pair of blue overalls was draped over one wing. Sylvía recognized her father's working clothes. A van that had seen better days was waiting to one side. Further back, by a dingy window, stood the Impala, the Chevrolet her father had been working on as a hobby for the last three years. The car was in bits, the glass out of the windows, the body stripped down. Patches of black underseal made the flash roadster look like a crashed fighter plane.

'How do you think Haddi is getting on at school this term?' Einar looked at the girl and screwed up his eyes, creasing his forehead.

'I think I'll have to lend him a stick so he can bowl all those noughts home through the streets when the Christmas exams have been marked.'

'And is he going to get himself rechristened as well?'

'I haven't the faintest idea.'

'There's all this stuff about the new woman these days.' Einar looked at Tryggvi. 'But I can't see anything new about them. As far as I'm concerned they've always been like that. Do you know what my old witch of a mother used to do when I was a kid? She used to give me great bowls of porridge before I went to birthday parties.'

'Was she a sadist?' asked Sylvía.

'No, it was so I wouldn't embarrass her by eating like a pig.'

'What a good idea,' teased Sylvía. 'You're mother was one smart lady, Einar. Of course she must have realized what a horrible brat you were.' The girl went and sat down again in the staff room. One of the walls was covered with pictures of naked women. A pair of blond twins in little black panties hugged each other. Their bodies glistened. Sylvía took a cracker from the packet and bit into it. 'What they need here is a picture of a naked man,' she thought.

As she arrived home there were three men standing a little way away from the house in the falling snow. One of them was holding a black book and another a briefcase. They came with her to the front door. Sylvía rang the doorbell. The one with the briefcase put a foot on the bottom step. 'Do you live here, little girl?' he asked in a strong clear voice.

'Yes. What do you want?'

'Is your mother's name Dagný Gísladóttir?'

'Yes.'

'I need to speak to her.'

Dagný opened the door.

'I have here an order with regard to the debts of Tryggvi Thórarinsson,' said the man with the briefcase sounding very self-important.

'Oh no, you're not. We've just paid more than 10 million off our debts and more than 2 million of that was interest.'

Sylvía slipped through the door and stood behind her mother, peeping round her waist. The bailiff indicated behind him. 'I have a witness here and a court official. I have come here to list possessions to the value of the outstanding debt and put a distraint on them so they can be disposed of at public auction.'

'Of course you're free to do that but I must tell you I don't own a thing. Tryggvi's mother bought the house from us in order to pay our debts. Our part of the house is mortgaged to the hilt and our only possessions are an old sofa, a few chairs and the dining-room table. What's the debt for anyway?'

'For the purchase of a car.'

'What car?'

'A Chevrolet Impala 1961. Tryggvi paid for it with a hundred thousand kroner draft.'

'Why don't you repossess the car?'

'Because he's destroyed it.'

'Destroyed it?' Dagný repeated. She had still not budged from the doorway.

'Yes, destroyed it! I can't imagine he'll ever get it mended. It's in bits.'

'He'll get it mended.' said Sylvía.

'Don't you own a car?' asked the bailiff.

'No. I had to give it back when I lost my job. How much is the debt?'

The bailiff checked in his papers. 'With interest and charges, seven hundred and eighty-six thousand. And Tryggvi's put his car in his mother's name. You're a nice lot, I must say.'

'Don't speak to my mother like that,' said Sylvía from behind Dagný.

'Tryggvi owns nothing here,' said Dagný. 'Seven hundred and eighty-six thousand! Oh God!'

'But he does live here, doesn't he?'

'Yes.'

'Then I need to check out the flat to make sure for myself that there are no relevant possessions here,' said the bailiff, glancing at the court officer. Then he barged up the steps towards the woman who backed out of the doorway. The witness and the court officer followed. The witness was rubbing his hands as if he was very cold. Sylvía shut the door. She could see the men's footprints in the snow. They stamped the snow off their shoes in the hall.

The bailiff was an enormous man but his face, in contrast to his chosen profession, was that of a smiling doll. He looked round the living room, letting his eye rest on the table. It didn't look as if it would cover the debt. He went into the sitting room. The old sofa and the chairs weren't up to much. The cover was worn in the middle, but it looked to him as if the three-piece suite with its black-laqueured cut-out woodwork arms might fetch something. He pushed open the door to the bedroom. There was nothing to be seen except the marital bed which was protected by law from confiscation for debt. As he turned round, his eye was caught by the painting. 'Who owns the painting?'

'Neither Tryggvi nor me.'

'Who then if I may make so bold?'

'Do you think I'm trying to keep something from you? I'm looking after it for someone.'

The bailiff raised an eyebrow to his colleagues. 'A likely story. You've kept things back before now. You refused to open a garage for me in the summer of 1985 when you were living on Njálsgata. I remember you very well although you might not remember me.' He turned to the court official. 'Open the account.'

'There's no point in writing down that painting,' said Dagný, who had turned pale. 'My mother died recently and she asked me to look after it and make sure it was returned to the rightful owners.'

'Yes, I know your mother died recently,' said the bailiff. 'Everything to do with her death should make you feel ashamed.' The court official, expressionless, sat down and opened his account book. 'Then it is your responsibility to prove the ownership of the painting. I am making a note of this. What is the title of the painting?'

'I've never heard it called anything in particular.'

'Yes!' shouted Sylvía. 'It's called the *The Beached Boat and the Sandbank*.'

'It's not worth anything,' said Dagný.

'I'll get a valuation from someone other than you,' said the bailiff. The court official wrote down the title and the bailiff looked at Dagný. 'I want to make it quite clear that I've brought a witness with me. In your presence, he will now sign to the effect that this painting, *The Beached Boat and the Sandbank*, was hanging here in the sitting room at 28 Thingholtstræti on 3 November 1994.' The court official stood up and the witness sat down and signed his name. 'If you try to remove this painting, you will be breaking the law.'

'What right has this man to come here and accuse us of all these awful things?' Dagný asked the court official.

The court official looked a bit sheepish but did not answer. The bailiff looked straight at Dagný and said, 'I think it would be a good idea to pay your debts. Shame on you.' They stormed out of the house.

'You'll just have to get the people who own the picture to make a statement,' said Sylvía. Dagný had slumped into a chair, looking grey. Sylvía looked round the living room. She'd never noticed how ugly their things were before.

'Do you think I can take this endless humiliation?' Suddenly Dagný got up, went into the bedroom and stood on a stool to get a green suitcase down from the top of the wardrobe. She threw it on the bedspread and starting energetically throwing clothes into it.

'What are you doing?'

'I can't stand it here a second longer. With nothing to call my own and the old girl upstairs eavesdropping all day long. Don't you understand? I'm leaving and you're coming with me.'

'With you? Where?'

'Somewhere. I don't know where. Somewhere out in the country. I'd rather sell my body than stay in this house a moment longer!'

Sylvía ran upstairs to get her grandmother. Gunnhildur was not in but as it happened the door was unlocked. She dashed to the telephone and rang the garage. Tryggvi answered. 'Father, you've got to come home immediately. Mother's gone mad. A bailiff came because of the car. She's packing her things and leaving!' When

Sylvía came downstairs her mother had finished packing. Dagný had put her coat on, her hair was all over the place and she had patches of high colour on her cheeks. 'I'm now finally getting out of this cursed house,' she said loudly. 'Get your things on.' Sylvía put on her shoes and a coat and they both hurried out. Snow was still falling lightly but there were patches of blue sky. Dagný walked tall, taking long strides, and the girl had to skip to keep up with her. Tryggvi found them on Bókhlödustígur. He drove up and wound down the window. 'Dagný, darling, my love, what are you doing? Please don't do this. Please let me take you home.'

Dagný swung the suitcase into her left hand and looked at him without speaking. He parked the car and got out into the wet sleet. Then she put the suitcase down and took a sharp kitchen knife from her coat pocket. 'If you come any closer I'll cut my throat!'

'Dagný darling.' He walked slowly towards her.

'I mean it, Tryggvi. I'll cut myself.'

'Silla, get in the car.' Tryggvi backed off a little. 'Your mother's gone mad.'

'No, I'm staying with Mother.'

Mother and daughter walked on down Bókhlödustígur and across Lækjargata. At Idno, the old theatre, she put down the suitcase. Sylvía watched the ducks swimming in a hole in the ice on the lake by the bank. The water, black as lead, lapped at the thin film of ice. A young girl in a woollen sweater, a scarf flying out behind her, was skating near by, her skates rasping on the ice.

'Shall we go home?'

'Never!' hissed her mother. 'What time is it?'

'Nearly three.'

Dagný took her daughter by the hand and walked along Lækjargata, keeping an eye out for cars. She glanced at every face they met. Across the street a man was standing watching them, but it wasn't Tryggvi. Was he hiding in a shop she'd have to pass? They crossed Skólabrú. 'You're going too fast,' wailed her daughter.

'Don't be so feeble.'

At the corner of Austurstræti Dagný went into a shop and asked the girl at the counter to give her a drink of water. The girl was a bit taken aback but seemed concerned for her and talked a bit to Sylvía while her mother was drinking.

Dagný was breathing a little more easily once she had had a glass of water. She looked this way and that out of the window. They crossed Lækjargata opposite Government House.

'Where are we going, Mother?'

'Skúlagata. It's all I can think of at the moment.'

'Can't we get a taxi?'

'No, we'll need the money.'

Sylvía saw Tryggvi. He was standing at the top of Arnarhóll watching them with his hands in his pockets and the wind in his hair. The hill behind him was white but it had stopped snowing. 'Oughtn't we to go and speak to him?'

Dagný turned and pulled the child across Lækjartorg. Sylvía was half running half walking. She looked over her shoulder. As they passed the corner of the Courts of Justice, Tryggvi was crossing the square behind them. He was keeping a careful distance between them. Dagný ran across Pósthússtræti by the Reykjavík Pharmacy, dragging Sylvía behind her. She headed towards the parliament building and walked straight in through a back entrance. They went up an echoing spiral staircase and Dagný put down the suitcase at the top. A security guard was sitting on a stool by a small table. He glanced up from his newspaper and said hello. Dagný walked through the door without acknowledging his greeting. Sylvía followed her mother into the public gallery. There was one man there, looking down pensively into the debating chamber with his chin on his hands.

The debating chamber was smaller than Sylvía imagined from television. Every seat was occupied. Something very important must have been being discussed. Dagný looked across the members of parliament and gave a heart-rending cry of despair.

29

The Minister for Foreign Affairs was discussing the war in Bosnia. He was saying that it was not possible to give detailed descriptions of the atrocities committed by the Serbs as they were too horrific for words. He stepped down from the podium for a moment to hand a photograph to a member of parliament to look at and then pass round the chamber. The photograph reached Theódóra. It was a mass grave. It showed a pile of dead bodies in what looked like a room without a roof. The dead lay one of top of another. There was a flannel shirt, a training shoe, a foot sticking up out of the corpses, with nothing more to be seen of the body it belonged to. One body was propped up in a corner. Where there should have been eyes there were nothing but red holes. Another man, alive this time, was wading knee deep in broken bodies. He was supporting himself with a hand against the earthen wall of the pit. His head was thrown back looking up imploringly at those standing round the edge some seven foot above him. A man was crouching by the wheel of a truck over a body that was probably about to be thrown down on top of the others. There was a yellow excavator on the grass a little way away. A row of trees in the heat on the far side of the plain. Theódóra passed the picture on.

She looked up into the public gallery. Why didn't the fair-haired woman standing there looking to and fro across the members sit down? Who was she looking for? Theódóra thought she recognized her and fumbled for her glasses. 'Oh God, it's Dagný!' she muttered. The Minister for Foreign Affairs was leaving the podium. This was the moment that Dagný gave her heart-rending cry.

Theódóra sat there as still as a fossil. There was a deathly silence in the chamber. In the next moment she wondered, 'Is she really going to start screaming about me giving her the sack?'

The members of parliament jumped to their feet and bustled about. They stared up at the public gallery, whispered to each other, waved their arms about. One continued sitting quietly, untroubled, looking up with mild curiosity. The Prime Minister dashed out of the chamber and then reappeared a moment later beside the woman who was still staring out over the chamber and, by the look of it, seemed to be not fully conscious of what she was doing. She had her hands up to her face. A frightened young girl was tugging at her skirt.

The Prime Minister took the woman by the elbow and talked comfortingly to her. Two journalists had arrived, but he did not let them near her and said something to them under his breath. Two members of the Women's Party had also now reached the gallery but Hannes had things under control. Theódóra didn't move. She clenched her teeth when she realized how Hannes could make use of the incident. Yet, he couldn't know who Dagný had been working for and who'd sacked her. But it wouldn't be long before he knew all there was to know about it. She could see the headlines: 'Heidnaberg under fire again'; 'Theódóra Thóroddsdóttir – actions speak louder than words'; 'Single mother fired without notice'.

Hannes pushed the journalists back with paternalistic authority, asking them to keep their distance. The television cameras were filming the whole thing, including the faces of the members of parliament as they watched in shock and curiosity. It was over almost before it had begun. Hannes was seen to guide the woman down to a bright and beautifully decorated sitting room on the south side of the parliament building. This was known as 'the round room'. There were chairs placed under a window arch. The stills photographers and television cameramen were in a frenzy as Hannes helped the woman to a chair and then knelt beside her. The child hid her face in her mother's skirt. Hannes talked to the woman for a minute or so and when he stood up again to talk to the press he seemed to know almost everything about her situation. He gazed fondly on the flock of journalists standing a little way away waiting for news. Sometimes these people were his friends; often they were his sworn enemies, but today they were his dearest friends. The Prime Minister's face was shining. 'This woman has a few problems,' he said as he walked towards them. 'She hasn't anywhere to live. She has come here with her young daughter. She has brought her problems straight to the top, straight to parliament, to the members of parliament, and her problems will be addressed.'

'What's the matter with her?'

'She needs somewhere to call home.'

'Is that all? It's just that she's homeless?' The microphones surrounded the Prime Minister.

'No, that is a long way from being the whole story. Far from it. She has sought sanctuary in the parliament building because of a dispute with members of her family. It is not up to me to delve further into that side of things. I shall get my assistants to examine the details and come up with a solution to the woman's current difficulties.'

'Are you really going to do something to help her or are you just saying that?' asked a very pushy female journalist.

The Prime Minister cleared his throat. 'I can assure you that everything humanly possible will be done on her behalf.' He spotted one of the journalists trying to reach Dagný. 'You can stop right there!' said the Prime Minister. 'I'm sure you will appreciate that the woman is in no fit state to answer your questions as yet. Please show her some consideration. I'm sure she'll be happy to talk to you at a more appropriate time. But now I must ask you to respect her privacy.'

Later that day Theódóra saw something of this performance on the evening news bulletin. Since the opening of the parliamentary session that autumn she had felt the eyes of the Prime Minister constantly on her. Every single time she went up to the podium she could see him watching her out of the corner of her eye. On one occasion she had pretended to yawn to feign indifference. As luck would have it this had been caught on film and she had now seen it seven times on television.

In fact enmity between members of parliament was a rarity. Disputes tended to evaporate during coffee breaks even though, when on the podium, members could scarcely breathe for indignation and swore blind they'd never have anything to do with their right honourable opponents ever again.

But the enmity between Theódóra and Hannes was of a different order. It was ice cold. It was the hatred of a woman who had lost her husband and the hatred of a man who had lost control of a company. Each had imagined destroying the other politically and the whole of parliament knew it. But how could the Prime Minister of Iceland stand up and say, 'The honourable member took 300 million kroner from me. It was perfectly legal but completely unethical'?

And how could Theódóra Thóroddsdóttir stand before the Icelandic Parliament and say, 'The Prime Minister killed my husband'?

She felt that anyone with any power in the party had turned against her. She was not denied access to party meetings but no matters of importance were discussed in her presence. *Weekend* finally started hinting that she was considering crossing the floor and had had secret meetings with the leader of the Social Democrats. When journalists asked her about it, Theódóra restricted herself to a shake of her head and a smile.

She still hesitated to take that step, to leave the Independent Party. But how could she harm Hannes in any other way? She tried when the Parliamentary Accounts Committee announced a 40,000-kroner bonus for members of parliament. She went on television and said she would not be accepting the bonus. It was a bad move. It seemed like some kind of joke, an insult even. She was, after all, the richest woman in the country. A little later she was appointed to the Treasury committee that would examine the national budget. There was no way to avoid considerable cutbacks, but she missed the fine print. How could she have been so stupid as to agree to a delay in paying compensation to victims of sexual abuse? How could she have been such a fool? She could not remember it being discussed in any meeting she attended but there was her signature on all the documents. There was a great furore and some-how all the journalists on the story wanted her to comment. She had to do all she could to hide her irritation from the cameras.

Once the news bulletin was over, she phoned Vilhjálmur.

'Were you watching the news?'

'Yes.'

'It's appalling, isn't it?'

'It's absolutely vile.'

'You know what'll happen next?'

'She'll sell her story to the press, but that's the least of our worries. I've been trying to get hold of you all day.'

'What about?'

'The National Bank is foreclosing on Nesja Salmon.'

'But how?'

'They're calling in all the loans and insisting on all outstanding debts being paid immediately. We're talking more than a billion kroner here. As you know, they've had the administrators in. I was getting it all sorted but they're not taking any notice of me any more.'

'How does this affect us?'

'I'm not sure yet. There could be some cash-flow problems.'

'Could we transfer funds from United Fisheries?'

'I'll look into it, but it's not as if we're the only ones with a vote.'

'We'll talk this through tomorrow morning.' Theódóra nodded as Ester put a cup of coffee in front of her and at the same moment the doorbell rang. 'I'll be in at nine tomorrow and we'll go over it all then.'

'I've been thinking about it all day,' said Vilhjálmur.

'And have you come up with any answers?'

'You remember the people who came over from Shadrak a few months ago? I can't say I exactly warmed to them, but when I was discussing fish-farming with one of them and talking about the temporary difficulties in the industry, he said they were always interested in diversifying. What do you think? A billion kroner is peanuts to them.'

'I don't know. We could think about it.' She looked towards the hall. 'I've got guests arriving.' She picked up a cigarette lighter from the table and absent-mindedly flicked the flame on and off.

'There's something else . . .'

'What now?' Theódóra took in a deep breath. 'Vilhjálmur, I am rather busy . . .'

'The foreign lad you're bringing over with the Lions and the Red Cross. The Indian boy. He's arriving on Thursday. There was a fax about it today.'

'We'll talk about it in the morning.'

Ester had set out the cups on the living-room table, brewed some coffee, opened a box of chocolates and a bottle of port was standing at the end of the table. Ester had been making herself useful round the house over the last month and was again on the payroll at Heidnaberg. The women shook Theódóra's hand one by one very formally as they arrived. The eldest was about sixty and the youngest scarcely twenty. She invited them to sit down and took her place at the head of the table. The twenty-year-old, Birna, gazed adoringly at Theódóra as she announced her decision. She was going to form a new political party, just like Albert Gudmundsson way back when: the Citizen's Party.

'We can confirm that we're all right behind you,' said the oldest woman, whose name was Elísabet Sigurdardóttir. 'We know what happened with Axel.'

Theódóra looked down with a resolute expression and smoothed her skirt.

'When you think of the election results, it was outrageous that no woman was brought into the government. We insist on something being done about it.' said Birna.

'We've a lot of work to do,' said Theódóra. 'We shall make the announcement between Christmas and the New Year, or perhaps at the very beginning of January.'

30

Father Bernhardur was expecting a man to come at about ten to connect the telephone in the young people's home. It was not impossible that the press might put in an appearance before midday. He had followed the Bishop's instructions to ring the papers and tell them what was happening. As he strolled down Túngata the priest looked around him. On a day like today the world seemed fresh and new, as if the city had been built overnight. The sun was shining but it had not yet melted the fine crust of snow on the cars.

He had visited Vilhelmína one evening a few days earlier. She was determined to convert to Catholicism but was wanting to take everything far too quickly. The first thing she wanted to talk about was her husband and children. Would the priest talk to Trausti, make him see sense, make him see he wasn't really a homosexual? And, as for Ester, she'd told her time and again that she wasn't going to look after that child any more, and yet she still turned up every single day and dumped the child on her. 'I want her to get married. There's a good man wanting to marry her. A real catch! Villi. He works for my sister Tedda, you must know him, he worships the ground she treads on. But she won't have anything to do with him. I can't understand it, he's so tall and handsome. I wonder, would you look into it for me, Father Bernhardur, just see whether we couldn't use the Catholic church for the wedding. I wouldn't even consider letting them get married in our church.

There's nothing but arguments all the time. The minister is always going against the wishes of the parish council. I don't think he's really quite up to the job.'

'I'll have a word with the Bishop,' said Father Bernhardur, careful not to promise anything. 'But I doubt he'll want to let the church be used like that.'

The woman was hardly listening to him. When the priest explained the Sacrament of Confession to her she laughed out loud and said, 'Well, that won't take long! I don't think I've ever committed a sin in all my life.' Father Bernhardur could see a thorny road lay ahead of him with this woman.

The telephone engineers were waiting for him at Sudurgata, two of them in a car. He looked up proudly at the sun-yellow building. The house was freshly decorated inside. They followed him up the steps. It was chilly indoors as all the windows were standing open to get rid of the smell of the paint. He turned up the radiator. They checked along the skirting board. There was a lot of old wiring. 'No problem,' said the older telephone engineer. It took them no time at all to connect the phones and test the lines. The older engineer handed the receiver to Father Bernhardur. 'Now you can phone the Pope.'

When they had gone, the priest sat down in the living room and looked around with a deep satisfaction. Tryggvi had kept his promise and surveyed the house from top to bottom. 'No wood rot,' Tryggvi reported happily. 'No rot of any kind. This house is in even better condition than Thingholtstræi was when I bought it, much better.' He stretched up and released the catch on the loft access. The steps swiftly slid down towards him. He looked round the roof space with his flash light. 'The beams are fine. No rot. It's a magnificent house!' They went down to the basement. 'No damp. It's just as if it was built yesterday. It might be an idea to double-glaze the windows but that could be expensive. I'm thinking of doing it at my place when I can afford it.'

They went out into the garden through the basement door and Father Bernhardur felt that despite his happy exterior, something was weighing heavily on Tryggvi. Finally Tryggvi volunteered as much to Father Bernhardur. 'Oh, Dagný!'

'What is it now?'

'She's a good woman, you know that. She's gone again and I don't know where she is.'

Father Bernhardur kept silent and waited.

'She says it was all my fault that that painting got written down in the bailiff's book the other day. Everything's always my fault! If they take that painting away she says she's going to kill herself.' Tryggvi sat down on the steps and clasped his hands together.

'What do you want me to do?'

'Could the girl and the two boys come over here during the day for the time being? It's too much for my poor old mother to look after them. Then I can try and talk some sense into Dagný. Perhaps she'll come back home. Then she'll have more peace of mind. She'd be free to do her acting. Perhaps she'll get given a role. They're so big now she has trouble controlling them, especially Haddi, and I'm sure it would do them good.' Tryggvi looked round. 'They could do their homework here.' He thought for a moment. 'It would do Haflidi no end of good to get some discipline for once. Have you got any children lined up yet?'

'As a matter of fact we have. One. A girl.'

'What's the problem there?'

'Nothing really. She just hasn't got anywhere to go.'

'Why?'

'Her mother works.'

'That's the way it is. That's the way it is. The world's gone mad. Women refuse to take any responsibility for their kids. They shoot their mouths off about equality and all I can see is injustice. Why don't they go rushing off studying to be mechanics, can you tell me that?'

Father Bernhardur scratched his beard.

'And then people are surprised when the town centre is full of drunk teenagers at the weekend. Do you know what I'd do if I was the mayor?'

Father Bernhardur shook his head.

'I'd turn the water cannon on them and drive them off the streets. Of course in the old days we all used to go driving round and round the town centre eyeing the birds but we were still decent law-abiding citizens.'

Father Bernhardur looked at his watch and stopped thinking

about Tryggvi. A doorbell rang in the silent, cold house. He was startled and he jumped to his feet. A journalist from *Today* walked in and glanced round the ground floor for the sake of appearances but was too lazy to bother going upstairs. The priest asked casually, after he had filled him in on the plans for the young people's home, 'Do you know anything about stocks and shares?'

'What about them?'

'You journalists know so much. Someone I know lost a lot of money when shares in United Fisheries were sold off cheaply.'

The phone rang. It was the first phone call to the home and the priest was thrilled to be answering it. 'Good day, Father Bernhardur.'

'Oh, it's you!' exclaimed the priest. 'It's so right for you to be the first person to ring. We'd never have got this place open without your help.' He remembered Axel's death and became rather solemn. 'I hadn't wanted to disturb you,' he said. 'But you have my sympathy. I hardly knew Axel personally, but he was very kind to me and I have prayed for him every day since he died. Who is going to take over the business?'

'That will fall to me,' said the woman, sounding tired and sad.

Father Bernhardur noticed that the journalist was looking at him with freshly kindled interest. 'I have someone with me just now. Is it all right if I ring you back in a few minutes? Where are you?'

'At Heidnaberg. Where else should I be?'

'Theódóra of Heidnaberg,' said the journalist. 'The member of parliament. She picked up those United Fisheries shares for a song. It's the business deal of the century. It's unbelievable, simply unbelievable. Do you know what she did?' The journalist didn't wait for a reply. 'She phoned from overseas and let an associate of hers, a man called Vilhjálmur, deal with it over the Whitsun break. He gave them a cheque for 7 million kroner but asked them not to present it before the banks opened for business on Tuesday morning. Naturally everyone trusted him. After all he's an executive at Heidnaberg. These people were really loaded, one of the richest families in the country, part of the cartel running everything in Iceland. But what do you think the chap did?' The journalist looked at the priest, his eyes full of admiration.

'I wouldn't know . . .'

'The first thing he did was to phone the cashier at United Fisheries when they opened on Tuesday morning after the holiday and got the share purchase settled by the company itself.' The journalist looked at the priest, his mouth open with the pure joy of it all.

'I don't understand.'

'Effectively he bought the company with its own money. He didn't actually cough up one single kroner. Just to humiliate them. Have you ever heard anything like it? He's one smart son of a bitch.' The journalist thought about it for a moment. 'Although, come to think of it, I'm not sure he is that sharp an operator. I reckon the old girl was pulling the strings. I'm sure it gave her a buzz to get hold of the company like that.'

Father Bernhardur saw the man out. 'I enjoyed talking to you. When do you think it'll be in the paper?'

'Never,' said the journalist. 'We don't print stuff like that.'

'I meant about the young people's home.'

'Oh, in a few days, I expect. You've got to understand it isn't exactly front page news. But tell me something. You're a priest. What do you think of that sort of deal?'

'Gathering riches is against the will of God,' said Father Bernhardur quickly. 'It says in the Book of Revelation: "Babylon the Great is fallen, is fallen, and is become the habitation of devils . . . and the merchants of the earth are waxed rich through the abundance of her delicacies."'

'Babylon? Wasn't it razed to the ground thousands of years ago?'

Father Bernhardur pointed to the city spread out below them. 'Babylon the Great is right here in front of us.'

The journalist looked out where the priest was pointing as if he was seeing the city of Reykjavík for the very first time.

Father Bernhardur called down the steps, 'Will there be a picture as well?'

'I'll send a photographer either later today or tomorrow and get him to take a few snaps of you and the home.'

The priest phoned Theódóra back determined to have it out with her over the purchase of the shares. 'Hello again.'

'You were saying . . .'

'Yes. We were talking about my husband's passing. I wanted to thank you, Father Bernhardur, for your words of comfort. I've just buried myself in work since Axel died. It makes me feel better somehow.'

'How is business?' he asked quickly.

Theódóra hesitated. 'I didn't think things like that were of any interest to you. Yes, business is good, thank you. How about the home?'

'I suppose you could say everything's going well. At least we haven't actually got any children in it yet,' said Father Bernhardur rather crossly.

'Yes. That's why I phoned,' she said gently. 'The thing is, in a few days a boy from India will be coming here to stay with us. It's connected with the people I do business with overseas. And I was wondering if he could stay with you during the daytime? I simply don't have the time to look after him, what with parliament and the company.' She sighed. 'And then there's the chairmanship of the Committee for Foreign Affairs and that's really a full-time job in itself.' She cleared her throat. 'It's very difficult for me. I need Ester at Dyngjuvegur every day because of Linda.'

'An Indian boy! Yes, that'll be perfectly OK. What's his language?'

'English, I assume. But that's not the only thing I wanted to ask you.'

'Yes?' Father Bernhardur frowned. Immediately the home was open the woman was ringing to get something back for her 100,000-kroner donation. Shall I never understand the ways of the world?' thought the priest and struggled to gain control over his temper. He looked at his watch. It was twenty to twelve.

'It's Linda,' said the voice on the phone.

'Your daughter?'

'Yes.'

'What about her?'

'She's really being going through it since her father died. She has terrible trouble sleeping. She blames herself for his death. Of course that's rubbish, but there seems to be no way I can talk her out of these feelings of guilt. It makes no difference to her to be told she couldn't have had anything to do with his death. She went out for a walk yesterday and I was so scared for her. She didn't come back until late in the evening, soaked through. I'd be so grateful if you'd

304

pop in and have a chat with her. You have such a way with people.'

'Oh, I think you have a much better way with people than I do,' said the priest, trying to strike a merry note, but his voice still revealed his irritation.

The woman remained stubbornly silent and the priest gave in. 'OK,' he said. 'I'll try to come over after Mass this evening.'

'Thank you so much, Father Bernhardur. I'll make sure there's some hot coffee waiting for you.'

He put the receiver down. At that moment the clock struck twelve. 'And then these people think it's all too much of an effort to come to church,' he thought. 'But I'm meant to dash hither and yon doing their bidding.' He went into the living room. It was bathed in sunlight. There were now to be four children. And they were expected any minute. It was a good beginning and you hardly needed more than that to start with. The mills of God grind slowly and they grind exceedingly small. He thought about Linda. Did it not occur to Theódóra that she might bear some of the responsibility herself?

He walked over to the window to see if it was possible to see the Midbæjarskóli. No, the view was obstructed by the houses on the other side of the street. It wasn't far. The boys would be arriving any minute. 'Perhaps I should pop up to the presbytery and get something to eat?' No, that was silly, he wasn't at all hungry. He turned on the radio. It always took him forever to tune in to the right station. The priest found highly complex technical equipment such as dials and push buttons almost impossible to master. This would of course be a simple matter for the children. After many snatches of pop music he eventually found what he wanted. He sat and listened. The newsreader was reporting the latest events in Bosnia. The siege of Sarajevo was continuing. The Serbs had exploded a bomb in the marketplace, killing thirty-two outright. The injured were lying all over the street. The hospital had come under bombardment. Snipers were picking people off. The United Nations could do nothing. 'Still, it does no good to surrender,' thought the priest. 'God has promised victory over evil. The world cannot be a mistake since it was created by God.' He turned off the radio and dozed. 'How strange to live in a time of peace,' he thought.

31

He woke with a start when the doorbell rang. He jumped to his feet and shook himself. It was just not right to have the good children arriving and finding him half asleep. He went to the door. It was the two brothers. 'Hello, Jökull. Hello, Haflidi.'

The brothers came in. Jökull looked a bit more sure of himself than he had when they'd first met. Haflidi looked around suspiciously as if he might come face to face with a nun or be made to kneel in prayer at any moment. They dumped their schoolbags in the hall. Haflidi walked into the living room without taking off his shoes and Jökull followed in his stocking feet. Father Bernhardur looked at the older brother's shoes but decided against saying anything. Haflidi was wearing a leather jacket and jeans. His long fair hair was grimy and unwashed. In contrast, Jökull looked quite smart. Haflidi knelt down by the music centre, glanced expertly at the controls, twiddled a few knobs with practised fingers and soon found the station he wanted.

'Keep it down, man,' said Jökull.

'Piss off.'

'Now, now, boys,' said the priest.

'So are we meant to hang around here all day scratching ourselves?' asked Haflidi. 'What for?'

'No, that's not the idea at all. You're to do your homework and then we'll have some lunch together . . .' Father Bernhardur pretended not to see the boy puffing out his cheeks to show how unimpressed he was. 'First of all, you could get me a copy of your timetable.' He turned to Jökull. 'Perhaps you could sort that out?'

'I'm not staying cooped up here day after day like an idiot,' said the older brother, 'even if the old girl has taken herself off to some women's refuge with Silla.' He grinned. 'The whole family's in shelters now. We just need to find somewhere for the old man. And Granny of course.' He looked round the living room. 'Are there only going to be the three of us in this big house?'

'No. I'm expecting two girls.'

'Wow, girls, man!' Haflidi winked at his brother.

'Let's go upstairs, shall we?'

'What are we doing here?' asked Haflidi. 'Everything was all right at home and life was fine until you stuck your oar in.'

'Your father asked if you could come here during the day so your mother could have more time to herself for her acting.'

'That's shit! She can't act! She's just into all this feminist nonsense. Nothing's ever good enough for her. It's always the same whatever poor old Father does. I think it's Mother you ought to have here. You should be bringing her up properly.'

'Cut it out, Haddi.'

'Boys,' interrupted the priest, 'come along upstairs. I want to show you over the house.'

He walked into the hall and to the foot of the staircase. Jökull followed him. Haflidi hung back and didn't answer when the priest called. Father Bernhardur went to see what was causing the delay but as soon as he stepped into the living room, Haflidi grabbed him by the hair, brought the priest's face down smartly against his knee and then spun him round into an incapacitating half-nelson. The speed of the attack took Father Bernhardur by surprise. 'Let go of me, boy!'

But the boy did not let go of him. The priest, bent double, turned in a circle, catching sight of the other brother's terrified face. 'Let him go, Haddi!' shouted Jökull feebly, but Haflidi was not to be reasoned with and tightened his hold. Father Bernhardur heard the doorbell ring. He struggled to free himself but could not get a purchase on the slippery leather jacket. The doorbell rang again. His nose was hurting. 'Let go!' he hissed. 'Do you want to suffocate me, you little sod?' The boy did not answer but tightened his grip further. Father Bernhardur's neck was hurting him and his back and stomach were also painful. Who was it at the door? The Bishop? A photographer from the paper? This was a fine way to be discovered on the first day. Suddenly he summoned up his energy, ran as hard as he could towards the wall and slammed the boy into it. Haflidi yelled but did not loosen his grip. By now Father Barnhardur was so desperate he made a lunge for the boy's feet, scraping his neck against the studs on the boy's sleeves. He could not get free of the boy's hold, so he grabbed Haflidi's hair and smashed his head twice into the doorpost. The boy let him go and kicked his shin. Like lightning, Father Bernhardur swung his fist up into his jaw and followed it up with a heavy punch to the diaphragm. Haflidi grabbed his stomach with both hands and looked at him in stunned amazement.

The priest was standing facing him with his fists up like a boxer. He expected the boy to turn the other cheek to mock him, but, as it happened, Haflidi was not conversant with biblical allusion. 'If you don't stop it, I'll knock you out cold,' hissed the priest.

'There's a girl here,' said Jökull.

There was a thin trickle of blood at the corner of Haflidi's mouth. He looked at the blood on his finger and, as soon as he could breathe again properly, said, 'I'd never have believed it.' There was admiration in his voice. 'Wow! A priest with a decent uppercut.'

'Yes, why don't you run off and tell your father?'

'Your nose is bleeding,' said Haflidi, laughing.

'You've got no chance, taking me on,' said Father Bernhardur as if they were of an age and he wiped his nose with the back of his hand. He looked at Haflidi. It didn't seem as if the boy was going to hold the punch against him. In fact it seemed as if he had already forgotten it, as if he was under some spell, watching the small, delicate girl who was standing out in the hall. Her name was Ingibjörg and her beautiful dark colouring made her look vaguely Oriental.

'What's happening?'

'You should take the boys upstairs and show them the house.'

This time Haflidi needed no second bidding to go upstairs. Father Bernhardur rubbed his neck, furious with himself. How had this happened? Hitting a boy! But how could he have freed himself otherwise? The Lord Our God remembers every blow. The whole venture was getting off to a wonderful start, he thought.

When the youngsters had looked over the house and even crawled up into the loft, he made them sit at the table in the sun lounge. Sudurgata was visible through the mass of tiny panes in the arch window. Jökull took some things out of his schoolbag. He looked rather subdued and seemed a little afraid of the priest. Father Bernhardur treated him gingerly. Haflidi did not take his eyes off Ingibjörg as he reluctantly took things out of his bag. The priest set them to work. He was quite comfortable with Icelandic, History, English and Danish. These were subjects he taught at the

Catholic school. Mathematics, however, defeated him. As a boy, mathematics had been his Achilles' heel. Algebra might have been Egyptian hieroglyphics for all he understood of it. A maths textbook appeared on the table. He looked in terror at a diagram of a circle. Beside the circle was a cat with its tail curled round. He was hoping for the doorbell to ring or conversation to turn to matters of religion.

And, extraordinarily enough, doorbell did ring. 'Carry on working, children. I'll see who's at the door.'

Sylvía was standing there. 'Just take off your coat and come into the living room. Don't you have some work to do?'

'No, our teacher was ill.'

'Perhaps you're good at maths?' the priest asked with hope in his heart as he touched his swollen nose.

The girl nodded.

'There you are,' said the priest. 'God is with us today. I've never understood how you can subtract a cat from a circle, add a farmyard goose and come up with the answer 21.'

'You've got it all wrong,' said the girl guardedly, squinting at him as if she wasn't sure whether he was serious or not.

'No, but you can show us how it should be done,' said Father Bernhardur, clasping his hands together and smiling at her.

'Yes, you show us, Silla. You know how to do it.' Jökull looked affectionately at his sister.

Sylvía clambered up on to the chair and pulled the maths textbook towards her. She kept looking down as the presence of Ingibjörg made her feel shy. Father Bernhardur walked over to the window. The city was bathed in sunshine and a large lazy-looking raven was sitting in a tree in the garden. It was strange to see it there. How had it found its way to the city centre? The doorbell rang. It was a nun from Landakot with a plate of pancakes and four pints of milk.

'Well,' said Father Bernhardur. 'Let's have some pancakes and we can look at this a bit later.'

'Great!' said Ingibjörg, and Haflidi agreed with her.

'Turn on the radio,' said the priest. 'Jökull, put out the plates, and Haflidi, go and fetch the glasses. We men shall wait on the ladies and show how sincerely we subscribe to the equality of the sexes.'

The boys laid the table. A trailer for a film blared out from the radio. 'I'm going to see that,' said Haflidi. He looked at his watch. 'Why don't we all go and see a film?'

'I don't hold with violence in the cinema,' said Father Bernhardur.

'Adults don't understand teenagers.'

'Teenagers have always been the same,' said the priest.

'No,' said Ingibjörg. 'Adults have no idea what it's like to be a teenager today.'

'Shall I tell you something that was written on a five-thousand-year-old slab of stone dug up in Egypt?' Father Bernhardur helped himself to a pancake. The nuns had put sugar on the top ones and rolled them up. He was talking with his mouth full. 'It took archaeologists years and years to work out what the symbols meant and when they were finally able to read it, what do you think it said?' He looked from face to face and but there were no takers. '"The world is going to the dogs. Children have stopped obeying their parents."'

'No,' said Ingibjörg. 'Teenagers today are different. There is far more violence and the kids get drunk and take drugs. And girls start having sex at, what, twelve, thirteen years old. And kids kill themselves. They can't stand how meaningless everything seems. And some of the girls become prostitutes.'

Jökull looked awkwardly down at the table. Haflidi grinned broadly, put some sugar on a pancake and said, 'That's true. I'm sure it wasn't like that in the old days. You know, when you were young. You never know, I might kill myself one day. That would be really cool.'

'Have you gone mad, Haddi?' asked Sylvía.

'I'm not as old as all that!' said the priest, offended. 'Actually, sitting here with you like this, I don't feel much older than you.' He looked round the group. The expression on their faces indicated that they did not share his opinion.

'How can you know what teenagers are like? You, a Catholic priest.' asked Ingibjörg.

'I think there are very few things in life that escape me. How many people do you think come to me for confession? I know most of what goes on.' He thought for a moment and then smiled. 'If I produced a magazine, it would knock *Weekend* into a cocked hat.'

'Tell us something,' said Haflidi.

'No, I can't do that. Confession is a secret between the priest and the penitent and mustn't be revealed, not under any circumstances. That would be a terrible sin. The priest would be breaking his vows before God. But I remember something awful that happened in Germany once. It was worse than any film you'd see today. And it involved a priest. Catholic priests don't always have such an easy time of it, even if you think they do. Do you want me to tell you that story?' He glanced at Sylvía, a little concerned. 'Perhaps you're a bit young . . .?'

'I'm eleven. Nearly twelve.'

'You shouldn't get people all excited and then bottle out on them,' said Ingibjörg.

'Well, don't tell your families I told you this story.' He looked at the children waiting in silence for him to begin. 'I went to Rome,' began Father Bernhardur, 'to study for two years and I spent a month at the Vatican. While I was there I got to know a priest, much older than me. He always ate at a table by himself. He did some light work, but I never found out what it was. Once I sat down next to him in the dining room. Over a period of time we became friends. On Sundays I used to go out walking. I fell in love with Rome. It's the most magnificent place on the face of the earth. Well, to get back to the story. At first, Father Werner – that was his name – wouldn't join me on my walks, but one Sunday he gave in and came along. Over the next few Sundays we covered every inch of Rome together. In 1974 he'd been a parish priest in a small town in France. One Sunday he told me his story. Father Werner was French, even though he had a German name. His father was German and his mother was French. Late one day a young boy came to make his confession. Father Werner would go cold when he thought about the strange sound of the boy's voice as he described how he had set about murdering a young girl. He tried every argument he knew to get the boy to go to the police and tell them what he'd done, but the boy would have none of it. The priest had no choice. He could not break his vow of silence. The best detectives were brought in to help the local police, but no one apart from Father Werner knew who the killer was. Three months later there was another murder. This time an eleven-year-old girl was tricked into going into the wood and was murdered. The boy came to the priest again and asked for absolution. When again the boy refused to go to the police, the priest went to his bishop and then to his archbishop but they both said he could not betray the confidence of a penitent. It was not until the boy tricked a thirteen year old into going into the wood and she escaped from him that the boy was arrested. At this point, the townspeople, who of course all came to the trial, learned the truth. The parents of the murdered girls took it in turns to sit on the steps of the house where the priest lived. The parents of the second girl to be murdered accused the priest of being responsible for her death. "You knew", said her father, "that the boy had committed one murder and it must have been obvious to you that he was likely to kill again. You had a duty to warn the police, even if you had done it anonymously. Nothing could justify your silence, which led to another girl being killed."

'Father Werner asked to be transferred and he spent three years living in a monastery in Switzerland. Then he was invited to go to a parish in Germany. First he was a parish priest in Frankfurt and then he moved to Langenberg. In both these parishes he earned the love and respect of his congregation. He had grown old before his time because of his experiences in France. His hair, which had once been black, was now white and he had deep lines on his face, even though he was only about forty years old when he took up his appointment in Langenberg.'

'How awful,' said Ingibjörg. The priest looked round at the children. The brothers were waiting eagerly for the next episode, but Sylvía was looking a little uncomfortable. Father Bernhardur fell into an embarrassed silence.

'Silla, go upstairs and have a look round the house,' said Haflidi.

'Yes. I think I'd like to do that.' The girl got up.

'Perhaps this story is just too horrible,' said Father Bernhardur. 'Perhaps we should leave it there.'

'No, go on, go on,' urged the teenagers.

The priest waited until he could hear Silla safely upstairs. 'Ten years went by. Father Werner gradually regained his peace of mind and soul after his sufferings and was not expecting any further evil when a nineteen-year-old boy, Hans Jürgens, came to make his confession one autumn evening in 1984. He described how he had killed a young boy. "I couldn't help myself," said Jürgens. "I took the boy into a garage in the middle of nowhere and was suddenly overwhelmed by an uncontrollable urge to kill him. I suffocated him and then lit candles around the body." The priest realized he was facing the same thing all over again. This boy, to look at him so tender and innocent, was by his own account a murderer, but the priest could do nothing unless the boy could be persuaded to give himself up.

'Father Werner struggled with his conscience. "The only advice my colleagues could give me", he said, "was to pray. I wondered about sending an anonymous letter to the police telling them what I knew. When I look at what then happened, I have to kneel down and beg God's forgiveness for not having done so. Three more boys were murdered and I kept silent. If, on the other hand, I had sent that letter, no one would have known except God and myself. Of course it would have caused my soul great agony. I would have had to have renounced the priesthood and entered a monastery, but probably I would have saved three boys' lives."

'Soon after the confession Hans tricked a ten-year-old boy into the garage, tortured him and strangled him. Then he went back to Father Werner, confessed and asked for absolution for the second time.

'"I was nearly out of my mind," said Father Werner. "Here was a boy standing in front of me needing psychological help rather than punishment. Yet all I could do was beg him to give himself up to the police. But all my prayers were in vain. I prayed to God that I might be allowed to pass on to the police the knowledge that was destroying me. I now wish that I had disgraced my vestments and been driven from the Church.

'"Hans Jürgens murdered a third boy and then a fourth, but he did not return to the confessional. I knew about both these murders," said the priest. "I knew who had committed them as the manner of them was the same as for the other two. The police too knew that they were looking for only one killer.

'"One evening, the mother of one of the murdered boys came for confession. She cried as if her heart would break when she told me how she had punished her twelve-year-old son for something quite trivial just before he disappeared. He left the house, saying he was going to a walk, and never returned. I begged God that Hans Jürgens should be arrested before he killed anyone else. I begged and begged as intensely and honestly as I could. It was the only way for me to stop him."

'Towards the end of 1985, Hans tricked his fifth victim, a boy of fourteen, into the garage. Hans was very strong, overpowered the boy, tied his hands behind his back and tied his feet together.

'He had brightened up the garage with lots of different coloured candles. While he was torturing the boy he chanted in Latin. About midday he started getting tired and went home for lunch. He told the boy he'd come back after lunch and strangle him.

'But the boy he'd chosen this time was more spirited and courageous than he'd bargained for. As soon as Hans had left the garage, the boy managed, with great difficulty, to crawl over to one of the candles and knock it over with his shoulder. As if by a miracle, the flame did not go out.

'The boy held the rope tying his wrists together in the flame, even though he got badly burned. He managed to burn through the rope, untied his feet and ran to the police station. Hans went back to the garage, where the police were waiting for him. He did not deny that he had killed the other four boys and that he was planning to kill the fifth. He also said he had confessed the first two murders to Father Werner. When the police questioned the priest, he admitted he had known that Hans had committed the first two murders and that he had probably committed the third and fourth as well.

'The townspeople made their position clear immediately. They insisted on the priest being charged as an accessory to murder. But the prosecutor would not have it. He said that the silence of the confessional was well established in law. The priest was bound by a vow that he could not break.

'Things did not change much for the better for Father Werner, although Father Bruning, the official spokesman for the Catholic Church in Germany, said that a Catholic priest could never, in any circumstances, repeat a single word spoken to him in the secrecy of the confessional. As the priest is the intermediary between God and the believer, the sanctity of the confessional cannot be put at risk. If it were to be jeopardized in any way, that would destroy the integrity of the confessional for ever.

'Hans Jürgens was taken to court, charged with four murders, and sentenced to life imprisonment. The prosecutor thought it unlikely he would ever be released. Father Werner decided to settle in Rome. "I am going to stay here for the rest of my life," he said. "I cannot bear the thought of sitting in the confessional and risking again hearing that a member of my congregation has committed a murder. I don't know of any other priest who in the course of his ministry has had to face what I have done more than once. The deaths of those children will always weigh heavily upon me, even though as a priest I know I am guiltless. I trust that God will lead me towards quietness of soul because it was in his name that I kept silent." That is the end of the story,' said Father Bernhardur. 'What do you think?' He looked round the faces of the children.

'It's horrible,' said Ingibjörg and Jökull nodded.

'It's odd,' said Haflidi, 'that that devil of a boy couldn't take his faith away from him.'

'Why should he?' asked the priest. 'He must have looked on it as a baptism of fire. Perhaps it brought him even closer to God.'

32

'On the day the young people's home opened, I, the priest himself, hit one of the children,' thought Father Bernhardur. He felt shocked and anxious as he explored his tender nose with his fingers. 'And to cap it all I told them a horror story full of violence and murder. Why? There must be something wrong with me. I planned to look after the children, listen to them, try to teach them something that would be of benefit to them, and then what did I do? Rabbit on endlessly about some nonsense.'

He wondered about making a confession but Bishop Lambert was watching a video with Father Otto and Father Bernhardur did not feel he could disturb them. Father Otto was in a particularly good mood as his favourite team, Manchester United, had thrashed Everton earlier in the day. He was now watching the match for a second time, pausing and rewinding to show the Bishop all the best bits.

Father Bernhardur walked across to the church and asked God to forgive him for hitting Haflidi. Then he asked St Joseph, the father of Jesus, to guide him in his care of the children.

He remembered he had promised to see Linda that evening. He had completed forgotten about it. 'What does that woman expect me to say to the girl?' he thought. 'What could be more natural than her grief at the death of her father?' At Axel's birthday party Linda had simply seemed a perfectly ordinary young woman, if a bit intense.

He went back into the presbytery and picked up a warm over-coat as it was frosty outside. There was a phone call for him. It was Tryggvi wanting to come and see him straightaway, to talk things over with him and get him to try and find Dagný.

'I'm very busy this evening. It's been a long day.'

'But this is really very important.'

'OK then. Come about eleven if it's really that urgent. There are people expecting me. Yes. Goodbye. Yes, we'll meet then.' He put down the receiver. Suddenly it occurred to him that it was not surprising if the woman wanted to get away from this extremely demanding man. He was disturbed to find he felt a little afraid of Tryggvi himself.

He was anxious about seeing the children the next day. What tricks would they play on him? Would they attack him the moment he came through the door? He turned on the ignition and drove along Skúlagata beside the sea. There wasn't another car to be seen anywhere. The arctic chill seemed to have emptied the world of human life. The heater was still blowing out cold air nearly all the way to Dyngjuvegur. The Toyota was just beginning to warm up by the time he parked outside the house. He rang the bell. Ester opened the door. 'Yes. How are you? Theódóra is expecting me.' An enchanting little boy was peeping out from behind Ester. 'And whose child is this?'

'This is my son. He's nearly three. Gauti, say hello to the gentle-man.' Gauti put the back of his hand up to his mouth and it came away glistening with saliva.

'Will you have a cup of coffee with us, Father Bernhardur?' Theódóra walked smartly into the hall. 'How are you finding the car?' She didn't wait for an answer. 'I just want to see the evening news and then we can talk.' She walked quickly over to the television, turned it on and sat down with her glasses on the tip of her nose. 'There he is!' she cried. The Prime Minister appeared on the screen.

The Prime Minister gazed solemnly across the massed ranks of Parliament and said with an emphatic flourish, 'Let us pray that that the Parliament of Iceland will never see such a day!'

'What's he talking about?'

'How should I know?'

The camera panned across the chamber. 'There's you, yawning,' said Father Bernhardur.

'Oh, that's an old shot they're always slipping in.'

Suddenly the sun shone on the white walls of Government House. The interview with the Prime Minister had been recorded earlier in the day. The journalist's voice was crackling with excitement, as if an important decision was about to be taken then and there on the steps of the building, 'Last spring Parliament agreed that the government would guarantee compensation payments to victims of physical violence, as it is often the case, obviously, that the perpetrators of such crimes are rarely in a position to pay compensation to their victims themselves. Now it has been agreed to postpone the introduction of his measure.' The journalist turned to the Prime Minister. 'Why is that?'

The accusatory tone was clear from the way the question was framed. The Prime Minister looked away as he replied. 'It's unavoidable. I don't think anyone could foresee for a moment there would be cuts in the field of law enforcement.' The Prime Minister smiled weakly. 'But I think the question would be better addressed to the member of parliament who was elected third as representative of the Independent Party. She is in a much better position than I am to give you a full response.'

'And what about taxing investment income?'

'It is still under consideration.'

'Is there any truth in the rumour that the coalition is about to collapse because of disagreement about the taxing of investment income?'

'Not that I'm aware.'

'It's what everyone's saying.'

'I think you'd better address your questions to the Radical Left. I have nothing more to say on the matter.' The Prime Minister turned his back on the journalist and walked towards the door of Government House.

'My sources are impeccable!' shouted the journalist scurrying after him.

The Prime Minister waved him away. 'As I said, I have no further comment to make.'

'Well, what did I say?' said Theódóra. 'He really dumped me in it this time. The man's obsessed with me.' Theódóra pouted and kept tapping her pen against her chin. She turned from the television to Father Bernhardur. 'How reckless and brilliant he is. But I have one more trick up my sleeve. Let's wait and see. And I had nothing to do with that budget cut. It's a lie, like all the rest of it.' She looked at Father Bernhardur with her mouth open. 'Don't you think it's appalling treating people like this? Rape victims? People who've lost their job and their income after some senseless act of violence? There's a man who lost an eye and along with it his pilot's licence. And not one of these people gets compensation. Father Bernhardur, isn't that unspeakable?' He nodded and she turned back to the television screen. 'But did you see', she said, 'how he nearly lost his temper when he was asked about the coalition?'

There was a filmed report from Bosnia. A small white United Nations tank was driving along an asphalt road with bushes on both sides. The Serbs were retreating. A voiceover warned viewers that they might find some of the pictures disturbing. A Muslim soldier returned to his family home. There were bullet holes in the white walls and the house was a burned-out shell. Its former resident picked up a red coat with the barrel of his gun and looked at it. The film showed a clearing in a wooded area, with tall fir trees close together, the grass rippling in the wind, a patch of brown earth. A spade was driven into the ground and turned up a skull with rotting flesh still clinging to the nape of the neck. Where the spade had cut into the soil, there was a wet, black sheen on the surface. The earth around the skull was tinged grey by the decaying flesh. The reporter said there were more than five hundred people murdered by the Serbs in the autumn of 1992 buried in the mass grave.

'It's horrible to see these things in your own living room night after night.' Theódóra sighed. 'It puts one off one's dinner.'

Ester leaned forward over the back of a chair and watched the television. Her tight curly hair didn't move at all. She said, 'You're right, Tedda, it's too much for people to bear.' They both turned to Father Bernhardur, almost apologetically, as if they were expecting him to make sense of the world for them. He was about to give them an appropriate biblical quotation when he remembered how he had hit the boy earlier in the day and he felt unworthy to be bringing the word of God to the women.

The little boy had been wandering around while the news was on. Now, determined and dangerous, he was heading towards a piece of Venetian crystal standing on the floor by a radiator. His mother leaped up to intercept him.

'I was quite forgetting why you're here, Father Bernhardur. I was wanting you to have a chat with Linda.'

'I think she's asleep,' said Ester.

'Then she'll have to wake up,' said Theódóra firmly. 'She didn't come and have dinner with us.'

'Well, Gauti,' said Ester to her son, 'I think it's about time we were going home.' She looked at her watch. 'I'll ring for a taxi.'

'Can't you hang on for a bit? Villi's coming over to discuss something rather important. He'll drive you home. You don't need to spend money on a cab. You're doing me such a favour, Ester my dear, I don't know how I'd manage without you. Go and talk to Linda, Father Bernhardur. I must know what's going on. All she does is talk nonsense.'

'Where's her room?' Father Bernhardur looked round.

'Come with me.' Theódóra led the way. The night lights in the floor were on. 'Here, at the end of the corridor. I did wonder about suggesting you asked her to come and help at the young people's home,' she whispered. 'I could pay her salary without her knowing. It would be our little secret. You could consider it a donation. If she had something to do it would give her a purpose in life and as far as I can see that is precisely what's missing. She can't face going abroad now Axel's dead.'

'Could you tell her I'm here, so I don't just barge in on the girl unannounced? We can discuss the other matter later.'

Father Bernhardur was curious to see the room. Theódóra knocked on a door and opened it into darkness. She said quietly, 'Linda, my dear, there's a man here come to have a word with you.' There was a brief rustling from the bed, as if someone had turned over quickly.

Father Bernhardur walked into the darkness. He couldn't see a thing. Theódóra followed. She did not turn on the top light, but yanked back the curtains on the north side to allow the light from a lamppost to fall across the desk. She drew up a chair and, a little embarrassed, the priest sat down. Theódóra left, closing the door quietly behind her. The girl sat up awkwardly and turned on a small lamp on a chair at the head of the bed. There were dark circles under her eyes. When she saw who it was she sighed wearily. 'What do you want?'

Father Bernhardur was sitting by an old teak writing desk. There was an office lamp bracketed to one edge. There were a lot of toys on a shelf. The room was like childhood preserved in aspic. He asked, 'Is it all right if I turn on this lamp? I feel rather uncomfortable sitting in the gloaming like this.'

'Feel free,' she said.

He turned on the light. The room was surprisingly small. Apart from the bed and the desk the only furniture was a chest of drawers painted blue by the door. Above the bed there was a large framed picture of Jesus Christ. He had let his white gown fall away from his chest and was revealing his Sacred Heart to mankind. It delighted Father Bernhardur to see the picture and gave him strength. So, the girl had taken his words at her father's birthday party seriously! Linda sat up in bed with the duvet covering her legs. She said, 'I found this picture downstairs among Grandmother's things. I remembered what you said and I decided to hang it up.'

'What am I being told about you?' joshed Father Bernhardur. 'That you've taken to your bed?'

'It's been so hard coping with Father's death,' she said, sounding like an exhausted old woman. 'And I've been having such weird dreams. Actually I've been having strange dreams for a long time.' She pushed her hair away from her face and the priest was taken aback. She looked haggard and her cheeks were sunken. 'And then I accused Mother of having killed Father. But she's forgiven me. Tedda is amazingly strong.'

'Dreams?' he asked carefully. 'What kind of dreams?'

'I can't tell you,' she said sullenly.

'Try!'

'I can't.'

'Look on me as your father confessor,' he commanded her.

'But I'm not a Catholic.'

The priest said nothing as he did not know the correct thing to say to her and looked at his shoes in embarrassment.

'Some of the dreams are terrible nightmares but the other day I dreamed that a man came to me and told me to pick up some clay which I started kneading. The clay came to life in my hands and turned into a bird which flew away.'

The priest clasped his hands together, rested his elbows on his thighs and listened attentively. 'Was it a dove?'

'Yes, I think so.'

'What did the man say?'

'He said, "Christ does not come for the clay. He moulds it."'

'That's beautiful,' said Father Bernhardur.

'What does it mean?'

'I don't know, probably nothing.'

'Does it mean God is sending his spirit to me?'

'Yes, possibly. Probably. There you are! You know far more about it than I do.' He looked into her face. 'So why are you so sad?'

'When we met in the summer you said we shouldn't take too much notice of dreams.'

'The Church warns against investing too much in dreams because people can become' – he tapped his forehead – 'a bit dotty because they don't think about anything else. And we can never be sure what dreams mean. But this dream is a good dream! It's a very beautiful and very good dream.'

'You also said that the devil might try and lead one astray in dreams,' she said, looking scared.

'I said he lies in wait when we aren't conscious, when we're not ready for him and our defences are down.' He nodded and she told him about the vision in great detail, about the beast standing on the horizon, marking the nations of the world for itself, and involuntarily Father Bernhardur crossed himself. 'Sometimes it feels as if I'm damned. As if Christ doesn't care about me.'

'My dear Linda, that's ridiculous.' He laughed but he was a little afraid. 'Christ did not take on human form because he did not care about us, but because he cared about us so very much. He invited us to be one with him in the Holy Eucharist and in his blood, the everlasting covenant that was shed for the redemption of sins. How could you be damned? Anyone who repents of their sin belongs to Christ. The only ones who don't belong to him are those who don't want to! That is the sin against the Holy Spirit, the only sin that cannot be forgiven. Forget about the nightmares. Concentrate on the good dream. Perhaps Satan has been trying to deprive you of your sanity, but now he will have to give in. The devil could never send you the spirit of God! How could that be? He would not be being true to himself. Linda, what I am trying to say is this: such a good and beautiful dream could be sent to you only by God. So don't worry. Just remember what Christ said: "Are not two sparrows sold for a farthing? and one of them shall not fall on the ground without your Father. But the very hairs of your head are all numbered. Fear ye not therefore, ye are of more value than many sparrows."'

'But why is God sending me this sort of dream?'

'I don't know why God calls people,' he said, a little abstractedly and with some sadness. 'But he has called people throughout the centuries. "Follow me," Christ said to the Apostles.'

'Does he have some special task for me?' asked the girl. She had sat up straight and was looking at him in amazement.

'One can never be sure of something like that,' he said guardedly. 'If he has some special task for you I would think it is most likely to be that you should simply strive to be a good human being. Perhaps he wants you to come to Mass and stop locking yourself away in your room. Or to help your mother. Religion is not the same as sentimentality or dashing off in all directions with no good reason for it. It is to stick with it and try to do the right thing! You read the Bible. Everything you need to know is written down there in black and white.'

'I was reading it earlier today.'

'So,' he said, sounding relieved, 'what were you reading?'

'The Book of Revelation.'

'Oh, that,' he said, and sighed.

'Isn't that good?'

'Yes, of course it's good, but the Book of Revelation is an account of the vision of St John and it's very easy to interpret it in the wrong way. It's defeated better brains than ours. Read the Gospels instead. This is too complicated. We've no way of knowing with any certainty what St John is getting at in the Book of Revelation. It doesn't do to think too much about it. People have gone off their heads and done terrible things. Do you remember that man in Waco, Texas, whose sect went up in flames in order to live out some prophecy in the Book of Revelation?'

The girl slumped back on the pillow. 'Should I take any notice of this or not? Was God calling me or wasn't he? It's got to be one way or the other.'

'Let's say he was calling you,' said Father Bernhardur carefully. 'I can't see that it would do any harm to believe that. But then I'm a very ordinary person. How can I be expected to answer all these questions? Follow the advice of Jesus Christ and everything will be well. The Church exists for the good of the people within it. It was established on this earth for mankind. But as for dreams and visions, there's no way of knowing where they come from. Sometimes Satan appears as an angel of light. He could send a beautiful dream. But, be careful, Linda. The moth is drawn to the flame and its wings are singed.'

Father Bernhardur threw wide his arms, thrilled by the dangers that lie in wait for people when they are asleep.

'What would you do if you were me? I'm so confused. It's almost as if I can feel the feathers fluttering in my hands when I close my eyes. I dreamed this dream the night Father died.'

After a moment he said wearily, as if he had been obliged into it, 'If I were you, I would believe this dream had been sent to me for my own good.'

She stroked her duvet shyly, looked up at the ceiling and then said, 'Everything fits together in this world, everything is connected and has a meaning, doesn't it? And God is everywhere.' She lay her head on the pillow and smiled. 'Even right here. Right now. I can feel his presence so strongly.'

After a while Father Bernhardur said, 'That's good. I have never felt the presence of God like that.'

A little earlier he had heard the doorbell ring. 'I suppose that was your guests arriving,' he said. 'Aren't you going to show yourself?'

She shook her head. 'I want to be left alone for a bit.'

'You promise to come to Mass?'

She nodded.

'Then let's say goodbye for the moment. I'm spending my evenings at Vilhelmína's at the moment. She's considering converting to Catholicism.'

The girl seemed to find this idea rather amusing. Father Bernhardur stood up, left the room and closed the door behind him. He felt strangely lighthearted, as if he had done some good deed, recovered an atheist or something of the kind. From the hall he could see into the living room. Vilhjálmur was standing in the middle of the room taking his orders from Theódóra. He glanced at Ester nervously now and then and patted her son who was leaning against him, looking admiringly up at this tall man.

'Well, here comes the priest,' said Theódóra. 'How's my daughter?'

'She's fine.' Vilhjálmur stretched out his hand to Father Bernhardur and they shook hands. Vilhjálmur's hand was large and warm and his smile struck the priest as open and boyish.

'But did she say anything to you? Should I get on to a doctor? Or a psychiatrist perhaps?'

'I don't think there's any need for a psychiatrist. Losing her father has come as a great shock. It's not unusual for grief to have this effect on people. At the same time she's been thinking about her life and what she wants to do with it. She hasn't made up her mind yet. I think she's quite capable of working it all out on her own. This phase will pass. She's promised me she'll come to Mass. And so did you, Theódóra,' he said accusingly, 'earlier this year.' The priest could not resist poking her playfully in the stomach and she looked down at his finger in astonishment. 'Why haven't you come? I've been watching out for you on Sunday.'

'I've been far too busy. The political life and all its ramifications. And then Axel dying. Tell me, do you speak German?'

'Like a native.'

'That boy from India I told you about. Of course I'd never have got involved if I'd thought Axel was going to die, but you can't always see these things coming and now it's too late to get out of it. The boy's arriving tomorrow and as I understand it German's the only European language he speaks. Could I possibly prevail on you to go to Keflavík Airport with Vilhjálmur to collect him?' She looked at the priest imploringly but somehow at the same time there was an imperious quality to the request.

'Why don't you just put me on the Heidnaberg payroll and have done with it?' He laughed and winked at Ester and Vilhjálmur.

'That might be a good idea. I regret it's just not possible for me to attend to this matter in the way I'd've liked, but even so, and my German, it's fairly good, what do they say, good enough . . .'

'". . . to pick up a prostitute,"' quoted Vilhjálmur, finishing her sentence for her and then becoming embarrassed when he noticed the annoyance of his managing director.

'Please don't use such language in the presence of a man of God!' said the scandalized Theódóra.

'Is there anything to eat?' They all looked round. Linda had come into the living room. She was wearing a thick brown dress.

'Yes!' said her mother, surprised. 'Have you got up, darling? There's plenty to eat.'

'Let me warm something up right away!' Ester leapt out of the leather chair in front of the television. 'Can you wait a little?' she asked Vilhálmur nervously.

'Yes, of course. I'm not in a hurry,' said Vilhjálmur eagerly, as if he couldn't believe his own ears.

'It's all right. I can do it myself,' said Linda.

33

Father Bernhardur parked the car outside the house on Vatnsholt. He bounced from one foot to the other in the cold and pressed the entryphone buzzer rather abstractedly. He was mulling over his conversation with Linda. What had he got himself into? He had made it a firm rule a long time ago to warn his congregation off anything mystical or 'New Age'. A boy's sulky voice answered, 'Yes?'

'It's the priest.'

'I don't want anything to do with any priest,' said the voice.

'All right, mate.' Father Bernhardur pressed the correct buzzer and introduced himself once more. The door opened. Vilhelmína came to the top of the stairs to greet him.

'I pressed the wrong buzzer,' he said when she had shut the door to the communal hall. 'And the people there don't want anything to do with a priest.'

'Please make yourself comfortable and take off your coat.' She shook her head impatiently. 'I don't know who does need a priest if the people downstairs don't. If anyone needs a priest, they do,' she repeated forcefully.

In the living room there were two chairs by a coffee table.

'Please sit down.'

He looked round. On his first visit the flat had made him feel sad and he hadn't known why. Everything had been selected with great care, the furniture was immaculate, the paintings on the walls even more expensive and grand than at Theódóra's and the neatness almost obsessive. Father Bernhardur did not realize what was inspiring this sense of melancholy until the woman started to pour tea into his cup with tremendous care. All the love and devotion that had gone into his surroundings was going completely unappreciated. He almost stood up and hugged Vilhelmína.

'I've just been to see your sister.'

'And what did she have to say for herself?'

'Only good things.'

'You wouldn't believe how tough Tedda is. I adored Axel. He was a good man. And now she's got all these problems with her politics.' Vilhelmína sat down and looked round her. 'She's so ambitious. I've never been ambitious like that.'

'Is there a big gap in age between you?'

'Seven years. I was born in 1948. People were always saying – I remember it like yesterday – "Is this Theódóra's sister? I'd never have guessed! They're so different."' Vilhelmína turned to the priest. 'Tedda was very beautiful.'

'What did we talk about last time?' asked Father Bernhardur.

'Did you speak to the Bishop for me?' the woman asked quickly. 'Can we use the Catholic church if everything turns out right?'

'I'm afraid that won't be possible.'

'Oh!' said Vilhelmína, immediately taking offence.

Father Bernhardur flicked through his copy of the catechism. 'I've talked to so many people recently I'm losing track. What did we discuss last time?'

'The differences between the Lutheran and the Catholic Churches. We talked about the Sacraments and then you told me about the Resurrection.'

'Yes, that's right. And tonight I want to talk about Christ sending the Holy Spirit to the Apostles. I was discussing this with the children in the young people's home earlier today . . .' Father Bernhardur waited while Vilhelmína poured more tea into his cup and pointed him in the direction of the milk jug. He poured a little into his cup while still holding his catechism in his left hand. He was sure that his initial instruction had gone straight over the woman's head.

'Hördur!' she said, sounding worried. 'My husband. Now it would really do him good to confess. I must ask you to talk to him if you get the chance. He really does need a priest. I've tried all I can to be a good influence on him.'

'And how have you done that?' he asked, keen to hear her answer.

'I took both children to the clinic for the families of alcoholics, so that we can learn how to help him fight his addiction.'

'Does he really drink as much as all that?'

'Yes,' said the woman. 'He's been drinking heavily for years.'

'Can he hold down a job? Where is he tonight?' asked Father Bernardur, anxiously.

'Oh, it's not that sort of drinking,' she said impatiently. 'He doesn't get unsteady on his feet. But it's constant. A couple of drinks every night. Cognac with his coffee. And we've let him carry on like this,' she said wearily. 'We've been "co-dependants", as they say.'

The priest interrupted her. 'I want to talk to you about Whitsun.'

'Luckily Hördur isn't drunk tonight. He's on the locum night shift. I pity the poor driver that has to go out with him. The one who testified against him. I expect he's having quite a night of it. Hördur's very keen to work with him.'

'Well, there we are,' said Father Bernhardur, sounding sad and pensive. 'Theódóra asked me to go to Thingholtstræti. I'm sorry I wasn't able to bring about a reconciliation there.'

'It'll have to run its course. He's appealed to the High Court. I can't understand that Dagný being like this about it. What's the matter with the woman?'

He let the question hang in the air and then said firmly, 'The Apostles were a disorganized and fragmented group before Whitsun . . .'

'What's been happening to Trausti this summer? Hördur talks of this being his supreme humiliation, his son being gay. And of course it's all supposed to be Ester's and my fault that the boy's carrying on like this. As I understand it we're supposed to have made him this way by being so dominant.' She laughed. 'Me? Me, dominant! I never get my own way about anything.'

'But Ester looks as if she could stand her ground if she chose to,' said the priest impatiently.

'Yes, and her father backs down then,' said the woman, nodding her agreement. 'And he didn't say a word when she had little Gauti by that dreadful little man,' she said, insulting me, your narrator.

Father Bernhardur again attempted to address the issue of the evening. 'As I was just saying,' and he opened his Bible at the Acts of the Apostles and started reading: '"And when the day of Pentecost was fully come, they were all with one accord in one place. And suddenly there came a sound from heaven as of a rushing mighty wind, and it filled all the house where they were sitting. And there appeared unto them cloven tongues as of fire, and it sat upon each of them. And they were all filled with the Holy Ghost, and began to speak with other tongues, as the Spirit gave them utterance."'

'Tell me, Father Bernhardur,' said the woman, brightening up, 'do you believe in reincarnation?'

The priest tugged at his beard impatiently. 'No,' he said. 'Far from it. As far as I'm concerned it's blasphemy and nonsense.

There's nothing in the Bible to support it.' Father Bernhardur was getting warm and he unbuttoned his jacket. When Vilhelmína noticed, she got up and opened a window. A cool draught entered the living room.

'Well,' said the woman, erupting with repressed yearning, 'I wouldn't want to be so narrow-minded as to deny all possibility of reincarnation. I'm still on a spiritual quest myself. I once went with a friend to see a woman who had second sight as they call it. She was firmly of the opinion that I had suffered greatly in a previous existence.'

He frowned, stared at her and waited.

Vilhelmína sighed. 'Yes, I went through a lot in the Nazi concentration camps.'

'In the Nazi concentration camps?' whispered the priest in stunned amazement. 'Haven't you just seen too many war movies? There have been films on television about all that for over thirty years.'

'Father Bernhardur,' said the woman, rather offended, 'I never watch television and certainly not those Nazi films. No, I was in a concentration camp. That woman said so and I've occasionally had inklings of it. Once I was out with this friend of mine and we went to Café Hressingarskálin for a waffle. We were sitting facing each other, looking into each other's eyes and suddenly we both burst out laughing. Do you know what was so funny?'

The priest shook his head.

'She had realized that she was a countess from the time of Catherine the Great and the extraordinary thing was that I was her personal maid. Just at the very moment she was remembering this, I was telling her about a vision I had of her in a long yellow dress, covered in pearls, in a magnificent palace. I described the dress to her and she recognized it. Don't you think that's extraordinary? That our previous lives had brought us together?'

'What? What's extraordinary? What brought you together?' he repeated, nonplussed.

'What I was saying.' The woman voice rose with her excitement. 'I'd been her personal maid. If that's not divine proof I don't know the meaning of the word. But there is something I don't understand. It's this. Why do I have to suffer so much in this life when

I've already suffered so much in the concentration camp? I was born in 1948, so I can hardly have had another existence in between unless I died in early infancy. I suppose I could have been reborn as an animal. Is that possible?'

'What's all this rubbish, Vilhelmína?' asked Father Bernhardur. He was on the edge of losing his temper. 'You all talk about nothing but dreams and seances, reincarnation, previous lives, visions . . . Everything is upside-down and everyone is prepared to believe anything except the one thing that truly matters to us all: God and the Son he sent us. The Church is the important thing!' He waved his hands. 'Christ is present in the Mass! No one wants to believe that, but if some old lady claims to be a rice farmer in China two thousand years ago then the whole country seems to find that easy enough to swallow.' Words failed him. 'The only life you have is this life.' He brought his fist down on the coffee table. 'The only means of communication the Almighty gave you is prayer and' – he laid his large clenched fist on the book – 'the Bible.'

'Oh, why do you say that?' said the woman as if overcome by an overwhelming sorrow. 'You make me feel my life is worthless and I am nothing.' She looked at him in desperation. 'Absolutely nothing!'

'But you can't mean that,' he said, shocked. 'You are created in the image of God. God created man in his own image.'

'Yes, *man*,' she said, bowing her head in agreement. 'Man!'

'"Male and female created he them."'

'Try telling that to Höddi.'

'We keep coming back to Hördur. Stop thinking about him. Concentrate on yourself.'

'He's the one who ought to become a Catholic and have his sins forgiven,' said the woman.

'Try to look on the bright side. Isn't it good to be married to a doctor?' he said, smiling. 'You don't have far to go if you need help when you're ill.'

'I'd never let Hördur examine me!' said Vilhelmína, shocked at the idea. 'I have no confidence in medical science at all. And he'd never dream of it. Doctors don't like treating their own families. Tumi, Tedda's family doctor, looks after me. But I never take anything unless it's absolutely necessary. I'd rather go for natural healing, especially homeopathy.'

'Well,' he said firmly, 'let's look in a bit more detail at the arrival of the Holy Spirit at Whitsuntide.'

'When Ester, Trausti and I went to the Alcohol Clinic, Hördur said he'd prove to us he had no problem with not drinking and he hasn't touched a drop for three weeks. Ever since that evening he went to the Prime Minister's and came home drunk.'

'They know each other?'

'They're thick as thieves these days, or so I'm led to believe. Don't ask me how it happened. He's meant to be asking Hördur out for dinner.'

'And did the family join in this bet?' Father Bernhardur shut his Bible and gave up all hope of instructing her.

'Of course! And no wine has passed our lips since. Hördur will give in before I do.' She hit the table with her fist.

'Well, I think it's time I was going home,' said Father Bernhardur, looking at his watch. 'I'm dog tired. It's been a difficult day. I'll come back tomorrow or the day after.'

34

The Prime Minister left the Parliament building by the main door, wrapped his scarf round his neck and set off home. He enjoyed his morning and evening walk when he could call his time his own.

It was nearly eleven and the debate in the chamber had gone on for an extraordinarily long time. There seemed no possible resolution to the dispute over taxing investment income and it had been flogged to death by the opposition. Earlier in the evening members of the Nation's Watch Party had filibustered for almost three hours and completely without justification had attacked the Prime Minister during his speech and accused him of bringing his own personal financial dealings into Parliament. Hannes was obliged to say that such an insinuation on the member's part was beneath contempt. Then a member of the Women's Party had stood up and accused the Prime Minister of paying only lip service to the equality of the sexes. 'Give them enough rope,' muttered Hannes.

There was a sharp frost. It was a still and starry night. It reminded him of the evening he'd invited that doctor back home. What a boring, long-haired creep he'd turned out to be! Hannes was irritated at the memory. Why didn't the man get his bloody hair cut? Now he wouldn't be able to get him out of his mind all the way home. Then he heard a voice behind him: 'Excuse me.'

He turned round, scarcely able to believe it. Was that bore lying in wait for him so he could go on and on begging him to intervene in his court case?

But it was a big-built, fair-haired man with an aquiline nose staring at him. It struck the Prime Minister how little security Icelandic politicians were given. It was an easy matter to make an assassination attempt whenever you fancied it. His foreign opposite numbers would never put up with such a lack of security.

Hannes waited without saying anything and stared back at the man.

'Forgive me disturbing you,' the man said, becoming more meek as the Prime Minister looked at him. 'I was on my way out to Landakot to try and see that Father Paternoster or whatever his name is and then I saw you coming out of Parliament and I thought I'd speak to you. Forgive my rudeness, but what I have to say really does concern you . . .'

'I hold open surgery once a week.'

'I was going to speak to you. I wasn't lying in wait for you. It's just a coincidence that I saw you. How's your new car?' The man beamed at the Prime Minister and held out his hand.

'My new what?'

'Your car?'

Hannes looked around slowly, out towards the open green area of Austurvöllur and back to the door into the Parliament building. He was wondering how he could avoid having this conversation. Would it be possible to slip back into Parliament?

My name is Tryggvi Thórarinsson. I work at GM Service. I checked your car over before delivery. The new Buick. It's great, isn't it?'

'Oh, right, OK, my friend,' said Hannes, relieved. He grasped the outstretched hand. The man seemed to him a typical Icelander, of the type he had constantly had to deal with when he had his law practice. 'Yes,' he said. 'It's the best car I've ever driven.'

'Isn't it just!' Tryggvi's face broke into joyful grin. 'I checked it over before delivery to make sure it was OK. It's as responsive as a speedboat.' Tryggvi put his hands in his pockets and stood facing the Prime Minister, radiating an extraordinary energy.

'Well, it was good to meet you,' said the Prime Minister, turning aside and starting to walk towards his home.

'Can't I walk with you? I'm going to the west side of town too.'

'Feel free,' said the Prime Minister, but he didn't sound very friendly. 'The streets are yours as much as they're mine.'

'Indeed they are. We're both Icelanders and I'm a member of the Independent Party just like you. I've been an Independent since I was a toddler, just like my old man before me. Our household was Independent through and through.' Tryggvi suddenly became tongue-tied. All he had to do was to get to the point. They walked on in silence for a while. Involuntarily the Prime Minister came to his assistance.

'What did you say you were going to the west end for?'

'I'm meeting a Catholic priest.'

'Everyone seems to be turning Catholic these days,' said the Prime Minister, down in the mouth. 'It's the fashion.'

'No, I'm not joining the congregation, although I suppose I might later. It's just that one of the priests has been helping me. He's a good man, Father Bernhardur.'

'Yes, I know him.'

'Do you? Yes, he's a good man, but this whole business affects you more directly than that. It's to do with my wife.'

The Prime Minister turned and looked at the man's profile as they carried on walking and said, surprised, 'Your wife?'

'Yes, you know who she is. Actually she's under your protection at the moment.'

'But, my dear man,' said the Prime Minister feeling increasingly uneasy; he was beginning to find this strange man rather frightening, 'I've got nothing to do with your wife. I don't make a habit of getting involved with other men's wives.'

'Don't get me wrong,' said Tryggvi chattily. He laughed. 'I don't mean anything by it.' His tone changed and he became serious and intense. 'In fact I ought to thank you for what you did, looking after Dagný like that. I saw it all on the evening news that night, even though it was edited down for the eleven o'clock bulletin. But it's impossible for me to find out where Dæja is. No one'll tell me. Dagný, the woman who was screaming in Parliament. That's my wife.' Tryggvi flung his arms wide in his excitement.

'Oh, I see. That's your wife, is it?' The Prime Minister started to walk a little more quickly.

'Yes. Where is she now? No one will tell me anything.'

'Well it's not me you should be speaking to.'

'But you took her under your wing. The whole country saw you do it.'

'Yes, I tried to help her,' roared the Prime Minister. 'But then I passed the whole business over to my colleague. Phone Government House tomorrow and probably he'll tell you what he knows.'

'What's the name of this man?'

'Haraldur Sumarlidason.'

Tryggvi repeated the name several times. 'What's he look like?'

'Tall, fat, red hair.'

Tryggvi was excited. 'Yes, a great big fat bloke. I've seen him on the box.'

The Prime Minister stopped. They were standing at the intersection of Túngata and Hólavallagata. 'This is where we say good night,' said Hannes. He looked at the man and then at the Catholic church.

'You've got to understand,' said Tryggvi excitedly, putting a hand up to his hair. 'Dagný's an actress.'

'Is she now? I thought I recognized her.'

'The thing is I want to do everything I can for her. I don't want to lose her.'

The Prime Minister couldn't avoid smiling. 'My dear chap, you'll have to discuss your marital difficulties with somebody else. I've got quite enough problems of my own.'

'Why should I do that?' said Tryggvi stubbornly. 'You're the Prime Minister, aren't you?'

'Evidently so, but . . .'

'There's no "but" about it. We can't all duck our responsibilities.'

Tryggvi was waving his arms about. 'You took her under your wing. I was waiting outside Parliament, ready to take Dæja home with me once she'd calmed down a bit. She screamed at me, "I'm a woman! I'm a woman!", as if I didn't know that. I bet I'm the only person who doesn't have to be in any doubt about it. There was a bit of a misunderstanding over a bloody painting. The sodding bailiff was going to get his hands on it. Now, when I run into you by accident and want to talk to you about it all, you just make out you don't know anything about it and palm me off on some assistant. If I cock something up at the garage I have to deal with it myself.'

'I'll phone Haraldur first thing in the morning and ask him to find out what happened to your wife.'

'Would you do that?' Tryggvi looked as hopeful as a child. 'I'd be so grateful. If there's something I could do for you some time? Just ring me if your car breaks down. Ask for Tryggvi Thórarinsson. And that fat bloke, Halli or whatever he's called, get him to tell Dagný that I'll be happy to have her back.' In spite of the cold Tryggvi blushed scarlet and was mortified with embarrassment. 'It isn't the first time she's walked out. She left me in the spring. She went to a friend who'd been putting ideas into her head. I had to work out what to do. I couldn't have that. And that friend of hers, I tell you, Hannes,' said Tryggvi forcefully, 'she's no better than a whore.'

'You can't go saying things like that about people.'

'It's only the truth. It's what you do all day in Parliament, tell each other what's what. How can Dagný do this to me? She's got three kids. We've been together for twenty-five years.' Tryggvi grimaced and his eyes flashed with the tension. 'She's a lovely woman. She made out she came back because she lost her mother but I know better,' he said triumphantly. 'I'm not an idiot. She came back because her friend came back from overseas and wanted her flat back. You see? She can't pull the wool over my eyes.' Tryggvi grinned. 'And she was well pleased to be back home, I can tell you. And things were OK for a bit. Those bloody friends of hers,' he said bitterly. 'One day her friend Jóna rang. It was lucky I was there. "Jóna, if you show your ugly mug at 28 Thingholtstræti, you'll be sorry, I can tell you." "Are you going to

335

ban my friends from the house?" Dagný asked me. "No, that's not the way I see it, Dagný," I said. "I just don't want you hanging about with whores." "And who says Jóna's a whore?" she asks. "I say she's a whore." "What reason do you have to say that?" I say, "Because I've seen the way she carries on."' Tryggvi looked at the Prime Minister as if he was telling him a secret. 'She really puts it about a bit, if you know what I mean. Well, the next day was a Saturday and she leaves me with the kids and says she's got to go out for a bit, get her hair done. A bit later there's a knock on the door. It's Jóna come round again. "Hello, Jóna," I say.' Tryggvi, his voice now hoarse, paused for a moment in his story. '"And what do you want?" She's got her nose in the air, all narked that I'm interferring. "Dæja sent me to get her ear-rings." "Her ear-rings?" "Yes."' Tryggvi looked at the Prime Minister. 'I tell you, Hannes, this put me right off my stroke and I couldn't say anything. When I could speak again, I said, "Well, you'd better go and get them then." She stomps into the bedroom, noses around in Dagný's stuff and then off she goes. Then I started to wonder. A mate of mine lent me a car and I hung around outside Skúlagata. I didn't want to use the red Ford. I knew she'd spot it at once. I saw them come out and take a taxi and I followed them to Café Ingolfs. I parked the car and wanted to go in. But along comes this bouncer. He thought he was really something. "What do you want?" he says. "I've come to get my old lady," I says, quite calm and polite. "You're not going in dressed like that," he says, getting shirty with me. I was in my working gear. I didn't say anything but just gave him a shove. Then three of them jumped me and gave me a thorough going over. I went home to change but the fucking bitches had got away. I went into bar after bar and I couldn't find them. It was nearly morning when she came home. "Where were you then?" I asks her. "I slept at my friend Jóna's," she says. "You think I'm stupid? You think I'm going to believe that?" "Deep down, you're vile, Tryggvi," she says. "You always believe the worst of people. You think everyone's as vile and mean as you are!"'

Tryggvi looked at the Prime Minister as though expecting him to give a verdict. 'Just imagine someone saying something like that to you! "How do you think I can bear being cooped up in this building site?" she says. "And with you!" "With me?" I says. "Yes, with you!" she screams at me. "Do I live with anyone else but you? Why's it so strange if I need to get out and have a bit fun once in a while?" "Well," I says.' Tryggvi stared straight into the Prime Minister's face. 'I'd had it by now. I said, "Dagný, I've had all I can take. If this house isn't good enough for you, built entirely out of redwood, from that fantastic ship that was washed up a hundred years ago, well then, you can sling your hook." But she never went. Not until she got all upset about that painting and came running to you. Now she wants to change the child's name and have our daughter called by her name. I'm not good enough to be Silla's father any more. Sylvía Dagnýjardóttir. How can anyone put up with that?' Tryggvi was silent for a moment and looked sullenly at Hannes. 'Are you going to give her a job or fix her up with a flat?' he asked. 'Do you think there's no limit to what I can put up with? Well, there is a limit. I've got friends. I've got a lot of friends from when we all used to be into cars and all that. Now they're all family men but I'm going to get them together, ten, twenty of them and we'll come up to Government House and we'll storm the place. Once I decide to do something, no one on earth can talk me out of it.'

'There's no reason for you storm Government House,' roared Hannes. 'You know what women are like these days. They want their freedom.'

'I know what play you'll have seen Dagný in. *Medea*. It was on for a month last autumn. Ridiculous thing. A really screwed-up old woman kills her kids to get even with her old man. Have they all gone mad? How can killing her kids make a woman free?'

'If I remember my mythology from school, she was made to drink gall for all eternity by the gods. But it's all above my head, I'm afraid, my friend.'

'Yes. And mine. But that's what they say! They do! That's what they say!' Tryggvi spread out his arms. 'Drink gall! Serve her right! And then they all went and floated candles on the lake to show solidarity with Medea. That was all down to Dagný. Don't you think it's crazy?' Tryggvi put his hand on the Prime Minister's arm. 'And do you think they've got any interest in us having equal rights, you and me, Hannes? No, what they want is power!' Tryggvi stared at him. He was electric with energy. 'That's what you've got to understand. What? Hannes, my dear old mate, Hannes! Don't you get it? You, the most powerful man in the country!' Tryggvi was astounded by the Prime Minister's apathy. 'When was the last time you heard a woman talking about men's rights? No, all they talk about is women's rights and that means only one thing: power. Power for them. Don't you see, the Battle of Stalingrad is being fought again in our front rooms!'

'It's a tough old world, my friend,' said the Prime Minister. 'But now I must be getting home.'

Tryggvi lifted a hand and waved goodbye. He walked away up the street with long loping strides. 'Thanks for the chat,' he called. 'If you can have a word with Dagný and get her to stop all this nonsense and come back home then you can count on me. You ring Tryggvi Thórarinsson and I'll come and fix your car any time. I must go now and talk to the priest. I'll ring the fat bloke first thing in the morning. If you tell the fat bloke not to sort her out with a flat I'll see you all right, you can count on me.'

'Hey you!' he called, when they were some distance apart.

The Prime Minister turned round.

'See the Northern Lights?' Tryggvi pointed.

Hannes looked at the sky. A wide band of Northern Lights stretched across the city. Irritated, Hannes shook his head and hurried on home.

Haraldur Sumarliðason was waiting for him there, twitching his shoulders nervously. He wore a pained expression. 'Yes, give it to me straight, Halli,' said the Prime Minister sternly as he hung up his overcoat.

'There's no way to get at them through the fish farm.' Haraldur puffed up his cheeks and blew out the air. He unbuttoned his jacket, straightened his tie and hitched up his trousers.

'Why not?'

'Because the vodka dealer is planning to put 15 million dollars into the fish farm. An Italian guy flew in in a private jet this morning. Vilhjálmur fixed it all. So it'll make no difference whether the bank calls in their debts or not. I've never in my life been persuaded to eat trout,' he added as an afterthought. 'It beats me how anybody with any sense at all can want to eat those slimy little buggers. How was Parliament?'

The Prime Minister smiled benevolently at his assistant. 'No real news from Parliament except the bloody Left won't budge. But I met a party member and political ally on the steps of the Parliament building. We went for a little walk together. And what that man has to cope with is no laughing matter. The poor bloke deserves all the pity he can get. Our problems are as nothing compared to his.'

When Father Bernhardur returned home after seeing Vilhelmína he was told he had a visitor waiting for him. Tryggvi was looking at the photograph of the old wooden church. 'There must have been some wonderful wood used in the construction of this church,' he said when Father Bernhardur came to the door. 'It's a shame it was demolished. It would have been fun to do it up.'

'Go ahead. It was moved up to the corner of the street. It's now the home of Reykjavík Sports Club.

'What? They turned a church into a gym? Isn't that sacrilege?'

'No. Why? You can't have come to talk to me about old buildings. I don't want to be rude but I've been dashing about from one end of town to the other all day. What is it you want?'

Tryggvi sat down. 'It's Dagný. Could you go and see the Prime Minister's assistant tomorrow and find out where she is? I happened to run into the Prime Minister in the street. Thanks be to God! They're sorting everything out for Dagný, getting her a flat and everything. Did you see it on the television? Well, my girl finally got herself a starring role! They're getting a lot of good publicity out of it, of course, that was obvious all along. You've got to go and see her for me and try and talk some sense into her.'

Father Bernhardur sat down. 'Try and talk some sense into her?'

'Yes, she's determined to leave me. They're getting her a job.'

'You can't force someone to live with you if they don't want to, Tryggvi. If people can't live together, they can't. You mention her getting a job. What's wrong with that? Isn't it a good thing if she gets a job?'

Tryggvi stared at him expressionlessly but in the silence that fell over them Father Bernhardur sensed his surprise. 'But you're a Catholic priest! I thought you didn't allow people to get divorced,' said Tryggvi at last accusingly.

'It's got nothing more to do with Catholicism than with any other denomination. People are not allowed to and shouldn't get divorced. But if they can't live together, then they can't. And that's an end of it.' Father Bernhardur was going to say he was very tired and offer to show Tryggvi out but there was no need as he had already stood up.

No sooner had Tryggvi left than the priest was called to the telephone. It was Vilhelmína to say she was not prepared to receive any further instruction in the near future. She wanted time to think it all over. Becoming a Catholic was a major step. And she was very cross with the Bishop for not letting her use the church if she succeeded in talking Ester into marrying Vilhjálmur.

35

Vilhjálmur was very anxious about going to Keflavík Airport with the priest to collect the Indian boy. He was expecting him to start talking about the Sacred Heart and all sorts of things no one understood, but to his great relief Father Bernhardur didn't mention religion once as they drove out to the south-west tip of Iceland. Vilhjálmur was a friendly sort and he chatted about all sorts of things that were of interest to him, notably the financial stability or otherwise of the country in general and of Heidnaberg in particular. There were dark clouds in the sky over the south coast and a storm so intense the jeep sometimes trembled. 'We have eight different lines of alcohol in the Duty Free shop.' He looked searchingly at Father Bernhardur as if expecting him to be teetotal. Suddenly he declared, 'I'll never understand Ester. The more I show my feelings for her, the more distant she becomes. I just don't understand it! I was convinced we were twin souls.' He drove a few hundred yards in silence. 'I'm expecting to become managing director of the company very soon.' Vilhjálmur beamed at the priest. 'But that's strictly between you and me, top secret.'

'The only twin souls I've met in the course of my priesthood have been when one party, husband or wife, has had to relinquish their own soul completely,' said Father Bernhardur. He pointed. 'Look! It's as if Michelangelo has painted the vault of the heavens. I lived in Rome for a few years,' he added by way of explanation.

'Yes. I wonder how the south coast will look to an Indian? All you see on television are temples and small still lakes.' Suddenly Vilhálmur realized he had forgotten to buy some flowers and that it was not right to receive a guest on his arrival in the country without presenting him with a bouquet. They took a detour into Keflavík. Vilhjálmur asked directions and they found their way to a florist. The jet was just landing as they entered the Lief Eiriksson Terminal. 'He must be one of the first Indians to visit Iceland,' said Vilhjálmur. 'I don't expect he'll want to go into the Duty Free shop.' He put the palms of his hands against the glass dividing the entrance hall from the terminal itself and scanned the incoming passengers. 'Look for a little Indian boy with a stewardess. That'll be him.'

Father Bernhardur stood by the window and from time to time put his hands to the glass barrier and looked through it.

A group of passengers streamed through and went straight into the Duty Free shop. Vilhjálmur chatted up a customs officer and tried to talk him into allowing him in on the pretext that he had to check the drinks stock in the shop. The customs officer wasn't particularly friendly and wouldn't let him in. 'Give a man a uniform and he thinks he's God,' said Vilhjálmur to the priest.

The conveyor belt jerked into action and a row of suitcases came sailing into the arrivals hall. At long last a stewardess appeared. She was carrying a bag and holding a young boy by the hand. He didn't look remotely Indian. Father Bernhardur and Vilhjálmur waited. The boy and the stewardess walked through the hall without the bag being checked. They stared in surprise at the boy. He would be about fourteen, a bit short for his age, with dark hair. His ears were a bit on the large side, but his hair hid them almost entirely. He looked rather ashen but very brave. There was a small dark mark on one cheek and his eyelashes were like black feathers.

'Here's your consignment,' said the stewardess.

'Were you asked to look after another lad? This one isn't from India,' said Vilhjálmur.

341

'Obviously not. He's from Yugoslavia, or Bosnia as we've got to learn to call it.'

The Serb boy had a label tied round his neck on which was written in big black letters: SALTYKOV.

Vilhjálmur stepped forward and introduced himself to the stewardess. 'Vilhjálmur Kalmannsson, executive director at Heidnaberg.'

'Well, here he is,' said the stewardess. She turned to the boy and spoke in English, 'These men are going to take you to your Icelandic hosts.'

'How did you get to London?' asked Vilhjálmur.

'I flew from Paris. The Red Cross got me to France.'

'We were under the impression', Vilhjálmur said to the stewardess, 'that we were collecting an Indian boy.' He was not yet used to the idea of taking delivery of the child.

'Well this is all I can offer you,' she said, laughing. 'There's obviously been some sort of mix-up. Aren't you going to take him?'

Vilhjálmur put the vast bouquet of red and white roses into the Serb boy's arms. He removed the label from his neck and reached for the boy's bag. The stewardess shook hands with the child and said goodbye. Then Father Bernhardur stopped daydreaming and welcomed the boy. They shook hands energetically and then the three of them walked outside together and headed for the jeep. Vilhjálmur opened the hatchback and put the bag in it. Father Bernhardur watched the boy. He was a long way from being cowed by all the horrors he had undoubtedly witnessed. On the contrary he was poised and confident with his companions. He was wearing a smart new suit. 'And what's your name?'

'Bosko Dragutin.'

Vilhjálmur repeated the name several times as if he was fixing it in his memory and slammed the hatchback shut.

Father Bernhardur held the door open for Bosko and the boy sat in the middle of the back seat. Vilhjálmur quickly slid into the driver's seat. 'I've nothing against the child. It's just not what we were led to expect. We had an agreement. I'll send them a fax.' He started the engine.

'Isn't it likely the Red Cross chose those in most need?' asked Father Bernhardur. He turned to the boy as soon as Vilhjálmur had backed out of the parking space. 'We are talking about the Red Cross.'

'Is there a problem?'

'No, no. It's just that we were expecting someone else. But you're very welcome here.' Father Bernhardur smiled.

'Who were you expecting?'

'A little boy from India.'

'What went wrong?'

'I've no idea. Have you?' Father Bernhardur looked at Vilhjálmur and he shook his head.

The Serb boy nodded gravely and looked out at what he could see of Iceland. As Vilhjálmur reached the main road and headed for Reykjavík, he asked, 'Is all of Iceland like this?'

'Like what?'

'All stones and snow.'

Vilhjálmur gave a little speech about the Reykjanes peninsula. Father Bernhardur had the impression that he had given it many times to foreign visitors. He covered the geological history, the volcanic eruptions out of the sea during the seventeenth century. He explained the reasons for the siting of the NATO base. The boy looked over his shoulder at the populated area round the airport and talked loudly about the barrenness of it all. Vilhjálmur maintained that there were denser areas of vegetation in other parts of Iceland. He discussed the relationship between Heidnaberg and Shadrak Inc., the distillers of Saltykov Vodka. Father Bernhardur thought this paragraph too had been thoroughly rehearsed. 'The lady who brought you to Iceland is managing director of Heidnaberg,' Vilhjálmur concluded.

'Am I going to live with her?'

'No, with him.' Vilhjálmur indicated Father Bernhardur with his thumb.

'But I was told in London that I was going to live in a large house with an older lady, the managing director of an Icelandic company,' the boy said, sounding irritated.

'Yes, but since this was arranged,' said Vilhjálmur firmly, 'the husband of the lady you mention has died and the lady is in no position to entertain guests. You'll live with the priest for the time being. You'll be fine there.'

'With a priest?' gulped the boy.

'A Catholic priest!' said Father Bernhardur and smiled into the rearview mirror.

'A Catholic priest,' said the boy sullenly. 'I'm not a Croat. I'm a member of the Orthodox Church.'

'He won't try and make a Christian out of you,' said Vilhjálmur, who was not very well up in the ramifications of the religious world. 'You'll just be living there for the time being. It's a young people's home run by the Catholic Church. Heidnaberg, Saltykov Vodka's Icelandic agent, helped to set it up.'

'There are some kids there you can make friends with,' said Father Bernhardur, looking over his shoulder.

'I don't much like the idea,' said the boy, frowning.

'You think you're doing a good deed,' said Vilhjálmur, 'and then you find the people you're doing the good deed for don't quite see it like that.'

'What's he saying?' asked the Serb boy.

'I was saying, just you wait until you see the house you're going to be living in. It's one of the nicest houses in the old part of Reykjavík.'

The boy didn't answer and they drove a long way in silence. Suddenly the boy said, 'At least the sea round the island's very beautiful. Can you see whales?'

Vilhjálmur and the priest looked at the sea. A column of light broke through the storm clouds and lit up a circular area of the greeny-blue turbulent ocean. 'But the countryside is ugly,' the boy added. 'In Serbia there are mountains and woods,' he said proudly.

'Whaling is banned at the moment, but 76 per cent of Iceland's gross national product is derived from the sea,' said Vilhjálmur. 'It used to be even higher. At one point it was 97 per cent, I believe.'

'Have you been in England long?' asked Father Bernhardur.

'Three weeks. I didn't want to come here. But there was no choice.'

'I can see Theódóra Thóroddsdóttir getting fed up with this little chap very quickly,' commented Vilhjálmur.

Father Bernardur could see the outline of the aluminium processing plant at Straumsvík. He feared Vilhjálmur was about to

344

launch into a dissertation on the production of aluminium, so he said firmly, 'But now you're here I'm sure you'll soon settle in. You'll be meeting boys of your own age at the house.'

'Are they refugees as well?'

'No, they're all Icelanders.'

'Are they all Catholic?'

'No. They're with us during the day.'

'Why aren't they at home?'

'Various reasons.'

'Is there much poverty in Iceland?'

'Not much. Some.'

'What kind of government is it? Communist?'

'No, this is a democracy. The Communists have never been in power here.'

'What about the police? Are they very brutal?'

'No. The police are thought to be really rather gentle. They don't even carry weapons.'

'No weapons!' The boy laughed.

They drove up a hill and the town of Hafnarfjördur lay spread out below them. Up the side of the valley there were a few houses, stacked one on top of the other.

'Those could be Bosnian houses,' said the boy.

Vilhjálmur drove through the suburb of Gardabær. The boy was looking out of the window. As they drove down the Kringlumýrarbrautin road he pointed to the flats and said, 'There are apartment blocks like this in Sarajevo.' Vilhjálmur took the Miklabraut route into town. The lake was frozen over and people were skating. 'I can skate well,' said the Serb boy. 'Will I be living near here?'

'Just a stone's throw from the lake,' said Father Bernhardur.

'Could someone lend me some skates?'

'I don't have any myself but I'm sure we can arrange something.'

'You'll be able to buy some skates tomorrow,' said Vilhjálmur. 'Come to think of it,' he turned to Father Bernhardur, 'I've got fifty thousand kroner for you in case there was anything the boy needed.'

'Let's go and get you some skates tomorrow,' said the priest.

The Serb boy smiled. Vilhjálmur turned on to Sudurgata and

into the parking area by the house. Father Bernhardur got out of the jeep and tipped his seat forward so the boy could get out. Vilhjálmur handed Bosko his bag, shook his hand and said goodbye. Then he stepped over to Father Bernhardur, took his wallet out of his jacket pocket and took out a cheque. It was a Heidnaberg cash cheque signed by the company cashier. 'Would you be good enough to get a receipt for anything you buy?' He smiled. 'We mustn't forget the accountants. Well, I'll pop by and see you all some time soon.' He waved goodbye and got into the jeep. Father Bernhardur and the Serb boy looked at each other. Father Bernhardur was holding the bouquet and smiling. He pointed towards the house. The Serb boy took a few steps up the path ahead of the priest and looked at the house. Then he looked over his shoulder. He seemed afraid and hesitant.

'What's the matter?'

'Nothing. It just looks like some of the houses in my village.'

'There's no need to feel anxious. Just make yourself at home.'

Jökull came to the top of the steps to meet them. He was the same height at the boy from Bosnia. They were a bit awkward with each other. 'There are two men waiting for you in the living room,' said Jökull.

'Who are they?'

'I don't know. One's a photographer. I think the other one must be a reporter. I haven't said anything to them. I've been doing my homework.'

'Where's your brother?'

'Upstairs somewhere. I think he's asleep.'

'Go and tell him to get up and say we've got a guest. Reporters! How's this happened?' muttered Father Bernhardur. 'They came and saw the house ages ago and they've photographed it from top to bottom.'

The reporter and the photographer were waiting for them indoors. They hadn't bothered to take off their shoes and were tramping around the downstairs rooms. The reporter was very curious about Ingibjörg. Was she a Catholic? What was she doing there? 'I'm not in any trouble if that's what you're getting at,' said the girl.

It was the same chap who had interviewed Axel back in the

summer. His name was Steindor. Now he was working for *Morgun-bladid*. I'd have put money on him trying to dig up some story quite apart from the visit of the boy. Probably he was hoping Ingibjörg was a drug-crazed child prostitute. He was always on the look out for stories he could sell on the side to the tabloids. I know precisely the kind of reptile he was.

'Ingibjörg, come and say hello to our foreign visitor,' said Father Bernhardur. 'And put the roses in a vase for me.' He turned to the newspapermen. 'And what can I do for you?'

'We've come to welcome your guest,' said Steindor cheekily, making himself at home. 'He's a refugee, isn't he? Here on charity from the Toyota agency?'

'Who told you that?'

'You'll have to ask our editor.'

Father Bernhardur turned to the boy. 'These gentlemen are from *Morgunbladid*, an Icelandic newspaper. They want to ask you a few questions. He speaks English,' the priest told the reporter. 'You were here very promptly,' he said and scratched his beard. 'Wouldn't it have been better to let the boy settle in a bit? Couldn't you come tomorrow instead?'

'We go to press at half past seven and we're not doing some in-depth interview. It's just a small news item. Where's he from?'

'Bosnia.'

'Tell me,' said Steindor under his breath, 'is he badly injured?'

He glanced at the door when he heard the floorboards creaking in the hall. Haflidi appeared, bleary-eyed, and came towards him. 'Look at you, kid, you're half asleep.'

'I was just having a nap. What's all the fuss?'

'Come and say hello to our guest,' said Father Bernhardur.

The photographer took a picture of the meeting between Haflidi and the Serb boy.

'Can we sit down while I make a few notes?' asked Steindor. 'I haven't got a tape-recorder.'

'Yes, feel free.'

'Get me some juice, Ingibjörg.' Haflidi slumped into a chair by the radio and stretched. 'I've got an awful hangover.'

'Get it yourself.'

The Serb boy had sat down at the table in the sun lounge.

Steindor called his name twice and then showed him the pad with his name written out in block capitals.

'Dragutin! That's a real tough name!' shouted Haflidi.

The boy repeated the story of how he got to London.

'And where's your family?'

'Dead.'

'Do you think you can tell us what happened?' asked Steindor, sounding friendly.

'Yes, OK.'

'I don't think we should be putting the boy through that,' said Father Bernhardur.

'My father was killed by a mad elephant,' said the boy. 'He was not killed in the war. I'm from a circus family. We're gypsies. I was brought up in the circus. Everyone knows elephants never forget when you do something bad to them. When my father was a young man he pricked an elephant in the trunk.' He raised his hand and seemed to be looking for the right word.

'With a knife?' asked the reporter.

'No.'

'A needle?' asked Father Bernhardur.

'Yes, that's it! The little baby elephant came every day and stuck his trunk through my father's window and my father would give him a lump of sugar. My father got bored and pricked him. Soon after that the baby elephant was sold. Thirty years went by. The circus bought an old elephant. As soon as he saw my father he took his chance and killed him. And my mother and brother. It was a miracle I escaped.'

'How did he recognize your father after all that time?'

'Don't ask me,' said the boy pensively. 'Elephants are highly intelligent and they have very long memories.'

'Lots of extraordinary things do happen in the animal kingdom,' said the photographer looking round at the others.

'Wow!' said Haflidi in Icelandic, sitting on the edge of his chair. 'A whole family killed by an elephant. I'd've loved to have seen that.'

'Yes, let's not ask him to go into details,' said Steindor. 'In the media we're always getting hauled over the coals for harassing people. Let's give a refugee a break.' He turned to the boy. 'How do you like Iceland?' The photographer took a picture.

'It's fine. I'm happy to be here. Us kids, we could choose which country we went to. Iceland was my first choice.'

Steindor looked up. 'Terrific,' he said. 'Toggi, have you got what you need?'

Steindor shook the boy's hand and said goodbye. 'Let me offer you my condolences.'

Toggi, the photographer, came and offered his condolences too.

When they had gone, Father Bernhardur said, 'You change your mind quite quickly. I thought you didn't reckon much to Iceland.'

'I was lying to him.'

'And the story about the death of your family? All lies?'

'Yes,' said the boy. 'It came into my head because you were expecting someone from India. Do you think you'd tell just anyone something as painful as how you lost your parents and younger brother?'

'Wow,' said Haflidi. 'I could really like this kid!'

36

There was a dangerous side to Tryggvi that Haflidi was the only one of his children to recognize. It was not that Tryggvi had ever been violent towards him, it was just that all he had to do was to look inside himself. When he was angry his chest hurt. And the only way to get rid of the pain was to let it come bursting out.

Haflidi woke up to find Tryggvi complaining to Gunnhildur. 'I can't bear it,' the boy heard his father saying calmly and deliberately. 'She'd got no right to take my daughter away.' There was a quality to Tryggvi's voice that made Haflidi feel suddenly cold beneath his duvet. He was absolutely certain something terrible was about to happen.

Then he remembered he was due to go to Mass at the Catholic church and sighed at the prospect of the boredom to come like an old man in great pain. Then they were meant to be taking a drive out into the country with the priest to look at nature. 'Examining

Our Environment', it was called. Incredible! As if he'd never seen grass and lava. Insane!

He was fully awake immediately, but managed to empty his mind completely and go straight back to sleep.

His shoulder was poked hard and his grandmother said, 'Come on, get up, my lad. How many more times do I have to tell you?'

'You've only told me once,' he grumbled.

'No, I called you a little while ago and you were talking nonsense. Jökull's up and dressed and has had his breakfast.'

'Leave me alone,' shouted Haflidi violently.

'You should be more like him, or you'll end up in Little Hraun Borstal,' muttered the old woman to herself as she turned on her heel.

He looked out of the window. It was still outside, but even so black clouds were scudding across the moon like smoke from a bonfire. He had been praying for bad weather. When he had been disturbed in the middle of the night the house was creaking in the wind. He got dressed, went into the kitchen and sat down. Jökull was sitting in their mother's chair, looking angelic. 'I'm too old to go to that place with this little brat,' he said, indicating his brother with his spoon. He looked at his plate and offered up a prayer of thanksgiving that it contained cornflakes and not porridge.

'Don't you start anything, Haflidi,' said his father. 'I've got enough to cope with as it is.'

He stood over them, his shoulders hunched, terrifying. There had been a bad smell in the flat since Dagný left. Tryggvi hadn't shaved, his cheeks were sunken and his eyes were dull and lifeless. He prowled round the living room, grimacing, constantly scratching his beard. Gunnhildur was out in the kitchen clearing the backlog of dirty dishes.

Haflidi shovelled down his breakfast. They were going to be late. He dashed to the bathroom, brushed his teeth and splashed his face. When he came out the Ford's engine was running and Jökull was scraping ice off the windscreen. The corrugated iron was creaking in the cold. The tower of the building known as 'The Turnip' was clear against the sky. The stars were shining.

'Look,' said Jökull, pointing at the tower. 'We could be in Russia, in Red Square.'

'And here we have Lenin's Tomb,' Haflidi said, looking up at their house. 'It's all Mother's fault,' he said bitterly. 'It's her fault! He's gone crazy since she left. Bonkers.'

Jökull stopped scraping and looked at his brother in amazement.

'Are you blind or something? Can't you see the man's nearly lost it altogether?' He stopped as Tryggvi was crossing the street with a box of tools and a coil of rope. He handed the box to Jökull and opened the scarlet boot of the Ford. As Jökull was about to put the box in the boot, he nearly scratched the shiny chrome cover of the spare wheel. Tryggvi snatched the box out of his hands and flung it violently into the boot.

They drove along Skálholtstígur, turned north into Fríkirkjuvegur, down Skólabrú and along Túngata beyond Kirkjustræti. The Catholic church stood pitch black against the night sky. Haflidi shivered, he thought it looked horrible. 'Listen,' he said to his father, dramatically. 'The old bat who sacked Mother, the one who owns Heidnaberg, she put money into the young people's home on Sudurgata. Did you know that? Her daughter's working there now. Do you think it's right for us kids to carry on going there, in the circumstances?'

'Stop that right now. I can't see it makes any difference. I haven't got any argument with that woman. Talk to your mother about it if you see her.' Tryggvi dropped the boys off and glared at the church. The sky was beginning to turn blue.

When Haflidi walked into the church he felt as if he were travelling overseas for the first time. Dark pews, enormous pillars holding the vaulted stone roof aloft, brilliant lights shining round the altar, where Father Bernhardur was busying himself. Sylvía and Linda were there. Ingibjörg was ignoring him like before, but so what, his attention was taken up with Linda and her glorious golden hair. Women like her sometimes had a thing for boys like him. There was a group of nuns sitting in the front pew. The boys sat near the front not far from the Serb boy. There was a large crucifix hanging above them, Christ with black hair and a pink body carved out of wood. The altar was covered with a white cloth and there was a vase of yellow flowers standing on it. Haflidi leaned back in the pew. Behind the altar there was a golden cabinet and on the top of the cabinet yet another figure of Christ, this time standing on the globe. 'Who are these old geezers?' whispered Haflidi, pointing to the statues and reliefs dotted round the walls.

'Saints. Shush.' Jökull put a finger to his lips.

'Mother says to say hello,' whispered Sylvía from behind them. 'Shush, shut up you,' said Haflidi harshly and assumed his role as elder brother as Father Bermhardur appeared in a white robe. The Mass was beginning. The priest approached the altar and everyone stood up. Father Bernhardur spread out his arms and intoned, so that it echoed round the building, 'Peace be with you!'

The congregation mumbled something Haflidi could not make out. It was all very strange. The nuns were now crossing themselves, downwards from their mouths and crossways over their chests. He glanced at Linda. She was doing the same thing, so he copied her. The nuns and everybody else sat down. Father Bernhardur nodded to Linda and she walked up to the pulpit. She read from the Bible open in front of her on the lectern: '"But when the morning was now come, Jesus stood on the shore: but the disciples knew not that it was Jesus. Then Jesus saith unto them, Children have ye any meat?"'

The Serb boy did not understand a word. He let his mind wander and again he saw the leather boot. The laces were caked solid with clay and grass. He watched his mother kiss the boot. They had been running through the forest when a group of soldiers had caught the family and arrested them. It was their second day in captivity. They were a long way from the village and his six-month-old baby brother wouldn't be comforted, no matter how much they bounced him up and down or sang to him or his mother gave him the breast. The Serb boy saw again the circle of thick dark hair at the crown of his brother's head. The soldiers were unshaven and their clothes were dirty and they had run out of cigarettes.

He looked up at the pulpit again where the fair-haired woman, Linda, was reading. He listened to the strange language again for a moment without being able to make out a single word. '"They answered him, No. And he said unto them, Cast the net on the right side of the ship, and ye shall find. They cast therefore, and now they were not able to draw it for the multitude of fishes. Therefore that disciple whom Jesus loved saith unto Peter, It is the Lord. Now when Simon Peter heard that it was the Lord, he girt his fisher's coat unto him, (for he was naked,) and did cast himself into the sea. And the other disciples came in a little ship; (for they were not far from land, but as it were two hundred cubits,) dragging the net with fishes. As soon then as they were come to land, they saw a fire of coals there, and fish laid thereon, and bread. Jesus saith unto them, Bring of the fish which ye have now caught. Simon Peter went up, and drew the net to land full of great fishes, an hundred and fifty and three: and for all there were so many, yet was not the net broken. Jesus saith unto them, Come and dine. And none of the disciples durst ask him, Who art thou? knowing that it was the Lord. Jesus then cometh, and taketh bread, and giveth them, and fish likewise. This is now the third time that Jesus shewed himself to his disciples, after that he was risen from the dead. So when they had dined, Jesus saith to Simon Peter, Simon, son of Jonas, lovest thou me more than these?"'

The Serb boy could see a wooded hillside. Far below them, through the trees, they could see an asphalt road. His brother's constant crying was getting on the nerves of one of the soldiers, a tall bearded man with a long face. He was getting more and more aggravated, really angry now. His mother tried to give her breast to the baby to keep him quiet. 'Get that fucking kid to button it!'

Now someone was digging an elbow in his ribs. It was that fair-haired boy, Haflidi, trying to get him to listen. He'd probably forgotten he couldn't understand Icelandic. '"He saith unto him, Yea, Lord; thou knowest that I love thee. He saith unto him, Feed my lambs. He saith unto him again the second time, Simon, son of Jonas, lovest thou me? He saith unto him, Yea, Lord; thou knowest that I love thee. He saith unto him, Feed my sheep. He saith unto him the third time, Simon, son of Jonas, lovest thou me? Peter was grieved because he said unto him the third time, Lovest thou me?"'

He pretended he was listening so Haflidi would leave him alone and then his eye was caught by the stone in the grass. A bird's song

*was ringing through the wood. The other soldiers were pointing
their guns at his father, his sister and himself. His mother was on
her knees kissing the leather boots of the man who was holding his
baby brother by one leg so his head hung downwards. The soldier
kicked himself free of her, swung his arm round and dashed what
he had in his hand hard against the stone.*

'"And he said unto him, Lord, thou knowest all things; thou knowest that I love thee. Jesus saith unto him, Feed my sheep."'

When Linda had finished the reading Father Bernhardur placed
the bread and the wine on the altar, stretched out his hands and
said, 'Lord, we ask you to bless these gifts with your Holy Spirit so
that they will become for us the Body and Blood of Our Lord Jesus
Christ.'

He took the white host, the consecrated bread, in his hands and
said, 'Take, eat, this is my Body which is given for you.'

Father Bernhardur showed his congregation the consecrated host
and he took the Chalice and said, 'After supper he took the Cup;
and, when he had given thanks, he gave it to them, saying, Drink
ye all of this, for this is my Blood of the New Testament, which is
shed for you and for many for the remission of sins: Do this, as oft
as ye shall drink it, in remembrance of me.'

After the congregation had received the Holy Eucharist there
was a meeting. Father Bernhardur wanted to change the plan and
take a walk up Mount Esja but the Bishop was reluctant to do this.
Linda suggested they might drive out to Heidmörk. They did not
get going until nearly eleven. The sun was rising and it was getting
warmer. They took two cars. 'I must be going soft in the head,
doing this,' thought Haflidi.

Father Bernhardur, Haflidi and Jökull went in one car and Linda
followed in the Toyota with Sylvía, Ingibjörg and Bosko. There
were two concentric circular walks in the park. They set off. There
were tall pine trees on both sides of the path.

Thrushes sang and insects, woken by the sun, hummed. The
leaves on the birch trees were gold and black and the leaves on the
currant bushes were red. They walked quickly and soon reached an
open area but then the undergrowth grew thick and tangled again.
The air was perfectly still. Linda was out of breath and fell behind.

354

'I think we should go back. I'm shivering all over. I didn't realize how out of condition I was.'

They stopped. Bosko was tired too. He was blowing on his hands, even though Father Bernhardur had lent him his scarf and his woollen gloves.

'Can't you carry on a little longer, Linda, and then we could take the shorter circle back?' asked Father Bernhardur.

'Yes, that's a good idea.'

After a while they came to a signpost. 'I'll go this way then. Would you come with me, Bosko?'

'No.' The boy shook his head.

'Bye, Linda! See you by the cars in a bit,' said Sylvía.

Linda had gone some way on her own when Haflidi came running to catch up with her, calling, 'Wait!'

'I want to be on my own,' she said, irritated.

'Don't be like that. Do you think I don't know how to behave with the ladies?' He'd heard his father say this and it pleased him when the gambit appeared to have its required effect.

Haflidi tried to start up a conversation but couldn't think of anything to say. He felt like a little kid beside a grown woman and he was cross with himself. The path joined another.

'They'll come this way later,' said Haflidi, pointing to the south. They walked northwards for quite a time and reached a clearing. 'Oh,' sighed Linda and sat on a stone slab. 'I'll have to rest for a bit. My heart's pounding.'

He stood and looked down at her. She was sitting there with her eyes closed, her face almost white, her hair not moving at all in the still air. The sun was high. 'Isn't it odd what a wimp that Serb boy is with a bit of cold? On television it looks as if it's always snowing there.'

She took hardly any notice of him and muttered something under her breath. She looked round the clearing. There were massive blocks of lava rising through the heather and strong pine trees sheltering the smaller birch trees in their autumnal glory. 'Can you hear anything?' asked the girl, looking straight ahead.

'No.' He listened along the line of the path.

'I didn't mean that.' She stood up.

'What then?'

'Shush!' She looked straight ahead with her mouth slightly open, listening. She pointed across the lava in the direction of the mountains.

They saw the wind coming from a great distance, disturbing the leaves as if it was trying to make its path visible, passing across where they stood, rustling the birch leaves, shivering the pines, stroking the cheeks of the boy and the young woman, scattering a few drops of rain over them. Then it was gone. 'Did you see?' whispered Linda.

'Did I see what?'

'Didn't you see the wind?'

'Yes.'

'Didn't you feel the drops of rain?' she asked, ecstatic.

'Yes.'

'It was the dew of God,' she said in a quiet low voice.

'It was what?'

'The dew that's mentioned in the Mass. Weren't you listening in church? I asked God if he wanted me to do his will for as long as I have left to live. I asked him to speak to me. I asked him when we were in church and again now when I was sitting here with my eyes closed.' Linda looked at Haflidi with her eyes shining.

'I didn't notice anything. Just a passing breeze.'

'But it was still before!'

'There's often a breeze when it's calm and still.'

'No, Haflidi. Not like this, not wonderful like this. Not when you pray with the kind of desperation I've prayed with. Rain doesn't fall out of a clear blue sky. It was the dew of God. He set me free because I have found favour with God, like it says in the psalm. Now I know I am forgiven.'

'Forgiven for what?' he asked, feeling embarrassed.

She didn't answer, but looked round the clearing. He heard the murmur of voices and the crunch of gravel beneath tramping feet. Haflidi realized he would have to keep this secret. There was a chance she'd lose her job if the rich old woman got to hear about it and that mustn't happen. He looked at Linda. She was bending down for some delicate-looking berries, but they turned to juice in her fingers. Then she clambered up on to one of the slabs of lava, looking round, and that was where she was when the others found them.

37

Theódóra had repeatedly asked Hördur to take a look at Bosko and finally, a fortnight after the boy had arrived in Iceland, the doctor called in at Dyngjuvegur. Theódóra had given instructions that the boy should have the best-quality clothes, even though she didn't have time to see to it herself. He was wearing a pale suit, a white shirt and a blue tie. His shoes were brown leather.

Hördur asked Bosko to take off all his clothes except for his underpants and took a medical history from him. The boy had spent months in a French hospital. As he stood there on the parquet floor he still looked painfully thin. Hördur touched the scars on his body. There was a ghastly wound on his back in the shape of a half-moon. Then he took both the boy's hands in his and squeezed them gently, as he always did when examining children. 'You're getting along well,' he said in English, sounding very kind.

'What happened to him?' asked Theódóra in Icelandic.

'Didn't he see something terrible happen to his family?' said Linda.

'What?'

'I've no idea, Mother. He doesn't want to talk about it. I imagine he saw his sister raped.'

To start off with the sisters had agreed that it was only fair that Trausti, just like Linda, would be given the opportunity to work at the young people's home. They suggested it to Father Bernhardur, but he was rather worried about the expense. Theódóra then agreed that Heidnaberg would bear all the costs involved. The day before Trausti was due to start he rang his cousin and asked her to collect him in the morning. 'There's one or two things I have to do in town first.'

She honked her horn outside Vatnsholt at eight o'clock. Trausti had moved into Ester's old room in the basement. He kept her waiting. Linda had expected this. They were of an age and they'd played together as children. She knew perfectly well just how lazy Trausti was. While she was waiting she thought back to the drops of rain the wind had showered over her. Had God really been speaking to her? Doubt set in. For a time she had been convinced that she had been repulsive in the eyes of God and banished from his presence, that she was marked with the mark of the beast, of the devil, and was on her way straight to hell. In her desperation she turned again to the words of Christ in order to steady herself and repeated, 'But the very hairs of your head are all numbered. Fear ye not therefore. But the very hairs of your head are numbered. Fear ye not therefore.'

She felt better when Trausti at long last dragged himself up the basement steps. She had expected to see him bleary-eyed and with his hair all unkempt, but instead he just looked sulky and had obviously been up for some time. He got into the car and slammed the door, saying, 'Where do you think my old man's sending me now?'

She shook her head.

'If I don't go, he says I'll have to move out of the room. He wants me to go and have a blood test at the City Hospital.'

'When?'

'Now.'

She looked at her watch. 'We haven't got time.' She backed out into the road. 'What's he think's the matter with you?'

'He thinks I've got Aids.'

She sniggered. 'That's ridiculous. How does he think you got it?'

'He thinks I'm gay. And probably deep down I am.'

'Why's he think that?'

'Don't ask me! Probably so he can tell us we've all made his humiliation complete.'

'Please come in with me,' he said as she drove into the car park at the hospital. 'I hate needles.'

'I can't be bothered.'

'Please.'

The name of the doctor who saw them was Helgi. He had gone to school with Hördur. He was a thin, friendly man. Hördur had rung him the night before. 'Oh, so you're Doctor Scab's son,' he said brightly.

'What?' Trausti didn't know what to say.

'Yes, well, that was when your father started doing the night locums for the City. He was only a young man then.' The doctor rolled up Trausti's shirt sleeve. 'He was told by the City Mayor that

358

he'd have to be on duty for the whole month because the doctors in Reykjavík had gone on strike. Well, of course, his colleagues weren't too happy about it and gave him this nickname. Hadn't you heard that before?'

'No.' Trausti smiled politely as the doctor slid the needle into his arm, having enjoyed telling the old story again. He drew blood into three phials. 'So, there you go, my friend.' He turned to Linda brightly. 'And what about you? Do you want me to test you at the same time?'

She looked at him in amazement. 'Yes, why not?' She held out her arm.

'When will I get the result?' Trausti watched the needle sinking into the crook of his cousin's elbow.

'Two or three weeks. Now don't you go letting your father know who told you about that nickname.'

On the way to Sudurgata Linda filled her cousin in about the job. 'It's very easy. There aren't many kids. Four, sometimes five. Although I understand there's going to be more soon. All the job involves is giving them something to eat at midday, keeping them company, sleeping there overnight from time to time. Father Bernhardur sleeps there now. Ingibjörg is living there twenty-four hours a day for a while. There's some awful trouble at her home. We help them with their homework. Just generally help and sup-port them. There's also that sweet little Serb boy. He's completely harmless and nothing like what you expect Serbs to be like. He's quite shy. I understand he's suffered terribly. Mother was rather put out that he wasn't brought off the plane on a stretcher. Then she could have turned up with a million photographers. It would have looked great in the papers.

'Aren't you Tryggvi's boy?' asked the postman as Jökull was just about to open the front door.

Jökull turned round. The postman, an old man with a large nose and a leather flying helmet, was standing on the pavement. 'Yes.'

'I've got a letter for you.'

Gunnhildur opened the door. 'Nothing for me?'

'Yes, some brown envelopes.' He passed the bills to Jökull and Jökull passed them to his grandmother.

There was a pile of bills waiting for Dagný on the radiator.

'I think you ought to drop those over to your mother when you get a moment,' said Gunnhildur. 'Your father's got quite enough bills as it is.'

Dagný had moved out of the women's refuge and was now back living in her friend's flat on Skúlagata. Jökull walked over there with the letters. Would he get the computer? Everything depended on him coming top of his class. His mother opened the door. Father Bernhardur was sitting at the living-room table. 'What! You here!' exclaimed Father Bernhardur.

'Just a moment, Jökull darling,' said Dagný. 'We've nearly finished.'

Jökull sat on the sofa and waited.

'There's really nothing more I can say on the subject,' said Father Bernhardur very firmly. 'Man does not know what lies in store for him. We have to abide by the will of God, as the Church teaches us. People can't just do what they want. We're always doing wrong. And it's the children who suffer most.'

Dagný mumbled something under her breath the boy couldn't quite catch. She beat her fists on her thighs to emphasize her point.

'People can never do more than it is in their power to do,' said Father Bernhardur finally and sighed. 'If they cannot live together, they cannot live together. I've said this over and over again. Go ahead and divorce the man if it's completely impossible for you to remain in this marriage.' The priest looked at Jökull apologetically. Dagný flicked through her mail and then threw the envelopes away. 'Nothing but bills and bother.' She saw the priest out. Jökull could hear them talking in the hall.

'Aren't you going to come home soon?' Jökull asked Dagný when she returned.

'No! Even if any of you kids were dying I wouldn't come back. Oh, I'm sorry.' She put her hand over her mouth and looked ashamed. 'Has anyone been asking questions about the painting?'

He shook his head.

'If anybody comes, you tell them that I've now got papers to prove that we don't own it but are looking after it for somebody,' said Dagný quickly. 'I went and dealt with it myself. It was embarrassing. I never expected to have to do that. The people thought I was barmy or something. None of them remembered the painting.

I'll phone in a few days and ask you boys to drop it over in a taxi.'

'Stop all this nonsense, Mother, please, come home. Father's going mad. He hardly sleeps. One night I heard him crying.'

'No, I know you're in good hands. Your grandmother's looking after you. Sometimes one has to be brave and put oneself first.' She looked solemnly at her son. 'That's what I'm doing.'

He tried to tell her about the Serb boy but she interrupted him. 'Yes, I read all about it in the paper. Has your father no pride sending you to a place like that?' She lifted up her head awkwardly. 'With Theódóra being involved.'

'Then why do you send Silla there?'

'That's different. That's because of Father Bernhardur.'

He looked at his watch. 'Well, I must be getting home. We get our results today. Father's promised me a computer if I come top.'

'Oh, so he's not broke then?' said Dagný, irritated. 'Will you ring and tell me how you got on?'

The brothers went to get their results after lunch. The computer! Jökull was sick with worry. One of the girls was getting marks closer and closer to his in classroom tests. Not many had turned up in Midbæjarskóli schoolyard when the boys arrived. They walked down to the lake. Lots of people were skating in the sunshine. The Cathedral clock stood at nearly half past twelve. 'Dear God,' prayed Jökull silently, 'please let me be top of the class.'

And as he prays he sees the clipper *Jamestown* tossed by a violent storm, its sails tattered and torn, driven by the tumultuous waves towards the southern end of the city lake, where it is stranded with a great roar in the shallows by the bridge. Wave after wave pounds the ship, splashing high in the rigging. Suddenly it breaks in two and the redwood spills out and is swept up the beach. 'Did you know,' Jökull asked his brother, 'that in its day the *Jamestown* was the largest clipper sailing the seven seas? There was only one ship that was larger: the *Great Republic*, and that was burned to a cinder before its maiden voyage.' Haflidi looked at him and didn't say anything. 'Come on,' he said, 'let's go and get the results. You'll get your computer all right. Don't worry about it.'

There were now lots of people in the schoolyard. A tall boy called out to Haflidi, 'Oi, you!'

'Yes.'

'Fuck you!'

'Shut your mouth, Audunn! You're a divvy!' screamed Haflidi. 'Don't you come here with your lies about all the old cars your father's got. Your father's a stinking poof and your mother's a tart!'

'Go screw your grandmother!' screamed Haflidi.

Audunn came over to them with a spring in his step. He did both weight-training and karate. Jökull was frightened. Audunn had two mates with him. They did whatever he told them to do. Haflidi was saved by the headmaster striding across the schoolyard towards him. Audunn and his mates hovered to one side looking tough and threatening. The headmaster bore down on Haflidi, wagging his finger at him. 'I heard what you said. Give me your name!'

'Haflidi.'

'And what class are you in, Haflidi?'

'Year 10.'

'And what are your parents' names?'

'Tryggvi Thórarinsson and Dagný Gísladóttir.'

'And is this the sort of language you use at home?'

'No,' said Haflidi.

'You're a disgrace to your parents. I shall let it go on this one occasion as the Christmas vacation is upon us. Otherwise I would be speaking to your parents.'

'What a prat!' muttered Haflidi as the headmaster disappeared indoors again.

The main doors opened and the youngsters ran up the steps. Jökull's heart was racing. The teacher walked round the desks, handing out their results.

'Who's come top?'

'Sigrídur.'

Jökull's vision clouded over. Bang went the computer. Someone was making out this was a terrible shock: 'Jökull, our resident genius, did he really only come second?'

'No. Third,' said the teacher. 'Eyjólfur came second.'

Jökull was amazed by how clear and intense everything in the classroom had become. Voices seemed to be echoing in the distance. He looked with horror at his grades. Icelandic Literature and Gymnastics had let him down.

The teacher wished them Merry Christmas and let them go. Jökull heard Sigrídur chanting, 'Jökull's come third, Jökull's come third. The professor's come third!' She drummed her feet.

What he really wanted was to get back to his bed. To pull the duvet over his head and let sleep take away the shame. He wanted to die. He noticed how disgusting the yellow paint in the corridor looked. It looked really dingy. He had to get home. But his grandmother, Gunnhildur, and Dagný wanted him to ring them. Jökull's come third! Jökull's come third!

He ran into Haflidi. His brother was grinning broadly. 'What's so great, Haddi?'

'The lowest grade I got was three, mate!'

'That's nothing to be proud of. I think you ought to use the Christmas holiday to try and catch up with your schoolwork.'

'What's the matter with you?' Haflidi looked at him, shocked. 'Where did you come?'

'I didn't exactly come top,' said Jökull sadly.

They walked down Laufásvegur and turned into Bókhlöðustígur. Suddenly Audunn and his mates jumped out from an alleyway.

'Are you going to take back what you said about my grandmother?'

'You've got your grandmother on your brain. Why don't you go and eat her?'

'My grandmother's dead,' said Audunn sorrowfully.

It was a gift to Haflidi. 'Then you can gnaw on her bones.'

Audun leapt at him and got him down on the ground. Haflidi was extremely lithe as well as tough and strong. He hit Audunn again and again in his side and managed to wriggle out from under him and get on top, but then one of Audunn's mates kicked his shoulder and knocked him over into the snow. Audunn sat astride Haflidi and kept punching him in the face.

Jökull wasn't brave enough to try and help his brother. He just stood there looking embarrassed. Haflidi glared at him from beneath Audunn, his long fair hair trailing in the snow. 'Take it back or I'll kill you,' hissed Audunn and smashed into Haflidi with his fist. Haflidi's lip was bleeding. He hissed back, 'Eat shit!'

An old lady appeared, waving and calling from some distance,

'Why are you all ganging up on the poor lad like this?'

Audunn stood up. 'That should teach you to watch your mouth, you wimp. Your mother's a dockside whore.'

Jökull knew he ought to do something. He ought to attack Audunn or his mate. But he couldn't do anything. He watched them walking down Bókhlödustígur.

'What sort of language is this?' The old lady watched Audunn and his mate.

Haflidi struggled upright out of the snow. Blood and snot were streaming from his nose. The side of his mouth was swollen.

He wiped his nose on the arm of his leather jacket and fixed his hair. 'Why didn't you help me, man? When the other guy piled in and kicked me? What sort of wimp are you? What's the matter with you, Jökull?'

'Are you badly hurt, young man?'

'Oh, leave me alone, you old bag.'

The school report was lying in the snow. It had got wet and the ink was smudged. 'Grandmother'll have a fit,' said Haflidi, looking at the report. 'You can't even make out the marks any more.' He laughed.

'Where's the envelope?'

'I lost it.'

'Did you manage to lose the envelope before we left school?'

'Yes.'

'You are amazing, Haddi.'

'I'll bring a knife and get them back tomorrow,' said Haflidi angrily. 'I'm sure I could throw it and get him in the eye. Shame I didn't have my knuckledusters with me. It would have been a different story then.'

At these words, the old lady headed off towards Lækjargata, muttering under her breath.

'Grandmother'll be furious with us,' said Jökull. 'I came third and we can't even read your marks.'

'She'll never believe me. She'll think I dropped it in the snow on purpose. Did you really only come third?'

'Yes.'

Haflidi voided each nostril in turn and wiped his face with snow. Hearing of his brother's feeble performance bucked him up a bit. 'What a pair we are!'

When they got home there was a note waiting for them on the table. 'Boys, I've gone to see a friend, Granny.'

'Thank God,' said Haflidi. 'I hope the old dear falls on the ice and breaks a leg.'

'Don't say things like that.'

'Relax. I'm only joking.'

When Tryggvi came home, Haflidi described the fight to him. 'And didn't Jökull help you?' asked Tryggvi, looking as if he was longing to have been able to join in himself. 'He's got no balls, that lad. How did he do in the exams? Was he top?'

'No, third.'

'Oh well, I don't have to find the money for the computer then,' mumbled Tryggvi, sounding relieved.

Tryggvi went upstairs to his mother's flat to grab forty winks in peace. He fell asleep immediately. He dreamed he was walking along Kirkjuvogur near Hafnir. This was where he had gone with Jökull a couple of times in the summer to find out about the red pine.

The *Jamestown* was washed up. The storm had died down. The ship was caught on the reef in the gentle breeze with waves lapping at the keel. Hardly a shred of rigging was left. A rough ladder had been lashed together with bits of redwood and fixed in the seaweed on the reef and many eager hands were offering to help the young ladies up on to the ship.

Tryggvi walked up to it. The gunwale seemed quite high but a man reached out a callused hand and pulled him up. He clambered over the gunwale and looked around the broad deck. The main mast was much thicker than he had expected and the aft mast was ripped apart. The three hatches were jammed with loose timber so tightly you couldn't even get the blade of a knife between the planks. Tryggvi walked down to the stern to look at the figurehead beneath the enormous bowsprit. It was a benevolent woman holding a ship's log and a pair of binoculars. Her dress was blue and her hair was gold, like unravelled rope. The sea was lapping regularly at the ship. More people were coming up the ladder. The girls were screaming. Someone said, 'Good God, this ship is enormous! Look at the mast!' Tryggvi looked up but the sun was in his eyes. There was a seagull circling above the mast, his cry sounding like laughter, looking for someone to tell about the ship running aground. Or was he shocked to see human beings milling about a ship that had been at sea for a thousand days in all kinds of weather? On deck you could smell seaweed, salt and tar. Tryggvi walked to the capstan and rested his hand on the great iron bar. It was cold and good to touch. In his dream he knew it was 1881. A world he'd long thought dead and gone came alive before his eyes. He saw the surface of the blue-green sea at Kirkjuvogur rippled by the wind and he heard the tender song of the loon as it ran across the lava and heather. He could feel the warm breeze on his cheek. But where was everyone? His mother with her stern look and fierce manner, his brother and sister, their father with the dirt under his nails? His father was now resurrected from his watery grave and was working on the timber. The wood, scattered along the shoreline, shone in the sun. He couldn't wait to see his father again, have a chat with him, ask him what it was like to be dead.

Then there was a knock at the door. In the dream this seemed strange to Tryggvi. He knew he was lying on a sofa on the second floor, but even so someone was shouting from the other side of the door, 'She's running aground!' He sprang off the sofa. They all rushed to the window to see: Dagný, Jökull, Haflidi and Sylvía. They got dressed and ran out in the rain, the dark and the storm. The ship was running aground all over again. The clipper was getting closer and closer to Hásteinar, where she would certainly run aground. There was a flash of lightning and Tryggvi could see the *Jamestown* clearly, every knot in the wood was visible in the white light. He could recognize the timber, he'd handled it often enough. The ship was shining white and you could see amidships as it pitched violently. In his dream he knew that the ship, which had been black the first time it ran aground, had now changed her colour. He looked round for his family but they had gone. 'Good God, is anyone on board?' someone shouted. 'The poor people will surely die!'

'No, there's no one on board, there's no one on deck,' shouted someone else.

It took a long time for the ship to rise up the beach. The black bowsprit sunk and then lifted up out of the cavernous waves. She edged along the coast and shook the water out of her rigging.

Tryggvi was soaking wet. He looked at the sky, hoping it would clear.

The sky turned to velvet and it stopped raining. The stars shone and surely the ship must run aground any time. But now the outgoing tide caught her and she turned outwards into the bay and faced the barrage of the incoming waves. Then Tryggvi saw that the ship was not without human cargo. In the bow of the *Jamestown* stood a child gazing at the people on the shore. Tryggvi shouted out in his anguish, 'There's a child on board! There's a child on board!' He looked down and was shocked to find the pavement beneath his feet.

He began to run along the beach. He knew he would have to reach the reef at Thórshavn further along Kirkjuvogur before the ship ran aground and the top mast crashed into the sea. But the *Jamestown* did not head out of the mouth of the estuary as she had a hundred and thirteen years earlier. Tryggvi stood still. Everything was intensely quiet. The sea was calm and darkness spread over the land. It was so black you could not see your hand in front of your face. He did not know where he was until the St Elmo's fire lit the deck with a blue light. The rigging was aflame and the fire was reflected in the calm black sea all around so that every piece of wood and every strand of rope shone. The ship bore down on him like a rock. The figurehead at the stern had changed. Now it looked like an evil spirit carved from wood, like the satyr on the sideboard downstairs in the living room, the hair thick and tangled, the face in a grimace with the full lips pulled back from the large teeth, the body painted yellow, the chest flat, but the arms strong and muscular. The figure was pointing angrily at Cape Reykjanes.

38

The following Saturday evening the brothers were on their way home from the young people's home – they spent nearly all their time there now, sometimes even sleeping there – when they thought they might pop into the town centre to see if any of their friends were out and about.

Snow was falling steadily in the still silent air. They walked down Sudurgata and turned the corner by the Salvation Army. There was a group of people hanging around outside the Odal club. Austerstræti would probably be jam-packed. The brothers wandered across the square and suddenly the group outside Odal began to break up. Two boys Haflidi recognized were running towards them. They were Audunn's mates. One of them knocked Jökull flying and, before Haflidi could do anything about it, the other had kicked Jökull in the head. As a reflex Haflidi found his knuckledusters, slipped them on and was soon dancing round his brother.

He knelt beside him once it was clear the boys didn't dare attack him again. Audunn was nowhere to be seen. Curious youngsters formed a circle round the brothers. The snow melted as soon as it came to rest on the pavement. Haflidi felt under his brother's head and found a piece of bone that gave to his touch. There was something soft underneath.

'Get an ambulance!' he screamed.

When Linda got to the hospital Father Bernhardur was already there in the waiting room comforting the parents. He stood up and came to her. He looked pale. Haflidi had gone to give a statement to the police. Jökull was in intensive care. Linda looked curiously at the parents. She had rarely seen two more attractive people. The father was whispering quietly to the mother. He was not as pale and shocked as she was. The mother snatched up a magazine from the table and flicked through it. A doctor came in. 'I'm not anticipating any change before morning,' he said. 'The boy is still unconscious, so it is difficult to ascertain the extent of his injuries. The head injury has caused some bleeding between the brain and the skull and in turn that's caused pressure on the brain. Why don't you go home now? We'll ring if there's any change in his condition.'

Linda and Father Bernhardur said goodbye in the entrance hall. They were both devastated. 'Jökull, such a quiet lad, who only wanted to get on with his studies,' said Father Bernhardur, shaking his head sadly. 'I just don't understand how such a thing can happen. We must pray for him.'

The snow on the pavement sparkled in the light from the hospital windows. Linda watched Tryggvi and Dagný talking. He looked like a man trying to persuade a woman he's just met into going home with him after a dance. In the end she gave in and went with him.

The next day when the police came, Trausti was standing by the window in the sun lounge at 14 Sudurgata. Haflidi and Bosko had gone skating on the lake. Trausti was surprisingly happy in his work at the young people's home. Perhaps he had found his calling. There was a knock at the door. It was a police officer and a man from the immigration department, both dressed in civvies. During the night two drunken youths had tried to break into the young people's home. They had heard there were girls there. Trausti had managed to keep them at bay, reasoning with them in a calm and relaxed way until they had left without any trouble. A bit later a drunk had woken them up to hand in a frozen leg of lamb for Bosko, so he could enjoy it the next day.

At first Trausti thought the police wanted to talk to Haflidi because they had come to tell him that Jökull was dead. Or perhaps it was because of the two lads who had tried to break in? He waited in the doorway for the police to tell him what it was about.

'Is the boy from Bosnia living here?' asked the other man.

'Yes.'

'I have instructions to take him for a medical.'

'A medical? But didn't he have a medical when he came into the country?'

'You'll have to ask somebody else that,' said the policeman. 'I had a phone call this morning instructing me to bring this to your notice. A letter's been sent to the person responsible, but nothing's been done about it yet.'

'The "person responsible" is my mother's sister.'

'That's all I know,' said the policeman. 'I'm only following orders.'

'But is there any need to "take him for a medical"?' asked Trausti, repeating the man's words. 'Can't we just take him over ourselves after lunch? Where's he meant to go?'

'The City Hospital.'

'Fine, I'll take him over. No sweat. That's OK, isn't it?'

'Yes, I suppose so. Yes, OK.' They said goodbye.

Trausti rang Linda at Dyngjuvegur. Linda tracked her mother down on the phone and in the end found her in the Ministry of Foreign Affairs. 'Mother, the police have been to the young people's home and Trausti's been told to bring our Serb boy for a medical. He said you'd been sent a letter. Do you know anything about it?'

'Yes, I got a letter. But I wasn't going to do anything about it. I've had so much on my plate. The police came?' said Theódóra, taken aback. 'What is all this? You didn't let them take him? I don't know how he might react when you think of all he's been through.'

'Of course we didn't.'

'How was it left?'

'Trausti said he'd take him to the hospital.'

'Good, then we don't have to do anything.'

'I thought I might take him myself.'

'We have to go for a medical,' said Linda when she arrived at the young people's home.

'Why?' asked Bosko. There was a slight glint of anxiety in his eye.

'It's nothing for you to worry about. I had a blood test myself the day I drove Trausti to the hospital. There's no need to be frightened. I'll come with you.'

She rang the City Hospital and tracked down Helgi, the doctor who had attended to Trausti and her. There was nothing to stop them coming straight away. Helgi met them. 'Would you like to stay with him? It might help him feel more relaxed?' he asked, sounding friendly.

'Any news of my cousin's test?'

'Not yet, but I'm expecting the results back in a few days.'

'And mine?'

'They'll come at the same time.'

Linda gazed affectionately at Bosko as the doctor inserted the needle into his arm. He didn't make a sound.

'There, what did I tell you? That wasn't anything to worry about, was it?' she asked, smiling. She looked at the doctor. 'Why are you doing a blood test? I thought this was just a medical.'

'They only asked me to do a blood test,' said the doctor.

She drove the boy back to the young people's home. Father

Bernhardur had arrived for the evening shift. Linda hurried back to Dyngjuvegur. Theódóra was looking unusually tired. 'Mother, what's wrong?'

'This morning I resigned from the Independent Party.'

'Why?'

'Because I can't face working for them after all that's happened.'

'It doesn't look as if the resignation's made you any happier. Will you have to resign your seat?'

'No, my position in Parliament doesn't change. I'll have my seat until the next election.' Theódóra's face clouded and she gasped for breath. 'No, it doesn't feel very good after all those years with the party, but I just didn't have any choice after those attacks on your father. But that's not what bothering me now.'

'What's worrying you?' Linda looked at her mother, surprised. Theódóra didn't make a habit of taking her stepdaughter into her confidence.

'I'd better tell you a bit about it, as I shall be having a meeting with the women later on.'

Linda waited.

Theódóra gulped for air. 'Early tomorrow morning I plan to announce the formation of a new party. Then, from my non-aligned position, I intend to place a motion before Parliament declaring the government unfit to govern.'

'That'll be quite something.'

'And how have you been lately, Linda dear?'

'Me? Fine. I'm perfectly OK.'

Theódóra pondered things quietly to herself and then said, 'I had a strange thought the other day when I finally made my decision.'

'What was that?'

Theódóra looked up, surprised at herself. 'I thought it might have been true what you said about me having killed your father. It was I who didn't want to take the political responsibility and blamed him. It was I who couldn't bear the thought that my mother chose to share my father with another woman of her own free will.' She looked round her, bewildered. 'Linda, did I lose my sense of reality somewhere along the line? When you're in Parliament, ordinary everyday life becomes unreal somehow.'

'I did ask you to forgive me for saying that.' Linda was about to sit down and put her arms round her mother but at that moment the phone rang. It was Father Bernhardur sounding very upset. Three policemen had come to the door. They had instructions to take away the Serb boy. The order had been signed by the Chief Physician. The priest read an extract from the letter: '"Bosko Dragutin, a Serb, registered domicile 4 Dyngjuvegur, Reykjavík, legal guardian Theódóra Thóroddsdóttir, has a serious medical condition. Consequently he is to be held in isolation."' Linda asked Father Bernhardur what this 'serious medical condition' was. Nothing had been specified and the police knew nothing about it.

'But it isn't possible. I only took him for his blood test today.'

'Yes. The police came back again a little while ago.'

'Have they taken the boy?' Linda looked anxiously at her mother. Theódóra stood there waiting.

'No. I think Haflidi was going to take him to the cinema or round to his mother's in Thingholtstræti. I tried to mislead the police as much as possible, although I realize that is not a Christian way to behave. I told them it was most likely that the boy was with you. They are probably on their way to see you now.'

'Hide the boy in a a safe place in the home as soon as he comes back. There's a cupboard under the stairs in the living room. Put him in there and put the music centre across the door so it won't be seen. It's probably all a mistake but it's best to be on the safe side and make sure the police can't get to him. Mother and I will come over as soon as we can.'

'What's going on?' asked Theódóra.

At that moment the doorbell rang. Linda didn't have time to explain.

'Is there a Serb boy living here,' the policeman looked at his piece of paper, 'by name of Bosko Dragutin?' The police car's engine was switched off and all the police had come to the door.

'This is his registered domicile, yes,' said Theódóra.

'We have orders to bring him in.'

'The child? Whatever for?'

'He's carrying a dangerous infection.'

'No, that's not possible.'

'He's from Bosnia, isn't he?'

'Yes.'

'What's so incredible about him having a dangerous infection? Didn't the black death break out there only the other day?'

'No, you're thinking of India.' Theódóra laughed. 'You can all go home and stop being frightened. The boy hasn't got the black death.'

'Have you studied medicine?'

'No.'

'Well then. You don't know anything about it.'

The three policemen stood there in silence, staring at her. A car drove by. Theódóra looked up at the sky, trying to master her temper. There were dark cumulus clouds with white edges. It was beginning to get warmer. She controlled herself. 'So that's it. My guest has got the black death.'

'That's not what we're saying, madam,' said one of them. 'We Icelanders don't know much about Bosnia except that there's this terrible war. It's a big country. A lot could be going on there and it's best to be on the safe side.'

'Are you some sort of expert on Bosnia?' asked Linda.

'He's as much an expert on Bosnia as your mother is on infectious diseases,' said the first policeman.

'We don't need to stand here arguing in the doorway,' said Theódóra. 'The boy's not here.'

'Then you won't mind, madam, if we take a look?'

'Be my guest.' Theódóra moved back from the door.

'No, Mother,' hissed Linda and she took a step forward and blocked the doorway. 'Yes, we do mind. They need a warrant to search the house. The boy is not here. And he can't have been found to have a disease so quickly.'

'And why not?' asked the policeman.

'Because he only had his medical at midday today.' She looked at her watch. 'Three and a half hours ago. I took him there myself. The results won't be back yet.'

'Isn't this to do with the results of an earlier examination? The Chief Physician knows what he's doing.'

'No. Today was the first time he went to the hospital. I should know, it's my job to look after him. It was me who took him there.'

'And he's not here?'

'No.'

'Where is he then?'

'He's at 28 Thingholtstræti. He went to visit some people. I'm going there later to collect him.'

The policemen raised their caps as they left. As soon as they'd gone, Linda grabbed the phone and rang Thingholtstræti. The boys had just left.

That evening Haflidi had taken Bosko to the cinema. Over the previous weeks they had become good friends and the boy had told him much of what he had gone through. Bosko had seen his father killed. His sister and his mother had been raped repeatedly. He had no idea of their present whereabouts. But he had however spoken to his mother on the phone before the Red Cross had airlifted him to London.

It was well after midnight when they returned to Sudurgata. Father Bernhardur told them what had been happening. The police were looking for Bosko everywhere and had only just left.

Father Bernhardur seemed distracted and was pulling at his beard, a clear indication of trouble. 'We've got to do something,' said Haflidi when the priest had told them what had happened, 'or they'll take the boy away. I know what the police are like!'

'But what can we do?'

'Ring Theódóra and see what she says. Take the boy to Dyngjuvegur. We've got to hide him.'

'I can't go against the police,' said Father Bernhardur and Haflidi was surprised by how jittery he seemed. 'Anyway, Theódóra and Linda have just left. I sent them home. They're both beside themselves with worry.' He looked at his watch. 'I don't feel I can ring them this late. Why were you so long?'

'Don't be such a wimp! Ring the old girl at once and get her over here. Now! Or they'll take him away. Just look at him. Can't you see how frightened he is? Get on the phone, man!'

Haflidi put on his shoes and grabbed his leather jacket from its peg. Something had to be done! He didn't know what. He had to make sure the boy was safe. He looked at his watch. It was gone three. People would be coming out of the bars. The streets in the town centre would be full of people. There was someone he had to find. He pulled on his leather jacket as he ran down the steps. As it happened, the weather was warm and a little gentle rain was falling. He ran as fast as he could towards Adalstræti. It was packed. When he reached Austurstræti he could see that the town centre was full of young people, thousands of them. He was frantic. How could he find his friends among all these people? He strode to and fro, looking round, running his fingers through his hair, an old habit he'd developed to look good for the girls. One girl glanced at him and frowned. She was sweet, thin, with round cheeks, black hair, just his type, but now wasn't the time to be picking up girls! He elbowed his way through the crowds. When he reached the corner of Pósthússtræti he still had little idea how he was going to get people to help him. Then he remembered the rock band that had hired a truck for the concert on 17 June and how the police had stormed the truck and put an end to the concert. He walked over to where there was a gaggle of youngsters and said, almost before he'd thought it through, 'The Assassins are going to give a concert at the young people's home on Sudurgata and the police are trying to stop them!'

The kids looked up. This was really cool!

He realized this was the idea he had been waiting for and was suddenly filled with courage. He shouted, 'A rock band is going to play at Sudurgata and the police want to stop it!'

He ran towards Lækjartorg, grabbing two boys he knew on the way and telling them the news. He was getting a positive response everywhere. He was waving his arms. 'A rock band's going to play near City Hall but the police are going to stop them! Come and help!' Haflidi looked round. The excitement had taken even him by surprise. The youngsters had nothing much to do. They were wandering up and down Austurstræti sharing a drink or, by the smell of it, a spliff by the wall of Reykjavík's old City Court House. Who had put this magnificent idea into his head when he had most needed it? Running round town shouting, 'The police are trying to take away a boy from Bosnia. They say he's got' – he thought a moment – 'Aids!' That would have been hopeless. But a concert outside a private house, that was perfect. Perhaps a lot of them would remember the last time when the police had put a stop to a concert and they wouldn't be likely to let the same thing happen again.

'Come on!' he shouted, wandering through the streets. 'The police are trying to stop a rock band playing at 14 Sudurgata! The next street over from City Hall. The Assassins!'

Haflidi had gone mad. He surprised himself with the level of hysteria and frenzy. He'd soon gathered a group around him, thirty or so, all watching what he'd do next. He didn't answer any questions, but kept on waving his arms about and confined himself to shouting the same sentence over and over as if it was burned on to his lips. Suddenly he found himself wondering whether it had been anything like this when the Holy Spirit came in the storm with thunder from the mountains and flames of fire alighting on the Apostles' heads. This idea brought him a sob-like burst of pleasure and the feeling that a flickering tongue of flame was burning in his hair. 'Come to Sudurgata! They're arresting a rock band!'

The town centre all around him was alive with excitement and the crowd followed him down Austurstræti. The news spread like wildfire through the youngsters. Not many of them had much idea what was happening where Haflidi stood in the eye of the storm. Someone was saying something about a rock band wanting to give a concert but the fucking police trying to stop it. 'But what am I meant to do when we all get to Sudurgata?' wondered Haflidi and he began to be afraid. But then quite suddenly he felt a tremendous sense of calm and it was clear to him that if God existed, like Father Bernhardur said, then God would be with him at this time and put something into his mind when he arrived at the house with the crowd behind him. To his amazement he found he was not without hope nor afraid, but full of inner strength. He knew there was no power on earth that could stand in his way at this moment. 'Tell everyone to come,' he shouted. 'Tell everyone to come. The Assassins are going to play.'

This was precisely what the people in the town centre had been waiting for. The bars were closing. The bands were packing up their instruments. The beer had all been drunk. Everybody was broke. And then the news came. A band was willing to play for free and the cops were going to impound their instruments. It was outrageous! Even those who did not have too clear an idea of what was going on followed the crowd because a hurricane like that could not be blowing through the town centre without something really cool being about to happen and they weren't going to miss out. Haflidi ran round the corner of Adalstræti and realized to his intense joy that he had gathered together several hundred very excited friends.

He ran past the Salvation Army followed by a great crowd of girls and boys, along Sudurgata and up the garden path. The large tree in the garden rustled in the dark, all the lights were on and the rain glistened on the yellow corrugated iron. When he reached the front steps he turned and shouted to the group in front, 'Wait here and get everyone else to wait!' They stopped at the bottom of the steps and Haflidi leapt indoors.

Theódóra was there. She was standing by the window looking at the lawn in front of the house completely covered with people. 'What's going on?'

'I've brought a few friends over. They're here to see no one takes the boy away from us.' He looked at her in amazement. Even she was showing some fear. Father Bernhardur looked much calmer. 'Where's the boy?'

'I hid him in the cupboard.'

'I will not be treated like this,' said Theódóra. 'Where's the phone? I'm going to call the Chief Constable.'

'He's the one who's attacking us, for God's sake!' Haflidi turned to Father Bernhardur. 'You've got to talk to them and make them help us.'

'What shall I say?' The priest seemed devoid of ideas so Haflidi himself walked to the door of the sun lounge and stepped out on to the veranda. 'Where's the band?' he heard someone shout.

He opened his mouth to speak. He had no idea what he was going to say. But there was no need for a flickering tongue of fire in his hair to give him the power of speech because at that moment two police cars drove slowly into the crowd of people out on the street. Eight cops got out. A couple had a few words with some of the youngsters but the other six elbowed their way through the crowd, trying to keep as low a profile as possible, reaching the steps up to the sun lounge and walking inside. A few people got into the hall, some drunk, curious and giggling. It was not clear to everyone that they were there to hear some band. Was that why they were there? One thing was certain, anyway, and that was that the police were trying to put a stop to it. When the police reached the steps, Haflidi backed into the living room. The one who seemed to be in charge was a big broad bloke and Haflidi had come across him lots of time before. The others were younger. One of them was tall and looked very strong. His face was boyish with high cheekbones. Haflidi reckoned he was a member of the 'Viking Squad'. 'We've come to get this sick kid,' said the member of the Viking Squad.

'"This sick kid",' snorted Theódóra. 'It's rubbish. There's nothing the matter with the child. You're exercising your power disgracefully. You're committing an appalling act that will bring shame on you.'

'As I told you earlier this evening, madam, I'm only obeying orders.'

'Do you know who I am?' she said, loudly. 'I'm a member of parliament. Do you think I don't know what I'm talking about?'

'I know exactly who you are. But I'm still going to take the boy. He's a foreigner. He's dangerously ill. He could cause an epidemic. He's going to be deported.'

'He's not going anywhere.'

'Aren't you a priest?' The older policeman looked at Father Bernhardur.

'Yes.'

'Can't you find a bit of common sense, even if the lady can't, and hand the boy over?'

'The boy isn't here.'

'Where is he, then?'

'Some of the youngsters who live here have taken him away with them.'

'We should still like to search the house.'

'Don't you need a search warrant?' called a young man from the hall. 'Do you think you can just come in here and do whatever you want?'

Haflidi tiptoed out through the sun lounge and squeezed his way down the steep steps from the veranda. The lawn was a sea of faces. 'What's going on?' someone asked. 'I thought the Assassins were going to play.' Haflidi found he was losing his courage. The excitement that had taken hold of him in Austurstræti had worn off and the group on the grass was a bit thinner than it had been. He walked down the lawn. The youngsters at the far end of Sudurgata were wandering off. A white Volvo drove up and two policemen got out. Why wasn't anything happening? 'If nothing's happening, it's my responsibility to make it happen,' thought Haflidi and he gulped a mass of disgusting green mucus from his nose and throat. He walked over to the white Volvo. The repulsive gunge flew through the air and landed on the bonnet.

'Oi! What do you think you're doing?' It was a woman's voice.

'I don't speak to morons,' said Haflidi. 'Aren't you a cop?'

The policewoman leapt over to him and grabbed hold of the sleeve of his leather jacket. Haflidi put up considerable resistance and hit her hard in the face with his elbow. The girl got him in a judo hold on the ground, flipped him over on to his stomach and forced his right arm up his back. Haflidi heard a click and knew she was about to put the handcuffs on him. He could see a mass of feet around them. He managed to get his wrist free and slip both hands under his body. A tiny grain of gravel dug into his palm. He pushed hard on the concrete pavement and managed to stand upright and get away. Another cop came bustling over and got him in a half-nelson. They were caught in a group of people pushing first this way and then that. He heard a howl of rage as the woman constable fell to the ground. Suddenly he was free and the other cop was trying to get back into the car, probably to get some CS gas and call for reinforcements. 'Don't let him get on the radio,' shouted Haflidi. A few of them jumped on the cop and made sure he didn't reach the handset. Suddenly he heard Father Bernhardur calling from the sun-lounge veranda, 'Now they've found the boy and they'll soon be coming out with him. He's in tears. We're not going to let him go!'

No sooner had the priest finished speaking than the tall young cop Haflidi was sure was a member of Special Forces came out on to the veranda with the Serb boy under his arm. Everyone in the garden looked in their direction. The policeman pushed Father Bernhardur so roughly that he almost fell over the railing and then he carried the boy down the steps. The Serb boy gave a terrible scream of grief and held both hands over his eyes.

'This is a foreigner!' cried Haflidi's shrill voice. 'He thinks they want to gouge his eyes out!'

There was some spare timber in a pile near Haflidi. It was left over from the renovations in the summer and Father Bernhardur had not had the heart to throw it away. Haflidi seized one of the sticks and was going to try and help the boy but he didn't make it that far. The other cops had come out of the house in order to clear the way to the car. But planks and posts were being grabbed from the pile of timber and used to beat the police. Poles were being passed back through the crowd. Haflidi was surprised to see Father Bernhardur holding a stake in his hand. The man of God was standing halfway up the steps hitting a policeman with all his might. He was aiming for the head, but the blow landed on the man's shoulder. The cop bounded up the steps and hit the priest square in the jaw. They had got Bosko down in the garden and were trying to force their way to the car. Haflidi went beserk. He scarcely knew what he was doing and was shocked at the sounds coming from his own throat. He had lost all control over his own voice and was yelling like a girl as he punched and punched. The grass was wet and slippery and he was finding it difficult to stay on his feet. The punches rained down on the police. Their caps went flying. Bosko screamed. With sheer grit and determination Haflidi managed to reach the Special Forces guy holding the boy in a half-nelson and give him a massive kick in the leg. The cop hit him hard, smack in the face, making his head spin. Just at that moment the cop was jumped by two youngsters and Haflidi saw Theódóra come running as fast as she could, hurl herself on to his back and try to scratch out his eyes. The Special Forces guy had to let the boy go in order to defend himself. Theódóra was hanging round his neck. Haflidi was punched in the back of the head and had to get off the lawn to avoid being killed if he lost consciousness and was trampled on. He couldn't move. Now a police car was being driven over the lawn into the crowd honking its horn. The cops didn't dare get out but simply stared at the mayhem around them. Haflidi looked back at the house. Father Bernhardur had disappeared. He saw Theódóra slip indoors with Bosko. The white railing on the veranda had come loose. Someone jumped up, ripped it away and threw it down to the crowd. He saw a policeman was holding Linda in his arms and her hair was tossing like a horse's mane. The policeman was trying to carry her through the crowd. He saw

Linda tear herself free. Then he couldn't see her any more. Had she fallen under people's feet?

'This is all my doing,' thought Haflidi and he turned round. He found an ugly face straight in front of him and received a heavy punch in his own.

When he came to he was lying on a mattress in a cell. A light bulb hanging from the ceiling burned bright. He had a throbbing headache. He sat up with a groan and felt his face. One of his eyes was all but closed and the right side of his mouth was swollen. He wanted to urinate and looked round. He had been in a police cell before and then there had been a can on the floor. There was no can on this particular floor. He was angry and stood up and hammered on the door. No one came. He beat on it again.

At last a tiny hatch was opened and a face appeared there asking, 'What do you want?'

'I need a slash.'

'There's a drain in the floor. Piss in there.'

'You think I'm as disgusting as you are?'

The guard slammed the hatch shut without saying anything. Haflidi walked round his cell, running his fingers through his hair and touching his face. He must look dreadful. To his surprise the door was opened and two of them were standing there. 'Take the boy to the toilet, Jón, and then bring him through,' the policeman said to the guard.

Haflidi followed them. The guard opened the door of the john. 'Where is this?'

'Hverfisgata police station.'

He walked over to the bog. When the man didn't close the door, he said, 'Saving yourself the cost of a cinema ticket, are you? You get off on watching guys piss?'

He tried to piss once the door was closed but he couldn't. He looked in the mirror and was shocked by what he saw. Although he had felt his face for damage he wasn't prepared for the sorry sight that greeted him. He looked like a prize fighter long past his best who'd hung in there for the full fifteen rounds. One of his eyes was completely closed, his mouth was swollen, his cheeks were scratched and he had a large bump on his forehead. He let water run into his cupped hands and threw it on his face. The door opened. 'Aren't you finished, boy?'

Haflidi followed the man into the corridor. There were pairs of shoes outside each door. The cells were full. 'Where are you taking me?'

'You've got to make a statement.'

'What about?'

'You'll know that better than me.'

He was shown into a room. A young policeman was sitting behind an oak desk. He looked at Haflidi in a friendly manner and pulled a piece of paper towards him.

'Name?'

'Haflidi Tryggvason.'

'Date of birth?'

'Nineteenth July, 1978.'

'Address?'

'Twenty-eight Thingholtstræti.'

'And you took part in the riot on Sudurgata?'

'What?' asked Haflidi.

'Why did you attack the police outside 14 Sudurgata?'

It was clear to Haflidi that there was so much confusion that the constable had very little idea of the details of Haflidi's part in events.

'Number what, Sudurgata?'

'You were arrested outside 14 Sudurgata for assaulting an officer in the course of his duty.'

'Sudurgata?' mused Haflidi. 'No, I'm not even sure where that is.'

'Don't be stupid,' said the policeman. 'You were brought here in a car from Sudurgata.'

'No,' said Haflidi. 'I was attacked by two boys in Adalstræti. I was on my way to some rock concert.' He tried to look as innocent as possible. 'Is that where Sudurgata is? Near the old graveyard? I didn't get that far. I challenged one of the boys to single combat. I shouldn't have done that. He knocked me senseless down at Grjótathorp.'

'This is all nonsense,' muttered the policeman. He pushed the button on the intercom. 'Jóhanna, can you come in for a minute?'

A policewoman came into the room. 'This boy is saying he had

382

nothing to do with the riot on Sudurgata. Weren't you in the reserve unit down there?'

'Yes.'

'Do you recognize him?'

'Not to be certain. The whole town was full of kids.'

'He says he got knocked out down at Grjótathorp.'

'Well, that could be right,' said the policewoman. 'A kid was found there unconscious.'

'That was me,' said Haflidi. 'I told you.'

'Well,' said the policeman, 'you can go. I've got your name. Do you want to make a complaint?'

'Of course I want to make a complaint,' said Haflidi. 'And I'm going to get some information about those guys who attacked me.'

The policewoman opened the door and let him out. 'I'm still feeling a bit wobbly,' said Haflidi. 'Could you run me home?'

She led him down the corridor. His shoes were waiting for him outside the cell door. He put them on. The guard gave him his leather jacket. The policewoman took him downstairs in the lift and even opened the door for him. She was a blonde not more than ten years older than him. He said, 'You're a real babe.'

She said nothing and drove him home with no expression on her face whatsoever.

He walked up to the front door. As luck would have it it wasn't locked. Haflidi tiptoed into the hall, locked the door quietly and peeped out through the peephole. He could hear voices coming from the living room. The police car was still parked in the street. He stood still for a minute and watched until it drove off. Then he went quietly down to the basement and out through the garden. He had to get to Sudurgata quickly. It wasn't right to leave Father Bernhardur to handle things on his own. The thaw had stopped and it was getting colder again. He decided to cut across the frozen lake. It was possible the police were watching the streets. Lights were on on the top floor of City Hall. There was a film of water over the ice and he was a bit afraid in case it wouldn't take his weight. The ice creaked in some places but he crossed safely and walked into a garden on Tjarnargata. He strode across the sloping lawn and peeped over the fence. There was not a soul to be seen on Sudurgata. He jumped the fence cleanly and ran across

383

the street. He expected there to be police on guard in the garden but there was nobody about. The railing that had been the glory of the veranda was lying in pieces in the grass, its white-painted wood gleaming in the dark. Two windows in the sun lounge were broken, but the lights were on in the house as if nothing had happened. He ran upstairs. He was surprised to find about twenty kids in the living room. The only two he recognized were Ingibjörg and the Serb boy. They told him that the crowd had been so worked up that when the fight had died down it had tried to take over the little police station in the customs house down by the harbour.

Father Bernhardur came to the door. 'Well, there you are, my friend!' he said. 'Good to see you!'

39

A young girl is on a secret mission in the early hours of the morning. Her heart is pounding. In one shoe she has a message for the priest on Sudurgata. It is an extremely important message written on a small piece of paper folded up several times. Sylvía's first thought was to cross the green at Landakot and get into the house from the back. The town centre is dark; it's a weird darkness, alive with voices. She walks along Hafnarstræti and suddenly she is engulfed in a snowstorm. It's like trying to walk through a snow-drift. She can hardly see the houses. Túngata, by the Salvation Army, is closed. She sees the headlights of a police car. She walks down Gardastræti and can see the outline of a police car parked on the other side of the street. She tiptoes into a garden. The snow-storm is at its worst. The grass is wet. The wall she tries to climb is slippery and covered in moss. There are lights burning low at 14 Sudurgata. The house looks different in the snowstorm. It seems to stretch out, change shape, become rhomboid. She knocks at the door by the kitchen, hands over the note for Father Bernhardur and hurries home again, even though the youngsters want her to stay. She walks down Sudurgata and Vonarstræti. As she reaches

384

the steps of 28 Thingholtsstræti, the snowstorm subsides. It is almost as if it has been protecting her.

It was a great relief to Father Bernhardur to hear the children's voices. They were moving about upstairs, talking quietly to each other. A big lad had settled down on the sofa in the sun lounge with an overcoat for a blanket and they had talked over the happenings of the night until the boy had started snoring. Then Father Bernhardur had gone down to the basement to check that all the windows and the door were securely locked. There was a blocked drain in the basement and the smell was overpowering. This was the second time that night he had gone down there. He checked all the doors on the first floor one more time, and then he crept up to the next floor, where he found two boys lying comfortably on mattresses, smoking. They both waved at him. He listened outside Linda's door. She had been quite badly hurt in the fight but there was no sound. Probably she was sleeping and it would be best to leave her in peace to get some rest. Father Bernhardur sat in a chair in the living room and a deathly silence crept over the house.

He was filled with anguish. Something close to terror. His heart raced. If he tried to sleep images floated into his mind. Haflidi, half crazed, in the crowd of people, his clothes bloody and torn. 'What have I got myself into?' thought Father Bernhardur. 'Here in Reykjavík, surrounded by the police! Me, a priest!'

He jumped to his feet when there was knocking in the hot-water pipes. In the end he fell asleep through sheer exhaustion. As drowsiness overtook him he thought, 'We're all sleeping here like in the Garden of Gethsemane. He felt as if he had slept soundly for a long time when he woke with a start, but when he looked at his watch he had been asleep for only a few minutes. And I hit a man in the head with a stake! And punched another one in the mouth. Won't they arrest me for that? What will the Bishop say? Father Bernhardur wondered about sneaking out of the door on the west side and creeping off home to Landakot. Then he shook his head at his lack of courage and stood up. He was so wound up, it felt as if he was seeing the interior of the house for the very first time. He glanced into the room at the west end where Haflidi and Bosko were sleeping. The door hinges creaked and the Serb boy reached out for Haflidi in his sleep.

As he looked at the boy a memory surfaced in his mind, almost without him being conscious of it. It was of Theódóra teasing him, saying, 'Are you brave enough to have dared to stand by your Saviour, Father Bernhardur? Or would you have been like Peter and denied him?'

He looked at the Serb boy and said quietly, '"And he took a child, and set him in the midst of them: and when he had taken him in his arms, he said unto them, Whosoever shall receive one of such children in my name, receiveth me: and whosoever shall receive me, receiveth not me, but him that sent me."'

Had the hour now come that he had asked God to send him? He thought about Peter denying Christ. How must Peter have felt when the cock crowed for the second time and the Lord turned and looked at him? Oh, I must not fail today. Father Bernhardur's hands were cold as ice and he rubbed them energetically on the arms of the chair to get the circulation going. Was the hour now come? Would he be tested today? Then he realized to his great relief, 'When it gets light we'll have to surrender. I can't see I'd be betraying anybody by doing that.' He put his face into his hands and rocked to and fro. 'O, dearly beloved Simon Peter, my friend. There are so many things in your nature that I understand so well.'

He dozed, then fell into a deep, dreamless sleep for nearly an hour. Then he sat on the edge of his chair, wide awake, and took out the note with the strange message from his breast pocket. It was a small typewritten note that Tryggvi had sent via Sylvía. It was just five words: 'Do what the Texans did.'

'Do what the Texans did'? What the hell was the man saying? Suddenly he realized what Tryggvi meant! It was a message in code. Those cult members in Texas had chosen to burn themselves to death along with their leader. Father Bernhardur clenched his fists with joy. I'll threaten to do the same thing! Immediately he was filled with hopelessness. They wouldn't be so stupid as to fall for that! 'But it's the only thing I've got left,' he thought. 'There are only about fifteen or twenty kids in the building.'

During the night, before they'd disconnected the phone, a police sergeant had rung and told him that the boy had got Aids and there was some question of him already having infected at least one girl in the young people's home.

'What! He's a child. He's not even fourteen.'

'Well, they're getting urges then, aren't they?'

'There are a lot of people with Aids in Reykjavík!'

'Not foreigners there aren't! And this kid doesn't have an extended visa.'

'He was entrusted to my care. I won't hand him over to you.'

'Then I'll just have to send in the Viking Squad.' The police sergeant cleared his throat. 'It's as simple as that.'

'When are they coming?' wondered Father Bernhardur and walked to the window.

There was nothing to be seen outside. The sky was black. He tried to stiffen his resolve. Lights were coming on in the neighbouring houses as if everything was normal. He could see into a living room on the other side of the street. The television was on in the middle of the room and people were watching a video. Odd at this time of night. There was not a sound to be heard except occasionally from above when a floorboard creaked as someone turned over. He undid the window lock, opened the window and propped it open. A cold wind stirred the curtain. There was no one outside in the street. He could see the snow had drifted over the broken railings on the lawn. A blessing from God that the storm had come up and protected the house.

Suddenly he was aware of a man walking towards him out of the dark. The man looked up at the window. Father Bernhardur withdrew. The man turned back down the street. The priest carefully closed the window.

He heard a voice from the floor above and came to himself quickly. Were the children awake or was someone talking in his sleep? He crept upstairs and looked at the group sleeping on a few mattresses and on the floor itself. Someone muttered something in his sleep. He went back downstairs carefully. Dawn was breaking but it was unlikely to get light much before eleven. He picked up the receiver. The phone was still cut off. So he would have to run out to meet them and threaten to set the house on fire with greater powers of persuasion than he had ever used in the pulpit if he was to have the slightest chance of getting them to believe him. He wanted Theódóra with him and he wanted a mobile phone so he could ring the media.

The Viking Squad arrived just before nine. Twelve of them came running out of two vehicles. As for myself, the scribe of this contemporary record, as you would expect, I too was present. As I drove past the Parliament building I saw a small Opel drive up and someone chuck a pig's head out on to the steps. The cheek of it! I was going to make a note of the number but I was too late and anyway I didn't have my glasses. A man saw me examining the pig's head and shouted at me, 'Oi, you! What do you think you're doing? Are you insulting our Parliament?' I ran towards the Salvation Army corner, but the road was blocked.

The phone rang in the young people's home. They were forever connecting and disconnecting the phone for fear that more kids would be summoned to the place. Father Bernhardur ran to take it. He was certain they would have got the Bishop either to come or to ring. It was fortunate it was a voice he didn't recognize. 'This is the police. We are about to enter the building. You have fifteen minutes to vacate the premises.'

'And if we don't?'

'Who's speaking?'

'The Catholic priest. I take responsibility for everyone under this roof.'

'The house will be attacked. There is a danger of the young people being injured. Do you want that on your conscience?' The voice was slow and spoke with great authority. 'Didn't you just tell me you were a priest?'

'Yes. And who are you?'

'The Chief Constable.'

'And what about your conscience?'

'I'm not going to quibble with you about ethical niceties. I am doing my duty. The building contains a young man who is dangerously ill and who, we are informed, has already infected others.'

'How can you know that from a blood sample taken only yesterday?' Father Bernhardur was angry with his own anxiety and hit his thigh with a clenched fist to try to stop his voice shaking.

'That is not a matter for me. However, when there's nothing

wrong, there can be nothing to fear from giving oneself up.'

'This is all political. People are arguing about who should run the country and who should have control of the money. It's shameful that good people should have been caught up in all this.' He swallowed and paused. 'The boy will be deported and sent back to Bosnia or God alone knows where.'

'The Viking Squad has the building surrounded. We can do this the easy way and you can all walk out of there, or they'll take it by force.' There was a moment's silence. 'They will be coming in in twelve minutes. Now you've got more sense than those kids. Just come out of there nice and easy.' The Chief Constable put down the phone.

There was a smear of yellow in the eastern sky. Father Bernhardur could not see anyone on the lawn or down the street. On the few occasions the Viking Squad had been on television, they had been dealing with things that were considered a bit of a joke. Nothing much ever happened in Reykjavík. A drunk shopkeeper firing a shotgun in his store and the Viking Squad would be outside armed to the teeth in their balaclava helmets. A guy drunk out of his skull shouting the odds at his home in the Fossvogur district – well, he'd been fast asleep by the time the Viking Squad burst in. He had thought then that the Viking Squad needed bigger and better incidents, a plane hijack, an armed siege, a bank robbery, a hostage taking. It had never occurred to him that he, an ordained priest, would offer them the very event they needed.

He looked at his watch and groaned. It was five minutes since his conversation with the Chief Constable. They would be here soon. 'Should I wake the children?' he thought. 'No, too risky. Good Father, guide me. How should I stop them?'

He had so little faith in the idea of the fire that he had forgotten to threaten the police with it. He picked up the receiver but the line was dead. He heard footsteps on the floor above. One of the children was awake. They'll be coming down any minute. I must go and talk to them. He opened the south door and walked out into the frost. The steps were slippery. He walked down into the garden. 'Hello?' he called. 'Is there anybody there?' He suspected his voice sounded weak and silly.

A man stood up from his position hidden behind a fence to his left. He was massive. He wore a deep-blue fine woollen sweater and a balaclava. He said, 'Are you coming out nice and quietly?'

'No,' said Father Bernhardur. 'And I strongly advise you not to storm the place because if you do I shall set the house on fire.'

'You haven't got time,' mocked the Special Forces guy and looked towards the south where another man was standing up out of hiding. He looked as if he was about to walk over to the priest.

Father Bernhardur put out his hand, warning him not to come any closer. 'I brought petrol into the house three days ago. It's stored in three locations. In the basement and on the first floor. If we're not allowed to live in peace, I'm setting fire to the house. The children are ready to do it on my signal. They are ready and waiting to pour gallons of petrol all over the place.'

'Don't be ridiculous, man! Do you expect us to believe that? I can't believe all those children are ready to die in a fire.'

'Not all of them, no. But two of them and myself. And more would be at risk,' he said with authority.

He walked back to the steps. He expected one of them to follow but he could not hear footsteps behind him. He needed to wake the children and tell them how he'd lied. 'Would they really be taken in?' he thought and felt like running away. He glanced over his shoulder before he reached the steps. They seemed to be hesitating. They were standing there talking about it, one of them watching him. Father Bernhardur called out, 'I want the phone back on.'

Then he ran up the steps. He looked round the house and woke up the boys in the west room. Bosko seemed to be in quite good shape. Haflidi scratched himself and yawned. The priest ran upstairs to wake up the people there. He counted his overnight guests. One after another kids got up. Father Bernhardur went to the window. He could see the street more clearly from the second floor. The Viking Squad was out in force. The phone rang. He shouted from the top of the stairs, 'Don't answer it, Haddi, I'm coming.'

The Chief Constable was on the line. 'What's all this talk of petrol?' he asked wearily.

'I've laid in stocks of petrol here. If you storm the house I'll set it on fire.'

There was a silence. Finally the voice said, with a dry little laugh, 'And you expect me to believe this?'

'I don't care whether you believe me or not. If you come any closer, I'll burn the place down.'

'Then go ahead, mate. We'll arrest you when you come out.'

'Not all of us will be coming out. At least three of us will go up with the house.'

'This is ludicrous! Simply ludicrous! Where did you get all this petrol?' he asked.

'Here and there around town. I thought something like this would happen. And when Theódóra told me she was calling for a vote of no confidence and was setting up a new party, I was sure about it.'

'I haven't the foggiest idea what you're on about. I shall be obliged to consult my superiors.'

'I shan't hesitate to start the fire if you try to take the boy away.' Father Bernhardur put down the receiver. He leaned back in his chair, stretched his legs out and let his arms hang loosely. He took deep breaths. He felt exhausted and his mouth was dry. 'I've got to be more forceful,' he thought. 'I've got to make them believe me!'

He had the telephone directory on his lap. He found the number for Government House, introduced himself and asked to speak to the Prime Minister. The girl seemed to know who he was and asked him to wait. She came back almost immediately. 'Here he is.'

'I'm not going to duck out of this,' thought Father Bernhardur. 'I'm not going to duck out of this!' The Prime Minister's voice boomed at him, 'Now what's all this then, my lad? You come and talk it over with me. I'll get Halli to tell the police to take a coffee break and you can pop on over here. But don't whatever you do tell the media. You know how they distort everything people say.'

'I'll come.' The phone was disconnected before he hung up.

At this point Linda staggered out on to the top landing. She sounded as if she was in pain, so Haflidi, blushing and happy, took her in his arms and, in spite of her protests, carried her downstairs. By the time he reached the bottom his cheeks were beginning to quiver with the strain.

When Father Bernhardur told Linda what was behind the siege she started kicking the wall and cursing with surprising facility. It hurt her to move. The priest crossed himself when he heard the language. Linda staggered over to the sofa.

391

The kids came thundering downstairs. One let himself collapse into a chair. Father Bernhardur called them to him like a group of students. He was used to this sort of thing. Everyone in that group had something distinctive about them. Some of them were badly hung over. Some had long hair, some crewcuts, one had his head shaved but still wore sideburns and looked rather scary. The next was completely bald except for an orange tuft growing above his forehead. He had a gold ear-ring. It was this lad who, with tremendous energy and fortitude, had held the north door when the police made their second assault. A little fair-haired runt had picked up a rock that had been thrown through the window of the sun lounge and dropped it over and over again on a policeman's foot.

The living room was nearly full. The priest looked round the group. Some didn't seem to be fully concentrating and others didn't seem at all sure of why they were there.

He spoke to them quietly and thanked them for coming to his rescue. In all honesty he had not expected a fight but since that was the way it had turned out there was no turning back. The police had perpetrated a great injustice. He told them what the Serb boy was being accused of. 'I am going to fight this to the bitter end,' he said. 'If anyone wants to leave now, he's welcome to do so. In a little while it'll be too late.' He watched the lads as they looked from one to another. Some had not quite made up their minds. 'Why don't the cops come for us?' asked the tall boy with the single lock of hair. He was so tall Father Bernhardur thought he'd never stop rising up out of his chair. 'They could take us, easy.'

The priest explained that he'd convinced them he'd soaked the place in petrol. One by one the kids started to smile. He saw he had acquired hero status in Haflidi's eyes. Everyone wanted to stay. 'If they're set on storming the place,' shouted a fat boy, 'we can make it nice and warm for them!'

This was received with applause. More comments were made. One guy was hung over and didn't think it was right to be facing a serious challenge like this without a cold Pilsner in his hand. Another said the Viking Squad would be far too busy giving the ducks a helping hand getting back into the lake. Ingibjörg came into the living room with her hair wet from the shower as if it was just like any other day. Some were asking the Serb boy about what he had seen of the fighting in Bosnia.

'Now, I've got to leave you for a while. So if you like to get dressed and so on. Linda, would you look after Bosko? Have some breakfast. Heat up some coffee. I'll be about an hour. If anyone tries to get close, the thing to do is to shout, "Don't come any closer or the whole place'll go up!"'

Father Bernhardur went out on to the steps and waited for the door to be locked securely behind him. There was a strange empty silence. He walked down the path.

40

Two fire engines were parked on Sudurgata and the firemen looked curiously at the priest. The sky was beginning to get lighter. They had believed him! The Viking Squad had gone. A large white van belonging to Television News was parked quite a way up the street. Thick black cables wound their way across the pavement. Television cameras and a powerful floodlight had been set up. A tall red-haired journalist walked across to Father Bernhardur and shook his hand, asking, 'Are you the priest?'

'Yes, but I can't say anything at the moment.'

The journalist became more forceful, demanding that Father Bernhardur give him an interview, but the priest was adamant. One of the policemen wound down the window of his car, beckoned him over and asked, 'Where do you think you're going?'

'To see the Prime Minister,' asked Father Bernhardur firmly. 'He has given me free passage. The young people will be looking after the house while I'm away. If anything, they're even more intransigent in this than I am.'

The constable wound up his window, smiled and said something to his colleague. They both laughed. Father Bernhardur couldn't see what was so funny. He looked up at the tower of the old fire station. A stocky bearded film-maker had installed himself there. He was making a documentary. Hordes of them descended on the scene over the next few days, but they were always in the wrong place at the wrong time.

Father Bernhardur was very anxious about the risk of running into the Bishop on the corner of Sudurgata. He knew if they came face to face he would simply follow him home without a word. He did not even glance up Túngata, so eager was he to disappear round the corner of Adalstræti. He walked down Austurstræti feeling threatened by the appearance of Government House up ahead. He had never felt so out of place on the streets of Reykjavík as he felt that beautiful morning. Men were working on the shop fronts. A lot of windows had been broken overnight. The town was still, strangely, very much itself. As he neared the corner of the Courts of Justice the priest felt more subdued. Government House loomed up before him, solid and brilliant white. He felt his knees go weak. He was surprised to have heard nothing from Theódóra during the night. Before the phone was disconnected he had tried to ring her twice, at Dyngjuvegur and at Heidnaberg, but there had been no reply. He crossed Lækjargata, went up the steps and along the pavement towards Government House, praying intensely all the time. He felt the building towering above him. The moment he walked through the door the girl on reception said, 'The Prime Minister's expecting you!'

An enormously fat, red-haired man stood beside her, looking very worried. It was Haraldur Sumarlidason.

The Prime Minister was sitting in his chair. He didn't seem overly excited and Father Bernhardur immediately relaxed. Hannes stood up, with an air of tolerant indifference and said, 'So, Father Bernhardur, we meet again.' Father Bernhardur held out his hand. The Prime Minister's hand was so warm that he could hardly be too worried. 'Your hands are so cold!' he said loudly. 'You're like a frozen fish! Listen,' he said, taking off his glasses, 'all this. Now don't you go running off to the press or the television or writing long articles once all this is over. I know of nothing more idiotic than people chewing things over in public in article after article.' He indicated for the priest to be seated, then sat down himself and waved his glasses airily over his desk. 'You and me, we're good friends, but we have a falling out. There's no way we can sort it out like brothers and then we embark on a public slanging match in the papers.' The Prime Minister seemed to be playing with him, pretending to be aggressive, imitating battle joined in newsprint: 'When I ran into you in Naust bar the other day, you looked pretty hung over to me. I offered you a hair of the dog and this is how you repay me, telling lies about me in our biggest-circulation national newspaper?'

Father Bernhardur said nothing. All this friendly banter was giving him confidence.

'Listen, what's all this about the wretched boy?' said Hannes, for all the world as if the kid had broken a window in Government House.

'You should know if anyone does,' said the priest, holding his ground.

'What's that supposed to mean?' Looking taken aback, the Prime Minister reached into an inside pocket for his cigars. 'I was going overseas. I was just getting on the plane when they called me back because of all this.'

'You started it! You wanted to attack the women in the party! You wanted to attack Theódóra because she was calling for a vote of no confidence in the government and was going to split the party. But things got out of hand. You didn't foresee this. That I wouldn't take it lying down. Do you think I don't know Theódóra got the shares and took control of your company?'

'What's all this about shares?' said the Prime Minister clicking his tongue. 'Why should there be a tax on the difference between the nominal price and the estimated market value of shares and why in God's name should that affect me, I, who don't have a single share to my name to collect a dividend on, as you've pointed out yourself? The only dirty trick I could pull on Theódóra would be to fight like a tiger alongside the Left and the unions. She's the one with the shares. I've got nothing to do with it, my good man. You ask my fellow party members and the Minister of Finance about share profits. Not me! Attack a woman?' he said guardedly and with emphasis. 'Who'd be stupid enough to try that in this day and age? Not me. I need the women's vote. I read in the paper the other day, straight from the horse's mouth, "I give my lover freer rein in bed than my husband because I don't want to lose the upper hand in my marriage." Just think of it! You can call that playing it safe in politics. I think you, a priest, ought to be looking into this sort of thing!' The Prime Minister looked out of the window, brooding. 'There are always lies, lies, lies being told about men in these rotten times, these rotten media-driven times.' He smiled warmly. 'You're a priest. You if anyone ought to know it's the way of things in our society just like any other for people to be accused unjustly. I think you'd call it "bearing false witness", wouldn't you? That's how it's been for me, just like for lots of others. I'm supposed to have had a hand in my friend Seli's death. And he was someone I did a lot of work for. He was a dear friend!' The Prime Minister sounded angry. 'Am I the kind of man who goes round killing people? Killing my friends?' Hannes looked into the priest's face and the gentle expression had gone. 'Tell me, am I a murderer? No. I didn't kill Axel. I haven't killed anyone. If anyone killed Seli it was the old girl herself. On the other hand, people have tried to do away with me, but no one cares about that, not even you, the man of God!' He cleared his throat, put on his glasses, took them off again almost immediately, folded them up and put them in his breast pocket. 'It's not the politicians who govern this country, it's the media. If the media decide to say I committed murder, then I committed murder and it's really of no consequence whether it's true or not. That's why I say: now what's all this about the boy? Am I supposed to be responsible for launching a military attack on an orphan? Wouldn't it be more to the point for you to lay this at the door of the Minister of Health? The Left runs that ministry. You can believe anything of that man. But then he has a way of being overseas at the crucial moment, just like he is now.' Hannes raised his voice. 'The best thing would be to send Theódóra to prison! Has she gone mad?' The Prime Minister leaned forward and lit a cigarillo, a lock of snow-white hair falling over his forehead. His skin had its usual pallor. 'And what happened to her anyway?' he asked sullenly as he exhaled the smoke. 'Did she run away?'

'She fought like a tiger when the police found the boy in a cupboard! No, she went to get a doctor. Her daughter was injured. Probably she was stopped from getting back to us.'

'You see!' roared the Prime Minister. 'Do you want to take responsibility for the well-being of the young people who were entrusted to your care?'

'This is simply a child all on his own in the world. A little boy who's afraid. He was brought here at the instigation of the Red Cross. Because this is supposed to be a good place to live. Because it is believed that Icelanders welcome those in need and treat them well. He's thirteen years old. He's suffered from malnutrition over a long period. Who's he going to infect?'

'As I understand it, he went for a medical and they took a blood test. Which revealed the situation. And what's so odd about people fearing infection?' The Prime Minister raised his voice. 'Aren't the kids having sex these days at ten or twelve? That's what they tell me! That's what it says in the newspapers. And isn't one of his carers, the doctor's son, isn't he a self-proclaimed homosexual? I have that on very good authority. I have it from his father. He came to me at his wits' end because of all the troubles he's got. And look at the legal position! It's treated as attempted murder if people with this condition go to bed with someone without informing them of their illness!'

'This is all lies,' said Father Bernhardur. 'It doesn't deserve an answer. And as for the Aids test, it takes weeks to get a result from a blood test, I know that.'

The Prime Minister looked at him in amazement. 'Don't be ridiculous. Perhaps you don't know much about it?'

'I'm afraid it's you that doesn't know about it. Get the hospital to make a statement acknowledging its mistake.'

'How can I go against the law and the justice system in this country?'

'Which particular law are you thinking of?'

'I'm in no mood to quote each and every article to you, but you can rest assured of one thing: the government is in the right on this. Hand over the boy. It'll cause the least trouble for all concerned.'

Father Bernhardur looked at him, unyielding. 'No.'

'Then he'll be got out of there.' The Prime Minister thumped the desk.

'Got out how? The house is drenched in petrol.'

Hannes laughed. 'For heaven's sake, nobody with a shred of common sense believes that. It took all my diplomatic skill to get the Special Forces to hold off. You do realize we have the resources to maintain law and order? People need to understand no one can behave as if the laws of the country simply don't exist.'

'If you try to seize the boy, I'll set the house on fire. And then it might be that those who have followed me will perish in the flames at my side.'

'You don't do things by halves, do you, mate?' said the Prime Minister. 'It's ludicrous, simply ludicrous!'

'Get the doctors to make a statement saying there's been a mistake and give me a document saying the boy won't be deported' – he looked at his watch – 'before six o'clock this evening. Then we'll co-operate and come out quietly.'

'I'll look into it,' said Hannes at last. 'If it'll save people from the risk of serious injury.' He took his glasses from his breast pocket and jabbed them repeatedly at Father Bernhardur. 'If you don't go running off to the media in the meantime. But I'm not promising anything.'

As he walked down Lækjargata, Father Bernardur could hardly believe that he had held his ground, that he had not been crushed, that he had not caved in in front of the most powerful man in the country, but that he had met him head on like some iron-willed union leader. He had to make a considerable effort to control himself and not burst out laughing with sheer delight.

It was nearly light now. As he passed the Salvation Army corner, the smile was wiped off his face. There was now quite a crowd in front of the house. A television reporter came running towards him with a large camera on his shoulder and there were three reporters with microphones jostling for position. 'Leave the man alone,' said the constable and Father Bernhardur was obliged to smile wanly as the police cleared a path for him through the crowd. He tried to ignore it, even when the journalists shouted questions at him. Someone who thought it was an established fact that all Catholic priests were foreigners shouted in English, 'Piss off home! We don't want your sort in Iceland!'

They escorted him to the front door.

All the lads were still in the house. One of them had made it to the baker's while he'd been out and come back with rolls and Danish pastries. There was coffee for those who wanted it and juice for the others. The music centre was playing full blast. The house vibrated from time to time with Metallica and AC/DC. With the load lifted off his shoulders for the moment, Father Bernhardur was ravenously hungry. But he still found it difficult to eat.

Haflidi was sitting in the middle of the floor playing a football game with Bosko. Every now and then he got up and went and checked on the house. The lad with the shaved head and sideburns was standing by an open window smoking a cigarette and watching the people outside. Haflidi had got guards posted on the windows and doors and had even climbed out of a window and up on to the roof ridge to see if anything dodgy was happening in the neighbouring gardens.

'I must have forty winks.' Father Bernhardur was completely exhausted.

The words were hardly out when the phone rang. It was the call he had been dreading. It was the Bishop ordering him in no uncertain terms to hand the boy over to the authorities immediately. Father Bernhardur couldn't believe his own ears when he heard himself refuse. He slammed down the receiver to bring the conversation to an abrupt end. He lay down on a mattress in the west room and felt he had burned all his bridges, cut all his ties to the outside world.

However hard he tried, he couldn't get a wink of sleep. In the end he dozed but one thing after another flashed in front of his eyes. Snatches of cartoons, Yogi Bear careering across thin ice with an anvil in his arms, but no vision from God as he'd hoped. He was delirious, lying there in a cold sweat, reliving the attack on the house. The tall policeman had pushed Theódóra into a wall when he'd found the boy and was preparing to carry him out of the house. He'd had to run out on to the veranda himself and shout for the kids to help.

At the end of the fight, there had been another attack and they'd shouted at the north door, 'Open up, this is the police!' The guy with the shaved head and the tuft of hair on his forehead had shouted back, 'It looks as if there's enough of you to do it on your own!'

When the priest gave up all idea of sleeping, the clock said six minutes past three. He went to the living-room window and was shocked by what he saw.

There were crowds of onlookers everywhere! Kids were sitting on the ruins of the garden wall oblivious of the ice beneath their backsides. His eye was caught especially by a little girl with curly hair and her legs dangling. Somewhere high above the house there was the sound of a helicopter.

41

Hördur Gottskálksson woke up in his surgery late that day. He turned on the light but there was no power. He went out into the hall and checked the fuses but there seemed to be nothing wrong with them. He looked out of the window. Other houses seemed to be affected in the same way. He sat on the couch, yawned and smiled a satisfied smile when he remembered that Gunnar Bragason the driver had taken to organizing a substitute whenever he was scheduled to drive Hördur on the night shift.

Vilhelmína had rung the night locum office late in the night and asked for a message to be passed on to him. Linda had got involved in a fight in the town centre and was injured, in bed, at the Sudurgata young people's home. 'Why are the sisters always so stupid?' muttered the doctor, irritated. 'Why phone me? Why don't they take the girl to A. & E.?' The new driver didn't say anything but shook his head and tried to assume a non-committal expression. He wanted to stay out of trouble as long as possible. Gunnar had given him a few tips on how to handle the doctor.

They looked in on A. & E., but Linda had not been brought there for treatment. The doctor who told them about the riots in town was called Thorsteinn. It was the same chap that Hördur had tricked into getting an unwanted haircut all those years ago. Thorsteinn's specialist field was viral infections. They hadn't seen each other for many years and Thorsteinn was rather nervous in Hördur's presence. Despite himself, Hördur felt increasingly confident in his company. His eyes met Thorsteinn's for a moment and he saw the other man register the fact. Hördur looked around and said something very quietly to the specialist in viral infections who was looking at him with sullen suspicion. 'The records are all computerized. They're not kept under the individual name but under the Social Security number. It's not as easy as all that. It's strictly confidential.'

Hördur kept on pleading and arguing. 'You've got access to the National Register upstairs. Can't you check the Social Security numbers on that?'

'What did you say their names were?'

Hördur again gave his colleague the names of Linda and Trausti with their addresses.

Thorsteinn went upstairs and returned from the laboratory some time later with two white envelopes.

Hördur tore open Trausti's letter and sighed with relief. The result was negative. He put his niece's letter in his pocket and decided not to do anything more about her injuries that night. Theódóra would have to arrange for a doctor to look after her own family. That hadn't seemed to present too much of a problem to her before. When his shift ended in the early hours of the morning, he drove down Túngata out of curiosity, but the police had closed off Sudurgata.

Hördur got up from the couch and put on his snow-white suit. He picked up the white hat with a black band and arranged his fair hair on his shoulders. He selected a wide yellow tie and slipped Linda's letter into his breast pocket. He switched on the news. 'There is currently a siege situation at 14 Sudurgata where a Catholic priest is refusing to hand a foreign boy over to the police. The boy does not have authorization to remain in this country and is understood to be HIV positive.' The doctor frowned, put on his white topcoat and went out. There was a large crowd on the corner of Vonarstræti. There were police cars with their lights flashing and two fully manned fire engines. Hördur spoke to a man on the street. 'What's happening?'

'Some nut is going to set his house on fire,' said the man. 'The Special Forces backed off earlier this morning so that the people inside wouldn't do anything stupid. They're scared shitless in case he actually does it.'

'What's the matter with him?' asked the doctor, shocked.

'He's a religious maniac,' said a woman.

Hördur stood in the crowd for a while. More people were coming all the time. He couldn't get to the front. He clambered up on to a garden wall by holding on to the iron railings. There was another group at the All Souls' gate into the old cemetery. The police were keeping the groups separate and the street between them was empty.

He decided to go back to the surgery, phone home and get Ester or Vilhelmína to come and get him.

As he walked past the Parliament building large snowflakes were falling from the sky like flowers and melting as soon as they touched the ground. He let himself in to the Skólabrú house. There was no answer from Vatnsholt. He rang Dyngjuvegur. Ester answered. 'Yes, Father. We're all here. What do you want? The car?'

'Why isn't your mother at home?

'She wants to support Tedda.'

'And where's your brother?'

'He's here too, Father. Do you want one of us to come and get you?'

'No, I'll get over there under my own steam,' Hördur said sourly.

He walked northwards along Lækjargata without being able to find a taxi. It was beginning to get dark. Lots of people were out in the streets and the shops were full of customers. In one window on the corner of Austurstræti there was a life-size mechanical Santa, holding a Christmas bell in one hand. The doctor had noticed it before. All day long it moved along a semi-circle track. Every time it reached the end and changed direction it jerked and the bell rang. It had a computer screen in its arms. Hördur stopped outside the window and rubbed his thigh. His leg was hurting him. Since he had got kicked back in the spring his leg stiffened up in the cold weather. The Santa was stuck without electricity. Its cheek was turned towards Hördur and its face set in an idiotic grin. The Santa looked straight at the shop owner who was lighting two candles on the counter. A line of cars drove down Austurstræti with their headlights on. People were annoyed and honking their horns. The doctor was surrounded for a moment by a gaggle of drunken kids. 'Sæmundur! Sæmundur!' For some reason they seemed to think that was his name. 'Let us have your old guitar!' one of them shouted and grabbed at him. 'Hey, you! Sæmi from Beatlemania! Come and talk to me! Come and join me over on Sudurgata for the fight. The police'll be bricking it when they see you.' Hördur tore himself free and swung at the kid, who immediately backed off.

'He's a bit wired, isn't he?' said someone in the group.

For a moment it looked as if the kids were going to go for him, but then one of them said, 'Hey, guys, let it go. Leave the old sod alone. We must save ourselves for the fight on Sudurgata.'

The doctor found a taxi by Government House. Every single light in the building was on.

A little earlier a group of women had met together at Dyngjuvegur. Theódóra sat at her dining-room table with her guests. One of them was speaking: 'Can you really not see that this is a conspiracy by the bastards to discredit women in the party and in Parliament, especially you, Theódóra, and to ruin your reputation with the public? They're trying to destroy the new party before it's even established. If you get involved with the kids in this riot and some of them are found to be in possession of drugs, you simply won't be regarded as a responsible person.' Elísabet Sigurdardóttir, who had been saying all this, had the unfortunate habit of bursting into fits of giggles at the most inappropriate moments and, as soon as she had got this off her chest, she exploded with laughter. It took her a moment to recover and then she reached into her bag and brought out a piece of paper and started reading. 'At noon today, 22 December 1994, the following agreement was reached.' She paused. 'Even though it is widely believed that the foreign boy living here in the temporary guardianship of Theódóra Thóroddsdóttir and the Catholic Church has been treated with gross injustice, we, the undersigned, still take the view that he should be handed over to the relevant authorities so that the grounds for his detention can be examined by the courts at a later date.'

In the autumn Theódóra had got rid of her old dining table and in its place bought a large oval shiny black mahogany table with extensions. In the centre there was a white vase with a black ring at the top. Round the base Roman soldiers were hunting a lion. Ester had brought out the yellow cups and saucers. It was getting dark outside and the stars were sparkling against a blue velvet sky.

'I just can't believe it! The injustice of it is appalling!' Theódóra looked round at her fellow party members perfectly calmly. They were sitting round the table with her in her rightful position at one end. 'You must be able to see it! Hand him over to the authorities!

He'll be whisked out of the country and no one will be any the wiser. I can't bear the thought of it and that bloody Hannes knows it!'

Ester brought in a coffee pot and served the coffee. There was a box of confectionery open on the table.

Vilhelmína sat a little apart and listened to the women. She was worried the police would come for Trausti and so she had sought shelter with her sister. Trausti was sitting on the sofa under the window, flicking through *Newsweek*. The police had let him go after asking him a few questions.

'Of course we can see what's happening, it's just that we don't see why we should be working for the Catholic Church, it's so anti-women,' said a young woman called Svandís. 'I'd rather not have anything more to do with it.'

'Yes, it undermines everything we've achieved,' said another, with a sing-song voice. 'Just at the moment when there's a realistic chance of getting a woman in as Prime Minister after the next election.' She looked round as if she had a job on her hands persuading the others. 'We're going for the no-confidence motion and calling for immediate elections!'

'But that's exactly why this has happened,' said Theódóra.

'Some people say the business with the boy is more to do with shares than with politics.' This was said by Birna, who had so admired Theódóra. She turned beetroot as she spoke.

'The whole world knows I made a killing at Hannes's expense,' said Theódóra sardonically.

'Isn't the best thing to go ahead and announce the formation of the new women's party straightaway?' asked Birna nervously. 'As things stand, do we have any alternative?'

'I need to sort out this mess first. The child is my responsibility.' Theódóra paused, deep in thought, then shook her head sadly and said, 'But it won't help to say that the whole thing has been orchestrated because of the imminent formation of the new party. People will only say that I'm trying to undermine the Prime Minister.'

'But we know he's guilty!' said Svandís with an air of moral superiority.

'Yes, but other people don't!' said Theódóra gently.

'Look! It's on the television,' said Vilhelmína from the sofa, putting on her glasses.

The television had been on without any of them watching it. The newsreader was saying that the electricity in central Reykjavík had gone off. The reason for this disruption of the supply has never been established. The lack of power caused considerable difficulties for businesses in town.

The screen was showing a picture of Sudurgata with a crowd of people being driven back. The street from Vonarstræti to All Souls' gate at the cemetery had been cleared. Then there was an aerial shot over the city. It showed the police surrounding the house. The people on Sudurgata reminded me of ants when I studied this footage some time later. The pavements were black with people. The camera came down to earth again and my face could be seen, pale and exhausted from lack of sleep. I was completely confused about what was going on and couldn't make head or tail of it. Of course at that time I had not followed all the threads back to the Icelandair jet and Haraldur Sumarlidson in mortal dread of dying of ebola fever. I managed to get to the front on the corner of Vonarstræti and waved my press card but no one was being allowed near the house. Theódóra had refused to give interviews to the television or the radio when it was realized that the boy was in Iceland as her guest. The phone rang continually and Ester was fully occupied keeping the media people away from the house. One or two lunatics kept ringing up and offering to die in the fire.

Then there was a live studio discussion. There were two women, one from Amnesty and one from the Red Cross and a man from the organization Child Concern. The Chief Physician had been otherwise engaged. The three of them were very animated. They were demanding an end to the persecution of the child, surely the public must see that the child was only a pawn in a very ugly game, the attack on him was simply ludicrous, it was a national disgrace, Iceland would be a laughing stock the world over. The interviewer pointed out to them that the authorities had the law on their side and quoted from a statute of 1965: 'If the continuing residence of a foreigner in this country can be considered inimical to the interests of the state or to the public or otherwise morally questionable, then it is permissible to deport him.'

There then followed a heated discussion about the injustice of this particular law and whether or not its application was appropriate in this particular case. Then there was a short interview with an immigration officer who said that of course there were aspects of the law that were open to interpretation but that as things stood it was the only guidance they had.

Government House appeared on the screen for a second or so. The Prime Minister was not giving an interview. Up to the time of writing the Prime Minister has been adamant in his refusal to discuss the matter of the boy in public. He usually declines with the phrase, 'I don't give credence to Falstaff's stories and neither should you.'

The studio guests threatened to obstruct the deportation of the Serb boy in any way they could. Their lawyers were already looking into his legal position.

'I should hope so too,' said Theódóra.

The women took up their discussion where they had left off and then it was time for the weather forecast. The unusually cold weather was continuing.

'Hannes killed my husband,' shouted Theódóra, banging her fist on the table. 'Now he's trying to kill me too.'

The women looked at each other, embarrassed. After a second or so Elísabet said, 'If we want to beat the bastards we've got to play by their rules.'

'Exactly,' said one of the others. 'We've got to play to our strengths. Women are used to getting what they want through deviousness and leaving all the stomping about beating their chests to the men.'

'It's all Father Bernhardur's fault,' said Ester, joining the discussion. 'He let it get out of control.'

'Someone told me the kids in town started it all because the police were going to stop a pop group playing on Sudurgata,' said Birna.

'Was that it, Trausti?' called Ester. 'Is that what happened?'

'Leave me alone!' shouted Trausti.

'We're going round in circles. We've got to be honest,' said Elísabet, getting red in the face with excitement. 'We've all come here, Theódóra, to give you our view that we believe that the law should be obeyed in this matter.'

'"The law should be obeyed"!' said Theódóra angrily. 'You sound just like the enemy.'

'We haven't got any choice,' pleaded Gudrún Samúelsdóttir. 'We'll lose public support otherwise. Our work will be wasted. And what for? Just because of some kid who's been sent here that we know nothing about.'

'Yes, that's true,' said a middle-aged woman quietly. She had been silent until now. 'Who is this child, anyway? Perhaps the blood test is correct. Millions of people all over the world have got Aids. Why not him? He comes from a country where it's rife. Couldn't he have got it in a blood transfusion?' She looked round as if apologizing for what she had just been obliged to say.

'There hasn't been enough time to do the blood test,' said Theódóra. 'It was only taken yesterday.'

'So what test did they go on then?'

'I've been ringing all round town all morning trying to find out but I haven't got any answers,' said Theódóra.

'I'm positive about one thing,' said Svandís, the youngest woman there. 'The country won't want a prime minister who doesn't abide by the law of the land.'

'All is not lost. Not if you go and persuade the priest to give up the boy,' pleaded Gudrún.

'Yes,' said Ester with real cunning, folding her arms. 'Then it would all look as if it was down to the priest. And it would be.'

'As long as we ignore the other possibility,' said Elísabet helplessly. 'What if he sets the house on fire? What then?'

'Yes, what then?' asked Birna, anxiously. 'Then there would be arguments for years about whose fault it was. They'd blame you. The child being here at all is your responsibility!'

'Some people say the priest's only bluffing, saying he's got all this petrol,' said Svandís.

'Trausti!' said Ester with some authority. 'Answer me. Is it all a bluff or has he got petrol in there?'

'Sis, it's like I told the police,' said Trausti wearily. 'Of course he's got petrol in there! Now shut up and leave me alone.' Trausti put the headphones on and concentrated on a CD.

'I'm sure the Viking Squad is itching for the kids in there to be armed,' said Gudrún coldly. 'So that they'd have a proper target. Then the poor guys would stop being such a joke.'

'They said on the radio news just now that a petrol-station

attendant's come forward to say he sold them lots of cans of petrol and even went to Sudurgata to deliver some of it,' said Elísabet, and they looked at one another.

'Yes, just imagine if some of those kids died in the fire,' said Gudrún, frightened. 'What then?'

'Well,' said Theódóra, 'whatever the situation, I'll have to go and talk to Father Bernhardur. Ester, would you just see if the phone's back on at Sudurgata?'

Ester rang the number, then shook her head.

The women stood up. Some of them had scarcely touched their coffee. 'This business of the boy, Theódóra, it's your own personal concern,' said Elísabet firmly. She was already catching her breath and you could see from her face that any moment now she would burst out laughing.

The doorbell rang. The women sat down again.

Ester opened the door to her father. Hördur looked round the living room and bowed his head in acknowledgement of the women's presence. Vilhelmína looked as if the riots in town were all her fault.

'How's Linda?' asked Theódóra quickly.

'I have no idea,' said the doctor, surprised to be asked. 'That's a matter for Accident and Emergency.'

'Didn't you go and look after her then?' said Theódóra, terrified.

'I tried to see her at dawn but the police were there ahead of me,' said the doctor, excusing himself.

'The phone's cut off. Oh God, the girl needs a doctor!' shouted Theódóra.

'We tried to phone you at the surgery,' said Vilhelmína quietly.

'You know I always pull the phone out when I'm sleeping there, Vilhelmína.' Hördur looked crossly at his sister-in-law. 'Are you trying to start a civil war? Turn everything upside-down? I haven't known anything like it in this country since the Vikings. What's the meaning of all this? If the child is infected, he should of course be deported like any other foreigner, whether you're responsible for him or not.'

'I'm afraid it's precisely because he's my responsibility that all this is happening.' Theódóra lit a cigarette.

'What! Taken up smoking, have we?' said the doctor. He put his

408

coat on a chair and sat down. 'You can't mean what you're saying. There is no one causing a fuss except you and your people. This maniac of a priest is trying to stop the police getting on with their duty. That's all that's happening!'

'How can you explain the results of a blood test being ready only a few hours after the sample was taken?' she asked him, putting out her cigarette almost immediately.

He screwed up his eyes. 'Is that what you think? Well, I'm not surprised a misunderstanding has arisen. The result is nothing to do with any test done here. The office of the Chief Physician got a fax from London. At least that's what I understand. That's where the HIV-positive result has come from.'

'No one at the office had heard any such thing when I rang this morning.'

'Well, perhaps it was the Immigration Office or the Ministry of Health, I don't know.'

'Anyone would think you were on the side of the enemy,' said Theódóra grimly.

'"The enemy"?' he repeated in surprise. 'My dear Tedda, you sound like a child. Who do you think is your enemy?'

She stared at him coldly. 'The Prime Minister and his cronies.'

Hördur glanced at Vilhelmína. 'Yes, what your sister has doubtless told you is true. I went and saw the Prime Minister to discuss a matter you've certainly become aware of. But if you think I'm involved in some conspiracy to destroy you, you'd better think again. That's more in your line,' he said firmly. 'I sometimes wonder if you shouldn't be sectioned.'

'For God's sake, let's not argue.' Vilhelmína put her hands up to her face.

The doorbell rang and Ester went to answer it. 'I suppose it's more bloody press,' she said and sighed.

Vilhjálmur had arrived, half out of his mind with worry in case all the business with Theódóra and the boy would adversely affect Heidnaberg's position. He followed Ester into the living room and stuck by her side, silent, pale and about to explode. He rubbed his large hands together and Trausti kept looking at him.

'Villi, do stop mumbling,' said Ester at last, exasperated. 'Have you got Heidnaberg on the brain?'

'I came to get my car,' said Hördur suddenly. 'It's the only property I can call my own and yet I seem to be constantly searching for it all over town.'

'Won't you go and check up on Linda for me?' asked Theódóra.

'I can't get into the house,' he said sharply.

'Tell the police who you are and that you're related to her,' said Theódóra, getting red in the face.

'We'd be very grateful if you'd have a look at her, Father,' said Ester. 'We're terribly worried about her.'

Hördur felt the eyes of all the women resting on him. He relished the power the title 'doctor' gave him. He looked round with a little grin. 'I thought you'd got other things on your mind today apart from a meeting of the sewing circle.'

'Let's go, ladies,' said Elísabet and got to her feet quite frostily.

Theódóra went with them to the door. When she returned Hördur said to her, nastily, 'Can't you at least call off your priest before the foreign child gets hurt? You're the only person who's got any influence over him and you're sitting on your hands.'

She shook her head and said quietly, 'The boy will be taken from us and then God only knows what'll happen to him.'

'What's the point of taking on a child and then not looking after him?' the doctor challenged her.

'I've had so much on my plate,' she said, helplessly. 'He's been well looked after by Father Bernhardur until now.'

He examined her. She looked tired and haggard. He picked up a sweet. 'Why aren't you with the priest and your foreign child now?'

'Because I couldn't get in. I was going to try again when the storm died down but by then the police had closed off the street.'

He beamed at her. 'My dear lady, you're just trying to save your own skin. It doesn't play well in an election when the voters see a candidate getting all tangled up with a drunken and drug-crazed rabble.' He stood up. 'Well, I haven't got time for all this. I've got to take care of your daughter!' He looked at Trausti. 'Trausti, can I just have a quick word with you in the hall. Yes, now, Trausti.'

Vilhelmína gave Trausti a dig in the ribs and he took off his headphones. He followed his father to the door sulkily. 'You're perfectly OK,' said Hördur once he had closed the door behind them. 'I picked up your results last night.'

'Of course I'm OK,' said Trausti, angrily. He looked at his father. 'I hope you're not mixed up in all this. If you are, then it's over between us.'

'You've all gone stark staring mad,' hissed Hördur. 'Mixed up in what? The police and the health services doing their job?' Then he smiled paternalistically. 'Threatening your father, eh? I was wondering when you'd finally grow up!'

42

It was about dinnertime when the phone rang. Dagný dashed to it and grabbed the receiver. She was expecting bad news from the hospital any moment. She could hardly believe her ears when she heard who it was and she handed the receiver to Tryggvi immediately.

It was nearly nine when Tryggvi stopped at the bottom of the steep hill up Bókhlödustígur. The clouds had come up as the day had gone on. The weather bureau was forecasting snowstorms. Reykjavík Electricity had still not succeeded in reinstating the power supply. The whole of the city was on edge, the same question on everybody's lips: would the priest set the house on fire? The television and press people were being kept back from the house in case anything awful happened. Rumour had it the Chief Constable had been sacked because he refused to have anything to do with it. There was a police car with its lights on at the corner of Vonarstræti and Lækjargata. The stark outline of the Alliance of Skilled Tradesmen's offices was visible. In the darkness Tryggvi walked straight into the arms of two policemen. 'I was told to come to City Hall. I've got a son in 14 Sudurgata. I have to go and talk to him. The stupid kids have got to be saved.'

One of the policemen lit a cigarette. His eyebrows met in the middle and looked like moss in the light from his match. His face was long and thin. Gravel creaked under his feet. The sound surprised Tryggvi, it seemed so high-pitched. 'I must be in a state,' he thought. 'Are there many people at City Hall?'

'Quite enough.'

'That Arab kid or whatever he is has got a good chance of infecting the girls.'

'They really go for foreigners,' said the one with the cigarette. 'The blacker the better.' Tryggvi hadn't yet seen the other one's face. It was too dark.

'So, don't the Muslims go for their own kind, then?' the one without a cigarette asked. 'Is that why the priest's got him there? I heard all Catholic priests are queer.'

'They're all poofters!' the one with the cigarette said. 'What's your boy doing in there?'

Before Tryggvi could answer, the other one said, 'I reckon I'd let them set fire to themselves. Then we wouldn't have to worry about them any more.'

'Couldn't we get NATO to help?' Tryggvi was immediately ashamed of himself for suggesting it.

'NATO!' laughed the one with a cigarette, inhaling deeply. The tip of his cigarette glowed yellow in the darkness for a moment. 'You don't expect NATO to actually *do* anything, do you? They looked the other way during the Cod War.'

A car drove down Lækjargata with its headlights on and turned into Vonarstræti. The three men fell silent and watched it. It parked opposite Idno, the old theatre. The engine was turned off and the doors slammed. Tryggvi heard voices but could not make out what was being said.

'Let's see what they're saying at City Hall,' said the one whose eyebrows met, as he and Tryggvi walked over to it.

There was a bridge over the lake to the eastern door of City Hall. They walked on to the bridge. A policeman was guarding the door. The glass door slid open. There was an emergency generator at City Hall. Tryggvi's companion explained why they were there and the policeman looked doubtfully at Tryggvi. Tryggvi spotted Hannes and walked over to him. The Prime Minister lifted a welcoming hand when he saw who it was and did not make any attempt to disguise the fact that it was he who had requested Tryggvi's presence. 'There you are, Tryggvi. It's good to see you, my friend. You're just the man we need!'

He took hold of his elbow and ushered him to a discreet corner.

Tryggvi looked across the hall. There were several dozen men there, some standing in groups deep in conversation. There were mattresses laid out on the floor and one man was asleep under a blanket curled up like a child.

'I heard your good lady had returned home and there's now no need for my colleague Haraldur Sumarlidason to do anything more about finding her a flat,' said the Prime Minister. 'All's well that ends well, then! But to come straight to the point, what I want you to do, Tryggvi, is this: go to 14 Sudurgata and get in to the lair of these old women and priests. Make a thorough survey, floor by floor, and see if they've got petrol there or not. Personally I don't believe they have, but it's best to make sure. And we'll act on your report. We have to establish the rule of law. There's one thing I want you to check out. Have they got any weapons? Guns? Knuckledusters? Flick knives? And how much of it? You might think it's strange I'm getting involved in all this but when the Chief Constable loses his bottle and turns tail and the whole town's in a state of siege then it's the man at the top who carries the can. Now, I don't want you to think I'm betraying your son.' The Prime Minister tightened his grip on Tryggvi's arm. 'That's not how it is! I know you see things the way I do and that it would be better to give those kids a clip round the ear and put a stop to this nonsense. I've looked into your situation since we had that conversation outside the Parliament building the other day, as you might imagine. Your mortgage . . .' The Prime Minister shook his head sadly. 'And all this interest you owe the government! I'll cancel it with a stroke of my pen.'

All the time Hannes was speaking Tryggvi did not take his eyes from his face. The Prime Minister's beady eyes were shining. On some level he was enjoying himself. Tryggvi looked away. By the door there was a tear-gas launcher and a pump-action sawn-off shotgun used for shooting out doorlocks. Tryggvi looked at the weapons. 'I'll start stuttering as soon as anyone says anything to me. Can't someone else go?'

'What's the matter, man? Don't you want to get your boy out of there? Aren't we comrades in arms, blood brothers? The bloody women will use this to blacken my name even more and we're both carrying the scars of attacks from that particular quarter. We've got

413

interests in common. You weren't afraid the other day when you were threatening to seize Government House with a few of your mates.' The Prime Minister looked at his political ally doubtfully.

'What if they won't let me in?'

'Then that's that,' roared the Prime Minister. 'This is a war. Can't anybody understand that?'

'I can't say I like the thought of it.' Tryggvi was trembling slightly with nerves.

'It's nothing to worry about, my friend! The time has come to stand up and be counted.' Hannes rested a hand on his shoulder. 'You said you were a member of the party. You came to me for help and I let Halli drag his feet getting your wife a flat so the precious woman wouldn't be lost to you. And now I need a favour, mate. I'm a man too! And you can scarcely want your boy to go up in smoke if they really have got petrol in there and that prat of a priest puts a match to it. Look what happened in Texas only the other day.'

There was banging on the glass door. Three men were wanting to get in and making a great noise about it. The moon was up and its pale reflection appeared on the film of ice covering the lake. One of the men was holding a bottle. The door slid open.

'No one with spirits is allowed in,' shouted Hannes.

'We're going to kill you, Hannes,' shouted one of the men standing outside as if they weren't going to risk coming through the door. 'It's all your fault! Everyone knows that!'

'What are the police up to?' asked the Prime Minister. 'I gave orders for the streets to be sealed off and yet any old drunk can wander in here and abuse me at will.' He was getting extremely angry and said, 'Is Iceland now a country utterly without law and order?'

'You're a dead man, Hannes. Just wait till morning.'

'Shouldn't we go out there and give them a good seeing to?' said one of the men.

'Yes, a few of you go and sort it, or at least get them off the bridge. And you, Tryggvi, go for it! And try and get back here within the hour.' Five or six men slipped out. A moment later the guard on the door let Tryggvi out too. There was some noise from round the Idno theatre area and then everything was quiet again. A bird

414

flew over the lake with the wind under its wings and was visible briefly by the light of the moon. He could hear voices beside Lækjargata. Tryggvi looked westward across the lake. There was candlelight flickering in lots of windows. The Parliament building was completely dark. His breath was visible in the silent arctic night.

He walked down Vonarstræti and as he passed the corner of City Hall the look-out tower of the old fire station was standing tall and white above him. He looked away for a moment and when he looked back he could make out an arm sticking out over the edge and he realized he was being watched. Tryggvi felt vulnerable and exposed in the darkness and was relieved to reach the shelter of the houses along Tjarnargata.

A police car was parked on the corner by the Salvation Army. The emergency lights were glowing deep red in the darkness. He couldn't see if there was anyone behind the wheel. It was as if the whole town was waiting to see what the priest would do.

He saw a young guy standing by a fence looking at him. Tryggvi crossed Sudurgata and the guy kept watching him. As Tryggvi passed him the kid fell in behind him. Tryggvi stopped and looked over his shoulder.

'What do you want?' asked the kid.

'I've come for my son.'

'What's his name?'

'What's it to you?'

'I'm the look-out.'

'He's called Haflidi.'

'Yes, he's in the house. It should be OK,' said the kid with great authority.

Tryggvi rested his hand on a fence post as he drew near 14 Sudurgata. There was only a short distance to the door now. 'They'll know the moment I open my mouth why I'm here,' he thought nervously. There were lights burning low in the downstairs rooms but no one was on guard outside. The sleepy-looking aura contrasted with the tension in the town. Wasn't this the house they were all talking about? He forced himself to imagine the roof exploding and fire bursting through all the windows. He listened. He heard the mumble of voices. He glanced up at the watchtower of the fire station, silhouetted against the clear bright sky, but he could see no movement.

He decided to knock on the door at the north side. He reached the steps. 'What the hell am I doing?' he thought, panting with anxiety. 'Am I losing it? I've got no business here with the poor kid. But then, cancelling all those debts!' Tryggvi was elated for a second. 'That would be wonderful!' He took a deep breath and started going up the steps. They shifted under his weight. He leapt up the remaining steps and knocked on the door. He heard footsteps and then someone saying, in a wary, sullen voice, 'Yes. Who is it?'

'It's Tryggvi.'

'Which bloody Tryggvi?'

'My name is Tryggvi Thórarinsson.'

'Are you police?'

'No.'

'I don't know you.'

'Well, that's not my fault.' Tryggvi was feeling more confident now.

'What do you want?'

'I want to speak to my son. He's in there with you.'

'Who is he?'

'Haflidi.'

'Where do you live, Tryggvi?'

'Twenty-eight Thingholtstræti.'

There was deathly silence on the other side of the door. As far as he could judge, the kid had gone into the house to give his name to those inside. Tryggvi found his hands were coming out in a cold sweat. He took to punching his fists into his palms while he waited. He heard footsteps and a voice saying, 'He doesn't want to talk to you.'

'Tell him I've got an urgent message to do with his brother.'

The footsteps went away again. After a while Haflidi opened the door and looked suspiciously at his father. 'What do you want?'

'I want you to come home.'

'What was that about Jökull?'

'Let me in so we can talk. I can't hang around out here.'

'Are you on your own?'

'Yes.'

The door was opened properly and Tryggvi walked into the hall. No fewer than five kids were waiting for him. Three of them had clubs. Haflidi locked the door and held on to the knob as a safety precaution. A large pimply lad with a fat gut looked suspiciously at Tryggvi. There was a large group of young men in the living room, some were hardly more than children. There were lighted candles everywhere.

'It's OK, guys, it's cool,' said Haflidi. He turned to his father. 'Is Jökull any worse?'

Tryggvi walked down the corridor without answering. He thought he might go straight to Father Bernhardur and greet him first to hide how nervous he was feeling. Father Bernhardur looked taller than he remembered him. His face was strangely pale. His hair was tousled and his beard standing out in tufts. The priest was wearing black trousers and a white shirt.

'Someone new,' said one of the kids who'd gone to the door.

'I know him,' said the priest and stood in the middle of the room waiting for him with an outstretched hand. 'Welcome, my dear Tryggvi.' Tryggvi said hello but he couldn't meet his eyes. He found the priest's hand was cold as ice and that comforted him somehow.

He looked round the living room. There were chairs here and there and a sofa under a shelf. All the seats were occupied. There was a sheepskin rug on the floor. There were too many faces for Tryggvi to remember them all. He looked round for the person at the centre of it all: the boy himself. He saw he was dozing on the sofa with a blanket over him.

'Many people out in the streets?' asked the priest.

'Not a soul. The electricity in the town centre's out and there's a problem getting it reconnected. It may have been a power failure, but no one seems to know for sure. The city centre's closed to everyone.'

'Then how did you get here?'

'No problem.' This startled Tryggvi a bit and he felt the lie must be obvious from the boyish voice that came out of his mouth. 'I walked east along Aegisgata and across the green at Landakot and then through the gardens. I couldn't see a thing. I was lucky the moon came out. Otherwise I'd never have found the house.' He hoped the guy on guard out in the garden wouldn't come in and blow his cover.

Father Bernhardur began to pull at his beard on the left side and pace about the floor. 'It's a conspiracy. They're fighting over power and money.'

'Politics.' This was said in a foreign accent. The Serb boy got up from the sofa. He walked over to Tryggvi and showed him the vein in his elbow and said something in English. Tryggvi looked around helplessly. He watched the pulse beating. The boy pointed to it with his index finger and shook his head to indicate his blood wasn't infected, He repeated the word: 'Politics.'

The kids around him all nodded.

'I'm told there's an Aids patient who's been living in the Breidholt district for the last six years,' said Father Bernhardur. 'There are people with Aids everywhere! There was never the slightest reason to deport the boy because people with Aids are not refused permission to remain in any country. Even in the United States, although foreigners with Aids and no health insurance aren't allowed to stay. Everyone knows they want to get rid of the boy because he's here as Theódóra's guest. There was never any reason to break into the house and search it. It was done only because she and I were involved. There was never any reason to hunt the boy down like some dangerous criminal and not simply a child all on his own in the world who had come all this way to enjoy Icelandic hospitality. Even if there had been some made-up reason, it doesn't hold good now because everybody knows there are lots of Aids patients in Reykjavík. And who knows how many other people in the country have it?' Father Bernhardur raised his voice. 'Can anyone doubt the justice of our cause? No. No one. Absolutely no one!' He fell silent for a moment, preoccupied with his own thoughts and then started speaking again. 'I am sorry to have to say that justice is not always victorious, but in this case it will be.' He raised his hand to emphasize his words. 'It will conquer, because many many people, whether they're Catholics or not, have banded together on the side of justice and are refusing to have anything to do with a party that wants to manipulate justice to its own ends. Justice will conquer because there are all these young people ready to defend it, ready to sacrifice their own interests in a good cause, willing to stand firm even though they face great injustice masquerading as law. The outcome of all this is assured. The boy will remain. God is with us.'

'The Viking Squad won't dare do anything,' said a boy who was obviously trying to impress Father Bernhardur. 'The kids won't let them take the boy. They'll come here from all over the city and defend the house.' Father Bernhardur nodded and looked round him. A deep silence fell.

Tryggvi walked over to a table in the corner of the living room. There was a pile of dirty coffee cups. Someone brought coffee and poured it into a cup for him. There were slices of bread and butter on a tray and he took one and sat down on the sofa, sipping his coffee. Now he was in the building and not arousing any suspicion, he could concentrate on the task he'd been given. What did they have in the way of weapons? Was there any petrol in the building? Suddenly his body was overcome with weariness and intense hunger. He wolfed down the bread and gulped down the coffee.

'Father, you look like you haven't eaten for a week,' said Haflidi, sitting close beside him. 'What was it you wanted to tell me about Jökull?' He sounded worried.

'It's nothing I can discuss here,' said Tryggvi quietly. 'Let's go somewhere private.'

Father Bernhardur kept looking at his watch. The deadline he had given the Prime Minister was long gone.

Tryggvi and Haflidi went down to the basement. 'What is it?'

'It's not about Jökull. He's still in a coma. I just wanted to ask you to come home before something happens here.'

'I can't,' said Haflidi, shocked even to be asked. 'It's a question of justice! The foreign boy is my friend. I feel my life's got some purpose to it now, Father.'

'But what if that mad priest really does set fire to the house?'

'Father Bernhardur! Don't talk about him like that. It won't happen.'

'But they say there's petrol stored here.'

'It's rubbish. Have you come over here to spy on us?' Haflidi looked at his father, furious and wary.

'How can you think that, boy?' Tryggvi managed to sound convincingly outraged. 'I came to ask you to come home, because I'm afraid for you. And because I love you. And because none of us knows whether Jökull's going to make it. I'm sick with worrying about him and I don't want to lose both my sons.'

'That's nice to hear, Father,' said Haflidi and he looked happy in the candlelight. 'I love you too, but I can't leave. Don't worry about it. I'm not in danger.'

'If you won't do it for me, do it for your mother.'

'Least of all for her,' said the boy vehemently.

'Then for your brother and sister.'

'No, not even for them. I can't let the priest down. He's been so good to me. And I won't abandon the Serb boy when everyone's attacking him.'

'OK then,' said Tryggvi and sighed. 'Then I'd better go.' He fumbled for the doorknob.

'And you promise not to tell anyone there's no petrol here?' whispered Haflidi as Tryggvi went outside on to the basement steps.

Tryggvi walked quickly in the darkness, trembling slightly with the tension. While he had been inside the police had moved the car from the corner by the Salvation Army on to the corner of Vonar-stræti. He could imagine how pleased the Prime Minister would be when he heard the news. 'And I'll give Haddi a good thrashing when all this is over,' he thought. Then he felt nauseous when he thought about how he had exploited his son's affection for him. 'I had permission from City Hall to go in and speak to my son,' he said as the constable wound down his window.

As he arrived on the west side of City Hall he almost felt as if he was attending some grand reception. He tapped on the glass door and it was opened for him.

Hannes was waiting impatiently for him in the front hall. The Prime Minister grabbed Tryggvi's arm and pulled him in. 'Well, my lad,' said the Prime Minister urgently, 'what did you find out?'

'They're sitting on gallons of petrol. If you try and get any closer, it'll be like when that religious maniac in Texas set his ranch on fire,' said Tryggvi without giving it a second thought.

43

Hördur did not arrive at City Hall until gone midnight. The night was pitch black. Two policemen were stationed at one end of the bridge to ward off sightseers. A group of young people had gathered there and were asking the police about the siege. The police weren't giving much away. Hördur felt they were there only out of curiosity. None of them was likely to go and help the people in 14 Sudurgata. They might be acting as if they supported them but it was all bravura. All the bars and restaurants in town had closed because of the electricity failure and the young people were enjoying themselves out in the Reykjavík suburbs. He stated his business and they escorted him to City Hall. From there he was taken to the corner of Vonarstræti and Sudurgata. Hördur was allowed through the cordon when his escort said why he was there. Hördur had not known a darkness like it since he had been a small boy out in the countryside. He walked along the street and up the path to the house with great care. He tripped over the broken veranda rail. He stumbled up the steps and knocked loudly on the door. It was opened almost immediately when he said who he was and why he had come.

He was escorted up to the second floor. Father Bernhardur was nowhere to be seen. 'I want to be alone with the patient,' he said, and walked into Linda's room.

It was dark in her room. Linda was lying on a bed to the right of the window and had turned to face the wall. On the table was a single thick candle with a tall, majestic flame. As soon as Hördur opened the door the flame flickered.

The Serb boy had given Linda his room. It was freshly painted and there were no pictures on the walls. There were lots of presents he had been given by well-wishers and various humanitarian organizations: a CD-player, a large collection of CDs, a video, a television set, a wardrobe, a chest of drawers. The wardrobe door was half open, revealing the new suit Theódóra had given him. In the bottom of the wardrobe was a pair of brown leather shoes. There was a table under the window, but the chair had been taken elsewhere. Apart from that the only furniture was a single stool.

Linda woke with a start. She turned and looked at Hördur and when she saw who it was she relaxed. The candle flame stopped flickering.

'How are you, niece?' asked the doctor.

She sat up. She had an elastic support round her midriff. She put the flat of her hand to her side. 'It hurts here but it's not too bad.'

He sat on the bed and examined her. 'It's probably a broken rib. It'll get better on its own and there's no reason to be too concerned about it. Just take a couple of codeine before you go to bed.' He reached for them in his bag. 'Won't you leave here with me and stop putting your mother through all this worry? You need to go to hospital for an X-ray.'

'My vision is coming true.' She hugged her knees gingerly and winced with the pain.

'Vision? What vision?'

'I was up in Heidmörk one day with the children. I was looking to the south, expecting to see the beast from the Book of Revelation appear over the horizon. The weather was beautiful. The stone I was sitting on was surrounded by heather. I was collecting berries in the palm of my hand. Haflidi, the boy I was with, told me there'd been a frost in the night and all the berries would be spoilt but I was certain that there'd be places where it would still be all right to pick them. There are lots of crevices in the lava covered by heather up at Heidmörk and maybe the frost wouldn't have got in there.' She paused. 'The sky was completely clear and I wanted to make cordial like they did in the old days.'

'And you thought you could gather enough?'

'No, Haddi was right, the frost had been too fierce. If I touched the berries, they burst and stained my fingers red. Then I saw that Christ was bleeding through the berries.' Linda looked at the doctor. 'God created the earth. And when the vegetation dies in the autumn it bleeds. You think that's strange, don't you? I don't think it's strange at all. When spring comes, the vegetation comes to life again and everything's new. I felt God's love for me. Then I saw it was no coincidence that my hand had turned red. There's no such thing as coincidence, even though sometimes that's how it seems! And when I felt God's love then I knew he had made his peace with me and forgiven me for the way I treated my father.' The girl stretched out her hand and described a wide arc. 'Suddenly a gentle breeze stirred the heather and it began to rain. A gentle rain fell over me from out of a clear sky and I knew that Jesus was washing me in the dew of his spirit. I clambered up on to a large slab of lava to see if I could see a cloud anywhere and saw pictures right across the sky, a long row of trucks carrying weapons from east to west. I was afraid and I wanted to go home.'

'You would still be exhausted from the traffic jam on National Day,' he said with a thin smile and fidgeted a little on the stool. 'That would explain the vision.'

'No. While we were driving back to town I was looking out of the window all the time. A storm was following us and the car was vibrating on the road. I started to doubt that God had washed me clean. I thought perhaps a shower of rain had been carried by high-altitude winds, I don't know where from, Thingvellir perhaps. And when I looked up into the sky again there were crowds of people fleeing where the trucks had been before. They were mostly children, with some women and old people. I remember the old people especially, how sad and cowed they were. I saw a group of young and middle-aged men looking into a grave that had been dug for them and I felt as if I was standing by their side even though I was driving along the Sudurlandsvegurinn. I remember a particular little boy. He was just a child and trembling so badly his teeth were chattering. We were in a clearing. The grass was tall and beautiful and some way away there was a row of tall trees. There was a mist in the forest and a large dairy cow was standing in the middle of the field. Suddenly the vision vanished and I was parking the car at Dyngjuvegur. I ran into the house. I went straight to the living-room window to see if the vision was still there. Everything was as it had been: the row of trucks, the old people, a girl giving birth, the men by the grave, the boy with the chattering teeth and then the sun grew dark.' She paused and turned to Hördur. 'Was there an eclipse of the sun last autumn, Hördur?'

'Not that I remember.' He shifted his feet because the stool did not feel very solid.

'There was an eclipse of the sun, because I saw it!' Linda clenched her fists. 'I saw the moon roll across the sun and darkness cover Reykjavík. I went out on to the balcony and the city was frozen and silent and the birds did not dare to sing and when I looked out into our garden, what do you think I saw?'

Hördur said nothing.

'Christ crucified on the front lawn. He was dead. I saw the blood running down from the cross and down the slope and down on to Laugarásvegur and then I understood why there was blood on my hands when I picked the berries. Do you know why my hands were covered in blood?'

Hördur shook his head without saying anything.

'Because I had crucified Christ.'

'Rubbish,' said the doctor.

'I tried to scream but no sound came out of my mouth and at the same moment the blood in the street caught fire as if it was petrol and the fire ran up the hill and burned under the cross and Jesus could be seen in the flames. I saw his profile so clearly. I saw that he was dead and then I heard a powerful, majestic voice saying, "Take care. He has entered your house and is standing behind you." I turned round and saw the tall man standing behind me. I stared at his chest because I was too scared to look up and then he tried to hit me and I tried to get out of the way but I couldn't manage it.' She leant closer and parted the hair above her forehead. 'Is there a mark?'

Hördur did not look at her forehead but sat completely still and stared at her coldly.

'Then when I came to I was lying on the floor. It was a bright day and the sun was shining but the vision was still there. All through the next day weapons were being transported across the sky and the clearing was still there, although it was further away. I tried to look at it in the way you look at the heat haze across the sands at Fljótshlíðin. It was as if the forest was consumed by fire, because the intensely hot wind shimmered above the grass and the people and the trees. And when Mother was sent the boy from overseas then I knew it was all for real.'

'My dear girl, this is all nonsense! You were hit on the head in the fight yesterday.'

'No. Someone kicked me in the side. What I saw in the sky is happening in Reykjavík now!' She fell silent and looked at Hördur. 'You're the man the voice in the sky warned me against.'

'My dear child, you've gone stark staring mad.' He was almost frightened.

'What are you going to do? This evening? After this?'

'I've come to try and help you.'

'No. You're going to do something evil. That foreign boy is Jesus Christ and you don't understand. I know why you killed the old woman. It wasn't anything to do with kindness and old age. You killed her so you could be someone!'

'Stop this idiocy,' he said, choking, and leapt to his feet.

'No,' she shouted. 'I won't stop it! Christ is here on Sudurgata and you are going to betray him, for the same reason you killed the old woman.' Suddenly her eyes bored into him. 'I can feel it. You've done it already!' She was yelling and her voice had become deep and hoarse.

'I'm not listening to this nonsense!' he shouted, red in the face and agitated. 'You've gone mad! Your mother said you'd slept with a black guy and some old man and you got a sexually transmitted disease from one of the them. Wasn't that why you were getting yourself checked out? I've watched you since you were a kid.' He was having difficulty finding the words to express his anger. 'You've always been spoilt. You're a spoilt little madam. Axel did everything you ever wanted and you never gave him one word of thanks! It killed him. If you'd been my daughter . . .' He was struggling helplessly to find the words. 'I'd've given you a good spanking, do you understand what I'm saying?' He was standing by her bed with his fists clenched. 'Besides, I can't imagine God wanting to have anything to do with you,' he said, stupidly.

She supported herself on the bed with both hands and winced as if she was expecting to be punched in the head. He regained control of himself and let his arms fall to his sides. 'Do you think I'm going to oblige you by fulfilling your prophecy?' he said, smiling wanly. 'So Christ is here in Sudurgata, is he, Linda? Right now? At this very moment?' A smile spread over his face. 'Does Christ come from Serbia?' He was smiling a smug, gloating smile.

In a quiet, calm voice, Linda said, 'Yes, he is with us!'

'I've dipped into your Bible, although that might come as a bit of surprise to you and your priest. It says there: "Behold, I have told you before. Wherefore if they shall say unto you, Behold, he is in the desert; go not forth: behold, he is in the secret chambers; believe it not. For as the lightning cometh out of the east, and shineth even unto the west; so shall also the coming of the Son of man be." I was outside a little while ago and the sky is looking pretty much its old self. Reykjavík is perfectly normal,' he said, smiling. He reached into his breast pocket and threw her letter on to the desk. He left, closing the door as he went.

44

He had to stop himself from bursting back into the room again. He expected her to stumble out on to the landing in order to have the last word. He waited for a moment outside the door. He heard the bed creak but she did not come out. His palms were moist with sweat and he was so angry he wanted to smash her face in. He looked into the next room and walked round it carefully as he regained control of himself. There was no one on the top floor. He went to the top of the stairs and could hear the young people talking downstairs but could not make out what they were saying. He jumped when someone laughed out loud.

A wooden ladder led up to the loft. Hördur looked up and could see wooden beams above him. He glanced along the landing but there was no one there. He took three steps up the ladder, put his head through the hatch and looked about him. The chimney obscured his view but otherwise all he could see was dusty floorboards, beams, a tired old mattress and a few scraps of silver paper, blackened on one side. He couldn't smell anything. There was no petrol or oil up here. If there was anything like that in the building, it would have to be hidden in the basement. He stepped down again lightly. As soon as he stepped off the ladder he could hear loud voices and he took a step or so backwards. 'I want to go home! I don't want to stay here any longer!' It was a girl's voice.

'But no one can go now!' said a boy.

'I'm going!' said the girl's voice stubbornly.

'No. No one can leave, Ingibjörg! As soon as anyone leaves here they'll get out of them that it's all a bluff.'

Hördur stepped back silently to make sure no one would see him. He was ashamed of himself. He'd been just as stupid as everyone else and he'd been taken in by the priest's lies. As soon as the young people had gone back into the living room, he went downstairs, furious with himself. When he appeared in the doorway the priest looked at him in surprise. 'Oh, it's you! I was told there was a doctor here and he didn't want to be disturbed.'

'Could I have a word?' Hördur beckoned Father Bernhardur. He saw the Serb boy waving at him. Hördur gave him a nod.

The priest stood up and went over to Hördur. As the evening had worn on, Father Bernhardur had become much calmer. He was now completely relaxed and examined the doctor with friendly curiosity.

'Just the two of us.'

Father Bernhardur opened a door into the west room and a curtain stirred. Everything was in total chaos. In one corner there was a pile of white boxes that had once held a music centre. They reached up to the ceiling. Against one wall there was an old teak couch with a yellow cover. There was a mattress on the floor beside it. The priest ushered the doctor to a seat and picked up a chair from where it lay on the floor and sat on it himself. 'Is there anything wrong with the girl?' he asked, concerned.

'There's not a lot wrong. A broken rib. That's about it.' Hördur let his eyes wander round the room. One of the windows was broken. The curtain did not move in the draught as the door closed, but he could feel the current of bitterly cold air finding its way into the room. He was still in a turmoil after the conversation upstairs. 'Do you imagine you are serving God by doing this?' he asked forcefully and looked at the priest's face with icy intensity.

'I'm doing my duty by acting on behalf of a child. That ought to be pleasing to God.' Father Bernhardur glowed with happiness.

'Do you think the government and the forces of law and order in this country will allow this situation to continue?'

'I place the needs of humanity above the law of the land,' said the priest by way of reply.

'You won't turn me into a lunatic like you have my niece,' spat Hördur.

The priest looked at him in surprise.

'Linda.'

'She has fallen into the hands of the living God,' said Father Bernhardur. 'I had nothing to do with it.'

Hördur sat there in silence for a moment, inspecting his hands, as if he was considering this as an idea. Finally he said, sounding rather offhand, 'I think you ought to laugh at yourself rather than sit there grinning like a madman.'

'What's so funny about me?' asked Father Bernhardur, curious.

'I need scarcely remind you of the long-established custom in France in the old days.'

'The Feast of Fools?' Father Bernhardur nodded impatiently. 'You mentioned it before.'

'Yes, when the Catholic Church turned itself upside-down just before Christmas.'

'But this was centuries ago,' said the priest impatiently. 'What are you getting at?'

'Well, it's been re-established in Iceland.' Hördur met his eyes.

'What do you mean by that?'

'What happened at the high point of the festivities?'

'The Lord of Misrule was chosen. And in that moment he knew who he was.'

'Exactly,' said the doctor, brightening.

'Exactly? What exactly?'

'The Lord of Misrule has been chosen.'

'And who is he?' The priest looked rather sulky, as if this discussion had nothing to do with the matter in hand.

'My dear friend,' said Hördur, spelling it out to the priest, 'it is you.'

'What do you mean by that?' asked Father Bernhardur, looking straight at him.

'You're surrounded here. There is absolutely nothing wrong with the boy.'

'How do you know that?'

'I've substituted an infected blood sample.'

Father Bernhardur waited for him to go on. 'What will you say when I make that public?' he asked finally. He did not seem to be taken aback by the news.

Hördur smiled in a friendly fashion. 'You can tell whoever you like. Feel free! No one will believe you. It was the Prime Minister's assistant who had the idea for the best way to get at you all. We lied to the police that the Chief Physician had received a fax from England notifying him that the boy was infected. Then I switched the blood samples. That was all there was to it. There is nothing whatsoever wrong with that child. The infected sample came from someone else.'

'How did you think you could keep this up? As soon as the boy's DNA's tested, it'll all come out.'

'But then time will have passed and no one will care. Every year there are innumerable mistakes in hospitals and people forget about them and cling to their limitless faith in the medical profession. Who do you think is going to speak up for the boy? Everyone hates the Serbs anyway.'

'Who did you do this favour for? You made Trausti go and have a blood test. Aren't you ashamed to use your own son like that?'

'My son? Who mentioned him? A favour? Isn't it obvious? The Prime Minister. I've come straight from a meeting with him. He wants to destroy Theódóra. She ruined him financially and she's trying to take his job if she possibly can.' Hördur's face hardened. 'She has humiliated me in every way she can ever since I married into that family. She won't give me what's rightfully mine! The Prime Minister is doing me a favour in return. I've been forced to defend myself.' He looked at the priest. 'There is no sympathy for you in the town at all, Father Bernhardur. The whole world hates the Serbs. They belong to a nation the great family of nations can unite in loathing. In the company of Serbs, everyone can feel gloriously self-righteous.'

Father Bernhardur was silent. Then suddenly his face lit up.

Hördur looked at him, but it was beyond him why the priest should look so happy.

'When you stand before Christ and you have to account for your actions, what will you say? No one should treat the weak among us like this. Remember what he said about those who do harm to children. Attacking a child is attacking God. It is an attack on the Saviour himself. "And whosoever shall offend one of these little ones that believe in me, it is better for him that a millstone

429

were hanged about his neck, and he were cast into the sea.'"

The doctor smiled a thin smile and stood up. 'Would you see me to the door? I fear I shall not be able to leave because of all your children. This', he said, looking around him and shaking his head pityingly, 'will not bring you closer to God.'

They went out into the corridor. 'And you can tell the police I haven't lied to them,' said Father Bernhardur, quite excited now. 'There is petrol stored in both the basement and the loft. There's not much of it, but quite enough to set a hundred-year-old tinder-box like this on fire.'

Two boys came out of the living room to see what was going on.

'I'll pass on that message.' The doctor smiled at Father Bernhardur. 'You've got that same pained expression on your face you did on Axel's birthday. It's just as I suspected when I first met you. The only human being with any faith at all in this house is the girl on the top floor.'

The priest gave a signal and one of the boys unlocked the north door. Father Bernhardur followed Hördur to the door and said in a shaking voice as the doctor went out on to the steps, '"Sinners will find an inexhaustible source of mercy in my heart." That is what Christ promises.'

Hördur and said calmly. 'You cling to your priesthood if you want. But if this limitless grace is on offer to all of us, then I think you'd better start asking for some of it yourself.' And he smiled, mocking him.

The kid by the door didn't seem to know whether to intervene or not.

The doctor walked down the steps and when he reached the garden path he could smell the sweet smell of the trees. The frost must be lifting.

A policeman accompanied him from the corner of Vonarstræti to City Hall. 'Anyone injured?'

'Not in need of an ambulance anyway. But there isn't a drop of petrol in the building. I checked from top to bottom. You can go in and get the boy whenever you like.'

'Better tell City Hall and see how they want to handle it. This whole thing seems a bit iffy to me.'

'Iffy? How? Why?' Hördur didn't understand what the man meant.

'You feel a bit ashamed being involved somehow. He's only a kid. I can understand why the Chief Constable went on unpaid leave. I don't think I've ever been involved in anything so dodgy in all my life.'

They walked in silence the short distance that was left to the brightly illuminated City Hall. When they arrived the policeman passed on the news to the superintendent. 'He says there isn't a drop of petrol in the building.'

'We don't need any highly qualified doctors to tell us that.' The superintendent tried to make it seem as if Hördur wasn't telling him anything he didn't already know. 'No one was stupid enough to believe that! We just need an official statement for the records.' Hördur looked at him, aware that he had himself gone up into the loft.

'I think the best thing to do is go in as soon as it's light,' said the superintendent.

45

Theódóra was no further forward at daybreak. She was fighting for her political life. If she couldn't find a way out it was the end for her. She rang Vatnsholt again, but Hördur had not come home. At long last, some time around dawn, Vilhelmína phoned with the news that, according to Hördur, Linda was in fairly good physical shape but her mental condition was, to say the least, heartbreaking. It was foolhardy to leave the girl unattended and in fact Linda herself was desperate for her mother to be there.

The car windows were covered in ice and she couldn't find the scraper. She had to go back in the house and get the keys for Linda's car. There she found the scraper. The stars were still shining and to the north the outline of Mount Esja could be seen in the darkness. As she drove along Skúlagata the sea looked like a sheet of black glass. Theódóra parked her car on Túngata. On the corner of Vonarstræti there were a few policemen standing about. The road was closed off with a wooden yellow barrier. There were very few people watching and the policemen's shoulders were hunched against the cold. The night had been quiet, despite the anxiety of the authorities. I was numb with cold. I'd passed the night in an old Ford I'd found unlocked in a nearby run-in and I hadn't had a wink of sleep. I'd spent all night trying to keep a patch of windscreen clear in order to see out. Unfortunately there wasn't a radio in that pile of junk. Father Bernhardur had got hold of a mobile phone the evening before and had explained his position to the nation. At a later date I was allowed to listen to the recording and everything he said on that broadcast has already been said in so many words in this narrative. A little later he came outside and gave a statement live to a television reporter. I was in the town centre at the time and missed it, but I got hold of a video copy later.

'No one except residents is allowed access,' said the policeman as Theódóra approached him.

'I think I might have the solution to this problem,' she lied.

'Let the lady through,' said the Deputy Chief Constable. 'She's the next prime minister.'

Theódóra's smile was a mite weary. She ducked under the yellow tape between the two roadblocks and walked up to the house. It was so still and quiet her footsteps echoed down the street. The lights were on on the first floor. She put her hand on the door knob. The door wasn't locked. She walked into the living room. Father Bernhardur was sitting on the sofa. Haraldur Sumarlidason was sitting on a chair facing him, nervously tapping his foot. He was wearing black patent-leather shoes. He was red in the face and glistening with sweat. From time to time he tugged at his shirt collar below his Adam's apple. Theódóra looked at the priest. 'What's he doing here?'

Haraldur Sumarlidason looked at Theódóra as if he was deeply hurt and betrayed. 'I'm here to ask him if he'll just be a good chap and come out. If he doesn't they'll storm the house. We don't want anyone to get hurt. Theódóra,' said Haraldur in a kindly tone of voice, 'you're a sensible person. Can you talk some sense into him?'

'I'm in charge here,' said Father Bernhardur. 'And you can tell your boss the responsibility is all on his own head. We'll never come out of our own free will and betray the boy.' The priest looked at Haraldur, defying him. There was a slightly insane glint in his eye.

'I hear a lot of things in my line of business,' said Haraldur Sumarlidason. 'Hannes has to put up with a lot because he would rather smooth things over between people even when they seem to prefer confrontation.' Haraldur looked accusingly at Theódóra. 'Even when he's nurtured a viper in his bosom.' He looked at Father Bernhardur as if he was something he'd found on his shoe. 'The sort of vile insinuations you made about Hannes to me now and in public on the radio and television simply reflect on the person making them. As I think you'll find! All my superior desires is to be a harbinger of peace. The country that made him its leader knows all about his good work in Parliament and recognizes the justice of my words.'

'Haraldur,' said Theódóra, 'will you get out before I spit in your face?' Haraldur Sumarlidason stood up with an assumption of weary tolerance, picked up his jacket from the back of a chair and left the room.

Theódóra turned to Father Bernhardur. 'What did he offer you?'

'Money, as far as I can make out. They're very frightened of public opinion.'

'And where's Linda?'

'Upstairs.'

'How many are there here now?'

'Haflidi and a few lads.'

'Where are they?'

'On the top floor and in the loft.'

'What about the boy?'

'He's with Linda.'

Father Bernhardur went over to the window. 'I think you should go upstairs. They'll be coming in any moment.'

Theódóra dashed upstairs.

Father Bernhardur was standing by the window when the Special Forces came running up the garden. They came in groups of four aiming for each corner of the building, two pointing their guns at the house and two in front of them running for cover. They were all wearing balaclavas. Father Bernhardur sighed deeply. He heard running footsteps at the north door. At that moment the door to the sun lounge was kicked open and two men barged in. Two more came running down the hall and another two broke in through the kitchen. Father Bernhardur smiled benevolently at them and said, 'Gentlemen, please make yourselves at home!'

He was holding a cup of coffee and a saucer with a stale Danish pastry on it. As he spoke he was thrown violently to the floor and the cup and saucer flew out of his hands. 'Get down!' one of the Viking Squad yelled over and over again. This struck the priest as ludicrous as he was already lying face down on the carpet. 'Get down!' The cameraman from national television caught this moment on film and it was broadcast repeatedly for all to see.

Father Bernhardur felt strangely elated. His arms were pulled behind him and he was handcuffed. Then he was yanked to his feet. He heard the thunder of feet as the Special Forces ran upstairs. Two of them led him out between them across the lawn. A police van was standing a little way down the street with its rear doors open. A cameramen from Channel 2 had positioned himself in the tower of the old fire station on the opposite side of the street after a violent argument with the documentary film-maker. A substantial number of policemen stood in a line on the lake side of the street waiting for the storming of the house to be completed. As Father Bernhardur was led to the van he had the opportunity to meet the eyes of each and every one of them. Only two could meet his gaze. 'Poor wretched cowards,' thought the priest.

He was driven to the holding cells at Skólavördustígur. He sat, straight-backed, in the middle of the back seat between two members of the Viking Squad. I can still see him in my mind's eye, sitting on the edge of his seat. Almost immediately I got a lift with a mate in a rickety old Skoda. We zipped through town and arrived at Skólavördustígur before the van. There weren't many people out and about. There was a crowd standing outside the prison. There was only one I recognized: Haraldur Sumarlidason. He leaned forward and watched the priest as he was led inside. 'Make yourself at home, Father Bernhardur,' said Haraldur Sumarlidason.

I tried to push into the building in the group around the priest and flashed my press card but the guards wouldn't let me in, any more than they would any other reporters.

Quite a few members of the Viking Squad and their fan club were standing out the front. A lot of the people were still drunk after hitting the bars the night before and were quite lively. They were stopping people outside Skólavördustígur and making them account for their presence. Most of them doing this were thugs and vigilantes. I decided to go back to Sudurgata. There was a good chance I'd come across something, a scrap of paper say, that would explain everything. Two policemen appeared, escorting an elderly man into the slammer. It was Ingibjörg's father. He was covered in blood. It was obvious he'd been hit over and over again before they'd put him in the car. He kept saying, 'I'm not letting you lock up my daughter! I'm not letting you lock up my daughter!' I learned later that Trausti had arrived shortly after I was taken away. He was looking for Linda. Some thugs who knew he was gay hustled him away and beat him up. 'Fucking queer!' they kept shouting. Linda had been taken to hospital. I tried to help Ingibjörg's father but was then sprayed with CS gas. They took me to the little police station on the first floor of the customs house. I had to stay there, blind as a bat. I was able to exchange a few words with a boy who'd been at Sudurgata. He told me most of his friends had been arrested on the top floor before they'd gone into the loft. It's strange how your hearing is sharper when you can't see: the slightest movement, the jangle of keys, a squeak from a grain of sand beneath the sole of a shoe, water bubbling in a radiator, sounds from out in the street, police chatting to each other in the distance. In the run-up to Christmas there hadn't been much action in Reykjavík. A man was stabbed on Fellsmúli. Two boys were arrested for stealing from parking meters. A drunk had rear-ended a police car. A tough guy (also drunk), trying to impress his woman, had laid down on his back under a car, planning to lift it. Things did not go according to plan, he got trapped under it and the car had to be lifted off him with a hydraulic jack. An old woman fell and hurt herself on Bergstadastæti and a little girl had fallen from a veranda in the Breidholt district. Thank God, neither of them was seriously injured. There were six attempted rapes. The police were notified of eight burglaries. In the west end of town two men vandalized a statue with welding equipment. A drunk stole a small fishing boat and sailed off towards Videy island before anyone could stop him. Later in the day the scales were beginning to drop from my eyes a little, although physically I could not see again properly until quite late that evening. I couldn't see a thing when they had me in for questioning. It emerged that the police had been looking for me. It was utterly ridiculous. Someone had fingered me as a witness to the incident with the pig's head on the steps of the Parliament building. He'd said it could even have been me who'd done it. I told them the truth, that I hadn't managed to make a note of the index number of the car involved. When the idiots finally let me go, I headed straight back to 14 Sudurgata. The lights were back on in the town centre. The floor at the young people's home was knee-deep in rubbish. The furniture was broken, the music centre smashed up. Nothing like this had ever happened in Reykjavík. A clock was hanging at a drunken angle on a wall. For some reason it had been spared the general carnage. I can still visualize the hands. It was getting on for one o'clock.

At about midnight Haflidi was let out of Skólavördustígur. He was the last of the kids to be released. He ran straight home. He had thousands of ideas running round his head for rescuing Bosko from detention. He had fought a rearguard action in the loft for as long as he could. He'd found an enormous heavy iron strongbox full of junk dating from the time the wholesaler occupied the building. He instructed the others to drag the box across the door to the loft and wedge it under the beams of the slanting roof so it was absolutely impossible to get up there. When the Special Forces had started to tear off the roof, he realized it was all over. Theódóra and Bosko were the first to go downstairs. As soon as Haflidi appeared on the ladder he was handcuffed, as were the others as they came down, one by one.

He walks past the windows at his home. Both the downstairs rooms look empty. The front door is standing wide open. He hears a strange sound. His mother is laughing; it is the enchanting sound of her laughter. He hangs his coat up in the hall and listens. From the hall he can see the clock on the sideboard. It is seven minutes to twelve. It seems odd that there's no one home except his mother. Still, Dagný is happy. What's so funny? He walks into the living room. Dagný is curled up in the bedroom doorway. Her wet hair is tumbling over the hands covering her face. 'Mother, what's the matter?'

She doesn't hear him. She sits by the door crying quietly. 'Mother, it's me.'

436

She doesn't hear him. He touches her shoulder. Suddenly she's scared and puts a hand up to protect her head. When she sees who it is, she pushes her hair away from her face. Her face is swollen and puffy. One of her eyes is closed and her lower lip is swollen. It looks to him as if the corner of her mouth has been ripped. It upsets him so much he sits on the sofa and stares at his mother. She tries to stand but she is too weak. She crawls over to the armchair and clambers into it.

'God, look at you. What happened?'

'Tryggvi went crazy. Completely crazy.'

'Where's Silla?'

'She went out with your grandmother.' Dagný feels the corner of her mouth. 'Einar came over with some brennivín and they had a terrible argument. I told Tryggvi it was all over. That I was only staying here because Jökull was hurt.'

'It's awful to see what he's done to you.'

She nods and screws up her face as if she's about to cry like a little girl.

Haflidi feels the anger surging about his brain like a tempest. Fear and powerlessness take over. Perhaps Tryggvi will come back. He dashes to the front door, slams it shut and locks it. He shuts the door into the hall and double-locks it. He goes over to the window. Two men pass by talking. He can't make out what they're saying.

A police car drives along the street. 'Wonder if they've come for me,' he thinks. At this point the phone rings.

'If it's Tryggvi, I'm not speaking to him.'

Haflidi picks up the phone. 'No, Grandmother, Tryggvi isn't here. He went off somewhere with Einar. They're drinking like fish.'

'You've been locked up! The way you've been brought up!'

'Grandmother, we can talk about it later.' He puts down the receiver and turns to his mother. 'Where's Father gone?'

'I don't know, but I'm not going to be here when he gets back. It really is over this time! I swear it on my life!' Unsteadily, Dagný manages to walk to the bathroom and examine her face. She looks at it closely. She touches the most painful places. She tries to open the eye that's closed but it's too swollen. She wets a flannel and dabs her face. She rubs her hair dry quickly and picks up a towel. She puts on some red lipstick. She checks her white shirt carefully.

Amazingly there are no bloodstains. 'Please will you get my coat?'

'Where are you going?'

'I'm going to go out and have some fun.'

'Now! Looking like this? In God's name please don't go, Mother.'

'I'm going anyway. I'm not going to sit here and wait for either your bloody father or the old woman to come back.'

'Where are you going?'

'Me?' She laughs. 'Clubbing, of course! Where else?'

'Then I'll come with you.'

'Are you out of your mind, boy? I'm going by myself. Give me my coat.'

'Please, Mother, don't go.'

He gives her her coat and shuts the door. She changes into a dress and teases her hair on her shoulders to make it look better. She gets a small handbag, puts on her high heels, stands by the door of the living room and says, 'Let me out right now!'

'No.'

'Why was it Jökull had that accident? Why wasn't it you?' she sighs.

He gets the key out of his pocket and opens the door. He leaves the key in the lock.

He watches her walk down the slippery steps. The clock says twenty past twelve. The frozen street sparkles in the moonlight. Haflidi puts on his shoes and takes his leather jacket off its peg. He unlocks the doors so he'll be able to get back in later and follows his mother. He thinks she's gone mad. Mad! Dagný walks along close to the houses, supporting herself by holding on to the walls. He walks in her footsteps the length of Thingholtstræti. In Bankstræti there are lots of people milling about. It's Christmas Eve. The electricity is on again in the town centre. Cars are driving slowly down the street into the centre. There are people everywhere and some of them are drunk. There's a gang of kids shouting and carrying on. He follows his mother up Laugavegur and down Ingólfsstræti. On the corner of Hverfisgata there's a queue of people going into Ingólfs Club one by one.

'What happened to you, love?' asks a kindly looking young man.

'In there,' says Dagný, pointing to the door and the long queue of people slowly easing their way into the building. 'I want to go in there.'

The man takes her arm and they go in. Haflidi is standing on the other side of the street watching. He stands there a long time, perhaps half an hour, perhaps a little less. He can't be sure. It tough standing there in the cold out on the street. Some older kids pass him and don't cause any trouble. He crosses the street and looks at the display in the opera-house window. Haflidi wonders about running round to Einar, who lives near here, and telling him that Dagný's at a club and in a bad way, but then perhaps his father's at Einar's and then God only knows what might happen. He has to rescue her himself. He has to get in there and bring her out. There's no one waiting outside now. A short stocky middle-aged doorman looks at him blankly. 'Is it OK if I take a look inside?' asks Haflidi. 'My mother's in there.'

'No, mate, no way. You're too young.'

'Please,' begs Haflidi. 'She walked into a door and her face is all bruised and swollen. I need to take her to the hospital. I can't have her wandering about looking like that.'

'Oh, the lady with the swollen face. Is that your mum?' The man's big, flat face gazes at him and the look in his eye is more friendly. 'Well, go in and see if you can get her to come out, but be sharp about it.'

'Thank you very much.'

The man on the door deals with a newly arrived couple. It's a young woman with black hair and a rather beautiful-looking young man in a pale brown suit. Haflidi runs down the steps into a carpeted corridor. The music gets louder. He looks round the dance floor but he can't see his mother. He walks through the tables. 'Oi, you, boy!' shouts a drunken woman. 'Come and talk to me!'

Haflidi sees a man sitting at the table in a corner and with him in the shadows there's a fair-haired woman. He recognizes the way her hair falls over her shoulders. He walks over to them. 'Excuse me. Mother!'

The man turns from the woman. He is a powerful-looking man. His eyebrows meet in the middle. His forehead is high and his jaw is square. Haflidi is sure this man is a member of the Special Forces. Dagný has a finger to her forehead to hide her swollen eye.

'Mother.'

Dagný looks up. There is a glass of vodka on the table. A slice of lemon floats in the alcohol. The man leans back in his chair and looks blankly at Haflidi.

'Mother, we can't stay here. Come home with me now!'

Dagný doesn't seem to be at all surprised to see her son in this place. 'Can't I stay here?' she asks, wide-eyed. 'Haflidi darling, why can't I? I can do what I like now. I've left your father.'

'Is this your son?'

'Leave her alone,' says Haflidi. 'She's a married woman.' The man smiles. Dagný puts a hand over her face and waves Haflidi away.

'Let's go home, Mother.'

'How could you imagine I would want to go home with you?' Dagný sounds as if she is arguing with a tiresome lover. 'Leave me alone! I think that arsehole of a father of yours has finally got it through his thick skull that I've really left him this time.'

Couples are sitting at nearby tables. The music fades away. He walks out of the club, going slowly up the steps and passing the doorman without so much as a glance. He walks out into the cold and crosses Ingólfsstræti. He plans to pop in on Hverfisgata and see if his father is with Einar. They've got to get Dagný away from that man. It distresses him that he's not bigger and stronger. He sees in a flash, as if a door were suddenly opened into a vast dark hangar, that then he would be capable of murder. The gate is open. He walks up the path. There is a light in the window. Einar is at home. He lives on the top floor of an old black brick house in the second row back from the street. The door to the top floor is standing open. There's a narrow hallway, partitioned with wood from old brown boxes. The wallpaper is peeling off and '4/11/29 MS Godafoss' is stamped on the partition. Haflidi goes upstairs. There's a radio on. He reaches the top of the stairs and goes into the flat. Everything is upside-down. There are oil-stained clothes in a pile on the floor. A 'Russian chandelier', a naked lightbulb, is on, light flaring in the air around it. The DJ on the radio is introducing a fresh track. There's a bad smell in the flat. A smell like turpentine. Petrol! It makes Haflidi nauseous. Somehow the smell of petrol is associated in his mind with his mother and father. It seems to Haflidi that this is the smell of hatred, of evil itself. 'This must be how hell smells,' he thinks. He senses somehow that his father is lying in one of the other rooms, drunk as a skunk. He peeps into a boxroom. No one there. Another room is full of rubbish, dirty clothes and tattered books. In the largest room there is a put-you-up with grubby bedding. Einar's bedroom. Einar is sitting on a chair in the kitchen. He is very drunk and his speech is so slurred that it is difficult to understand what he is saying and Haflidi is not even sure he recognizes him. Einar looks up with glazed eyes. 'Pe'rol!' He looks at Haflidi, puzzled. 'Haddi! Drygvi go' pe'rol. Gone mad.' Einar tries to shrug. 'Got petrol day before yesterday. Took it home. What's he want with petrol? Is there going to be a strike? Afraid he won't be able to drive his fancy car?'

The phone rings. Haflidi picks up the receiver and says, 'Yes.'

'What are you doing there?'

'I was looking for you.' All he can hear is his father's voice. Stone cold sober.

'Why did you think I'd be there?'

'Mother said you and Einar had gone off somewhere together.'

'Where's your mother?'

'I don't know.'

Tryggvi is amazingly calm. 'Are you coming back soon?'

'Yes.'

'Be quick. I need to speak to you. It's father-and-son stuff.'

Haflidi is about to put down the receiver when his father takes a deep breath and says, 'Is Einar there?'

'Yes.'

'Tell him from me he can fuck off.'

Tryggvi put down the receiver.

Haflidi runs down the stairs and heads for home. He is surprised to find the lights on the ground floor are off. So are the lights upstairs. Gunnhildur has stayed out at dinner longer than she planned. The front door is unlocked. He walks into the hall. There's something different about the familiar place. Is it the smell? It's so bad it's hard for him to think straight. It's a smell he's only just left behind. The dense, suffocating smell of petrol. He opens the door on to the street to let in some fresh air. He goes into the dining room. The smell's even worse in there. It's pitch black in the room but his father speaks calmly out of the darkness. 'Haddi, lock the door.'

Haflidi turns the key without the door being properly shut and pushes it close up against the door frame. He turns on the light. The living room is soaked in petrol. Splashes of it up the walls. Petrol in a bowl on the living-room table. Petrol on the floor. The sofa and the chairs soaking wet. Tryggvi is standing in the large doorway that separates the two reception rooms. He does not look at his son but is trying to strike a match. He succeeds at the second attempt. As soon as the flame forms, Tryggvi shouts, 'I am a human being too!'

His voice is strangely high and shrill.

The shout and the slight pause preceding it save his son's life. Haflidi flings himself out into the hall and runs through the open front door. He leaps into the street with his feet scarcely touching the steps. He does not look over his shoulder until he has reached the pavement on the other side of the street. It's as if 28 Thingholt-stræti is holding its breath.

Then fire surges like molten metal out of all the ground-floor windows.

46

It so happened that I was on the second floor of 14 Sudurgata and saw the fireball on the other side of the lake. I knew it must be somewhere near 'The Turnip' because the tower was silhouetted against the flames. I ran into the Thingholt district but Midstræti and Thingholtstræti had been sealed off. The fire was in the house next to 'The Turnip'. A vast crowd of sightseers was gathering. A chap I didn't recognize shook his fist at me and screamed in his moral superiority, 'You disgusting purveyor of filth! You news-paper people are vermin! It's all your fault!'

I avoided this lunatic and melted into the crowd. To this day I haven't a clue what the bloody man was on about! A stiff breeze had got up some time in the early hours and the firefighters were having problems protecting the neighbouring houses. A cameraman from Channel 2 put himself in terrible danger by creeping up an alleyway when he had been expressly forbidden to do so by the police.

I dashed up Grundastígur. The sky was glowing with the fire. I ran down Spítalastígur hoping to get through that way, but there was a crowd of sightseers at the bottom of the hill and it was hopeless. All that week they kept showing the fire on television and trying to work out the reason for it.

A few days later the Prime Minister was glowering at his television set. They were still going on about that bloody fire. The newspapers were all blaming the priest. Theódóra Thóroddsdóttir had arrived on the dot to give the television reporters an interview. She looked stunning, smartly dressed and with her red hair shining. The reporter had adopted an attitude of respectful sympathy which infuriated the Prime Minister. 'How have the police been treating you since the attack on 14 Sudurgata?'

'When the Special Forces took the lad I was up in the loft with him and the other boys. We offered no resistance whatsoever. They'd put a ladder through the hatch and I asked the men to stand back while I came down but they wouldn't.'

'Yes, and you tried to kick their faces,' muttered the Prime Minister.

Theódóra continued: 'As soon as we came down the ladder one of them grabbed the boy's arm very roughly. The boy was very distressed and when I asked the officer to be more careful he ignored me. The boy started crying and I wanted to comfort him, but the man grabbed hold of me and ordered me to stand back. As we were walking to the car I had hold of the boy's other hand. The men made us run so fast I was almost thrown to the ground time and again. They pushed me into the car. I wasn't resisting in any way.

'They drove us to Reykjavík City Hall. A police guard was put on the boy and myself. The police were deeply upset by having to do this. Then Dr Thorsteinn Gunnarsson turned up and asked me whether I wanted to accompany the boy to the police station on

Hverfisgata. I said I wanted to go with him to see what was happening. Then we were driven over there and the boy and I were given rooms and treated reasonably well.

'The next day the appalling behaviour on the part of the police began in earnest. I was deeply concerned about my daughter who had been injured in the affray outside the house, but when I went to the office to use the phone, I was not allowed to do so. In the end I was permitted to speak to the Acting Chief Constable and I asked him whether or not I was being detained. He told me I was not. I then demanded to be allowed to go wherever I wanted, but this was not granted. I was, however, given permission to phone my daughter. There were other people I needed to speak to on the telephone. Every time there was a change of shift I encountered the same problems with regard to access to the telephone. No one told me how Father Bernhardur was and when I asked the Acting Chief Constable he felt it was not appropriate to give me this information. I further pointed out to him that in accordance with Article 49 of the Constitution, as a member of parliament I had immunity unless I had committed a criminal offence or stolen public funds. This was ignored and I have to ask, "Was it a crime to try to protect an orphaned child?"'

'What about the boy? How is he?'

'The boy was examined by a doctor but neither he nor I was informed as to what was to happen to him. In the end, at noon on Tuesday, I was obliged to write to the Prime Minister requesting a meeting to get any information at all. The Acting Chief Constable told me I was being granted a interview with the Prime Minister and I was driven to his office. I asked for a delay in the travel arrangements for the boy as he was deeply distressed and had been hoping to be able to stay in the country until the spring, but I was told it was a matter for the doctors. The Prime Minister insisted he had no authority in the matter. When it became apparent that the demands of the humanitarian organizations and their lawyers were being completely disregarded, I demanded to be allowed to arrange an appropriate host country for the boy myself. The boy has consistently refused to leave and fears for his personal safety. He is desperate to speak to Father Bernhardur. In my opinion he would be the best person to comfort and counsel the boy. I consider the haste with which it is planned to deport the boy grossly irresponsible. He needs time to adjust and I fear the effect the trauma will have on him. Besides, in the short time available, I cannot prepare him for the journey or make any arrangements concerning his future myself.'

'When did you return to the young people's home and what did you find?'

'I visited yesterday at about six. The building's in complete chaos. Previously everything had been taken good care of and now many things are broken and smashed to bits in all the living areas. Documents have been taken or are lost and some papers have been scattered on the floors.'

'How is your daughter?'

'So-so.'

'Theódóra, what will happen to the Serb boy?' asked the reporter eagerly.

'He'll go back to London. What happens to him then I don't yet know.'

'You sentimental creep,' the Prime Minister addressed the face of the reporter on the screen.

'It is obvious,' pursued the reporter, 'that recently there has been a great deal of tension between yourself and the Prime Minister. It is interesting that you chose to meet with him even though it is not clear that he has any authority in this matter.' The reporter's manner softened. 'The priest has repeatedly claimed in the media that this whole business is essentially a political attack on you personally. Some commentators have even hinted that the man is not entirely sane. Is it your view, Theódóra, that the Prime Minister was directly involved in all this? Is there anything to substantiate that claim? Is it your view that the boy's nationality affected the outcome? Many people think that the way the authorities reacted, given that we are dealing here with a minor, a child really, was disproportionately harsh. Does all that the boy has had to endure while in this country reflect badly on us as a nation?'

'Yes, of course the Prime Minister was behind it all,' said Theódóra. 'He set out to destroy my reputation at the moment when I was about to form a new political party!'

The reporter became solemn and rather portentous. 'These are grave accusations with serious implications. Are you in a position to substantiate them here and now?'

'I will present the evidence at a later date and in another forum. This is neither the time nor the place.' She lifted her hand to forestall his next question. 'But I will deal with one aspect you raise. I don't think the fact that the boy is a Serb had anything to do with it. Icelanders are a hospitable people, deeply egalitarian in their attitude to other nationalities. I am not aware of any racism in this country. I trust our people.' Theódóra turned to the nation and smiled. She looked a little tired and strained, or at least that's what this particular commentator thought.

'Damned bitch!' muttered the Prime Minister. 'She's still fighting her corner.'

The reporter went on, 'Here on *Newsdesk*, we were curious about what the average Icelander has made of recent events and so we decided to find out.'

There followed a series of vox-pop interviews and they all said the same thing. People thought a mountain was being made out of a molehill, that it was all a bit weird to say the least, and weren't quite a lot of people in Iceland HIV positive anyway? Why hadn't the boy been looked after in an isolation ward? People were guarded on the possible involvement of the Prime Minister. After all, what was in it for him?

One man said it was a funny time to be setting up a new political party. Wasn't there something in the papers about the women in her own party not supporting her? No, it's all made up to get at the Prime Minister. Hasn't there even been a rumour about him killing somebody? Everyone had to see how ludicrous the whole thing was! And why is the Catholic Church huffing and puffing about it all? Hadn't it been burning witches for hundreds of years? Is it trying to pretend it's more godly than the other denominations?

Hadn't that woman had her chance at the end of May? someone asked. Didn't she cave in during the negotiations? Most people were of the opinion that the law of the land should be obeyed. The final question was: 'Would you trust Theódóra Thóroddsdóttir as your next prime minister?'

Every single person, except for one girl who was below voting age, answered in the negative. 'A prime minister must obey the law,' said a middle-aged man. 'He mustn't let his emotions run away with him, or get involved with religious maniacs or get caught up in a riot with a drunken rabble.' Even so he thought the doctors, or someone else, must have made a mistake and there was a question of justice to be answered. 'Yes, of course the Prime Minister was behind it and she'd get my vote,' said an old man who, the Prime Minister seemed to remember, had once been very active in left-wing politics. 'On the other hand, it seems to me that the poor woman's a bit too caught up in financial jiggery-pokery.'

The reporter had an item of late-breaking news. The Workers' Union was considering dropping its demand for taxation on investment income in exchange for a one-off payment of 10,000 kroner to those on a low income – something suggested by the Prime Minister. A member of parliament representing the Women's Party was asked her opinion of this turn of events. She was short and stocky, not unlike Ester. 'Well, he's given the Radical Left a poisoned Christmas present and driven them into a corner.'

This comment had been put to the Prime Minister earlier in the day. He watched his own snow-white hair blowing in the wind. He was wearing a thoughtful expression, as if human nature was a great mystery to him. 'It is strange that the Women's Party can't bear the thought of the ordinary people of this country having a boost to their bank accounts at the beginning of February just when the credit-card bills arrive in a snowstorm. Well, that's a matter for them. But it does seem to indicate that Christmas spirit isn't exactly overflowing in the honourable member's heart at this holiday season.'

A closed door appeared on the screen. A frowning man opened it briefly and shook his head. The voiceover intoned: 'When the views of the Radical Left were sought on this development, the party leadership was holding a meeting and journalists were not allowed access.'

The Prime Minister reached for the remote control and switched off the television. He smiled to himself and put a finger to his temple to massage away the headache that was beginning to go of its own accord. Theódóra was finished in politics. There had been a time when he had worried about his own position and had almost given up hope that the witch could be tricked into going back to the young people's home. The intervention of the doctor, irritating creep that he was, had been like a gift from the gods.

He went up to the second floor and took a shower. The phone rang. When it wasn't answered he remembered his wife had gone out jogging. He cursed and walked naked out on to the landing, dripping on the floor. 'Hannes, you bloody old fox. They broke the mould when they made you, all right. A chap could almost consider joining your party. We'll drop the demand to tax investment income,' said the voice as soon as he put the receiver to his ear.

PART III

47

Between Christmas and the New Year sales of *Weekend* went through the roof because of all that was going on. A new magazine, *Soul of the Nation*, hit the streets in the New Year and sold in vast quantities but then went belly up in the spring. The arguments about what had really happened went on and on. What role had the Prime Minister played in events? Or Theódóra? Had she really intended to split the Party or was it all just a ruse? Did the boy have Aids or not? What was the Church up to? All investigation ran into a dead end. There were many fanciful theories that I won't repeat here. I did not go public on what I knew because I was still researching the facts. I wrote two articles for the new magazine and never saw a kroner for them as the publishing company changed its name to avoid liability for its debts.

But let us go back to New Year's Eve. I did not find out about this until later in the spring. It was all the fault of a small invitation card. There were only two copies of it printed. One of them is lost and the other came into my hands and is lying by my computer as I write this.

It was the day before New Year's Eve when Dr Hördur Gottskálksson received the invitation from Reykjavík City Council. Vilhelmína couldn't understand it. But then, when she thought about it, it didn't seem so strange after all. It was their turn! She thought about phoning her sister, lifted the receiver but then replaced it. Theódóra was always being invited to receptions and it would amuse her if her sister dashed to the phone the moment she got an invitation herself.

Vilhelmína realized immediately that it was hardly likely the gilt-edged envelope would be for them. For whom could the exquisitely embossed insignia of the City of Reykjavík in the bottom right-hand corner – the twin pillars of a Viking throne placed vertically across the waves of the sea — be intended? But then it *was* addressed to 'Dr and Mrs Hördur Gottskálksson, 56 Vatnsholt, Reykjavík'.

She ran her fingernail down the flap, ripping the envelope open. Although she could read the words and understand them she couldn't bring herself to believe what they meant. It was only on a third reading that it sank in and Vilhelmína felt a wave of joy wash over her and her heart pound with anticipation. It was an invitation from the Mayor. 'The City of Reykjavík and The Embassy of the United States request the pleasure of your company *honoris causa* at City Hall on Saturday, 31 December, at 4 p.m. Dress: formal.'

She leapt upstairs like a young girl and opened the other letters – the electricity bill and an abnormally high telephone bill. She decided from the goodness of her heart to spare Trausti a roasting. He had recently taken to using the phone late at night talking to someone he called 'darling'. It delighted his mother that he was now beginning at long last to take an interest in girls. She read the invitation yet again. It only confirmed what she already knew.

She managed to resist phoning Hördur immediately and relished the moment for herself alone. Then she rang him. He answered straightaway. She asked how he was and if he was in the middle of something and before he had a chance to reply she had called him 'darling', an endearment she hadn't used for years. She sensed his surprise in the silence between them.

'Darling,' she said, 'I've got something to tell you.'

'They've dropped the civil action,' he said. He sounded optimistic.

'Who has?'

'That tart from Thingholtstræti.'

'What? No, nothing like that. Is it really bothering you?'

'Of course it is. How are we going to make ends meet if I'm struck off? The way things look at the moment, it could go either way. We're still waiting for a ruling from the High Court and yet the case could be dropped any day. And you still seem unwilling to insist on your sister handing over what's ours by rights.' There was an edge in his voice. 'I've got patients waiting. What did you ring me for?'

'We've been invited to City Hall by the Embassy of the United States.'

452

'That's odd,' he muttered.

'What's odd about it?'

'What business can the City of Reykjavík and the Embassy of the United States have with me?'

'With us. We're both invited, don't forget.'

'Perhaps they're inviting people who studied in the States.'

'It doesn't sound very likely. That would mean thousands. Do you think it's because the Mayor asked you to take on the night locum work when all the other doctors went on strike?'

He thought for a moment. 'Hardly. It's ridiculous. They wouldn't involve the American Embassy in something like that.'

'Well, I don't know then.' She was feeling uncomfortable and all her joy had evaporated. 'Perhaps it's a mistake. Do you want me to ring them up?'

'Ring who up?' he said sourly.

'The American Embassy or City Hall. Either one should know if it's all right. At least we'd find out why we'd been invited.'

'That's not how things are done, Vilhelmína. You only lay yourself open to ridicule. A guest ringing up because he doesn't think he's important enough to be invited. It's laughable.'

Suddenly she knew the answer. 'Listen. I know why we've been invited.'

'Why?'

'It's because you were the first Icelander to take part in a heart-transplant operation. Your colleagues may have found it easy enough to forget, but the American Embassy's quite another matter. It needs to maintain good relations with Iceland.'

He wasn't entirely convinced. But he didn't say anything and she took the silence as indicating he thought her explanation was worth considering.

'Anything else?' he asked, sounding relaxed and happy.

It was so long since she'd heard that tone in his voice she was sorry not to be bringing him more good news. She was convinced he was in line for recognition because of the anniversary. It was twenty-five years since that remarkable transplant operation had taken place. Hadn't Hördur been sent a questionnaire by some international directory five years ago for the selfsame reason? The book now stood on its shelf, a book as thick as your hand:

Practising Physicians. It had cost fifty dollars plus postage and packing. The edges of the pages around G for Gottskálksson were slightly discoloured where the entry was repeatedly consulted. 'Born Kirkubearklastur, Iceland, 1941.' Couldn't the bastards even get the spelling right? He often used it as an example of how bad foreigners were at spelling Icelandic place names. Then whoever he was demonstrating the point to would feel obliged to read the whole entry.

They had been talking so long that Vilhelmína suddenly realized there couldn't be many patients waiting to see her husband at his surgery. She asked, 'Much to do?'

'Look how you've held me up, woman! The waiting room's full of people. I only hope they haven't gone. See you tonight.'

He asked her to read the invitation to him just one more time before they said goodbye. '"Dress: formal", eh? Are they worried we'll show up with our arses hanging out?'

As Hördur walked down the surgery steps at five o'clock that evening, the air was still pleasantly warm. He paused a moment and looked across to the Parliament building. Father Bernhardur was in prison but the old girl had escaped a custodial sentence because she had parliamentary immunity.

The doctor breathed deeply. Two women had brought a sick girl to the surgery after Vilhelmína had rung. He had been in such a good mood he had reached under the couch and brought out the toybox to give some toys to the child to play with. It must have been years since he'd got it out and it was covered in dust and hair. The child didn't like any of the toys and called them 'horrid'. But nothing could cloud the doctor's happiness. He walked down Austurstræti with a light step towards the garage on Kalkovnsvegur. There was just one thing irritating him. They had not been given enough notice of the reception. It was actually rather insulting to be given only twenty-four hours' notice. It was common practice for things like that to be sent out a week beforehand. He tried to stop himself feeling too aggrieved. Americans were famous for their generosity and decency, they gave people their due and acknowledged their true value and were relaxed and easy-going in their dealings with other nationalities. Icelandic prickliness was incomprehensible to them.

Dusk fell swiftly. Hördur suddenly felt that life is finely ordered, that everything falls out in the end as it is meant to. Then he was seized with melancholy. 'I must be really dissatisfied with my life if such a small thing can make me happy,' he thought and he resolved to get his wife to ring up first thing in the morning and decline the invitation. But as he passed Government House he smiled a thin smile because he knew who had engineered the invitation. And why.

A delicious smell met him as he opened the door at Vatnsholt. The flat was golden in the candlelight. Next to the candle-holder stood a bottle of red wine and the label seemed whiter than ever in the light from the candles and the wine an even richer red. The table was laid for two. Hördur asked whether the children were planning to eat with them but Vilhelmína said she had rung Ester and Ester had said she was going out with a friend but Vilhelmína didn't know where. She had slipped Trausti some cash for pizza and a film, so they would be left to themselves until about ten. Hördur asked what they were eating and his brow creased with delight when she showed him the recipe for an American dish, the turkey legs cooking in the oven. She had gone out straight after lunch and been lucky to find turkey legs, which were something of a rarity. She suggested that Hördur dress for dinner. He had a bath and put on the dark blue suit he wore for special occasions. She was wearing a dress that revealed her back. She thought it was a bit common herself, but she knew he thought it made her look good.

There were no plates on the table. She was warming them in the oven in the American way before laying them on the table. He sat and waited, looking at his own reflection and twisting the elegant silver ring round the damask napkin. Neither mentioned the invitation, although Hördur was certainly keen to see it. The cooking had been remarkably successful. They finished the bottle of red wine between them and talked in the way they used to long ago. Vilhelmína could almost believe that they were happy. Hördur put his rather formal self to one side and told her an anecdote he'd recently heard. An American married an Icelandic woman and moved to a village deep in the country. He threw everything out of kilter with his free and easy ways and his 'hail fellow well met' attitude. The Icelandic villagers, all silence and sullenness, hadn't a clue what was going on. Hördur chuckled at this point. Then they threw a Viking feast. The poor American bloke was invited. Everyone was having a high old time, yelping at him like dogs and wanting to stuff the poor bastard and even his pockets as well with sheep's head and potato stew and sharkmeat and drown him in brennivín to show how welcome he was in their village. Well, the Yank assumed he'd really cracked it with the villagers and when he ran into one of the most friendly of the fellows at the bank a few days later he greeted him warmly, only to find the chap make a face like he'd swallowed a litre of starch. Isn't that just typical of us Icelanders?

They laughed at the ways of Icelanders. Vilhelmína opened another bottle.

'Hey, we're getting plastered.'

'So what?' said the doctor.

And they went to bed before dessert.

On New Year's Eve a strong wind blew up as dusk fell. Vilhelmína had had Hördur's evening suit cleaned. When he put it on she couldn't help but say he should never be seen wearing anything else. He complimented her too. And with good reason. She was a considerable beauty. He could still see traces of the twenty-year-old beauty queen he had fallen in love with. Trausti was at home and his mother wanted him to drive them in the Chrysler but Hördur would have none of it.

'We'll take a cab, woman. I won't hear of it.'

'Why spend money on a cab?' she said, astounded. 'I wouldn't dream of it.'

This got on Hördur's nerves. In his mind's eye he saw his father-in-law, standing stiffly in front of the mirror in evening dress, grimacing as he tried to fix his tie.

'And how did your father travel to the Doctors' Ball?' he asked, glancing at the photo of old Thóroddur hanging on the wall. 'He always took a taxi!'

But it was not a matter for discussion. Vilhelmína's mouth was set. He knew that look. It was sheer stubbornness. One thing could lead to another and before he knew it they would be discussing the

456

ten days he moved out to live with his secretary. Normally he would not back down and would dig his heels in but this evening he decided to give himself a break. He had no doubt any more that a US government decoration was awaiting him. That would show them, when his photograph appeared in the press with him holding up his citation. It would knock spots off the usual photograph of a doctor standing beside some piece of equipment some benefactor had obliged the hospital to accept. Sauerbruch and his low-pressure chamber indeed! It's about time that lot saw what I'm worth!

'Well now, Trausti,' Hördur said. 'How about running your mother and me into town?'

'What's all this then?' the boy said. 'It must be some party you're going to!' He couldn't escape being affected by the relaxed atmosphere now infecting his home. He looked admiringly at his father. He could never understand how such a handsome man could find so much in life to make himself miserable. Gauti, the little boy he was looking after, was pulling at his grandfather's trouser leg. 'Grandad, Grandad, goody!' (This translated as 'Grandfather, I'd like some sweets.')

It was taking Vilhelmína for ever to get ready. She kept changing her dress. Then she decided her hair-do had completely fallen out, although both Trausti and Hördur reassured her that her hair looked as good as it had ever done. She tried on blouses and skirts and gowns. They seemed to arrive at a decision together and then the whole thing started all over again. It was getting late. Hördur was getting restive and his son could feel it. But as luck would have it Ester arrived and sorted everything out. In less than ten minutes she had talked some sense into her mother.

'How long will you be gone?' she asked.

'Not more than an hour,' said Hördur.

'That's a bit of an underestimate!' said Vilhelmína.

'Well, two at the most.'

'I can hardly wait for you to come back and we'll eat together. I'm so excited about it all.' Ester was standing there with the invitation in her hand, reading it out for the whole family to hear. 'It says "*honoris causa*". This is really exciting. What do you think it means, Father? "*Honoris causa*"?'

'Let me see,' her father said and stretched out his hand to take the card. But in actual fact he had already taken a peek at the card as it lay beneath the crystal bowl on the sideboard the night before while Vilhelmína was asleep and he had got up to go to the toilet.

The white Chrysler was waiting for them in the dusk. Trausti wanted his father to sit in the back seat but he wouldn't hear of it. In Lækjargata Trausti made a U-turn. His father wanted to get out of the car and walk the last few yards. 'I need some fresh air in my lungs before facing the festivities,' he said, laughing.

Earlier in the day he had rung City Hall and asked which door was used as the entrance to official functions.

'Do you have some reason for wanting to know?' he was asked.

Hördur had lied. 'I'm a journalist.'

As they said goodbye to their son, the wind from the south was blowing up. They walked along Vonarstræti along the sheltered side. Guests were not expected to approach City Hall from the bridge over the lake on the east side; all the windows on that side of the building were dark. They had to walk slowly because the dress Ester had chosen for her mother was full length and Vilhelmína had to hold the hem up. No one had warned her how uneven the pavement was around here. She commented that it didn't reflect well on the city to have the pavement in such a poor condition near its civic buildings. Hördur was convinced they were meant to arrive at the Tjarnargata entrance. You couldn't expect them to take care of all the pavements in the area.

'How do you know that?'

'Know what?'

'Which entrance we're meant to use.'

'I just know,' he said. Vilhelmína didn't pursue the matter. In Tjarnargata they were met by locked doors. Hördur cupped his hands round his face and peered inside. The corridor was dark. There was not a living soul anywhere. 'What's going on?' asked Vilhelmína. She looked up at the façade of the building.

'Don't ask me,' he said. He raised one arm and tapped lightly on the glass with his index finger. It was all he could think of doing.

'There's a light on the third floor,' said his wife.

'Yes?' Hördur bent backwards and squinted at the light far above him.

'Perhaps we should try the entrance on Vonarstræti?'

'Do you really mean that?' Hördur was irritated by her stupidity. 'It's the same bloody corridor.' Still, they gave it a try. Again he cupped his hands against the window and put his face close to see inside. It was more a gesture to please her than anything else. The corridor was just as drab and dreary from this side of the building.

'Have you got the invitation with you?'

She opened the little black bag with its gold clasp and handed him the card. He read it and checked the date on his wristwatch. There was no mistake. They were in the right place at the right time. 'Could they have printed the date wrong?' he asked.

'Surely not,' said Vilhelmína. 'The City of Reykjavík never makes mistakes like that.'

'Well, we must be expected to enter from the east side,' said Hördur. Mentally he relived the conversation with the Council employee. Suddenly he couldn't trust his own memory. Wasn't there a distinct possibility the man had said it was the east door they used for official functions? Before they turned into Vonarstræti Hördur scanned the side of the building but couldn't see the faintest glimmer of light. The lit window on the west side probably belonged to the nightwatchman.

They walked on to the bridge. The wind was stronger now. There were a few lights actually in the water and the broken surface of the lake made it look like an underwater smithy with flashes of hot metal. They crossed the bridge and the wind caught Vilhelmína's dress. Hördur was getting anxious. Vilhelmína put both hands up to her hair and cursed the weather. This time the doctor did not try to see through the glass door for the simple reason that all three doors opened on to the same corridor.

'Perhaps we should go round to the west door and ring the bell,' said Vilhelmína. 'There was a light in that window.'

'There's no point.' Suddenly he realized what had happened. 'They must have got the venue for the reception wrong. If this is to be given by the United States, surely they'll be holding it at the American Embassy.'

They were both enormously relieved and left the bridge. The dress whipped against the iron railings. Vilhelmína looked round and was pleased there was no one about to see. They must look ridiculous, all dolled up on the bridge with City Hall dark and deserted. A firework ascended slowly into the sky from the Thingholt district and burst into a desultory shower of sparks. Vilhelmína was glad they had reached the shelter offered by the Idno theatre. The American Embassy was situated in Laufásvegur. They did not have far to go. As they crossed the corner at Laufásvegur she saw there were some parking spaces left empty. The building had the same sleepy aura as City Hall. Hördur seemed to hesitate, unsure whether to knock or not. She glanced at his face and saw he had lost his anxious look. Now he looked scared. She did not follow him up to the door of the Embassy. He tapped lightly on the door with his index finger. A young man – obviously an American – came to the door looking friendly and solicitous. Hördur spoke to him in English. He said he had heard there was to be a party there tonight but the official was completely mystified. Hördur moved closer to him. 'Oh well,' Vilhelmína heard her husband say and then at the same time become both more deferential and pull himself up to his full height to try to maintain his dignity. 'Oh well, there must be some mistake.' She saw him bow a little too deeply, as if to give the man to understand that he had had nothing to hide when he had seemed to be giving himself airs. He turned away from the door and the expression on his face was so terrible she felt afraid.

'What I thought is probably right,' she said. 'It'll be the wrong date.'

'Things like that just don't happen.' Hördur Gottskálksson looked up and down Laufásvegur. His face had turned grey and he was muttering to himself. Vilhelmína could understand what he was saying but she was so shocked she asked him to repeat it.

'You heard what I said.'

'A practical joke? No, it can't be!' she exclaimed idiotically and looked into his face with an expression of abject misery. 'Let me go and talk to the man.' And she started to walk towards the Embassy door.

'Let's not make bigger fools of ourselves than we already have,' he hissed and grabbed her arm.

'At least let me ask where the Ambassador is tonight.'

He did not reply but kept a firm grip on her arm as he looked up and down the street. A small car drove by. Hördur looked through the windscreen but didn't recognize the man behind the wheel. The driver did not look at them.

'I want to go home, Hoddi,' said Vilhelmína, using his pet name. She winced as if he was hurting her and he let go of her arm.

'We can't go home now,' he said as he released her. 'It's only five o'clock. What would we say to the children? And don't call me "Hoddi". I wouldn't insult an old dog by giving it a name like that.' He grabbed her arm again and they walked along Shálholtsstígur to the corner of Fríkirkjuvegur. As City Hall came into view they looked up hopefully but there was no change to be seen.

'Go and find a cab,' she said.

'I'm not going home yet,' said Hördur. 'The children will know at once what's happened. Let's go to the surgery for a while.'

'I can't bear it there. It's so dull and dreary. Perhaps the reception's being held at Government House, or at the official government residence in Tjarnargata?' She let a flicker of hope stir within her.

'Let's go to a bar and have a drink. I can't let the children see we've been had like this. They're so looking forward to us coming home.'

'I can't go to a bar in this dress. I look like a Christmas tree,' said Vilhelmína.

'Then come to the surgery on Skólabrú.'

'I've just said I can't face it.'

'It's still better to wait there than hang around in the street. It is possible we're being watched.'

'Do you really think so?' She felt scared and looked around her.

Mentally Hördur was planning his battle strategy. He would visit all the printers, one after another. Someone would recognize the invitation card. And when he discovered the forger, he would commit murder. 'Whoever has done this', he said out loud as he stood in Lækjargata, 'will regret it. He has taken me into a dark place and a way out of that dark place may not be easy to find.' He realized he was sounding pompous and fell silent. Vilhelmína did not respond.

As luck would have it he had his keys with him, including the key to his surgery. It felt good to enter the shelter of the dark hall at Skólabrú. Vilhelmína snuggled up to him and whimpered, 'Perhaps it's all a mistake?' He patted her shoulder gently and strained to hear any sound from his surgery. He was expecting a phone call. Deep down he was still hoping for a miracle. Someone from City Hall or one of the Embassy staff would ring, or it would be one of the children to say that people were searching desperately for them all over town. There were lots of people waiting for them to arrive at the Saga Hotel. But there was dead silence in the building. He opened the door to the surgery and they went in. Hördur sat at his desk and Vilhelmína sat on the couch. She looked round the dimly lit room. He did not turn on the light but stood at the window peering down into the street. She looked down at her lap and smoothed her skirt. 'Surely this is a mistake? No one could be so cruel. The printers must have got it wrong. There was a confusion about the date.'

He drew the curtains and opened the old white cabinet with the glass door where his father-in-law used to keep his surgical instruments. He took a bottle of liquor from the bottom shelf – he had acquired quite a supply from a dentist friend of his – and poured the strong spirit into two glasses, one an ordinary tumbler he kept on the shelf above the washbasin. He mixed the drink fifty–fifty with water. He had not let the water run cold and it made Vilhelmína feel nauseous. Still, she took a mouthful and fought the urge to bring it back up. Hördur sat in silence at his desk and sipped his drink. Then he turned on the desk lamp, pulled the arm downwards, took the invitation card from his pocket, bent his head over it and studied it with grim determination. He picked at the embossed gold lettering with his thumbnail but it didn't flake off. 'It doesn't look like a forgery,' he said.

'Oh?' said the woman, with a glimmer of hope. She thought he was discovering some officially recognized wisdom with regard to invitation cards that had hitherto eluded her. He turned the card over and inspected the reverse.

'If someone is trying to deceive me, they've gone to a lot of trouble.'

'Ring home,' she said. 'Perhaps someone's been trying to get us.'

He drank the best part of his glass in one gulp, picked up the phone, cleared his throat and rang home. 'Ester, my dear,' he said and smiled, revealing his large teeth. 'It's Dad. Yes. Mother and I are fine. I just wanted to check in case anyone had tried to ring us tonight and asked about me. What? Nobody. Of course everything's all right. The party's in full swing. I'll tell you all about it later. We're quite likely to be a bit late. Yes, my dear. No, there's no need to delay dinner. Yes, I'll tell her.'

Hördur stood up again and fixed himself another drink. His face was flushed and suddenly he was quite drunk. 'Can I offer you something?' he said, waving the bottle carelessly in front of her. He was still full of the false bonhomie he had put on for the phone call.

'No, thanks. I've still got some.'

He sat down and flicked through the phone book for quite some time.

'What are you looking for?'

He said nothing but carried on leafing through it with his head bent low into the pale circle of light cast by the desk lamp. He had to close one eye in order to read. She needed the toilet. When she stood up she realized she was quite drunk. They couldn't have been there more than twenty minutes. She walked unsteadily to the door.

'Don't turn on the light,' whispered the doctor. 'It's of paramount importance that the building is in complete darkness, so no one will know we're here.'

When she returned from the toilet, he was on the phone.

'Yes, I understand. So it's all a mistake. No, I was told the City was planning a reception to honour a few doctors. I take it you know nothing about it?'

He sat stock still with the receiver to his ear and picked at a scab on his temple. She leaned against the door frame and watched him. She looked round the room. The door of her father's old steel cabinet was half open. When she was young she had thought that all the wisdom in the world was needed to use the tools it held. She walked over to the cabinet and looked at the surgical instruments on the top shelf. They looked like ancient artefacts. She turned and looked at the old couch. It had belonged to her father. She could picture Hördur there with his secretary. They must have made love many times, although he denied it whenever she brought it up. Once he had even laughed and said, 'You've been watching too much rubbish on TV, Vilhelmína. That girl didn't want anything to do with me. The only thing she fancied was my car.' Vilhelmína sat down on the couch again. Hördur was inclining his head with great dignity again and again. Finally he said, 'I shall have to take this matter further and get to the bottom of this. Yes, indeed. I beg your pardon? Yes, and a Happy New Year to you!'

Vilhelmína picked up her drink and drained the last drop. 'Who was that on the phone?'

'A City Councillor,' he said proudly.

'"A City Councillor"!' she mimicked. 'And what did he have to say?'

'We were at school together, this chap and me,' the doctor said. The conversation had left him feeling elated.

'And did he remember you?'

'Of course he remembered me, Vilhelmína!'

'And was it a mistake at the printer's?'

'A mistake . . .?'

'On the invitation.'

'He didn't know anything about the invitation. I didn't bring it up. I'm not that stupid. I said I'd heard the City was giving a ball for doctors. I didn't mention the American Embassy, nor . . . nor . . .' He tried to lift up the card with one finger. It was difficult. 'Nor "honoris causa".'

'Give me another drink.'

He stood up drunkenly and held out a hand for her glass. She was amazed by the simple joy he took in some City Councillor remembering him from their schooldays. 'He's a fool,' she thought and realized how desperately tired she felt and how much she suddenly wanted to lie down on the couch. She laid her hand on the leather upholstery and looked at the foot of the couch. It was up against the big white filing cabinet Hördur had bought at the American Navy Surplus Store. There were dark marks on the cabinet that looked as if they had been made by someone's feet.

'Why's the cabinet so grubby by the foot of the couch?'

'It's probably my feet when I have a snooze during the day,' said Hördur and winked. 'What are you getting at, Villa? That cabinet wasn't even here ten years ago.'

'What do you mean?' she said, her voice loud and coarse. She held out her hand for her glass. '"That cabinet wasn't even here ten years ago." What are you trying to say? What are you talking about?'

Hördur sat down on his chair. The anxiety had gone. The alcohol had worked its magic. He wasn't a heavy drinker but when he did drink he could consume vast quantites and the effect was reinforcing rather than debilitating. He was fine now. The humiliations of the evening had receded far into the distance for the moment. On the other hand, Vilhelmína had no head for drink and was now considerably the worse for wear. When she had finished the glass he was now handing to her, she would become confused and start talking nonsense.

'Who do you think did this?' he asked.

'Did what?'

'The invitation.'

'Puh!' she said, waving her hand airily and shaking her head. 'I haven't the foggiest idea. It's nothing to do with me.' And she made the 'puh!' sound again.

'I'm positive it's Theódóra. She wants to get even.'

'Tedda?' Vilhelmína pulled a face to indicate her contempt for his foolishness. 'How can you think that? Get even for what? I can't bear it when you go on about my sister like this.' She took a drink from her glass and laughed. 'How could we be such idiots to believe it? How could we be so stupid?'

'Believe what?' Ice cold, Hördur suddenly felt a desire to commit murder.

'That we were invited. That you were invited. That I was invited. Some joke, huh?'

'What's so funny about that?'

'You know what they used to call you? "Doctor Scab".' She raised her glass to her lips. 'You're so stupid,' she said, and drained her glass.

He looked at her and felt as if he was facing some evil witch he had never seen before. He was too angry to speak. When finally he managed to say something, it was 'Shut your mouth, you filthy bitch!'

Vilhelmína taunted him. '"The first heart-transplant operation in the United States"! Gee, how swell!' She was trying to mimic her husband's voice: '"Won't they give me an honour of some kind?"'

465

She glared at Hördur scornfully. 'You idiot! Can't you get someone to give you a certificate that says what an idiot you are?'

The desk lamp on the table was the old-fashioned kind. It had a moveable arm and a thin metal shade. The shade was yellow with a dark rim and looked rather like a clam shell. The flex ran down the side of the desk and across the floor. Hördur always took great care not to trip over the flex as he moved round to his chair behind the desk. His father-in-law had used the lamp when he was doing minor operations in the surgery, mainly on the face, when the patient would be seated at the desk. Hördur seized the lamp and held it up high, threatening her.

'What are you doing?'

'I'm going to throw this lamp in your face,' he said, his hatred boiling over.

'Please, Hoddi, stop this ridiculous business at once and put the lamp down,' she said and sighed.

'Don't call me that!' He hurled the lamp across the room. The flex was not long enough, the plug was ripped out of its socket and the woman screamed in the darkness. His anger evaporated as if by magic and he sat motionless in his chair, full of self-justification. She had it coming. 'Am I a fool for thinking I might be entitled to a little recognition for a job well done?' he said. His voice was steady in the darkness.

Vilhelmína was rocking to and fro whimpering. 'What have you done? Oh, my God, what have you done? You've really hurt me. What have you done? Put the light on. Put the light on this minute!'

He tried to read her tone and recognized it immediately. She was stoking up the tragedy in order to get the upper hand.

'Put the light on,' she said, her voice dark with drama. 'What have you done?' She began to cry.

'Put it on yourself,' he hissed angrily. 'You called me an idiot. Whatever I've done, you certainly deserved it.' His voice was no less dramatic.

She did not respond as he had expected but carried on whimpering. In the end he got fed up and turned on the light, if only to drag the woman to the mirror, demonstrate to her she wasn't hurt at all and get her to stop all this play-acting.

She was sitting on the couch, rocking backwards and forwards.

Her top lip was a mess, her chin was covered in blood and her mouth was full of dark, thick blood.

Hördur was so shocked he almost sobered up. 'What have I done? Darling, I didn't mean it.'

She moved her tongue and push the blood out of her mouth. The action irritated him. Just like her to make the most of it. Blood was trickling down her neck. He turned on the cold-water tap. He was too agitated to find a flannel and dampened the towel from the radiator instead. He wiped the blood from her chin and dabbed gently at her top lip. There was an ugly cut but the blood was beginning to congeal. There was no getting round it. She needed two or three stitches. There were bloodstains on the front of her dress and in her lap.

'I'll have to stitch you up,' he said drunkenly.

She lifted her bloodied face slowly to him.

'I'm leaving you. You won't get a penny. I was going to tell you at dinner: we're rich. Theódóra wants to give us our share of the company, of Heidnaberg. Villi is going to be managing director. She wants to move out, so we're getting the house on Dyngjuvegur. You're a man of means, Hördur! You're stinking rich! Ester's decided to marry Vilhjálmur now she won't be dependent on him financially.'

'So her bad conscience got to Theódóra in the end, did it?' he said.

She put her hand to her mouth and the blood trickled between her fingers.

'You shouldn't have made me so angry,' he said solemnly. He handed her the towel. 'Hold this to your lip, my dear.' She let the pink saliva run into the towel. He took it away from her, folded it and held it to her lip. 'Hold it like this,' he said, sounding professional. 'You need to press quite firmly.'

She pressed the towel to her face and waited. He decided to give her a local anaesthetic before suturing the wound. He found a syringe and took a while to lay hands on a needle on the glass shelf in the cabinet. He found the cartridge and held the syringe and the drug up to the light while he drew off a few millilitres. 'That should do it,' he said. 'You won't feel a thing, Vilhelmína. Moving to Dyngjuvegur, eh! Well, that's quite a bombshell. The beginning of a new life. My dear, I'm so sorry this happened.' He was going to say, 'Forgive me', but managed to stop himself. He knew from bitter experience that if he used that particular word, she'd immediately have the whip hand.

He stepped towards her, brandishing the needle. He took the towel away from her face and gave her a number of injections around the wound to numb the whole area. Vilhelmína sat there with her eyes half closed. She was feeling dazed and hardly noticed the injections. He pushed a bit too hard.

It would take the anaesthetic a moment to take effect. He made her hold a white dressing over the cut and prepared to suture. He found a needle and suture and threaded it with surprisingly steady hands. He moved a chair up to the desk for her to sit on, glanced at his watch, drummed impatiently on the top of the desk with his fingers, finished his drink, took the bloodstained towel, soaked it and wrung it out on the washbasin. While he was busy doing this she was rocking backwards and forwards. He took the dressing away from her face and plucked gently at her lip on each side of the cut. Did she feel anything? No, she was completely numb. He asked her to move over to the chair. But he had forgotten that he had ripped the lamp out of its socket. It was lying at the foot of the couch. The bulb was broken and there was a fine dusting of glass on the worn leather. There were two lights in the ceiling, both equally faint. Hördur did not feel up to suturing in such poor light. He asked her to tip her head back as far as possible, but it did not make a lot of difference.

Out in the stairwell there was a window facing east. There was a light in the ceiling. Hördur went upstairs and tried the door to Ester's flat but it was locked. The bulb was the only light in the building bright enough for him to suture by. He turned it on and took a chair from the surgery up on to the landing. Then he went back for his wife. 'Come on,' he said. 'I need to be in a place where I can see what I'm doing.'

'Where are you taking me?'

'Up to the landing. That's the only light bright enough.'

He guided her into the hall, upstairs to the landing and helped her sit down. Then he began to work. He pressed the needle against the flesh, which yielded to it, and it didn't take him long to complete the three sutures. He admired his handiwork, quite proud of himself. 'An excellent job.'

In an instant the wooziness left the woman. She was fully alert. 'What did you say!' she exclaimed. '"An excellent job"!'

'Yes,' he said and then added, 'There'll be hardly any scar to speak of.'

He never did understand why she laughed. She had to tense her lip and hold it away from her teeth and guard the wound with her index and middle fingers to stop the sutures tearing. It hurt to laugh even with the anaesthetic.

'You'll ruin the suturing if you don't stop this nonsense,' he said in desperation.

'But it's so funny,' Vilhelmína said through her nose. 'Perhaps I should award you a certificate to commemorate your excellent suturing. You could have it framed and hang it up in the surgery.'

He saw her rolling down the stairs and her head hit the bottom step. He watched this happen with mild surprise, as if it was something taking place a long way away, even though it was he who had hit her. He stood on the landing under the bright light thinking that when all was said and done the whole thing was simply a terrible misunderstanding.

48

Just wait till he found out who was responsible for this! His anger was so extreme he could not follow the thought through to its logical conclusion.

He snatched the invitation card from the desk, stuffed it in his pocket and ran out of the door. The card was stiff and the edges were as sharp as a knife. Outside, to his great surprise, the ground was completely white and this seemed to soothe him. It was eight o'clock. He did not know where to go. All the bars were closed at this time on New Year's Eve. He was optimistic about the Harbour Bar on Hafnarstræti but even that was closed. Then he ran into a group of men on the same quest. They pooled their funds and

bought a bottle from a taxi driver and ended up drinking in a basement room on Hallveigarstígur. The contents of the bottle evaporated like dew in the sun and another was purchased at Hördur's
expense. Before you knew it, there was only a dribble left in that
one. It became clear to the doctor that the winos were taking more
than their fair share when he wasn't looking.

He went outside and set off for Vatnsholt. He walked for a long
time. In the end he flagged down a cab and asked the driver to take
him to the nearest New Year's Eve bonfire. A shopping centre was
sponsoring an enormous bonfire out on Ellidavogur and the driver
took him there. On the spit of land reaching out into the river
estuary there was a large group of people lighting fireworks. There
was a dark pyre on the grass the size of a house. At ten o'clock they
set it alight. The fire roared through the pile of timber. On the very
top there was an old fishing boat. Dozens of men and women were
silhouetted against the fire, their shadows stretching far away from
them. The bonfire was one of the largest in town and lit up the
surrounding area as far as Heidnaberg. The spectators stood in
wonder and obeyed the safety rules, holding their children close to
them. Even though there was a stiff breeze, it was very warm on
the grass. Hördur took a swig of the brennivín he had brought with
him from Hallveigarstígur and offered it to the man standing
beside him. The man wiped the mouth of the bottle before taking
an almighty gulp. Hördur felt as if he knew the man but he couldn't
quite place him. He had a large nose and rough cheeks. He was
wearing a beret and holding a small fair-haired boy by the hand.
Suddenly Hördur realized who he was. It was a politician! A
member of parliament! He was almost overwhelmed by an urge to
tell the man the full 'inside story'.

The bonfire collapsed beneath the boat, which, burning, sailed
downwards into the flames.

Hördur was bored watching the bonfire and the politician, who
was fed up with people always wanting to strike up conversations
with him, wasn't exactly talkative. People began to wander off.
Hördur had to walk all the way along Miklubraut. You couldn't
find a taxi for love nor money. Over Reykjavík there was a storm
of fireworks. Suddenly he realized what had really happened. He
stood stock still. He suddenly realized who it was who had played

the practical joke on him: Dagný! It wasn't enough for her to get him struck off. She had to destroy him completely, make him a public laughing stock. He could clearly remember the address, just as if it was written in front of him: 58 Skúlagata. The fucking bitch! The thing to do was to go there and kill her. What could it matter to him what happened? He set off down Kringlumýrarbraut, determined to kill her. *En route* he looked out for shops whose windows he could kick in. What he needed was an axe! A weapon to despatch his nemesis!

There were no shops in this part of town. The streets were now a mass of slush. She had the greatest justification. Why hadn't he seen it before? He remembered telling her about the world-famous heart transplant. That he wasn't treated with proper respect. Even so, he wasn't sure. He'd told so many people about it. Everywhere you looked there were cars and people milling about. Fireworks in the sky, rockets shooting skywards from private gardens. His feet were soaking by the time he got to Skúlagata.

The door was unlocked. On the second floor there was a man with a drink in his hand. He was wearing a dunce's cap. He looked at Hördur and swayed as he did so. Behind him a door stood open to a lively party. People were wishing each other a Happy New Year. 'Where's Dagný's flat?' asked the furious doctor.

'At the very top.'

Hördur fingered the faithful invitation card. Now he had no occupation, no honour. Nothing mattered any more. He rang the bell. A woman he didn't recognize came to the door.

'Yes?' she said to him.

He told her who it was he wanted to see in a harsh voice, which startled the woman.

'Who? No, she doesn't live here any more. She's got fixed up with a flat.'

'Do you know where?'

'No, sorry.'

'Can I use your phone?'

'Yes, be my guest,' she said grudgingly.

There was a party going on in the flat and an old Beatles record playing on the record-player. He rang directory enquiries to find out where Dagný Gísladóttir lived. No one by that name was registered with the phone company. When he put down the receiver the music had stopped and the people in the room were staring at him in silence.

When he left the building calm had settled over the town. He was worried that he might have killed Vilhelmína, so he took a taxi to Skólabrú and asked the driver to wait. She was no longer lying on the hall floor. It was nearly ten o'clock.

All the windows at Vatnsholt were dark. She wasn't there either. Probably she would have run to her sister's. He found a bottle of whisky in a cupboard and gulped down half a glass before collapsing on the sofa, exhausted. Just before sleep overtook him he saw Dagný's face in front of his eyes. He'd find out on New Year's Day where the bloody cow lived.

He hadn't been asleep very long when he was woken with a start. It was still dark. He decided not to answer it but the phone kept on ringing with a merciless implacability. He was about to roll out of bed on his left side as he usually did when he encountered the back of the sofa. He opened his eyes and looked into the dim light afforded by a nearby lamppost. The phone just kept on ringing. Hördur scrambled off the sofa and found his unsteady way over to the phone. He lifted the receiver. He had not yet allowed himself to remember the events of the previous evening.

'Did I wake you?' teased the voice.

'Who is this?' He thought he recognized it.

'My name is Thorsteinn Gunnarsson. Your old friend. We were students together.'

'So?' The events of the previous evening were now returning to Hördur and a chill ran down his spine.

'Don't you remember me?' asked the voice.

'Yes, of course I remember you,' said Hördur roughly. 'What do you want?'

'You sound horribly shaken up, mate,' said the voice.

'It's nothing.'

'One all,' teased the voice.

'What do you want? I was asleep.'

'I hope you don't remember your sins for a long time,' said Thorsteinn, laughing aimiably, then he pulled himself together and

472

said seriously, 'Yes, it's OK if you do remember this, Hoddi. But I'm sorry your wife got involved.'

'Was it you sent the invitation? Damn you.'

'Just paying you back for old crimes.'

'And of course you'll have enjoyed watching me tramping the streets done up to the nines?'

'Nothing I'd've enjoyed more.'

'But why? Don't you think I've suffered enough? A man found guilty of a mercy killing?'

'Excuse me,' said the voice. 'But it gets to me every single time someone puts his hand to his head and grins as he says he needs a haircut. Then I think back to when we were students and you forged that letter and I went running off to the barber. One all!'

'You bastard!' Hördur managed to laugh. 'It would serve you right if I killed you.'

'Happy New Year,' said Thorsteinn and wished him goodnight.

49

OUR TALE CONCLUDES

It was late in the spring when the High Court finally delivered its verdict. Father Bernhardur was sentenced to eight months' imprisonment but his co-defendants, the teenagers who had resisted the police, were given much lighter sentences. I attended the trial, both in the Magistrates' Court and in the High Court. A lot came out that has proved very useful to me in the writing of this chronicle. Much was still appearing in the press and people held a variety of opinions about it all. I kept all the cuttings, but there is little point in quoting from them at length. Many humanitarian organizations thought the assault on the child was beyond the pale, as might well be imagined. The man in the street was generally of the opinion that the boy was carrying the virus and that the priest and the young people had simply overreacted. Others thought that Theódóra couldn't really be held responsible for her actions. She had been hit hard by Axel's death and the way she had behaved demonstrated that she wasn't entirely in her right mind. Some wanted her stripped of her parliamentary immunity but it didn't come to that. When she had lost her position and contacts, she made her peace with me and told me many details about the whole business. You came across people who believed the Prime Minister knew far more than he was letting on, but they were few in number. In my narrative I have stuck to established fact.

Along with the majority of the population, I was surprised when the accused were granted pardons. When Haflidi heard about it he immediately went to see Father Bernhardur.

Father Bernhardur was still allowed to serve as a priest but I gathered Bishop Lambert was determined to send him overseas for a few years. Perhaps even to Rome. The Church had been vilified in the press. The priest had lost a lot of weight and looked a wreck. I heard many people rang him up and he would never recount these conversations but they always left him even more sad than before. Everyone thought that if he hadn't made the mistake of threatening to set fire to Sudurgata then Tryggvi would never have got the idea of committing suicide by burning his house down with himself inside it. *Weekend* had been hinting at this relentlessly for weeks and people were getting fed up with it. There were new scandals to cover: a man had managed to mortgage a derelict house for 60 million kroner.

The Chief Physician finally defended himself in a long article and posed the question: had a fax been sent from London giving the results of the tests on the boy's infected blood? Not to his office it hadn't. Yes, he had heard this rumour but why did people think the fax was in his possession? Wasn't it more likely to be at the Ministry of Health? Why were people talking about a 'mistake'? The results of the DNA test would soon be available. On the other hand, and it was to be much regretted, there had recently been a number of instances that threw some doubt on the reliability of tests such as this.

No documents could be found at the Ministry of Health, although they could not issue a categorical statement that such papers had never been there. But even if they had, then they must have been mislaid.

Father Bernhardur maintained a steadfast silence on the fact that it was not he but Tryggvi who had had the idea of threatening to set Sudurgata on fire. He decided that no matter what consequences he faced he would never reveal it in order to make things easier for himself. Even though, in this situation, he was not bound by the secrecy of the confessional.

Father Bernhardur was sitting in the living room of the presbytery when Haflidi arrived. They moved into the small room because Father Otto was watching basketball on television. The boy had expected to be send to prison for a just cause. As he talked and talked Father Bernhardur tried to imagine the burning house. It had said in the papers that 28 Thingholtstræti had literally disappeared in an instant in the blaze. The task of the firefighters was made almost impossible by a sudden strong wind placing the neighbouring houses in great danger. Father Bernhardur could easily picture Tryggvi in his mind's eye. 'How could I not have ministered better to this man?' he bitterly accused himself. 'But the truth is, if I am completely honest with myself, as I got to know him, I thought him a rather reprehensible human being. I became rather wary of him, afraid even.' The priest rested his head on one hand. 'When all is said and done, the fact remains, I did advise the woman to leave him.'

Haflidi went on and on about the Serb boy. He had written to London to try to find out about him but had not received an answer. 'Pardoned!' said Haflidi. 'We were pardoned because of a petition by people who said they were "concerned about us". Who were they? People who don't want to be looked at too closely, I should think.' Haflidi clenched his fists. 'I can't bear it! I don't want to be pardoned! I don't want anything to do with it!'

All this talk of the boy made Father Bernhardur tired. The whole business had become the cause of intense pain to him. He had sat in prison for four days refusing food and taking only the occasional sip of water. In prison he had meditated on the sufferings of St Peter who had asked to be crucified upside-down so he could not be likened to his Saviour. He tried to imagine the saint's spiritual suffering and his physical suffering and how long it would have taken him to die. But hadn't he himself asked God to touch him? Yes, he had certainly done that. Now he was set about with dread.

Father Bernhardur dozed while Haflidi held forth about justice and injustice, but even so he could not stop the thoughts in his mind. Was it not extraordinary that the Creator kept watch over the entire earth and knew the thoughts of all men and saw the movements of every living thing? But why had he given that self-same power to the Evil One? As the Devil could tempt all men, then he too must know the mind of man no less than did God himself.

He came to himself as he heard Haflidi say, 'When the blood sample comes back from the test overseas, then our case will be proved. DNA doesn't lie.'

'I'm afraid that sample is likely to be lost in the post or the tests will prove inconclusive,' said Father Bernhardur carefully and he yawned. 'I'm afraid it's all over now.'

'And the bloody insurance people tried to get out of paying Grandmother. But she'd already had the good sense to have the house signed over to her legally at the land registry. It's bad to feel ashamed of my own father,' said Haflidi seriously.

'Why do you say that?'

'He betrayed us.'

'What?' The priest didn't understand.

'I told him there wasn't any petrol in the building,' said Haflidi, visibly distressed.

'Oh, that! It all had to end somehow.' He made a dismissive little clicking sound with his tongue. 'Forgive your father, if that's what he did. You and me, we did all right.' Father Bernhardur changed the subject. 'How's your brother?'

'He's OK. His speech is coming back.' Haflidi seemed happy. 'The doctors were worried about permanent loss of movement or brain damage, but he'll make a complete recovery. Just imagine, he was unconscious for three weeks! He missed the whole business and Christmas and everything. Do you know why those kids said they attacked him?'

Father Bernhardur shook his head.

'That it pissed them off when he didn't have the balls to help me when I had that fight with them.'

'What will become of your brother and sister?'

'Everything's OK. And we'll be seeing each other, you and me.

The Bishop's going to take care of things for me and perhaps make a grant for my education overseas later on. That's what he said the other day, anyway. I've just got no idea what I'd want to study. And Mother's got a job in the old post office in Austurstræti. Ester's now the major shareholder in Heidnaberg. She wanted Mother to go back to her old job but she wouldn't hear of it. But the High Court rejected her action. One judge gave a dissenting judgment and said the doctor was guilty of criminal negligence. But she didn't get any compensation because the doctor was cleared of liability.'

'But how is she?'

'She never mentions Father if that's what you mean. She doesn't think you were responsible for the fire and neither do I. After all it was her idea to use the threat of fire and she sent you that note with Sylvía.'

'What?' said the priest and looked at him in stunned surprise. 'It was your mother's idea?'

When Haflidi had gone Father Bernhardur went into the living room. Father Otto stood up and turned off the television. He looked at Father Bernhardur with considerable distaste. 'You, Father, always the reason for trouble be,' said Father Otto. 'Always different from the other priests be.' He bent down awkwardly and turned off the video. He looked accusingly at Father Bernhardur. 'Nothing in this to happen if you my advice follow. You should a Subaru have buy. Obey superiors. That is all. Tell me,' he said, sounding rather more friendly, 'this nonsense, all a conspiracy is?'

'Of course it was a conspiracy.'

'Today the woman to Catholic convert, yes?'

'Yes,' said Father Bernhardur, nodding. 'The doctor's wife.' He had told neither Vilhelmína nor Theódóra of Hördur's part in the affair. It served no purpose to create more bad feeling and unhappiness in that family than there already was.

The bloody things gather in the pine trees, fly round, get together in gangs in the sky and then divebomb the park. The doctor was sitting on a bench in Miklatún cursing the starlings.

He stretched his legs and sighed. Soon they would be moving

away from the area and he would miss the park. Ester and Vilhjálmur had just got married with great pomp and ceremony in Háteigskirkja. The doctor was returning from the service. He had offered to sell them the flat at Vatnsholt but Ester didn't want to live there. They had recently bought, for cash, a villa where they planned to live with their son. Ester had been given custody in a recent hearing. I mention this only in passing. Please note: I made an undertaking to keep my own business out of this narrative as far as possible. Ester became chairman of Heidnaberg in the new year. Vilhjálmur seemed to her a more sensible choice for this degree of reponsibility, so she suggested that he become managing director. It was said that Ester was making a very good job of it. The doctor snorted. It did not surprise him that this should be the case.

Over the last few months Vilhelmína had been studying her catechism with the priest. Tomorrow was to be her first confession when she would be accountable for all her sins. She would be anointed with oil, receive the Holy Sacrament for the first time and become a Catholic. He had done what he could to talk her out of it. But since Vilhelmína had given up on reincarnation, she thought she'd rather be a Catholic like Theódóra. It might be thought that one element in this decision had been her older sister's decision to pass over all her shares in Heidnaberg. The doctor lit a cigarette, grinned and shook his head. It was all nonsense.

Recently the sisters had spent more time together than they had for many years. According to Vilhelmína, Theódóra had finally 'faced up to the truth'. 'What truth?' the doctor had asked. 'That's between Tedda and me,' said Vilhelmína, sounding very self-important.

He smoked and thought for a while. A woman with a pushchair came along the path. She let the little brat out of the pushchair and allowed it to run on the grass. The doctor watched as the child ran about wherever its feet took it, squealing, holding its hands up in the air. Probably Theódóra had realized that she was responsible for Axel's death and that it was her who had driven the girl into permanent insanity.

Hördur had given up the idea of joining a group practice. It was doubtless all over town the way Thorsteinn had got one over on him. He had his eye on a solid old stone mansion in the west end of town. He looked up at the sky. The birds were still shrieking as they flew between the tops of the trees. In olden times such an occurrence was meant to presage 'the age of the wolf'. But the woman with the pushchair and the children playing football far away on the grass did not take any notice.

Vilhelmína and her family appeared an hour before Mass. She and Father Bernhardur went off for the confession. Mass was sung and the woman said the Creed. Father Bernhardur walked along the altar rail and served the Holy Sacrament in a silver chalice to the kneeling congregation. The chalice that had been stolen a year earlier had still not been recovered. The priest felt the doctor's eyes boring into him.

There was to be a small gathering with coffee and cakes at Vatnsholt later that day. 'You must promise you'll come, Father Bernhardur,' said Vilhelmína as they came out on to the steps. He nodded.

'Of course he'll come,' said Theódóra. 'As it might have been predicted, Father Bernhardur, it came to pass that you brought a little lamb of God into the bosom of Holy Mother Church.' She kissed her sister's cheek. Then she and Vilhelmína walked over to the car with Ester, Trausti and Vilhjálmur. Vilhjálmur was carrying Gauti. They got into Hördur's Chrysler and drove off.

The following day Father Bernhardur took a letter to the post office. There had been a sudden flurry of snow that morning. The sun was shining, glinting on the frozen snow and ice. He had decided to take up the Bishop's suggestion and live in Rome for a year or so while the matter of the boy was forgotten. He had friends there and he wanted to warn them of his imminent arrival. He felt uncomfortable out on the streets. He felt he was marked down as the man who was responsible for the fire. He saw Dagný as soon as he went into the post office. He joined the queue at her counter and waited, even though another girl indicated that she was free.

He passed the letter to her. He felt the moment he had been waiting for Î was nearly upon him. When Dagný had sorted out the stamps, stuck them on the envelope and he had paid for them, Father Bernhardur still stood facing her without giving any sign of being about to leave. A large group of people had now gathered in the post office. A number were waiting in line behind the priest. Finally the woman, sounding a little embarrassed, said, 'Aren't you now, in spite of anything, just a little bit fond of me? The idea of threatening to set the house on fire kept everyone off your back.'

Father Bernhardur's eyes were on Dagný, but they seemed to be looking through her. It was as if he was preparing to speak to someone who had not been there but who had suddenly appeared behind her and was looking towards him because the hour he had been waiting for had come. He raised both hands for emphasis, as if he was holding the chalice that had been stolen from the church the previous spring and he shouted in his anguish: 'But you know I love you!'

Everybody there looked at him in surprise and those who recognized from his clothing that he was a Catholic priest shook their heads tolerantly when they saw what an extraordinarily attractive woman he was addressing.

50

EPILOGUE

A little before Easter Theódóra passed the Dyngjuvegur house over to the Vatnsholt family and moved into Skólabrú. She found the change comforting. 'I don't need the big house any more,' she said to her friends. 'And the walk from here over to the Parliament building is very convenient. I shall see out the present parliament.'

When her health permitted it, Linda would stay with her.

After the move, Hördur decided he and Vilhelmína would take a short break in Benidorm. It so happened that Theódóra was overseas at the same time on behalf of the Foreign Affairs Committee. The Prime Minister took the opportunity to ask, 'Does anyone seriously believe that I set out to damage a woman the government is currently sending to a conference on Peace and Security in Europe?'

If anyone was indeed that stupid he had the good sense to keep quiet. The country as a whole seemed to have entirely lost interest in the matter except of course for myself and the odd obsessive.

Trausti took the opportunity to have Linda to stay. He let her sleep in her old room and slept in the living room himself.

He awoke suddenly the first night she was there. Linda is standing by the living-room window wearing her white nightdress. She stands on tiptoe and is stretching her arms up to the heavens. Trausti gets up and moves silently across the floor. Now he is standing right by her. Her hands move a fraction. There is a deep frost outside, a yellow moon in the clear sky and the stars are shining. Reykjavík is alive with light. The Laugarsdals Stadium is flood-lit and the grandstand is in darkness. He looks down, beneath the hem of her nightdress, at her tensed muscular calves. It surprises him how long she can stand there on tiptoe. He rests a hand on her shoulder but she does not appear to notice. Her sleeves have fallen back halfway down her arms.

'Linda,' he says, 'you can't stay here.'

She relaxes her feet and stands normally. Her arms drop. She turns round and takes a moment to recognize him.

'Come,' he says. 'Come to bed.'

She shakes her head like a little girl. 'No, no. I can't! He says that we must go and tell all the people that a sea of fire is coming and it will engulf the whole world.'

Trausti holds her shoulders fairly firmly. Not too tight. He feels the tension in her body evaporate. 'Who is talking to you?'

'Jesus Christ is showing me the Day of Judgment. He ordered the earth to give up its dead. And I saw the dead rise up out of the earth and look towards him. He ordered the sea to give up its dead. And I saw the dead rise up out of the sea and look towards him. And I heard the cry go up from all over the earth: "Master! Master!" And I saw his anger was terrible. And he shouted so that the mountains crumbled: "You have betrayed the body that I gave to you so that you might live in me and I in you!" And the next moment I saw him crucified. And his mother knelt at the foot of the cross and shouted: "My son, forgive them that have offended against you!"

'But Christ bowed his head and yielded up his spirit and did not heed her words. A road led up to the cross. And suddenly that road was a road of fire and no one could walk along it any more. This time is coming and so we must go out together now, you and me, and warn the people! We must warn all of Reykjavík. All of Iceland! Before it is too late! We stand here in the eye of God. All our trespasses are committed there. And he is threatening to destroy the earth.' She turns her eyes slowly and carefully up towards the night sky, frightened, as if the vision is still there.

'Linda, come to bed. I'll go with you into town tomorrow. I am brave enough to do it. Just like you, I'm not like other people.'

She nods at the sky. 'We must make our peace with God. I am to warn the people. I am to tell the people what Jesus told me. Before it is too late.' She struggles in his arms.

'People go to church on Sunday. They'll be in the right frame of mind. Next weekend.'

He leads her to her room. He puts the duvet over her. He finds a mattress for himself. He draws the curtain so it is dark. He kneels by her bed in the darkness and strokes her hair until she is calm. After a long time he crawls under his own duvet and listens for her breathing to become steady and calm. Then he falls asleep on the floor.

And where is he? It is dark in the house, a shimmering darkness that writhes like a serpent around the house. Trausti knows that he should wake up. That he must wake up! He tosses his head this way and that but he cannot tear himself free of this dream.

Suddenly there is the scream of the doorbell. He thinks he is at home on Vatnsholt. There is another fierce ringing. He reaches clumsily for the bedside lamp. The heat. Who has closed the door into living room? He had left it open. There is something the matter with the radiators, he couldn't turn down the heat before. He switches on the light and looks across to Linda's bed. It is empty.

He throws aside the duvet and runs out into the hall and, terrified, shouts at the top of his voice, 'Who's there?'

The door is too solid for anyone on the outside to be able to hear him. There is another ring and then the ringing is continuous. Out on the steps there is a taxi driver. He has left the engine running. The driver is nervous and apologetic. 'I came across this girl on the corner of Langholtsvegur. She says she lives here. But perhaps she's got it wrong?'

Linda is standing behind the driver in just her nightdress. She is wearing waders. Her legs are bare. She is blue with cold, ecstastic with victory. 'I have done as I was bidden,' she says.

MARE'S NEST

Mare's Nest brings the best in international contemporary fiction to an English-language readership, together with associated non-fiction works. As yet, it has concentrated on the flourishing literature of Iceland. The list includes the three novels that have won the Icelandic Nordic Prize.

The poetic tradition in Iceland reaches back over a thousand years. The relatively unchanging language allows the great Sagas to be read and enjoyed by all Icelandic speakers. Contemporary writing in Iceland, while vivid and highly idiosyncratic, is coloured and liberated by this Saga background. Closely observed social nuance can exist comfortably within the most exuberant and inventive magic realism.

BRUSHSTROKES OF BLUE
The Young Poets of Iceland

Edited with an introduction by
Pál Valsson

112 pp. £6.95 pbk

'Exciting stuff: eight leading northern lights constellated here'
Simon Armitage

Sigfús Bjartmarsson   Gyrdir Elíasson   Einar Már Gudmundsson
Elísabet Jökulsdóttir   Bragi Ólafsson
Kristín Ómarsdóttir   Sjón   Linda Vilhjálmsdóttir

A representative introduction to contemporary poetry in Iceland,
Brushstrokes of Blue is full of surprises, from startling surrealist
juxtapositions and irresistible story-spinning to gentle aperçus and
the everyday world turned wild side out.

EPILOGUE OF THE RAINDROPS

Einar Már Gudmundsson

Translated by Bernard Scudder

160 pp. £7.95 pbk

'A fascinating and distinctive new voice from an unexpected quarter'
Ian McEwan

Magic realism in Iceland is as old as the Sagas. Described by its
translator as 'about the creatures in Iceland who don't show up
in population surveys', *Epilogue of the Raindrops* recounts the
construction (and deconstruction) of a suburb, the spiritual quest of
a mouth-organ-playing minister, the havoc wreaked by long-drowned
sailors, and an ale-oiled tale told beneath a whale skeleton, while the
rain falls and falls and falls.

JUSTICE UNDONE

Thor Vilhjálmsson

Translated by Bernard Scudder

232 pp. £8.95 pbk

'Thor Vilhjálmsson's hallucinatory imagination creates an eerily beautiful vision of things, Icelandic in far-seeing clarity, precision, strangeness. Unique and unforgettable.'
Ted Hughes

Based on a true story of incest and infanticide and set in the remote hinterland of nineteenth-century Iceland, *Justice Undone* is a compelling novel of obsession and aversion. An idealistic young magistrate undertakes a geographical and emotional journey into bleak, unknown territory, where dream mingles sensuously with the world of the Sagas.

ANGELS OF THE UNIVERSE

Einar Már Gudmundsson

Translated by Bernard Scudder

176 pp. £7.95 pbk

'Einar Már Gudmundsson, perhaps the most distinguished writer of his generation, is generally credited with liberating serious writing in his country from an overawed involvement in its own past, and with turning for inspiration to the icon-makers of the contemporary world.'
Paul Binding, *The Times Literary Supplement*

With humane and imaginative insight, Gudmundsson charts Paul's mental disintegration. The novel's tragic undertow is illuminated by the writer's characteristic humour and the quirkiness of his exuberant array of characters whose inner worlds are gloriously at odds with conventional reality.

NIGHT WATCH

Frída Á. Sigurdardóttir

Translated by Katjana Edwardsen

176 pp.   £7.95 pbk

'She has written a book that has no equal in recent Icelandic
literature. It is remarkably well written and tells several stories
that all merge into one . . .'
Susanna Svavasdóttir, *Morgunbladid*

Who is Nina? The capable, self-possessed, independent,
advertising executive, the thoroughly modern Reykjavík woman?
Or is she the sum total of the lives of the women of her family,
whose stories of yearning, loss, challenge and chance absorb her
as she watches by the bed of her dying mother?

TROLLS' CATHEDRAL

Ólafur Gunnarsson

Translated by David McDuff and Jill Burrows

304 pp.   £8.95 pbk

'It is a vagrant, morally unsettled form of story-telling on the same
wavelength . . . as Dostoevsky.'
Jasper Rees, *The Times*

'*Trolls' Cathedral* is a formidable work, mesmerically readable.'
Paul Binding, *The Times Literary Supplement*

The architect yearns to create a cathedral echoing the arc of a
seabird's wing, the hollows of a cliff-face cave. His struggles with
debt and self-doubt appear to be over when a seemingly random act,
an assault on his young son, destroys him and his family. Obsessions,
dreams and memories lead, inevitably, to violence.

Nominated for the 1998 International IMPAC Dublin Literary Award

THE SWAN

Gudbergur Bergsson

Translated by Bernard Scudder

160 pp. £8.95 pbk

'For many days after reading *The Swan* I remained preoccupied and enchanted with it. Here is a great European writer who has, with extraordinary subtlety and in a unique way, captured the existential straits of an adolescent girl.'

Milan Kundera

A nine-year-old girl is sent to a country farm to serve her probation for shoplifting. This is no idyll: she confronts new and painful feelings and faces the unknown within herself and in her alien surroundings. By submitting to the restraints of rural life, she finds freedom.

Z – A LOVE STORY

Vigdís Grímsdóttir

Translated by Anne Jeeves

280 pp. £9.95 pbk

' "I want you to know the real me" resounds tragically through this novel . . . To be afraid to finish reading a book is a strange feeling, but Z grips the reader with peculiar force.'

Marín Hrafnsdóttir, *Dagur-Timinn*

Two sisters, Anna and Arnthrúdur, seek to understand themselves, each other, their lives and their relationships with their lovers – with Valgeir, semi-detached from his wife, and with Z, the journalist named for the flash of lightning that attended her birth. Approaching death casts issues of independence and commitment into sharp focus as the women's contemplation achieves a blistering and loving honesty.

THE BLUE TOWER

Thórarinn Eldjárn

Translated by Bernard Scudder

192 pp.   £9.95

'*The Blue Tower* is picaresque . . . serious . . . entertaining. However one chooses to approach the novel, Eldjárn's language runs through the mind like a clear stream, shimmering with vitality.'
Sigrídur Albertsdóttir, *DV*

'A minor miracle . . . *The Blue Tower* is a masterpiece.'
Ármann Jakobsson

'A really stunning jacket and an unusual setting promise good things for this Icelandic novel.'
Guardian

Gudmundur Andrésson is incarcerated in the Blue Tower. With fine wit and rich bawdy he reflects on the calamity his talents, appetites and taste for satirical verse have brought upon him. As a poor but transparently clever boy, Gudmundur is sponsored by a kindly scholar but his desires for high office and a socially advantageous marriage are frustrated by the jealousy and rank-closing of powerful Icelandic families. The birth of a child out of wedlock, counter to the Great Edict – the oppressive morality law imposed by Denmark, the occupying power – and the circulation of a scurrilous thesis seal his fate. Yet ultimately his subversive history is outweighed by his loyalty to his few friends and his intellectual integrity.

The Blue Tower was shortlisted for Aristeion 1998 – the European literature and translation prize.

WILLIAM MORRIS

ICELANDIC JOURNALS

216 pp.   £15.99 new edition, cased

The *Icelandic Journals* are pivotal in Morris's aesthetic,
political and literary development. He was fascinated by Iceland and
his experiences there helped to clarify his ideas of the relationships
between function and beauty in design and between art and labour.
His translations of the Sagas and the vocabulary he evolved for them
influenced his late fairy tales.
The *Journals* were last published in England in 1969.

The volume has a foreword by William Morris's biographer,
Fiona MacCarthy, and an introductory essay by Magnus Magnusson.
The illustrations include facsimile pages from the original edition and
endpaper maps of Morris's routes.

'For Morris enthusiasts these journals are invaluable. For one thing,
Morris kept a diary only occasionally, and this document of his
thoughts on a day-to-day basis, during a critical time of his life,
proposes one of the most accurate portraits available to us . . . the
journals are an engrossing and sympathetic insight into one of the
planet's most fantastical countries . . .'
Simon Armitage, *The Spectator*

'The Sagas alone people Morris's Iceland. His beautifully simple but
detailed accounts of the landscape are heightened by his knowledge
of what happened there . . .'
Glynn Maxwell, *The Times*